Shattered Covenants Book VII

Twilight & Endgame

By

Dwight E. Foster

This book is a work of fiction. Places, events, and situations in this story are purely fictional. Any resemblance to actual persons, living or dead, is coincidental.

ISBN: 1-4140-0566-0 (e-book)
ISBN: 1-4140-0565-2 (Paperback)

This book is printed on acid free paper.

Art Cover by Brian Kappel

1stBooks - rev. 11/05/03

Dedication

TO: Dorothy Choitz Foster, the former comma queen of Penn State University, who suffered through proofing the entire seven volumes of Shattered Covenants. She certainly has surpassed Mrs. Tolstoi.

TO: All of the Partners, management group members, professional staff, and administrative employees of a firm once known as Peat Marwick Mitchell & Co.

6:15 AM, January 7, 1992

Baxter had the alarm set for seven o'clock. It represented a logical time to rise in order to catch the 9:39 Metroliner to Philadelphia. He reached across the bed and found he was alone. The space on the bed next to him was still warm. Apparently she was up. Baxter stared through the darkness at the outline of the ceiling light fixture. It was an older apartment building erected in the 1920's with high ceilings and dark wood baseboards.

Baxter slid out of the bed, flipped off the alarm, and ran his hand along the floor for his pajama bottoms. He generally slept in his tee shirt and shorts, but the last four evenings represented a special occasion. He had entertained a lady from out of town. It was the kind of event that called for the black silk pajamas that girl had given him four years ago at Christmas.

At age 57 Baxter had given up running in the early morning streets of New York City. His knees had given out according to his doctor. He was advised to quit running on the city cement.

Baxter slipped off his pajamas and stepped into the shower which distributed water unevenly through the ancient shower head onto the art deco tile shower floor. He shaved quickly after his shower, and started to re-don the black silk pajamas only to conclude they were starting to smell after four consecutive nights of use.

Linda! That was the girl's name who had given him the pajamas. She had quit two years ago following Monica over to the actuarial, benefits, and compensation firm. Baxter could never recall the firm's name. Linda and he had been hot and heavy sexual partners during the period after Bridgette had left him through the following summer. The black pajamas were his lone trophy of the encounter. Perhaps he'd buy an alternative pajama set in dark blue and rotate them. But then again, who need pajamas for an old sleeping companion? New sleeping companions required silk pajamas. New sleeping companions for Baxter at this time of his life were rare.

Shaving the face in the mirror, Baxter estimated that his hair was now an equal mix of red and grey. Ernie Grey, with Toni's assistance, had maintained his jet black hair over the years. Today Ernie would be buried with his jet black hair. The coffin reviewal had been on Monday, but Baxter had skipped it. Ernie Grey had died on Saturday, January 4th, in a roller blading accident in Naples, Florida.

According to Toni, they had been innocently roller blading on Saturday morning, and Ernie had dodged a motorcycle bolting out of the driveway, lost his balance, and careened into a stone fence that cracked his head open. Ernie had been knocked unconscious and pronounced dead at the hospital. Toni had called Baxter that Sunday evening and announced in a calm voice that Ernie had been killed in a freak action. Could Joe be in Philadelphia for the reviewal?

Baxter could have done it, but he chose not to. What could he add? Looking back, Baxter believed that Ernie had let him down on the Harwell transaction. Still he might have gone if Rusty hadn't stayed over. Baxter had been admittedly lonely over the past two years, and Rusty Collins had represented good company.

Baxter slipped on the bottoms of one of his old running suits and padded his way out of the master bedroom. Rusty sat in his study at his Macintosh punching in data with a steaming cup of coffee at her side. She was wearing one of Baxter's tee shirts and her red hair reached down to the middle of her back. Rusty apparently had her contacts out and she was wearing her dark rimmed glasses.

"Son-of-a-bitch! Son-of-a-bitch!" she addressed the computer screen in a soft, low impatient voice.

"Good morning. Is that coffee you have there?" he greeted her.

"It's instant," she responded without looking away from the screen. "I couldn't figure out how to work your coffee grinder, high tech coffee pot out there."

"How long have you been up?" Baxter asked.

"Maybe an hour. I was on a roll. But now I'm afraid I've screwed something up." She wheeled around in the chair from the computer. "Good morning. I know I look like hell, but I've got to get this project done today. Every time I started to work on it over the past few days, you've pulled me off to bed."

"I'm going to make a pot of coffee. Can I fix you some breakfast? Then I'm going to get dressed and should leave here no later than nine o'clock if I'm going to make the 9:39 Metroliner."

"Coffee will do. I'll have some dry toast later," Rusty replied and turned around to face the computer screen. Baxter padded away from the study through the hallway to the kitchen. His den was in actuality the second bedroom in the apartment. It was lined with books, contained desks at each side of the room and there was a hide-a-bed in the middle. There was a second bathroom across from the den. The remainder of the apartment consisted of a large L-shaped living room and a long narrow kitchen. Baxter had moved into the apartment two and one/half years ago at the same time Linda had moved out.

The apartment house was an older brick building erected in the 1920's, and situated near the corner of Madison Avenue and 35th Street. His living room looked out on Madison Avenue while the kitchen provided a view of 35th Street. Baxter poured beans into his German manufactured combination coffee grinder and coffee pot. He decided he would have what the Metroliner offered as breakfast. He wanted to talk to Rusty and persuade her to stay one more day. Baxter did not want to return from Philadelphia to an empty apartment.

Rusty Collins had shown up on Baxter's phone mail somewhere near the end of the third week in December.

"Joe Baxter, Rusty Collins here. I'm going to be out in New York on Friday, January 3rd, to complete a market survey on an Electronic Commerce study we're doing. Could we meet for a drink on Friday evening post five o'clockish? My last appointment is down on Wall Street at 3:30. 5:30 should fit. I'd like to get caught up. Give me a call over the holidays. 213-551-9027."

Rusty's given name was Marie and she disliked her name. 'Rusty' had been a natural nickname and she had legally changed her name to Rusty after she had joined McKenzie Barber from Stanford.

Rusty had transferred to Los Angeles in June 1988 after Jack Baldwin's practice had imploded. Baldwin, presumably Floyd Piper's successor, had turned from the New York Office star group partner to the "dog" practice in seven short months. Lon McMasters had reorganized the New York Office

Group system, and Baldwin had been placed under Jon Grunwaldyt, who was acknowledged to be the newly recognized New York Office "star" after the Hortense Foods MBO group had acquired the company. Baldwin was offered 'start again' transfers to either Chicago or Los Angeles and accepted Los Angeles. He had been scheduled to relocate to Los Angeles effective October 1, 1988, but resigned in August to join Robson Allen in San Francisco as a direct admission Partner responsible for its Western Region Financial Services practice.

Baxter had initially consented to have drinks with Rusty Collins in January 1988. They had met briefly at the 1987 McKenzie Barber Christmas Party, and she left a voice mail on New Year's Eve. They had two rounds at the Sunset Club in mid-January. Rusty had impressed Baxter at the time as a competent, attractive, female management group consultant who was beginning to worry about her future with McKenzie Barber. Baxter concluded that he liked Rusty when he signed the cocktail check. He tried to put Rusty at ease regarding her McKenzie Barber career, and she seemed upbeat when Baxter escorted her to a cab. He lost track of her after the cocktail session.

Baxter next encountered Rusty at the Admiral's Club at Chicago O'Hare a year later in the midst of a blizzard. Baxter had been making calls to downtown hotels after he had exhausted the O'Hare area hotels. He recognized Rusty at the outer edge of the bar peering out at the falling snow. He waved twice and she recognized his second wave. At the same time, he located a hotel room in a small North Side hotel where McKenzie Barber had a relationship.

"Hi, stranger," she greeted Baxter. "The airport is closing and my travel agent tells me that I ought to try Milwaukee for a hotel room tonight."

"I have just secured a room downtown," Baxter said, tired but triumphant.

"Anymore where that came from?" Rusty stood in front of him with a half glass of wine. Tall, with her red hair tied in a pony tail, Rusty wore a dark suit and black pumps.

"I got the last one. It's a small hotel on Delaware Street where McKenzie Barber puts up visiting Partners, and I just got the last room. Now comes the challenge of getting downtown," Baxter explained.

Rusty perched on the arm of Baxter's chair. "Are you into weather, Joe? Did you know this stood a chance of happening?"

"I assumed that I could beat the storm. When things get backed up at O'Hare, they stayed backed up. Sleeping downtown is better than sleeping on the floor here. You airline carrier is required by law to find you a hotel room for the night."

"Did you get a double bed?" Rusty asked.

"Did you ever see *It Happened One Night*?" Baxter asked.

"Let's get our bags," Rusty said.

The room at the Blackford Hotel thankfully offered twin beds. Baxter and Rusty had a nightcap in the downstairs bar.

"I probably should have waited for American Airlines to get me a hotel room, but I jumped at having a room in hand. I would hope that we could keep any kind of physical relationship under control, and just be good roommates this evening," Rusty offered.

"I just hope you don't snore," Baxter responded. "There's only one cure for it."

Rusty did snore, but Baxter managed to drop off. Rusty allowed him to use the bathroom first as she did her exercises.

"We'd make a pretty good brother and sister routine," Baxter commented over breakfast.

"You're probably the only Partner in McKenzie Barber that I'd risk something like last night with," Rusty had responded. She sent Baxter a dozen roses the next day.

They met again in the spring of 1990 in the Los Angeles office. Baxter had borrowed a cubicle which turned out to be two doors down from Rusty.

"What brings you to town, Mister?" She was in a white dress this time and perched on the edge of the desk crossing her legs dramatically.

5

"I'm speaking tomorrow morning on US compensation practices to a consortium of Japanese companies. Today I called on California banks and explained to them what was going on in the outside world."

"Spoken like a true arrogant New Yorker," Rusty acknowledged. "You should let a girl know when you're coming to town. Doing anything for dinner tonight?"

"I'm having a dinner with the Chairman of the Compensation Committee at Empire Electronics. I'm catching a noonish flight back to New York."

"There's a lesson here. You spend a night with a man and he won't give you the time of day after that."

"When will you be at O'Hare again? We seem to have better luck there."

"My career's going better. Things always go better after I talk them through with you. I don't care much for living in LA, but this is a good office. Jack is killing us in San Francisco, regrettably."

"Do you still see Jack?" Baxter asked.

"From time to time. He'll swoop in here and suggest that I come over and sleep with him."

"That's called sleeping with the enemy," Baxter commented. "Has he offered you a job with Robson Allen?"

"I'm not talking. By the way, I hear you're divorced."

"It's a work in progress. But I'm pretty much abandoned now," Baxter said. He wondered how many people in the firm knew that Linda had moved out the week before.

"Well, when I'm out in New York again, I'll let you buy me another drink." Rusty slid off her perch on the side of the desk. "You'll have to excuse me, Joe. I have to get back to work to make money for the greedy Partners of this firm."

Baxter invited Rusty to meet him, at the Sunset Club on January 3, 1992.

"Long time, no see," she greeted him walking confidently across the floor wearing a green suit and matching pumps. Rusty's smile was broad and her handshake firm. They were seated in front of a window looking out on the West Side.

"We had drinks here four years ago at this time. You gave me quite a pep talk as I recall."

"I try to be inspiring on all occasions," Baxter answered and they began to talk. They were two drinks down when Baxter suggested dinner.

Rusty went on to describe her Electronic Commerce project.

"It could well be my last project for McKenzie Barber, because I expect that I will be offered a job by the client when I make my report next week. If they offer me enough money, LA base or not, I'm taking the job."

"You'll be a great loss for the LA office."

"No, I won't. There are a number of people behind me. I'm competent in what I do, but so are the people coming up behind me. I'm not going to be nominated for Partner unless I can personally bill a million or so. It's time for me to call it a day with McKenzie Barber. I really wanted to get your insight into the merger. It's going to get very serious now isn't it?"

"You're referring to the grand old firm of Robson Barber?"

"It's hard to say it, isn't it. I called both the New York and LA offices today and I almost hung up both times when I heard the word Robson."

"The word McKenzie is gone forever from the masthead of the combined firm. I'm willing to bet that John McKenzie's picture disappears from every office. They'll probably put up Charley Robson's picture next to Eric Barber," Baxter predicted. "To McKenzie Barber!" Baxter raised his glass and they brushed wine glasses.

"I may just start bawling, Joe. For a long time I believed in the firm. It was ten years for me last July."

"That's just a cup of coffee. I started on the day after Labor Day in 1967. I'm 24 years worth, fully vested and, for some reason, still here."

"Could you see the merger coming?" Rusty asked.

"I knew something had to be done. The firm had failed miserably under Buzzsaw's stewardship. I thought he gave up around the fall of 1988. That's when General Pritchard implied that he was considering public service after he had fulfilled his leadership commitment to the Partners of McKenzie Barber. That's when Fitzgerald and Pinker started organizing their coup d'etat. No one saw them coming, and suddenly they had a movement."

"Were you involved in their election campaign, Joe?"

"No. I did 1984 and that was quite enough. I voted for them though, because I knew they had to clean house. And Jesus did McKenzie need a housecleaning with all of the incompetents that Buzzsaw and Clyde Nickerson installed."

"Did you know Glen Fitzgerald or Jack Pinker very well?"

"Fitzgerald was someone out in Chicago who took himself very seriously. He was an IT Partner that Gene Richards hired from one of the accounting firms. The guy took off like a house of fire, and suddenly had the largest practice in the firm and did it through internal growth. Fitzgerald added 50 consultants in one year and kept them all busy. Information Systems has never been a strength of McKenzie Barber, and all of a sudden we had this guy with his act together. Pinker, I knew from the New York Office Financial Services practice. He was an ambitious second year Partner when I got to know him back in 1983. We served on a committee charged with the hire of a Director of Communications. I didn't see him as Deputy Chairman material at the time, but time disguises all flaws."

"He used to work for Jack in New York. Jack considered Jack Pinker as average."

"There's the flaw to your thinking, Rusty. We want our best people out serving clients. Leave the running of the firm to the dumb and inept."

It was over dinner that Rusty announced that she was going back to LA the following morning.

"Why don't you stay through Saturday and go back on Sunday?" Baxter offered.

"Because I could not stand a third night in that dreadful fleabag Broadway hotel the firm put me into. All non-Partner consulting personnel must be booked through the executive office travel agency. If you book yourself into an unauthorized hotel, you get your expenses bounced."

"How long has that policy been around?" Baxter asked.

"Since a month after Fitzgerald and Pinker took over. They created this central executive office travel bureau that negotiated special rates with the worst hotels in the country. By having dinner with you, I'm postponing the time I have to spend in that dreadful room."

"Why don't you check out after dinner and you can spend tonight and tomorrow at my place. I'll get theatre tickets for Saturday night, and we can enjoy a memorable weekend together."

"Mr. Baxter, I thought I would ask you out for a drink. You bought the drinks. Next you throw in dinner. Are you now proposing bed and board?"

"I'm proposing that we get you out of that dreary sounding hotel and into my sparkling clean apartment. I know it's sparkling clean because the maid visits on Friday. I'm proposing that you postpone that six hour flight for 24 hours."

"And I recall that you and I have spent the night together before without complications."

"I will commit to no guarantees regarding contact this time around."

"Now, you're trying to make yourself interesting. You also make a case for getting out of that hotel room." Rusty extended a hand toward Baxter which he accepted. "Joe, I'm very flattered, but I had better get back to LA in the morning. I have a relationship back there, and I'm expected back for a dinner party Saturday night. Maybe a raincheck is in order."

They were out in the street at a quarter to nine.

"How about a nightcap? The evening's young," Baxter suggested.

"One drink. I really have to pack, Joe."

Baxter hailed a cab. "I know a place that's quiet with good music where you can get a full sized drink. I'll take you there for a nightcap," Baxter said holding the taxi door open for Rusty. "The corner of 35th and Madison," Baxter instructed the driver.

"It's only going to be one drink," Rusty said as Baxter hung up her coat.

"You can have two if you like." Baxter took Rusty's arm and led her into his black Eames chair adjacent to the sound system in his living room.

"Let me look around. This is an interesting room. It resembles a library. It's all books and a large desk."

"Are you sticking with Scotch?" he asked.

"A very light Scotch. I'm leaving here within the hour and I'm going back to my hotel and pack."

Baxter turned on some Satie and left Rusty to roam through the room that had been originally designed by a 1920s architect to be a living room. He poured a light Scotch into a high ball glass and added a brandy in a snifter for himself. He found Rusty perched on the ottoman of the Eames chair with her glasses on looking through one of his McKenzie Barber ring binders.

"What is this? Is this some kind of scrap book?"

Baxter presented the Scotch and Rusty muttered a "Thank you" and continued. "This is quite interesting. It's all about McKenzie Barber."

10

"I'm preparing to write a history of the firm now that its life and identity are virtually ended," Baxter explained. "I've been accumulating material for the last year or so and organized it into ring binders."

Rusty closed the ring binder and placed it on the Eames chair. She rose to her feet and stepped out of her pumps. Baxter noted that she had quite large feet.

"This certainly isn't a conventional living room. No woman has had anything to do with the decorating in this room. Is the rest of the apartment as bad as this?"

Baxter followed behind Rusty as she moved slowly around the book shelf covered walls.

"Are these your children?" Rusty asked when she came to a picture shelf.

"My son and my daughter," Baxter acknowledged.

"They are very nice looking," Rusty said lifting each picture individually from the shelf for closer inspection. "What are they doing now?"

"My son is dead. My daughter is up in Vermont working this winter in a ski resort. She's taking a year off from college to regroup herself. She took her brother's death and a couple of other setbacks pretty badly."

"I'm terribly sorry, Joe," Rusty said facing him. "Is that Debussy playing?"

"Satie," Baxter corrected her.

"Can I have a tour?"

Baxter led Rusty through his narrow kitchen back to his second bedroom. "This looks like an office too." Then he led her into the master bedroom.

"Well done, Mr. Baxter. This room resembles a bedroom," Rusty commented and took a long drink of Scotch. She handed the glass to

Baxter. "This could use a topper." Rusty left the master bedroom in long strides.

Baxter prepared a slightly stronger drink for Rusty, and found her looking through another ring binder. "This book is nothing but obituaries," she observed.

"When you reach my age, Rusty, the people around you begin to pass out of sight. You begin to maintain records on who's checked out."

Rusty carefully replaced the ring binders back on the bookshelf.

"I take it that you live alone, Joe."

"My last wife left me in December 1987. I've been in this building for about three years now. I have a country place in upstate New York where I generally spend my weekends. I like to have books and music around me and I consider this apartment as an extension of my office where I can sleep."

"You sound very lonely. Do you have a number of women friends?" Rusty asked.

"Not really. There's a woman I see from time to time when I'm up in my country place." Baxter seated himself next to Rusty on the ottoman. They sat in silence for a moment listening to Satie's piano music and then Baxter kissed Rusty lightly on the forehead. She turned her mouth up to meet his and there was a long kiss that evolved into an open mouthed exchange of tongues. "I should go back to my hotel right now," she protested.

"I ask you to consider staying the night," Baxter offered. "I'll help you get off in the morning."

"Joe, I have a relationship back in Los Angles."

"I could be a very interesting one night stand."

"Joe, I'm very careful of my relationships these days. A woman can't be too careful."

Baxter rose from the ottoman and unlocked his living room desk drawer. He had had a physical examination in November. He produced the Physician's report letter.

"As of November 21st, I was clean as a whistle. Read for yourself." Baxter handed the letter to Rusty. "I really hate to be reduced to providing comfort letters from my Doctor, but I recognize that these are troubled times for one night stands."

Rusty scanned the letter, pushed it back to Baxter, and put her shoes back on. "Thank you for the drink and the opportunity to review your medical report, Mr. Baxter." She rose to her feet.

Baxter enclosed his arms around Rusty. "I so rarely get women up here that I hate to see them drink and run." She seemed to relax in his arms. Rusty pecked Baxter on the mouth. "And how can you be certain that I'm free from life threatening diseases, Joe?"

"You have an honest face, Rusty."

"As I recall you were more peaceful that night at the Blackford in Chicago. I didn't get a sexual peep out of you that night."

"I'm dangerous and reckless on Friday nights," Baxter said releasing her. "I'll get your coat and see you into a cab," he offered.

"I'm in no hurry, Joe. It is Friday night and I've always liked your company."

"We could have a wake for the passing of McKenzie Barber," Baxter suggested.

They returned to the Eames chair, removed their shoes, and settled in with their feet on the ottoman. He extended an arm around Rusty while she loosened Baxter's tie and opened his collar button.

The sound system changed into a Debussy CD and Rusty turned her long body against Baxter. "I feel very comfortable right now, Mr. Baxter. This has been a bummer of a week. You bought me a very nice dinner this evening, and now you have me relaxed and vulnerable with you in your living room. Tell me, Joe, do you own a reliable alarm clock?"

Baxter set the alarm for six AM and when the buzzer sounded, Rusty shot upright in bed. "What the hell time is it?"

"Six AM, lady. I am prepared to get you off to your hotel and onto the 9 o'clock flight to LA."

"I'll go back Sunday. I need my sleep. I allowed some man I barely know to ravish me last night. I need my sleep now. Thank you very much." She rolled over on her side. Baxter touched her bare shoulder and received a pat on his hand. "Ring me up later," Rusty said. "I need my sleep now."

Baxter was out of bed before seven and left a snoring Rusty behind him. He showered, shaved, and donned his black silk pajamas. He had lived in the apartment for nearly three years, and Rusty had been the first woman to spend the night. His sex life had dropped off dramatically since Linda had moved her things out from the apartment on 38th Street after she had become engaged to the cardiologist. Rusty's green suit had been hung in the front hall closet as a trophy around half past twelve. Her slip and panty hose lay across his desk on top of his physical examination report.

He made a pot of coffee and planned a Saturday to be spent with an unplanned companion.

It was during the second bottle of Bordeaux over lunch at an East Side French restaurant called Fouquet's that Rusty announced that she wanted to stay another day. She wore a sweater and pants with the ski jacket they had purchased that morning.

"I'm getting comfortable with you, Mr. Baxter. I'm really enjoying New York with you, and the best I could do was standby on the morning flight. If you'll have me, I'll go back Monday morning. I'll need some time Sunday afternoon to get my report on disk. I have to deliver a draft to the client on Thursday afternoon. I expect to get an offer on Friday and hopefully I can safely resign from McKenzie Barber on Tuesday, January 14th. I'm going to consider this weekend an interlude before I resume the rest of my life. So, am I good for one additional night?"

"You're on American plan through Sunday night," Baxter affirmed.

"I thought I was on French plan this morning. You have the most innovative ways of waking a lady up, Mr. Baxter."

"Do you have a job offer coming?" Baxter asked.

"On Friday, the 10th. It's with CCCS, California Credit Card Services. It's a non-bank credit card issuer. They are offering me a Group Product Manager's job in affinity marketing. I'll take it on the spot if the money's right and they make it a SVP. If it's at a VP level I'll negotiate them up. I don't want to leave McKenzie Barber at the ten year level for a VP job. I'll have a decent travel budget. Maybe we could do this again sometime. Now what are you going to do? Will you stay at Robson Barber?"

"I expect to be offered a package when I show up again. There's a guy named Dr. Gilbert Ranglinger at Robson Allen, now Robson Barber, who has the equivalent of Nickerson's old job. His secretary has been leaving me voice mail since mid-December. I pretended to go along with the spin-out of the Benefits practice, but pulled out in November. It added another year and 4% on my retirement pay. There's no place for Joe Baxter at Robson Barber."

"Then what will you do?"

"I'll go write my book about McKenzie Barber, move out of New York City and live up in my country place in Brinker's Falls, New York. With proper encouragement I could be persuaded to take an occasional trip to Southern California."

Rusty's right hand settled on Baxter's left hand. Her red hair was tied in a pony tail. She wore dark glasses, a red sweater, and dark stretch pants. Baxter had enjoyed Rusty's tall thin body, small breasts, and wonderful long legs. They would walk some more after lunch, dress for the theatre, see Phantom of the Opera, enjoy an after theater dinner, and return to his apartment to make love. He had completely forgotten Rusty Collins until she telephoned him for drinks. Now he was forming an affection for her. It was a little like that weekend so many years ago in Paris with Dominique.

"Joe Baxter. This is going very fast. I called you in the middle of December to invite you out for a drink and talk about the firm. I had no plans for dinner, and certainly no plans to spend the night with you. Now here we are sitting over a leisurely New York lunch in a French restaurant and behaving like star crossed lovers. And I'm loving it. Now you tell me who's in your life and I'll tell you who's in mine."

"No one really," Baxter answered. "My wife moved out in November 1987. I took up with a young woman for a while, but she left me for someone her own age. There's a woman that I see from time to time when I'm up in my country place. That's nothing serious or binding, but it's convenient. I guess you could classify me as aging and alone."

"I would also classify you as rather interesting," Rusty responded.

"Your turn," Baxter prodded.

"I'm 36 years old, divorced without children, and seeing a man three years younger than I am. He's an Associate Professor at USC and operates a market research firm on the side. I met Win through one of my clients. I've been seeing him for two years, and it's a comfortable relationship. Win is very bright, charming and generally entertaining to be with. He was a little miffed when I told him I couldn't make the dinner party with him tonight. Win's always been a little in awe of me because I've been with McKenzie Barber and doing strategic work, while he's been all business and market research. I doubt whether Win could make it much past Associate with McKenzie Barber. The question is, what does a career minded lady in her mid-thirties want to settle for?"

"And what do you want to do with your life, Rusty?" Baxter asked.

"Wife and mother no! I believe I can run a business in the financial services sector by the time I'm 40. Have you ever seen my personnel file?"

Baxter shook his head.

"Well, I taught for a couple of years in Menlo Park before I went on to Stanford. My father was a junior high school principal and my mother was an elementary education teacher. I got interested in business through a Junior Achievement project my Junior year. I met Jason, my first husband, at Stanford. He was in Law School and we were married at graduation, selected San Francisco firms and moved to the Bay area. I was in the pool for about four months when I was assigned to a Financial Services Practice on one of Jack Baldwin's engagements. I did reasonably well and was asked to transfer permanently to the Financial Services Practice. I was the first consultant in the class of 1982 to be promoted out of the pool. I was full of myself. I was promoted to Associate in one year."

"Jack Baldwin was like a God to me. He was the brilliant Jack Baldwin, who had been elected a Partner at age 28. He selected me to work on some of his engagements, and suddenly I was one of Jack's entourage of fast track consultants. Sleeping with him seemed to be a natural pattern in career progression. There were two or three of us that he liked to rotate. I outlasted the other two. Jason and I went sour and we decided to go our separate ways after four years of marriage and my invitation to transfer to New York."

"Joe Baxter is a legend among the women consultants of McKenzie Barber. You pick up a lot of talk in the Ladies Room and over cocktails. Legends are passed over time. I heard about you before I went up and introduced myself to you at that New York Office Christmas Party four years back. I can remember the time you took me out for drinks in 1988. You gave me time when you were busy and listened to my career anxiety. I've never forgotten that. It really meant something to me. Now we've become lovers which was certainly not my intention. Let's enjoy each other and see where this relationship goes. I feel very mellow about you right now, Mr. Baxter," Rusty said squeezing Baxter's hand.

Their common bond, of course, was the firm. The firm that had ceased to exist on January 2, 1992. Whenever their conversation ebbed, the topic of McKenzie Barber would revive it. They walked through the damp streets of the grey New York afternoon down Madison Avenue with arms extended around each other's waists. Rusty had no name recognition of Ernie Grey or Hamilton Burke. She could remember Bob Friedman, and Rusty had greatly admired Floyd Piper.

"Jack assumed that Floyd would move up to Chairman over time. He was in shock when they shelved Floyd. McMasters didn't help at all. Jack believed that Lon McMasters had an agenda to replace all of the Floyd Piper's people. Then when they replaced McMasters with Brett Williamson from FSO, everyone was in shock. I heard you were a big factor in getting Williamson out. Is that right?"

"Brett Williamson was a big factor in getting himself fired. I'd like to say that I helped, but I can't take credit for dumb personnel moves and natural selection," Baxter answered.

17

"Were you high up in the firm at one time?" Rusty asked.

"Never really that high. I did some special work for the Chairman and was slated to be Administrative Partner if Burke had won the 1984 election. That was eight years ago, and now we have a different firm. It's time for Joe Baxter to move on. Just as it's time for Rusty Collins to do something else."

"You have a way of cutting through issues," Rusty said and she drew Baxter into a doorway of a shop on Madison and 45th Street. "Something that pleases you?" Baxter commented as they studied the mannequins.

"Hardly. I want you to kiss me. Right here and right now." They shared a long kiss in front of the display window while Baxter sensed that customers were passing by them into the shop.

"I'd like to make love to you before we dress for the theatre," Baxter requested.

Rusty's dark glasses were on her forehead skier fashion. "I want you Joe. This day is going like a wonderful dream. I'm so glad that I stayed behind to be with you."

"I'll get a cab," Baxter said.

Rusty asked about Joel when they shared a drink before the car service arrived to take them to the theatre.

"He's a nice looking boy. How long ago did he die?" she asked studying the picture.

"About a year ago. Joel died of AIDS," Baxter answered. "My son was gay and he was more than a little reckless. He died in a hospice a year ago last Christmas."

"Were you close to him?" Rusty asked.

"Not really. Joel was a product of my second marriage. We didn't seem to fit together very well. I'd like to tell you that I tried my best to make it work, but I wouldn't be telling you the truth."

Rusty squeezed Baxter's hand. "I'm sorry, Joe." Then she moved to the book shelves. "You seem to have every book Beth Gold has written."

"Beth is a friend. We go back almost 40 years. I have most of her books but I really haven't read many of them."

Rusty pulled out *An Interlude of Discontent* from the book shelf. "I tried to get through this book and I couldn't. It was too depressing. Generally I've liked her books."

Baxter opened the book for Rusty. It was inscribed:

TO JOE BAXTER WITH LOVE

BETH July 1988

"I couldn't get through it either. Beth put her heart and soul into this book and it bombed. The critics hated it and I don't think she has done much writing since. She's been fooling around researching a book on Alice Dungler, but Beth has been taking too long. There's a little tart who used to write for *Enterprise Week* who's going to beat her to it."

"How often do you see her?"

"Every six weeks or so, we have a Saturday luncheon. She has a friend named Stephany who's an unemployed Securities Analyst. We have outrageous luncheons together. They both tend to drink like fish," Baxter explained.

"Are they girlfriends?" Rusty asked.

"They are middle-aged lady friends," Baxter corrected Rusty.

Their relationship began to wear thin on Sunday. Toni Grey's call came shortly after nine in the morning.

"Joe, this is Toni," a solemn voice greeted him. "Ernie died on Saturday. We're having the reviewal on Monday and we're burying him Tuesday. Can I count on you to help?"

"How did it happen?" Baxter asked. He had seen the former Chairman of McKenzie Barber in November at an IPCO Analysts presentation. Ernie Grey had conducted himself in the manner of a chief executive in his early fifties.

"Ernie was roller blading. A motorcycle came out of a driveway didn't see Ernie and hit him. He was sent flying into a wall and it was believed that he was killed instantly. His body will be flown up this evening. Can you come down and help?"

"I'm tied up, Toni," Baxter responded. Actually he was angry with Ernie Grey. He hadn't supported him on the Harwell transaction and cost Baxter a lot of money.

"I will be down for the funeral on Tuesday. Have you contacted Millie?"

"Millie's been most helpful, Joe. Pres should be down here on the noon train, and Millie and Kathleen will be here this evening. My brother and his wife are driving down in the morning."

Now, with all of those people coming to Philadelphia, Baxter reasoned, what in hell did Toni Grey need him for.

"I have to be in New York today and Monday, Toni. How can I help?"

"McKenzie Barber must have an obituary ready. I'm at the Four Seasons in Philadelphia. I have a fax in the suite. I'll give you the number. Would you see that I get a copy to review as soon as possible. Can you also see that an internal firm-wide announcement is made about the funeral arrangements. You should have someone get out an E-mail first thing. Who's the Chairman of McKenzie Barber now? I've forgotten."

"Toni, there is no McKenzie Barber anymore. It's been Robson Barber since January 2nd," Baxter reminded Toni.

"Joe, I've been on the phone already with the Director of Public Information at IPCO. They committed to having a fax obituary to me within the hour. I'm counting on you, Joe Baxter, to handle McKenzie Barber."

"Are you shooting for two separate obituaries, Toni?" Baxter asked.

"Joe, a great business leader has died suddenly. McKenzie Barber people need to be informed of Ernie's passing. They will want to attend the funeral. Philadelphia should be quite manageable for all of those New York people. I need your help on this."

"Give me your telephone and fax number, Toni. I'll get on it now. I will be down on Tuesday for the funeral."

"I would think you would, Joe. I would think you would be able to come tomorrow in order to help. Ernie was your friend," Toni scolded and recited her telephone and fax numbers.

"I'll get on it and be back to you," Baxter said and hung up.

Rusty was behind his chair and placed her hands on his shoulders. She kissed him on the ear and the neck.

"Good morning, Mr. Baxter." She was wearing one of Baxter's tee shirts and slid into his lap. "Now what was that phone call about?"

"Ernie Grey died."

"Who's Ernie Grey?" Rusty asked innocently.

"He was the Chairman of McKenzie Barber for twenty-four years. He was Chairman of IPCO until 1991. He died Saturday morning while roller blading in Naples, Florida. That was his wife on the phone. The funeral's on Tuesday and she wants McKenzie Barber contacted."

"There is no McKenzie Barber anymore," Rusty reminded Baxter.

"There's got to be someone at Robson Barber who will get something out to the interested McKenzie Barber people."

"Who's going to be interested? The man retired eight years ago. McKenzie Barber has gone through so much change and chaos, I doubt whether there's anyone left who will remember him."

"Rusty, the man was Senior Partner and Chairman of the firm for twenty-four years. A lot of people will want to turn out for the funeral to pay their last respects. I remember how angry Ernie got when Harvey Randolph died and he had to learn it from the *New York Times* obituary column."

"Another new name."

"I'm expected to call someone. Who do I call?"

"It's Sunday. The office is closed. There's no one there to talk to. Were you and this Ernie Grey close?"

"Not really. He talked and I listened."

"Wasn't he the one who screwed up the firm?" Rusty asked.

"No that was Buzzsaw Pritchard. Ernie should have crushed him in the 1984 Chairman election, but he got mad at Burke."

"More names I've never heard of."

Rusty's arms were around Baxter's neck and she sat in his lap clad in his J.C. Penney tee shirt. He could feel her nipple through cotton material and her pubic hair was in plain view.

It was the first time Baxter had had a willing woman in his apartment for this extended period of time and Ernie Grey had screwed it up by becoming a roller blade fatality.

"Rusty, I've got to get on the phone," Baxter explained.

"So I'm being dismissed?" She bolted out of Baxter's lap and extended the tee shirt down to the middle of her thighs. "I'm going to take my shower and then I'll start on my report. I'll leave you to your duties. I may try to get out of here this afternoon. Do you have an airline guide?"

Baxter produced his OAG and Rusty left the room skimming the pages. He was now alone at his desk.

Baxter really hadn't paid much attention to the internal workings of McKenzie Barber since the spring when the team of Fitzgerald and Pinker concluded with Richard Fairbrother's help that the best way out of the mess in the US was to enter merger discussions with Robson Allen. Normally a new Chairman/Deputy Chairman combination would be putting their team in place. The Fitzgerald and Pinker combination spent their first three months trying to estimate how deep a ditch had been dug by the Pritchard team, and concluded by March that a merger combination was the logical way out.

Jobs that should have been filled were left vacant and Executive Office responsibilities were doubled up. Floyd Piper had taken early retirement in 1989 after being stained with the blame for sinking the New York Office. Baxter skimmed through the 1990 McKenzie Barber Directory. To the best of his knowledge, the firm had never issued a 1991 Directory. He identified a public relations manager position which was presumably held by a Symantha Dugan. Ms. Dugan had a New York number.

A voice mail greeted him. "Hi. You've reached Sym and Chad. We can't come to the phone right now. If you'll leave your name and number and a brief message, we'll be right back to you."

"Joe Baxter, a McKenzie Barber Partner now Robson Barber, calling Symantha Dugan. Miss Dugan, you have been identified in the firm Directory as Manager of Public Relations for the firm. Ernie Grey, the Chairman of McKenzie Barber from 1960 to 1984 died on Saturday. I know the firm will want to inform Partners and employees and may wish to contribute an obituary. I hate to bother you on a Sunday, but this is a communications emergency. My number is 212-983-1129 and my name is Joe Baxter." His message fit the recording window. Now what would he do next?

He decided to dial Pinker at his Greenwich home number. A teenage girl's voice answered the telephone.

"Pinkers!"

"Is Jack Pinker in?"

"Can I tell him who's calling?"

"This is Joe Baxter. I'm one of your Dad's Partners and there is an emergency."

23

"Hold the line. I'll see if he's available."

Baxter waited until the voice returned to the phone.

"My Dad's busy. He asked if it could wait until Monday when's he's back in the office."

"You tell your Dad that Ernie Grey died on Saturday and will be buried on Tuesday in Philadelphia. The firm must get a communication out."

"What's that name again?"

"Ernie Grey," Baxter repeated.

"Okay, I'll tell him."

"It's okay to tell him, but I want to talk to him and I want to talk to him right now."

"Hold the line," an impatient youthful voice instructed.

Baxter waited nearly three minutes. A woman's voice came on the phone. "This is Annette Pinker. May I help you?"

"Mrs. Pinker, this is Joe Baxter. I'm a Partner well acquainted with your husband. I just received news that Ernie Grey, who was Chairman of McKenzie Barber from 1960 until 1984 died on Saturday morning. The funeral will be in Philadelphia on Tuesday. The firm should get out a notice right away."

"Jack's on an overseas call to England right now. He can't come on the phone. Suppose you give me this man's name. The one that died. I'll tell Jack and he can call you back when he's off the phone with Mr. Fairbrother. You are aware there has been a merger and there is no more McKenzie Barber. Now what was your name again?"

Baxter repeated his name and left a telephone number. The phone rang again as soon as it was returned to the receiver.

"Joe?" A voice Baxter didn't recognize greeted him. "This is Pres Grey. I'm on the Metroliner with Mom. Can you hear me all right?"

There was some static, but Baxter could hear the voice of Ernie Grey's son clearly. "I'm very sorry about your Dad, Pres. It certainly must be a great loss to your family," Baxter responded.

"Thank you, Joe. Mother wants me to take charge of the funeral arrangements. I buried my Uncle Arthur two years ago and Paula Webber last year. I know that Toni has called and asked you to help on some matters, but I'm taking over from here on. It's the way Mother wants it. Do you understand?"

"Pres, I've just been innocently answering my phone on a Sunday morning. If the volume of calls continues, I may miss church," Baxter explained.

"Let me give you the details, Joe. Dad had a will. Certain parts regarding his personal estate have changed over the years, but there is a section in his will that has never been amended. That pertains to his funeral arrangements. Did he ever discuss this with you?"

The question baffled Baxter. It implied that he was some kind of close buddy to the former McKenzie Barber Chairman.

"No."

"My Dad wanted the service to be conducted in the Greystone Academy chapel. Then he is to be buried in the family plot next to his parents, sister, and brother at Franklin Farms Cemetery in Wynnwood. I know that Toni has called you and asked you to do certain things. Just ignore her instructions. For example, we have the IPCO Public Relations people working on the funeral announcement. That will suffice. They will make contact with the McKenzie Barber people and see that announcements are made."

"Pres," Baxter interjected. "There is no McKenzie Barber anymore. It merged with Robson Allen Harbridge. The firm is now called Robson Barber."

"Goodness. I hope that IPCO people have kept track of this. You might stand by your telephone this afternoon. There may be some things for you to help with. But just assume that I'm going to take charge of things from here on in."

"You just go ahead and do that, Pres. Good-bye," Baxter said hanging up the telephone.

Baxter located Rusty at his Apple Computer in the study. She was still wearing his tee shirt and had donned her glasses. There was a mug of coffee at her side. Baxter placed his hands on her shoulders.

"Don't touch me, I'm inputting market share data."

Baxter placed his mouth over Rusty's right nipple and kissed her through the tee shirt. She allowed him to linger for a minute and then pushed Baxter's hand away gently.

"You're out of control, Mister. Please let me get the rest of this page in and I'll take a break. I need to run market share." Rusty's hand guided Baxter's head back on her mouth and she ran her tongue in his ear. "Give me fifteen minutes, please."

They made late morning love through at least four separate successions of telephone rings. "My God," Rusty said in the shower. "We must be both sex-starved. I can't keep my hands off you."

"As I see it," Baxter said soaping Rusty's long body in the shower. "We simply get on well together."

"I'm going back on Monday for sure. Can we visit the Metropolitan and the Whitney? We can have an Art break," Rusty suggested.

Baxter shaved, dressed and returned to his phone mail which announced he had four messages.

"Joe Baxter, this is Symantha Dugan. I'm returning your call. I don't believe I can be of any help to you. I was terminated from McKenzie Barber in March 1991 and I'm also in litigation with the firm on claims of wrongful dismissal and sexual harassment. Good-bye and have a nice day."

Flipping onto the next message, Baxter heard Jack Pinker's voice. "Joe, this is Jack Pinker returning your call. Fitz heard from the IPCO PR person about an hour ago. They will have funeral announcement details over to my secretary, Ginny, first thing in the morning and she'll get out a firm-wide "E" mail first thing Monday morning. I called Richard Fairbrother and he was confident that there would be a Barber representative at the funeral. Charley Robson may want to come. I'm going to see that he's notified. It's good to know you're still out there somewhere, Joe. Gil Ranglinger tells me he's been trying to catch up with you since mid-December. As you know Gil's trying to sort out the merged organizations. I'd appreciate it if you could give Gil a call on Monday and get with him this week. I assure you, Joe. The Ernie Grey thing is being taken care of.

Pinker clicked off without a good-bye.

The third message was from Toni. Her voice seemed distinctly upset. "Joe, this is Toni. It appears that everything I tried to do was wrong and that Preston Grey will be bringing his extensive funeral experience to bear. Joe, I need someone with me. Millie is such a hateful person. I thought Preston was my friend, but he is obviously his mother's son. Can you come down to Philadelphia and help me see through this thing? Could you come this afternoon? I'm at 215-642-4000. Suite 2102."

The last message was from Andy Nickerson. "Joe, Andy here. Ernie Grey died on Saturday. Clyde and I are driving down for the funeral which is scheduled for Tuesday. Would you like a ride with us? Give us a call. 203-782-6121."

My goodness, Baxter observed. Andy Bourke Nickerson out of the blue. The passing of the old Chairman certainly relinked a lot of people. He had seen Andy last at Buzzsaw's farewell in October 1990. They had stood against the wall at the reception room fronting the main ballroom at the New York Hilton. Andy had been wearing a brown knit suit and appeared to have continued to gain weight. The room was only half filled and it was slightly after 12:30.

"Well, Andy, looks like the end of an era. 1984 to 1990 will be remembered as the Pritchard years."

"They were courageous years considering the shape McKenzie Barber was left in when Ernie retired," Andy had shot back. Baxter wondered how Andy's story would be altered for Tuesday's event.

27

"I have never walked so much in my life," Rusty observed as they crossed Fifth Avenue at 72nd Street. "Nor have I been so very thoughtfully indulged. I got a little miffed at you for lack of attention this morning when you were in the midst of all of those phone calls. But I'm over it now. You're really very mellow. Now tell me, were you and Ernie Grey very close?"

"Hardly. I had some exposure to him during his last term as Chairman. I also knew his second wife, Toni, pretty well. She had been a consultant at McKenzie Barber and Ernie left his wife to live with her and eventually married her. Now she's caught up in the dilemma of having Ernie's first wife, Millie, taking over the funeral arrangements?"

"How old is Ernie Grey's second wife?"

"Toni is in her mid-thirties."

"Have you ever slept with her?"

"God, no," Baxter responded.

"Is she attractive?"

"Toni's attractive in a sterile way. I'm not the lady's man you think I am, Rusty. I was completely faithful to my third wife during the five years of our marriage."

"How long were you two together?"

"Maybe seven years. We lived together a couple of years."

"Three wives is a lot of wives. When and if I marry again, it's the last time for me," Rusty commented. "Where are we going now?"

"I'm going to take you for a drink at the Sherry Netherland, then we're going to supper and we're concluding the evening by going back to the apartment and making love."

"There's a predictability about you that I'm beginning to appreciate. How would you take it if I stayed through Tuesday?"

28

Baxter maneuvered Rusty into the doorway of a closed store front and enjoyed a long kiss. When Baxter pulled away, Rusty leaned forward and began a new embrace. "We can have supper a little later if you'd like."

At the end of the evening, they enjoyed a brandy nightcap together nude in the Eames chair listening to Sondheim.

"I've never done anything like this before. I met this Joe Baxter for a drink on Friday night and shacked up with him through Tuesday. I am two days behind in writing up my Electronics Commerce Marketing study. The client is going to offer me a job after the report is delivered. The preparations and delivery of this report to CCCS may affect my coming in as a SVP over a VP. Now, I've just agreed to play hooky on Monday and Tuesday. You're like the Pied Piper, Mr. Baxter. Do you corrupt someone every Friday night? I've never had a weekend like this before?"

"I had one many years ago with a Paris Barber consultant. We had finished up a job in Paris and she corrupted me. I never believed I would match that weekend, but I think I'm there again with you," Baxter confessed.

"What's to become of us, Joe? Is all of this going to be over on Tuesday and go on to become a pleasant memory?"

"I'll have a lot of time after I go into the office on Wednesday to cut my deal. If you like, I'll come out for the weekend January 17-19 and stay with you in California. You, in turn, can come out and spend the weekend at my country place in upstate New York. We can go back and forth in two week intervals until we either get tired of each other, or want to make this a permanent relationship. Think about it."

"Is the often married Joe Baxter proposing to me?"

"The often married Joe Baxter is suggesting that we make every effort to continue the wonderful relationship we have struck up this weekend. The often married Mr. Baxter feels obligated to remind Ms. Collins that he is many years her senior."

"How old are you, Joe?"

"57. But I'm spry."

"You're two years younger than my father."

"We're a November/May relationship," Baxter estimated.

"I'd put myself in the July-going-on-August category. And then there's always the possibility that we may not like each other very much tomorrow night at this time."

"Then," Baxter said. "Let's always remember this minute. Just freeze you and me and the Eames chair in your mind. Snap a picture right now. Got it! Now store it! We will always have the picture of us snuggled up in the buff on the Eames chair."

"What will you do after you cut your deal on Wednesday?'

"I will promptly clean out my office and place my personal possessions in boxes. I will do this by myself or in the company of some of those security guys who wander around the office in cheap suits carrying beepers. I can sense that they have been eyeing me for the last six months. Security has been the one growth department of the old New York Office of McKenzie Barber. Then property exited, I will return to my Rusty-less apartment and begin to work on my history of McKenzie Barber. On Thursday, I will corral my good friend Beth Gold into a three martini lunch and review the entire literary project which I have tentatively titled *McKenzie Barber-The Rise and Fall of a Management Consulting Firm.* There's something about the title that is uncatchy. I'll work on it over time."

"You're serious about writing a book about McKenzie Barber?"

"It's either go off and be a consultant with some firm as a senior associate, or write a book about McKenzie Barber. I know that Robson Allen has some restrictive covenants about competing with them while you're drawing retirement. The spin-out human resources consulting firm that Dilger formed has a one year restriction for consultants who didn't join their buy-out group. I could write for a year, and then start consulting again. Besides, I believe I represent the one person in the world who could really write the book. That's what all of those scrap books and ring binders are about," Baxter confessed. "I've been rigorously collecting documents and clippings over the last few years. Sometimes on weekends I'll go through the files at 311 Park and Xerox Executive Office memoranda. My access card is still coded back to the days when I had the run of Executive Office, so I can go anywhere in the building. Those days are probably over with the Robson takeover. I have a lot of paper in boxes up at my country place. I just wish I would have begun saving papers from the time I was a consultant."

Rusty looked at Baxter quizzically. "You're serious about writing a McKenzie Barber book. I would think you would want to get on with your life rather than look back at it."

"I'm determined to write the McKenzie Barber book while it's fresh in my mind. Then when the book is done, I will get on with the rest of my life. If I'm terminated as expected this Wednesday, I expect that I will have the book completed by late fall 1993."

Rusty shook her head. "This certainly is a side of you that I hadn't expected. I was simply going to have a drink with Joe Baxter, a congenial senior partner of my firm, and now I find myself seduced by a closet archivist and historian. One week from tonight both of us will be history with McKenzie Barber. It's almost as if this were some kind of a farewell weekend. Next I have to ask myself. Will this thing with Joe Baxter ever be this good again?"

"We'll just have to see about that, won't we?" Baxter began kissing Rusty about her neck and shoulders and then on the hard nipples of her pointed breasts.

"I don't want this to ever end," Rusty groaned. "I just want to stay in this Eames chair for the rest of my life and let you touch me."

Monday started with a 7:30 call from Toni. Baxter had the answering machine on and checked his messages when he left the back bedroom shortly after eight o'clock.

"Joe, this is Toni. I'm about ready to go downstairs and meet Millie and Preston for breakfast. I had hoped that you would be here with me. When will you be coming to Philadelphia? My sister and her husband are here, but they're not much help in dealing with the Greys. They are determined to run the funeral arrangements. I'm just being pushed aside. Please call me, Joe. I'm at 215-782-6161. Suite 642."

The situation appeared to be a tar baby waiting for his touch. He would show up for the funeral services and that would be the end of it. Ernie Grey would be gone from his life, as would McKenzie Barber, and he could begin his history.

Rusty emerged from the bedroom shortly after ten.

"I shouldn't be here. My report is barely started and I don't have all the back-up I need to write the report. I should go back today." She picked up the OAG from Baxter's desk and began to pour through the pages for LA flights. "I never should have let myself get involved with you. My career's on the line."

"I'll get out of here for a while," Baxter offered. "If you're still here when I get back, I'll buy you dinner."

Baxter showered, shaved and put on a suit. Rusty emerged from the back bedroom where she had been working on her report.

"Are you angry with me? Last night was so wonderful, but I've got to get on with my life and career." Again she was clad only in one of Baxter's tee shirts. Rusty placed her hands on Baxter's shoulders and he could feel her breasts against his suit coat.

"Get your report done. I'll come back in the late afternoon. I understand. I'm in the consulting business too. I'm going by 311 Park Avenue to retrieve a few things in advance of my Wednesday final visitation."

They exchanged a light kiss and Baxter left the apartment. It was an overcast grey January day with the morning temperature in the mid thirties. Baxter decided to walk up Park Avenue. Robson Allen's offices were at 101 Park Avenue two blocks south of Grand Central. He walked into the lobby and studied the building directory.

Robson Allen occupied five of the upper floors and appeared to house the services functions in the basement level. They appeared to represent a mirror of the New York Office of McKenzie Barber. He hadn't thought about the London plane ride with Charley Robson for some time. It had been back in January 1988 in the start of the crazy period of his life that had started after Bridgette had left him.

Linda had insisted on seeing him off and had carefully packed Baxter. He was going to be gone a week beginning Sunday, January 10th, and was scheduled to return on the following Saturday. There was an international conference in Frankfurt, preceded by client briefings in London, and followed by a visit to Zurich, and concluded by client meetings in Paris. On the agenda was a Friday luncheon with the de Hartogue senior management which was to include the Baroness de Hartogue. The Paris office had arranged the luncheon among a full day of meetings with French clients who had US interests.

They settled into the first class lounge where Linda sipped a Coke while Baxter had a glass of champagne. Linda had spent most of the previous week trying to make amends for not making it back to him on New Year's Eve. She had come to his apartment at noon bringing a luncheon packed by the deli at the corner, a bottle of white wine, and a file folder which contained the action items related to the move to his new apartment. After they had covered the items on the list, Linda went upstairs and disappeared into the bathroom. She emerged wearing only a bathrobe padding down the steps in bare feet.

"Come," she said extending a hand to Baxter. "This is the last time we have to be together for a week."

Baxter watched Linda's reflection in the large glass mirror as she flipped through the pages of a *New Yorker*. She appeared to be an attractive, flawlessly groomed, conservative young woman who was young enough to be his older daughter. Three hours earlier she had been an aggressive sexual acrobat. It was now fifteen minutes before boarding. Two chairs down, Baxter recognized a familiar face that he couldn't identify by name. The man appeared to be in his late fifties. He stood up from his chair and looked around the room settling his eyes first on Baxter then on Linda. He then looked at his watch and walked across the room to refill his coffee cup. The man wore a dress shirt, open at the collar, a tweed sport coat, tassel loafers. Another man greeted him at the coffee urn and called him Charley. They stood in front of the coffee urn chatting amiably for a few minutes.

"Linda," Baxter said softly. "I believe that's Charley Robson of Robson Allen standing in front of the coffee urn."

"That man is the Chairman of Robson Allen? He certainly doesn't look like a Chairman. The man is a little shrimp."

"He's a founder shrimp. They're usually smaller than the shrimp who come after them," Baxter explained.

Linda accompanied Baxter to the gate and they exchanged a long kiss with her body rubbing against Baxter before leaving him at the rampway. Baxter turned to wave and found himself facing a grinning Charley Robson.

"With that kind of good-bye, fella, you're probably going to want to return on the next flight."

"She's a very encouraging friend," Baxter replied and led the path down the rampway to the first class section. He held 5B. Charley Robson held 5A.

The flight attendant noted their names as Robson and Baxter and took beverage orders. Charley Robson ordered an orange juice while Baxter continued with champagne. Each dropped their trays and produced file folders from their brief cases. Out of the corner of his eye, Baxter spied several black RAH folders. Nothing on Baxter's tray had a McKenzie Barber logo.

"That was quite a send-off you got at the gate," Charley Robson said raising his glass. "I haven't had one like that in a long time."

"Here's to send-offs and happy landings," Baxter said touching his champagne glass against Robson's orange juice glass.

"I take it that wasn't your daughter," Robson continued.

"She's too young to be my daughter."

"Known her long?"

"A while."

"Does she work for you?" Robson asked bluntly.

"No. And I don't beat my wife anymore either," Baxter answered.

Robson grinned. "Touché. My name's Charley Robson."

"Joe Baxter," Baxter said gripping the extended hand. "I should tell you right now that I'm with McKenzie Barber." Robson pushed his glasses up on his forehead and grinned again. "I always prefer to sit next to a potential client rather than a competitor on a transatlantic flight, but you'll just have to make do."

The flight attendant retrieved the glasses when the plane began to back away from the gate. Baxter adjusted his watch ahead to London time.

Once up in the air, Robson began to talk again. "And how's my old friend Ernie Grey doing?" he asked.

"I was at his Christmas Party a couple of weeks back. He appeared to be in mint condition."

"I assume he's doing better in the oil business than he was doing in the consulting business." Robson switched to Scotch when the flight attendant returned.

"Ernie's doing very well in the oil business," Baxter commented.

"People are always giving Ernie Grey things to do. John McKenzie made him Chairman of McKenzie Barber and now Cornelius VanderKelen has given Ernie the family oil company to run while he goes gallivanting around Latin America. Ernie Grey has fallen into it all his life. The rest of us have to had to scrap to make it, while Ernie simply coasted ahead."

"Ernie Grey ran McKenzie Barber very successfully for eighteen years. His last term was a bit of a test, but the firm is stronger than ever now," Baxter lied.

Robson nodded his head skeptically and laughed. "Good for McKenzie Barber." He took a sip of Scotch and looked Baxter over. "You must be twenty-five or thirty year man at McKenzie Barber. Right?"

"1967. I had a job in industry first," Baxter qualified himself.

"What do you do at McKenzie Barber?"

"I head the Executive Compensation practice."

"Alvardi's old job. When he came back, he mentioned a chap he wanted to bring with him. Was that you?"

"Frank never mentioned recruiting me to Robson Allen. I know that I certainly wasn't interested."

"Frank failed with us after we brought him back. He just didn't have the Robson Allen style of competitive energy. I suspect that he picked up some bad habits during his years at McKenzie Barber. Frank just didn't like to work that hard."

"I believe he brought that work ethic with him from Robson Allen."

Charley Robson slid his glasses down on his nose again. Baxter noted that Robson had a small wiry body, and an unusually large head.

"I have to confess, Joe, that the two firms were very similar in talent through the 1970's. We have pulled away in the US in the 1980's, but you're still way beyond our reach overseas. I should also announce to you that I'm stepping down after our March meeting. No Chairman Emeritus bullshit! I'm going effective March 21, 1988. This is my last European trip for Robson Allen Harbridge. You will note that I'm not traveling with a gaggle of young lieutenants. I'm going off by myself to personally say good-bye to our overseas Partners, managers, and professional staff. I'm going to thank them for their fine efforts in making our firm stronger, and then I'm going to remind them that they broke their covenant to me to eclipse Barber in Europe and the Middle East. As you probably know, we're having Barber for lunch in the Pacific Asia Basin."

Baxter nodded his head. Actually, the US McKenzie Barber Partners were poorly informed on the world-wide performance of the firm. There had been a succession of press blurbs about Robson Allen's Hong Kong and Singapore offices being involved in overseas consulting work.

"Now, Charley, are you the last remaining member of the founding Partners of Robson Allen?"

Charley Robson took a long sip of Scotch. "That's right, Joe. I am the last of the founders. Ab, Jason, and I started the business after we escaped from the Pentagon in December 1945. We had been at MIT together in the class of 42, and our draft board numbers were up. Jason had this uncle in Washington with heavy duty connections and he got wind of this new unit that was being formed with mathematicians. Jason graduated first in our class, Abner was second and I was third. We had a bunch of interviews and cut a deal to enlist as privates in the Army, go through basic training at Fort Dix, and then be assigned to this lab in Virginia. The work was challenging and we were identified as the 'whiz kids' because we could do all this mathematical modeling on top secret projects. They promoted us all to Sergeants after a year or so. We were all single, and Jason had enough trust money coming to fund an apartment for us." Charley Robson took another sip of Scotch. He appeared to be warming up to telling his story.

"That might have been the happiest days of my life. We were single, had the pick of the women who were left behind, and had all of these neat projects to perform. We did some projects with your outfit, FSO, and that's when I got the idea of forming a consulting firm. Jason wanted us to hire out as a team to some large corporation and Abner wanted to go back to MIT, get his doctorate and teach. A whole bunch of people offered us jobs. Your Mr. Mac offered Abner and me jobs, but believed that Jason would be better off going back to MIT. Mr. Mac wanted us to start at the bottom in kind of an apprentice program. We talked with some of the senior IE Partners at McKenzie Barber, and Ab and I concluded we had worked with smarter people in the Army. Jason was affronted when McKenzie Barber didn't offer him a job too. There we were in February 1946 living in New York off our mustering out pay and Jason's inheritance and getting bored. Over a couple of beers one night I outlined my plan to form our own consulting firm. I recommended that we go back to all of those corporations and say, 'Why don't you just rent our brains.' My name would be at the front because it was my idea and I would go out and get the business to keep us busy. We would be equal Partners, but I would be the Managing Partner."

Charley Robson took another sip of Scotch. His highball glass was now only a third full and he flagged the flight attendant for a refill.

"Well, I got us a bunch of work. We were early into modeling in the days before computers. We could do things that those old IEs from McKenzie Barber never dreamed of doing. We worked seven days a week for about six months before Abner came to me and pleaded with me to start hiring people. 'Charley' he said to me one morning. 'I'm working so hard, I can't screw anymore.' And that's when I figured it was time to add consulting staff fast. All of a sudden we had staff, facilities people, payrolls that had to be met, accounts payable and clients that didn't pay very fast. Abner and Jason wanted no part of that side of the business. They just wanted to run projects with a lot of smart people to help them. Their attitude was, 'Take care of it, Charley.' Pretty soon all I was doing was selling and administering and they were having all the fun."

"Mr. Mac tried to buy us twice. Once in 1949, and he took one last shot in the early fifties. Ernie Grey was his bag man then. The first time, Mr. Mac had his secretary call me and summon me to a breakfast meeting. I accepted like a docile little lamb. Did you ever meet Mr. Mac, Joe?"

"No. He had been retired many years before I joined the firm. I've seen pictures of him, of course."

"Well, the man had a commanding appearance and a seductive voice. He belonged to some downtown club that reserved a cozy corner for Mr. Mac's breakfasts, lunches and dinners. He knew all about us. He knew about me. Mr. Mac knew I was a Brooklyn second generation, Polish Jew who had gone to MIT on an Isaiah Broadbaker scholarship. He knew that Jason and Abner were from well placed Boston families, and that I was the business getter. He knew the jobs we had taken away from McKenzie Barber, and saw that we were doing things with a statistical design concept that his IE's couldn't touch. He proposed hiring our whole firm for a raise in pay and a signing bonus. I told him that Abner, Jason and I would have to come in as Partners, and we would expect that McKenzie Barber would pay us something for our firm."

"'Young man,' he said to me. 'My information has you at 29 years of age.' Actually I was 27 because I graduated from high school at 16 and I was 20 when I finished up at MIT. Mr. Mac shook his head and said, 'Mr. Robson, you're far too young to be a Partner with McKenzie Barber.' I look back at that overpowering old man and said, 'Then you had better recontact me when I'm old enough to be a Partner with McKenzie Barber. But we may be the larger firm by that time.' The old man just looked at me and said, 'Rubbish!' He went out and bought FSO the following year."

The flight attendant distributed menus and Charley Robson scanned the menu and began to talk again.

"Then Ernie Grey came into my life. He called me out of the blue sometime in the winter of 1953. He identified himself over the phone as Mr. McKenzie's assistant and invited me to a breakfast meeting with Mr. Mac. I told him that I was pretty busy and gave him a date some four weeks out. We were growing pretty fast, and were continuing to take work away from McKenzie Barber but it wasn't coming as easy as it had been. McKenzie Barber had been growing fresh talent after the war and was opening offices around the country. I had one of my people check out Ernie Grey. The information came back that Ernie Grey was some kind of HBS golden boy who had been a naval air ace in the Pacific and was married to some Philadelphia department store heiress. He had worked in consulting briefly and had been Mr. Mac's bag man for about three or four years."

"We met for breakfast in a private room at Mr. Mac's club. There was Mr. Mac in a tweedy brown suit wearing the brown hightops that he liked to wear in the winter months. He looked like someone out of 1910. And standing beside him in a dark navy Brooks Brothers suit was this striking young man who looked like Tyrone Power with an air about him that reminded me of all those self important young Pentagon naval officers I had grown to love during my Washington tour. Ernie looked me up and down and gave me a condescending look and a handshake to match."

"We sat down and began to talk a little business. I told them that our business was sensational, which incidentally, was true. Mr. Mac said that McKenzie Barber's US business was excellent, but that he and Mr. Grey had been required to spend a good deal of time in London over the past two years in order to straighten out Barber. That was the way Mr. Mac was. Opinionated as hell, but direct. There was no bullshit to the man! He was always professionally candid. He went on for a few minutes talking about the European and UK economies and Barber's steady decline since the end of the war. Ernie Grey looked at him as if he were telling family secrets to a total stranger."

"Mr. Mac lectured the both of us on the global future of management consulting. Ernie Grey had heard the lecture before, but it was new to me and the old man was thrilling. He was brilliant that morning. Mr. Mac predicted the sixties and seventies flawlessly. He was a man with formidable wisdom and vision. I never forgot what he said that morning about the emerging world-wide market for management consulting services. Then when Mr. Mac finished his little speech, we ordered and Mr. Mac announced that Mr. Grey had a few things to say."

"Ernie began with what he probably considered were flattering comments about Robson Allen. He had made a careful study of our growth over the years since 1946. Here it comes, I told myself. McKenzie Barber is going to make a pitch for the firm we have built, and Mr. Mac is having this young man present the deal. Looking back, it always angered me. This kind of discussion should have been held between senior partners. I hadn't brought a bag man. Ernie Grey complimented Robson Allen on our growth and stability over our seven year firm life. When he stated that our business strategy had been to date efficient, effective and productive in his typical Ernie Grey condescending manner, I was ready to say, 'And what the hell have you been doing all these years, pussycat? Getting coffee for your boss?' But I held my tongue."

"It was Ernie's conclusion, and Mr. Mac's too, that Robson Allen had gone about as far as it could go under our leadership. It was clearly time to fold Robson Allen under the McKenzie Barber umbrella. The three founding Partners would be direct admission Partners at McKenzie Barber and there would be a handsome earn-out opportunity for all of us."

"That was before the word 'organizational culture' had entered the business communications lexicon. There was no cultural fit for our firm with this old line IE firm trying to come grips with the 1950's. I told them that I regarded McKenzie Barber as part of the past of management consulting, and that Robson Allen represented the future. 'Rubbish!' the old man snorted back. 'Mr. Robson, what you have accomplished is admirable, but you are simply a fly speck in the history of management consulting. Whatever you have the capacity to accomplish you will achieve more quickly on a grander scale with McKenzie Barber!'"

"Ernie then went on to provide an overview of McKenzie Barber's expansion plans in the US and world-wide growth plans. He had obviously done it before and he was good at it. I asked Mr. Mac why he had bought FSO. It was the only identifiable acquisition McKenzie Barber had ever made."

"'We made that acquisition, young man, because the government wanted a responsible party to take over the management of FSO. It was in serious financial trouble in the spring of 1950. Shortly after the Korean War began in June 1950, there was a surge of new contracts, and the business has been stabilized. FSO does not represent a long term strategic holding for McKenzie Barber. As soon as Mr. Grey and I have completed our reorganization of the Barber side of our firm, Mr. Grey will proceed on the sale of FSO to a qualified buyer. The Partners of McKenzie Barber will then have fulfilled their obligation to the US government.'"

"Then Ernie started in about coming over and spending some time at Robson Allen. All I could think of was that these guys weren't much on foreplay. I asked Ernie Grey, 'Have you ever been a consultant, Ernie?' He said something about being a consulting for a year or two and then taking on his current assignment. 'Well,' I turned and said to Mr. Mac, 'If someone from McKenzie Barber is going to come around and visit us, I would prefer a well experienced consulting partner.'"

"'Mr. Grey is my designated emissary in these kinds of discussions.' And I said, 'I'll certainly entertain calling Mr. Grey when I believe discussions are merited.' Then we broke off breakfast and went on our way. Ernie Grey called me periodically every six months and asked me how things were. I told him they were sensational and finally he quit calling when he was named Senior Partner. We started to send Ernie a Christmas card every year."

Charley Robson ordered the haddock while Baxter selected the airplane veal. Charley Robson began to talk again when the salads were served.

"Ernie sure got a snoot full of publicity that summer he split from his wife. Did he finally marry that consultant he was living with?"

"Yes, and they seem quite well matched," Baxter responded. "Toni's a very attractive, intelligent young woman and gives a good holiday party."

"I've never had much luck with wives," Robson said. "They've had pretty good luck with me though. I was paying three sets of alimony for a while, but the second one got remarried. How many times have you been married, Joe?"

Baxter held up three fingers. Robson nodded his head knowingly. "Typical consultant marital patterns. Getting married is something I'm never going to do again. Nobody gets married anymore. I mingle with our young consultants from time to time, and they're all living together. Are you going to do anything with that little lady who saw you off?"

"Not anything more than I'm doing right now," Baxter answered:

"Did you ever meet Ernie Grey's wife?" Robson asked.

"Once or twice."

"I used to see her around at functions. I thought she was the perfect CEO wife. She was gracious, self confident, outgoing, and had a hell of a sense of humor. I guess she had to have one having been married to Ernie all those years. What did this second little lady have that the first one didn't have?"

"I have no idea," Baxter obfuscated.

"I haven't had much luck with wives. I take you haven't either, Joe."

"They're not with me anymore and I'm not paying alimony to any of them," Baxter replied.

"I'm doing two. I'm good at negotiating in business, and very poor at negotiating in post-marital matters. My reasons for marrying were generally dictated by emotions emanating from below my belt buckle. How about you?"

"The first time the lady was pregnant, and the next two times I thought I was in love," Baxter assessed.

"Hell, I always thought I was in love. Two of my wives were from Robson Allen. How many have you married from McKenzie Barber."

"Not one."

"How about the young lady who saw you off tonight? Was she with McKenzie Barber?"

"No, she's a Robson Allen consultant."

Charley Robson guffawed. "Maybe that's my problem. I should have taken up with McKenzie Barber women consultants." Salads were taken away and replaced by entrees, and wine flowed.

"What ever happened to Allen and Harbridge?" Baxter inquired.

"They're retired. They were a lot smarter than I was. They let me take the lead and they sat back and did what they wanted to. Jason went first. He left in 1971 after twenty-five years, and now serves on the boards of a number of high tech companies around the Boston 128 beltway. He's made some good investments and hit a couple of home-runs. Abner became the firm's computer guru. He took us way out ahead of McKenzie Barber in the information technology area. Abner attracted and built the stars that we have in information technology. He stayed in the background and orchestrated. Abner left in January 1976. I went to his New Year's Eve party with my second wife. Jason guided me into his study around 10:30 that night. 'Charley,' he said. 'Thirty years is enough. I'm getting out. I've got good people behind me. We're doing well. You can pay me out over ten years. But I want to get out. I planned to give this business five years and I've stayed thirty. It's time to get out.' So we worked it out."

"What's he doing now?" Baxter asked.

"He's dead. Jason knew he was dying of cancer when he told me he wanted to get out. So there I was alone. But in reality, I had been alone a long time. I had been running the firm since we started in 1946. We had good people coming up who wanted to be assured of a future, and sure as hell we were going to pass McKenzie Barber in the US during the 1980's. I was the one who personally brought along Al Carmichael and Brian Philbrick as my successor leadership. My succession was well planned, orchestrated, and executed, which is one hell of a lot more than I can say for the mess Ernie left behind in a contested election. We never would have elected a Buzzsaw Pritchard as Chairman. I also thought that Hamilton Burke was a smart ass. Your Partners had lousy choices. Burke was a loose cannon, but would have been better than Pritchard. Your business strategy in the US is dumb, and plays right into our hands."

"The US firm has struck off down some new roads, but the payout should be considerable for us three years out," Baxter responded positively masking his considerable personal doubt.

Robson simply grinned and picked at his salad in silence until the flight attendant served the entrees.

"Bon appetit," Baxter said, with a wave of his wine glass. Robson nodded his head and appeared to be skim reading through a sheaf of papers with the Robson Allen log in the corner. The papers were organized into columns of numbers and tables. Robson had produced a yellow highlighter pen from an inside pocket and began to make marks and notations on the papers while he picked at his entree with his fork. After the entree had been cleared, Robson produced a notebook computer from his brief case. It was the first notebook computer Baxter had ever seen. Robson noted the interest and began talking again.

"This is an advance model of a notebook computer. Some people at IBM gave me this to work with. Five years from now everybody will be carrying a notebook computer in their briefcase. We're way ahead of McKenzie Barber in systems and computer technology. That's how we left you in the dust. McKenzie Barber stayed too long in strategy and back office industrial engineering and didn't move quickly enough into technology. We moved aggressively into technology and became the consulting firm of choice to clients with technology issues. Then we married technology to business strategy, and McKenzie Barber was history. You tried to buy talent while we developed and nurtured it."

"I can't help but recall that Robson Allen, in the mid 1980's, was aggressively bidding for the same acquisitions McKenzie Barber was pursuing," Baxter countered.

"We looked at them, but no offer was ever made. McKenzie Barber made the offers and overpaid every time. You chewed up resources acquiring untested consulting firms while we reinvested in our own business. I expected that your Partners would take Ernie Grey to task sooner or later. And they did when they rejected his protégé as Chairman. Maybe he's better at running an oil company."

"Have you ever met Hamilton Burke?" Baxter asked.

"Several times. I met him socially for the first time at some Historical Society black tie dinner up at the VanderKelen estate. He was condescendingly cocky, and had this icy French babe with him. I remember talking to Ernie that night. He was hanging around with Cornie

VanderKelen, and I guess that he was in board talks back then. I ran into Burke a couple of times on planes like this, but never shared a seat with him. He'd always come over and greet me cordially as one statesman to another. I couldn't help but feel though, that Burke regarded me as a third world country. Then I had a couple of meetings with Burke after he had resigned from McKenzie Barber. I assume you knew Burke."

"I worked for him on a couple of projects," Baxter answered.

"Burke wanted me to hire him as Chairman of Robson Allen Europe. He called me one week after he had resigned. We agreed to meet in Paris." Robson signaled the passing flight attendant to refill his wine glass.

"I met him, maybe six weeks later, in his suite at the George V. Later, I found out that the suite belonged to his wife's company. Burke had no sooner poured coffee when he announced, 'Charley I am prepared to come to Robson Allen under the following conditions.' I sat there and asked myself, 'Who in the hell has invited you, Burke?' But I thought I'd hear him out. I knew I didn't want him making acquisitions. 'These are my conditions, Charley' he said. 'I want to come as Chairman of Robson Allen Europe. I would expect to be on the Robson Allen board. I would live in Paris, but commute to London. I will work for one dollar during 1985, but would expect to be paid as the second ranking officer of Robson Allen for 1986. When it's agreed that I'm performing to your expectations, I would like to be regarded as a possible and logical successor. You were born in 1922. I was born in 1937. I'm certain that I can bring Robson Allen into a fully competitive stance with Barber within a three year time horizon.'"

"There I am sitting in this guy's George V suite and he's announcing that he is willing to take over Europe for Robson Allen and wants to succeed me as Chairman in the firm I built. The only upside I can see is that he's willing to work for a buck the first year. I looked at him and said something like, 'Look, Ham, I'm very flattered that you would consider Robson Allen. I barely know who you are. You certainly aren't that well known in the marketplace. All I know is that you were Ernie Grey's number two, and your Partners didn't elect you as his successor. Tell me about yourself.'"

"All I had to do for the next forty-five minutes was sit back and listen. The man was one of the most splendid orators I ever heard, and I've listened to the best. Burke has the most melodic, seductive voice I've ever heard. The man clearly has a persuasive command of the language. He's like an

English gentleman who grew up in the South. I was impressed. We must have talked for two hours after he finished with his oral history of Hamilton Burke. I told him I needed some time to think over our discussion. We agreed to meet in New York in mid-December, and he agreed to send me a CV. Burke really started me thinking. I had some good senior leadership behind me, but I wasn't sure. This guy could give me another option. I decided to have my people check him out. What I found out was not good."

"Did you meet him again in December?" Baxter asked.

"Of course. And I squeezed enormous competitive intelligence out of him. I learned where every wart and weakness was at McKenzie Barber, and all it cost me was a few ounces of insincerity and the price of a dinner in a private room at my club. I wrote him a very nice note in January and said our timing was not good."

"What did you find out about Burke that dissuaded you?" Baxter probed.

"You'll have to excuse me, Joe. I believe it's time for me to visit the washroom and brush my teeth."

Baxter unbuckled his seat belt and stood in the aisle while the Chairman of Robson Allen Harbridge squeezed by him. He was small, wiry, and looked his sixty or so years. He carried a shaving bag with him.

Burke again! He had altered Baxter's life and cast him in the place he occupied in the world. His only escape route was through Harwell Management.

There was little further conversation with Charley Robson during the remainder of the flight. He returned in ten minutes, smiled at Baxter, snapped off his reading light and announced that he was going to try to get some sleep. Baxter put on his head set and slipped off to sleep listening to Beethoven's Ode to Joy. He dreamed for a while of Dominique and was making love to her when he awakened to the muffled sounds of the flight attendants serving the breakfast snack. Charley Robson slept peacefully and awoke thirty minutes before landing. He shook hands with Baxter as they departed from the plane. Nothing more was said about McKenzie Barber or Burke.

Charley Robson had stepped down in the Spring of 1988, and his successor had been Alan Carmichael, a man in his early 50's who was now going to be the Chairman of the combined firms. The last year had been a blur for Baxter. Where under Burke, Baxter had been close to the inner circle of McKenzie Barber, he was now on the outer rim of understanding. The space at 101 Park Avenue would have to be combined with 311 Park Avenue. The signs on the building directory remained intact. What would it look like a week from now?

Baxter stayed away all day to allow Rusty to work on her report. He walked up to the Whitney and roamed through a French Impressionist exhibition. All through his McKenzie Barber career, he had been early into the office and one of the last to leave. Now it was the last place he wanted to be. Two days from today it would be all over. He would keep his appointment with Dr. Gilbert Ranglinger, and walk out the door for the last time with his severance and settlement in hand.

Baxter had left the apartment with an empty brief case. He had a second briefcase in his office, and assumed that he could clean his office of any critical materials today. It was the first Monday in January, a time when the old McKenzie Barber typically bounced back with vigor to attack the marketplace. On this day the area around his office on the 30th floor seemed very quiet. He had been moved in the Fall of 1990 after Monica and Linda had resigned. Mrs. Bunker had been retired at the same time, and Baxter now shared a secretary with a Partner in the Benefits practice. She was an Italian lady named Rose Marie who lived in Mount Vernon. Rose Marie had been the secretary of Ray MacGruder, a Benefits Partner, and had received the additional assignment of Baxter and his shrunken practice. She generally placed the Benefits correspondence ahead of the Executive Compensation practice. She was a fortyish woman with dyed black hair who wore dangling earrings and chewed gum on the sly.

"Hi stranger," she greeted Baxter. "Are you ever coming back to work?"

"I'm nearly through with my vacation time, Rose Marie. I was going to come in tomorrow, but as you may be aware, Ernie Grey died and his funeral is on Tuesday in Philadelphia."

"Who's Ernie Grey? Was he a consultant here?" Rose Marie asked.

"He was the Senior Partner and Chairman of McKenzie Barber from 1960 until 1984."

"I don't know the name. I didn't come to McKenzie Barber until 1985. The only Chairman I can remember were Mr. Pritchard, and now Mr. Fitzgerald. Now we have a new Chairman named Mr. Carmichael and the McKenzie is going from our name. All the support people are scheduled for training on video conference next week. There was a lady who came by to see you today. Her name is Brenda, and she said that she was Dr. Ranglinger's administrative assistant. She asked me to call her the minute I saw you in the office. She said it was an emergency."

"Call her back, Rose Marie, and tell Brenda that I will be by to see Dr. Ranglinger at 9:30 on Wednesday. I have some personal matters to attend to and must serve a pall bearer at Mr. Grey's funeral on Tuesday."

"What kind of a Doctor is Dr. Ranglinger?" Rose Marie inquired.

"I believe he is a Proctologist," Baxter said, brushing by Rose Marie into his office.

Baxter maintained certain strategic files in his office. He had discs which held data files and significant report drafts. He was able to cram the last five years of his work into his brief case. Before 1987, he had to rely on hard copy. He piled client reports into the large briefcase that he kept in the chair well of his desk. The final report squeezed into the brief case was Pennsylvania Steel. On Wednesday, he would be certainly accompanied by someone from Security. On his credenza were pictures of Joel and Muffin. He decided to leave them for his official departure on Wednesday. The light on Baxter's telephone indicating he had calls waiting. He picked up the phone, but decided to ignore the phone mail and called Beth Gold instead.

"This is 212-288-9671. I can't come to the phone right now. Leave your name and number at the sound of the multiple beeps and I'll return your call." Beth's voice sounded very sexy to Baxter.

"This is an obscene phone call," Baxter said. "I'd like to buy you lunch on Wednesday." He knew that Beth liked to play possum on incoming phone calls.

Beth's voice cut in. "Joe, I'm having lunch with Stephany on Wednesday. You're welcome to join us, and it's good to hear from you."

"And where are you having lunch?"

"The Giaconda Smile on 51st between 8th and 9th. It's in the Theatre district, but remarkably good in spite of its location. Stephany could use some cheering up. She's been unemployed now for fourteen months."

"How's your book coming?"

"Slowly. Everything goes slowly now. According to my agent, I'm a writer of declining stature."

"Sounds like you should change agents."

"I've had three in the last five years. I better stay with this one. He's competent, but brutally honest."

"A wonderful combination, Beth."

"And how are you doing? I read that Ernie Grey died roller blading. That was my laugh for the day. Are you okay in this merger with Robson Allen?"

"We'll talk about it on Wednesday, Beth."

"Joe, I'm very glad you called. Now be damned sure you show up on Wednesday. Stephany's unemployed and my stature is declining. We're going to need someone to pay the check."

"I'll be there oneish."

"We won't order without you. Is there anything special about Wednesday?"

"It's likely to be my last day with McKenzie Barber."

"Then the next day will be the first day of something else, Joe dear. Stephany, you and I are indestructible. I'm going back to work now until I receive my next obscene phone call."

Beth clicked off and Baxter scanned the office for anything additional to take with him.

Beth had turned out to be a loyal friend over the past few years. She had been especially helpful and comforting during Joel's time in the hospice, his eventual death, and through the funeral services. Linda was gone by then, and Baxter had leaned heavily on Beth to get him through. Forty years had elapsed since that Christmas in Iron Creek. What an innocent he had been at the time! He had no idea then that so much of his life was to become entwined with the rise and fall of a single organization of people.

Rusty was on the phone when Baxter returned to the apartment.

"No, no, Maureen. That's the wrong file. I'm leaving on a 10:30 tomorrow morning flight which will put me in shortly after one. Line up a word processor from the report section who can work until eight tomorrow night, and fax me those graphics from the other reports. Don't forget to fax me the executive summaries from West Coast Data and California Credit Services reports. That's a fax number in a private home where I have been staying in New York. Call this number for confirmation just after you've faxed."

"You could grab a late evening flight at 9:30 or so and land in LA shortly before midnight," Baxter suggested.

"I'll go in the morning when I'm fresh. I've been thinking about you today and how wonderful this weekend might have been if I hadn't had this report and my career change hanging over my head." Rusty extended her hand to Baxter which he first clasped and then kissed. "I need another hour or so to finish up. Then I can get gussied up and you can take me to a snazzy restaurant, and we'll celebrate our last night in New York together. We can complete the evening listening to one of your Eames chair concerts. What I don't get done tonight, I can finish in the morning. I assume if I leave at nine, I can make a 10:30 JFK flight. Now here comes my fax."

Later, when Rusty was dressing for dinner, Baxter read through the first draft of Rusty's report. It had a great many information gaps and he estimated that it was about one-third done. Rusty had placed herself in an exposed position by staying over. Over dinner they talked about their future together.

"I called a resort place up in Big Sur and made a reservation for us the weekend of January 25, 26, and 27. Let's see if what we've had together these four days in New York can translate out to California. Then I'll come East two weekends later in mid-February. Maybe you want to take some time off and spend a week or so with me in LA. As you have found out, I'm very grouchy in the morning, but very affectionate in the evening. You seem to be very even-tempered and cynically cheerful."

"And I'm twenty years older than you," Baxter reminded her.

"That's bothering you?"

"It hasn't so far. Let's plan ahead, but not too far ahead."

"Do you expect something to happen to you? Do you have a terminal disease that you haven't told me about?"

"I feel I'm at the end of something and I can't see a beginning right now. It's hard to plan ahead when you can't see a future."

"And what will you do after your Wednesday meeting with the mysterious Dr. Ranglinger?" Rusty asked.

"I'm going to have an outrageous multi-martini lunch with Beth and her friend Stephany, go home, sleep it off, and drive up to my country place where I will stay until Monday morning. By the time I get back to New York, I expect to have a clear vision for the next 57 years of my life."

Baxter selected a blue pinstriped suit, a white button-down broadcloth shirt, wine colored braces, and a burgundy club tie to wear to the funeral. Rusty was out of her shower wearing only a towel around her head as she packed her bag.

"I need to borrow a bag, Joe. I'm leaving with far more things than I brought out. You can reclaim it when we get together in Big Sur two weeks from now."

Baxter sat on a chair and watched Rusty carefully fold clothes and pack them standing in the nude. He thought back to that morning in Paris when Dominique had packed him. New York cab drivers lacked the romantic sensitivity of Paris taxi drivers, he concluded. Rusty was a rangy woman with long legs and a good mind. The three days he had been with her were about as good as any Baxter had ever spent with a woman. How many more like her were likely to drift into his life?"

"I'll order you a car for JFK from my car service," Baxter said rising up from his chair "I would suggest nine o'clock if you can be ready."

Rusty caught his arm at the doorway. "First kiss me. I don't have any lipstick on." It was a long kiss and embrace featuring a naked body pressed close to a blue winter suit. Baxter's watch reported 8:25.

Rusty was dressed in her green suit with matching pumps when Baxter placed her coat on her shoulders at 8:50.

"Should you have the driver drop you first?" Rusty asked when they reached the lobby.

"I'll take a cab. I don't want you to get caught in cross town traffic. You might miss that JFK flight."

"There's always one more flight. Would you like me to come to Philadelphia with you?" she asked as they paused in front of the revolving door.

"It's time for us to take a break. We'll pick up things in Big Sur on the 25th, 26th, and 27th. You've got to get me the details. It's time for you to pick up your career again," he said.

"Why are you always so damned sensible?" They kissed at the sidewalk and Baxter helped the driver load the bags. Rusty rolled down the rear window as Baxter stood beside the Sedan. "You be damned careful how you use that Eames chair while I'm gone," she called out and she waved from the back window of the car. Baxter watched them make the turn at 35th Street and then waved down a cab for Penn Station. It was time to say good-bye to Ernie Grey.

The Metroliner ride to the 30th Street station in Philadelphia consumes approximately one hour and ten minutes. Baxter would arrive approximately ten minutes to eleven, take a cab to Toni's hotel, and presumably travel with the Alters by limousine to the Greystone Academy Chapel for the service. Then there would be another limousine ride to the Grey family plot for the internment. The internment would be followed by refreshments at a place called the Schuykill Club. Baxter assumed that he could safely plan on a train back to Penn Station by half-past eight, and that he would return to his empty apartment by ten PM.

He produced the *New York Times* obituary from his inside jacket pocket after he had settled in his club car seat. The copy had obviously been based on material from the IPCO communications people.

ERNIE GREY, 70, RETIRED CHAIRMAN OF INTERNATIONAL PETROLEUM COMPANY

Ernest Grey II, who retired as Chairman and Chief Executive Officer of International Petroleum Company (IPCO), died on Saturday in Naples, Florida, in a roller blading accident. Mr. Grey had retired from IPCO following the December board of Director's Meeting.

Mr. Grey was a native of suburban Philadelphia, where five generations of the Grey family were shareholders and Chief Executives of the Pennsylvania National Bank. He graduated from Greystone Academy, the University of Pennsylvania, and the Harvard Business School. Mr. Grey interrupted his undergraduate college years when he enlisted in the US Navy in December 1941. He completed cadet training and was assigned immediately to the Pacific War Theatre where he distinguished himself as a fighter pilot in the Battle of Midway and the Battle of the Coral Sea. Mr. Grey flew over fifty missions and was credited with shooting down twenty-one Japanese planes. He returned to the US as a flight instructor in Pensacola in the summer of 1944, and was discharged as a Lieutenant Commander in 1945.

Mr. Grey joined McKenzie Barber, an international management consulting firm, following graduation from the Harvard Business School. He was singled out early in his McKenzie Barber consulting career by John McKenzie, the firm's founder, and served as a special assistant to the Senior Partner. Mr. Grey succeeded Mr. McKenzie in 1960 upon his retirement, and served as Chairman of the consulting firm until his retirement in 1984.

He was invited by the late Cornelius VanderKelen to join the IPCO Board of Directors in 1979 and succeed Mr. VanderKelen as Chairman in 1985 when the latter accepted a Presidential appointment on a special mission to Latin America. Mr. VanderKelen then served in a succession of Executive branch appointments and left Mr. Grey behind to serve as the Chairman and Chief Executive Officer of IPCO.

Jack Donohue, IPCO, Chief Executive Officer and successor to Grey, hailed Ernie Grey as a "man who had distinguished himself in several walks of life. Ernie was a war hero, he made important contributions to the profession of management consulting, and served as Chairman of his firm for twenty-four years. Ernie capped his career through his successful leadership of IPCO through a period of international dissonance. He retired from IPCO leaving behind a clear vision for the future and well planned executive succession." In addition to Mr. Grey's service with McKenzie Barber and IPCO, he served on the Board of the Pennsylvania National Bank until mid-1991 when the bank was acquired by Bank West. Lastly, Mr. Grey served as Chairman of the board of Trustees of Greystone Academy.

Mr. Grey was married in 1948 to Millicent Stockbridge of Philadelphia. This marriage ended in divorce in 1985, and he was remarried to Antonio Alter, a former McKenzie Barber management consultant. Mr. Grey is survived by his wife, a daughter, Kathleen Grey of New York, and a son, Prescott Grey III of Greenwich, Connecticut. Funeral services will be at the Greystone Academy Chapel at 2 PM on Tuesday, January 6th.

Baxter read through the obituary twice. They had left out Paul Reynolds, the man who had actually succeeded John McKenzie and was the forgotten Senior Partner. Calling Toni a consultant was a bit of a stretch, and the picture of Ernie Grey which accompanied the obituary appeared to be the same picture McKenzie Barber had used in firm publications at the time Baxter had joined the firm in 1967. Today would be the long good-bye for Ernie Grey. The train lurched forward and Baxter placed his head on the head rest and closed his eyes. When was the last time he had gone to a grand scale funeral? The answer was Leon Harwell's internment.

Baxter and Harwell had begun discussions about Harwell Management in the last week of January in 1988 after Baxter had returned from Europe. They met for breakfast in a private room at the Gotham Club. Leon Harwell appeared tanned, but his eyes seem fatigued. Baxter briefed him on the five assignments being conducted for Harwell's board committees. He nodded his head in acknowledgment and picked at his scrambled eggs as Baxter highlighted the progress of the work.

"Looks like you're on top of things as usual, Joe," Harwell commented. Baxter braced himself for Harwell's customary peppery questions but none came.

"How was your European trip?" Harwell asked.

"It was cold and wet. I concluded my visit with a management compensation briefing for the de Hartogue holding company senior human resources people."

"Was the Baroness in attendance?"

"It was posed to me that the Baroness de Hartogue would attend the briefing if she could fit it into her schedule. Apparently she could not."

"The de Hartogues are going to make a great deal of money on the Hortense Foods buyout. It appears that the management group has their financing arranged, and we should close by the end of February. We made a good deal of money along with the de Hartogue interests. The Baroness's probably out trying to buy something else so that she can provide a CEO job for her boyfriend, Hamilton Burke."

"Burke?" Baxter questioned. Burke again! Burke and Dominique!

"I received that information from Hakim. He's close to all of the transaction gossip. I never was interested in who was sleeping with whom. I wanted to know whether a company could sustain their earnings level. Now I understand that Ernie had a chat with you about coming over to Harwell Management. You have had better than a month to think it over. Are you interested?"

"It's not clear to me, Leon, as to what I'd be responsible for at Harwell Management," Baxter probed. Actually he had thought quite a bit about Harwell management over the past four weeks. He had also closed off discussions with Alvardi.

"You would work for me as kind of a general manager. I'd want you to look after things for me. I don't want to make you a president, but I could call you executive vice president and general manager."

"Who would report to me?"

"Everyone except me. Ned, Dan, Hakim, and everyone would report through you to me. If something should happen to me, you would hold things together until Spencer is ready to take over. You know more about Harwell Management than any outsider. If something were to happen to me tomorrow, Harwell Management would be in Hakim Selim's hands. I need someone to counter-balance Hakim. I believe you could accomplish this. I've given you the general mission of the position. You go write yourself a job description and a contract, and we'll meet again in two or three weeks."

"Ernie and I talked about compensation. Did he share that part of our conversation with you?" Baxter continued his probes.

"He mentioned that you wanted me to entertain $500,000 a year and some kind of bonus. I find that a little rich for my blood, Joe. We're paying Selim quite a bit of money, and for now he's contributing a great deal. He likes to take risks and with risks comes losses. I would like you to start around $400,000. I would expect that we will have to fund an accelerated retirement benefit for you to work until you reach a retirement age. Those funds will have to come from somewhere. What you give up in direct compensation will be made up in deferred income. Also, I would have no objection if you were to do some occasional consulting on the side, unless it started to require an excessive amount of your time."

"Have you discussed this position with your family or Harwell Management?"

"No. I want our arrangements confirmed and I will announce your appointment as a fait accompli."

"What do you anticipate will be their reaction?" Baxter asked.

"They will be outraged. It may be unpleasant for a year or two, but then it will settle down once when they recognize they're stuck with you."

"The job sounds high risk to me, Leon."

Harwell shook his head. "Nothing high risk at all if we develop an iron clad employment agreement for you. You will have far more security with Harwell Management than you have today with McKenzie Barber. Ernie verified that for me. He told me that meeting the retirement vesting schedule is likely to be very critical for you. When will you vest?"

"On September 4, 1988, I will have twenty-one years service and I will be 53 years old. That will equal 74 exceeding the rule of 73. It also means that I will discount my normal retirement by 20%. Harwell Management should be prepared to make up the difference, and set aside an additional amount for enhanced retirement benefits. I would also require a minimum term employment agreement of ten years duration," Baxter negotiated.

"Put your terms on paper, Joe. I'll review them and get our outside counsel involved when we're ready for a final draft. We should plan on you starting with us in mid-September."

"Leon," Baxter responded. "I have to think long and hard about making this move. I'm very flattered that you would consider me for this position. I've treasured our consulting relationship over the years. I am prepared to hold earnest discussions with you relative to coming to Harwell Management. I must tell you, however, that I'm not certain that coming to Harwell Management would be in my best career interests. We both must give the matter considerable sensitive and constructive thinking."

Leon Harwell folded his napkin neatly and placed it on top of his plate indicating that their discussion has been completed. "I should tell you Joe, that I'm resigning from all of my boards after the spring meetings. Those projects you're working on now are likely to be the last that I will be in a position to refer to you."

"You're cutting back, Leon?"

"I've had my run at board service, and my fill at creating incentives that would motivate management to perform for the shareholders. My time as a stock picker is past. The future belongs to the market opportunist Selims of the world. I need someone like you to provide oversight until Spencer is ready. I would also like to spend more time with Mrs. Harwell." They paused out on the street in front of the club.

"Please move this matter along, Joe," Harwell cautioned Baxter. "I have some other names to consider, but you are my first choice."

"I understand, sir," Baxter replied. They shook hands and Harwell headed for Park Avenue, while Baxter walked briskly to Lexington Avenue. It was obvious to Baxter. Harwell was dying, and this represented Baxter's prime opportunity to escape from the ugly McKenzie Barber world of Buzzsaw Pritchard, Clyde Nickerson, and Brett Williamson left behind by Ernie Grey.

It wasn't easy for Baxter to move matters along in the pre-spring months of 1988. His practice was busy. He was involved in divorce negotiations that had turned ugly, and he allowed himself to be drawn into an affair with one of his staff consultants. Baxter felt pulled in all directions.

McKenzie Barber had been engaged by Planters & Commerce Bank following a succession of presentations which included a final presentation to the Compensation Committee of the board of Directors. Harry Devonshire's transfer to the Atlanta office was announced in February, and Harry began immediately to lobby for the work to be an Atlanta Office engagement with Baxter serving as an advisor.

Harley Dimon called Baxter the day after it was announced the McKenzie Barber had been selected. Baxter had answered his phone to "Joe, one moment for Harley Dimon, the Managing Partner of McKenzie barber, Atlanta." It was a new voice with a crisp Southern lilt to her voice. Baxter waited for nearly thirty seconds while he pondered a sassy response.

"Joe! Harley!" A voice finally came over the phone line.

"Is this the Harley Dimon who's the managing Partner of the Atlanta Office of McKenzie Barber?"

"None other."

"That's good. I do business with another Harley Dimon in Brinker's Falls, New York. He's a taxidermist. He's been handling a succession of raccoon stuffing's for me. That's real smart of you to have her announce exactly who you are to folks you call up." There was silence on the other end of the line. Then Harry continued in a very serious voice.

"There are several items I need to discuss with you, Joe. First, I was very pleased to learn that we had won the Planters & Commerce executive compensation work. I was more than a little disappointed though, when I had to learn about our success from someone outside our firm. I ran into Jasper Mitchell, one of the Planters & Commerce Board Members, at the Commerce Club yesterday. He was the one who told me we had the work."

"Mr. Mitchell is the Managing Partner of Barnes, Mitchell, and Stallard. He chairs the Compensation Committee of the Board of Directors. You were copied on a memo last week that announced the meeting. You were copied again on a memo mailed yesterday, Harley."

"I'm quite aware of Jasper's role on the Planters & Commerce Board, Joe. I would assume that the work will be an Atlanta engagement with you in an advisory role. I would expect that Harry would be heavily involved in the work for Planters & Commerce. It will be a great start for Harry in Atlanta."

"Harry won't be working on Planters & Commerce. It's a New York engagement, and I'm using well experienced New York consultants in the early phase of the work," Baxter explained.

"Harry is still a New York consultant, Joe. He won't officially transfer until April 1."

"We'll get Harry involved later. I expect that our work for Planters & Commerce will be a multi-year engagement. Jesse Durham wants a complete overhaul of the bank's compensation plans. He's looking at changing the name of the bank and making a number of acquisitions. I expect that Planters & Commerce will be a more substantial engagement than Pennsylvania Steel. There will be plenty of work for Atlanta over time, Harley. In the early stages, I plan to use Marty Dunlap, a New York Office Manager with considerable experience in mathematical modeling, and a smart young woman named Linda Green. Then we'll bring in other people, and I believe we could use some Atlanta Banking practice people a little later on in our work. This should be a great relationship building opportunity for the Atlanta office," Baxter predicted.

"When exactly do you expect to have Harry involved in the Planters & Commerce work, Joe?" Harley's voice betrayed a wisp of Southern skepticism.

"When the time is right, Harley. Now I understand that Bonnie Grow has been on leave of absence, and that has delayed the start of our work for Rikuns Companies," Baxter probed. He had called Bonnie over the holidays and reached a message on her answering machine that she was on holiday and not returning until January 11th. Baxter had tried to reach her twice during the week, January 11-15th and had been informed that Miss Grow would be on leave of absence until the end of January.

"That's another matter I wanted to discuss with you, Joe. We sent Bonnie up to spend a week in the New York Office and she's been out ever since. What happened to her up there?"

"What have you heard, Harley?"

"Clyde called me around Christmas, and said that Bonnie had picked up a bug and needed a lot of tests. Harry said that he saw her at the New York Office Christmas Party and she seemed fine then. Clyde has her on an administrative leave of absence with her pay charged back to Executive Office. I've never seen anything handled like that before."

"Have you discussed it with Neil?"

"He told me something about a transfer to another office. All I know is that I sent a healthy Bonnie Grow up to New York for a week of training in your practice and I haven't seen her since. I also have been given to understand that we can't start that work with Rikuns Companies until Bonnie comes back. So I'm a little confused, Joe. Why don't you fill me in? What happened to Bonnie in New York?" the voice now seemed arrogant to Baxter. Bonnie had implied that she and Harley had been lovers.

"How hard have you pushed Clyde for a straight answer, Harley?" Baxter pressed.

"Pretty hard. But you know Clyde, Joe. He can be evasive when he believes it's in the best interests of the firm. There's something going on there that I haven't seen before in this firm. I'm the Managing Partner of the Atlanta Office, and I should be informed on all Atlanta personnel matters. I demand, Joe, that you level with me on what happened to Bonnie up in New York."

Baxter had a choice,. He could evade Harley Dimon's question with a plea of ignorance, or he could set a tied of retribution in motion. Baxter concluded that he was close to a deal with Leon Harwell. Why not?

"Harley, this is on the ugly side, but I agree, you should be informed on this matter. Can I count on your confidentiality?"

"Damn it Joe, get on with it!"

"Bonnie met Brett Williamson at the McKenzie Barber Christmas Party. She accompanied him to his room after the party and Brett sexually abused her and beat her up pretty badly. We got her off on a plane back to Atlanta on that Saturday afternoon and informed Clyde as to what happened. I haven't been able to reach Bonnie since that Saturday." Harley was obviously shocked. "Joe! Do you swear that what you told me is absolutely true?"

"I wouldn't make a thing like that up. The Chairman's golden boy is a bad person. Clyde, like a good McKenzie Barber cover-up artist, is trying to make the thing go away for a while until Williamson strikes again. The guy is sick, Harley."

"He's on the Operating Committee, Joe."

"That doesn't make him well, Harley."

"Who else knows about this, Joe?"

"Clyde, Bonnie, Monica Graham, one of my managers, and of course, Brett."

"If you're lying, Joe, there's no place for you in this firm," Harley threatened.

"Harley, I'm here to serve clients and create operating profit, not to tell despicable fibs about members of the Operating Committee. Monica Graham took pictures of Bonnie's battered and abused body. Give her a call and tell her that she has my support is talking openly with you. We have a very sick person in the firm to whom we have awarded a good deal of power. He needs psychiatric help badly. You're on the Board and the Operating Committee. Step up to your responsibilities!"

There was a near forty seconds of silence of the telephone line. Then Harley said, "All right, Joe. I'm going to make a few calls to check out this story. I hope to hell for your sake that what you've told me is true."

"Grow up, Harley," Baxter said and hung up. At least there was no more discussion about Planters & Commerce being an Atlanta Office engagement.

The call to Harley had established the impregnability of Brett Williamson. Baxter received a call from Clyde Nickerson on the Thursday after the Tuesday he had talked with Harley Dimon.

"Joe, Clyde here. Does this Monica Graham work for you?"

"Yes. She's at the Director level, very competent, and most certainly Partner potential."

"Get rid of her! I'd like her out by the end of the week. She's been making outrageous and unsubstantiated accusations about the leadership of this firm. If she's resistant, tell her we're ready to take legal action."

"Whoa, Clyde. What in the hell are you talking about?"

"That's all I can share for now, Joe. This decision is coming right down from Ross."

"No deal, Clyde. You've got to tell me what Monica has done as just cause for separation. If you can't, I'm going to McMasters, and then I'm going to the General Counsel's office. As a Partner of this firm, I'm not going to be a party to capricious acts that will leave McKenzie Barber vulnerable to legal actions."

"Look, Joe, this is for the good of all of us. I handle her severance as an executive office expense and I can come up with some money for a search fee for her replacement."

"Clyde, I know how all this started out and I want it dropped right now," Baxter said defiantly. After all, he had one hell of a backlog, was practically vested, and the job with Harwell was his for the asking. "You weren't straight with Harley Dimon on Bonnie Grow. He pressed me the other day and I told him straight out what happened. He wanted some corroboration and I gave him Monica's name to call in confidence."

"How did she come to know about this matter?"

"She was present that Saturday morning. I needed someone to help me get Bonnie Grow dressed and off to the airport."

"I thought you had some woman doctor with you."

"Dr. Irene Rabbinowitz, my neighbor. She examined Bonnie, took some pictures, and concluded that she was well enough to travel. Irene, I believe, is required by law to file a police report and had a plane to catch. She had no idea of Bonnie's identity. She just observed the body of a young woman that had been brutally abused. I don't believe that any useful purpose could be served by involving Irene further," Baxter said hoping to retire his mythical neighbor and doctor from the conversation.

"I'd like to see those pictures, Joe."

"The pictures are securely tucked away in a safety deposit box. They are, if it makes you feel better, sealed in a McKenzie Barber envelope marked private."

"Joe, I've made a thorough investigation of this whole unfortunate incident. This young woman led Brett on. She visited his suite. Brett's a fairly macho fellow who had too much to drink. She teased him and he lost his control. Then she tried to blackmail him, and Brett acknowledged that he slapped her a couple of times. She became hysterical and he saw her back to her hotel. Brett said that she was in control when he put her on the elevator at her hotel. He suspects that someone cooked up this rape with her."

"Clyde, have you ever considered that Brett may be a perverted liar?"

"Brett Williamson is President of FSO and on the Operating Committee of this firm. He may, one day, become Chairman of this firm. Brett is a man of great integrity and leadership ability. He has one major weakness. Women! We know it. He knows it. Women know it! They use this weakness to take advantage of him."

63

"What's happening to Bonnie Grow, Clyde? Is the firm going to press charges for reckless endangerment of a member of the Operating Committee? Is there a chance of some kind of mercy on the part of the firm?"

"This isn't a humorous matter, Joe."

"You're making it humorous, Clyde. What in the hell is the firm doing for his poor, battered well meaning young woman who visited someone's hotel room anticipating a little honest conventional sex and wound up in the clutches of the Marquis de Sade. Your whole premise that the woman consultant is always wrong stinks. I'm ready to call Buzzsaw's office, get on his calendar, and blow this thing wide open," Baxter threatened.

"Joe, the firm has its adjustment problems right now. It doesn't need this kind of distraction. Bonnie Grow has signed a properly worded affidavit that had been reviewed by her legal counsel. The firm will pay her for better than two years through September 30, 1991, in addition to a lump sum payment. Additionally, she has been reimbursed for legal and medical costs, and I will personally handle her references. Brett has also sent her a hand-written letter of apology. Now you tell me, that's a pretty fair settlement for a one night of bad judgment. Isn't it?"

"You're missing the point, Clyde. Bonnie Grow has gone away, but what have we done to ensure that Brett won't repeat this kind of behavior?"

"Look, Joe, this is an Executive Office matter. It's been handled. You just remind this Monica Graham to keep her mouth shut." Clyde Nickerson clicked off without a good-bye. Now he's off screwing something else up, Baxter had reflected at the time.

The Rikuns work never really started. Bonnie Grow had accumulated some time and a week of New York expenses that totaled $7,000. Baxter had tried to call Bill Rikuns four times during the month of January, and his calls were not returned. At the end of January, Baxter received a short letter on Rikuns Company stationery.

Dear Joe:

I'm sorry that I have been too busy to call you back. I have talked over the project you proposed, and my Dad and I agree that it is not the time to start such a project.

We appreciate the time you spent with us and would be glad to reimburse any properly documented expenses you may have incurred.

We will recontact McKenzie Barber if we should want to consider revisiting the project at some time in the future.

> Yours very truly,
> William Rikuns, Jr.
> President

Alvardi was furious with Baxter. They met for drinks in the front bar of the Pierre where Alvardi greeted him with a snarl.

"You're either gutless or plain stupid, kid."

"Nice to see you again, Frank. Enjoy your holidays?" Baxter said after ordering white wine to accompany Alvardi's martini.

"I have waited two months for you to make up your mind. I have to be out at Western Pacific Spring quarter full time. Now I'm going to have to spend the next year or so in a plane hopping between LA, Atlanta, and New York. I have some new work in from Brimmer Industries. You passed up a gold mine, kid, for an opportunity to hang around with McKenzie Barber a little longer until they ask you to walk the plank. You could have picked up my business with a personal loan from Lorna Brimmer. You wouldn't have had to come up with a dime."

"Wouldn't that represent a conflict of interest for Lorna? That is to have an investment in a supplier of services to a company where she serves on the Board of Directors."

"It wouldn't have been a conflict. Lorna was prepared to make you a loan from her personal investment firm. She calls it Brimstone Ventures. Brimstone Ventures is a separate legal entity. You blew it, kid, unless you're gong to tell me tonight that you've thought it over and want to settle a deal. I have to be frank with you, Joe. I've had a lot of nibbles lately."

"Frank, I'm in the middle of negotiations in another situation. I was ready to get serious with you but this other situation developed, and we're working out the contract now."

Alvardi's eyes widened. "Another consulting firm?"

"No."

"Not some human resources job. Those guys are either pansies, parasites, politicals, or whores. It's a dumb but necessary job."

"No."

"Not the Federal Government?"

"No."

Alvardi shook his head. "Jesus, kid, I can't figure out what the hell else you could be good for."

"I'll let you know when it's finalized. But I guarantee you it's going to happen," Baxter affirmed.

"I heard you split with your last wife. How's that going?"

"I thought it was going to be an amicable divorce."

"There is no such thing, kid. I went through one. I never want to go through another. Find relationships with women who don't want commitments. Married ones looking for a little action on the side have worked out well for me over the years. Beware of young women on their way up. They're full of tricks, and are more likely to take advantage of you than you are of them. It's a matter of strike zones, kid," Alvardi lectured. "They should be no younger than 38 and no older than 48, have their own careers, and have a husband who travels a lot. Stick to that profile, kid, and you will enjoy a long and fulfilling series of relationships."

Alvardi had been all too right. No divorce was amicable. Baxter anticipated a painless distribution of property. Bridgette had been the one to exit their relationship. Baxter anticipated that Bridgette would simply keep her newly acquired place in the Hamptons, while Baxter would be responsible for the lease on the New York apartment. Bridgette wanted the furniture, and expected that Baxter would pay for the movement of the furniture. She also wanted a cash settlement on her share of the house on Brinker's Falls. Further her attorney, Irving Milch, proposed to Baxter's attorney, that Bridgette be awarded a portion of Baxter's McKenzie Barber retirement pension.

Baxter had Zach Blum threaten to sue Ward Bowman for alienation of affections, and demanded his fair share of Bridgette's $7.3 million on the Florida Group buy-out. He sat in a Chrysler Building windowless conference room with Zach Blum on a cold mid-February afternoon. Blum was a short, fat, greying man who sported a goatee. He appeared jacketless with an unknotted tie in each of his meetings with Baxter. He had a thick file on his desk that was labeled J. Baxter.

"I've talked to Milch about the alienation of affections suit and your share of the buy-out money. He just laughed. I told him that Bridgette's requests were excessive, and that if she wanted to pick up the furniture, she could hire her own truck. You still have this furniture?"

"It's in storage just waiting for her truck," Baxter answered.

"I know Milch. I've been on the other side of the table from his before. He's a reasonable man but he usually attracts unreasonable clients. Rightly or wrongly, Milch works very hard for his clients. Your wife seems very vindictive. Did she find out that you had something going on the side? This dark haired girl who keeps dropping off things? Did Bridgette find out about that?"

"She works for me, Zach. I was married to Bridgette for five years, and was absolutely faithful. She became full of herself the last three or four years. She believed she had outgrown me and left me to carry on with Ward. I'm the one that was dumped. I just want to get on with my life."

"You're not in a hurry to get a divorce so you can marry someone else?" Blum probed.

"I have no plans to marry anyone."

"Then you're willing to let this divorce action take its course?"

"I'm willing to settle in for a period of extended negotiations in order to keep what is rightfully mine. I don't want anything of Bridgette's."

"Are you still involved with her emotionally?"

"What do you mean?"

"Are you still in love with Bridgette?" Blum asked.

Baxter stood up from the conference table and paced a few steps. "I probably am. She's truly a one of a kind."

"Would you take her back?"

"I don't believe she would ever come back."

"I believed your Bridgette has a hidden agenda in her demands."

"What's that?"

"She wants to leave the door open for her to come back. If there's no pre-trial agreement on property settlement, it's going to wind up in a judge's hands. Milch has probably told Bridgette that she's being unreasonable. By reputation, she's a smart cookie. She may be having some doubts and may be stalling to see if a reconciliation is in order."

"Did Milch imply that?"

"Milch is very careful in his choice of words with me. But I think he would like to get the four of us in a conference room and get this settlement resolved. My best estimate is that you're going to get a call from Bridgette one of these days, and she's going to propose that the two of you get together."

"I'd have to think about that," Baxter said rising again from his chair. "Are we done for today?"

"For the time being. You'll be getting a progress bill from me shortly."

"I understand about billing," Baxter replied.

Linda Green really didn't move into the 38th Street apartment with Baxter. Rather she kept clothes there, and would periodically appear. Linda continued to date for what she termed 'appearance's sake' and continued to exhibit an incredible work ethic. She seemed to have social events to attend on weekends with an endless succession of uncles, aunts, and cousins. Baxter was never asked, nor was he invited to accompany Linda. Linda Green had evolved into Baxter's capable, lead consultant whom he would socialize with in bed one or two times a week. He would visit Brinker's Falls alone on weekends, and find Linda waiting for him in the 38th Street apartment on Sunday evening, sipping tea and prepared to accommodate his preferences.

"Linda Green," Monica remarked over spring evening drinks at the Sunset Club. "seems to have moved herself into my old job, Baxter. You're the only one she works for anymore."

"I'll get her rotated a little more after the Planters & Commerce work settles down. She is a talent, Monica. With Harry moving to Atlanta, you have become my main man in New York," Baxter explained.

"I'm not complaining, Joe. It would seem to me that Harry's transfer has cleared out barriers in front of me to be made a Partner. I would expect that I would be on the Partner nomination list for this fall." Monica never let up. She always wanted more money, and now she was sending out Partner ultimatums. He had not placed Monica Graham's name in nomination for the fall of 1988. It wouldn't be supported by McMasters. Monica's time would be October 1, 1989, at the earliest.

"1988 may be a tough year for Partnership nominations, Monica. The firm is unlikely to enjoy a banner year. I am, however, considering putting through a mid-year promotion to Associate for Linda. What do you think?" Baxter said testing Monica's reaction.

"Don't make her wait until September, Joe. It's the right thing to do. Get her at least a 15% raise. That poor kid is close to the line financially."

"What's her personal life like? Is Van Hoeven still trying to romance her?" Baxter tested.

"She's not interested at all in Bill Van Hoeven. Linda has a great many boyfriends. She goes to movies with some guy who's a cardiologist in residency. I don't know how serious that is. She may have a sugar daddy out there. She's a hardworking, smart, ambitious young woman. We are lucky to have her, and we should take good care of her. She's grown three years of experience in five months working with you. Sometimes Linda even sounds like you, Joe. Linda's a keeper."

Baxter paused and looked out at the lights in the Manhattan sky. He wondered how many men he was sharing Linda with? How many suspected his existence?

"Now tell me, Joe. How is the Exec Comp practice doing?" Monica began again. "It looks like we were identified with the wrong side on the Hortense Food buy-out. Jon Grunwaldyt is the New York Office star for bringing in the Hortense Food MBO group as clients. I also note that we were not used on the management compensation piece. The rumor is that the Benefits practice is bootlegging the compensation work. You've got to step in, Joe."

"What do you hear from Dominique?" Baxter asked to change the subject.

"de Hartogue is going to clear about seventy million on the MBO offer. Harwell will get about half of that. She doesn't believe the MBO group will make it. She'll have de Hartogue ready to pick up the pieces she wants in a couple of years. Dominique is on the hunt for new acquisitions."

"Does she ever mention her relationship with Burke?"

"Ham Burke is a kind of business advisor. She planned to have him run Hortense if the offer had gone through," Monica responded.

"Their relationship runs a little deeper, doesn't it, Monica?" Baxter probed.

"I don't know what you mean by that question, Joe," Monica responded innocently enough.

"I had head that Ham and Dominique had developed a special relationship," Baxter pressed.

"He's become an ongoing business advisor to the de Hartogue group. I believe Dominique has him on retainer. I know she planned for him to run Hortense Foods if it would have been acquired. She also has told me that Ham is biding his time waiting for his father to die so that he can run Burke Farms."

"How's Ham getting along with Henri?"

"There's no need for them to get along. Dominique runs de Hartogue, and Henri attends to the children and household matters. He has an office and a secretary, and shows up once a week to check his mail. He's a charming man. He and Erik used to be international playboys together. Erik eventually had to go to work. Henri didn't. The old Baron trained Dominique to run the business, and she produced grandsons for the Baron and the de Hartogue line. Dominique can't stand Burke's wife. They don't socialize. There was a scandal when Yvonne left her husband years back to live with Burke. She's really quite spoiled and arrogant. Yvonne regards Dominique as an adventuress from the provinces. The relationship between Hamilton Burke and Dominique de Hartogue is strictly business. It could never amount to anything more than that. There's been talk, of course. But Dominique has always been focused on what had to be done. She'd never allow herself to be sidetracked on some kind of physical/emotional issue. She's really a very determined person. She knew exactly what she was doing on the Hortense Foods transaction. I believe she paraded out Burke as a stalking horse. Now de Hartogue will be loaded up financially to make new acquisitions. Now, Baxter, answer me one question very truthfully."

"We were never an item," Baxter said anticipating the question. One day, Baxter decided, he would disclose in his memoirs that he once made love to the great French conglomerator in a taxi cab on the way to Charles DeGaulle airport.

"We worked together for a week which turned out to be her last week at McKenzie Barber. Everybody remembers their last consulting engagement forever."

"Well Dominique has a warm spot in her heart for you, Baxter."

"How often do you talk to her?"

"Every ten days or so. If she doesn't call me, I call her. She always calls back within a day or so. We would have been wired for big work if the Hortense deal had gone through. I provided her a lot of data on Hortense Foods before we knew what she was up to. Dominique knows she owes us one. She always asks about you, and was disappointed that she missed you in January when you were in Paris. She is very interested in how your life is coming along. She wanted to know if you were seeing anyone. So I'll ask. Are you?"

"Tell her that I've thrown myself into my work and could use some more," Baxter responded.

"Why don't you tell her? Give her a call." Monica pulled out a business card ands crawled a telephone number across the back.

"This is Dominique's private line. It's a 24 hour phone mail. I believe she checks it three times a day. Call her. It might be good for business."

Baxter studied the number and slipped the card into his wallet.

"I'll catch up with her one of these days," he pledged.

Lon McMasters was not a happy man in his position as Managing Partner of the New York Office. Baxter was summoned to a dinner meeting in late April to review his practice. They met in a back corner table in a remote corner of a French restaurant called Boulevard Francaise that was nestled in the bottom floor of the East side high rise where McMasters had taken up his New York residence. Marveen had called Baxter to schedule the dinner. Lon McMasters had discontinued the Group Partner meetings in January with an announcement that the New York Office was in the process of reorganization, and the new organization would be announced in the spring. Baxter knew that periodic meetings were being held but that he was not invited to those meetings. Baxter was ahead of plan for the period ending March 31, and was reasonably confident he would make plan in New York, and anticipated that he would miss the national plan by less than 5%. That performance level certainly wouldn't get him fired but was unlikely to get him any more units.

"He's meeting with all the Group Partners one-on-one, Joe," Marveen explained. "That's the date he wants to see you and he wants to meet you for dinner. He's doing breakfasts, lunches and has got dinner reserved for you."

"What will we talk about over dinner? How can I prepare myself in advance for this historic meeting, Marveen?"

"The way you always have, Joe," was Marveen's response. "I got another call coming. If seven o'clock's OK, I'll put you down." She clicked off. Marveen, once an ally, was now in the camp of another power.

Baxter estimated that he had talked personally with Lon McMasters twice since the first of the year. They had exchanged some voice mails relative to the perfunctory details of Harry Devonshire's move to Atlanta, and reassurance calls on Baxter's backlog position.

Baxter arrived shortly after seven at the Boulevard Francaise and was escorted to the McMaster's far corner table. He rose half way up in his chair to shake Baxter's hand and sat down again. A half empty bottle of red wine was on the table which indicated to Baxter that his Managing Partner had arrived early.

"This is very good claret, Joe, if you would like to join me."

"Sounds fine, Lon," Baxter said, pleased that he was not being offered Red Mustang beer.

McMasters waved a waiter over instructing him to pour Baxter a glass of the claret and to bring another bottle.

"Well, Lon," Baxter began. "Long time no see. How's everything going?"

"You gonna make plan this year?"

"New York for sure. National, maybe."

"Can you make the profit plan if New York carries Devonshire through the end of third quarter?"

"There is no reason why I should carry Harry in the third quarter after I did in the second quarter. He operates from the Atlanta office now."

"Can you get him more active in the Planters & Commerce work?"

"In due time but not for the moment."

"What if I order you to do both?" McMasters threatened.

"I would tell you that what you're proposing is neither good for the New York Office, or especially good for the client right now."

McMasters swished the wine in his glass and stared at it for nearly a minute without speaking. Baxter decided to wait him out.

"The New York office is not performing, Joe," McMasters began after his minute of silent wine glass gazing. "We've got to reorganize. I'm moving Grunwaldyt up to Deputy Managing Partner. We're going to divide the New York Office into two groups. The practices that are functioning and the practices that need a lot of day to day oversight. Jon is going to take oversight responsibility for the practices that appear to be running on plan. I'm going to personally concentrate on remedial actions on the underperforming practices. Executive Compensation will go under Jon. He wants it integrated into one practice under Walker. We're going to scrap the Group Partner organization for the time being. Maybe we'll reinstate it after the end of fiscal year."

"Lon, I refuse to report to Walker. Also, I have to tell you that I'm in employment discussions with someone else. The job is outside the consulting industry and I expect shortly to provide you the six months advance notice in compliance with the firm's Partnership agreement."

McMaster's eyes widened. "Are you vested in September?"

"21 years of service, 53 years of age equals 74, Lon. I'm not going off to a competitor but rather to a whole new career."

"What in the hell are you going to do that for? You're one of the best in the Compensation business. You make a real contribution to this firm. Now are you talking about a done deal?"

"There's been no contract signed but it's in draft."

"Who are you talking with?"

"It's confidential, Lon. I promise to keep you informed."

McMasters waved for the waiter. "Menus, se vous plais," he commanded in his best Texan French accent. "Let's get an order in, Joe, and talk about this."

The conversation that followed took a number of twists and turns. It had been a little less than six months when McMasters boldly and self confidently took over the New York Office.

"Christ, Joe," McMasters concluded with the arrival of a third bottle of claret. "You're one of the few guys around the New York Office who knows how to make money. Your practice isn't very damned big but you always throw off a decent amount of positive cash. You've got a reputation of being a smart ass, but the Operating Committee was damned impressed with your bringing in Planters & Commerce. You're not regarded, though, as a team player. Now I value individualism and believe this firm needs a few wild ducks like Joe Baxter. I don't want you to finalize any career decisions until I have had the opportunity to talk with the people around the firm about your future. For the time being, you will continue to report to me. Walker will report to Grunwaldyt."

"How bad is it, Lon?" Baxter asked.

"Pretty bad. I'm making a number of changes. Baldwin's going back to San Francisco. I'm putting Pinker in his job. We have tremendous write-offs in the Financial Services Group. Baldwin started a bunch of work with oral authorization, and didn't get the engagements documented. The guy who told him to go ahead got himself fired, and the bank which will remained unnamed, is trying to stiff us. Grunwaldyt has caught everybody's eyes by bringing in the Hortense Foods MBO Group as a client. That work will probably run $10 to $15 million, and it has to be completed by the end of June. The ongoing work will probably mean an annual annuity of $3 or $4 million a year. He's saved the second and third quarters for the New York Office. Jon believes you were on the other side with the Harwell Group. But he'll get over it. A number of people from the underperforming practices will have to leave by June 30th. I expect that we will have New York Office turned around by the fourth quarter and that we will be back on track in FY 89. You're needed around here, Joe."

"How was all this allowed to happen, Lon?" Baxter pressed.

"It started under Burke. Dirks helped him make things look better than they were. The Friedman came and was determined to look good. Dirks helped him and then left the country after the 1984 election. Floyd came in and implemented the firm's change strategy which made some faulty assumptions about how quickly strategic change could be effected. Floyd completed his grace period and still couldn't find the bottom. Now it's my job. By the way, I'm dealing with Neil Schmidt now on the Harry Devonshire transfer. It seems as though Harley Dimon is resigning."

"Resigning?" Baxter questioned. Harley had been one of the chosen ones following the 1984 election.

"You haven't heard the story?" McMasters questioned.

"What story?"

"Harley took a couple of swings at Brett Williamson after an Operating Committee meeting. They broke it up, but Buzz had Nickerson court martial poor Harley. We were all pledged not to talk about it, but it was all over the firm the following week. I guess they were both seeing the same woman. Brett kept his cool, but Harley made an absolute fool out of himself. Clyde cut him a decent package, and Harley's been gone now for a couple of weeks. Neil, officially, has his office back but then again, he never really let loose of it in the first place. There are going to be a lot of changes at McKenzie Barber over the next year or so, Joe. You should stick around to see the fun."

The dinner represented the last discussion regarding the integration of Baxter's practice with the Benefits practice during McMasters' tenure as New York Managing Partner. He continued to report to McMasters, but never met with him personally, and Baxter was no longer invited to the Group Partners meetings. Jon Grunwaldyt invited him out one week later for one of their front bar of the Four Seasons drink-on -the-way-to-the-train sessions.

Jon was resplendent in what appeared to be a British tailored brown herringbone suit and matching brown oxfords. He sat comfortably perched on the second bar stool next to the railing, and Grunwaldyt had obviously reserved the corner stool for Baxter. He waved across the room to Baxter and patted the empty stool. As Baxter drew closer, he noted that the Grunwaldyt blonde mane was a little shaggy, and he appeared to have gained some weight. As the newly minted Deputy Managing Partner, Jon Grunwaldyt had been proclaimed the new young Siegfried of the New York Office. He was credited with single-handedly bringing back Hortense Foods into the client fold.

"Joe," Grunwaldyt greeted him with an enthusiastic handshake. "It's been too long."

"Well, I guess we've both been on the go, Jon." Baxter slid into his place on the end bar stool.

"Murray," he addressed the bartender. "A glass of Sauvignon Blanc for Mr. Baxter." Turning to Baxter, he explained, "I personally find the French white wines superior to the California's. I find this place has become my office away from the office." Baxter remembered bringing Grunwaldyt to the Four Seasons for the first time. It had been way back when he drank California's.

"First, Joe, let me congratulate you on the Planters & Commerce engagement. I understand that Neil arranged for you to meet Jesse Durham and that you have parlayed that introduction into a major client service opportunity for the firm. When your work is completed, we can position the banking practice into Planters & Commerce for strategic work. That's the kind of teamwork that's going to be required to put this firm back on track."

"You're right on, Jon," Baxter pretended to agree. "But let me set a few details straight so that you can strengthen your senior management vision. I was introduced to Jesse Durham when Harley Dimon had me down to Atlanta as a speaker. Neil had nothing to do with it. I don't believe that Neil has any kind of influence at Planters & Commerce. Harley was reasonably helpful, but I understand that he has just resigned from the firm."

"I believe Harley's on a leave-of-absence, Joe. He's been through a difficult divorce along with the pressure of taking over from Neil in 1984. Neil will now be spending virtually all of his time in Atlanta. Harley could well be back with us in October."

"Jon, I heard a story about some kind of a tiff between Harley and Brett Williamson at an Operating Committee meeting."

Grunwaldyt shook his head. "I haven't heard anything like that. I believe they are very good friends. Harley simply had a lot of personal problems, was under a lot of performance pressure, and asked for a leave of absence. The firm's new strategic direction has made a lot of demands on the Partners, and particularly the Managing Partners."

"I recall you and I discussing that strategy on these very barstools, Jon," Baxter responded.

"And the strategy is coming around, Joe. As you are aware the new New York Office reorganization plan has placed the underperforming practices under Lon and the practices performing at or above plan under me. Lon proposed that we combine your practice with Walker's. I felt that this was wrong, Joe. I think he got the idea when I had to use Dilger on the Compensation work for Hortense Foods. You were too closely identified with Harwell Management."

"What was the nature of the work that Dilger's people performed for Hortense, Jon?"

"They recommended pay levels, annual incentive plans, the stock option plans and drafted the management contracts, in addition to reviewing the employee benefit and pension plans," Grunwaldyt responded.

"And what qualified the Benefits practice to work on the pay and capital accumulation plans for Hortense Foods?"

"They had Carl's people in Chicago work on that phase of the work," Grunwaldyt explained.

"And why wasn't I informed? As I recall, I am charged with the national responsibility for Executive Compensation. I should have had a final review on the recommendations presented to Hortense Foods. We had just finished up a limited engagement for Hortense's Bakery Services Group."

"I believe that Carl conferred with Harry about that engagement. Let's face it, Joe. McKenzie Barber was in trouble with Hortense Foods because of our relationship with that French woman and your relationship with Harwell Management. The only way we could work for them was to shut Joe Baxter out. I didn't particularly like shutting you out of the Hortense work after all we've been through together over the years, but it was a necessary consideration to properly serve the client."

"Who reviewed Carl's work? He tends to be very technical and highly inflexible."

"It's been delivered, Joe, and the client is satisfied. You will continue to report to Lon, unless you request to report to me. Your national role may be recast at the end of this year. I expect that the firm will be reorganized dramatically for the beginning of FY '89. FY '89 will be the beginning of McKenzie Barber's new era of growth. We've had a rocky year, but we're on the road back."

Baxter raised his glass. "Here's to a successful return for Harley Dimon around October 1."

Leon Harwell's law firm was Asher, Gardner, Willingham, a white shoe law firm whose relationship dated back to the late 19th century days of Big Bill Harwell. Their offices were downtown on Liberty Street. Baxter began to meet with Harwell's lawyers in late spring with the objective of structuring the arrangement. While Baxter had developed Hakim's employment agreement, the final document had gone to Asher Gardner for review. Now Baxter was in the queue with Asher Gardner. He was instructed by Leon Harwell to meet Stanford Asher, the Managing Partner, and grandson of one of the founding Partners. He turned out to be a slight, very stiff, humorless grey man with arthritic hands. Stanford Asher met with Baxter in a conference room accompanied by a middle aged attorney called Chalmers and a heavy set woman stenographer referred to as Grace.

"I wanted you to know, Mr. Baxter," Stanford Asher said in the opening of their initial meeting. "That I have gone on record with Mr. Leon Harwell that your pay demands are excessive. They are not as excessive as those that you recommended for Mr. Selim, but certainly excessive. I also find your choice of legal representation somewhat unusual. Mr. Blum's legal reputation is that of a divorce specialist."

"Mr. Asher, I consider compensation as a matter of personal negotiation between Mr. Harwell and myself. I'm here to work out the legal language of my contract. Mr. Blum had been engaged to review certain matters relative to my estate, and I want him to review the final document that these discussions produce. I am a Partner with the management consulting firm of McKenzie Barber. Leaving this firm to join Harwell Management will require careful crafting of a suitable role to assure me that this change is desirable."

They met four times over the space of two months, and a final employment contract was ready for review by Blum by the end of June.

"Looks to me like one hell of a deal," Blum concluded. "You got your McKenzie Barber pension protected, and you're walking away into what looks to me like a high paying cushy job with a fat eleemosynary client. You've got some tax planning on your hands based on the payout of your interest in unrealized receivables. You should get this divorce settled before you announce this move. The contract reads September 15. That means you leave McKenzie Barber a couple of days before and report to Harwell Management on September 15th as Executive Vice President and General Manager. Now, how many of the family have been informed that you're coming on?"

"None," Baxter answered.

"When is Mr. Harwell going to inform them?"

"Probably the day I show up. I believe Leon Harwell wants me announced as a fait accompli. I don't believe he's even confided in his wife."

"How's his health?"

"I believe he's slipping a little." Baxter thought back to the succession of breakfasts and luncheons at the Gotham Club over the past months. Harwell was in the process of resigning from all of his boards. There would be no more consultant recommendations from the Chairman of the Compensation Committee of the Board of Directors. The Leon Harwell of today lacked the energy of the times past. His eyes seemed tired, and he had a consistent slight cough.

"Could anyone question if Leon Harwell was of sound mind when he negotiated this contract with you?"

"They could, but I assure you that Leon Harwell is in full control of his faculties."

"And he's doing this because he doesn't trust the Chief Investment Officer you helped him recruit?"

"Hakim Selim is a great talent. Leon recognizes that talent. Hakim loves the risk and high rewards. Leon regards his nephew and son-in-law as marginally competent. He has great hopes for his youngest son, Spencer. Spencer is slated to become the successor family leader of Harwell Management. Spencer is being trained under Hakim. He even served two summer internships at Broadbaker as a Trading Assistant. Spencer graduated from the University of Chicago in June, and is now working as an Analyst at Broadbaker where he is being molded as a Selim clone, Spencer is scheduled to join Harwell Management in January 1991, following an obligatory three years at Broadbaker. Leon wants me there as his agent and buffer."

"It doesn't sound Joe that you're bringing a lot to the party. I can see why you need a contract," Blum observed. "Let me give you some advice, Joe. Make sure the family knows you're coming before you quit McKenzie Barber and sign up. If Leon Harwell should check out ahead of schedule, you may have a problem."

Baxter brought up the family notification issue to Leon Harwell over dinner in a private room at the Gotham Club. Leon invited Ernie Grey to attend. Leon had maintained his fatigued look while Ernie, with his chemically supported jet black hair and exquisitely tailored Bond Street blue pinstriped suit, appeared, in contrast, to be early fifties youthful. The contract had been finalized and required signatures. Ernie Grey, apparently, was there to witness the signing. He had recently been elected the first non-family board member of Harwell Management.

"This has been be a very historic moment for all of us," Ernie observed. "It was a little over 46 years ago when I encountered Will Harwell in a Pensacola BOQ during Navy flight training. I met Leon for the first time in 1945, some 43 years ago. Now, Joe Baxter, one of my boys at McKenzie Barber, is going to Harwell Management after concluding a significant consulting career. I really feel good about this."

When the hell was I ever one of your boys, Ernie? Baxter asked himself.

"Joe has been an outstanding consultant to Harwell Management, better than anyone with the exception of you, Ernie. I believe I will sleep better each night, Joe, knowing that you will be the family watch dog at Harwell Management." Leon signed his name with his fountain pen across both copies of the contract and passed the pen for Ernie Grey to sign as witness.

"I have been mulling this move over and over again in my mind," Baxter interjected. "Leon, when do you intend to inform Spencer, Hakim, and the rest of the family that I'm coming?"

Leon Harwell peered back grimly at Baxter with his tired eyes.

"On the day you come to us. I don't want your selection marred by family intrigue. What we're doing is for the benefit of all members of the Harwell family. I don't want any discussion of this matter to occur before Joe comes to us. There can be plenty of discussion after Joe has been announced."

"Leon," Ernie suggested. "Why don't you give a family dinner the evening of Joe's announcement. If you like, Toni and I will attend. It will give you an opportunity to introduce Joe and his new job to the family."

"That seems like a good idea. I want time to think about it. I don't want to hold a dinner of that kind until after Labor Day. It goes without saying that Joe's appointment at Harwell Management remains confidential until we are prepared to announce it. Your idea of a family dinner, Ernie, is really rather good. Let me work it through in my mind," Harwell responded.

"Who will succeed you at McKenzie Barber, Joe?" Ernie asked.

"The practice should best be positioned under Bob Dilger and Carl Miller in Chicago as the practice leader. I can probably position my major relationships with existing staff, and my contract with Leon allows me four days a month availability to perform consulting work up to a maximum of 48 days a year. I'm at a time in a major engagement with Planters & Commerce Bank when the Atlanta office has been clammering and politicking to take over the work," Baxter explained.

"Who's there now?"

"I transferred down a New York Manager named Harry Devonshire this January. He really needs the Planters & Commerce work if he's going to survive."

"Who's' running Atlanta?" Ernie asked.

"Neil Schmidt."

"He's supposed to be Deputy Chairman isn't he?"

"Harley Dimon resigned this Spring and Neil is serving as Acting Managing Partner in addition to his Deputy Chairman responsibilities. I would expect that Neil will remain an Acting Managing Partner of the Atlanta Office until he retires. He really has abdicated his Deputy Chairman responsibilities to Clyde Nickerson."

"That's really appalling. How's the firm doing?"

"About as expected under the leadership team of Buzzsaw and Clyde," Baxter answered.

"How's this McMasters fellow doing in New York?" Ernie probed.

Baxter carefully folded his copy of the signed Harwell Management contract and placed it in the inside pocket of his suit. It was his ticket out of the firm. "McMasters is seeking to bottom out the New York Office."

"Floyd Piper cratered the New York Office," Ernie commented to Leon. "He was one of the key opposition Partners."

"It must be very unfortunate for you, Ernie, to look back on a business that you so carefully built and see it unravel."

"It is, Leon. But I have the IPCO shareholders to worry about now. I did the best I could for the Partners of McKenzie Barber for twenty-four years." Turning to Baxter, Ernie asked, "Joe, the firm has a chairman election coming up in 1990. Has there been any election talk?"

"Not that I have heard, Ernie. McKenzie Barber is over for Joe Baxter. I'm going to finish my career with Mr. Leon."

"And that's how you should finish your career, Joe," Leon Harwell commented. "Let's toast to that." The three touched wine glasses. Baxter noted the slight tremor in Leon Harwell's hands.

Baxter secretly developed an exit plan from McKenzie Barber. His Leon Harwell sponsored work was gone forever, but he had an installed base of clients that required periodic plan maintenance. The Penn Steel plan had not paid off at management's expectations. The stock had spurted slightly but really was only trading 2 3/8s higher from the period of implementation. LBO interests were beginning to make shareholder threats to break up the company. May Wilson had resigned from both the IPCO and Penn Steel Boards replacing them with a Bank and a retailing Board. The newly formed Penn Steel Compensation Committee of the Board had not invited McKenzie Barber to propose, but instructed Baxter to cooperate on providing information to proposing compensation consulting firms.

Planters & Commerce had gone well, however. Baxter was now completing his third phase of the assignment, and had been working Monica into the interface over Linda. While smart and hardworking, Linda demonstrated immature judgment and had been abrasive with some of the bank human resources staff that had been assigned to them.

"They're just not very bright, Joe," Linda had protested as they reviewed materials in Linda's Atlanta motel room. "They are dumb Southern crackers just like that Bonnie you had up to the New York Office and managed to get herself raped by that fascist, Brett Williamson."

"Where in the hell did you hear that?" Baxter demanded. Had Monica let the cat out of the bag?

"It's all over the firm. That's why Harley Dimon left. He was supposed to have slugged Williamson after an Operating Committee meeting in Washington."

"Where in the hell did you hear that? Not from Monica?"

"It was discussed on at least three different occasions in the Ladies room at 311 Park Avenue, and I heard about it on different floors. Some of the women have written unsigned protest letters to Pritchard. Someone from Clyde Nickerson's office usually intercepts them and there's an active hunt for the writers. Nickerson wants them fired."

Baxter slid out of the bed and pulled his shorts on. "I had better get back to my room. It's pushing eleven o'clock," he said stepping into his trousers. Linda rose from her side of the bed wearing only her glasses. Baxter had learned that Linda took out her contacts from time to time.

"Are you upset about something? Maybe it's that I'm getting tired of Planters & Commerce. If you want to replace me with someone else, I would welcome it. I miss New York."

Baxter buttoned his shirt and pulled up his braces. "Maybe it's time to get Harry involved."

"I won't be able to be with you this weekend. My mother expects me to spend the weekend with her out on the Island. We're having a family thing. I'll be back with you Sunday night." Linda stood naked in front of Baxter and wrapped her arms around his neck. "I'm going to miss you this weekend, but I'll make you very happy on Sunday night." Her lipstick was off and Linda kissed Baxter on the cheek.

"You've had your mind on something else lately, and you have been spending a lot of time lately with Mr. Harwell. You're not planning to leave McKenzie Barber are you?"

"I'm several years away from retirement age, and have no clear successor."

"That bothers a lot of us."

"You've been holding meetings?"

"Consultants always talk. I take a lot of calls from other offices for data. You've been out of the office on Planters & Commerce two days a week. We don't seem to have any new Harwell sponsored work coming in. Monica believes that you're making a half-hearted effort on the Penn Steel proposal."

Baxter looked down into Linda's dark, hard, ambitious eyes. Getting involved with her had been a big mistake. They had both been getting tired of the relationship, but neither wanted to break it off while it was still useful. Linda wanted the relationship with Baxter to advance her career, while Baxter needed someone young and attractive whom he could mentor and screw.

"I believe that it's time to get you off Planters & Commerce and onto other things in New York."

"Any specifics?"

"We'll talk about it the week before Labor Day," Baxter kissed Linda on the forehead, opened the door, peered down both directions from the hallway, and walked briskly to the elevator. He had added another night without detection in his relationship with Linda Green.

Baxter had tea at the Ritz Carlton with Lorna Brimmer the following afternoon.

Lorna was seated regally in a large wicker chair at the rear of the lobby, and wore a beige linen suit with matching pumps. Her hair was pinned smartly, and a tuxedoed maitre-d stood at her side in conversation with his arms folded.

"Here's Mr. Baxter now, Claude. Would you have someone serve us some tea and biscuits?"

"Right away, Mrs. Brimmer," he said with a slight bow and pulled Baxter's chair out.

"Well it took us a while but we've managed to get together," Lorna began. "I was in a meeting with Jesse Durham the other day, and he said that you were doing some work with Planters & Commerce. We talked about me going on the Planters & Commerce Board."

"Are you going to do it?"

"I've got to talk it over with Paul. He's in Southeast Asia until after Labor Day. As I've probably told you, Planters & Commerce cut us off our first year here. Paul has yet to forgive them. Jesse believes I was some kind of high flying consultant at McKenzie Barber. How closely does a bank like Planters & Commerce check out incoming Board members? I'm on the Brimmer Industries Board, and three large local charities. I'm on those Boards because I'm Mrs. Paul Brimmer. Jesse wants women on his board. I've built a life here as Mrs. Paul Brimmer."

"How important to you is going on the Planters & Commerce Board?"

"I'd like to do it. I like business and Planters & Commerce is at the center of business in the Southeast. I just wouldn't want to embarrass Paul if someone would find out a few things about my earlier life."

Tea was served and Lorna remained silent until the waiter was of earshot.

"Did you talk it over with Frank?" Baxter asked.

"His advice was to walk away. Frank believes that I should explain that my husband does not want me to serve on a bank board. He believes that Planters & Commerce will become the largest regional bank in the country, and that over time they will acquire a money center bank."

Baxter had been given an operational understanding of the Planters & Commerce strategic plan as well. Lorna had been briefed.

"What do people around here know about Mrs. Paul Brimmer?"

"They know I came down with Paul from the Chicago office of McKenzie Barber ten years ago. I worked for three years with the company as Vice President and Corporate Secretary, and then went on the Board and began to get into the community. I've implied that I attended private schools and told a few people that I hold degrees from Beloit and Northwestern. After you tell it a few times you begin to believe it. The ladies and their husbands gave me careful scrutiny and I passed the test. Paul believed someone from the officer group had to be active in the community, and I was the obvious choice to him."

"How are you described in the proxy and 10k materials?"

"It shows my age as 47 and that I was employed previously with McKenzie Barber, an International consulting firm. I used to prepare those documents when I handled investor relations."

"And you're afraid that if you should go on the Planters & Commerce Board, you'll be exposed."

"Yes."

"Then why don't you fess up with them and see if Jesse still wants you."

"I want to keep my persona just as it is."

"Then take Frank's advice," Baxter recommended. Lorna Brimmer reflectively sipped on her tea.

"I would be honored to serve on the Planters & Commerce Board. But it's not an imperative."

"What do you want out of life, Lorna?"

"More than what I have, but I don't want to put where I am at risk. I've become a great lady. I play golf, attend teas, raise money at charities, and serve the community. Most of it is due to becoming Mrs. Paul Brimmer."

"And what's it like to be Mrs. Paul Brimmer?"

"That story is best told over a late evening drink at some future time and not told over tea. When do you go back to New York, Joe?"

"I have a six something or other Delta flight to LaGuardia. We're pretty far along with our work and it's time we involved Atlanta consulting staff. We have a new practice manager here who used to work with me in New York. I'd like to get him introduced to Paul some time this fall. His name is Harry Devonshire."

"I could try. We use Frank exclusively but we may put him on our Board next spring. You really should have bought Frank's practice last January. He sold it to Hiller and Randolph, an actuarial firm with a compensation practice. Frank, more or less, runs his business through them. It's worked out reasonably well, but Frank would have been more comfortable selling his business to Joe Baxter. The arrangement with Hiller and Randolph runs three years. It could be transferred in February 1991. You should be well vested with McKenzie Barber by that time. Now it's interesting that you should mention the transfer of the person from New York to Atlanta. I understand that the young lady you introduced me to has left McKenzie Barber and is engaged to Bill Rikuns."

"Do you mean Bonnie Grow?"

"I believe that's the name. I understand that she resigned from the Atlanta Office shortly after the first year of the year."

"I believe she was disappointed with her progress with the firm," Baxter explained.

"I sat at the same table at an opera fund-raiser with Mr. Harley Dimon. He told me that he had resigned from the firm. In fact, he came out to Brimmer Industries to have a sandwich with Paul. Paul told me that Harley was looking for a job. What's going on at McKenzie Barber?"

"The firm, as always, is going through a number of changes. Harley's had a good career, but I believe he wants to try something else. Bonnie Grow is in the same boat."

"Bill Rikuns is regarded as something of a joke around town," Lorna commented.

"Well apparently Bonnie Grow has taken him seriously," Baxter responded.

"Do you and Frank talk?"

"Not a lot."

"I hear your wife has left you."

"She wanted to try somebody else."

"Good old Joe Baxter, carefully editing each word in every sentence. I can remember a time when we used to talk more openly."

"That was before you became a great lady. I always couch my language in front of queens and duchesses."

"Paul believes that McKenzie Barber is falling apart."

"The firm has never been stronger, Lorna," Baxter responded.

"Are you going to continue to visit Atlanta regularly? I know Paul would like to see you. He appreciated that introduction you arranged last December with Leon Harwell."

"It's time to transition the Planters & Commerce work to the Atlanta office. I'm going back this afternoon and I'll be back the week after Labor Day to facilitate the transition."

Lorna produced a business card from her purse. "Then why don't you call me a week in advance and I'll check Paul's schedule. We can have a quiet dinner at our home. Paul isn't much for going out to dinner unless there's a business reason."

Baxter studied the card. It read:

LORNA KING BRIMMER
VICE CHAIRWOMAN OF THE BOARD OF DIRECTORS
BRIMMER INDUSTRIES

"The bottom number is my private line at home. Call a week in advance and so I can schedule Paul. We have built a very lovely home in Buckhead. It could be quite a show place if Paul was into entertaining. We hold an annual holiday party where Paul is a very reluctant host. Now, when do you go back to New York, Joe?"

"I'm leaving this afternoon," Baxter replied. It was September 1st. He planned to announce his resignation from McKenzie Barber on the Tuesday after Labor Day. He would be the newly appointed Executive Vice President and General Manager of Harwell Management when he returned in September.

"Come and see us." Lorna stood up from her chair and extended her hand. "It was so good to see you, Joe."

Lorna had a firm handshake with strong fingers. The finger strength, Baxter assumed, was developed from her years of typing documents. The maitre'd rushed to Lorna's side to offer parting felicitations as they left the restaurant. Lorna King Brimmer walked briskly away from Baxter toward the entrance to the parking area. Baxter concluded that she had evolved from an attractive thirtyish woman to a striking, handsome and self-confident society matron. Lorna waved and smiled back from the revolving door entrance. Possibly, there may be a future relationship a two hour flight away. He certainly was growing weary of Linda Green.

Baxter settled in with the newspapers and a Canadian Club in the first class section of the 5:17 Delta flight to LaGuardia. He scanned the *Wall Street Journal* and moved on to the Obituary Section of the *New York Times*. It had been his favorite form of junk reading since his 1977 flight to New York in the company of Beth Gold. Now let's see who's packed it in, Baxter thought as he turned to page A 19.

Taking a sip of Canadian Club, Baxter began at the left hand side of the page scanning the names.

MARSHALL BOUCHER, 3D BALTIMORE CIVIC LEADER, 76

SIDNEY LIPTSHITZ, 94, EDUCATOR AND ADVOCATE OF YIDDISH STUDY

BOYD LYONS, A VETERAN CIVIL-RIGHTS LAWYER IS DEAD AT 87

LEON HARWELL, 64, LEGENDARY INVESTMENT MANAGER CHAIRMAN OF HARWELL MANAGEMENT COMPANY

Baxter re-read the headline three times before proceeding to the narrative.

Leon Harwell, who was universally regarded as an icon of the investment industry, died in his sleep yesterday in his Greenwich, Connecticut home on Tuesday evening. The cause was a cerebral hemorrhage said his wife, Adele.

Mr. Harwell was the grandson, of "Big Bill" Harwell, a famous and notorious late 19th century Coal Baron, who was reputed to have accumulated an enormous fortune during the development of the US coal mining industry. Mr. Harwell was the second son of William Harwell, II, who is credited with selling off the coal assets of the company and forming the Harwell Trust, a forerunner of the Harwell Management Company. Mr. Harwell and his older brother, William Harwell, III assume management control of Harwell Trust in 1945 following the conclusion of the Second World War. They continued to jointly manage the assets of the Harwell Family trust until 1958 when the elder brother died in a commercial plane crash in Latin America. Mr. Harwell assumed the Presidency of the family investment trust in 1958, changed its name to the Harwell Management Company in 1964, and ran the family investment company for the next thirty years. During that time, Mr. Harwell became revered and respected as a skilled and secretive investment manager. He additionally served on the Boards of Directors of over fifty large and small public companies during this period, limiting himself to no more than six board seats at any one time. Mr. Harwell generally liked to serve on the Compensation Committee of the Board of Directors. He was a passionate believer in providing stock ownership opportunities to senior management.

While the Harwell Management Company releases no performance data, outsiders who have charted the Harwell Management investments in public companies, rated their performance as superior. Mr. Harwell, outside of his public company board service, was described as a reclusive individual who had little time for the media or civic activities.

Mr. Harwell attended the Fieldcrest Prep School and earned a degree from Yale University in 1944. Exempted from military service by a history of poor health, Mr. Harwell joined the Harwell Trust in September of 1944. He married Adele Busler in 1950, whom he often described as "the family's representative in charity matters".

In addition to his wife, Mr. Harwell is survived by two sons and a daughter. The eldest son, Wilson of Culver City, California, is an independent film producer in addition to serving as professor of cinema arts at UCLA, a daughter, Claudia, of Greenwich, Connecticut, and a son, Spencer, of New York. Private funeral services will be held on Saturday, September 3rd.

Baxter could only think of one word as he read and re-read the obituary. Shit!

The flight attendant collected Baxter's drink and the window seat passenger, a man with greying hair dressed in a pinstriped business uniform, squeezed by him.

Baxter was numbed. Harwell was gone. He had a contract that had not been announced to the family. Ernie Grey had been the only one privy to the contract. Baxter had checked his phone mail before getting on the plane. The calls had been routine. What was wrong with people? Was he the only one who read the *New York Times* obituaries? He'd have to get to Ernie from the airport.

Baxter ordered a second Canadian Club when the plane was up and his seat mate ordered a white wine.

"Do you live in Atlanta?" the man in he window seat asked conversationally after their drinks were served.

"Just visiting. I've lived in New York for several years," Baxter answered.

"I see you have the Times obituaries there. Can I borrow them for a minute?"

A man after my own heart, Baxter concluded.

"A rather important figure in my industry died suddenly earlier in the week. I just flipped through the Times at breakfast. It came as quite a shock."

Baxter passed the obituaries. He watched the man fold the paper around the Harwell article.

"Were you acquainted with Leon Harwell?" Baxter asked.

"I met with him on several occasions. Did you know him too?"

"I worked with him on several projects over the years," Baxter responded.

His seatmate looked Baxter up and down in a new light. He was a lantern jawed man in a tailored white shirt, the initials, GMW on his breast pocket, and wore a blue Hermes tie with blue silk braces.

"Are you in investments?"

"Management Consulting. Joe Baxter, McKenzie Barber," Baxter said offering his hand.

"Gardner Jamison, Fletcher Berwick & Co. I run the equity advisory group. Quite a shock wasn't it? Leon Harwell has been around a long time. That icon of the industry comment is very accurate. Although a lot of us in the industry thought something might be up when Harwell brought Hakim Selim over from Broadbaker as Chief Investment Officer. Do you know Hakim?"

"Reasonably well."

"We couldn't fathom why Hakim would leave Broadbaker to go to Harwell Management. The reason is right here. He's going to be running the place, isn't he?"

"I believe that will be contingent on his level of support from the family," Baxter advised.

Gardner Jamison raised one eyebrow. "You know the Harwell family?"

"I've met most of them. In addition to being a client, I regarded Leon Harwell as a close personal friend," Baxter said with a tone of sincere finality.

"I understand and offer my condolences for a loss of a close personal friend," Jamison said.

Baxter ordered another Canadian Club and worked his way through the *Wall Street Journal* hoping to avoid further conversation with Jamison. Unfortunately Baxter had identified himself as someone who knew people to a man whose life's work could well be getting to know people. Jamison ordered a second white wine and resumed the conversation.

"Didn't Ernie Grey, the Chairman of IPCO, used to be with McKenzie Barber?"

"He was the Chairman of McKenzie Barber for twenty-four years. Ernie was on the IPCO Board when Cornelius VanderKelen was called off to Latin America."

"Do you know Cornie VanderKelen, Joe?"

"No. I was at one of his homes for a black tie fund raiser and shook his hand. I was a guest at the Harwell table."

"Ernie has had a bit of a marital turn hasn't he? Our home is in Greenwich. We've used GreyWebb, his son's firm, for some interior design work. We got to know Millie Grey pretty well. Apparently Ernie took up with some young consultant."

"The second Mrs. Grey is a very close friend of mine. I wasn't acquainted with the first Mrs. Grey," Baxter answered coldly in the hope he could break off the conversation.

"Do you know some of our senior people at Fletcher Berwick?" Jamison probed.

"I was Stephany Hart's guest at your Christmas Party at the Pierre last December. I know Chet and Sybil Stone. Sybil was a literary agent who used to coordinate the McKenzie Barber Press publications. I was liaison to her for a couple of years."

"Chet's retiring this December. He's bought a ranch out in Wyoming. Chet says he and Sybil are getting out of the rat race."

Baxter took a sip of Canadian Club and recalled his nooners with Sybil McCarthy before she had taken on the role of Sybil Stone. He remembered that she was partial to black underwear.

"Stephany Hart," Jamison continued, "was away with the SEC in Washington for a number of years. I believe she's a Securities Analyst now, covering the retail industry. My people know her well, and she has an excellent professional reputation. She's a very knowledgeable and well respected in the retail industry."

"Stephany is a very old friend. It's been nice talking to you." Baxter slid back his seat and closed his eyes. He needed relief from this relationship manager. He needed a career game plan that he hadn't had when he boarded the airplane.

The funeral service was held at St. Marks Church at 10 AM on Saturday, September 3rd. It took Baxter a frantic hour of calling from the Delta Crown Room in LaGuardia on Thursday to locate the time and location of the ceremony. He finally found Toni Grey at a place called Lake Wampum in the Pocono Mountains of Pennsylvania.

"Oh Joe, it happened so quickly. We've had Labor Day plans for months. My brother and sister-in-law are down with us. Now we have to drive to Connecticut on Friday afternoon for the reviewal on Friday night and the funeral Saturday morning. Apparently, Leon went to bed on Tuesday night complaining that he was very tired and Adele woke up next to him in the morning and found him cold and dead. It must have been a horrible experience for her. They had been married 38 years. I offered to help, but the oldest nephew, Ned jumped in. He apparently took over arrangements, but Spencer, his youngest son stepped in. There was quite a squabble. I got two or three calls from Adele, and Ernie was out of town, as usual. But I got a hold of Ernie in Los Angeles and he stepped in and got things under control. He told me to, 'Get to Joe' and I planned to call you first thing on Friday morning."

"Did Ernie give you any other message for me?" Baxter asked.

"None other than to tell you the funeral arrangements, Joe."

"Where can I reach Ernie tonight?"

"You can't. He's on a plane back here that will land in Philadelphia. I have to leave very shortly to pick him up. I can have him call you in the morning," Toni offered.

Ernie returned Baxter's call mid-morning at McKenzie Barber.

"Joe, I know you have heard the news about Leon," Ernie's voice sounded resonantly over the line. "It's pretty chaotic right now. There's a major split between Ned, Gasdan, and Spencer on succession. But the main thing is to get everyone civil long enough to get Leon buried. Poor Adele is caught in the middle."

"What about my arrangements, Ernie? I have a signed contract to join Harwell Management on September 16. I planned to resign from McKenzie Barber on Tuesday. What shall I do?"

"Joe, all of this has happened so suddenly. The first thing we must do is to get Leon buried. Then we have to get the family sorted out. I'll need some time on that. We can talk on Saturday. I'll see you then." Ernie clicked off. It was obvious to Baxter that he would not be resigning on Tuesday from McKenzie Barber.

St. Marks Episcopal Church was located in Old Greenwich and Baxter was lost twice in the wooded winding back roads of Greenwich, and finally Old Greenwich, before he sighted St. Marks Church. The church was a large, white frame, single spired building with a cornerstone that had been inscribed 1892.

It was surrounded by a grassy lawn and to the right of the church was a large parking lot that appeared to be approximately half filled with cars. The sky was overcast and Baxter felt scattered drops of rain as he quickly walked from his rental car.

He took a seat on the aisle in the rear of the church. It was bright and airy with beamed ceilings and a huge mahogany cross over the altar which was surrounded by flowers. The organ was playing some familiar Bach which Baxter could not name. A large left front pew contained the members of the Harwell family. Baxter could make out Adele Harwell flanked by her son, Spencer, and Ned Harwell. The pew appeared to have a capacity to seat eight parishioners. Was it a Harwell family pew that dated back to the erection of the church? The people in the pew were representative of the people he would be working for in the absence of Leon Harwell. How many were there of them? Leon Harwell had promised Baxter a complete briefing the week before he joined Harwell Management. Leon's death had changed everything. Baxter had counted on Harwell having a life expectancy of three to five years.

An Episcopal priest emerged from a door in full clerical regalia and the church assembly rose to their feet. The priest said some words Baxter couldn't make out and then motioned for them to sit. The ceremony began.

There was some liturgy interspersed with songs and another short Bach piece. Had Harwell been going to church all these years? Baxter knew him only as the steel-willed, understated man who ran Harwell Management. The client who had taken an interest in him. It had been Baxter's relationship with Harwell that had singled him out and had influenced his New York transfer. How would his life and career have progressed if he hadn't met and hit it off with Leon Harwell? Baxter had slowed his pace to accommodate his transition from McKenzie Barber to Harwell Management. The job had been his to start in twelve days time. Now what was his future?

The priest began to recite his words now. He was summarizing the life of Leon Harwell much in the manner that the *New York Times* had two days earlier. He added that Leon Harwell had been a loving father and a benefactor to the less fortunate. There was a commercial for life in the hereafter followed by one last hymn of five stanzas length. The ceremony was concluded and Baxter stood outside the church in a light rain as people departed from the church. The first familiar face was that of Spencer Harwell. In his dark suit with wire rimmed glasses and cold chiseled features, he seemed to Baxter to resemble a young Leon Harwell.

They gripped hands and Baxter said his condolences.

"Mother spotted you in the back of the church." Spencer pulled out a three by five card from the inside breast pocket of his suit.

"Here's directions to the cemetery and you're invited to come back to the house after the burial. This all happened so suddenly, and we couldn't get to all of Dad's close friends. Thank you for coming." The card with the directions was thrust into Baxter's hands, and Spencer darted back into St. Marks Church.

The burial service went quickly. The rain had become heavy and the funeral goers stood in a semi-circle of twenty or so open umbrellas while the priest said his last words over Leon Harwell's casket. Baxter stood under his newly acquired K-Mart umbrella. He could make out the faces of Ned Harwell and Spencer Harwell flanking the frail form of Adele who wore a black hat and veil. Ernie and Toni Grey stood closely together in Burberry raincoats. Across from the grave site was a young man whom Baxter recognized as Preston Grey accompanied by a dark-haired mature woman with her icy eyes trained on Ernie and Toni. That had to be Millie Grey,

Baxter concluded. Hakim Selim stood to the right of the casket with a trench coat over his shoulders holding an umbrella. The body was lowered into the grave, and Adele Harwell emptied a spade of dirt over the casket. She was followed by Spencer with each member of the family adding a spade-full of earth. Adele led a slow silent procession of mourners through the rain and back down the walk to the parking lot.

Baxter caught up with Selim in the parking lot. "Will I see you at the Harwells?" he asked when he caught up to Selim at the door of his candy apple red MG.

"I think not, Joe. It's quite edgy among the family members right now. It should settle down by Wednesday. A meeting with Stanford Asher, the family attorney, has been set for ten in the morning. I understand that you have done some work for Leon in management succession. I assume you will be invited. My track record as Chief Investment Officer and my contract make me invaluable to the family. I've paid my respects, and I certainly don't want to overpay them by lingering among the power prowling Harwells. I'm going into New York, have a nice dinner, and make love to a woman. I would suggest that you consider something similar." Selim opened the car trunk and placed his coat and umbrella inside.

"I'm going to miss Leon," Hakim said placing his hand on Baxter's shoulder. "He was, in his own way, a brilliant investment manager. Antiquated perhaps but nevertheless brilliant." Hakim slid into his MG, closed the door behind him, and jumped the engine. Baxter noted that his license plate read SELIM 48972 X.

The funeral guests were assembled in a large sitting room that looked out on the garden. A buffet table had been set up with finger sandwiches, salads, large urns of coffee and hot water. At the far end of the table was an assemblage of brandy and port bottles placed around two large bottles of Irish Whiskey. It was an eclectic group. Some were accustomed to being welcomed into the Harwell estate, while for others it might have been their first and final visit to the private world beyond the Harwell front gate.

Baxter poured some brandy into a coffee cup and found himself in a conversational trio comprised of Dan and Susan Gasdon and the Episcopal priest, who was introduced as Dr. Martin. Baxter was introduced as a close professional friend of Leon Harwell.

"I'm very glad you could make it, Joe," Dan Gasdon, the Harwell son-in-law and General Counsel said to Baxter after the introductions. Baxter had been introduced to Susan Harwell on other occasions. She had inherited her mother's plain features and her father's reserve. She remembered Baxter as someone who had done some sort of work for her father over the years. He could either be a groundskeeper or an accountant as far as she was concerned. Dan Gasdon knew better. He viewed Baxter as his father-in-law's confidante who was privy to information which was excluded from him. He placed his hand on Baxter's shoulder and asked in a soft voice. "Joe, has Stanford Asher reached you? He was at the church and the gravesite, but had to be back in New York this afternoon."

"No he hasn't." Baxter recalled the meeting with Asher over his contract. Had he informed the family?

"Who is this Stanford Asher again, dear?" Susan Gasdon politely demanded.

"He's Leon's attorney."

"I presumed you were my father's attorney, Dan?"

"I'm the General Counsel for Harwell Management, dear. Mr. Asher and his firm have served the Harwell family for three generations. His grandfather was Big Bill Harwell's attorney."

"Big Bill, indeed, Dan. You make our great grandfather sound like a plant foreman," turning to Dr. Martin. "Our great grandfather was one of the leading industrialists of his day. Everything the family has today is rooted in his leadership and vision."

"And Leon safely stewarded the family assets," Dan added. Baxter wondered how well the Gasdons got on.

"I thought your service was very thoughtful and professional," Baxter said to Dr. Martin.

"Why would Mr. Asher need to see Joe?" Susan Gasdon persisted.

"I believe you have been working with Leon for some time relative to his retirement plans. Joe helped Harwell Management locate Hakim Selim and had some private discussions with Leon about his plans for stepping down one day."

"Why would Leon talk over a matter like that with you? Is that what you do? Retirement planning?"

"I had the pleasure of working with your late father on a number of projects over the years. One issue that he wanted to review outside the family was the time when he would step down either through retirement or untimely death," Baxter replied. He conceded to himself that Hakim was the smart one having fluidly made his exit.

"Dear," Dan Gasdon said taking his wife's arm. "It's been a very long day. Why don't we say good night and last condolences to your mother, and get home to the children."

"Dr. Martin," Susan Gasdon said to the priest. "You have been so helpful and inspiring to our family over the past few days. We are very grateful to you for your kindness."

Then turning to Baxter. "Dan is the only one qualified to succeed my father. Don't you forget that."

Baxter nodded his head and then bowed slightly hoping that Dan Gasdon would maneuver and get his wife away from him.

Dr. Martin stood in front of Baxter continuing to nurse his half glass of what looked to be sherry.

"It's been a trying few days for everyone involved. Leon and Adele have always been major supporters of St. Marks. I believe Dan and Susan were married in the church several years before I was called here."

"Leon was a regular church goer?" Baxter questioned.

"He seldom missed a Sunday, and he seemed to love joining in on the hymns. His health appeared to be slipping a bit over the past year. No one expected God to claim Leon this prematurely. Now do I understand that there's some question as to who will succeed him?"

"The family will have to work that out, Dr.," Baxter said slipping from the clergyman. He greeted Adele Harwell in the center of the room where she held Spencer's arm for support.

"Oh, Joe, it was so good that you could be here to say good-bye to Leon." She squeezed Baxter's hand and he kissed Adele on the forehead. "I believe I've said hello to everyone now, Spencer. Do you see anyone that we have missed?"

"No, mother. I believe that it's time for you to get your rest. I'll see after the guests."

"Hakim. I haven't greeted Hakim," Mrs. Harwell realized.

"He had to head right back to New York, Mrs. Harwell. I believe he had an important overseas investment call to make," Baxter reported.

Bennett nodded his head in agreement. "It's time to get you off to bed, mother."

"Don't shoo our guests off now, Spencer. They stood in the rain to say good-bye to Leon. Isn't that just like Hakim, running off to look after the family's money." Baxter heard Adele Harwell chatter as she moved through the room. He saw Ernie and Toni at the doorway exchanging hugs.

"Now isn't that an adorable couple?" He heard a voice next to him say. The voice belonged to the woman Baxter had identified as Millie Grey. Her son, Preston, was at her side.

"Go over and say hello to your nice Daddy and his girlfriend and get it over with. If he comes over here, I'll talk to him, but I'm certainly not going to seek him out."

Preston Grey started across the room. Millie made eye contact with Baxter. "I know you from some place. Do me a favor. Run over and get me a fresh brandy. I'm on number two, and I don't want to get a reputation as a hard drinking lady at wakes."

"Any special brand?"

"What ever is pouring," Millie replied.

102

Baxter poured a large snifter of brandy and worked his way across the room to Millie Grey. She looked like a woman of thirty from across the room. It was only up close you would guess her age in the mid 60's.

Millie accepted the brandy snifter and held it up to the light.

"You certainly didn't spare the horses on this one. You wouldn't be trying to get me drunk so that you can take advantage of me, would you?"

"It never entered my mind."

"Well you might think about it. That's my ex across the room with that little lady in the black pants suit." Millie nodded her head in the general direction of Ernie and Toni where Preston held them in conversation.

"That's my son, Preston, over there. He's an interior designer. The dark haired man is his father," Millie explained.

"I know Ernie Grey and I've met your son a couple of times in the past. My name is Joe Baxter and I'm a Partner with McKenzie Barber. We met years ago at a New York Historical Society Ball on the VanderKelen estate."

"You're right, that was many years ago. Good old Vandy, the man who took a powder on his Chairman job so that he could be a roving ambassador. And when I say roving, I mean roving. He doesn't call. He doesn't write. He just roves."

"And how is your daughter doing? I met her last December at a holiday party. She had taken a job as house counsel with an apparel firm."

"They're in Chapter 11 bankruptcy, but she's getting paid and she's found a nice married man twenty years her senior with three children to spend her free time with. We're very proud of our Kathleen. Hell, she was always Daddy's girl anyway. Pres is a go-getter. He worked in his uncle's decorating business until Arthur died. Pres took it over and tripled the business in five years. He may not have graduated at the top of Greystone Academy or got into Harvard, but he's going to be very successful. How did you get to know Leon?"

"He was a client. I've worked with him for years. He's been a very special person to me over the years and I will sincerely miss him."

Millie took a long drink from her brandy snifter. "Leon was all right. I think his youngest kid is all right too. The rest of them are losers. Leon was brilliant and Adele was so right for him. We go back all the way with the Harwells. Ernie flew with the older brother, Will, in World War II. Will was married to Laura. See that big blonde cow over there by the sandwiches?"

Baxter observed a heavy set woman in black nibbling on a finger sandwich talking to a thin balding man who was tieless and wore dark glasses. "That's Wilson Harwell she's talking with, the mysterious and little known film producer. He's in from California to take an estimate of what his cut of the estate will be. You can bet he's got it spent already. Laura will be trying like hell to nudge her little crown prince, Ned, into Leon's job. Laura's a hard-headed German, and she let herself get fat and stay fat. I used to refer to her to Ernie as the Graf Zeppelin. Will decided to die in a plane crash and left the whole bag on Leon's shoulders. Leon's grown their wealth and their egos. On the other hand, Leon loved being Leon. He loved making money, and he was damned good at it. He was a faithful, loving husband, and he tried to be a good father. I know Ernie's on their board now because Leon wanted him around to sort things out if something ever happened to him. This Moroccan investment manager they hired is reputed to be a smart little shit, but nobody trusts him. Ernie could probably run Harwell Management, but he's making a couple of million with IPCO. He doesn't need Harwell Management in his life." Millie took another long sip of brandy. "I'm running off at the mouth to you, aren't I? I hope you won't repeat what I've just said. You have the face of a bartender. Did anyone ever tell you that?"

"Come to think of it, my last wife did," Baxter replied.

"Well," Millie Grey said with resignation, "It's time for me to pay my respects to my ex-husband and his wife. What's her name? Do you know it? Is it Polly or something like that?"

"It's Toni," Baxter corrected her.

"She sure looks like a Polly. Well here goes. One hearty 'Isn't this tragic and what a beautiful funeral' and I'm out of here. Nice to talk to you."

Baxter watched Millie Grey move across the room in aggressive steps toward the husband of her earlier years and Baxter saw Ned Harwell wave and start toward him.'

"Joe, isn't it?" Ned Harwell extended his right hand and balanced a half-filled teacup in the other. He had to be in his mid-fifties. Ned Harwell maintained a cheerful upbeat appearance with his bald head, suntan and well tailored clothes. He appeared to be trimmer than the Ned Harwell Baxter remembered from his luncheon at Pietro's three years earlier. Baxter had, over the years in between, seen Ned Harwell's picture periodically in the *New York Times* society section. He was always in the company of his fashion model wife who apparently was still unwelcome within the closed circle of Harwells.

"Joe Baxter," he said accepting Ned Harwell's firm handshake. "You and I had lunch at Pietro's a few years back when I was doing some work for Mr. Leon."

"And very good and timely work it was. You brought us Hakim, and that has worked out very well for the family. It's worked out well for Hakim too. Lord knows we're paying him a bundle, but he's worth it." Ned Harwell seemed to Baxter to be in ebullient spirits for a man who had suddenly lost an uncle.

"Uncle Leon was very much like a father to me. While I don't and never will have Leon's head for investments, he counted on me to coordinate certain family and philanthropic matters for Harwell Management. He also kept me briefed once a week on the status of the investment portfolio and administrative matters, while I kept him up to date on the family and the charity work. Leon and I were a very close team. He had a lot of confidence in you Joe. He'd always say, 'I'm going to get Joe on that'. Leon's health began to slip about two years ago. The whole family was pleased when he persuaded Ernie Grey to come on the board. Ernie was my late father's closest friend. They were fighter pilots together in the second war. Ernie was the friend of the family who jumped in to help Leon after my father's sudden death."

Baxter nodded his head. He had heard these tales of Harwell before. Ned Harwell had an agenda.

"And wasn't Aunt Adele a trooper, today?" Ned Harwell continued. "The two of them were so devoted. I didn't think she was going to make it through the last three days, but she rallied very nicely and made it through the funeral service. Aunt Adele is made of strong stuff. In fact, the Harwells are made out of pretty strong stuff. Now I understand that you have been doing some recent work for Leon and that Ernie Grey was involved." Ned Harwell had come to his point.

"Leon was concerned about his succession. This goes back to our lunch at Pietro's. I've had periodic discussions with Leon about succession plans," Baxter replied in his best bedside manner consultant's voice.

"I would think that succession would be all settled when Hakim was brought in. We had our Chief Investment Officer successor to Leon. Now it's simply a matter of the family to pick a successor to Leon and that can be accomplished through the principles of lineage. Everything should be in place for succession thanks to your previous work."

"I'm certain everything will be resolved in your meeting with Stanford Asher," Baxter responded.

"What will be resolved? There should be no question in the lineage for succession. I'm prepared to succeed Leon as the Chief Executive of Harwell Management Company. When I reach retirement age, Spencer should succeed me. It's as simple as that. There's nothing to be resolved that I know of in the Stanford Asher meeting. Do you know of anything, Joe?"

"I have no idea of what's in Leon Harwell's will. He simply asked me to study certain matters affecting Harwell Management CEO succession."

"And what were your conclusions?" Ned Harwell demanded in a soft voice.

"I made my report to Mr. Leon and Ernie Grey. I would recommend that you take it up with Ernie."

"I plan to. And I will also take note of your lack of willingness to disclose information this evening."

"I understand, and I hope that you will understand the consultant's proprietary confidentiality that I'm required to adhere to as a McKenzie Barber Partner," Baxter bluffed.

Ned Harwell nodded his head. "Of course, Joe. I understand. Ernie Grey pleaded with me to join McKenzie Barber when I wanted to leave the bank. But I just believed that the tie lines between Leon and Ernie were too close. I wanted to go to a place where I could make it on my own steam. I'm glad we could have this chat, Joe. And thank you for coming to say good-bye to my Uncle."

Baxter accepted Ned Harwell's hand. "Your uncle was more than a client. He was a friend and mentor."

Ned nodded his head appreciatively and Baxter proceeded across the room to Ernie Grey. Millie Grey stood with a fur coat over her shoulders while her son, Preston, was writing something on the back of his business card for a distant Harwell mourning cousin. Toni Grey was talking animatedly to Millie Grey, while Ernie stood in silence with his hands clasped surveying the room.

"May we have a moment alone?" Baxter said softly to the retired Chairman of McKenzie Barber.

Ernie continued to stare off into space.

"Could we have a moment alone?" Baxter repeated.

Ernie's dark eyes settled on Baxter and it seemed to take a few seconds for him to recognize his questioner.

"Not here. Let's stop for coffee. Do you know the Holiday Inn just off the freeway. We can talk there. We have to get back to Lake Wampum. Toni has her brother and his wife down for Labor Day weekend," Ernie replied laconically.

"Is anything wrong, Ernie?"

"It's this room." Baxter watched Entire take in the room with a wide angle glance. "I remember it from the housewarming. It must have been back in the mid 1950's."

Suddenly the two of them became a threesome. They were joined by the tieless balding man whom Baxter recognized to be Wilson Harwell. It was Baxter's first look up close at the eldest son of Leon and Adele Harwell. The son who went West and was rarely mentioned.

Wilson Harwell had his father's spare body frame. His eyes were obscured by blue tinted glasses and he wore a blue blazer, white turtleneck sweater, grey trousers, and loafers without socks. My God, Baxter reflected, he went to his father's funeral sockless.

"I know you're Ernie, but no one's introduced me to this gentleman," Wilson said with a half smile.

"Joe Baxter. I was a consultant to your Dad." Wilson had rough skin and a soft handshake.

"In investments?"

"No, I worked with him on organization and other matters." Wilson couldn't be more than 5 feet six and Baxter seemed to tower over him.

"Joe worked with Leon on Harwell Management organization and helped your father hire Hakim Selim, the Chief Investment Officer. Joe is a Partner at my old firm, McKenzie Barber."

"My accountant tells me that the little Arab is making a lot of money for the family, maybe even more than dear old Dad. You do good work, Joe." Wilson spoke in a relaxed California style tenor voice. Wilson turned to Ernie. "I understand that you are the only non-family member on the Harwell Management Board."

"Your Father asked me to come on the board about two years ago. I believe he planned to ask other outsiders into Harwell Management to assist in the transition process in the event of his retirement or death."

"Well we got the latter as opposed to the former. What happens now?"

"I assume that you have been informed that a meeting of the immediate family members has been scheduled in the Stanford Asher law offices on Wednesday." Ernie's jaw was set, and Baxter sensed that he had taken an instant dislike to Wilson Harwell.

"I was considering having my lawyer fly out for that meeting. Are the others bringing their lawyers?"

"I would check with Mr. Asher's office. The meeting will be confined to family members," Ernie explained. "Mr. Asher would probably not object to having family members attorneys as either designated representatives or on call from some anteroom in the Asher offices, but I doubt whether we will allow family members and their attorneys to be present in the meeting room."

"Who's going to run Harwell Management now? Is the family going to vote? I guess Ned is next up. It's a good thing that Dad hired that little Arab. I certainly wouldn't want or expect Ned to run the Harwell money."

"Well, I believe your father arranged for a competent succession. You'll have to excuse me. I have to look after my wife." Ernie left Wilson Harwell with Baxter and without a handshake, "That's the Holiday Inn, Joe," he said in passing.

"How about a last drink, Joe?" Wilson offered.

Baxter wanted to leave, but here was an opportunity to cultivate another family member. Perhaps an extension of the conversation could be useful.

"Port okay?" Wilson asked and poured two glasses upon Baxter's nodded agreement.

"Were you allowed in the house often?" Wilson asked.

"I worked with your father professionally. Most of the time we met at the Harwell Management offices or at his club. Your father and mother held a very nice annual Holiday Party each year in mid-December that I always attended and I was invited out for diner a few times. I admired your father."

"I'm the family black sheep. Spencer represents the model they really wanted in a son, and they got it right on their third try. They kicked me out of Yale, and I went off to USC to study film making. I wasn't what they wanted in a son and they certainly weren't what I wanted in parents. I made a deal with my father. Keep the money coming and I'll do my thing on the other side of the country. Now my concern is about the money continuing to come in. I've produced some very commercially unsuccessful movies, and have some alimony costs out there to ladies who managed to get pretty good lawyers. This Ernie Grey seemed to be a real stiff. Do you know him well?"

"He's rather upset over the death of your father."

"I note that he managed to have both his first and second wives show up for the funeral. It reminded me of a script I read last week."

"I believe Ernie Grey and his first wife, Millie, go back a long way with your mother and father. Ernie flew in World War II with your late Uncle Will, and at one time all three couples were very close."

"Ah yes. The incredible disappearing Will Harwell. The man who's been declared dead, but may be alive. You don't suppose he'll show up at this Asher's office on Wednesday and want his old job back?"

Baxter finished half of his port glass in one gulp. He wanted to be free of this little turd.

"I take one look at you, Joe, and I can tell that you were my father's kind of professional. I can look in your face after listening to you talk, I know your whole life story. Your father was either a doctor or a lawyer in some small Connecticut town. You were Captain of your prep school football team. You either went to Dartmouth, Yale, or Williams College. You served as a Naval Office and then went on to take an MBA at Columbia. You joined McKenzie Barber after Columbia and have been there ever since. You married a girl from either Wellesley, Skidmore, or Vassar one year out of business school and you have three children of which two are in college and a third is in his last year in prep school. You're going to retire in five years and ask yourself what did I accomplish in my life other than holding my place in the social chain? My father liked the tall, smooth, with good manners and social grace. How am I doing?"

"Amazingly on the mark, old fellow," Baxter replied and downed the rest of the port. "I really have to be going. My son, Lance, is expecting me to pick him up after his lacrosse match. I really have to run. Have a nice inheritance."

Baxter looked in the coffee shop of the Holiday Inn first. Toni located Baxter near the cash register.

"Ernie's in the bar, Joe. Something really upset him back there. I'm going to let you spend 45 minutes together and then I'm going to come in and get Ernie. We've got to get back to Lake Wampum."

"How did you get along with Millie Grey?" Baxter probed.

"We get along famously, Joe. She regards me as a little nothing that her husband took up with, and I regard her as a deceptive, mean spirited, and selfish person. Both of us seem to understand how the other feels, and we were very civil."

Ernie Grey sat in a booth near the door with a half-filled straight up martini in front of him.

Baxter waved, ordered a Port and joined Ernie Grey in the formica covered booth. It was a quiet Labor Day weekend bar with a few beer drinkers watching a televised baseball game.

"Well it's over," Baxter said sliding into the booth.

"It was a sacrilege to Leon Harwell's memory. I'm tempted to resign from the Board at the end of the year. Poor Adele. What greedy, self-centered people. Wilson was too much for me. The first time I visited the Harwell estate was for their housewarming party. Adele was carrying Wilson at the time. Will Harwell II was alive, but fading, and it had been decided that Leon and Adele would move in permanently."

"What kind of a son was Wilson? He told me that he was a blacksheep," Baxter questioned.

"In those days I was closer to Will. Leon reached out to me after his brother's plane had gone down. We exchanged a lot of confidences over the years. Wilson was always a problem. He was virtually expelled from Yale. His Harwell name required withdrawal. He's gone through millions over the years. I wanted to throttle him back there, Joe. I'm worried about Adele.

111

There had better be some kind of separate personal trust for her. Damn it! We have no time. I believed Leon had a minimum of two years and five years on the outside. Now he's gone."

"And I have a contract to join Harwell management as Executive Vice President & General Manager," Baxter reminded Ernie Grey.

"That will never work now, Joe. You have two options. One is to call Stanford Asher and tell him to void that contract. The second is to settle the contract with the family. Reporting to Harwell Management in the EVP & General Manager job without Leon as President would be a disaster. I believe you better forget about Harwell Management, Joe."

Baxter leaned back against the red naugahyde padding of the booth. The dream of leaving McKenzie Barber to join Harwell Management Company was over with Leon Harwell's death. It was salvage time.

"Ernie, who will be the next President of Harwell Management?"

"The bylaws, as I recall, will require the family shareholders to vote on succession. This Wednesday meeting could be very messy. I have had to reschedule operating review meetings to be available on Wednesday. At this time in my life, I don't need this kind of aggravation. Asher will convene the meeting but I'm going to have to run it. I would rather that the issue of your contract not be introduced until we have selected a President. Thank God we have Selim running investments."

"But wasn't my selection by Leon related to his need for oversight of Hakim?"

"The family respects Selim. They won't be able to place the same value on you that Leon did. I would plan to complete your career with McKenzie Barber, Joe."

"Thank you for your thoughts in this matter," Baxter said rising up from the booth. "Have a good weekend and I would appreciate being updated on the family meeting." He left the Port behind untouched. Baxter found Toni talking to her brother on a lobby pay phone. He tapped her on the shoulder.

"We're done now. I would get him out of that bar as soon as you can." Toni patted Baxter's hand and continued to talk on the telephone. He heard her say, "I've got to run," as Baxter reached the revolving door.

Baxter had two choices as he drove his rental car out of the Holiday Inn parking lot. He could drive back to the apartment in the city and wait for Linda to show up, or he could head up to Brinker's Falls and nurse his wounds quietly. He chose Brinker's Falls.

After stopping at the A& P for groceries, Baxter drove up the driveway in the late afternoon Labor Day weekend sunlight to find the battered blue Chevrolet that he had come to identify with Darlene. He could make out the strains of Brahms 4th Symphony as he opened the car door only to have the music turned off as he approached the kitchen door steps. Darlene appeared at the door in a tee shirt, shorts, and sweat socks holding her low-cut tennis shoes in one hand.

"Oh, Joe. I hadn't expected you. I lost track of time. I must be going." She held the door as he entered the kitchen.

"Are you alone?" Baxter asked.

"Rob is off with his father and some other men and their sons on a fishing trip up in the Finger Lakes. I came over to clean and thought I'd stay awhile. I should be going," Darlene said stepping into her tennis shoes. "I just get so relaxed here, I hate to leave."

"Then stay a while," Baxter invited her.

Darlene's face flushed. "Oh I couldn't impose on you."

"I could use the company." Baxter placed the grocery bags on the table and stepped into the living room to return to the sound of Brahms. He found an open hardback book which turned out to be Edith Wharton's *Ethan Frome*. Next to the stuffed chair was a blue canvas overnight bag.

Baxter turned to see Darlene framed in the doorway to the kitchen. She was tall, blonde, long legged, bosomy, and sad faced. "You haven't been by all summer. I hardly expected you to come up on Labor Day. I have the weekend off and I planned to stay here and read and listen to your music."

"There's really no need to totally alter your plans," Baxter said. "Why don't you put away the groceries and we can have dinner together." He rapidly made his way upstairs without another word to change clothes.

Baxter heard the strains of Brahms 4th Symphony as he buckled the belt to his khaki trousers.

Outside Baxter's upstairs bedroom the sun had moved to a lower mid-quadrant toward sunset. A soft breeze brushed the white curtains of his bedroom window. It was five-thirty in the afternoon the Saturday before Labor Day, and it appeared unlikely that he would be leaving McKenzie Barber to join Harwell management. His wife, Bridgette, had dropped from sight. His mistress, Linda, had another agenda which probably included a liaison with another lover. His daughter was in Italy visiting her mother. His estranged son was someplace in the Village pursing his gay creative life. The long legged Darlene was downstairs sipping iced tea, while reading Edith Wharton and listening to Brahms. Her husband was presumably 200 miles north in the Finger Lakes region on a fishing trip with her son.

The image of Darlene would run through Baxter's head from time to time. Comely, plodding, gentle Darlene with her well chiseled Nordic features, trapped in an unhappy marriage with a strange twisted semi-crippled ex-jock who fancied himself as the Assistant Sheriff. Baxter's house had become Darlene's escape and sanctuary from the ugly drab life she shared with Luke.

Darlene closed her book and stood up from her chair when Baxter returned to the living room. "I put away the groceries and I really should be going now. I know you want your privacy."

"Stay for dinner. I could use the company," Baxter said.

"Oh I really couldn't," she protested in a soft voice.

"I also could use a little exercise," Baxter said extending his hand. "Come and take a walk with me."

Darlene placed her book on the coffee table and took Baxter's hand. He couldn't remember ever taking Darlene's hand. It was obviously that she applied lotion to soften her skin, but Baxter could feel the hard callouses of a woman who worked with her hands. She donned a pair of drug store sun glasses from her purse, and they walked into the late September afternoon sun down the path through the high grass.

"You really should have someone come in and mow the grounds once in mid-June and once in early August. Luke said that your property runs 40 acres."

"That sounds about right," Baxter agreed. He continued to hold Darlene's hand and her thigh brushed against him from time to time as they walked.

"Luke has studied up on the Dopman case. He believes there are bodies buried out here someplace."

"And how is Luke these days?" Baxter knew he would have to ask sooner or later, and he thought he would get the question out of the way.

"He's studying very hard on his correspondence courses. Sheriff Clowson will let him study in the office when they're not real busy. He can't pass the physical exam for the Highway Patrol or most of the big city police forces. Sheriff Clowson thinks that Luke would make a pretty good #3 man in a small town public safety department. He promised Luke that he would write letters of recommendation after Luke finishes his correspondence courses. We would probably have to move then, and I wouldn't get to be your housekeeper anymore."

"I'm certain you would find work easily enough in a new community."

"Do you know how long I've been your housekeeper?"

"Some years. Five or six years perhaps." Baxter could remember a time when he did not own the Brinker's Falls house and Darlene had practically come with the house.

"It was in January of 1982. You had been up with your wife, although I don't think she was your wife then. You had gone to see Sheriff Clowson about those calls, and came over to the Inn for lunch. I thought you both were sophisticated New York City people, and I never saw so many books, records, and cassette tapes before in my life. At first I would come mid-morning two Saturdays a month, depending on how often you came up, and I would be out by one o'clock in time to fix Rob his lunch. One time you left the stereo on when you left in a hurry and I let the music play through. I liked it and played more music. Then I started to look through your books. All I ever read in the way of books after I left high school were the paperback romances that were for sale in the drug store. I started to come earlier and stay later. I started paying the woman in the trailer behind us to watch after Rob. On cold days I would build a fire in the afternoon, brew a pot of tea, listen to your music, and read books. There were so many words I didn't know the meaning of. I bought a notebook and would look up the words in the dictionary. I filled up two notebooks the first year. I read your book twice, and I understand parts of it. You figure out how to pay big shots a lot of money."

"Stick to Edith Wharton. She's far more interesting," Baxter recommended.

"I'm enrolled in a literature class in the community college this fall. I can't wait for it to begin. It's about the Twentieth Century American novel. It's a morning class that I can take while Rob's in school. Luke thinks it's a waste of time. He doesn't think women need any education beyond high school. But I know that there are many very well educated women who hold very responsible positions in New York. I read about them in the business magazines you leave around. Sometimes I wish I could start my life all over again."

"Many of us do," Baxter added.

"You're very well educated and successful. But I suspect that you haven't had much luck with women in your life. But that's certainly is none of my business."

"And have you had a lot of luck with men in your life, Darlene?" Baxter asked pointedly.

Darlene drew to a stop on the path and stared down at her tennis shoes for a moment. There were tears streaming down from under her sunglasses when Darlene raised her head.

"I believe it's time for me to go home. This walk was a mistake." She started to run by Baxter, but he grabbed her forearm. Darlene placed her hand on Baxter's chest to push him away. He pulled Darlene up against him and kissed her on the forehead. "I'm sorry," he whispered.

Her hand moved up Baxter's chest and around his shoulder to the back of his neck. He tilted up her sun glasses and kissed the tears on Darlene's cheeks. Her mouth found Baxter's and her body was suddenly against his.

Baxter placed his hands on Darlene's buttocks and she rubbed against him sensually. Suddenly he swelled into a hard erection. Darlene squirmed against him rubbing herself against his erection. They kissed with open mouths and Baxter noted that Darlene's eyes were closed.

He placed his hand under the elastic of Darlene's shorts and into her underpants. She was quite wet and writhed her hips and thighs after the insertion of his finger.

"Please. Please," she gasped and gripped Baxter's member with her hand. She climaxed with a rapid series of groans and chest heaves. I seem to have ignited the fires of rural womanhood, Baxter observed to himself.

"Thank you, Joe. Thank you," she said dropping to her knees and fumbling with Baxter's zipper. He pulled her by the shoulders to her feet. "I suggest we walk back to the house now."

"Yes. That's the thing to do," Darlene agreed. They walked back to the large white frame house with arms locked around each other's waists. Baxter on impulse stepped to kiss Darlene at two points on their return journey. She pulled his hands up over her breasts at the first stop, and ran her tongue into his ear by the large oak tree on the edge of the backyard clearing. They walked apart as they approached the house, but once inside the screen door, Darlene placed her hand around Baxter's swollen member. She went to her knees again and this time drew it out of his trousers. She kissed him twice on the head and then lowered her mouth half way down his stem. "There, I've even made you bigger," Darlene said pulling her mouth up and away from him.

She led Baxter to the bear rug. "This is where you like to bring your women, isn't it? I've cleaned up the stains."

Darlene slipped her tee shirt off and unsnapped her brassiere.

"I want you inside me. I've wanted you for so long. I've dreamed about making love with you."

117

"Just a few technical questions, Darlene," Baxter posed. "One! Do you use pills or wear a diaphragm for birth control? Two! When do you expect Luke back from the Finger Lakes?"

Darlene stepped out of her white underpants and appeared naked before Baxter. Her body reminded Baxter of calendar girl drawings that were posted on the locker walls of plant workers. The hard nipples of her large well formed breasts were pointing at him. There was a white line across her belly and her pubic hair was bushy and grain colored. Darlene's thighs were large and muscular, while her calves were thin and shapely.

She pointed to the white line on her lower belly.

"This is a hysterectomy scar. I had one after Rob was born. Luke won't be back until Labor Day morning. We have tonight and Sunday to be together if you want."

Baxter entered Darlene missionary style on the bear rug. She enjoyed an early orgasm and then rolled over on top of him. "Now I'm going to love you, Joe," she said placing her body on top of him. Darlene was beginning to remind Baxter of Alice Dungler.

The temperature went down to the high sixties after the sun went down, and Baxter built a fire. She nestled her naked body into Baxter's arms as they listened to Chopin. Darlene sipped Coca Cola while Baxter consumed Canadian Club.

"It was very good for me, Joe. I hope I was good for you," Darlene said as she kissed Baxter about the neck.

"You certainly improved my day. It was going very poorly until we took that walk."

"I'll have to go home soon, but I'll come back in the morning. I'll be here very early. You stay in your bed and I'll crawl in with you. I'll make you a nice breakfast and we can have a picnic together. I'll bring a nice blanket and we can love in the grass in the afternoon.

Baxter's watch said five minutes to eleven. "Why don't you spend the night here?" There was something very relaxing about the warmth of

Darlene's naked body against him. He didn't want to give it up for the moment.

She shook her head. "I'll have to go in ten minutes. It's important that my car be parked outside of our trailer. There would be a lot of talk in the trailer park if a night passed and no one saw a car in front of our trailer at any time." Darlene stood up from Baxter and slipped into her panties. Her dressing aroused him and he stood up to embrace her.

"No, Joe. I have to go now. We must be very careful. I'll be back tomorrow. Please don't see me to the car if anyone should be passing by or watching."

"What time will you be back in the morning?" Baxter asked as he watched Darlene lace her tennis shoes.

"I'll try to be here by 8:15. Luke will call me at 7:30 and I want to be there to answer the phone. It's only a twenty minute drive from the trailer park to here. Stay in bed. I'll come to you. This has been the most wonderful day of my life."

Baxter watched Darlene apply make-up in the mirror over the kitchen sink. Then she pushed by him and was out of the screen door.

"Good night, Mr. Baxter. I'll finish up tomorrow. Sorry it took so long." Then he heard the sound of the Chevy engine turn over. The car was gone when he arrived at the screen door.

Baxter was awake with the morning sun. He was showered and shaved by 6:15 AM and sipping his morning coffee in the kitchen by 6:30. The smart thing, Baxter concluded, would be to leave immediately and drive back to the city. He could leave Darlene a note indicating that he had been called away on a client emergency.

The possibility of sex with Darlene had been at the back of Baxter's mind for at least three years. He knew that the prospect of a relationship was his for the taking. Now that he had taken it, the question remained as to what was he going to do with it? Baxter's life had turned 180 degrees since he had boarded the Atlanta flight Thursday evening. It was unlikely he would be resigning from McKenzie Barber to join Harwell Management. His major client sponsor had died. He had been planning to transition

Planters & Southern Bank to the Atlanta office and gently fade away. Baxter had been ready to propose Carl Miller as his successor, and allow the Exec Comp practice to fold into the Benefits practice.

Wednesday would have been such a good day to resign and retire from McKenzie Barber and move on the next phase of his life. Bridgette had been gone ten months, and Baxter had promptly taken up with a consultant some twenty-five years his junior. He had renewed acquaintances with Beth Gold, and now he had bedded his housekeeper. Poor lonely Darlene, who had adopted Baxter's country house as her private sanctuary from her weirdo husband and ugly drab life, had moved up four spaces on the gameboard of Baxter's life. Now he questioned as to whether he should wait for Darlene or immediately retreat back to New York. Baxter was tempted to bolt. He decided to check his phone mail before making a decision.

"JOE BAXTER. YOU HAVE FIVE NEW MESSAGES." The robotic female voice greeted him.

"Message #1, 2:45 AM, Saturday, September 3."

"Joe, this is Jennifer. We have a complication with Muffin. She's pregnant. 17 years old and two months pregnant. The father is someone named Gabe who's she's been seeing from Joel's theatre group. I suppose you don't know a thing about it. An abortion is clearly the answer, but she needs to hear from you. I can get it taken care of over here. Please call me. We have a six hour time difference. My number's 39-2-67-9190. I would hope to hear from you within twenty-four hours. I'm leaving this message on both your office and home answering services. I know it's Labor Day weekend, but I must hear from you soon. This matter has got to be resolved quickly."

Baxter hung up the telephone and stared at the high kitchen ceiling for a long time. His Muffin was apparently pregnant by that little theatre twirp Joel had introduced her to. He had sent Muffin off to Europe to visit her mother. She had been scheduled to return home the following weekend in time to return for her senior year at St. Marks on Monday, September 12. Baxter had a warm dinner at the Rainbow Room with Muffin in mid July, the night before she left for Milan. It had been Gabe-this and Gabe-that. Baxter had promised to accompany her to Milan, but had been knee deep in the wrap-up and repositioning of Planters & Commerce Bank.

"We'll visit colleges together in the spring," Baxter had promised.

"Daddy, you'll never have the time. McKenzie Barber fathers rarely have the time. The ones that did were fired," Muffin commented matter-of-factly.

"I'm going to have more time with you after the first of the year. You just watch." Baxter had been certain that the move to Harwell Management Company was going to permanently alter his lifestyle.

Now his favored child and hope for the future had managed to get herself in the same fix her father had gotten himself into some twenty-five years earlier.

Baxter dialed Italy.

A voice answered and said something that sounded like 'pronto'.

"Jennifer Washburn Baxter, please?"

"The senora. Momento. I get her." Baxter clocked a forty-five second pause before Jennifer's voice came on the phone.

"Hello." The voice seemed to have lost its quality of mellowness since the last time Baxter had heard it. Had it been ten years?"

"Jennifer? This is Joe. I got your message on Muffin. Can we talk about it?"

Jennifer shouted something in Italian which Baxter interpreted as 'clear-the-room! "You certainly took your time in calling back,' she greeted Baxter.

"I'm at my country place. I just checked my phone mail. Are you absolutely certain Muffin's pregnant?"

"I had her examined a week ago and the medical report came back on Thursday morning. She's approximately eight weeks pregnant. How could you let this happen?"

"Muffin is in and out of the city and I've been traveling. I haven't met this Gabe. Have you talked to Joel about him? What did he say?"

"What Joel says about this Gabe fellow will have little affect on Muffin's pregnancy. She is definitely pregnant and this Gabe is apparently her only lover. How could you let this happen?"

"Jennifer, this is not a time to discuss past events. We must review Muffin's future options. What does Muffin want to do?"

"She wants to have the damned baby she's carrying. I believe she should get an abortion fast. She can rest up over here and I'll send her back in November. She'll miss some school and may have to graduate late, but it all seems manageable to me. We'll need you to wire transfer us some money."

"May I speak with Muffin?" Baxter requested.

"She's still a little emotional, but you may be able to talk some sense into her."

Baxter heard the phone being set down and experienced another wait. Finally a familiar voice spoke into the phone.

"Daddy?"

"I'm here, Muff."

"Mother has told you?"

"Is she in the room with you, Muff?"

"She's out on the balcony reading the paper."

"How are you feeling?"

"I was feeling great until the nausea started. Now I know I'm pregnant with Gabe's child. I want to have this child, Dad. Mother wants me to get an abortion."

"Have you talked this over with Gabe?"

"I can't find him. He's directing a summer theatre up in the Poconos. It ends with a K. Could you find him for me? I cant' reach Joel either. I think he's with a bunch of friends out on Fire Island, but I have no idea whose name the phone is listed under."

"How long and how often have you been sleeping with this Gabe?"

"Daddy, that's my own business not yours."

"It wasn't until you got yourself pregnant." Baxter waited through a thirty second transatlantic silence for an answer.

"I became intimate with Gabe last Christmas probably about the same time you took up with that Linda person. I have been spending most weekend nights with Gabe in his apartment in the Village."

"St. Marks allowed you to do that?"

"I forged your name in January on a letter to the school requesting weekend privileges. I want to go to NYU next fall so that I can live with Gabe. He is a brilliant talent and will be a coming voice in the American Theatres."

"Muff, you must talk to Gabe and tell him about your pregnancy. Then the two of you will have to determine what makes sense."

"He can't marry me right away, Daddy. He's not divorced yet from his last wife. She was an ambitious English faculty bitch, and he moved out on her a year ago last Spring. I thought that I could move in with you for a while and then have the baby in March. I've been thinking and thinking and thinking about what to do over the last 48 hours. Mother wants me to have an abortion here and go back to America in December. That way, I'll miss the Fall semester at St. Marks."

"Were you planning on going back to school this Fall?"

"School starts on the 12th. I have my ticket. I won't begin to really show until November. Then you can have a grandson."

"Muff, I believe I had better run down Gabe. What is his last name?"

"Rothman. His mother is French and his father is Jewish. He's originally from Portland, Oregon."

"And he goes by Gabriel Rothman?"

"It's Gabe, Dad, not Gabriel."

"Then I will track down Gabe Rotham and have him call you."

"Dad, tell him that I love him and miss him."

"I'll find him. I love you, Muffin."

"And I love you, Dad. Help me, please."

"Would you please put your mother on the phone again?"

"Well, do you know where this boy came from?" Jennifer asked after an interval of silence. "Muffin is downstairs now. We can talk."

"Gabe is someone Muffin met through Joel. She started to see him on her Christmas break," Baxter explained.

"She said that you were going to have this Gabriel call her. That's all very nice, but she needs to get an abortion scheduled."

"Do you know how to locate a responsible physician?" Baxter asked.

"I've had experiences with abortions, Joe. I know two reliable doctors in Milan. But it must be done very quickly. We have to be together on this and getting this Gabe to agree with us will help. I believe Muffin should stay out of school this semester and spend the fall with my parents in Naples. I assume you can fix it with her school. She'll simply graduate six months behind her class. Now, I hold you accountable for this, Joe. Muffin was in your charge and she was, as usual, totally neglected. She also tells me that your third wife has left you. You're probably the most self-centered person I've ever met over the course of my life," Jennifer announced.

124

"Jennifer, let me talk to this Gabe and do what I can from this end. This is no time for finger pointing and recriminations. Let's do the right thing for our daughter. Good-bye."

Baxter replaced the receiver and stared at the phone in silence as he sipped his morning coffee. It was seven o'clock on the Sunday morning before Labor Day. Darlene was scheduled to arrive in one hour and fifteen minutes. If Baxter were going to make his escape from Brinker's Falls, he'd have to do it shortly.

He poured himself a fresh cup of coffee and called Joel, reaching him at the Fire Island weekend place he shared. Baxter roused him from bed with a family emergency announcement to the young man who answered the telephone.

"What's up Dad?" a tired Joel answered.

"I need to reach Gabe Rothman. Where is he?"

"Why?"

"Muffin's pregnant by Gabe. She's in Italy with your mother."

"Oh my God. That son-of-a-bitch! Muff's only 17. Damn him! He's married."

"How do I find him?"

"Dad, I'll get the number of the resort where he's working. I'll get his number to you right away. How can I help, Dad? She should get an abortion. Don't you agree? Can I call her?"

"Let me get to this Gabe first," Baxter cautioned.

Joel called back within fifteen minutes with the number of Krautshimer's Lake Wampum Resort in the Poconos. Gabe Rothman had a "Do Not Disturb" on his room phone, but Baxter informed the front desk that he was Mr. Rothman calling from Portland regarding a family emergency.

A young woman's sleepy voice answered the telephone with a "Hello."

"Gabe Rothman, please."

"Who's calling him?"

"This is his father."

"This is Mrs. Rothman. I recognize Cy Rothman's voice. You're not Cy Rothman. I'm going to hang up."

"I'm someone else's father. My daughter is pregnant by Gabe Rothman and I want him on the phone right now. She's seventeen years old. If Gabe Rothman is unwilling to talk to me right now, I will call the Pennsylvania State Police and make a statutory rape complaint against him. My name is Joseph Baxter, Jr. and my daughter Martha has just finished her junior year in high school. I would advise you to put him on the telephone immediately."

The telephone was placed down and Baxter could hear a voice saying "Gabe" over and over again. "There's some weirdo on the phone that says you have his daughter pregnant. He says his name is Joseph Baxter."

"Good morning, this is Gabe Rothman. May I help you?" A fresh male voice called into the phone.

"This is Joseph Baxter, Jr. I believe you are acquainted with my daughter, Martha, whom the family calls Muffin. I also believe you know my son, Joel."

"Those names are familiar to me."

"My daughter, Muffin, has informed me that she's pregnant, and you're the father. What do you have to say for yourself?"

There was a nervous laugh on the other end of the telephone.

"Your daughter has quite an imagination, Mr. Baxter."

"She has the kind of imagination that will put you behind bars for one to three years in the state of New York. I've been in touch with my New York attorney. He says that Rikers Island beckons. Now if you should wish to avoid the unpleasantness of incarceration, I want you to fully cooperate with me. What's your decision?"

There was a ninety second silence on the other end of the phone before a voice agreed. "What do you want me to do?"

Darlene bounced in the kitchen door shortly after Baxter had finished his conversation with Joel. She was wearing a white sun dress, white pumps, dangling earrings and drug store sun glasses."

"You're up and awake," she smiled. "I'd hoped I'd find you upstairs in bed waiting for me."

"I had some business to take care of," Baxter explained and stood up from the kitchen table. Darlene pushed her body against him. Twenty-four hours ago, she would have sadly waved. Now her arms around Baxter's waist and the fullness of Darlene's body rested against him. He could see and feel his way through Darlene's white summer dress. Across the world in Italy, a case for abortion was being built for his daughter. Darlene's mouth was kissing Baxter about the face. Her mouth found Baxter's mouth and her hand found his fly. He had assumed that he would be unable to involve himself in a physical relationship at this time in the morning. To Baxter's surprise, he found himself immediately ready.

"And did you talk with Luke this morning?" Baxter asked at 8:55 while propping himself at the side of the bed in the upstairs master bedroom.

"He seemed to be having a good time and Rob caught a fish yesterday. He was very excited. Luke said they'd head back after breakfast tomorrow. It's about a two hour drive."

Darlene's back was perched against the large hand carved headboard and the bed sheet covered her naked body from the waist down.

He reached across and stroked her bare breast.

"I love your touches," she said. "I've wanted us to be together for years and it's wonderful."

"How do you feel about Luke?" Baxter asked.

127

"He's my husband and I've been stuck with him. He's a very unhappy man. Luke once dreamed of being a very famous football person. Then he was going to be a Marine and work his way up to the Commandant of the Marine Corps. Then after his disability forced him out of the Marines, Luke got a job at the paper mill and was going to work his way up to superintendent. When the mill closed, Luke was out of work a long time before Sheriff Clowson took him in as his clerk. Police work is now going to be his life. He's determined to solve the Dopman case."

"What's to solve about the Dopmans? They're dead and I bought the house and inherited a crank caller as a legacy. It's more of a project for an investigative reporter than a local police clerk."

"That's Luke. The Dopman case is an obsession with him. Sheriff Clowson has told Luke to back off and not waste his time. The only thing that keeps the house talked about is the crank calls you get."

"Can you remember the Dopmans, Darlene?"

"As a little girl. They used to come into the drug store when they visited town. One of them bought me an ice cream cone once. I could never tell them apart. They smiled, but never really talked to people much. You usually saw them together. They made most of the furniture in this house. The Dopmans were wonderful woodworkers. It was the furniture and books and music that you added that has made this house so wonderful for me. I would rather be in this house than any place in the world. I've always wanted you to be my lover. You're such a sophisticated man of the world. You're like the men in some of those books I've been reading."

"Have you had lovers before, Darlene?"

"Yes."

"Does Luke suspect?"

"I'm very careful. Luke gets jealous of people who pay too much attention to me. He's not very affectionate. When I put on too much weight, he moo's at me and calls me a cow."

"Who have been your lovers?" Baxter asked.

128

"I won't tell you. Just as I will never tell anyone that you and I have been together." Darlene pulled the sheet back and took her place on the side of the bed next to Baxter. Her arms were extended around his neck and she started kissing Baxter about his neck and shoulders.

"There are a lot of men who come through the diner, but none of them like you, Joe."

Baxter sensed that there would soon come a time when he preferred that Darlene limited her activities to scrubbing floors, dusting, and vacuuming.

"I really should check the rest of my phone mail at the office," he said easing his way free from Darlene's arms.

"JOE BAXTER, YOU HAVE FOUR NEW MESSAGES", his old girlfriend with the robotic voice greeted him.

"Message #1, 10:09 AM, Saturday, September 3."

"Joe, this is Linda. Are you aware that Leon Harwell died? What does this mean for our business? My mother has made big plans for this weekend. We have cousins, aunts, and uncles assembled. I won't be back on Sunday night and we have a family picnic planned for Labor Day afternoon. With traffic on the LIE the way it is, I doubt whether I'll get back until late Monday night. I'll see you bright and early on Tuesday morning. I assume we have a staff meeting."

"Try to get some rest this long weekend, you poor dear. And leave a phone mail if you get a chance. Sorry to desert you, but Jewish mothers rule in these matters."

"Message #2, 10:49 AM, September 3."

"Joe, this is Lucy Tweetman. It's Labor Day weekend and Tommy is setting a booth for some kind of trade show in Las Vegas. I'm in our temporary apartment in White Plains. I dropped our daughter off at Kenyon College this week and drove on out there. Tommy believes I should stay in White Plains until things are settled in Washington. We closed on our house in Indianapolis in July. The apartment in White Plains is small and I'm quite bored. I would like to come into New York and see you. You have changed phone numbers in New York. Have you moved? I left my number on your answering service on Friday night. Tommy thought I should leave word on your office phone. So, Joe Baxter, if you're in listening distance, please call me. Let's have dinner or lunch and talk. I need to see a friendly face. My number is 914-653-8751. I'll say it again very slowly. 9-1-4-6-5-3-8-7-5-1. Please call me. I'm a desperate lady."

Women, women, everywhere. Baxter observed to himself. They zipped in and zipped out of his life and generally used him to their advantage. Now he had taken on another one.

"Message #3, 10:35 AM, Saturday, September 3."

"Joe, this is Ernie. I've been thinking over the situation at Harwell Management. I believe that the best course of action for all concerned is for you to write a letter to Stanford Asher on Tuesday morning requesting that your contract be rescinded and have it messengered over first thing. You might say something to the effect that the untimely death of Leon Harwell has caused you to reconsider your employment with Harwell Management at this time and you respectfully request that you be relieved of your contractual obligations. I've talked to Asher about an hour ago, and he believes he is bound to inform the family members of Wednesday of Leon's contract with you. He agreed to maintain his silence on the matter if he has a release letter from you. Wednesday will be a very difficult day for the Harwell family factions. The subject of your contract would represent a serious distraction from the main business at hand of selecting Leon's successor. Therefore, I'm asking you, Joe, to get this matter taken care of by Tuesday morning. I will personally see that you get some substantial consulting work at IPCO and make a concerted effort to open a few more doors for you. I'm sorry that things have turned out this way, but I believe that this is the only course of action to take."

There was no good-bye. Ernie Grey had had his say.

"Message #4, 8:47 AM, Sunday, September 4, 1995."

"Joe, this is Jon. This is short notice but we're trying to organize a Group Partner's meeting for Tuesday morning. We're shooting for 8:45. We have a fantastic announcement to make. A leadership change that will substantially strengthen the firm. I won't keep you in suspense, Joe. Lonnie McMasters is going to FSO as President. Brett Williamson is coming to New York as his successor. I would expect Buzz is prepping Brett to move into Neil Schmidt's job by October 19?. I believe we need a full turn-out to welcome Brett. If for some reason, you can't make it, Joe, leave me a voice mail. I want every Group Partner present, or at least accounted for to welcome our former Marine leader. See you Tuesday, Joe. Have a great Labor Day weekend."

Darlene returned to the kitchen topless in white shorts with bare feet.

"Good news?" she asked.

"I'll have to return to the city first thing in the morning," Baxter announced.

Darlene brushed her hand across Baxter's head. "As long as we can have this day together. I've planned a picnic. I've brought ham sandwiches and potato salad and there's beer in the refrigerator. I have some Indian blankets in the car and a radio where we can get the SUNY classical station from Albany. We'll have such a wonderful day. It's gotten of to such a good start." Darlene kissed Baxter lightly on the mouth. "I'm going to get some clothes on now. I'll just be a minute, Joe."

Baxter poured himself a fresh cup of coffee. It was now eleven in the morning. He had been up six hours. During that time he had learned that his daughter was pregnant, confronted her seducer, made love to his housekeeper, heard the death knell for his escape to Harwell Management, been informed that his high school sweetheart required companionship, and that his boss, Lon McMasters, a reasonable ally, was being succeeded by Williamson, his evil nemesis. What the hell, he had the picnic to look forward to.

He dialed the White Plains number of Lucy Albright Tweetman and was greeted by a cheery hello.

"Lucy, Joe Baxter here. I've been traveling. I just picked up your SOS. I will be in the city on Labor Day if you want to come in for a late lunch."

"Oh, Joe. How wonderful to hear your voice. I was rescued from my despair when a good friend came in from Indianapolis to keep me company. His name is Howard Brunger and he has business meetings in New York next week and came in early to keep me company. I'd love to have lunch with you and will bring Howie with me. He's heard about you and would love to meet the famous Joe Baxter. Howie runs the Brunger Company, a large insurance agency in Indianapolis. He and Tommy were in Kiwanis together. We had an excellent dinner in Greenwich last night and we're going for a drive today. You called just in time. He's picking me up in fifteen minutes. Now where would you like us to meet you?"

"The Palm Court in the Plaza at 1:30. The reservations will be in my name."

"Now where's the Plaza again?" Lucy asked and Baxter followed with directions. After calling the Plaza, Baxter tried Grunwaldyt's home number and got his answering machine.

"Jon, Baxter here. I have client commitments, but I'll try to be there. The news was so surprising. Lon's only been in New York for ten months by my count. Fill me in if you get a chance. A brief phone mail will do."

Baxter considered calling McMasters but held back. McKenzie Barber's leadership churning was a certain sign that the firm was in trouble. If only he could have retired on Wednesday as planned.

It was a decent enough afternoon with Darlene. There was a spot nestled between two poplar trees that overlooked the creek. The creek served as the dividing line between Baxter's property and the neighboring dairy farm. He had made no attempt to meet his neighbors over his years of residence. Baxter could not recall ever seeing his neighbors on either the east or west side of his property. He had seen cows, presumably belonging to his westerly neighbor, from time to time. They would be grazing near the barb wire fence and would on warm days futilely lower their heads to reach for the water under the lower strand of wire. The creek curved to the west at the rear of Baxter's property and according to local maps turned north. Their spot was located on a slight rise looking down on the creek. They were observed through the afternoon by two Guernsey cows who had settled in the shade on the far side of the creek.

"Do you know the people who live next door to me?" Baxter asked settling down on the blanket.

"The farm next door belongs to the Leftstroms. Those cows belong to the Leftstroms. They settled here in the 1920's from Sweden. You could see their large white house from the road if you ever came that way. You always drive up Creek Road past the Alicks. They live in the house with the fake brick siding. The Alicks are very poor and have been on relief. The Leftstroms make ends meet and that's about all. You would have nothing in common with them. In fact you have nothing in common with anyone around here. A lot of the local people refer to you as the rich guy from New York at the Inn."

"I'm talked about."

"There's not so much talk about up here, Joe. Everyone knows I'm your housekeeper, and they think I've got it made because you so rarely come."

"And what they say about me?"

"What they know about you is what I tell them. The town people are in awe of you."

"Why?"

"Because I have described you as a rich, private man who lives in New York City with a very important job who travels all over the world. Sheriff Clowson describes you as a very cultured man with a good sense of humor."

"And what does Luke have to say about me?"

"He doesn't like you. But he likes the money you pay me. Rob adores you. He tells his friends about your maps and he has the map of London you brought back for him up on the wall of his room."

Darlene had unbuttoned the two buttons of her white blouse and ran her hand up from his calf to the top of his Bermuda shorts.

"How long have you known Luke?" Baxter asked.

"I guess—all my life. Our fathers both worked at the paper mill together. Luke is five years older than me. He was the star athlete at BFH. That stands for Brinker's Falls High School. I was in eighth grade when he was a senior. Luke was like a prince in those days. He went off to college to be a football star and came back the next summer and went to work in the mill. But, come September, Luke didn't go back to the same college. He went off to a junior college in California. He stayed there maybe a year and a half and then came back. Luke went back to work at the mill and started to hang around in the drug store where I worked my junior and senior years. I let him walk me home a couple of times. He talked to me about his life and I was flattered that someone like Luke would take an interest in me."

"I was always big for my age, and I probably wasn't as pretty as a lot of the other girls around town. But I had the figure that they didn't have. I started to have sex with Luke. I became pregnant with Rob, and Luke joined the Marine Corps. He had this accident with a hand grenade where he hurt his knee and got out on a disability. We get a check for $839 every month from the government. Luke came back to the paper mill, but it eventually closed. We had some hard times after that. I took the waitress job at the Inn and Luke finally went to work as a clerk to Sheriff Clowson. That's when I ran into you."

"You must recognize that what has happened between us is not a permanent arrangement," Baxter cautioned.

"I love the way you say things, Joe. You don't talk like the people around here. I'm a married woman with a child, and I'm your housekeeper. It would suit me fine if we could be together when you come here. I could never stay overnight or anything like that. I would just want to be with you when you have time for me. That's all. I could never be a part of your New York world. But I want to continue to improve myself. Sooner or later, Luke will get his chance, and either I'll move with him or stay here."

"Do you love Luke?"

"No. I used to be in awe of him. We both need each other, but one day I expect that I will leave him. Now is not the right time."

"And you see other men from time to time?"

"Yes. But they're not like you. They're lonely married people like me. None is as cultured as you. Some of them are passing through and spend time at the coffee shop. I'm starting a night school literature course in the community college next week. I need to meet people outside the cafe and Luke's bunch of buddies who hang out at our trailer, drink beer and watch endless games on television."

"And what did you want when you were seventeen or so?" Baxter asked, thinking back to his own daughter pregnant in Milan.

"I wanted to meet a nice boy who would take care of me and raise children. Leaving Brinker's Falls was scary. I could see moving maybe one or two towns away. But going off to live in some place like Albany or Syracuse was unthinkable. Now I want to leave Brinker's Falls as soon as I'm ready."

Darlene continued to talk and stroke Baxter's leg while he rested his head against a pillow and stared at the bright September sky. He thought back to that afternoon he spent with Alice Dungler in the Spring of 1978. If he had gone with Alice, and would have been able to stick it out, he would be worth millions today. Possibly he could be running the place now in Friedman's job. Instead, he was drinking Budweiser on an Indian blanket learning more about his full-bodied housekeeper than he really wanted to know, while being observed by two dairy cows. Baxter believed he preferred Darlene quietly vacuuming.

Baxter arrived early at the Palm Court and settled in with a martini. There was something about the Plaza that connected Baxter with gin. He spotted Lucy and her escort at the maitre'd stand at a quarter to two. Lucy, from a distance, looked the same. Blonde hair cut shorter, dark glasses, a white suit with a blue scarf. She was accompanied by a balding man with shell rim glasses in a light blue suit. The maitre'd nodded and assigned a waiter to guide them to Baxter's table.

Baxter rose to greet them and noted that Lucy's escort was wearing white shoes. Bridgette would have described him as a 'full Cleveland'.

"Joe, this is Howard Brunger, a good friend from Indianapolis." Lucy pushed her sun glasses up to her forehead and offered her cheek to be kissed. "How wonderful to see you again, Joe." Howard Brunger appeared to be a man slightly north of fifty with a firm handshake.

"Howard Brunger, the Brunger Company, Indianapolis," he introduced himself. "I've heard a lot about you over the years, Joe. I've read some of your stuff. It's very good. The Brunger Company writes more than its share of key man life insurance in the Indy marketplace."

Baxter nodded his head knowingly and held a chair for Lucy. Brunger picked up the wine list. "I'm not much for cocktails in the middle of the day. What do you say to little vino?" he smiled.

"As long as you can hold it to choices of red or white," Baxter responded.

"Howard saved my weekend, Joe. I was absolutely desperate when I left that call at your office on Saturday. No sooner had I hung up from trying to reach you, when the phone rang with Howard calling me from the car rental at LaGuardia. He was coming in for an insurance seminar in Hartford that was to begin Tuesday, and he decided to come early. We're late because Howard insisted on driving in."

Brunger snapped his fingers for the waiter. "How about a California Chardonnay, guys?"

"Howard has one of the most expensive wine cellars in Indianapolis, Joe," Lucy added.

"Had. I'm going through a divorce right now, Joe. My soon-to-be ex is contesting the wine cellar. Things are little testy back home right now. I'm scheduled to speak at this Agents seminar up in Hartford and this is my first Bachelor Labor Day in a long time. I'd decided to come away early and see if I could find this lady for company. And," he said patting Lucy's hand. "I got lucky."

Baxter looked to Lucy. At 53, she looked 40. He hadn't seen her since their 30 year Iron Creek High School reunion some five years earlier. She appeared bright, vivacious, and desirable to Baxter.

Brunger ordered an overpriced California Chardonnay that he put through an exhausting taste and smell examination before allowing it to be poured. Baxter winked at the waiter who recognized him from previous visits.

"Well here's to new friends," Brunger toasted. "Now, Joe, fill me in a little. I know that you grew up with Lucy in northern Minnesota. But how long have you lived in New York?"

"Ten years or so. I have a place in upstate New York where I spent this weekend."

"And how are your children?" Lucy asked.

"I talked to both of them this weekend. My son, Joel, works in the New York theatre community as a stage manager. My daughter will be a senior in Prep School this fall. She's been in Milan this summer visiting her mother."

"Now the children are from your second marriage to Jennifer, the girl you married in Racine. Tommy told me something about you being separated from Bridgette," Lucy probed.

"Bridgette and I are separated, but not divorced," Baxter explained.

"Well this is marriage and divorce number one for me," Brunger added. "I have been married twenty-five years to the same woman. Although she certainly isn't the same woman I married back in 1963."

"Howard runs the largest insurance agency in Indianapolis," Lucy said.

"In Indiana," Brunger corrected her. "I'm the third generation of Brungers to run the Brunger Company. I once bought a computer system from Lucy's Tommy. My soon-to-be-ex wife, Eloise, was very active with Lucy in a number of civic organizations." Brunger's hand reached for Lucy's as he spoke.

"And Tommy's in Las Vegas at a trade show for Re-plen-o-link?" Baxter asked.

"I would not abandon this lady on Labor Day weekend if she were my wife," Brunger said as he patted Lucy's hand.

"Sometimes a man's got to do what a man's got to do, Howard," Baxter responded.

"Joe, what kind of company is this FRS? I took a look at their prospectus, and the company looked a little shaky to me. Is Tommy involved in some high risk venture?"

"High risk, high reward," Baxter responded. "Re-plen-o-link is a software product with considerable upside potential. FRS needs sales right now. Tommy has everything on the line during this fall quarter."

"That's what Tommy has been telling me," Lucy said. "And that's why I'm supposed to be patiently waiting for him in White Plains until Tommy tells me it's the right time to move to Washington. But tell me, Joe. Why is it necessary for this woman Elyssa to travel with Tommy?" Lucy questioned.

Baxter turned to Brunger. "Our work with FRS was completed last Spring. Elyssa, as I remember, is Dr. Horgcost's executive assistant and very familiar with the general operations of the company. I would see her as someone very valuable for Tommy."

"I've been to Washington twice to see the FRS offices, Joe, and this Elyssa woman looks like quite a little number."

"I can't comment on that, Lucy. I suspect, however, that she enjoys a special relationship with Dr. Horgcost, and represents his eyes and ears on the Las Vegas trip. In short, Lucy, I wouldn't worry about Elyssa. She's somebody else's squeeze." Brunger was now holding Lucy's hand.

"I offered Tommy a job to be one of our Account Executives, but he turned me down to take this transfer, and then resigned from World Computer to take this job at FRS last January on your recommendation, Joe."

"I didn't recommend any course of action for Tommy, Howard. He told me that he was unhappy with his situation at World Computer, and I suggested that he contact Dr. Horgcost. The decision to go to FRS was Tommy's," Baxter said. He wondered how this weekend would have gone if he had checked his phone mail after leaving the Harwell funeral. Would Lucy be patting his hand? Baxter had loved Lucy since he had been twelve years old. Now someone else had beaten him to her window of availability. He had screwed his housekeeper instead.

"You know, Joe," Howard Brunger said as he scanned the menu. "There must be a way that McKenzie Barber and the Brunger Company could work together."

"We, at McKenzie Barber, have some unique independence problems relating to relationships with insurance industry providers, Howard," Baxter said dismissing Brunger. He looked across the table to Lucy Albright Tweetman. Was she in play again at last?

"Taking into account that you're being neglected by an absentee husband, why don't you come in town next week, Lucy, and we can reserve an evening for dinner and the theater," Baxter offered.

"That sounds wonderful, Joe," Lucy said and slipped her hand away from Brunger's to pick up the menu.

Joel called around 6:30 in the evening on Labor Day.

"Dad, I'm at a pay phone about two blocks away from your apartment. Can I come over to see you?"

It was the first time since Joel had gone off to Prep School that he had asked permission to come by. He presented himself at Baxter's door dressed casually in a black polo shirt and blue jeans and sporting a black eye. He asked for a beer.

"This is smaller than the upper East Side place," Joel remarked.

"But more manageable," Baxter answered. "Have you taken up prize-fighting, Joel?"

"No, I'm a victim of personal dramatics. I got a buddy of mine to drive me up to the Poconos where I confronted Gabe. I made a fool of myself and have gotten a shiner for my trouble."

"You were avenging your sister's honor?"

"Something like that. That asshole took advantage of my younger sister. He lied to her, deflowered her, and knocked her up. I was steaming, but my execution was off. I'm afraid Gabe got the better of me and I was thrown out of the resort by the manger who threatened to call the police. I feel pretty stupid right now. I had to take the bus back to the Port Authority and decided I wanted to see you on the way back."

"It's good to see you, Joel," Baxter said snapping off the top of a Heineken.

"I mean—my God, Dad, Muffin pregnant! Where was I as her brother?"

"Where was I as her father?"

"Dad, what time is it in Italy? Should we call her?"

"I believe it's two in the morning in Milan, Joel?"

"We've got to get her through this period. You and I are really all she's got. We can't count on mother. I'm very depressed, Dad. I feel very powerless."

"Look, Joel, the world is an unpredictable place full of a lot of twists and turns, and we don't see them all coming. We have to be up on the balls of our feet ready to deal with events as they come at us. You and I have got to represent a united support system for Muffin at this time. I'm very proud of the way you stood up for your sister today, and I'm pleased that you have come to me tonight."

Joel nodded his head and took a swig of beer. "Dad, I want to repair my relationship with you. I had dinner with Dean Bain and his wife last week. They came in to see our play. We talked it through and I agreed to take the first step. I planned to call you after Labor Day."

"Dean Bain?" Baxter questioned.

"You used to call him Bwana. He told me some very funny stories about when you were in the Army together. I wish I had known you then. They talked a lot about Beth Gold, the writer. Mrs. Bain once traveled to Europe with Beth Gold. Did you know that?"

"I remember. They showed up together at Fort Gately."

"And you had met Beth Gold two years earlier in Iron Creek. What on earth was someone like Beth Gold doing in Iron Creek, Minnesota over Christmas time?"

140

"She had been Lucy Albright Tweetman's roommate the year before at a private school in Duluth. Lucy invited her down for the holidays and I was paired off with her. I believe she regarded me as a playful juvenile at the time. Beth has been in and out of my life for some thirty-five years now."

"I'm reading a book of her short stories right now. Dean Bain recommended it to me. Mrs. Bain said that she was quite famous at one time, but that her readers have drifted away. Were you and Beth Gold lovers, Dad?"

"Just friends of long standing, Joel."

"I got the impression that she snubs Mrs. Bain."

"Beth has a limited amount of time for socializing. She's a writing machine."

"They said she had married a guy who ran a hot New York disco and that he died of AIDS. Did they adopt some Vietnamese children?"

"I don't think they are with her anymore. I believe she got them through high school. They tried college and then drifted off. The only time she hears from them now is when they want money. Does that behavior sound familiar?"

"Dad. I've been confused all my life. Part of it is that I never had a decent father and son relationship with you. You were always off pursuing your career. You may look down on people like Dean Bain, but he's done a lot of good for young people. I don't know how I would have made it to where I am today without Dean Bain. I understand that Bridgette's gone for good?"

"She's out of my life at present. I would estimate that the possibilities of her returning are remote."

"And that young woman we met last Christmas is your new girlfriend?"

"She comes and she goes. Linda's quite ambitious and I suspect that she decided she'd taken a turn at sleeping with her boss. I suspect that we are in the twilight of our relationship, Joel."

"Do you think we could call Muffin now?"

"It's 2:30 in the morning in Milan. Why don't you stay over? We'll set the alarm for six AM and we'll call her at noon time."

"Dad, let's suppose that Muffin goes ahead with the abortion. Is the plan for her to go down to Grandma and Grandpa in Naples for a month and then return to school in January?"

"That would be one way. Possibly we can arrange for her to take some classes through correspondence. Muffin has been a good student."

"Then I have an idea. Why don't the three of us spend the Christmas holidays at the house at Brinker's Falls. We could be together as a family. Do you still have that big blonde housekeeper?"

"I saw her just this weekend."

"What do you think of my idea?"

"It has merit."

"Dad, I'm not certain, but I'm going in for tests next week. I may have contracted AIDS."

"Jesus," was all Baxter could say in way of reply.

"It's probably my imagination, Dad, but I've experienced some of the symptoms lately. I'm going in for an examination on Thursday."

Baxter studied his son in silence. Joel was an attractive young man. He had his mother's saucer eyes and sculptured features, and his slender body had grown to be an inch or two over six feet. He was twenty-two years old and potentially facing a life threatening disease. He remembered the child that waited patiently beside his sister for him at the front door of the house on Palmer Street. Baxter generally arrived from Chicago between seven-thirty and eight on Friday evening. Joel and Muffin were in their pajamas after their baths with freshly combed hair kneeling on a rug.

"Daddy!" they would greet him as they ran to the door. They represented bright little pieces of sunlight in his dim life as an alienated husband and traveling consultant.

They would assemble in the kitchen where Agnes would pour him a Canadian Club and they would talk about their weeks. They would close off the evening with a game of twenty questions, and Agnes would lead them off to bed at nine o'clock. Baxter would go up to tuck them in twenty minutes later and then settle back with a late evening sandwich and drink with Agnes, until she went to bed at 10:30 after the conclusion of the early concert on the local culture FM station. Now those bright shining faces and young bodies had grown into near adults, and their lives had become troubled.

"What are you thinking about, Dad?" Joel interrupted Baxter's reverie.

"I was thinking back to the days on Palmer Street when Muff and you used to wait for me at the front door."

"And Agnes? God how we loathed Agnes, Dad."

"She loved both of you."

"You didn't have to spend the time we did with Agnes. She was a fussy old tyrant. Mother was fun when she was around. She had a lot of boyfriends, and that British guy from the company that bought Washburn was always trying to hang around. Mother used to refer to him as a low class Brit. What ever happened to him?"

"I would assume that they are getting ready to knight him as a captain of British industry. I believe he's done pretty well with Henry Wiggins PLC and is back in London now."

"I wish sometimes that we could have stayed in Racine, Dad. I would have come to New York sooner or later, but maybe later would have been better. But then I never would have met Dean Bain, and he's been very important in my life. In some ways he's been the father to me I wanted you to be. He accepts me as I am. You always wanted me to be Joe Baxter #2 and that simply wasn't me. I tried to be like you today when I confronted Gabe. I made a fool of myself. You were the famous brawler."

143

"You've got me mixed up with my father, Joel. My last fight was in the Iron Creek locker room when I was a junior in high school. It was related to the defense of a lady's honor. I've never been a fighter, Joel, and I quit being a basketball player when I came to McKenzie Barber."

"Dad, I believe our life in New York would have been a lot better if you hadn't taken up with that Bridgette woman. I take it she's left you for good."

Baxter shrugged his shoulders. "Not everything is final in this world, Joel. Look at us. We're having a cordial conversation for a change."

"Is that Linda living with you now?"

"She comes and goes. It's not a long term relationship. She had the weekend off. You can sleep here tonight on the couch if you like," Baxter offered.

"I'd like that, Dad. Do you suppose I could have another beer?"

Baxter and his son talked into the night. They compared reminiscences about the house on Palmer Street, his annual Naples visit to his grandparents, and his infrequent correspondence and contact with his mother.

"I love mother, Dad. But the reality is that she abandoned me to live in Europe. Dean Bain has helped me work through that. All Muff and I really wanted from her was to be our beautiful mother and be with us when we needed her. You were our big business man Dad who traveled all over the country, but was with us every weekend. Then you abandoned us, too and moved to New York. You finally brought us out and you were with that woman. Muffin loved her. But she loves everyone. And then Bridgette abandoned Muff. Muffin gets pregnant by Gabe and he abandons her. Grandfather and Grandmother Washburn put up with us once a year. They ask about you, Dad. They thought you were good for mother. When it gets down to is Dad, just about everyone has abandoned the Baxter kids. Do you talk occasionally to your other daughter, the religious nut?"

"She writes me occasional little notes and says that she remembers me to Jesus Christ regularly. Lenore and her husband live in Duluth, and she tells me that they are in the process of adopting two children. She is a well meaning young woman with whom I have nothing in common."

"You've always been a cold hearted son-of-a-bitch, Dad. What ever happened to your brother? The one that had the wedding reception in the Chinese restaurant who married the black stripper? Muff and I still get the giggles when we talk about that night. There was your uptight Lenore in the middle of a bunch of criminals and sinners. Where is your brother now?"

Baxter shrugged his shoulders. "Gordy just disappeared. He's been missing ten years. I had some calls on him and some cop from Duluth came by and asked me a lot of questions about six years ago. Gordy's gone, and so is his wife, Honey. They were last seen in Duluth."

"I suspect, Dad, that I will go on to become a great theatre artist because my family background is so weird. Is it true that my great grandfather sexually abused my mother?"

"Where did you hear that?"

"Agnes told us that one night when she was drunk. She used to get drunk every night and listen to classical music in the kitchen. I told mother and that's when Agnes was banished permanently to the carriage house. Well how about it? Did he?"

"He did. The experience made your mother different."

"She was crazy, wasn't she?"

"Your mother was mentally ill. She was treated and she worked out her adjustment to life."

"Did you love her?"

"At one time."

"She always talked about you coming from the lower classes."

"She had a point there. Joel, I believe that I became infatuated with your mother the first time I saw her. She was sitting on a desk outside the conference room at Washburn Manufacturing. Jennifer Washburn was the most beautiful woman I had ever met. I suspected that there was a dark side to her that I couldn't understand, but I ignored it. Your grandparents encouraged Jennifer to take me seriously. I thought I was marrying the boss's daughter, and that I would wind up running Washburn Manufacturing. Those are pretty heady ideas for a working class kid from Iron Creek, Minnesota."

"I guess you're someone who's supposed to be looked up to. You know how to get ahead. Dean Bain told me that you were far better at the Army than he was. I know you're some big time Executive Pay expert at McKenzie Barber. Are you happy with your life?"

"Some days, yes. Some days, no. This weekend has been a bummer, Joel."

"It's been a bummer for me too, Dad. And I've gotten a shiner for my trouble. I have a Labor Day weekend wish."

"What's that?"

"I want things to go better between us. You know, father and son stuff. Can we work on it? If I'm sick, I'll need your support. Muffin needs both of us."

"I've always been here for you, Joel. Sometimes reluctantly, but always here," Baxter replied.

"Can we have one more beer together, Dad? I really feel good talking to you this way. You're really overpowering. I swear sometimes I feel like you've read every book ever written and you always put me down. I know you feel awkward about me being gay, but that's who I am. Just as you feel compelled to take all these women to bed. But then mother was the same way I guess. I just like talking to you openly like this. I wish we could have started earlier, and I hope we can keep it up."

Baxter made up the sofa bed for Joel shortly after one o'clock. He discovered Linda at the foot of his bed in the six AM morning light.

"Are you aware that there's someone sleeping on the living room couch?" She was wearing a white tee shirt that was stenciled Columbia

Business School, Bermuda shorts, white sweat socks, and tennis shoes with sun glasses parked on her forehead.

"That's my son, Joel. We had a father and son Labor Day," Baxter explained.

"My dry cleaning didn't come back to my apartment. Most of my office clothes are here. I'd like to take a shower and dress."

"I believe Joel's a late sleeper. I'll let you shower alone for the sake of appearance."

"You're an impossible man." Baxter watched Linda slide open the closet door and produce a blue bathrobe that she kept at his apartment. Linda untied her shoes and pulled off her sweat socks carefully placing them in her tennis shoes. Next she pulled her tee shirt over her head and placed it over Baxter's reading chair. Her black brassiere followed and lastly Linda slipped off her bikini pants and stood before him in the morning light. She slowly donned the blue bathrobe.

"It's shower time. I won't be a minute. You'd be a dear if you'd make some coffee."

Baxter rolled out of bed and Linda kissed him lightly on the cheek as she passed by him to the bathroom. He stepped out into the kitchen area which looked out at the living room Joel seemed to be sleeping soundly. Baxter thought back to Linda's recent strip tease show in the bedroom. She had probably been with someone over the weekend. The underwear had been a give away. At the same time she appeared to want to keep Baxter interested. Raises at McKenzie Barber would be announced in two weeks time. Today the Brett Williamson era was scheduled to begin at the New York Office of McKenzie Barber. Baxter had to get on with his life, such as it was.

9:37 AM, Tuesday, January 8, 1991

The Metroliner stopped briefly at the Trenton Station. Baxter reclined in his first class seat, sipping his coffee and reflecting back to that eventful 1988 Labor Day weekend better than two years past. That particular weekend clearly marked the beginning of his steep decline at McKenzie Barber. Baxter's life, like most lives was filled with what-ifs. What-if Leon Harwell had lived another year? He would have been too far into that General Manager job for the family to nudge him out. What if he had gone back to the city after the Harwell funeral instead of heading up to Brinker's Falls? Would the relationship with Darlene have ever started in the first place? What if Joel hadn't contracted AIDS? How would Joel have developed? Did he really have talent? Or was he another one of those young men and women with limited skills who migrated toward the theatre scene and hung around until they were pushed out by the next wave?

Joel had gone in for tests the week after Labor Day and two Labor Days later, he was dead. Observing his son slowly die had been a long emotionally draining experience for Baxter. Joel had seemed well enough in the beginning and he was prescribed drugs that promised remission. His illness seemed arrested on the first Labor Day anniversary, but Joel slipped badly after that time point and entered a hospice the following spring. Baxter tried to visit his son each Saturday, and pleaded with Jennifer by letter to return for one final visit with her son. Jennifer finally agreed to come over Easter week in the spring of 1990.

Baxter met Jennifer for a late breakfast on the Thursday before Good Friday. She was registered in a small, genteel, but seedy hotel north of Lincoln Center. Baxter walked slowly through the small lobby to the coffee shop. He concluded from the assortment of languages used by the guests at the hotel catered to visitors and tourists from southern Europe.

"I'm joining Miss Washburn for breakfast," he announced to a heavyset woman who wore a red blazer over her waitress uniform. Baxter watched as she scanned a list of names on the clipboard. "No Miss Washburn here," she said shaking her head.

Baxter looked over the long, narrow dining room with checkered table cloths and observed a woman wearing a beret and dark glasses at a window table facing Broadway Avenue.

"Who's that woman in the table by the window?" Baxter asked.

"That's Senora Palmetti. She's waiting for a Mr. Baxter."

"I'm Mr. Baxter." He brushed by the hostess and made his way to the table.

Jennifer was smoking a long cigarette and gazing out at the eight AM upper Broadway street scene. She wore a red blouse with a brightly colored designer scarf, black slacks and long black boots that reached two inches above her knee.

"Good morning, Jennifer," Baxter greeted his ex-wife.

She looked Baxter over and then raised her glasses to her forehead. "Hello Joe." Jennifer held out a hand, but didn't rise from the table. Baxter accepted her hand and squeezed it. The hand was smooth, and her saucer eyes had retained their allure. Jennifer had to be nearly fifty and remained an attractive, desirable woman. He pulled out the chair across the table and faced his wife for the first time after an absence of a dozen or so years.

"You've put on some weight, Joe," she greeted him.

"And you look the same Jennifer, although I understand that you go under the name of Senora Palmetti now."

"I was married to a man named Carlos Palmetti in the mid-1980s. We're divorced now, but I continue to use his name. I had a favorable divorce settlement which helps out some. I also understand that your last wife left you a few years back. Are you divorced yet?"

Baxter signaled the waiter for coffee. "I'm separated. My former wife has some other business matters on her mind. She was President of a retailer who went through a major bankruptcy and there were several issues related to shareholder suits. Bridgette has other things on her mind these days other than the administrative details of a divorce," Baxter explained.

"I understand from Muffin that this Bridgette person left you in the Fall of 1987. Three years seems like a long time to complete a divorce."

"The property settlement is in agreement. There are no issues relative to support or financial assistance. Bridgette has been a very well paid executive. It's simply a matter of taking the time to get the divorce actions scheduled in the courts."

"Do you still see her?"

"We talk by telephone from time to time. Bridgette prefers to call me from car phones and the communications are always a little flawed."

"How's Muffin? I'm more than a little concerned about her not being in college," Jennifer probed.

"She's working up in New Hampshire in the gift shop of a ski resort, and reasonably happy with her life. She may be ready to try college in the Fall."

Jennifer took a long pull from her cigarette and stumped it out in the ash tray. The waiter brought coffee and took Jennifer's order for a croissant and Baxter's order for bacon and eggs.

"Well we have one child dying of a social disease and the other a college wash-out. Tell me more about Muffin first. I pretty well know Joel's status."

Baxter knew that Muffin dutifully wrote her mother every four weeks and rarely received a reply.

"As you know, Jennifer, Muff came back from Italy in November of 1988. She spent some time with your folks in Florida and she was back in school in January 1989. Muff's grades slipped a little in her senior year. We didn't have the choices that we would have had if Muff had enjoyed a conventional senior year. She was admitted to Adams College in New Hampshire for the spring term. Muff did very poorly at Adams and she was placed on probation after one year and dropped out to get her head together last Christmas. She has a job in the gift shop of a ski resort. If you like I can drive you up there on Saturday and we can spend the afternoon with Muff. She very much wants to see you."

"A college drop out! What the hell's wrong with her? She must be over this Gabe boy by now."

"That's long over. Muffin has experienced a lot of difficulty in adjusting. She was shattered over Joel's illness. Our children are very close to one another even if we aren't. The abortion was a setback for Muffin and I pushed her through Prep School. I don't believe she was really emotionally ready to begin college when she enrolled in Adams."

"And was Adams absolutely the best you could do in the way of a college for Muff? Did you really try to get her into Vassar, Skidmore, or Wellesley?"

"Muff didn't have the grades or the SAT scores to get in. Adams was the best we could do. I anticipate that we will have her back in Adams this fall."

"What will she major in?"

"Communications."

"What in hell is communications?"

"It runs the spectrum from Journalism to Electronic Communications," Baxter explained vaguely. He had no idea what a Communications major was about and doubted whether Adams College did either.

Jennifer shook her head. "I was a liberal arts graduate and the best I could do after graduation was to go to work for a failing department store. I would hope Muffin could do better than that."

"What Muffin does in life is more or less up to Muffin. I believe she will do very well over time."

"And Joel has no future?"

"As long as Joel is alive, he has a future, Jennifer. There is a lot of research going on relative to AIDS and perhaps a cure will be developed in time. Until then, the hospice is the best place for him."

"How much time does Joel have?"

"His doctors tell me that Joel could be gone by this Labor Day, or he may be around by next Easter. He could recover and go on to lead a normal life." Baxter waxed with false enthusiasm.

"Do you really believe that?"

"I'd like to believe it. Joel and I had our differences in the recent past, but I've grown close to him over the past two years."

"And have you accepted him as a homosexual?" Jennifer produced another cigarette from a silver case. Baxter made no move to light it.

"Joel has a sexual orientation that I don't agree with. He now has a life threatening disease that is probably related to his choice. I have accepted where Joel is in his life. Jennifer, I have a major point of contention with you. I believe that it was very ill-timed to tell Muffin during her recovery period that you doubted as to whether I was her real father. That theory caused Muffin some serious emotional adjustment problems. She's been seeing a therapist trying to work out matters. I don't like you, Jennifer. You're simply not a nice person."

"And you have always been a crude, lower class, pompous ass who helped to destroy the company my grandfather built." Jennifer lit her own cigarette with a silver lighter that matched her compact.

The waiter served their breakfasts and refilled their coffee cups while Baxter and Jennifer exchanged glares. Baxter thought back to the first time he had kissed her following a concert on a snowy Racine afternoon. He had innocently viewed her as the beautiful, snobby, boss's daughter, as opposed to a vicious, self-centered, selfish woman with dark family secrets. All his life, Baxter concluded, he had been serving as a pawn on someone else's chessboard.

"How did you locate this hotel? I've never been here before," Baxter said to break the silence.

"It's cheap and clean. Some friends of mine are importers and recommended this place. This trip has been very expensive. I live comfortably enough in Milan but my funds have limits."

"What ever happened to Mr. Palmetti?" Baxter asked.

152

"It didn't work out. Carlos was a painter and fifteen years younger than me. He thought I had more money than I had and I believe he loved me. Fortunately the paintings he produced during our marriage have begun to sell. The Italians aren't high on divorce. I had a clever attorney and now have an income stream. I have concluded that all future relationships will be with independently wealthy men in their late fifties to early sixties. That could include your old friend Basil Crowley who calls me from time to time when he's near Milan."

"Basil was a brief acquaintance. He is hardly an old friend," Baxter corrected.

"He was very successful with Washburn, and he's been back in England for several years now. The Henry Wiggins company is headquartered in Birmingham but Basil maintains a flat in London. He's invited me over several times for long weekends. Basil tells me that he's next in line for Chairman."

"I have only a vague recollection of Basil. I just remember him as a vicious, mean spirited, little Brit with a ridiculous mustache. He probably likes you because he favors Italian women. You would make a very nice couple."

"He remembers you as a very immature and idealistic young man."

"Tell Basil, when you see him again, that I've lost my idealism."

"We're going to have an arduous day together aren't we, Joe?"

"We're together to be with our son who may be close to death."

"Call Muffin and ask her to come to New York City if she wants to see me. I looked at the map this morning. New Hampshire must be three or four hours north of New York City. I have no intention of spending that amount of time alone with you." Jennifer opened a compact and applied fresh lipstick. "Besides, I'd like to get some shopping in while I'm here. Let me get my coat from my room." She stood up from the table.

"Let's get this time behind us. I'll meet you in the lobby." Baxter watched Jennifer move out of the dining room taking aggressive steps in her high heeled black boots. She caught the eye of every man in the room.

TRENTON MAKES. THE WORLD TAKES said the sign on the bridge over the Delaware River. The Metroliner pushed out of Trenton Station bringing him closer to the 30th Street Station in Philadelphia where he could assume his role in the pageantry of Ernie Grey's funeral.

Baxter hadn't thought about that 1990 Easter weekend with Jennifer in a long time. He didn't like to think about Joel. Those last two years between Labor Days had been very painful for Baxter and lethal for Joel.

As it turned out, Jennifer had behaved very well. She was an actress at heart. They spent two days with Joel in the lower East Side hospice. Jennifer played the beautiful, charming, brave, loving, sophisticated woman of the world, and was the center of attention for Joel's friends and fellow patients. She discovered a piano in the recreation room on the afternoon of the first day and began to play. Soon she organized a sing-a-long among the patients. Baxter had no recollection of Jennifer playing the piano. He estimated that there were at least twenty middle-aged and young men clad in blue bathrobes and assembled in a loose semi-circle around Jennifer at the piano.

Joel stood happily next to the piano leading the singing. He had his mother's Washburn saucer eyes. He had grown very thin with a steady weekly weight loss. It would be their last time together, Baxter concluded. The other men who also lived in the house of death with Joel were, for the most part, cheerful and seemed in good spirits. They attended a religious service on Good Friday and concluded their visit after Saturday family hours.

Baxter had met Muffin's bus Friday evening at the Port Authority. She was hostile in the beginning with her mother, but again Jennifer turned on her actress charm. The two had gone off shopping together on Saturday morning and returned mother and daughter bonded. The three had dinner together on Saturday night after leaving Joel. Jennifer extended an invitation to Muffin to spend the summer with her in Milan.

"We can visit the antiquity sites and then sail to the Greek Islands. I have a friend who owns a lovely cruiser. Then you can return to that Adams

College rested and with a European perspective. I know we can squeeze in a side trip to Paris. Your airplane ticket will have to be your father's responsibility. Think about it."

"Oh mother, that will be so wonderful," Muffin said taking Jennifer's hand.

Muffin slept on Baxter's sofa bed that evening. She perched at the foot of Baxter's bed in shorty pajamas with a glass of wine and full of talk.

"Today was a wonderful day. I had forgotten how beautiful Mother was. She cheered me up when all I could think about is that Joel will die. Would you send me to Italy for the summer? Last time there was such a cloud over my head. It was a scary time for me. This time I could relax and enjoy myself."

"You may go if the invitation is solid," Baxter agreed.

"Do you still see that Linda?"

"No. She resigned to join another firm. She's also engaged to be married to a young man her age."

"And what do you hear from Bridgette?"

"Not a good deal. The Florida Group is in Chapter 11 bankruptcy and the entire senior management was fired by the trustee. Bridgette's name has been included in some of the shareholder suits. She also has some problems with the IRS. Bridgette's recently been named as President of a small California headquartered specialty chain. She said that we'd get a divorce as soon as things settle down for her."

"I really don't understand what you just told me, Dad. Did Bridgette do something wrong or dishonest?" Muffin asked.

"She didn't do anything that a lot of other people didn't do in the late 1980's, Muff. Except Bridgette got called on it."

"Will you ever get back together with her?"

"I really doubt it, Muff."

155

"Were you ever happy when you were married to mother?"

"To be honest with you, Muff, I was never very happy when I was married to your mother. Before we were married, I believed I loved her, asked her to marry me, and I thought I could be happy with her. It was a mistake."

"She told me when I was in Milan that she was pressured by her Grandfather into marrying you. Grandfather believed that the family needed new blood, and you were the right kind of person. He believed that you and mother would produce the right kind of children who would eventually run the company. Isn't that a laugh?"

"We used to call your Grandfather, Mr. Tom. He was not in full command of his faculties when I came to Washburn Manufacturing."

"And he abused mother when she was a child? She told me all about it when I stayed with her. She also told me that my real father was some one night stand she met in the peace movement. Was mother always highly promiscuous?"

"I believe she was always sexually aggressive. I wouldn't take that peace movement lover story too seriously, Muff."

"Dad, it's okay." Muff moved down to Baxter's place on the bed and wrapped her arms around his neck. "I didn't feel right at first, but I thought it through. You're my father, not a piece of stray sperm. You're the one who's there for Joel and me." Muffin kissed him about the face with fierce little pecks. "I have an idea," she offered. "Why don't you come with me to Italy to visit mother? You wouldn't have to spend the whole summer. Maybe just a week or ten days. Maybe you could pick things up again and get back together. I think she'd take you back if you asked her. She really likes New York and she asked me a lot of questions about how well you were doing at McKenzie Barber. I even pointed out a copy of your book in the business department at Barnes & Noble. Mother seemed to be very impressed."

Baxter remembered helping Jennifer on with her coat as they were leaving the restaurant that evening. He could smell her perfume as she whispered in his ear.

"Why don't you get Muffin settled in and come by my hotel for a nightcap?" Baxter had begged off. The actress was plotting.

Jennifer left on a 6:30 PM TWA flight on Easter Sunday evening. They had an expresso together at the JFK Ambassadors Club. Jennifer was wearing her outfit of Thursday morning with her high booted legs crossed, inviting looks from passerby. They had returned from a final meeting with Joel in the hospice.

"I'm exhausted. I'm going to take a pill and sleep through to Milan," she said lighting a cigarette.

"Joel and Muffin treasured your visit."

"Joel looked bad today. He won't last the summer, will he?"

"It doesn't look good," Baxter agreed.

"Muffin looks good. She's going to grow into a very attractive young woman."

"We talked at dinner last night about Muff coming to Europe this summer. I believe she's very excited over the prospect."

"I slept on it, Joe. It's really not a very good idea for this summer. Perhaps next summer. I have a number of commitments this summer. Muffin will just have to wait a year or two."

"Will you write her and explain?" Baxter requested.

"Of course. My plans changed a little this morning when I received a call. It looks as though I'll be in Cannes this summer with some friends. You explain to Muffin and I'll write her a letter a little later this week."

"Will you write Joel, too?"

"Of course. I'll write him regularly." Jennifer ashed her cigarette. "I've been meaning to ask you. Do you suppose those men in the hospice have sex with each other? Or do they put something in the food?"

"I've never thought about it," Baxter answered.

"Well, I have." Jennifer stumped out her cigarette. "I'm off to the departure lounge." She extended her hand. "There's really no sense in having you see me past security."

Jennifer waved after she cleared the metal detector. Baxter wondered at the time if he would ever see the actress perform again.

Joel died during an August hot spell in 1991. Baxter had dropped in at the hospice on his way out to LaGuardia. Joel seemed listless. He had received a long letter from Jennifer saying that she would try to visit him over Christmas.

"Everyone asks about Mom," Joel said. "They remember her from the sing-a-longs. Even the people who weren't here ask about here. Now I've got something to look ahead to."

His saucer eyes appeared drowsy. He fell asleep in his chair as they talked. Baxter had a plane to catch. He remembered stroking Joel's hair and kissing him on the forehead.

Bwana caught up with Baxter two nights later at a Detroit airport motel. There was a call from Godfrey Bain with Bwana's home telephone number.

"Joel's gone, Joe. I can make the arrangements if you like," Bwana said in a flat emotionless voice.

"Please do. I'd like to leave the thing if your hands with full discretion."

"I'll handle everything, Joe. We'll have the service in the school chapel. Is Saturday morning at 10 AM okay?"

"Fine. Thank you, Bwana."

"Then good night, Joe. Give me a call tomorrow night and I'll provide you the details. Needless to say, I've done this before."

"Let's just get it done. And thank you," Baxter added.

He wired Jennifer about the funeral arrangements, but didn't hear back from her until late September. Grandfather and Grandmother Washburn sent flowers. There was a small turnout of friends and former teachers, and Baxter hosted a buffet luncheon at a Princeton hotel, which seemed to include a great many faces that he hadn't seen in the chapel nor at the gravesite. Muffin broke down and wept uncontrollably in the rental car ride back to Manhattan. His son had exited Baxter's life.

The Metroliner came to an unscheduled halt fifteen minutes out of Trenton. A gruff conductor's voice came over the speaker and announced that there would be a delay of twenty minutes because of a track problem. There was some grumbling among the club car passengers about twenty minutes meaning an hour. Outside Baxter's window was a clump of leafless trees planted in dirty, hard packed snow under a sullen sky. What a day for Ernie Grey's funeral.

His life over the last three years had evolved into a succession of reorganizations, termination's, and funerals. All around Baxter people seemed to be either fired or have died. It became obvious to nearly everyone at McKenzie Barber that the firm was slipping. Robson Allen had forged well ahead of McKenzie Barber, and suddenly new competitors had emerged and were taking business away. Baxter found his own practice first surrounded and then overrun by competition. The competition was willing to cut fees in order to position themselves with clients. Baxter found a colder competitive world without the sponsorship of Leon Harwell.

In the early 1980's when he had been hot from the Pennsylvania Steel engagement, Baxter had been interviewed by a young reporter from *Enterprise Week* named John Baker. Baker went on to write a book called the *Paymasters* which featured Baxter and Alvardi along with other senior practitioners. The book enjoyed a reasonably long good press run and catapulted Baker into a frequently quoted expert on executive compensation matters. Baker, a lean wiry young man who hid a weak chin behind a beard, was frequently on the telephone with Baxter and quoted him from time to time. Baxter regarded John Baker as superficial, naive, and useful. Baker was infuriated when Alvardi published his book, *The Over Paid Executive and Other Examples of Incompetency in Executive Compensation Consulting.*

"Have you read it, Joe?" Baker demanded in an early morning phone call.

"Read what?"

"Alvardi's book."

"I wasn't aware it was out." He remembered the book from the year earlier when Alvardi had been trying to sell Baxter his practice.

"You're in it. He has a chapter on your consulting work at Pennsylvania Steel. He calls it, 'Pandering to Shareholder Value'. He's not very flattering. I'll be reviewing it. I'd like your input, Joe. Can we have a quick lunch or breakfast?"

Baxter agreed to breakfast and met Baker in the Helmsley in late September of 1988.

Baker was now wearing tinted glasses and reminded Baxter of a young James Joyce. He held out a copy of the book which had each page marked with a paper clip or a yellow posting tab.

"Frank has written the book as an expose of greedy executives and whore consultants. It's an insult to your profession." The book was passed across the table while Baker continued to talk. "I'm reviewing the book for the magazine and trying to locate the reviewer for the *New York Times*. This book is dangerous and must be discredited from the beginning. You're in Chapter Nine."

Baxter flipped through the pages of the book. Someone, presumably Baker, had written in felt tip pen in the margins of every page. On the top of Chapter Nine "See Baxter!" was written.

PANDERING TO SHAREHOLDER VALUE AND OTHER CORPORATE FOOLISHNESS

Baxter scanned the page. It read:

Joe Baxter of McKenzie Barber is a former protégé of mine. He's a big, charming, redheaded Irishman from the Iron Range of Minnesota who somehow turned himself into a New Yorker. Joe has the gift of gab. He can sell clients and he can sell himself on the crazy things they want to do. He is not very technical, but put him in a room with a compensation committee and Joe can sell them anything they want to be sold.

Let me tell you about Joe's adventures at Pennsylvania Steel—

It was all there in black and white. The Pennsylvania Steel plan had paid off marginally because the stock had not advanced. The plan had been abandoned and the Grace Group was back in as consultants.

Baxter returned the book to Baker. "That Frank. He has such a way with words. Do you suppose there will be a film?"

"Are you going to sit there and take it while the man reviles your work?" Baker demanded.

"Hell no. I plan to write a damned snotty letter to the editor of every magazine that reviews this book."

"Joe, I need your help to attack this book. People tell me that you know Frank Alvardi as well as anyone in the world. How long did you work with him?"

"Maybe a dozen years." Baxter thought back to Dwyer's illness in 1969. Baxter was supposed to go into Executive Compensation on an interim basis and somehow he made it into a career.

"Was Frank fired from McKenzie Barber?"

"No. He was doing very well. The firm wanted more and Frank believed that in light of what he was being paid, he had given enough."

"Was he fired from Robson Allen?" Baker had a small pad out and was taking notes.

"Robson Allen got out of the business. They went through some kind of practice portfolio review and concluded that they wanted to be #1 or #2 in every practice segment. Executive Compensation was competing in a very fragmented business market. I guess they just let Frank take the practice, and he had some kind of an alliance with Robson Allen."

"Were you aware that he was trying to sell his practice last December and nobody would buy it?" Baker probed.

"I'm not surprised. It would be pretty difficult to operate his practice from California. I know he maintained his consulting relationship with Brimmer Industries."

"What kind of man is Frank Alvardi? To tell you the truth, Joe, I found him both manipulative and condescending." Baxter sipped his coffee and thought. Did anyone really know Frank Alvardi? He rarely talked about his personal life. He was a good looking Italian who resembled Joe DiMaggio. Alvardi had been married once and then divorced, and enjoyed a succession of relationships with women. He had been close to Dirks and Dwyer, and had tolerated Baxter as a protégé.

"Frank has always been a very private person. I know very little about his personal life."

"He's unmarried. Is he gay?"

"Anything but. He once told me that he had married his college sweetheart but hadn't been cut out for marriage. Frank has had a number of quiet relationships with women over the years. My advice, John, is to attack the premise of the book, not the man."

"Normally, I would never consider attacking anyone on a personal basis. But things have been said in this book that are outright objectionable and will discredit American business. Joe, you know most of the top Compensation practitioners. I want to get them on board of this. Can I count on you?"

"Of course."

"What do you know about Alvardi's connection to Brimmer Industries? He's some kind of Brimmer Industries Scholar at this university."

"Paul Brimmer was the former Managing Partner of the Chicago Office of McKenzie Barber. He's used Frank as a consultant for years."

"He dedicated his book to Paul and Lorna Brimmer."

"Mrs. Brimmer has been the mother Frank never had."

"Are they elderly?"

"I have no idea. I believe they are," Baxter said and started in on his eggs.

Baxter read his copy of Alvardi's book that evening in one sitting. It was brassy, clever and funny. Throughout the reading, Baxter noted attack and rebuttal points. Baker's issue was that Frank Alvardi had written a book that he had hoped to write. Alvardi had written a better book and had beaten him to it. Controversy would make the book sell. Frank had gotten even with Baxter by including the Pennsylvania Steel work. Baxter went to his word processor. It was counter attack time. The words flowed from him.

IN DEFENSE OF SHAREHOLDER ALTRUISM
PENNSYLVANIA STEEL REVISITED

I was very pleased to be included in Frances Alvardi's book, *The Overpaid Executive*. Frank, over the years, has done more to contribute to the over Compensation of Chief Executives than any living American. He has flattered me in singling me out in his book as a consultant who put the shareholder's interests ahead of Executive Management. For that he will have my undying gratitude. For many years, I had the privilege of serving as a consultant to the late Mr. Leon Harwell, one of American's foremost investors. Let me share with you some of the points on executive compensation that Mr. Harwell emphasized over the years—

Baxter had hoped his letter would be placed in the *New York Times Op-Ed* but it didn't make it. He was picked up by Enterprise Week.

Baker vigorously attacked *The Overpaid Executive*. But it was Frank Alvardi who made CNN and the talk shows.

Baxter left several calls for Alvardi in his office at Western Pacific University and received a return call two weeks later on his phone mail with an Atlanta number.

"Alvardi," the phone answered on the second ring.

"Baxter here. I wanted to talk to you about the wonderful plug in your book."

"That's fine kid. I always try to help. Are you still at McKenzie Barber? I hope you're calling me to tell me that you've taken early retirement or quit."

"I'm still with McKenzie Barber, Frank, doing what I do so well. Now, did I reach you in Atlanta?"

"Buckhead to be exact. I'm doing some work for Brimmer Industries and operating out of some office space in one of their subsidiaries."

"And how's your teaching going?"

"I'm teaching two sections during the day and one Saturday a month in their executive program. I'm king of the mountain out here kid. I have some good long legged graduate assistants and celebrity status among the profs. You should be grateful to me. My book will have everyone on their toes. The Exec Comp business was getting pretty moribund. Every actuarial and accounting firm is starting a practice sucking up to management and cutting prices while turning out very pedestrian work. My book may have saved the business. If I were you kid, I'd buy up a thousand copies from my publisher and mail them out to every client you got. Now I heard Harwell kicked over. What are you going to do for a deep pocket now?"

"I'll get by nicely, Frank."

"Lorna is setting up a dinner with Jesse Durham. I'll give him a free critique of your work to date. I'll be sure to let you know if there's a problem."

"As an educator, I would assume you have limited time to serve new clients, Frank."

"Yes and no, kid. I now have an unlimited source of cheap labor in graduate students. I may become the low cost producer."

"And how are Paul and Lorna?"

"You make them sound like a nightclub act, kid. Mr. Brimmer is in the midst of buying back his stock. He wants to take out Harwell Management, but that little Arab wants a premium price for Harwell's block. Brimmer tried to call Ned Harwell to set up a New York visit, and wound up with the Arab calling him back. He gave Brimmer a lecture on the conglomerate discount and advised him to restructure Brimmer Industries. You can imagine how well that went over. You know Brimmer. The company is his life. He works 14 hours a day, seven days a week."

"And how is Lorna?"

"A very foxy lady who is always there for her husband, but knows how to make time for herself. Usually women deteriorate with age, but Lorna just seems to get better and better."

"Well, give her my best."

"She liked my description of you in my book. 'That's Joe all right' she said."

"Well, Frank, I just thought I'd call you and compliment you on your book. You certainly have become the Xaviera Hollander of Executive Compensation. Readers over the globe are always interested in what one whore says about the other whores."

"Kid, I'll make it up to you. I'll fix you up with some California seminar time in the dead of winter. You can represent the shareholder's point of view."

"Have you heard from Dwyer or Dirks, Frank?"

"Dirks is retired and living on a boat. Dwyer's in trouble. He was fired from the accounting firm and is some kind of adjunct professor and part-time consultant in upstate New York. I wrote him a glowing recommendation. He should just plain retire but he's never saved a dime. The only ex long term McKenzie Barber guys who ever found jobs and kept them were Ernie Grey and Bob Friedman. Nice to talk to you, kid." The phone clicked off.

Baxter had a farewell drink with McMasters in the Four Seasons on Friday, September 30th, 1988, the final day of the fiscal year for McKenzie

Barber. He had purposely cut the introductory Partners Meeting for Brett Williamson. Baxter's feedback was the Williamson had been relaxed, but direct. He had said that he was going to weed out the non-performers very quickly and continue the restructuring work that Lon McMasters had initiated. After making a stop with Buzzsaw and Clyde after the meeting, Williamson apparently had returned directly to Washington. He was to assume his new duties on Monday, October 3rd.

McMasters was waiting for Baxter on a stool facing the railing. When Baxter requested the meeting, Marveen had informed him that it would have to be a quick drink. McMasters had placed his shoulder bag on the neighboring bar stool reserving Baxter's place.

"Sit down, Joe," McMasters greeted him coldly. "White wine, I assume." McMasters had a bottle of Perrier in front of him. "This is move weekend and I've got a lot of bases to cover. What's on your mind?"

"What are these moves all about?"

"You should have come to the Partners meeting on the Tuesday after Labor Day. It was all spelled out very clearly. You want me to repeat what was said then?"

"Lon, I don't want to review the bullshit that was passed out in the Partners meeting. I want to know why you're being transferred after one year when it was expected that you'd be in place for three to five years. I had gotten used to you. What can I expect from Williamson?"

"He likes you. I brought you up the other night when I went over the New York Partners. He said that Joe Baxter was the least of his problems. You had a decent year. Nothing that will get you more units but nothing that will get you fired. There's a lot of others who ought to be shaking in their boots. I see Brett drawing a bead on Walker whom I'm sure isn't your favorite Partner. It should take Brett at least a year or two before he's worked his way down to you, Joe."

"Why is this switch happening, Lon?"

Baxter's wine arrived and he raised his glass. McMasters simply stared at the bubbles in his Perrier. "Joe, if I were you, I'd just keep my head down and do my job, and not worry about the why of things. What is going to happen at McKenzie Barber is going to happen, and the Partners selected to run this firm don't want a lot of input from the rank and file of the general partnership."

"This firm is owned by the Partners, Lon."

"I didn't say I agreed with it, did I?" McMasters snapped back. "That's just the way things are. There's an election in two years. That's the time to take a stand if you don't approve of the firm's leadership."

"The morale of the Partners around the firm seems to be very low. The numbers look cloudy. There could be a clean sweep in the 1990 election," Baxter predicted.

"I'll leave that to you politicals. I've always been an operator," McMasters countered.

"And how will you like operating in the government business?" Baxter probed.

"Look, God damn it, Joe. All throughout my career, I've wanted to be the Managing Partner of the New York Office. I never thought I'd get the opportunity. Then it came. The office was messed up and the firm's strategy was faulty. I told the Operating Committee that I need the first year free and I'd have New York completely turned around by the third year. There was more wrong than anybody knew. I was on track, and Buzz and Clyde called me in at the end of August and told me that Brett was coming to New York and that I should go to FSO in his place."

"Why, Lon?"

"Brett will probably be Buzz's running mate in the 1990 election. They want him to have New York Office operating credentials at the time of the election. The credit for what I've managed to accomplish in the last ten months will go to Brett. Now you and I have never had this conversation. But that is the why. I also suspect that the numbers have been run up the last couple of years to make Brett look good. I may have the New York Office all over again. When the unit run comes out, you will see that I have been well rewarded. Now you and I have exchanged our piece and I have to go."

McMasters slapped a twenty dollar bill on top of the bar check. "Have a second drink on me. You're a good Partner. Good luck, Joe."

Baxter caught McMaster's arm as he slid off the bar stool.

"Lon, would you vote again for Buzzsaw in the 1990 electron."

"Hell, Joe. I didn't last time," McMasters said brushing quickly by Baxter.

Lucy Tweetman was meeting Baxter at 6 PM. He had instructed her to meet him in the front bar of the Four Seasons. He planned a pre-theatre dinner in the Pool Room followed by *Phantom of the Opera*. She arrived at ten after six in a smart looking green sleeveless dress with her hair pinned up. Lucy moved through the room to him followed by the envious eyes of the men assembled around the bar. She had remained a looker.

"Joe, I managed to get myself lost," she greeted Baxter. "I thought I knew what I was going, but I went out the wrong door of Grand Central Station. Then I took another wrong turn and wound up on Third Avenue." They exchanged kisses on the cheek and Baxter led Lucy to the maitre'd stand.

"This is wonderful," Lucy gushed as she looked around the pool room after they were seated. "I read up on this place and understand it's one of the best in New York. It would be wonderful just to have a leisurely dinner here but I wouldn't want to miss the play. Howard, you remember Howard Brunger, said he'd take me here the next time he came to New York. And now I'm here." Lucy's reviewed the menu intensely. "This is a little awkward, Joe but do you suppose we could skip the theatre and just talk tonight?" She extended her hand across the table to Baxter which he accepted.

Baxter waved down the waiter. "We're going to skip the theatre this evening. Please bring full menus and a wine list and ask someone at the maitre'd stand to cancel my car service pick-up," he said extending a five dollar bill.

"You've really become the masterful New Yorker, Joe. I assume that the theatre will just let you exchange the tickets for a night you can come."

"They're a warm hearted bunch here in New York."

"I was on the Board of a community theatre back in Indianapolis. We had a very liberal ticket exchange policy."

"How's Tommy?" Baxter asked after he had placed the wine order.

"That's one of the reasons I wanted to talk tonight. I'm stuck up in White Plains and Tommy's off running around the country. I really never wanted to leave Indianapolis. Then we had no choice if he wanted to continue to have a job with World Computer. So I put the house up for sale, and braced myself to move to White Plains. Then Tommy takes this job in Washington with FRS which he tells me will make his career. Joe, I think I want to leave Tommy. I need to talk it through with someone who really knows me."

Baxter nodded his head and they remained silent while the wine was served. Baxter could hardly be classified as a person who really knew Lucy Albright Tweetman. She was someone in the middle drawer of his Iron Creek memories. Lucy Albright, who lived up on Pine Hill, and once sang the Arkansas Traveler while wearing a bare midriff blouse at a seventh grade Junior High School assembly. His senior year love now sat across the table from him in the Four Seasons thirty-five years later and announced that she was considering leaving her husband of 30 years duration. Cracks had developed in the marriage of the perfect couple of 1958.

"We haven't exactly been next door neighbors over the years, Lucy," Baxter replied.

"No, we haven't Joe, but just to spend a few minutes with you and those days in Iron Creek all come back. You were very shy with girls in those days. And now look at you."

"Tell me about Tommy and you, and why you believe you are where you are now?" Baxter ordered them both the duck as an entree and the watercress soup to start.

Lucy began to talk when they were alone again. "I almost didn't marry Tommy. I would have loved to have you pay a little more attention to me over the years. But you had that mess of a marriage with Maggie, and there was always Tommy. I dated a little when I was at UMD and Tommy was over at Bay State College but he was always my fallback. My father believed that Tommy would do very well in business and would wind up the President of any company that he went to work for. My mother and father and Tommy's parents just assumed that we would be married sooner or later." Lucy took a long sip of wine for encouragement.

"This is hard for me to say to another person, Joe. Tommy and I have never been physically right for one another. He's a man who other women find very attractive. I found him attractive but I always found it very difficult to adjust to his physical needs. We went into sexual therapy when we were living in Lansing. And I went quietly for years to a psychiatrist in Indianapolis. Tommy once had a transfer to Los Angeles posed to him. It would have been a big promotion but I couldn't bring myself to move our family or leave the care of my psychiatrist. You see, Joe, I was sexually frigid for years."

Baxter nodded his head in support. The watercress soup was being served. 'Ah the stuff you learn over dinner' he observed to himself.

"Because I could not fill Tommy's needs, he looked outside our marriage to fill his needs. Sometimes these women were in his own branch office. I've always tried to be sympathetic and understanding to Tommy but he embarrassed me several times over the years. Now I know that there is something going on between Tommy and that Elyssa down in Washington."

The watercress soup was very good. It was a shame that he had agreed to pass on the theatre. He wouldn't have had to listen to all of these intimate secrets during Phantom, Lucy would have been soundly shushed.

"Do you continue to have this frigidity difficulty?"

"Only with Tommy. It's been very good with Howard and me. Now Howard wants me to leave Tommy and come to Indianapolis and live with him. He's coming off a bad marriage. It was a lot like my marriage with Tommy. They looked good to outsiders but they hadn't gotten along for years. What did you think of Howard?"

"He impressed me as the pride of Indianapolis," Baxter answered. "Obviously he has carried the family business to a new level."

"That wasn't the real Howard Brunger who was at lunch with us at the Palm Court. He was trying to impress the world famous Joe Baxter, and made a bit of a fool of himself. Howard's a lot different when he's back in Indianapolis."

"There's home games and road games Lucy. It's hard to get used to the court in the first half on road games."

"You sound like Tommy with your sports metaphors, Joe." Lucy smiled across the table. She was a fine looking woman who had recently overcome her personal struggle with frigidity. Perhaps passing the theatre wasn't a bad idea after all.

"I know you're going through a divorce, Joe. But are you seeing someone right now?"

He considered replying that he was down to a consulting associate and a housekeeper and there certainly was room on the schedule for one more. Especially someone he had desired since seventh grade.

"My personal life is in a state of turbulence just now, Lucy."

"Poor Joe."

"Poor Lucy." They held hands as the waiter sliced the duck.

"I'm not used to drinking," Lucy announced after her second glass of wine had been served. "Tommy drinks quite a bit. More than what's good for him. Howard drinks a lot of wine. I always remember you, Joe, as a big drinker. This wine is very good, though. Joe, do you remember how many times you kissed me over the years?"

Baxter ran through the event files of his mind. Kisses from Lucy was a small file rarely reviewed.

"I believe four times. Once on New Year's Eve in 1953 at the Iron Creek Country Club. That was a social peck. The second time was in front of Bud's place the night I learned that Maggie was pregnant. The third time was when I was home on leave from the Army in 1955. I kissed you on your front doorstep. And the last time was on the dance floor at the 30 year reunion. That's the sum of it, Lucy, four kisses in 36 years."

"And you remembered each one. That's amazing. I knew there were more than two. Because I remember that kiss out in front of Bud's. You could have carried me off after that kiss. Tommy wasn't paying any attention to me that night. He was just full of himself as usual. Then I compared you with Tommy at the thirtieth reunion, and I wondered what my life would have been if I had waited for Joe Baxter to court me."

"Lucy, looking back produces a lot of fantasies. We have to look ahead at the time we have left and how best to use it. What might have been is an abstraction."

"Joe, did you ever question as to whether Lenore was really your child? Maggie must have slept with 20% of the men in Iron Creek."

"I was the only one with red hair. Lenore is definitely my child, and she is as different from me as I was from my father. Marrying Maggie was the proper thing to do. Remaining married to her would have been a debacle for me. I would have spent my life in Iron Creek."

"It really has become a dreary place, Joe. I was so happy to transfer to Glenbrook Hall in Duluth for my sophomore year."

"And you had to come back your senior year to take care of your mother," Baxter recalled.

"That wasn't the whole of the story, Joe." Lucy leaned forward toward Baxter and lowered her voice. "Beth was the reason I came back."

"Beth Gold?"

"Are you still in touch with her? I understand that she lives right here in New York."

"I saw a lot of Beth last winter. She's in the midst of writing a new book, and tends to be reclusive when she's working hard."

"What's she like now? I never saw her again after that Christmas vacation in 1952. We used to write, and then we got down to Christmas cards, and then we quit getting Christmas cards. I've read all of her books with the exception of that Vietnam book. I just couldn't bring myself to finish that book. What is Beth like today?"

"She could be classified as a literary icon whose peak creative period is past. Beth is looking to reposition herself back into the literary mainstream. *"An Interlude of Discontent"*, Beth's Vietnam book, bombed with the critics and in the marketplace with her readers. She poured her soul into that book after her husband, Lester, died. Beth is tall, thin, intense, not very attractive, and she dresses outlandishly. When she wants company, she'll let you know. Her best friend is a lady named Stephany Hart, who's a Securities Analyst with a Wall Street firm."

"Do they live together?"

"No, but they drink together regularly."

"Joe, I had a lesbian affair with Beth at Glenbrook Hall. It was my idea to come home and take care of my mother. Did you ever suspect that Beth was a lesbian?"

"I assumed that Beth had a number of male and female relationships over the years." Baxter thought back to Beth's 1955 European trip in the company of Laura Bain, but decoded not to offer it up as anecdotal information.

"I was Beth's roommate and we became intimate. But she also developed relationships with older men, and encouraged me to do it too. I dated a little and liked to kiss, but I couldn't stand to have a boy touch me. I knew I had to get out of Glenbrook Hall and used my mother as an excuse. Beth came out to collect me, and I had found Tommy. You wound up with Beth. Tommy and I broke up once over sex."

Baxter nodded his head in understanding. If they had only gone on to Phantom. He wouldn't have had to listen to all this drivel.

"Well, I appreciate your sharing this with me, Lucy," he said, gesturing for the check.

"Joe, is there a chance for us after all of these years?" Lucy asked extending her hand across the table to Baxter.

"Let's see where this takes us," Baxter said squeezing her hand.

They walked down Park Avenue on a cool September evening. Baxter felt an occasional brush of Lucy's breast against his arm as they walked down the east side of Park Avenue. It was Baxter's intent to see Lucy off on the train to White Plains.

"I told you some things about myself tonight that I shouldn't have. Didn't I, Joe?"

"You've got them said and your relationship with Beth is thirty-five years back."

"Do you live near here, Joe?"

"Five minutes by taxi."

"I would love to see your apartment. I've never been in a New York apartment. Also I have no place I have to be in the morning."

"We can go there for a nightcap. But I must warn you, there is a young lady I see from time to time, and she has a key to the apartment. She may drop in."

"She spends the night with you?" Lucy asked.

"When she can fit it into her schedule."

"And how long have you been seeing this woman?"

"It started shortly after my wife walked out on me. We're at the ten month mark, but the flame of our relationship is flickering out."

"Does that mean you have room for a new relationship in your life?" Lucy pulled on Baxter's arm.

"Lucy, I'm a middle-aged man whose life is a blend of discontinuity and ambiguity. You and I are back in a 1952-1957 time warp. I've experienced a lot of things in my life, but I've never been to bed with you. If we're going to do it, let's get at it."

174

Lucy pulled to a stop in front of 277 Park Avenue. Her body, which had been relaxed, had turned rigid.

"I don't like to be talked to in that manner, Joe Baxter."

"Then let's get you on the late train to White Plains," Baxter countered.

"Why must all men have the same thing in their minds every hour of the day?" Lucy protested.

"You're being unfair, Lucy. I have loved you since you sang the Arkansas Traveler in that bare midriff blouse at seventh grade assembly. Now we've come together for this evening in the autumn of our lives. I have proposed to fulfill a life long dream of making love to you. We may never find time for this moment again."

Lucy kissed Baxter on the cheek and whispered in his ear. "Will you promise to be gentle with me?"

Baxter hailed a cab. "I promise to be the most gentle lover you have ever known," he replied, opening the taxicab door.

"What if that woman is there or shows up?" Lucy whispered as the taxi pulled away.

"We'll simply ask her to join us."

Lucy explained in the elevator of Baxter's building that she had her tubes tied after the birth of her daughter eighteen years previously. There was a note from Linda saying that she was going to a movie and would not be back that evening. Two file folders had been left on his desk for review. Baxter poured two brandies, a small snifter for Lucy and a large snifter for himself. He served Lucy in the living room and watched her take a furtive sip.

"Joe, I can't do this. Could you call me a taxi?"

"In New York, we hail taxis in the street, Lucy. If you changed your mind about tonight, I'll accompany you down to the street and hail you a cab."

"I just freeze up in situations like this, and I'm embarrassed. I'm still Tommy's wife and the mother of his children."

"I understand, Lucy," Baxter said setting his glass down on the desk. Lucy stepped forward and he took her in his arms. Baxter kissed her once on the forehead, then on the cheek, and then on her neck before moving into a full mouthed kiss. His fingers found the zipper at the back of Lucy's dress, and everything fell into place after that. His hand on her bare skin seemed to excite Lucy and she stepped out of her dress peaceably. She was well past the point of no return by the time Baxter unsnapped Lucy's brassiere.

Baxter had a stiffness problem that evening that he had experienced over the past year. Lucy feigned an orgasm after a mechanical coupling, and said that it had been truly wonderful. She produced a tooth brush from her purse which she had carefully placed on Baxter's bed stand and proceeded to the bathroom.

Baxter rose from his bed and stared out at a deserted 39th Street. He had finally made love to the girl with the bare midriff in seventh grade. One more check mark on the things-to-do list of his life. His career was falling apart. His son had tested HIV positive. His daughter was recovering from her Italian abortion, and he had just engaged in a modest act of adultery with the wife of his former 1953 Cougar teammate. To top it off, Beth Gold had scored with Lucy some thirty-six years earlier.

Lucy returned to bed with a Colgate mouth and a nestling naked body.

"Was I good for you? You were wonderful for me. You were so gentle. We've got to get our lives straightened out and have our time together. We both deserve it. I'm so glad I came back with you tonight. I love you, Joe. Do you love me?"

"Let's see where this goes," Baxter said and Lucy settled in his arms for sleep.

Baxter put Lucy in a cab in the morning. Two weeks later after several calls, Lucy left a voice mail saying that she was returning to Indianapolis and was staring divorce procedures with Tommy. She hoped Baxter would visit her in Indianapolis.

Baxter made it a point to visit Tommy Tweetman's Alexandria Offices when he passed through Washington in late October. Re-plen-o-link now operated with a suite of offices separate and adjacent to FRS. The plaque next to the door read:

REPLEN O LINK DIVISION
FRS CORPORATION
SUITE 1410
THOMAS A. TWEETMAN
VICE PRESIDENT & GENERAL MANAGER

"This business is moving, Joe," Tommy said from behind his oval shaped desk in the 14th floor office. "We had a great show in Las Vegas, and bookings are flowing in. We're going to have just one hell of a 1989."

Elyssa stood in the office doorway.

Tommy, may I see you on something?" She wore a blue knit dress two inches above the knee and retained her attractiveness of 1987. "Elyssa, you remember Joe Baxter?"

Elyssa entered the office and extended her hand with a confident smile.

"Of course. I worked with Mr. Baxter and Dr. Dunlap last fall on the executive compensation plan. I understand that Tom and you go back a long ways. I have to borrow him right now for a few minutes on a shipping problem that has come up."

Tommy followed Elyssa out of the office, and Baxter looked around the room. There were pictures of Tweetman's son and daughter on the credenza behind his desk, but there was no sign of Lucy. The walls contained sales trophy plaques from IBM and World Computer. Tommy's desk was clean except for two large stacks of paper. One appeared to be a tall stack of order form copies. Baxter stepped over to the credenza for a closer look at the Tweetman offspring. They photographed well, as did Baxter's own children. Kevin was the oldest at 23. In the picture he had his mother's blonde hair, which was close cropped, and his father's eyes. Kevin had just graduated from his father's school, Bay State College in northern Wisconsin. He had captained the basketball team as a point guard, and had finally graduated in the summer with a low C average. Kevin had just secured a job as a management trainee with a mass merchant discount chain.

Jill, the daughter, looked like Tommy. She was unhappily enrolled in a small Indiana liberal arts college and had been described as a Daddy's girl. Jill was also a basketball player.

"Good looking kids aren't they, Joe?" Tommy said upon returning to his office.

"You must be very proud of them."

"I am. They are going to be living with me out here next fall. Kevin started his last two years at Bay State, captained the team his senior year, and made second team all conference."

"Did he have his father's shot?"

"No, but Jill does. She was All State in women's basketball. Jill had some scholarship offers from big team women's programs at major universities, but Lucy would have none of it. I heard you were out to dinner with Lucy last month in New York. Did she talk about us?"

"Some."

Tommy closed his office door and seated himself on a chair next to Baxter's.

"Some! What the hell does that mean, Joe? This is your old buddy, Tom here. I told Lucy in August that I wanted a divorce. I told her that she should get a lawyer the week before Labor Day. I got one in Washington who has a connection in Indianapolis. Lucy has been a millstone around my neck for over thirty years. Replen-o-link is probably my last chance for me to make it big time. If I fail here, I'm just another ex-IBM, ex-World Computer has-been. I've got to succeed and I will succeed. We've got something that nobody else has. This is way beyond selling mainframe computers. It's licensing the world with a unique intellectual property. I'm in the fourth quarter of my career, Joe, and I've got my shot back. If I were you, I'd get into the stock very quickly. We're at 3 7/8's now, but Doc Horgcost and I are going to put on a hell of a road show in December. We're going out for a secondary. There should be some work for you, too. Horgcost is out of town today."

"How are you getting along with Dr. Horgcost?"

"I can manage him. He's as slippery as the day is long. He spends his time mucking around in the body shop side of the command and control business. In fact they do some sub contracting with FSO, your Washington outfit. Doc Horgcost is smart enough to stay the hell out of my business, and I'm negotiating a three year contract on my anniversary date."

"I see you have easy access to Elyssa, Dr. Horgcost's executive assistant."

"Elyssa's been my Manager of Administration since July. The Doc has a new executive assistant now. Elyssa's been a big help this last year, Joe. We hit it off from the beginning. When do you go back tonight?"

"I want to catch the nine-thirty shuttle, Tom."

"Give me fifteen minutes to clean things up and we'll have a quick dinner, and I'll drop you at the Delta Shuttle. It's just damned good to see you, and we've got to get caught up."

Fifteen minutes turned into forty-five. Baxter was provided a desk and phone in what appeared to be a customer service area. He found himself surrounded by young men and women wearing headsets and responding to buzzing telephones. Elyssa dropped by to talk with Baxter briefly.

"This is a busy part of the day for us. We developed a number of new distributors on the West Coast as a result of the September Las Vegas trade show. Thank you for sending Tommy to us," Elyssa said, patting Baxter on the shoulder.

They ate in the back booth of a neighboring cafe where Tommy appeared to be a well known customer.

"I eat here when I'm in town, Joe, and I have a peanut box efficiency apartment around the corner. Replen-o-link is a full-time, seven day a week job. I burned my bridges when I walked out on World Computer last January. This has to be a big success for Tom Tweetman or my career's in the dumpster. That's why I didn't want Lucy down here. Let's get an order in, Joe. I can have you in front of the shuttle in fifteen minutes from the time we're in the car. This place isn't like one of your fancy New York restaurants, but they're fast and I'm used to it." Tommy ordered a coke and a rib steak sandwich while Baxter settled for coffee and a clubhouse sandwich.

"Let's get it out on the table first thing. Lucy and I are splitting. It's a final decision for both of us, and we should have done it ten years ago, but it wouldn't have been the right timing for our kids. It was a mistake for us to get married in the first place, and we allowed it to last thirty-one years. How many times have you been married, Joe?"

Baxter held up three fingers. "Technically, I'm still married to Bridgette, but we're having difficulty in getting our lawyers in sync."

"Somebody told me that the Florida Group wasn't doing very well," Tweetman observed.

"I'm not close to retailing, Tom," Baxter responded.

"This is my first divorce and I know I'm going to get screwed. Lucy keeps on saying that we must have an amicable divorce in the interests of the children. They're adults now and anything but children. Kevin is trying to stay neutral, but he's never really liked his mother. Jill has always tangled with Lucy. It came to a head when Lucy insisted that Jill turn down NCAA scholarships so we could enroll her at St. Scholastica in Indiana, which was exactly where Jill didn't want to go."

"Why would Lucy do that?" Baxter asked innocently.

"Lucy sees a dyke behind every athletic bench. She's got a real hang-up on lesbians getting to Jill. My kids grew up on basketball hoops. Jill has played in organized basketball since she was eleven. She's always been the kind of stand-out that every coach treasures. Lucy used to third degree Jill every time she got close to a woman coach. Lucy's got a mess of hang-ups Joe, and I knew about most of them when I married her." Baxter sipped his coffee and nodded his head.

"Do you realize that Lucy's mother lived with us for a dozen years before I managed to get her into a long term care facility?"

Baxter shuddered at his recollection of Mrs. Albright, Tommy's wheelchair mean mother-in-law.

"Twelve years, Tom?"

"Twelve years, Joe. She came to live with us in Grand Rapids and moved with us to Indianapolis. And after you made your mark, all I ever heard about was Joe Baxter. Lucy would always go through the *Wall Street Journal* and *Enterprise Week* looking for the pithy sayings of Joe Baxter. She kept a Joe Baxter scrapbook that she would pull out for the neighbors to see. You were Saint Joe Baxter, the brilliant consultant, and I was Tom, her working stiff, computer peddling husband."

"Did you remind her that you outscored me back at Iron Creek?"

"Iron Creek! Joe, I often wonder what my life would have been like if I had never seen that place. My Dad wanted to run a clinic and there was his chance. I pleaded with him to let me stay behind at Ginter Lake for my senior year. 'No dice' my Dad said. 'We move as a family'. So I came to Iron Creek and tried to make something out of the Iron Creek Cougars. You guys would have been lucky to win three games a season in our conference in central Indiana."

"We're not going to replay the Darwin game again, are we Tom?" Baxter looked purposely at his watch.

"All I'm saying, Joe, is that Lucy was about as good as a guy was going to get in Iron Creek. She was the best looking woman in town, although the one you knocked up had the best body."

"I haven't thought about Maggie's body for a long time, Tom. She's quite middle-aged and fat now. Based on my dinner with Lucy, I'd say she'd kept herself up pretty well," Baxter commented.

"Outsiders have always considered Lucy as the ideal wife. I've been told for thirty years how lucky I was to have such a great wife."

"What's exactly wrong with her, Tom?"

"Joe, Lucy is an all-controlling, selfish, frigid bitch. I thought she'd loosen up a little on sex after we got married. But she never did. It took me about ten years to figure her out. But then we had Kevin, and Lucy was pregnant with Jill. I calculated that I was on the fast track with IBM, and divorce would look like hell. Remember Joe, that was back in the Tom

Watson/white shirt days at IBM. There I was, Joe, a hot shot young branch manager who always made the 100% Club, who probably needed one staff marketing assignment in Armonk, and Lucy said, 'no way'. We couldn't move her mother. Then the next call came for Chicago on the District Manager job. Lucy wouldn't budge. Then my old boss defected to World Computer and he offered me the Indianapolis branch. No move involved and more money. I took it, and two years later I was offered the District Manager job in LA. 'No way', said Lucy. I stayed in the Indianapolis branch, my boss got fired, and things began to slide for me. What if my Dad would have stayed in Ginter Lake and I never saw the light of day in Iron Creek? Then where would I be today, Joe?"

"Back at IBM."

"You're a smart ass, Joe."

"And you're spending too much time looking back, Tom. Get your divorce and get on with your life and career," Baxter advised. He debated as to whether he would ask Tommy why he had fled the University of Kentucky Wildcats.

Tommy bunched his hands into fists, squeezed three times, and reopened his hands.

"You're right, Joe," he acknowledged.

Tommy's eyes grew hard. "Joe, did you screw Lucy the night you took her out to dinner?"

Baxter took a sip from his coffee. Should he risk his ride back to the airport.

"Lucy spent the night at my apartment, Tom. She told me her side of the divorce plans."

"Was that the first time you slept with her?" Tommy was clenching and unclenching his fists again.

"I hadn't seen Lucy since the 1983 reunion until I had lunch over Labor Day weekend with Lucy and her Indianapolis friend, Howard Brunger. Then Lucy and I had our dinner a couple of weeks later."

"Brunger and Lucy deserve each other. He's a guy who inherited the family business and managed, through dumb luck and a long term broker sales organization, to grow the business. Howard believes he's a management genius. I sold him a computer system when I was with IBM, and later convinced him to convert to a World Computer and throw out IBM. We used to do things socially with Howard and his now ex-wife, Barbara. Barbara had gone through two tennis pros by the time Howard caught on. Lucy could be very comfortable with someone like Howard. Joe, I always regarded you as my friend. Why did you have to screw Lucy while she was still married to me?"

"Tommy, have you ever been unfaithful to Lucy?"

"Whenever I could get it in. I remember your last wife, Bridgette, from the reunion. She impressed me as a handful. But I sure as hell didn't try to screw her."

"Tom, accept what happened between Lucy and me as an accidental relationship. It certainly wasn't anything premeditated."

"Joe, nothing is accidental with Lucy. She planned to be in your bed that night. I'll bet she even faked an orgasm to make you feel good. Do you plan to visit Lucy in Indianapolis over the holidays?"

"Tommy, I don't have time to get involved in a relationship with Lucy at this point in my life. I was candid with you when you asked me a direct question. That's all I have to say on the matter."

"Let's get you out to the airport, Joe."

"Why don't I get a cab?" Baxter offered.

Tommy Tweetman waved down the waitress. "Ernestine, will you please get this gentleman a radio cab for Washington National?"

Baxter rode back alone in the taxi to the airport. He concluded that full disclosure was not always the best policy in matters of infidelity.

Brett Williamson officially assumed his New York Office Managing Partner responsibilities effective October 3, 1988, the first day of McKenzie

Barber FY 1989. He asked Baxter to join him for a late afternoon coffee on Wednesday, October 7th. Marveen held forth as the Managing Partner's gatekeeper from Charlotte Bunker's desk.

"Hello Marveen," Baxter greeted her. "Brett wanted me to drop by for coffee this afternoon."

"Sit down, Joe," Marveen responded coldly. "Mr. Williamson is on a conference call."

"How's it going, Marveen?" Baxter asked cheerfully.

"We're in transition, Joe. All of us have to adjust."

Marveen slipped on a headset and began to type from a recording.

The door of the New York Office Managing Partner's office opened, and Brett appeared in the doorway.

"Com'on in, Joe."

"Marveen!" he said sharply. "Hold my calls with these exceptions. Chairman Pritchard, Mr. Nickerson, and Lon McMasters. No exceptions!" Marveen nodded as Baxter stepped into the office. He had spent a lot of time in the New York Managing Partner's office over his career. The first time had been with Bruce Dinsmore who had been in the twilight of his career. That had been followed by Hamilton Burke, Bob Friedman, Floyd Piper, and Lon McMasters. Now the office was occupied by Brett Williamson, ex-Marine, and protégé of the Chairman. Baxter quickly noted a newly hung picture on the wall with Brett in his Marine dress blues posing with a sabre.

Brett motioned for Baxter to sit. His desk and table were covered with piles of papers. Brett wore dark suit pants, a white shirt with military creases, and a dark tie with a USMC tie bar. He wore military style oxford shoes that were highly polished.

"Sit down there, Joe," Brett greeted him cold motioning Baxter to a side chair across from his massive desk. With his gleaming black short hair, short side burns, and dark somber face, Williamson reminded Baxter of a company commander of a disciplinary barracks.

"Do I understand that Marveen, out there, used to work for you at one time?" Brett had retained his Southern accent, but his words didn't flow out melodically as they did from Burke. Rather they shot out of his mouth like short bursts of automatic weapon fire.

"Yes, Brett, she was my secretary before her transfer to Lon."

"How would you like to take her back?"

"When Lon asked me to transfer Marveen to the Managing Partner's office, I agreed to take Charlotte Bunker in return for one additional department secretary."

"It's time for Mrs. Bunker to retire, and you to take your Marveen back. She's just plain not qualified to be the New York Office Managing Partner's secretary."

"Why's that?" Baxter asked.

"Because she's an ignorant black lady. That's why. I don't know what got into Lon to take her as a transfer. My Human Resources Director from FSO is transferring up here effective the 10th of October. Her name is Druanne Smithers. I can't understand how Piper and McMasters operated without a Human Resources Director. They tried to use Bill Richardson's New York Office Administrative Group. He's got a Personnel Manager named Isabell Mirana down there at the Lex Level. Know her?"

Baxter shook his head. He had seen the name on various forms over the years, but delegated all contact with the Lex Level administrative people to Marveen and now Charlotte.

"I put Richardson on notice yesterday that the Lex Level bunch had better get their act together, or I'll outsource them effective 1, January. Druanne is a 20 year retired WAC Major. She knows how to take action, and we think alike on personnel matters. She really likes that incentive plan you put in place for us at FSO. I'll be back to you after the Partner's meeting. I want something similar developed and installed in the New York Office no later than Q-3. The first thing I want Druanne to get into is the secretarial situation. She should get me a classy New York executive secretary who's worked for a CEO before. Then I want a production secretary to get out my hard copy and e-mail correspondence. You will find that I'm in constant contact with my Partners, but I always maintain the chain of command. The next thing we're going to do around here, Joe, is to increase efficiency. The New York Office is unbelievably over-secretaried. A partner with a practice your size needs only one administrative secretary. The rest of your work should go through an assigned word processing section. At FSO, I have often been referred to as the Henry Ford of the government contracting business. The first thing we're going to do in the New York Office is to take the ship in for maintenance. Then we're going to sail out and blow all of our competitors out of the water."

Brett stared at Baxter with hard, cold eyes. He obviously expected Baxter to say something. Baxter searched for words and thought back to the good old days of Floyd Piper.

"Brett, what would you like to know about the Executive Compensation practice?"

"Here's where I come out, Joe." Brett twisted slightly in his swivel chair. "You got a piece of business that makes a little money, but really isn't going anywhere. If you want it to remain separate and independent, you've got to get some growth this year. I've seen your plan, and it's just not good enough. We need a minimum of 30% growth from the New York Office, and 25% around the firm. And it seems to me that you should get it with the same amount of people. I want you to resubmit your plan with those growth assumptions, and have it on my desk for final review by the end of this week. This has been a country club around here, and the New York Office Partners are going to find me a little more demanding than Lon McMasters. Baxter knew he had two alternatives. He could say, "Yes, Brett," and exit the room or he could take his stand now. His life would have been less complicated if Leon Harwell had lived.

"Brett, did you thoroughly review the narrative of underlying assumptions and actions that supported the National and the New York office plans?"

"I scanned it, Joe. The numbers weren't worth shit. You give me the numbers I want and make 'em, and you write me another pretty little essay about all of the wonderful things you're going to do to make your plan."

"The numbers were built on the basis of marketplace and delivery of service assumptions, Brett. They represent a reasonable growth for 1989. I have New York at a 15% growth rate with a 28% net to gross." With the loss of Harwell and the tail down of Planters & Commerce, the numbers that had been submitted in late August represented a stretch plan for the Exec Comp practice. He had not expected to be around to achieve the plan. Now Baxter was stuck with it and Brett Williamson wanted still more.

"Your numbers are unacceptable at your unit level, Joe. If you hit the numbers I want, I'll get you some more units. If you just hit the plan you submitted, I'll take some units away from you. If you don't grow your practice, I'll merge you in under the Benefits folks."

"I won't work for Walker, Brett," Baxter reacted.

"Walker's gone, Joe. I gave him his walking papers on the Thursday after Labor day. He's retiring. We're announcing it at the Partner's Meeting next week. Like I said, we're cleaning up the New York ship. I like you, Joe. I want you to be part of the solution around here, not one of the causalities. Who's your number two man in the New York practice?"

"My number two is a woman named Monica Graham. She's at the Director level. I'm placing her on the Partner's nomination list in December. We need a second Partner in the New York practice, and she's ready."

"Hit the numbers I want and you've got her." Brett placed a hand on his forehead and closed his eyes. "Monica Graham. Monica Graham. Did I meet her last year at the McKenzie Barber Christmas party? I had FSO running like a top since I took over from Buzz in 1984. My mission is to clean up the New York office in two years time and pick out my successor. Then I expect to take Neil Schmidt's place on the ballot in 1990. Joe, I expect to run this firm in 1996. You do right by me now, and I'll reward you. Underperform and your time will be short." Brett looked at his watch. "This is all the time I have for you today. You're getting your colored lady back in November, and Druanne will get Mrs. Bunker retired for you."

They exchanged grips in a handshake. "Get your revised plan in to me by Friday. Good to have you on my team," Brett said with a cold smile.

Baxter waved at Marveen as he walked by her desk station. She didn't look up from her word processor.

It was that Fall at the Partner's Meeting at the Boca Mirage Hotel & Yacht Club that Baxter observed the beginning of the buzz of a Partner's revolutionary movement. He arrived late on a Tuesday evening, and went down to the back bar for a nightcap. There were five men gathered around a circular table located against the window facing the moonlit canal. They were dressed in gold shirts and wash pants in contrast to Baxter's now rumpled blue pinstriped suit. A bald heavy-set man with shell glasses waved at Baxter as he approached the bar.

"Hey, Joe Baxter, come over and join us."

The face was vaguely familiar and he wore a McKenzie Barber name tag. "We need a little New York office input."

There were four occupied chairs and two empty ones around a table that contained an assortment of bottles of imported beer, and several small bowls of popcorn. The popcorn was littered across the table. Baxter concluded the group had been together for several hours. Baxter read his greeter's nametag as he drew up to the table.

It read, Ed Grinsigle, Dallas, and Baxter placed him as an Information Technology Practice Partner. The other three rose up from the chairs and extended hands. One was a tall, athletic thirtiesh man who wore Bermuda shorts. His nametag read 'Schuyler Teaford, Los Angeles'. He introduced himself as Schuy Teaford, IT LA. A third table member was a powerfully built man with a mane of white air. His tag read 'Graham Spurgeaon-Atlanta'.

"Joe, Graham Spurgeaon, Atlanta, by way of Toronto and Sydney. I've read your stuff for years. Good to meet you at last."

The last member of the group was of average height with greying black hair and dark penetrating eyes. He reminded Baxter of a young Ernie Grey. His nametag was pinned on the right as opposed to being clipped on his left hand breast pocket. It read 'Glen Fitzgerald-Chicago'.

"Joe, Glen Fitzgerald. We haven't met before. This is only my third year with the firm, and the first occasion I've had to attend a Partner's meeting."

Grinsigle waved to the waitress for another round and Baxter ordered a Coors. "None for me right now, Ed," Fitzgerald said. Baxter noted Fitzgerald's glass was three-quarters full.

"Glen came to us from Andersen as a direct admit Partner three years ago, and completely rebuilt the Chicago Office IT practice. He maintains that he has been too busy with clients to take time off to attend the bloody Partner's meeting." Graham announced.

"I've been coming all three years and I didn't know it was optional," Grinsigle grumbled.

"You just have to show up if you're unprofitable or barely covering your units, Ed. That's why we expect a good turn-out this year," Graham Spurgeaon added.

Baxter placed his suit jacket over the back of his chair and loosed his tie. He was an outsider invited into an unfamiliar group. Did they have a collective agenda?

"I take it, Joe, you're joining this meeting following a client meeting?" Fitzgerald asked.

"Planters & Commerce Bank in Atlanta. We're on the final phase of an exhaustive overhaul of the bank's executive and management compensation plans."

"I believe that your work at Planters & Commerce has been well publicized throughout the firm in the Partner's newsletter. Carl Miller in a recent Chicago Partner's retreat, spent some minutes on it describing his role in the work."

"Planters & Commerce has kept a lot of McKenzie Barber people busy," Baxter responded.

"I'm relatively new to the firm, Joe, having joined just three years ago. Fill me in on the executive compensation practice. I know that you have a small practice under Carl in Chicago, and I've seen your name for years in the business magazines. I'm curious as to what your practice is all about." The faces around the table were attentively watching Baxter while deferring to Fitzgerald.

"Glen, I'm always delighted to talk about my practice, both to clients and colleagues." Baxter took a sip of beer and studied the faces around the table. Teaford was the youngest in the group, and had the urbane young Turk look about him. Grinsigle, in contrast, was a fifty-ish career Dallas Partner probably looking ahead to retirement by the end of the early 1990's. Graham Spurgeaon impressed Baxter as a typical expatriate McKenzie Barber Partner. They gypsied their way through the various global practices, setting down in one country for a few years, and then jumping to a new country. There was no going back to Australia for him.

"The Executive Compensation practice was one of Ernie Grey's mid-1960's initiatives to diversify the firm's scope of consulting services. The old Industrial Engineering practice had worked with pay systems for years, but really confined their work to the development of wage and salary systems and incentive bonus plans. Robson Allen really pioneered Executive Compensation consulting in the late 1950's. They developed a consultant named Arthur Perrin who became an instant luminary. McKenzie Barber got into the business ten years later when they recruited Frank Alvardi, Perrin's number two, to launch the McKenzie Barber Exec Comp practice in 1967."

"Frank was posted to the Chicago Office in 1967. I transferred into the Exec Comp practice in the Fall of 1969 from the Manufacturing practice. Carl transferred into Exec Comp from the pool about six months earlier. Frank Alvardi transferred to New York in 1973, and I succeed him. I was moved to New York in 1977, and Carl succeeded me in Chicago. Frank was recruited back to Robson Allen in 1980, and after a search, I was chosen to succeed Frank. The US practice totaled about $10 million in FY '88 with about 55% coming from the New York office. We have practice units in Atlanta, Chicago, Dallas, Los Angeles, and San Francisco. We're traditionally a 25% net to gross practice after Partnership accruals. Our work is primarily directed to the development of short and long term executive incentive plans for the senior levels of management."

"I understand that Robson Allen has exited their Exec Comp business. Why are we still in this business?" Fitzgerald questioned.

"You obviously weren't listening carefully just now," Baxter shot back. "We're a 25% net to gross practice. If you make money, you stay around here. If you don't, you had better be a crony of the Chairman or Clyde Nickerson."

"Your practice doesn't make that kind of money in Chicago, Miller's lucky if he's in the 14 to 15% range. I'm privy to the Chicago performance numbers by practice unit. I just see the New York office numbers in the aggregate, and they haven't been very good over the three years I've been with the firm."

"I'm hardly responsible for the entire New York office. As you may be aware, the New York Office is now on its third Managing Partner in four years."

"Who are your competitors, Joe? This Alvardi seems to be getting a lot of mention in the business press with this book of his."

"Have you read the book, Glen?" Baxter asked.

"Yes, I have. I found it very engaging. He described you as a master snake oil salesman."

"I'm hardly a master, Glen. The master snake oil salesman wrote the book. Frank has an amazing sense of market timing. Our competitors are boutique compensation consulting, the compensation practices of the actuarial firms, and the benefit consulting practices of the national public accounting firms. Last, but not least, is the Grace Group, a salary administration firm that extended into executive compensation in the early 1970's. When I transferred into the Exec Comp practice unit in 1969, Robson Allen and McKenzie Barber shared the high end of the market with Grace Group holding the middle. Then consulting boutiques were formed, followed by the extension into compensation by the actuarial firms. Today we have a very price competitive market in the general practice segments with the high margin work available only on large scale engagements like Planters & Commerce. Now, fellows what is this little committee of inquiry up to? I was invited over for a beer to provide New York input into some subject of great interest," Baxter said cutting off the discussion.

The group looked to Fitzgerald to respond. Fitzgerald formed a wisp of a smile on his expressionless face.

"That's only fair, Joe. As I said previously, this is only my third year as a McKenzie Barber Partner, and this is the first time I've had time to spend at this meeting. I've been confined to my own little world of computer technology, and I'm trying to get my arms around what's happening in the rest of the world of McKenzie Barber. I left a firm where I was on the fast track, to move to an opportunity at McKenzie Barber that was easily three years away for me at Andersen. Everything has worked out well for me ahead of expectations. Meanwhile, the great firm around me appears to have become a bit of a rudderless ship."

"So you thought you'd actually show up at one of these meetings and see what's going on first hand?" Baxter interjected.

Smiles formed around the table. "Touché, Fitzgerald!" Graham Spurgeaon added.

Fitzgerald responded with a broad, self effacing smile. "You've got me there, Joe. If I don't take time out to participate in the annual communications forum, what complaining do I have? Well, I'm here this year. As I understand it, McKenzie Barber is two years away from the election of the Chairman and Deputy Chairman. The last election took place in 1984, which was a contested election. Two years from now in 1990, the Partners will be faced with the re-election of Chairman Pritchard and his designated Deputy Chairman, or consider alternative leadership. As a fellow Partner, Joe, how would you assess the stewardship of Buzzsaw Pritchard and Neil Schmidt since their election in 1984?"

"Are you asking me if the firm is better off today than it was in 1984? Hell, you already know the answer. The firm has slipped badly."

"What's your assessment of the current leadership?" Fitzgerald pressed. "Can they deliver the results that they continue to promise and fail to deliver?"

Baxter took a long sip of beer. Were there more than this little corps of conspirators. "The group in power is both incompetent and corrupt. The only thing they have raised to a new level is cronyism. Now what are you proposing to do about it?"

"I'm trying to make up my mind, Joe. Ed tells me that you were fairly active in the 1984 election process. I've studied the Partner's agreement, and believe I understand the provisions for the Partners-at-large nominating alternative candidates. I have a few questions for you."

"Forget the questions, Glen. I was on the establishment side and we blew it. We should have won and didn't. Ernie Grey, should have demonstrated more support for Hamilton Burke, and he didn't. And what do we have today? An ex-general who delights in strategic planning, while isolating himself from the business. An unelected, undesignated Vice Chairman in Clyde Nickerson, who has no concept of the consulting business. I'm 53 years old. The Chairman election of 1990 is the last election I will participate in as a Partner of McKenzie Barber. With Brett Williamson's transfer to Managing Partner of the New York Office, Buzzsaw is positioning his protégé for nomination as Deputy Chairman in 1990. If Pritchard is re-elected, there may not be a McKenzie Barber in 1996 for the next election."

There was a silent nodding of heads around the table.

"We're being lied to by the regime, gentlemen," Schuyler Teaford said. "Either we take a stand, Glen, or we should get out of here."

Baxter finished his beer. "That's it for tonight, fellows," he said rising from the table. There were handshakes all around and Glen Fitzgerald rose from the table and placed his hand on Baxter's shoulder. "I want you to have breakfast with Jack Pinker tomorrow morning. How about 7 AM at the Golf Club?"

"That's a little early, Glen.

"Joe, please take time to meet Jack. It's for a good cause."

Baxter estimated that he ran into Jack Pinker on the street and in the 311 Park Avenue offices at least ten times a month. Occasionally there was a chance meeting in the airport, and last there was the old reliable quick exchange at the New York Office Christmas Party. Baxter had worked with Pinker back in 1983 during the Director of Communications recruiting project which resulted in the hire of Dave LeMire. Pinker had been a two year Financial Services practice Partner at the time. Baxter hadn't expected

Pinker to last under Jack Baldwin, but he had survived Floyd Piper's protégé.

Baxter arrived at the Golf Club at 7:03 AM and spotted Pinker drinking coffee under an umbrella at the furthest table in the patio. He wore a blue shirt, yellow golf trousers and loafers without socks. One leg was up on a chair and he was reading the *Wall Street Journal*. Pinker's black hair had greyed slightly. Baxter estimated that he was now in his mid-forties.

"Jack," Baxter greeted him as he drew up to the table. Pinker drew his leg off the metal beach chair and stood up to greet Baxter.

"Glen said that you were a late arrival last night. Thanks for coming out so early in the morning."

Baxter noted that Pinker's name tag was also pinned to the right hand side of his shirt instead of clipped to his pocket. Pinker waited for the waitress to bring orange juice and pour coffee before he began to talk.

"Joe, I understand that you had a beer last night with Glen and the IT boys. I thought it would be productive for us to meet and brief you about our collective concerns about McKenzie Barber. But first, let me ask you one very important question. Joe, how do you feel about the current leadership of the firm?"

"The question, Jack, should be, are we better off today than we were in 1984?" Baxter replied.

"I don't believe so and I don't believe you do either!" Pinker said empathetically.

"Well, Jack, now that we are one of one mind that the firm is mismanaged, what do you propose?"

"We want to take a run at the current regime in the 1990 election. We believe that it is time for new leadership at McKenzie Barber. Are you with us?"

"Tell me, whose us?"

"Anybody you see in today's meeting with their nametag on their right."

"What's your plan?"

"Glen is prepared to go to the microphone and call the Operating Committee to account. There will be some careers at risk in this morning's session."

"Why don't you wait until next year's meeting in 1989? You seem to be starting a year early."

"That has been debated, and the conclusion was that we had better serve notice in this year's meeting. Then we can negotiate change from a position of strength. There's a pent-up mandate for change. The Pritchard group won't expect a challenge in this meeting."

"What are your objectives?" Baxter asked.

"We want Ross Pritchard to step down prior to the 1990 election. He's been talking about running for Congress. A lot of Partners are upset about moving Williamson to the New York Office. Do you know anything about him and a woman consultant from the Atlanta office?"

"Are you seeking to discredit Brett Williamson?"

"We've learned that Brett's success at FSO may not be all it seems. There are some serious overruns on contracts. McMasters has a major clean-up on his hands. Williamson was moved to New York to move McMasters back to New York in 1990 where he can finish his career."

Baxter sipped his coffee and listened to Jack Pinker. These guys would certainly fail. If only he could have escaped to the Harwell Management Company. There was no way Baxter could meet Williamson's bogey for the Exec Comp practice. They wanted dirt on Williamson, but it might be a little early in the contest for Baxter to commit.

"I heard some rumors over the years about Brett getting out of hand with the ladies. Have you talked to Harley Dimon?"

"Harley's signed some kind of non-disclosure agreement that affects his severance deal. He hinted that we should talk to you. Talk to me about Williamson and some lady in the Atlanta office."

"What would I know about that? There was a young woman who worked for a fellow named Charley Higdon. We counseled out Charley to make room for Devonshire's transfer. I believe her name was Lonnie something. Let me check my notes when I get back to New York."

"You've heard that Walker Frederick has been pushed out? He's retiring effective December 31st. I suspect that it's just the beginning of Williamson's agenda. You could be on Brett's target list, Joe."

"I've vested, Jack, and I've already got a lawyer. Also, I make money for the firm."

"Are you ready for a change, Joe?"

"I would welcome it for the good of the firm, Jack," Baxter replied. They were goners, Baxter decided after he finished his breakfast with Jack Pinker. The Pritchard bunch would blow them away. Baxter was credited with knowing something about Chairman elections, which was untrue, and suspected of having information on Brett Williamson's misdeeds, which was true. The question was when and how to use it.

The year end numbers were reviewed and presented by Neil Schmidt followed by a request for questions. Fitzgerald stood up from his aisle seat and stepped to the microphone.

"Mr. Deputy Chairman. I'm Glen Fitzgerald from the Chicago office, and I have a question or two about FY 1988."

Baxter decided midway through Fitzgerald's third sentence that his appearance marked the beginning of a serious challenge. Glen Fitzgerald's voice calmly probed the FY 1988 results, asking for clarification on item after item.

Neil Schmidt became more uncomfortable with each question, and began to look at his watch.

"I believe we are overdue for a coffee break, Glen. I'll answer one more question. Then let's break for fifteen minutes and we'll begin the next session with Clyde Nickerson's report on employee benefits."

"No," an unidentified voice rang out. "Let's continue with the questions."

The auditorium thundered with applause. Baxter removed his nametag from its clip on his pocket and pinned it on the right side of his polo shirt.

The meeting was concluded two days later with promises of reconciliation and the creation of an at-large committee of Partners who would meet regularly with the Operating Committee. During the Friday evening black tie dinner, Walker Frederick and fifteen other retiring Partners were honored. Buzzsaw Pritchard thanked them for their service and loyalty to McKenzie Barber and delivered a ten minute speech on teamwork. The McKenzie Barber Partner's meeting ceremony had been concluded for another year. Notice had been served by the discontent, and a vow had been made to do better in FY 1989.

Baxter was settled on a moonlit bench overlooking the canal with a nightcap Canadian Club when he identified Brett Williamson walking toward him. Baxter quickly moved his nametag to the left hand breast pocket of his tuxedo.

"Hey, Joe. What are you doing out here by yourself?"

Brett held a full plastic glass of what Baxter concluded was some kind of Cognac.

"I'm having a nightcap before I turn in, Brett."

"How about coming into Fort Lauderdale with me tonight?"

"Not tonight, Brett. I've got an early morning flight out of Miami."

"I heard you're a bachelor again." Brett seated himself on the bench beside Baxter. He obviously wanted someone to talk to.

"It's been almost two years now, Brett. I'm getting used to it."

"I heard your wife was a real hot retailer. Did I ever meet her at one of the New York Office Christmas parties?"

"I don't believe you did." Baxter wondered how one went about causing Brett Williamson to go away.

"It was one hell of a meeting, wasn't it, Joe?" Brett slapped Baxter lightly on the shoulder.

"One I won't easily forget, Brett," Baxter replied. He considered the 1988 McKenzie Barber Partner's meeting a boring, programmed, milling-around event that had been briefly ignited by Fitzgerald's questioning and oratory in the mid-morning of the first day. It had represented the initial outburst against the Buzzsaw Pritchard regime. The Wednesday meeting had adjourned fifteen minutes behind schedule, and the coffee break had been an extended buzz about Fitzgerald's questioning. The Partners were finally herded back into the auditorium for a thirty minute oratory on the revised Partner employee benefit plans. After Clyde's presentation, the McKenzie Barber meeting plodded ahead, on the surface, according to schedule.

Baxter noted the migration of nametags from the left side to the right side of shirts and sport jackets. Baxter circled the room twice at the cocktail party that preceded the black tie dinner. He tried to tally the name tags. It appeared to be about even in support, but the total count for support was based on the individual Partner unit holdings. Still, for a revolution, it appeared to represent a reasonable start.

"I thought we made pretty good progress in this meeting," Brett commented. "How well do you know this Fitzgerald from the IT practice? I thought he made some pretty good points, even if he didn't have all the facts at his disposal. I liked what he had to say. He's been a success despite being buried under Gene English. I don't believe Fitzgerald paid much attention to Dr. Gene. He just went out and got it done. That's what we need around the New York Office, Joe. We got too many heavy unit partner bureaucrats. There's a lot to get done in New York, Joe," Williamson said slapping Baxter again on the shoulder. "You sure you don't want to go into Fort Lauderdale with me?"

"I've got an early morning plane, Brett," Baxter begged off again.

"You've got to take me out some night in New York and show me the hot spots, Joe."

"I've been out of circulation for a long time, Brett. You should cultivate some of the younger Partners. They'll know the hot spots."

"I don't intend to get too close to the New York Partners, Joe. An old timer like you, Joe, is different. You've been in the New York Office for ten years. I'd like to have some private off-the-record conversations with you from time to time. Buzz told me to pick out a senior New York Partner I could trust who I could talk to in confidence. I believe that someone is you, Joe."

"You could always have Clyde as a confidante."

"I've always had problems warming up to Clyde. I suppose every organization needs someone like Clyde to clean up personnel matters. That's why I brought in Druanne Smithers. She's my Clyde Nickerson. I sure don't need two of them."

Brett took another swallow from his plastic glass. "I can feel it, Joe. McKenzie Barber will leave its problems behind by this time next year, get rid of our losers, and it will be smooth sailing after that. Did you see Walker up there on the dais tonight? He's gone. My job is to clean out the losers. Gene English is next, but he isn't going to have time to hang around to take up a seat on the dais at the Fall 1989 meeting. Fitzgerald wants his job. That was obvious to me when he went up to the microphone to take on Neil. He's got those IT Partners in a little tight ring around him. You know, Grinsigle from Dallas, that Australian guy, and Teaford, the tennis star. I spotted them working the meeting. They were up to something. Then I figured it out. They want to take out English. I'm going to see Fitzgerald in a couple of weeks and feel him out on taking over as English's successor."

Then Gene English is as good as gone?" Baxter asked.

"Count on it." Brett emptied his glass. "You sure don't want to go in to Fort Lauderdale with me?"

"Can't do it."

"Well, then I'm gone. The fleshpots of Fort Lauderdale beckon. Be godamned sure you make your plan this year, Joe. The one I want! Not the one you're trying to defend." Brett slapped Baxter affectionately on the shoulder one final time, rose from the bench, and marched away to Baxter's relief. He was now rid of Brett for now, but Baxter would have to face him for the rest of FY 89 in the New York office. Baxter estimated that his probability of making the FY 89 plan was .10 without some form of divine intervention. Perhaps the impending revolution would save him for a while longer in order to build pension credits.

Bob Dilger was on Baxter's flight from Miami to New York. They were both placed in the main cabin, and arranged to sit together in the last row of the plane with the middle seat vacant. Dilger, the tall Indiana actuary, had been officially named as Walker Frederick's successor during the Partner's meeting.

"Did you behave yourself last night?" Dilger asked after he had settled in the window seat. He wore a sweater, golf slacks and docksiders in contrast to Baxter blazer, tieless blue button down shirt, grey slacks and loafers.

"Went to bed early, Bob. I have a big catch-up day at the office. I've been out more than a couple of days."

"We need a shorter meeting, Joe."

They settled in, scanning their copies of the out-of-town edition of the *New York Times*. Baxter moved to the obituaries.

GREG LIGAN JOHNSON, JR., INTERIOR DESIGNER, 45

MERRILL SLONER, CARTOONIST, 75

DANA HARRIS, DANCER, DIES AT 42

GEORGE DORSCH, 67, WRITER AND LECTURER ON THE ARTS

Three of the four had died of AIDS and were survived by companions.

"What did you think of the meeting, Bob?" Baxter asked as the plane began to taxi.

"Overall, I thought it was a very good meeting, Joe. I was a little sad to see Walker retire, but I guess it's best for the practice. Walker still has a little baggage from the 1984 Chairman election that the Operating Committee people remember."

"What will Walker do after retirement?" Baxter asked.

"Walker's pretty well fixed, Joe. McKenzie Barber paid a lot of money for us back in 1977. We did pretty well on the earn-out formula. Walker will never have to work again. He'll probably go on some boards, and it will pay off for both of us to keep close to him. He plans to stay in New York and the firm has committed to providing Walker an office through 9-30-89. I know that there was always a little bad blood between Walker and you, and I trust that our respective practices can get together now that Walker's retired."

"The practices should maintain steady contact, but don't belong welded together as a single practice, Bob," Baxter replied, establishing his position on the long time organizational debate.

"Well, Joe, it would appear that Brett Williamson favors your position on the separation of the practices. We had quite a talk two weeks ago on the 1989 plan. I assume that you experienced the same discussion, Joe. The man was quite unrealistic in his expectations for the Benefits Practice. We have an impossible plan for FY 89 and I can only assume that you do also." Dilger spoke in a slow Indiana drawl. His words came slowly and seemed measured.

"Brett may be asking us for a little more than we have the capacity in place to stretch us," Baxter responded. "He has a lot of loser practices in New York, and he's looking for the profitable practices to stretch in order to make up for the losers."

Bob Dilger nodded his black head of hair that was beginning to streak with grey.

"You may have something there, Joe. My people are getting a little tired of paying for the underperformance of other practices. Like you, we've always made money. A lot of the Partners around us haven't."

"Bob, are we better off as a firm today than we were in 1984?" Baxter asked politically.

Dilger placed his glasses on his forehead and looked at Baxter with bloodshot eyes. "What kind of a question is that, Joe? Are you in with the IT group that want to contest the 1990 Chairman election?"

"Bob, I'm the guy in the practice next door who has the same concerns as you, making money, and keeping my units. We've got an election coming up in 1990. How do you stand?"

"There's no question as to how I stand. Buzz Pritchard will be elected to another term and someone will be selected by the Operating Committee to succeed Neil, who is too old to serve a second term. I have no predictions. Anybody the Operating Committee chooses is good enough for me. I don't believe that the firm needs an election process like we had in 1984. The factionalism of that period had a lot to do with putting us where we are today. What we need right now, Joe, is for all of us to pull together, not separately."

"A good point, Bob. I'm going to get some shut-eye now," Baxter said and pressed his chair rest backward for a nap. Dilger clearly belonged to the nametag on the left crowd. He accepted the regime that was mismanaging the firm and he would do his job in spite of them. Dilger was well, but not excessively paid, by Benefits Consulting industry standards. The Bob Dilgers of the world didn't want to rock the boat. The question was: How many Bob Dilgers were out there in the Partner ranks of McKenzie Barber?

10 AM, Monday, November 27, 1989

Baxter waited alone in a conference room in Zach Blum's Chrysler Building offices. Today was divorce signing day. It represented the last official day in his marriage to Bridgette Morgan. Baxter had arrived 15 minutes early hoping to catch a word with Bridgette prior to the arrival of the lawyers. He had been ushered into the conference room by Blum's mini-skirted secretary, and settled in with a coffee.

Baxter scanned the left hand column story in the *Wall Street Journal*, sipped his coffee, rising occasionally to peer out at a rainy Lexington Avenue. There was no story on the Florida Group that day. The major coverage had begun in the spring of 1988. The Florida Group had remained in Chapter 11 until the spring of 1989. They were promptly acquired by an investment firm in Cleveland who fired senior management, hired an interim manager and began to liquidate the company. An investment group led by Mark Rosen promptly acquired Incognito and Incognito Too. There was no further mention of Bridgette, other than that she had resigned to pursue new business interests. Baxter looked each day in the WHO's NEW's column of the *Wall Street Journal* for an announcement on Bridgette, but none appeared.

Zach Blum nudged the divorce proceedings forward through continuous contact with his adversary, Irving Milch. The two regularly opposed one another in divorce transactions and respected the other's skill. The settlement seemed simple to Baxter. They had always kept their money separate and Bridgette could maintain her property and Baxter would keep his place at Brinker's Falls and his McKenzie Barber pension. They would divide the assets of the New York apartment which Baxter had subleased. There would be no alimony. Baxter had initially assumed that the divorce would be behind him inside of a year.

"She's dragging her feet," Blum would periodically report to Baxter. "Are you talking to her on the side? Has there been an overture for reconciliation?"

His only communication with Bridgette had been a Christmas Card which had been forwarded to his 36th apartment. It had read:

Joey,

All the best at Christmas time. Hope your life is okay. Send my love to Muffin.

Bridgette
XMAS 1988

In the early summer of 1989, the discussions began to pick up. Zach Blum called Baxter one morning and announced:

"Milch said that Bridgette was ready to settle. She wants the New York apartment back and for you to take responsibility for evicting the sub-lease tenants. Bridgette wants possession of the New York apartment by December 15th, 1989. You can keep your country home property and your pension. It sounds like your Bridgette is planning to move back to New York in mid-December."

It had been Linda, who had come up with the idea of the sub-lease. Baxter had been introduced to the Goldbergs, a husband and wife medical practice team, who bargained hard for a sub-lease through March 31st, 1990. Blum had represented Baxter in the lease negotiations. Baxter calculated the he incurred a monthly loss of $1,269 each month the Goldberg's occupied the apartment.

Blum's firm now handled Baxter's tax work, and was involved in his entire financial stream. Baxter had become a financial hostage to a Jewish divorce lawyer who officed in the Chrysler Building. During the past twenty-four months and over a succession of office conferences, breakfasts, and cocktail sessions, they became something that approached friends and Baxter came to trust Zach Blum. Blum explained early on in their relationship that he did not do lunch or dinner unless it involved a key negotiation. Drinks were limited to two cocktails, and Blum always held cocktails to 59 minutes.

"I've been divorced too, Joe. I have a young woman who lives with me now. I don't ever want to be married again. I'm a specialist in divorce law, and I do estate planning. You're a fun client because you need everything I've got to offer. I sure wish you would have let me sue Harwell Management for breach of contract. You impress me, Joe," Blum expounded over drinks one evening in the spring of 1989. "You're a nice

204

midwestern guy who has made it in New York, but you appear to be very vulnerable to people who want to take advantage of you. You have to remember, Joe, I deal with all kinds in my line of work. Most of my clients are greedy, vicious, and petty. You seem to be content to sit back and let the world screw you. Your wife has engaged Milch, and he can smell weakness on our side."

"They are dragging their feet to see how much they can get from you. We've got to be aggressive and mean, Joe. Your wife ditched you and left you behind with financial obligations. You should have gone after her two years ago. My only conclusion is that you're still in love with her, and wanted her to come back. Milch is using that to get what they want. Whatever you do, Joe, don't start sleeping with her again. I've done a little research on your Bridgette. She's got a tough reputation with the retail trade. This bankruptcy with the Florida Group isn't going to help her. A lot of her suppliers walked away with twenty-four cents on the dollar."

"There are a number of lawsuits that include your Bridgette. She's been hiding her assets. She sold that place of hers in the Hamptons at a loss. We've got to toughen up our stance, Joe, or Milch and your wife are going to take us."

Baxter agreed. Blum asked for a settlement on the New York apartment and an accounting for Baxter's share of Bridgette's assets. The negotiations began to edge forward.

Blum called Baxter on the Thursday before Labor Day. "I just got off the phone with Milch. I believe they've come around. Bridgette will reimburse you $32,283 for your costs in retaining the apartment, and reimburse you all costs related to evicting the Goldbergs. She will then be the sole owner of the New York apartment and assume responsibility for the mortgage. No alimony. No claims against your pension, and that place upstate belongs to you. It's the worst settlement I've ever negotiated. Do you want it?"

"It's exactly what I wanted," Baxter had replied. "All I want is what I brought to the marriage."

"I just hope you're tougher in collecting fees from your clients, Joe. You've given the store away to Bridgette. She walked out on you and the New York apartment ought to be yours."

"That's the deal I want, Zach."

"I'll get the papers drawn up. You haven't been living together for two years. Under New York State law, if both parties are agreeable to the divorce settlement and have been living apart for two years, a divorce is a shoe-in. We'll meet in my office, sign the agreement, and forward it onto the courts. It should be approved by the end of the year. You can be a bachelor by New Year's Eve. I'll set up the settlement meeting for the last week in November."

"Who will be at the meeting?"

"Bridgette, Milch, you and me. I assume that you two can share a conference room amicably. It should only last a half hour at the most."

"I'll be there," Baxter assured him.

Baxter stood up from the conference room table, sipped his coffee, and stared out the rainy street filled with sluggishly moving cars contrasted with people moving quickly under umbrellas. His watch said 9:58.

Baxter hadn't seen Bridgette since the November 1987 dinner at Le Grille. He hadn't realized how important Bridgette had been in his life until she had left him. Images of Bridgette flashed through his memory. He remembered his first sight of Bridgette on the steps of Brookline Fashions trying to push a large carton up the steps. Baxter had helped her with the carton and she had returned to a beat-up, fuel-less, convertible clad in a Yankees jacket. Then he rolled on the movie picture of his mind to the next day when they wound up in a long lunch in Brooklyn. She had driven Baxter to LaGuardia and kissed him in the car. Finally there had been the day he had run into her at the hot dog stand on Broadway and 38th Street. They had dinner that night and made love for the first time. She had been the indefatigable, outrageous Bridgette Morgan in that period of time.

The door knob turned and Zach stood framed in the doorway.

"Milch's office called and they said that Bridgette's car is stuck in traffic. She'll be about twenty minutes late."

Baxter asked for more coffee and the use of the conference room telephone.

Baxter came to Blum's office directly from his 38th Street apartment. He didn't particularly like to make an appearance at 311 Park Avenue. 1989 had been an ugly year for Baxter and the Executive Compensation practice on both a national and New York perspective. Baxter had come in at 65% of the New York plan and 70% of plan nationally. The only bright spot in the practice during FY 1989 had been Atlanta under Harry Devonshire, but that had been attributable to the additional phases of the Planters & Commerce work. McKenzie Barber was now in a phase-out stage of its work with Planters & Commerce Bank. In time past Harwell Management had come through with work recommendations. Ned and Spencer Harwell had no interest in the executive compensation plans of the Harwell Management Company's investments. Baxter had lost his confidential senior partner relationship with Brett Williamson by January when Baxter's performance numbers began to reflect the erosion of his McKenzie Barber practice.

Baxter had cooked up a shareholder value review product with Marty Dunlap. The product reviewed top management compensation of the stock against industry earnings performance, and the fair market value of the stock. Marty had become qualified as an industry expert in computer graphics and they developed sparkling exhibits. The issue was getting trigger time with the Compensation Committee of the Board of Directors. The December Board meetings represented the last shot to position work for the spring of 1990. They had approached every corporate client where McKenzie Barber had previously performed some form of senior management compensation work over the past ten years. About 60 percent had represented Harwell Management referrals. Baxter believed that they had developed a decent product, but recognized that the competition all had a similar product on the marketplace. He tried Ernie Grey for openers. Ernie agreed to a presentation. Marty and Baxter worked over the weekend to make a Tuesday morning presentation at IPCO. Cornelius VanderKelen died of a heart attack in Rio de Janeiro late Sunday evening and their presentation was canceled, rescheduled, and canceled again.

"Time is running out for you, Joe Baxter," Brett snarled at Baxter when they had their mid-year review. "You're looking at a big unit reduction and early retirement if you can't cut the mustard around here. You saw what happened to English, Walker, and McCarthy? This isn't a club anymore.

This is a business. This firm can't afford to carry unproductive old farts like you. You go make an appointment with Druanne and figure out how to immediately cut your staffing costs by 30%."

Druanne Smithers had quickly established a reputation as a horror in the New York office. She was allowed by Brett to operate with unbridled power over personnel matters. Druanne was a tall, thin, flat-chested woman who had retired as a Lieutenant Colonel from the WAC. She wore shell rim glasses, no make-up, and had a face that featured a beak like nose and a thin mean mouth. Baxter decided in their first meeting that Druanne Smithers was probably the ugliest woman he had ever seen. His first brush with her had taken place over the Charlotte Bunker/Marveen Scott exchange.

"Sit down, Mr. Baxter," Druanne had greeted him in her spartan cubbyhole office three doors down from Brett. Druanne did not offer to shake hands, but rather motioned with her hand for Baxter to sit. She reminded Baxter of the school nurse back at Iron Creek High School.

"You really don't have the problem you think you have. Marveen Scott does not want to return to your department. My Placement Administrator is attempting to interest other Group Partners in Marveen, but the reaction at this time is not encouraging. I don't like losing a qualified Afro-American, but I'm afraid we will have to settle a severance with her. Mrs. Bunker is another matter. She's way overpaid for serving as a Group Partner's secretary in a department the size of your practice. I'm going to terminate her this Friday. You're going to have to get by on temps until we find a permanent replacement."

"Wrong!" Baxter objected. "Mrs. Bunker is performing superbly and is a highly valued administrative associate. I had an agreement with Mr. McMasters when I accepted Mrs. Bunker's transfer. The office of the Managing Partner agreed to absorb the difference between Marveen Scott's salary and Mrs. Bunker's salary."

"That agreement is no longer in effect. Mr. McMasters, as you are well aware, now is part of FSO."

"We have the potential exposure of an age discrimination suit with Mrs. Bunker if we terminate her without cause. Let's call Mr. Nickerson and get his opinion," Baxter suggested.

"Why would we involve Mr. Nickerson in a New York office matter relative to a secretary? I know that Mr. Williamson wouldn't want him bothered."

"If you go ahead and terminate Mrs. Bunker without conferring with Mr. Nickerson, and the firm is sued by Mrs. Bunker, your own career with McKenzie Barber could be threatened. I filed a highly favorable performance evaluation in September for Mrs. Bunker. I recommended her for a 5% salary increase."

"Mr. Williamson wants Mrs. Bunker terminated, Mr. Baxter."

"Ask Mr. Williamson if he wants McKenzie Barber sued under his watch?" Baxter said rising from his chair.

Charlotte Bunker was terminated that Friday and Baxter arranged through Blum for introductions to three law firms. McKenzie Barber was no longer fun.

Bridgette arrived at 10:45 AM. She came with Milch, who turned out to be a short thin man in his sixties with grey close cropped hair. Bridgette followed him into the room. Baxter didn't recognize her at first sight. Bridgette's hair was long and she wore dark glasses. She wore a tan Burberry coat over her shoulders. Milch gallantly helped Bridgette out of her coat revealing a blue pants suit. Her pants legs were tucked into calf high black fashion boots. Bridgette pulled her glasses up on her forehead skier style, and extended her hand to Baxter.

"Hi, Joey. It's been a while."

Bridgette's hand seemed moist and somehow her fingers seemed longer. She had always worn her hair short. Now, it was draped down to her shoulders. Her skin was slightly tanned. Blum arranged for a coffee service to be set up. Bridgette and Milch took chairs on the far side of the room while Baxter and Blum seated themselves by the window, each facing their opposite number.

"You're looking good, Joey. You've put on a little weight and you're a little greyer, but you're looking good."

"And you're looking very California," Baxter responded.

"I'm going to be a New York lady again. I've got an appointment with Gunther tomorrow for a New York do."

"Gunther, apparently, is still hot." Baxter observed to Blum. Blum's secretary came into the room with four legal sized documents labeled Baxter v. Baxter. They appeared voluminous and were held together at the top by a metal fastener.

"It isn't as bad as it looks," Blum said. "There's a nine page summary covering all the major points where we reached agreement. The rest is written in legalese and represents the final draft of the document that will be submitted to the court. We expect an early action to confirm the dissolution of your marriage."

"We have a few additional negotiating points, Zach."

"At this late date, Sid?" Blum questioned. He slapped his hand on the file. "This represents two years of negotiation. My client came to this office today in good faith that the negotiations had been concluded and only had to be signed."

Bridgette lit a cigarette and stared innocently across the table at Baxter.

"Mrs. Baxter is unwilling to reimburse Mr. Baxter for costs related to the eviction of Drs. Leonard and Emma Goldberg from the penthouse condominium located at 220 E. 79th Street. Further, Mrs. Baxter wants Mr. Baxter to assume financial responsibility for all damages to premise incurred during the Drs. Goldberg tenancy at 220 E. 79th Street. I have prepared an addendum for your review." Milch passed copies of the addendum to Blum and Baxter.

"I find the introduction of an addendum at this late date highly unprofessional, Sid. Why is this demand being introduced now?"

"Mrs. Baxter was not involved in selecting the Drs. Goldberg as tenants. She has been provided information that the apartment may have incurred substantial damages over the past two years." Baxter shook his head to Blum.

"Mr. Baxter will not accept this financial demand," Blum stated.

"Dogs! Joey! The Goldbergs own a fucking pair of Yorkies. They have been tearing around in that apartment for two years. You sub-leased that beautiful apartment to people with dogs."

"Mrs. Baxter, the sub-lease document was reviewed in this office and I assure you that the document contained standard language regarding the recovery of damages."

"I just want Joey to financially guarantee that all damages will be repaired to the apartment's condition as of November 1987. He should also pay for the eviction costs. He's the one who sub-leased our home to irresponsible tenants."

Baxter looked to Sidney Milch. He was obviously uncomfortable with his client's outburst. Baxter assumed that Milch had been through similar scenes many times previously in his legal career.

"I must remind you, Mrs. Baxter, that you were the party who deserted the marriage. You placed Mr. Baxter under considerable financial pressure—"

"I'd like to speak to Joey alone for a few minutes, Zach. Listening to your sanctimonious bullshit is a waste of my time."

"I cannot recommend to my client to meet with you privately without the advice of counsel," Blum said and looked to Baxter. Baxter raised his hand. "Zach, let Bridgette and I have ten minutes alone, please."

Blum shook his head. Baxter repeated, "Please."

"Ten minutes only," Blum agreed reluctantly rising from his conference room chair.

"Com'on Sid," he addressed Milch. "I'll show you another view of Lexington Avenue."

"You just show me to a phone, Zach. I've seen plenty of Lexington Avenue over the years." At the door, Milch turned to Bridgette. "Ten minutes is tops, young lady."

Baxter faced his now long haired soon-to-be-ex-wife alone in the conference room. He wondered what Gunther, the hair dresser would have in store for her?

"Well, Bridg, here we are. Alone at last. Now what do you have in mind that won't hold until lunch? We had a deal according to your Mr. Milch and I'm just here to sign papers and say good-bye. There are no points for further negotiation, Bridg." Bridgette lit a second cigarette. "Is there someone in your life now, Joey?"

"No. How about Ward and you?"

"Ward's living in Zug, Switzerland now, Joey. He likes their extradition laws. I'm about ready to launch a new business. The new business will require me to be in New York half of the time. I need a New York address where I can receive people from overseas. I went over to see the apartment yesterday and got the super to let me in. Those damned dogs have ruined the place."

"Damage to the apartment is covered in the lease, Bridg."

"It will take years in the New York court system to get a settlement, Joey. I want an up front money commitment to cover the redecorating costs. Then you can sue the Goldbergs, and I can get on with things. It shouldn't run more than $40,000 or $50,000 at the outside. You should check the household insurance."

"Maybe there's some pocket money to be recovered. I could hang on to the $30,000 check I'm supposed to give you this morning as an advance credit."

"That's $32,283 and not a penny less. That money is owed to me and there will be no divorce papers signed this morning unless that money passes hands," Baxter said empathically.

"I'm a little stretched financially right now. I've had to spend a lot of money on lawyers this year and I have some IRS problems to settle by December 15th Joey, be a dear, and lighten up a little. You exhibited a terrible lack of judgment when you sublet that beautiful apartment to those dreadful dog owners."

"You're the one who ditched me, Bridg. I did what I had to do. You've been offered what I believe to be a very fair settlement. There is no more to it. Either we sign the settlement agreement this morning or we turn things back into the hands of attorneys." Bridgette took a long puff from her cigarette and blew a smoke ring at Baxter. They stared across the table in silence. Their ten minutes together was nearly over.

"Tell me, Joey, have you ever thought about getting back together again?"

"It might be something to look into after we're successfully divorced," Baxter answered.

There was a knock on the door followed by Blum's appearance in the doorway. "Ten minutes are up."

"Anybody got a pen. I'm ready to sign," Bridgette said and opening her purse, she produced an envelope. "I have a cashier's check made out to Joseph Baxter, Jr. Who wants it?"

"I'd like to inspect that, Mrs. Baxter," Blum said accepting the check.

The signing took ninety seconds. Blum passed the certified check to Baxter. "It looks like the real McCoy to me. I'd deposit it as soon as possible," he whispered to Baxter.

Milch discovered a typo on a page and insisted that all parties initial the correction while Blum offered to have the page reprocessed.

"I've got a car downstairs and I'm on my way downtown. Can I give you a lift, Joey? You can buy me lunch, if you have the time." Bridgette stood up next to Baxter and ran her hands through the lapels of his suitcoat. "I had forgotten how tall you were, Joey."

Blum stood behind Bridgette shaking his head. Bridgette excused herself to use the ladies room and Baxter exchanged a gruff good-bye with Sydney Milch. Blum pulled Baxter back into the conference room and closed the door. "Be damned careful of that woman, Joe. Milch was furious with her. Whatever you do, Joe, don't sleep with her until after the divorce papers are final. Your little Bridgette is a very dangerous woman."

"I have a lunch reservation, Joey. Want to join me?" Bridgette asked when they were settled in the back seat of her black stretch limo.

"Why not?" Baxter answered.

"John," Bridgette called out to the driver. "This gentleman and I will be running down to the Purple Dove in Chelsea. Please wait for us. Then pick me up at 2 o'clock, drop me at the World Trade Center, take this gentleman back to 311 Park Avenue, and come back and wait for me at the World Trade Center until my meeting's over. Then you can drop me at Newark Airport."

Bridgette turned to Baxter and kissed him on the cheek. "Do you want to fool around on the way downtown?"

"It will make the time go faster," Baxter answered.

Bridgette closed the driver's panel and slid under Baxter's extended arm. She tilted her mouth to meet Baxter's and they shared their first kiss in two years. Lips touched, mouths opened, and tongues touched. Bridgette's hand was on the back of Baxter's neck. Baxter opened Bridgette's Burberry and placed his hand on her neck. Bridgette's right hand gripped Baxter's hand and drew it down across her left breast. Was it possible, Baxter asked himself, that divorce negotiations were being reopened. He gently eased away from the embrace and settled into the middle of the spacious limo seat.

"You always were a good kisser, Joey. You're a little grayer and you've put on some weight, but you're still a good kisser. I remember you telling me about being friendly to a lady in Paris during a taxicab ride. I suppose you're out of practice these days."

"My wife left me for another man two years ago. What really hurt me was that it wasn't a precipitous act, but a carefully pre-planned and sneaky exit from our marriage. It was a shattering experience for me, Bridg."

Bridgette lit a cigarette and puffed silently as the limo moved forward in slow lurches over a rainy 42nd Street toward the entrance to the FDR Drive.

"You know, Joey, I came very close to staying. You were a bit of an ass that night in Les Grille. If you would have been a little patient and reasoned with me, I would have been back by the next weekend. But you had to

214

bluster at me, and go storming out of the restaurant leaving me with no other alternatives."

"That was the week I began to figure out that the Florida Group wasn't all that it was cracked up to be. For the first time in a long time, I had no Joey Baxter to help with advice and counsel."

"You lost the use of a telephone?"

"I had my pride, Joey. I wound up messing up my business reputation and career. I've been named in a bunch of law suits from suppliers. Now I have a chance to start my life over. I could use a Joe Baxter around."

They knew Bridgette well at the Purple Dove. There was a red awning that led through a brick facade into a cavernous two level room that appeared to Baxter's trained eye to have had an earlier life as a 1930's warehouse.

"This place is hot, Joey," Bridgette whispered as they approached the maitre'd stand. They were greeted by a maitre'd in his early thirties who exchanged kisses with Bridgette. He was introduced to Baxter as Emiliano. Behind Emiliano was a packed dining room with every table filled.

"We had just about given up on you, Mrs. Baxter."

"Traffic is impossible today. You know very well that when I say I'm coming, I appear. Something on second floor away from the din will do nicely, Emiliano, dear. Mr. Baxter and I have a few matters to discuss."

Emiliano intently scanned the table plan on the maitre'd stand. He pulled up his glasses which had been suspended from a gold chain across his blue blazer. Emiliano pulled on his ascot twice and then rose up from the stand.

"I will have a table for two on the main floor in ten minutes. Can I seat you at the bar?" he asked with a nervous smile.

"Emiliano," Bridgette glared. "I won't accept a table on the main floor. My secretary specified second floor when you accepted the reservation. Now, Emiliano, come up with a quiet table on the second floor right now or—," Bridgette lowered her voice to a whisper that only the three of them could hear. "I will never enter this fucking restaurant again and pass the word to all of my friends. It's your call, Emiliano."

Emiliano shook his head. "Mrs. Baxter, Mr. Golsen has a table on the second floor today. As does Mr. Fink. You instructed me to never put them on the same floor with you. The only table I have on second floor is between Mr. Fink's table and Mr. Golsen's table."

"I'm in Mr. Baxter's protection today. You just slip us right in between them. I want to be out of here by 1:55 dear."

Emiliano snapped his fingers and a young woman appeared in dark slacks and a tuxedo top bearing an armful of menus.

"Morgana, Table 208, next to Mr. Golsen. Mr. and Mrs. Baxter must leave by five minutes to two," Emiliano commanded.

"Nice to have you with us again, Mrs. Baxter," Morgana greeted Bridgette and led them through a room of New York's pretty people to a staircase that led to the more intimate second floor mezzanine area.

"People come all the way down to Chelsea for lunch?" Baxter questioned.

"Power lunch, Joey," Bridgette explained. "This place is hot."

Bridgette walked boldly past Sam Golsen's table. "How are you hitting 'em, Sam?" Bridgette smiled as she was seated by Morgana at their table. "Fink's the fat man with all the rings at the next table. Look like he's got the DMM from Fast Lane Lady with him. That's about one hundred fifty doors out of Memphis. Her name is Esther Shrimpowitz or something. She was a Gimbel's loser before she found her way to Memphis. With the whole fucking New York City to eat in, how did I manage to pick out a restaurant with two of my significant creditors?"

"You picked the restaurant and insisted on eating upstairs, Bridg." Baxter studied the aggressively priced nouvelle cuisine menu while the waiter hovered over them.

"Order, Joey. Have a drink. I'm just having a Pellegrino because I have a meeting to go to. Lunch is my treat."

Baxter ordered a martini on impulse. He hadn't had a martini in years. This appeared to be shaping up as a memorable day in his life. They both ordered seafood salads.

"Well, here's to the end of our marriage," Baxter raised his martini glass.

"And maybe the beginning of a new relationship, Joey," Bridgette said clinking his glass. "I sort of missed you."

"What happened at the Florida Group?"

Bridgette shrugged her shoulders. "We never really had the money behind us that Ward claimed we had. I can't talk about this in detail because I'm gagged by the courts," Bridgette lowered her voice to a whisper. She had a talent for speaking in the ideal voice octave which was unlikely to carry beyond the table.

"Ward had some money from Latin America investors that he believed was long term, but turned out to be short term. His investors wanted out unless they could sell us a lot of crappy ready-to-wear merchandise that came from their sweatshop investments. I got it diverted for them a couple of times, but we needed an October 1987 IPO and one hell of a Christmas season to pay off our investors. I stretched out our suppliers for terms and they shipped to me on my reputation. Joey, I'm not happy about anything that happened to me after the night we broke up at Les Grille."

"Were you in love with Ward?" Baxter asked draining his martini and signaling the waiter for a refill.

"I was. Ward was good looking, smooth, engineered a deal that paid me $7.3 mill, and made me a CEO. Ward did the things you didn't do. He played tennis, liked to disco and was a contemporary person. This was in contrast to Joe Baxter, the small town guy from Iron Creek, Minnesota, who grew to be a McKenzie Barber partner. The man lived in the 1960's and resented most of the culture of the late 1980's. You were getting middle-aged boring, Joey. Big time boring. I always was a little young for you, Joey. All of a sudden, you seemed twice my age. And, that's why I left you for Ward. Comprende?"

"Well, Bridg, better luck with your next boyfriend. I take it I'm a fill-in today for someone who couldn't make lunch."

"I've been working with a venture capital guy out of San Francisco on a direct marketing concept. He had to stop off in Chicago to see some investors and will be joining me at the World Trade Center meeting. I was free for lunch, and it seemed like a good idea. You're still an attractive man, Joey. I expect to be in New York 50% of the time, and I'd like to see you when it fits our schedules. I could still use some help on the apartment. It needs a lot of work. Who knows? Maybe you'll be moving back in one day. Now, how about you, Joey? Do you have another woman in your life? How's my little Muffin and that son of yours?"

Before Baxter could answer he looked up to see Sam Golsen leaning over their table.

"Are you two kids back together again?"

"On the contrary," Baxter spoke up. "We're celebrating our divorce. It's something we're always going to have."

"It's a very amicable divorce, Sam. Joey and I are still good friends. How's Esther?"

"Esther's doing wonderfully. Thank you for asking. And Motief is doing sensationally. Our spring goods are pretty well sold-out. We took the hit from Florida Group and absorbed it into our financials. Bridgette, I want you to know that I harbor no ill will to you personally. What are you up to these days? I recommended you for a senior merchandising spot at Saks and for the COO job at Grundhofers in Milwaukee. I assume you were contacted."

"I'm not in the market, Sam. I'm in the final negotiation stages for my own company, Sam. Watch for an announcement after the first of the year."

"Where will you be headquartered?"

"New York and LA. I'm moving back into my old New York apartment."

"Retail?"

218

"What else am I good for, Sam?"

"I hope we can do some business at some future date."

"Love and kisses to Esther, Sam." They exchanged kisses on the cheek.

"I love your hair long, Bridgette." Golsen looked back and recalled Baxter. "And good luck to you, Joe. I hope you make out fine without Bridgette."

"I've been practicing, Sam. I'm sure I'll manage," Baxter called out with a wave.

"Basically a nice man, Joey, but a putz. Florida Group damned near took him under, and I know that he'd ship me tomorrow." Baxter ordered half of a martini when Bridgette asked for a check.

"You're drinking more than you used to, Joey."

"I don't get divorced every day. Please have a little sympathy for an abandoned husband."

"Oh shit, Joey. Here comes Larry Fink. Protect me, please."

Fink was a large man that Baxter measured at five foot ten and two hundred fifty pounds. His black hair was slicked back and parted in the middle. He wore a brown, pinstriped double breasted suit that had been tailored to fit loosely over his girth. Fink had a deep resonant voice that carried.

"Let me catch up to you downstairs," Fink instructed his guests.

"I need to have a few words with this young lady," Fink glared down at Bridgette with a menacing stare. "You cost me a lot of money, Missy."

"The whole Florida Group matter was unfortunate for all of us, Larry. It wound up in the hands of the courts. I did all I could for you, Larry. We all have to live with the settlement," Bridgette said contritely.

"I'll never ship you again. You could go to May Company and I still wouldn't ship you," Fink said. "You knew Florida Group was in trouble and you lied to me!" Fink looked to Baxter. "Who the hell are you?"

"I'm Mr. Munker from the Investigations Section of the Internal Revenue Service. We're in settlement discussions on a number of matters. If you'll provide me your tax ID number, I'll be glad to review your settlement." Baxter produced a pen and a sheet from his pocket diary. "Just the name of your company, your title, and address will do. With our technology, I can have your entire file on my desk tomorrow morning," Baxter said with a straight face.

"And now you're hanging around with the tax Feds—," Fink stormed away from the table.

"I've got to hand it to you, Joey. You're quick. All of Seventh Avenue will know by lunch time tomorrow that the much maligned Bridgette Baxter is hanging around with the IRS." Bridgette signed the check. "I've got a meeting, Joey."

Bridgette was subdued on the ride to the World Trade Center. She smoked and stared out the window at the rainy streets.

"Something bothering you, Bridg?" Baxter broke the silence.

"I felt okay until lunch. I used to have a reputation. I was hot. I was pushy. But I was fair. Ward Bowman took that away from me."

"Are you on the ropes, Bridg?"

Bridgette shook her head and took a long reflective puff from her cigarette. "I might be on the way back after today's meeting. I've got a concept. If we can sell the investors and get them to pony up, I'll be back in a big way. Then watch guys like Larry Fink come groveling around. Jesus, I wish to hell I had never met Ward Bowman." Bridgette patted Baxter's knee.

"Well, we're practically free of each other, Joey. Do what's fair for me on the apartment. We'll talk." She was out of the rear door, retrieved a brief case, and exchanged some words with the driver. Baxter watched

220

Bridgette confidently walk toward the revolving doors of the World Trade Center. He waited for a wave but received none.

"311 Park," Baxter instructed the driver.

Baxter, in contrast to his ex-wife, Bridgette, was clearly on the ropes. Monica greeted him in his office after he had his jacket off and hung on a hanger behind his door.

"Where the hell have you been?" she said closing the door.

"Getting divorced."

"How does it feel?" Monica seated herself on one of the arm chairs across from Baxter's desk.

"I feel a little empty to be frank with you. I also had two martinis at lunch. I know now there's no going back."

"That's too bad, Joe." Monica shuffled in her chair and leaned forward to Baxter. "I've got a little more bad news for you. I want you to know that this is one of the most difficult things I've ever had to do."

'Oh, oh,' Baxter thought. She's quitting.

"Joe, I'm resigning from McKenzie Barber. I've been made a very generous offer by Bowers Merrin in their New York office. I will be responsible for serving International clients in the US. I'm coming in as a VP. They have a different title structure there. I'm working for Rob Moreland, the head of the Eastern Region Compensation. He said he knows you."

Baxter shrugged his shoulders. He had heard the name somewhere but had no recollection of the individual.

"I was head hunted, Joe. I told the headhunter the first two times he called that I wasn't interested. Then nothing happened for me here in October, and I got this piddling raise and bonus at the end of September. You said that was the best you could do for me. Well, I told myself, if that's the best Joe could do for me, I might as well talk to the Bowers Merrin guys. I had two meetings with them and they had an offer on the table that will increase my base by 25%, and they have guaranteed a bonus for 1990 that will double my McKenzie Barber bonus with no cap."

"Monica, Bowers Merrin is an actuarial firm that is primarily involved in employee benefits consulting. Their compensation practice has to be very small."

Monica shook her head. "Joe, Bowers Merrin is five times as large as McKenzie Barber in compensation in the US. They have proprietary analytical software that we can't touch. Bowers Merrin is at least six years ahead of us in hard core competency. They have invested in their compensation practice and can do what we do faster and at a discount in fees. They have sound leadership and know where they're going as a firm. McKenzie Barber has been a mess since they elected Buzzsaw Pritchard Chairman. I told you that I would leave unless I was elected a Partner in the fall of 1989. It didn't happen. So I'm leaving."

"You have some client obligations to be completed," Baxter reminded Monica.

"There's nothing outstanding that Marty couldn't pick up. The custom around here is that when someone resigns to go to a competitor, they are immediately out the door. I'd like my last day to be Friday. I'm not starting with Bowers Merrin until January 2nd, but I need some time off."

"Your Director agreement requires 90 days advance notice of termination. I know that Brett Williamson will want to enforce it. The earliest you could join Bowers Merrin would be February 27th, 1990, provided I receive a letter of resignation from you dated today," Baxter threatened. It had become Brett Williamson's standard policy to have Druanne Smithers threaten and harass any unplanned defections to the competition. Monica's face flushed.

"I would need and expect your support to get me out of here on my schedule, Joe. We have pictures on Mr. Williamson. I'm prepared to tell a few things I know about the man who considers himself the world's greatest and most virile lover. I've had to fight my way out of one cocktail lounge and two limo rides with him in the last three months."

"What's this again?" Baxter asked. "Are you saying that Brett Williamson has tried to hit on you since he came to the New York office?"

"Tried is the operative word, Joe. The man has zeroed in on me since he showed up in September."

"We haven't talked about this before. Why? When did this attention start? You know what kind of a man Williamson is? Did you encourage him?" Baxter demanded.

"The man had Marveen call me out of the blue last week in September. She said that Mr. Williamson wanted to talk to me privately about the Exec Comp practice. We met at 6 PM in his office. Marveen just ushered me into his office and announced that she was leaving to catch her bus. He's got some kind of automatic door closer and there I was in his office with this man. We sat down at that oval table. He told me our discussion was off the record. Williamson wanted to know why the Exec Comp practice wasn't doing better? Was it a matter of leadership? He also told me that you had deferred my nomination for Partnership which was news to me. Apparently he had reviewed my personnel file. Williamson knew all about me. He knew about Erik. He knew about Dominique. He said he wanted to get to know me better in the coming year. 1990 looked good for me if I continued my development. All I could think about was how battered Bonnie Grow had been that Saturday morning after the McKenzie Barber Christmas Party. We must have talked for about an hour before Williamson lapsed into a routine about how it was getting late and did I have dinner plans? I told him that my husband and I were entertaining clients, and I was running late. Williamson said he had a car waiting and asked if he could drop me? Dumb me. I said sure. Our famous New York office cost cutter has a limo on retainer. We talked about the Exec Comp practice country-wide on the ride home. It provided me an excellent moment to take some hard shots at Harry Devonshire. Williamson seemed to be listening to me and he started patting my knee in agreement."

"Suddenly, I realized what the man was doing. Luckily we were in front of our apartment building at that point, and I was able to bolt out of the car."

"Williamson called me directly the following week and suggested that we finish our discussion over a drink. Dumb ambitious me. I took him up on it. He took me to the top of the Beekman and we were placed around the corner where we had a view of the East River. We talked about my favorite subjects, my career and compensation. Then Williamson told me that he expected to be Deputy Chairman after the next election. He wanted to identify the up and comers. Next thing I knew he was on my side of the booth drawing organization charts with his right hand with his left hand moving up over my knee to my thigh. I told him that he was a very attractive man, but I was a married woman. That seemed to settle him down for a while. It was raining like hell outside and I accepted a lift from Brett in his ever ready limo. Traffic was terrible on 1st Avenue and Brett was all over me."

"Now, I've had some experience over the years with men, Baxter. They keep coming at me and I'm pretty good at getting them to go away. In addition, this man is the Managing Partner whose support I need to become a Partner at McKenzie Barber. I won't give you the details, but it got messy and I have some torn under garments as souvenirs. I finally caught him across the bridge of the nose with a judo chop and jumped out of the car at an intersection. He sent flowers the next day with some dumb note about it being too bad that last night's engagement got out of hand. I've avoided him ever since."

"Why didn't you discuss this with me?"

"I was so damned mad at you for lying to me about Partner nomination."

"We had zero chance of getting you elected. We just didn't have the numbers nationally. McMasters wouldn't support it. He counseled me to withdraw your name in the late spring without prejudice. He committed to me that we would get it done for you in the fall of 1990," Baxter lied. Actually, Carl Miller had written a long letter to the Operating Committee stating that Monica was not qualified for nomination to Partnership at this time. He had copied Baxter on the letter which cited Monica's failure on the Dungler Technologies work and her overall lack of quantitative technical skills.

"This, sure as hell, is going to sink your Miss Graham for this year," McMasters observed. "Withdraw her name and get Miller to write a nice letter next year," McMasters had counseled.

Baxter and Carl Miller had an explosive fight over the telephone with accusations freely exchanged until Baxter found the real problem. Carl, like Baxter, hadn't had a unit increase in five years. He believed that the election of an additional Partner would reduce his probability of unit increases.

Monica was right, Baxter concluded, it was time for her to escape from the world of McKenzie Barber.

"Joe, I want to get out of this place, and I want to get out as fast as I can. Should I consult a lawyer?"

Baxter processed the event of Monica's termination quickly through his brain. It was going to happen. There might be a way to use it to his advantage. His watch read 3:05.

"Let me work on this. There may be a way of drafting your resignation letter that will work to your advantage. Let's meet for a drink at the Four Seasons at six."

Monica pushed herself from the chair and then sat down again.

"Joe, there's one other thing." She looked away from him behind the window. "I'm taking Linda with me. She will be coming to you in the morning to resign. She doesn't want to stay either."

"I see," Baxter acknowledged with a nod.

Monica rose to her feet. Her expressive brown eyes appeared sad. She made a small wave from the doorway. "I'm sorry, Joe."

"We'll talk again at six."

Monica closed the door behind her and Baxter was alone in his office with a blinking red light on his phone that indicated phone mail.

"Joe Baxter," the mechanical voice greeted him. "You have twelve new messages." Baxter debated as to whether he should plunge into his phone mail. He, too, was weary of McKenzie Barber.

Baxter reluctantly pressed the 5 key on his phone and he entered the world of recorded phone messages. The first six were routine. The seventh was from Brett.

"Your numbers look like shit!" Brett's voice rasped. "First quarter is in the crapper for you, my man. I won't accept a second quarter like this. You goddam well better start chopping right now. I want a plan from you that will deliver operating profit of 31.5%. The hell with revenue. Start chopping people. Call my secretary and make an appointment with me early next week. There's no more buddy-buddy stuff, Joe. You have to perform or get out."

Baxter decided that he would save the other five messages for Tuesday. The challenge now was to salvage Monday.

Baxter, on an impulse, decided to call Glen Fitzgerald in Chicago. Fitzgerald's secretary explained that he was in a meeting. "Then pull him out," Baxter demanded.

"He's in a conference room leading a practice meeting. Mr. Fitzgerald can't be disturbed."

"This is a very important matter. It directly relates to his nametag on the right project."

"Mr. Baxter, I can't interrupt. Mr. Fitzgerald for something about nametags. He has Partners in from all over the country for a special meeting. The meeting started at 2 PM and it is scheduled to last until eight. They are having sandwiches brought in. I can have him call you in the morning."

"Morning will be too late. He needs the information I have for his meeting."

"Then why don't you E mail it to him? I can take it into the meeting."

"Young woman, go into the meeting, bring Mr. Fitzgerald to a telephone and have him call me immediately in the New York office." Baxter recited his direct dial number. "The information I have is vital for Mr. Fitzgerald's meeting. Go to him now and I will await his call."

Baxter hung up the phone and placed his feet up on the desk. He was still groggy from the martinis.

Baxter's private line rang twenty minutes later with Fitzgerald on the phone.

"Joe, this is Glen. I have been given to understand that you have something important to say to me. I have taken a break from what I consider to be a critical meeting to return this call. What's up?"

"Glen, I'm coming to you with a bit of guilty conscience. I've been keeping my silence on a series of incidents out of loyalty to the firm. I can no longer maintain my silence on these maters. I'm going to Ross Pritchard and I expect that I should offer to retire at the same time. In doing so, I believe that you should be informed in advance."

"Joe," Fitzgerald came back in a calm but irritated voice. "What in hell are you talking about?"

"Brett Williamson has been sexually harassing a number of women over the years at McKenzie Barber. I have just received the resignation from one of my key staff. She informed me that she is resigning because of Williamson's forceful and unwanted attentions."

"How forceful?" Fitzgerald's voice remained calm, but questioning.

"We're talking about groping at her undergarments in his limo. It's all in her resignation letter. Also there is an additional incident that I know of that involved rape, including forceful anal intercourse, with a professional staff member that occurred in December 1987."

"Was this young woman from the Atlanta office?" Fitzgerald probed.

"I have pictures of the young woman's battered and abused body. Clyde Nickerson covered it up."

"Are you certain of that?"

"He wanted to shield the information from Chairman Pritchard. I believe a settlement was made with the young woman. This afternoon was the last straw for me. I'm going to Pritchard with the documents and pictures. Brett Williamson is a very sick man. He needs professional help. Steps have to be taken immediately in the best interests of the firm."

"Why are you coming to me with this, Joe?"

"I regard you, Glen, as the leader of the loyal opposition. Clyde Nickerson has the skill to make recalcitrant Partners disappear. If I should be persuaded to retire very quickly owing to ill health, I want someone like you informed to continue the fight. This man is capable of miring McKenzie Barber in law suits and ultimately damaging the reputation of the firm."

"What are you going to do next, Joe?"

"I'm going to get on Ross Pritchard's calendar and show him the evidence. If I feel we're going to have another whitewash on our hands, I'd like to be able to pass the documents over to you. If the Chairman fails to act on what I'm going to bring him, my career with McKenzie Barber is over."

"Why didn't you come forward before, Joe?"

"I was overly concerned with my own survival, Glen. Now, I've said everything that I wanted to say, Glen. Please get back to your meeting."

"God bless you, Joe, and good luck. Let me know if I can help." Fitzgerald clicked off.

And now for the evidence, Baxter told himself.

Jon Grunwaldyt shared the elevator with Baxter at a quarter to six. They nodded and rode in silence for a few floors before Grunwaldyt spoke.

"Brett's on the warpath today. Has he gotten to you?"

"We shared a very cordial phone mail. The man is inspiring," Grunwaldyt smiled sadly. "The man is heartless, but I've got to hand it to him, Joe. Brett is getting the New York office turned around."

"Do you see him as the next Deputy Chairman, Jon?"

"He'd be very good, Joe. And as an extra benefit, he'd be out of the New York office," Grunwaldyt added. The elevator door opened and Grunwaldyt mumbled a good night.

Monica was ten minutes late, and they were seated against the far wall in the front bar of the Four Seasons. "I talked to my lawyer. He wants a copy of my management contract. He said people are moving back and forth all the time between consulting firms. He recommends that I indicate in my resignation letter that I have no plans nor intentions to have contact with McKenzie Barber clients for a period of two years following my last date of employment."

Damned lawyers! Baxter cursed to himself. They were always butting in where they were not needed.

"I would agree with him in most cases. McMasters wouldn't have contested it. Neither would have Floyd Piper. Williamson is different. He's a vicious man. The only way he'll let you loose without a fight is for you to go to bed with him a couple of times. But I've thought it out and I see a way that will put him on the defensive."

"How would I do that?"

"We will draft a resignation letter stating that you are resigning because of the Managing Partner's sexual advancements."

"Joe, I just want to get away from McKenzie Barber quickly to start my new career. I don't want to cause trouble."

"Monica, we need to write a letter. I will, of course, assist you in drafting the letter. How about some champagne?" Baxter offered.

"Baxter," Monica observed after the champagne had been served. "I see myself being pulled into one of your grand schemes. You're obviously out to get Brett."

"For the good of the firm. The team of Buzzsaw, Nickerson, and Brett and lesser incompetents have come close to sinking this firm over the last five years. Brett is being positioned as the next Deputy Chairman. He's got to be stopped. He's a very sick, deviant person."

"Baxter, I don't want to get involved in this. I just want out of McKenzie Barber to get along with my career and my life. I've watched you over the past year. You don't seem to give a damn anymore. Linda has seen it too. You've slipped badly after Leon Harwell died. I know that the last year has been difficult with your son dying. I understand your daughter had some problems too. You're just not the same. You've lost the old Baxter fire-in-the-belly style. The Exec Comp business got a tremendous shot in the arm after your pal, Alvardi wrote his book. Every comp consulting firm seems to be taking advantage of Alvardi's book, but us. You're looked at as Joe Baxter an Exec Comp icon from the early eighties. The compensation consulting industry has passed you by. You're perceived as slick, smooth Joe Baxter, the country boy, board room salesman from McKenzie Barber. Rob Moreland would like to meet you sometime. He thinks he could make a place for you at Bowers Merrin. I know you're vested. Maybe you could come over to Bowers Merrin after a while. Both Linda and I are going to miss you."

"You're missing the point, Monica. Do you believe that Bonnie Grow and you are the only women at McKenzie Barber that have been abused by Brett?"

"The man has a reputation passed through the ladies rooms of the firm. Every now and then Brett finds a woman who likes his style. That usually lasts a couple of months and some favorable pay treatment when the pay window is open. Then he drops them for a new relationship. I may be the first one to be honored with his attentions in the New York office."

"Have you discussed your adventures with Brett with Erik?"

"Do you want World War III to start? He'd demand satisfaction or something. That's another reason why I shouldn't write the letter. All I'm up to, Baxter, is a plain vanilla resignation letter."

"How about writing for Bonnie Grow and all of the women who have been abused by Brett? How about writing it for all of the future victims of this man?"

"Baxter, I'm not much for causes."

"Monica, the worst that could happen to you, would be a quiet severance and a quick release from McKenzie Barber. Nickerson will want a cover-up."

"What did Bonnie get as severance? Do you know?" Monica's interest in letter writing had suddenly piqued.

"I believe Bonnie got two years. But Brett did more damage there. You could get six months pay. I don't know whether you could get a year unless you got an attorney involved."

"Do you think I could get six months pay and a half year's bonus?" Monica asked.

"With a truly well written letter," Baxter said refilling Monica's champagne glass.

"How soon do we have to write this letter?"

"We must write it tonight." Baxter flagged down the cocktail waitress. "Miss, you must have a supply somewhere of white paper cocktail napkins."

"Have you spilled?" The clear faced young woman in the Four Seasons jacket asked.

"We need to begin the drafting of an important document," Baxter explained.

Monica's letter took up eighteen cocktail napkins which Baxter estimated would cover a page and a half of a letter size stationary. When the draft was finished shortly after eight, they returned to McKenzie Barber to prepare the letter. The final typo-less document was ready at 9:40. Monica signed the original. They made several copies and went out for Chinese.

The letter read as follows:

Mr. Joseph Baxter, Jr.
National Partner-in-Charge
Executive Compensation Services
McKenzie Barber & Co.
311 Park Avenue
New York, New York 10022

Dear Joe,

This is a very difficult letter for me to write. I have learned much over my seven year career with McKenzie Barber & Co. and it has been my goal to advance to Partnership and finish my professional career with the firm. I believe I articulated this to you in my annual review and the document is in my personnel file.

Since October 1988, Mr. Brett Williamson, Managing Partner of the New York Office, has expressed a personal interest in my career. He singled me out at firm meetings and invited me to his office for private meetings, presumably to discuss the practice. I had many reservations about meeting with Mr. Williamson privately. These reservations date back to December 1987 when Bonita Grow, a professional staff member from the Atlanta office, had been brutally abused sexually by Mr. Williamson following the McKenzie Barber Christmas party. At the time, several photographs were taken of Ms. Grow, and I assisted you in getting Ms. Grow dressed and on a plane back to her home in Atlanta. You said at the time you planned to review the incident with Mr. Nickerson. I remember you telephoning Mr. Nickerson from LaGuardia Airport to inform him. I never saw nor heard from Ms. Grow again after the incident. When making personal inquiries relative to Miss Grow's health and well being, I was informed that she was on an extended leave of absence. Ultimately she left the company. I began to become concerned about a similar fate to Miss Grow.

In October of this year, I accepted a ride home from Mr. Williamson in his limousine following a conference in his office. He began to fondle my legs in the car. I left the car immediately when it stopped in traffic near my apartment. A few days later, I received a dozen roses from Mr. Williamson with an invitation to join him for a quick drink on the roof of the Beekman Hotel. I was at a loss as to what to do, but I finally agreed to meet him.

After all, Mr. Williamson had been selected by the firm to manage the largest operating office of the firm.

Our evening began cordially enough and we had a very constructive discussion about the firm. It was raining furiously that evening and no taxis were in sight outside the hotel. I again accepted a ride in Mr. Williamson's limousine and this time he turned into a beast. He attempted to kiss and fondle me and tore my undergarments. Once again I slapped and scratched my way out of the car. I was too embarrassed to share the story with my husband of eleven years. Being of European temperament, I was concerned that my husband might take the matter of retribution into his own hands.

The following day, I sought help from a friend's analyst. I came to the conclusion that I must leave McKenzie Barber immediately. It was also my analyst's conclusion that Mr. Williamson immediately secure professional help.

After a brief and panicked job search, I have accepted employment with Bowers Merrin, an actuarial consulting firm. I will be starting over again in a foreign environment trying to rebuild my career. I request that the firm, in its wisdom, waive the competitor clause in my Director's contract. I am fleeing the firm rather than betraying it. I had looked to you, Joe, and the personnel polices of the firm to protect me from sexual harassment of this kind. I have no other choice than to resign. I wish to conclude my employment on Friday, December 1st. I need a month to recover from the emotional trauma attributable to Mr. Williamson's unwelcome advances. I hope to resume my career with Bowers Merrin on January 2nd.

My attorney has recommended that I sue McKenzie Barber. I would not want to be part of an action against a firm that has been so good to me. I ask only that Mr. Williamson, for his own good, be immediately relieved from his responsibilities and receive the professional help that he needs.

Thank you for everything.

Yours very truly,
Monica C. Graham

Baxter called Miss Billington, Buzzsaw Pritchard's secretary, first thing on Tuesday morning.

"Miss Billington," Baxter announced to the officious authoritative voice who answered "Mr. Pritchard's office."

"Miss Billington, this is Joe Baxter. I must have some time with Ross today."

"That will be quite impossible, Joe," Miss Billington said dismissing him. "The earliest you could see Chairman Pritchard would be in the early part of the week after next. He will require a brief summary of the subject of your discussion topic one week in advance. Our Chairman is very busy these days."

"Miss Billington. I am in possession of a document that must be reviewed with Chairman Pritchard immediately. It has to do with deviant behavior on the part of one of our Partners which could result in substantial litigation for the firm. I have a letter in my possession which I will have immediately hand carried to you. When is Ross due in this morning?"

"Late mid-morning. Possibly as late as noon," Miss Billington replied. Baxter suspected that she was lying. Perhaps a copy would do for an opening salvo. Originals had a way of getting lost if they should be shared with Clyde Nickerson.

"I'll have a copy of the letter delivered."

"Joe, I can't guarantee when Chairman Pritchard will find time to read it. It could be several days. He's quite busy."

"Miss Billington, we have a sexual deviant and rapist in our midst."

"Is this a New York Partner? Perhaps you want to take up the matter with Mr. Williamson?"

"Miss Billington, Mr. Williamson is the Partner I wish to discuss with Chairman Pritchard. He needs professional help immediately. A copy of the letter will be delivered to you shortly. You must, in the best interests of the firm, see that Chairman Pritchard reads the letter as soon as possible."

There was silence on the other end of the phone. Baxter decided to wait it out. He pictured Miss Billington in his mind. She was a tall imposing, controlled fiftiesh woman who dated back to Buzzsaw's Pritchard's days in the Pentagon. "I don't believe that you should send that kind of letter to Chairman Pritchard, Joe. He has received a number of similar crank letters in the past. He asked me not to bother him with those kind of·letters and simply send them to security."

Security? Baxter questioned. When the hell did McKenzie Barber establish a Security Department?

"Where does Security report?" Baxter asked.

"To Mr. Nickerson. Would you like me to transfer this call to Mr. Nickerson, Joe?"

"This letter must be read by Chairman Pritchard. Mr. Nickerson will simply cover the matter up for what he believes are the best interests of the firm. We have a major issue here, Miss Billington. I must discuss this matter with Chairman Pritchard or these letters will continue until the firm is awash with sexual harassment suits." Baxter raised his voice an octave for emphasis.

"Very well, Joe. I will call you the minute Chairman Pritchard arrives. You can hang on to the letter and deliver it personally."

Baxter placed his feet up on his desk, sipped his coffee and scanned the Wall Street Journal. He anticipated that his former protégé, Linda Green, would be by shortly to resign. There was a predictable tap on his door at 9:20, followed by a turn of the handle of his door. Linda appeared in his doorway.

"Joe, can I see you for a few minutes?" She stepped across the threshold and closed the door behind her. Linda was wearing a red knit suit with blue trim. Her skirt rested approximately an inch above her knee and she seated herself cross legged in the arm chair facing Baxter's desk.

How much time had elapsed since the last time they slept together? It had to be in early September. They had been in his apartment and Linda had perched herself on the side of his bed. She was fresh from the shower with a towel tied turban style on her head. Linda had stroked Baxter's head.

"This is the last time, Joe. You have known for a while that I have some other relationships. You and I have never talked about anything permanent. I believe that this is as good a time as any to call things off between us."

Baxter nodded his head in agreement. Obviously Linda didn't like her raise.

Baxter ran his eyes down from Linda's forehead to her red pumps. Her dark hair was piled high this morning revealing the neck that Baxter kissed so many times in dark hotel rooms. He usually began their lovemaking by kissing Linda on the neck. Next he would proceed to her shoulders followed by open mouth kissing. By then her nipples became hard little BBs that she liked to have kissed and gently bitten. There had always been an energetic mechanical quality to Linda's lovemaking during their two-year relationship. She put out well. But the question always lingered in the back of Baxter's mind.

Was her heart really in this?

"Joe, this is one of the most difficult moments in my life."

"But you're still young, Linda. I'm certain there will be more difficult moments."

Linda turned her hand to display a handsome diamond engagement ring. Baxter lacked the skill to measure carats, but it was obvious that some swain had made a big time investment to lock Linda into a relationship.

"I've become engaged to a very nice and talented young man who is completing his residency in June. We plan to be married in July. Therefore, it's clearly time to end our relationship and best that I leave McKenzie Barber. I've learned so much from you over the past two years and for that I will always be grateful. Now it's time for me to move on to the next phase of my professional career. I have written a brief letter of resignation." Linda handed a letter size sheet of paper across to Baxter. It read:

Dear Joe,

I have enjoyed an exciting career with McKenzie Barber since joining the firm out of Columbia "B" School in 1985. I have learned so much from you and the splendid management group of the New York Office Executive

Compensation practice. I feel privileged to have participated in engagements with major McKenzie Barber clients.

With my impending marriage, I believe it is best to lighten my load to take on a less demanding job with an actuarial firm. I would prefer to complete my obligations by the end of September. I am very proud to have been a McKenzie Barber consultant and advanced to Associate over my four year career. I would be pleased to direct any young man or woman graduating from a top MBA program to begin their business career with McKenzie Barber.

Thank you, Joe, for your mentorship during my career with McKenzie Barber. Best wishes to the firm on its continued success.

> Yours very truly,
> Linda A. Green
> Associate

Baxter read the resignation letter twice. Linda had clearly written the letter to a multiple audience.

"This is really a moving letter, Linda. Tell me, you're not going off to the same actuarial firm as Monica Graham. Won't you two make a dandy team? Bowers Merrin is the name, as I recall. They are not a direct competitor to McKenzie Barber in the field of executive compensation, but clearly trying to be."

"I wasn't aware that Monica was going to Bowers Merrin. I was recruited separately. I must confess that I'm a little shocked to learn Monica is going to Bowers Merrin. She was under a Director's contract, while I, as an Associate, am under no contractual relationship to McKenzie Barber."

"Bully for you, Linda. Monica told me last night that she was taking you with her. I can only assume that you have been co-conspirators in this relocation. Your resignation is accepted with regret." Baxter returned the resignation letter across the desk to Linda.

"Dress this letter up! Put an address block over the Dear Joe salutation."

Baxter's phone rang. It was Miss Billington. "Chairman Pritchard is in. Bring your letter, Joe."

"I'll be right there." He faced Linda again. "I have to run up to see Buzzsaw about something. I shouldn't be long. When I get back I want the two of us to go over your current engagement load." Baxter had brought one set of the Bonita Grow photos in an envelope and he had a copy of Monica's resignation letter in a manila file folder. Linda stood up with him.

"By the way Linda, have you ever heard any stories about Brett Williamson and ladies around the office?"

"What kind of stories?" Linda asked innocently.

"We'll talk later," Baxter said walking briskly out of the room.

Baxter knew that he had put himself in play by going on the attack with Brett Williamson. If he lost, he would go the way of Walker Frederick no later than late Spring of 1990. If Baxter won, he could probably buy two more years and build his pension credits by 4% a year. There was a 90 second wait for an ascending elevator that seemed like ninety minutes. There were two young consultants with familiar, but nameless faces. Baxter nodded in response to their greetings and pressed 38.

"On your way up to Mount Olympus, Joe?" a sandy haired young man in a Brooks Brothers suit asked.

"I have to see our Chairman about something."

"Give him our best," the other elevator passenger added. "We understand that he is rarely in the office these days. Ask him if he's really going to run for the House of Representatives in New Jersey?"

"Is that the rumor, fellows?" Baxter asked innocently.

"That's the rumor, Joe," the sandy haired young man confirmed.

They left the elevator at 37. Was Buzzsaw preparing to bolt? Baxter asked himself.

Mrs. Billington greeted Baxter somberly. "You can go right in, Joe. Chairman Pritchard has asked Mr. Nickerson to join him."

Baxter knocked and opened the door to find Pritchard and Nickerson seated in stuffed chairs around the coffee table. Buzzsaw Pritchard sat calmly in his chair, jacketless in a blue button down shirt, a yellow tie, and splashy gold braces with blue horses. Nickerson wore a brown three piece suit and gleaming brown wingtips displayed from his nervous crossed legs. His body language hinted extreme irritation.

"Sit down, Joe," Buzzsaw greeted Baxter with his hand pointing to the empty chair at the opposite chair across the coffee table. Neither Pritchard or Nickerson stood up to shake hands.

"Now what's so important this morning, Joe?"

"I'd like to read to you from a letter of resignation that I received last evening."

"I'd like to see that letter before you read it to anybody," Nickerson interjected.

"Listen first, Clyde. Then you can have your own personal copy," Baxter responded and proceeded slowly to read Monica's letter. Then he stood up walked half way around the coffee table and handed the letter to Buzzsaw Pritchard. Nickerson extended his hand but Pritchard waved him off.

"Who's this Grow woman, Clyde?"

"She was an ambitious little tart from our Atlanta office. She was up here for a few days over Christmas two years ago. She caught Brett's eye and you know Brett, our bachelor Managing Partner. They wound up in his suite. They had consensual sex and the next day she claimed that she was raped. I discussed the matter with Brett and he assured me that it was consensual sex. I stepped in and got the matter settled. The young woman accepted a modest severance and signed some papers clearing the matter up. That was the end of it. This Graham woman has been rumored to be Baxter's mistress for years. It looks like they've cooked up this matter to discredit Brett."

239

Baxter again stood up from his chair and passed the envelope with Bonnie Grow's pictures from the morning after the 1987 McKenzie Barber Christmas party.

"Take a look at these, Mr. Chairman. These aren't the pictures of a lady after consensual sex."

Pritchard winced after shuffling through the Polaroid pictures. He held them up for Nickerson to review and received a headshake.

"I suspect that these pictures are fakes. Besides the matter has been closed and is behind us."

"This isn't the first correspondence we've had of this nature about Brett, Clyde. Do we have a problem here?" Ross Pritchard asked calmly.

Nickerson shook his head. "The only problem we have here, Ross, is that we have a swashbuckling single Marine officer in a highly visible management post, with a lot of woman trying to draw a bead on him."

Pritchard turned to Baxter with calm grey eyes. "And you, Joe, believe that we have a problem."

"A big problem, Ross. A problem that's not going away unless the firm takes action. And for the record, sir, Monica Graham is not my mistress. She is very happily married to a French banker and Clyde's comments, just now, were totally inappropriate."

Pritchard nodded his head. "Yes, I agree. They were." He turned to Nickerson. "Clyde, why wasn't I informed about this Bonnie Grow matter? Those were very serious charges. You had an obligation to brief me."

"Ross, I have a written release from Miss Grow. She was very embarrassed about her behavior and quietly resigned. I can have my secretary send the document by this morning."

"I'm not interested in seeing a release form. I'm certain that you have one. I asked you a question and I want it answered. Why didn't you brief me? Brett was my direct report."

Baxter watched Nickerson squirm and twitch as Buzzsaw Pritchard stared at him with his General's stare. Baxter assumed he had learned it at West Point.

Nickerson cleared his throat. "Ross, you're a very busy man. We've had a major job over the last four years in putting this firm right after the mess we inherited. You didn't need this kind of distraction. You were about to go off on a well earned family vacation. I jumped in and resolved the matter."

"How many other of Brett's situations have you had to intercede in over the past few years, Clyde?"

"This is the first time," Clyde answered.

"Either you have a faulty memory, Clyde, or you're committed to keeping distractions away from me. You see, I had problems with Brett when I was in Washington. The problems continued after I became Chairman. I counseled him before he came to New York. Brett assured me that he has sought professional help and had made adjustments." Pritchard turned to Baxter. "Brett Williamson has always performed very well for McKenzie Barber and for me. He is mean spirited, but gets results. We needed that at FSO. We also need those qualities of leadership in the New York Office. Brett is getting the job done in New York. But Joe, you did the right thing in bringing this matter to my attention."

No one talked for at least two minutes. Clyde was sitting back in his chair and staring ahead at the wall behind Baxter. Buzzsaw Pritchard began to talk. He faced Baxter and ignored Nickerson. "I faced a similar situation when I was a young officer. We had a major, a man whom I greatly admired, who had raped a succession of Army nurses. We were stationed at a remote base of operations. The Head Nurse finally came to me, a newly promoted Captain, to seek redress. The major was a close friend of the CO who had a grade on him. We were on the edge of a combat zone. Every officer and enlisted man was needed. I was due for rotation as was the major. My dilemma was to either let the matter drop and transfer out or file charges. I decided to file charges. My CO tried to dissuade me. But I knew that there was only one course of action to take, Joe. Either we, as the US Army stood behind our regulations or we had nothing. I don't believe in cover-ups. If this Miss Grow matter had been covered up, then there have to be others. Did you serve in the Army, Joe?"

"Yes sir. Three years active duty."

"I was a supply officer in the Navy," Nickerson announced out of nowhere.

"What happened to the major?" Baxter asked.

"He took out a patrol the two days later supplanting a Lieutenant. He didn't come back. Well, we can't very well do that with Brett, can we?"

"I believe that Brett deserves a fair hearing," Nickerson demanded.

"He'll have a fair hearing and it will be with me. After that's concluded, you are going to have a fair hearing. To fail in business is unfortunate. To fail in morality is both unacceptable and unthinkable."

"Ross, I will have a letter requesting early retirement to you this afternoon," Baxter offered.

Pritchard shook his head. "No. No. We can't have that. You're needed here." The Chairman of McKenzie Barber stood up from his chair and moved to the telephone on his massive desk. "Miss Billington, I want you to reschedule all of my appointments and meetings for today. But first I want you to locate Mr. Williamson and have him come to my office immediately. Yes, I believe we will be ordering lunch in." Pritchard hung up the telephone. "Joe, will you stay in the office today. I may need you later on."

"Do you want me to sit in, Ross?" Nickerson asked.

"That won't be necessary, Clyde. My talk with Brett will be a private conversation." Pritchard walked to the door with Baxter and shook hands.

Baxter resisted winking at Miss Billington as he passed her desk on the way out. He returned in the elevator to the 35th floor and stopped for a fresh coffee in the kitchen, and briskly walked back to his office. Once inside, he closed the door, placed his feet up on his desk and looked out the window at Park Avenue.

"I got that son-of-a-bitch!" he said aloud. "And maybe I got both of them."

Wednesday, November 29, 1989

All was quiet in the New York office on Wednesday. Clients were not pestering Baxter with opportunities for new work and the interoffice mail and calls were astonishingly light. Baxter wondered if Buzzsaw Pritchard had relented.

He advised both Monica and Linda that their resignations were accepted subject to the fulfillment of their commitments to McKenzie Barber. Baxter was now down to five consultants with Marty as his most senior person. The New York practice unit would be marginally profitable for the first quarter ending 12-31 but would be far off plan. Barring some kind of a client new business miracle, Baxter forecasted that he would be fortunate to come within 50 to 60% of his annual profit plan and, at best, 50% of his revenue plan.

At an earlier time in his career, Baxter would have made a run for the plan confident that he would make things happen. Something had gone out of him. Baxter hadn't planned to be part of McKenzie Barber for FY 1990 and here he was at the end of November 1989 ready to throw in the towel with ten months remaining in the year. His department had little backlog. Baxter had lost his top business generator to a competitor. He was also losing the consultant who supported him on most of his personal engagements to the same competitor.

December would be unlikely to produce much in new business and the New York Exec Comp unit was likely to operate at a deficit during both January and February. There would be no windfall referrals from Harwell Management to bail him out. If he hadn't gotten Williamson, Williamson would certainly get Baxter. Carl Miller was off to an excellent start in Chicago. Harry Devonshire was mopping up in the Planters & Commerce work and beginning to bring in new clients. Harry and Carl seemed to be talking regularly and proposed that the two practice heads collectively talk with Baxter via telephone conference call on the first and third Mondays of each month. Dallas, Los Angeles, and San Francisco continued to be border line marginal practices.

Harry Devonshire volunteered to do a first draft of a white paper dealing with the future of Executive Compensation at McKenzie Barber. At age

54.5, Baxter questioned how much personal fire he had left to pull the practice forward.

Baxter really couldn't afford to retire. Joel's hospice bills had to be paid off. Muffin would require tuition money when she was ready to return to college. Harwell Management was behind him forever. Baxter's only option was to forge ahead as best he could until someone at McKenzie Barber came to Baxter with a favorable exit proposition.

On Thursday there was an "E mail" to all McKenzie Barber management group, professional, and administrative staff from Ross Pritchard. It tersely stated that Brett Williamson had submitted his resignation for reasons of declining health. The resignation had been accepted immediately with deep regret. The Operating Committee was meeting on the matter of succession and expected to make an announcement early next week. The "E mail" announcement went on to say that McKenzie Barber was off to a record year.

A private memorandum addressed to all Partners arrived in the morning mail on Friday. It read:

PRIVATE-TO BE OPENED BY ADDRESSEE ONLY

TO: ALL US PARTNERS - MCKENZIE BARBER
FROM: ROSS E. PRITCHARD
SUBJECT: SENIOR PARTNER RESIGNATIONS, RETIREMENTS AND APPOINTMENTS

IT IS WITH DEEP REGRET THAT I MUST ANNOUNCE THE RESIGNATION AND IMMEDIATE EARLY RETIREMENT OF BRETT WILLIAMSON, MANAGING PARTNER OF THE NEW YORK OFFICE AND MEMBER OF THE OPERATING COMMITTEE OF THE BOARD OF DIRECTORS. BRETT HAD A VERY SERIOUS MEDICAL PROBLEM IDENTIFIED EARLIER THIS WEEK AND OUR ONLY RECOURSE, REGRETTABLY, WAS TO ACCEPT HIS RESIGNATION AND ARRANGE FOR HIS EARLY RETIREMENT.

AS MANY OF YOU MAY RECALL, BRETT JOINED MCKENZIE BARBER IN 1980 AS VICE PRESIDENT OPERATIONS AT FEDERAL SERVICES OPERATIONS (FSO). HE SUCCEEDED ME AS

PRESIDENT & CHIEF EXECUTIVE OFFICER AFTER THE PARTNERS OF MCKENZIE BARBER ELECTED ME CHAIRMAN IN 1984.

BRETT TRANSFERRED TO MCKENZIE BARBER AS MANAGING PARTNER OF THE NEW YORK OFFICE EFFECTIVE OCTOBER 1ST, 1989. OVER HIS SHORT TWO MONTH TENURE AS MANAGING PARTNER, NEW YORK, BRETT TURNED IN AN OUTSTANDING PERFORMANCE IN THE IMPROVEMENT OF THE NEW YORK'S OFFICE'S OPERATIONAL EFFECTIVENESS.

PRIOR TO JOINING MCKENZIE BARBER, BRETT SERVED IN THE US MARINE CORPS WHERE HE ADVANCED FROM A NAVAL AIR CADET TO THE RANK OF MAJOR. BRETT SERVED WITH ME DURING MY FINAL ASSIGNMENT IN THE PENTAGON AND DEMONSTRATED REMARKABLE RESULTS ORIENTED LEADERSHIP IN EVERY ASSIGNMENT AND RESPONSIBILITY HE ASSUMED THROUGHOUT HIS BUSINESS AND MILITARY CAREER. BRETT WILL BE SORELY MISSED BY THE FIRM AND THE MANY FRIENDSHIPS HE DEVELOPED AT MCKENZIE BARBER. BRETT WILL RETURN TO HIS HOME IN MCCOMB, MISSISSIPPI, DURING HIS CONVALESCENCE.

CLYDE NICKERSON, PARTNER-IN-CHARGE OF EXECUTIVE OFFICE ADMINISTRATION, HAS REQUESTED RETIREMENT EFFECTIVE 12-31-89. CLYDE HAD BEEN A LONG TIME FIXTURE OF MCKENZIE BARBER HAVING JOINED THE FIRM FROM PENNSYLVANIA STEEL IN 1964 AND ABLY SERVING THE FIRM IN A SUCCESSION OF ADMINISTRATIVE POSITIONS. CLYDE WAS ELECTED A PARTNER IN 1975 AND LEAVES THE FIRM WITH A LONG LIST OF ACCOMPLISHMENTS.

EFFECTIVE 1-2-90, GLEN FITZGERALD WILL ASSUME MANAGING PARTNER RESPONSIBILITY FOR THE NEW YORK OFFICE. GLEN JOINED THE FIRM AS A DIRECT ADMISSION PARTNER FROM ANDERSEN CONSULTING IN 1985 WITH RESPONSIBILITY AS THE MID-MIDWESTERN REGIONAL PARTNER-IN-CHARGE OF THE INFORMATION TECHNOLOGY PRACTICE. GLEN HAS BUILT ONE OF THE MOST SUCCESSFUL PRACTICES IN THE HISTORY OF THE FIRM. GLEN RECENTLY AGREED TO SUCCEED DR. GENE ENGLISH AS THE FIRM'S NATIONAL DIRECTOR FOR INFORMATION TECHNOLOGY. THE

OPERATING COMMITTEE CONCLUDED THAT GLEN IS NEEDED MORE BY THE FIRM AS NEW YORK OFFICE MANAGING PARTNER THAN IN NATIONAL LEADERSHIP FOR THE INFORMATION TECHNOLOGY PRACTICE.

JACK PINKER, A NEW YORK OFFICE FINANCIAL SERVICES GROUP PARTNER, HAS AGREED TO SERVE AS THE FIRM'S PARTNER-IN-CHARGE OF ADMINISTRATION SUCCEEDING CLYDE NICKERSON. JACK WILL ASSUME HIS NEW RESPONSIBILITIES EFFECTIVE MONDAY, 12-4-89.

LASTLY, I WANT TO ANNOUNCE MY INTENTION NOT TO RUN FOR A SECOND TERM AS CHAIRMAN OF MCKENZIE BARBER. I PLAN TO CONCLUDE MY TERM OF OFFICE WITH THE ELECTION OF MY SUCCESSOR AT THE OCTOBER 1990 PARTNERS MEETING AND WILL RETIRE 12-31-90. IT IS MY PLAN TO COMPLETE MY CAREER IN PUBLIC SERVICE IN EITHER AN ELECTED OFFICE OR AS AN APPOINTED GOVERNMENT OFFICIAL.

I HAVE FOUND MY CHAIRMAN SERVICE CHALLENGING AND REWARDING BUT IT IS MY CONCLUSION THAT THE FIRM NEEDS FRESH LEADERSHIP FOR THE 1990'S. I HAVE DISCUSSED MY RETIREMENT PLANS WITH NEIL SCHMIDT, YOUR DEPUTY CHAIRMAN AND LEARNED THAT HE ALSO PLANS TO RESIGN WITH THE ELECTION OF HIS SUCCESSOR. YOU HAVE HONORED ME BY ELECTING ME YOUR CHAIRMAN IN 1984. I PLEDGE TO YOU AN OPEN ELECTION PROCESS TO ENSURE THAT THE PARTNERS OF MCKENZIE BARBER ELECT FRESH LEADERSHIP IN AN OPEN DEMOCRATIC PROCESS.

THANK YOU FOR YOUR CONTINUED SUPPORT.

ROSS

Baxter received his copy of the memorandum in the Friday 10:30 mailed drop. Grunwaldyt called at 10:55.

"Joe, have you read Buzzsaw's memo?"

"Just finished it."

"What do you make of it? Does Williamson have AIDS?"

"I have no idea."

"Have you tried to call Brett?"

"I did yesterday after the "E mail" came out. Can I come by? Call Brett's phone mail. I'll be right there." Grunwaldyt clicked off and Baxter dialed 6001, the dreaded phone number of the New York Managing Partner. The phone buzzed four times before it was answered by a phone message from Miss Billington.

"You have reached the office of Brett Williamson. Mr. Williamson has retired from active service at McKenzie Barber. You may leave a message on this line which will be forwarded to Mr. Williamson or you may press 6002 and talk with Miss Billington for further information." Baxter pressed 6002. Her recorded voice again came on the line. "This is Miss Billington. I can't come to the phone right now. Please leave a message after the beep." Baxter waited for the beep and a fresh booming male voice came on the line. "The storage capacity for this telephone line is full. Please call back."

Grunwaldyt entered Baxter's office without knocking. There were age lines in his golden face. He seated himself across from Baxter with a harried look. "Joe, what in hell is going on here? Last week I was bracing myself for Brett Williamson to be the next Deputy Chairman and ultimately the Chairman of McKenzie Barber. Now he's developed some mysterious sickness and vanished into retirement."

"It might be AIDS. As you may be aware, my son died of AIDS. The disease goes fast."

Grunwaldyt shook his head. "Oh God, Joe. I didn't know your son died. I'm sorry! Now what's this about Clyde retiring? He told me once that he had cut a deal with Buzzsaw to stay on to 1992."

"Clyde may want to spend more time with his wife and family," Baxter offered.

"But Clyde and Buzzsaw were very close. Buzzsaw wouldn't make a move without consulting Clyde first," Grunwaldyt argued.

"And that, Jon, explains why this firm is so screwed up. Maybe Buzzsaw thought he'd try it alone for his last year without Clyde and improve his outcomes."

"You've never liked Clyde, have you, Joe?"

"I have no comment on that matter, Jon." Baxter had quit trusting Grunwaldyt two years back. Now he just managed information flows through him.

"What about this appointment of Fitzgerald? What in hell does he know about being a McKenzie Barber Managing Partner? He's never been one. And finally Pinker being named Clyde's replacement. What's that all about?"

Grunwaldyt appeared agitated. His world seemed to have fallen apart with Ross Pritchard's memo.

"The firm moves in mysterious ways hopefully for the better, Jon," Baxter explained in his most statesmanlike voice. "Always maintain faith in the firm's leadership, Jon. Without that covenant, you, personally, will become lost."

Grunwaldyt stared at Baxter for over thirty seconds. "Joe, I had Brett figured out. I knew what I had to do to please him. He told me last week that he anticipated being the Deputy Chairman nominee next fall and that I was one of three Partners that he was considering for his successor as New York Managing Partner. He promised me a big unit increase if I made plan this year. He was doing great things with the New York office cost structure. Now he's vanished and a strange unlikely choice has been made for his successor. I've heard rumors that Fitzgerald and Pinker were organizing some kind of coup. Is it with us now? Brett Williamson was the hope of the future for a lot of the young Partners. What could have happened to him? I think Chairman Buzzsaw has some explaining to do to his Partners."

"Do you want to call him?" Baxter said placing his hand on his telephone. At the same time, Baxter's phone rang.

After he answered "Baxter" a woman's voice greeted.

"Joe, this is Remy, Jack Pinker's secretary. Jack would like to see you today. Could you come by his office at four thirty today?"

"Remy, what will Jack and I be talking about in our meeting? I want to be adequately prepared."

"I have no idea of the subject, Joe. Jack just instructed me to arrange meetings today with certain New York Office Partners. It shouldn't be too long. Jack wants to catch the 5:42 to Greenwich."

"I'll see him at 4:30 then." Baxter clicked off.

Grunwaldyt stared in silence at Baxter for at least twenty seconds. "Are you one of them, Joe?"

"One of what, Jon?"

"There's a network of Partners plotting to take over the firm in the 1990 election. Are you one of them?"

"Jon, my days of being a politicking Partner are behind me. Pinker may be having me in to announce my illness and early retirement. This could be an empty office on Monday morning."

Grunwaldyt pulled himself from the chair. "Well, I'm glad you've retained your sense of humor. A lot of careers have been tossed in the air by these changes."

"Ever considered concentrating on clients, Jon?" Baxter called after Grunwaldyt as he left Baxter's office.

A going away party had been organized for Monica and Linda that evening in one of the back rooms at San Miguel, a First Avenue Spanish restaurant. Baxter had assigned the party project on Wednesday to a young woman named Heidi who had transferred to the practice from the pool in October.

Baxter dialed her extension. "Heidi Marks," her phone was answered promptly.

"Heidi, Joe Baxter. Are all of the arrangements for the party set?"

"I'll be right in, Mr. Baxter." The phone clicked off. Baxter had been willing to settle for a "yes" or "no". But now he was going to have another visitor.

She had been a borrowed pool consultant who had worked on projects for Marty, Monica, and Bill Van Hoeven. Heidi was an exceptionally tall woman in her early thirties who had worked as a nurse before Columbia Graduate School. Baxter questioned why the firm had hired a thirty year old ex-nurse and had been told that she was expected to transfer into the Healthcare practice. Monica related to Baxter that the Healthcare practice after a few projects didn't want Heidi.

"She's an intelligent woman and just hanging around the pool. I know we could cut a deal for her," Monica recommended. Monica's judgment had been correct and Baxter agreed to take Heidi. She always called him Mr. Baxter, came to the office at 7:30 AM and rarely left before 7 PM. Heidi had a busy vitality about her. She was close to six feet tall, thin and always wore white blouses, dark skirts, and flat black shoes.

"Mr. Baxter." Heidi entered his open office door. "I have the details on the party." Heidi had a manila folder which she opened and placed at the edge of Baxter's desk. Continuing to stand, Heidi began to recite from the folder.

"6 to 8PM in the Alhambra Room at the San Miguel Restaurant, 1st Avenue between 52nd and 53rd, East side of the street. The maitre'd's name is Pepe."

"How many will be coming?"

"10."

"How did we reach 10?"

"Linda is bringing her fiancé. His name is Dr. Eli Wachler. Monica asked me to invite Marveen Scott and Charlotte Bunker to the party. I know Mrs. Bunker and I understand that Mrs. Scott was a secretary in this department for many years."

Baxter nodded his head. Marveen had elected to leave the firm rather than come back to Exec Comp. The party would be made up of a near equal amount of deserters and non-deserters.

"I have a meeting at 4:30 PM, I assume that I will be there in time, but please move the party forward if I should be a few minutes late," Baxter said with finality assuming that Heidi would stand up and leave the room.

"May I ask you a few questions, Mr. Baxter?"

Baxter made an exaggerated look at his watch. "Why of course, Heidi. I always have a few minutes to answer questions."

"First, let me say that I am very happy to be in the Executive Compensation practice. I'm fairly new to the firm and I wasn't very happy in the pool. The resignations of Monica and Linda were disturbing to me, but at the same time, I recognized that these losses may represent an opportunity for me. Now I understand that part of Monica's leaving was related to Mr. Williamson. Linda's leaving is related to her forthcoming marriage. My question is, will these resignations create an opportunity or will you hire replacements from the outside?"

"First, Heidi, I don't understand the relationship between Mr. Williamson and Monica's resignation. Can you elaborate on that connection."

Heidi seem flustered. "It is—" She searched for words. "Rumored that Mr. Williamson exhibited aggressive and excessive behavior toward women employed with McKenzie Barber."

"Where on earth did you hear that?" Baxter responded. "It was my understanding that Mr. Williamson developed a very serious illness."

"I believe you know exactly what I'm talking about, Mr. Baxter."

"Did Mr. Williamson ever make any unwelcome advance to you, Heidi?"

Heidi blushed and looked down at her shoes. "I have heard stories around the firm."

"We can't confirm rumors, Heidi. Let's say for the purposes of our discussion that Mr. Williamson has resigned from the firm for health reasons and leave it like that. No common advantage can be advanced for the firm unless there is internal and external agreement on that point. People frequently leave McKenzie Barber to go off to other careers. These losses create opportunities for people to advance. You must work hard to qualify yourself for internal advancement and not be concerned with peripheral events. Face the market not the rumor mill!"

Heidi looked up and made eye contact with Baxter. She stood up from the chair opposite Baxter. "I understand every word you've said. You can count on me, Mr. Baxter."

Baxter wound up waiting ten minutes outside Pinker's office exchanging pleasantries with Remy. Remy turned out to be a tall dark haired girl with middle-eastern features.

"Jack's had a lot of meetings back-to-back today and he's running behind," Remy explained.

"How long have you been with McKenzie Barber, Remy?"

"Two years. I used to be a secretary to a tax partner at a public accounting firm. I really like working for Jack because there's so much going on. This last set of changes have really set me in motion. All of a sudden we have a big organization to account for. It's going to be a big challenge for Jack. How long have you been with McKenzie Barber, Joe?"

"I've joined the firm in 1967 and was elected a Partner in 1978."

"That makes you an old timer. Congratulations, Joe."

"I'm part of a vanishing tribe," Baxter added.

Remy answered her telephone. "Mr. Pinker's office, Remy speaking. Yes, Nancy. Jack will meet Glen at 10 AM at O'Hare Admiral's Club tomorrow. I've got him on an eight o'clock flight. Yes, he's going to see Joe Baxter next. Okay, Nancy. Sure. Bye."

Remy turned her attention to Baxter. "That was Nancy. Glen Fitzgerald's secretary. We talk all the time, but I've never met her. We've been so busy today and we're moving tomorrow. I have to be in all weekend to supervise the move and unpack."

"Where are you and Jack moving to?"

"38th floor. We're moving into Mr. Nickerson's office three doors down from Mr. Pritchard."

"And where will Mr. Nickerson be moving?"

"To the Lexington level. He'll just need an office for a month because of his retirement. He and Jack spent two hours together this morning. There's so much to do in this kind of transition."

Remy's phone buzzed. "Yes, Jack. I have Joe right here. OK, I'll call your wife and tell her that you'll be on the 6:21." Remy hung up the phone. "I've got Peggy on speed dial," she said pressing a three digit code. "Oh, Joe. Jack says to go right in."

Baxter rose up from the side chair and carefully walked the six feet to Jack Pinker's closed office door. Was he about to be fired? Baxter knocked twice and turned the knob at the same time he heard a "Com'on in, Joe."

Jack Pinker had the standard McKenzie Barber "line" Partner's office. It was 14 by 18 with a large dark wood desk backed by a credenza. There was a smaller round table with four chairs next to the window. Pinker had his coat off and greeted Baxter in shirt sleeves with his collar button open and his tie knot lowered. His hair was salt and pepper now. Baxter remembered him as a naive, but opinionated, second year Partner from their work together in 1983 on Burke's communication task force.

"Let's sit over here at the table, Joe," Pinker gestured without any effort to shake hands. Baxter removed his suit jacket and placed it over the back of the chair he selected. There was a small pile of blue McKenzie Barber Partner's personnel jackets on the table. Baxter tried unsuccessfully to make out the names as he seated himself. He wished he had brought his calculator with him in the event this was going to be a severance discussion.

"It's been a busy day, Joe, and I've got a lot of matters to get through in the next hour. I won't keep you long. First, let me say that Glen and I are very grateful to you for blowing the whistle on Brett Williamson. We were prepared to launch our campaign right after the first of the year and figured we'd have to slug it out through September. We tried to get you to come forward at the Partners meeting. What finally made you step up?"

"I had two resignations of women consultants from my practice on Monday. I decided I had enough, Jack."

Pinker's face showed no emotion. "The firm is in a mess, Joe. According to Buzzsaw Pritchard, he has been lied to for five years. We believe Buzz is an honorable but naive man. He wants to step down from the chairmanship with a cleaned up firm properly focused for growth. We gained nine to ten months thanks to you."

"Where is Brett?"

Pinker shook his head. "Pritchard took care of that personally. He had Nickerson work out the details Tuesday night and got outside counsel involved. Brett's office was sealed Tuesday night around midnight. Part of the deal was for Brett to be out of New York by Wednesday noon. I know the details but that's all I can share with you."

"And Clyde?"

"Buzzsaw blew Clyde out right after Brett's deal was done. He's going to retire 12-31 but remain on call as a consultant until December 1990. Clyde's been in the middle of a number of specialized personnel transactions. He's been the executive office Rasputin for a long time. Clyde seemed to make up Partner personnel policy as he went along."

"And how long do you expect to serve as Administrative Partner, Jack?"

"As long as it takes to get things cleaned up. I will be running with Glen as his Deputy Chairman this fall. I found a copy of that Administrative Review that you performed back in 1983. It wasn't bad, but read like it was a bit of a whitewash. I assume that vested interests edited it for you. Then I found another study that you participated along with Dirks and Grunwaldyt for Ernie Grey. That was pretty objective."

"Hamilton Burke was the client on the Executive Office study. He was the editor and decided what he wanted and didn't want disclosed. Ernie

255

Grey was the client on the review of the acquired subsidiaries and that helped get Buzzsaw elected."

"When the hell did you find time to work on clients?" Pinker pricked.

"I didn't have any option, Jack. I did what I was told like a good Partner."

"Glen and I need a quick intensive review of Executive Office functions completed by the end of February. Do you want the job?"

"My practice needs me. We're damned near out of backlog. If I'm not out selling in January and February, we're not going to be close to plan in Q-II and Q-III."

"Joe, your practice is being merged in Dilger's effective 10-1-90. After the study's been completed, you're working for Bob Dilger. Executive Compensation is history as a freestanding practice at McKenzie Barber. If that doesn't suit you, there's always early retirement. You could, of course, be a candidate to succeed me as Administrative Partner. That would give you another three years pension credit and you're out at 58."

"Can I take the weekend to think this over, Jack?"

"There's nothing to think over. Glen and I want Executive Office Administration reviewed. You are our first choice to do it. This is an opportunity for you. It's also a payoff for you. Do I have to draw you a picture?"

"So, as I understand it, Jack, I don't have a lot of options here."

"You have three options, Joe. 1.) Jump on the Executive Office Administrative Study. 2.) Go to work for Dilger effective January 2nd. 3.) Take early retirement."

Pinker's phone buzzed. "Think it over, Joe. Give me an answer by the time I'm off the phone."

"Pinker," he shouted into the phone."

The conversation lasted three minutes and Baxter blotted out the words. He had gone from one set of bullies to another.

"I'll do it, Jack," Baxter announced after Pinker had hung up the phone.

"I thought you would see it our way. Give me a detailed work plan by Wednesday noon and we'll go over it at 5 o'clock."

Pinker wheeled in his chair turning his back to Baxter indicating that he was dismissed.

Baxter arrived at 6:15 at San Miguel. Pepe, the matire'd, turned out to be short, brusque, and on the edge of ill-mannered.

"McKenzie Barber, Alhambra Room. Up the stairs, to your right." San Miguel was one of Monica's hangouts. She was always meeting Spanish and Mexican bankers there for drinks. Baxter regarded San Miguel as a mediocre mid-town restaurant.

This night probably marked the last party that the New York Exec Comp practice would ever hold as a group. Baxter trudged slowly up the stairs after checking his coat. Monica was leaving after seven years and Linda after three. He had hoped to beat them out the door of McKenzie Barber. At the top of the stairs a great deal of noise sounded out of the Alhambra Room. Baxter suspected they had started early.

Baxter opened the door to find Charlotte Bunker with a martini glass in her hand. "Here's the man of the hour." She kissed Baxter on the cheek. Monica waved from across the room where she was sitting on Marty's lap. Linda was standing next to a tall young man with a beard who wore an open neck white shirt with a gold chain inside a blue blazer.

"Is there a Doctor in the house?" Baxter said extending his hand.

"Joe, this is Eli Wachler, my fiancé. Eli, this is Joe Baxter, my boss and mentor." They shook hands.

"Boy, have I heard a lot about you over the past two years," Eli said with a grin. "You sure have kept Linda on the run."

"And you've completed your residency?"

Eli nervously talked non-stop for a few minutes with Linda snuggling under his extended arm. He was trying to decide between three clinics and a public health position. Linda's new firm would give her more flexibility for transfer. Baxter watched Linda kiss Eli affectionately on the cheek.

"I better get myself a drink," Baxter said excusing himself.

There was a table of hot and cold hors d'oeuvres in the middle of the room, and a bartender in the far corner of the room. Monica reached out to Baxter from her place on Dr. Marty Dunlap's lap. He clasped her hand.

"Joe," Marty said very seriously. "I must confess that we started at 5:15. It was a slow Friday and seemed like the thing to do."

"You can make up the time next week, Marty."

Monica kissed him on the ear and whispered. "I assume you and I are going to get together for dinner."

"Where's Erik tonight?"

"In Miami. He's due back at noon on Saturday. It's up to you to keep me entertained tonight." Baxter concluded that Monica Graham was three drinks up on him.

Heidi stood in the corner talking in Spanish to the bartender, who stood nearly a foot shorter than Baxter's newest consultant.

"Mr. Baxter," Heidi greeted him somberly. "I'm afraid that the party started ahead of time. Dr. Dunlap, Mr. Van Hoeven and Miss Graham just put on their coats and went out the door. I told them that the room wouldn't be ready until six but they just left. I'm very new in the department. This is the first party like this I've had to arrange."

"Looks fine to me, Heidi," Baxter said and ordered a Canadian Club on the rocks from the bartender. "I really doubt we'll have this bunch out of the room until after nine."

Heidi held a tall glass filled with yellow liquid and ice.

"What do you have there, Heidi?" Baxter asked.

"It's grapefruit juice and club soda. I'm afraid I'm not much for alcoholic drinks, Mr. Baxter."

"We'd need someone sober to keep order, Heidi. Have you met everyone?"

"I believe I have. I talked with Dr. Wachler, Linda's fiancé. He's in Cardiology. I'm going over to talk to him again shortly."

Baxter looked around the room. Monica was now upright from Marty Dunlap's lap and was laughing with Linda. Bill Van Hoeven had his arm around Vera, the consultant that had transferred in from the pool the previous June. Baxter still couldn't remember her last name. With the resignations, Baxter was down to five professionals. He had allowed the department to run off. Was there someone he could use on the Executive Office Study?

Marty was too gentle and academic. Van Hoeven would never keep his mouth shut. Ed, the Carnegie Mellon June grad on loan from the pool, was way too naive.

"I hope, Mr. Baxter, that I didn't seem too forward to you in my comments this afternoon," Heidi continued.

"Heidi, how long were you in Nursing before you entered graduate school?" Baxter asked.

"Seven years."

"I suppose you worked with a lot of people who were pretty sick and had to become accustomed to a lot of unusual behavior?" Baxter probed.

"I was a psychiatric nurse at Bellevue while I was attending Business School. The pay was a little better to compensate for the personal risk."

"With the loss of Linda, I'm going to be in need of a key support consultant to assist me on a very sensitive assignment. It will require complete confidentiality."

"I'm very flattered that you would choose me to work directly with you."

"Your psychiatric experience may be very helpful. I'll brief you on Monday after the staff meeting."

"Thank you, Mr. Baxter."

Baxter stared off toward Marveen who had just entered the room.

"What will you have, lady?" he called down to her. Marveen pointed toward the bottle of white wine at the end of the bar. Baxter carried a glass of wine down to Marveen and kissed her on the cheek. "I understand that you've left the firm," Baxter said passing the wine glass to his long-time secretary.

"I'm working downtown in the corporate finance department at Broadbakers. It's a crazy place with a lot of big egos, so I got used to things right away."

"You didn't choose to talk to me about coming back to Exec Comp?"

"That was two years ago, Joe. After working for Lon McMasters, I didn't want to go back to a small practice like Exec Comp. I hear you took care of business with Mr. Brett this week."

"And what ever do you mean by that, Marveen?"

"Joe Baxter, I know you. I worked for you for more than five years." Marveen's eyes scanned the room. "When I worked for you, all I could see was the Exec Comp practice. Then when I went to work for Lon, I could see the whole New York Office and I saw that Exec Comp was just a freckle on the face of McKenzie Barber. You transferred Harry out, and now Monica and that Linda are going. What do you have left?"

"What I don't have now I'll go into the marketplace and get. I've hosted going away parties before, Marveen."

"How many years with McKenzie Barber do you have left, Joe?"

"As many as I choose to have, Marveen. So glad you could come," Baxter said beginning to move away. Marveen caught his arm.

"You did good by Brett Williamson. I don't know what you had on him, but the man was evil. Even more evil than Mr. Nickerson. You were good by me and good to take on Mrs. Bunker. You've been one of the few human beings around the firm. I was real sorry to hear about your son." Baxter patted Marveen's hand, nodded, and made his way around the table to where Linda was standing alone.

"Eli seems to be a fine young man," Baxter said.

Linda nodded as she observed Eli in a conversation group with Monica, Marty, and Bill Van Hoeven.

"He's ideal, Joe. He has a wonderful career ahead of him as a cardio-vascular specialist. I started dating Eli about the time we became friends. He's a gentle and brilliant man who will go far."

"And more your age," Baxter reminded her.

"I enjoyed our time together, Joe. Both personally and professionally," Linda said with the warmth of a wedding present thank you note.

Marty Dunlap was the first to leave. He was followed by Linda and Eli who were followed by Marveen, Bill Van Hoeven, and Charlotte Bunker. Baxter stopped Charlotte Bunker at the door.

"We haven't had a chance to talk, Charlotte."

"I believe you and I have said about everything we have to say. I expect a settlement from McKenzie Barber, and then plan to retire. Thank you for taking me in for a while."

Bill Van Hoeven took Baxter aside to ask about his expanded role in the practice and suggested that they arrange a breakfast. The room population had been reduced to Heidi, who remained silently stationed next to the bartender. Monica had placed her hand on Baxter's shoulder while she carried on in Spanish with the bartender.

Monica whispered to Baxter. "I'm ready for my dinner now. Let's get out of here." She bit him lightly on the ear.

"Heidi, let's call it a night. Can we drop you anywhere?" Baxter said while signing the bar check.

"No, Mr. Baxter. I prefer to walk home for the exercise." Heidi produced a pair of running shoes from her bag.

"Where do you live?" Monica asked.

"Lexington and 91st Street."

"That's on our way," Monica announced. "Mr. Baxter is buying me a dinner at a hotel on the East side."

Baxter had assumed that they would eat at the Sunset Club, and that he would place Monica in a cab which would take her out of his life.

Monica took Baxter's arm. "I have made 8:30 reservations at the Versailles on 63rd Street. Dominique now has a permanent suite there and I've gotten to appreciate the dining room." Heidi sat next to the far door of the taxi with Monica nestled in the middle.

"May I ask you how long you two have worked together?" Heidi asked.

"Seven and one half years," Monica answered while patting Baxter's knee. "And I'm going to miss him. I'm counting on you to eventually take my place, Heidi. You'll find him to be a great big teddy bear."

"I was asked this afternoon to do another review of the Executive Office, Monica. How do you think I should staff it?"

"This is where I came in, Baxter. I'd use Heidi here. It would be a great way for her to learn everything that's wrong with McKenzie Barber." Monica turned to Heidi. "Baxter and I did that little number back in 1982. You'd get a chance to see how the wheels of the firm turn, and Mr. Baxter's skills in the art of white-washing."

"I would be honored to work personally with Mr. Baxter," Heidi said sanctimoniously.

"It has been an honor, Heidi, to work with Mr. Baxter over these past seven years. You will learn from him and I'm going to miss him." Monica kissed Baxter on his cheek as the taxi pulled in front of the Hotel Versailles.

Baxter pressed a ten dollar bill into Heidi's hand. "Drop by my office after the Monday staff meeting and I'll brief you on the Executive Office review assignment."

"I plan to be in the office on Saturday. Are there any advance preparation materials I should review?"

"We'll talk Monday, Heidi," Baxter said stepping from the taxi. He extended a hand to Monica who pushed her body against him at the curb. Monica waved to Heidi in the departing taxi. "Oh boy, Baxter, she's going to be more fun than a barrel of monkeys. At least we can be confident that you'll keep your hands off her."

Baxter took Monica's arm slightly under the armpit of her mink coat. He could smell her perfume and could sense by her step that Monica had had too much to drink.

"They know me here, Baxter. I've had dinner with Dominique here three times since July." She led Baxter to a small formal dining room off the lobby where they were seated at a center table. The voices around the brightly lit room were in French.

"You've been seeing Dominique regularly?" Baxter asked after the waiter had taken a wine order.

"We talk once every two or three weeks. She has quite an acquisition war chest since de Hartogue was bought out of Hortense Foods. She still has Hamilton Burke on some kind of retainer. Now, if I can introduce a mercenary subject, what kind of settlement bonus am I going to get for my sexual harassment at the hands of the scurrilous Brett Williamson? I would assume I would get a deal equal to half of what Bonnie Grow got."

Baxter tasted the wine, a Sauvignon Blanc and studied Monica's face, subtle brown eyes, and a model's body. Her hands had been on him in the taxi. They had worked together over seven years, and maintained their professional distance. It was technically their last night together.

"Monica, I arranged for your release from the Director's contract. Should the practice meet its goals for FY 1990, there may be an appropriate bonus recognizing your contributions through December 31st, 1989."

"Baxter, it was my understanding that I would receive some kind of settlement bonus for the humiliation I incurred from Mr. Williamson's unwelcome advances. There's still time to get a lawyer involved in this, Baxter."

"Monica, leave well enough alone," Baxter counseled. They touched glasses.

"Baxter, you know that I embellished the description of Williamson's advances. To tell you the truth, I don't think he ever got much above my knee."

"Don't take more credit than you deserve, Monica. The pictures of Bonnie Grow were the clincher."

"I took those pictures, Baxter. You couldn't have taken out Williamson without me. Admit it!"

"You've been very helpful over the years, Monica. I will miss you." Baxter opened his menu.

"So you're not going to pay me out. You used me, Baxter."

"I used you for good, not evil, Monica."

"Dominique told me about the taxi ride in Paris, Baxter." Monica opened her menu.

"Which cab ride was that?" Baxter asked innocently.

"The one in the late 70's when you practically screwed her to death on your way to Charles DeGaulle. By the way the escargot is very good here. Anyway, I've heard about that cab ride for years. I will always remember our first meeting in your conference room. 'So this is the taxi cab lover' I said to myself when this large red-headed man came into the room. I knew you two had been lovers when I came to New York. I also picked up on Linda and you, Baxter."

"I have no idea of what you're talking about," Baxter said. "I will start with the escargot. How's the snapper?"

"Linda has never fessed up, but I could see the two of you were up to something."

"You're quite wrong, Monica. Linda has been like a daughter to me," Baxter countered.

"Oh Christ, Baxter. I'm done with McKenzie Barber as of now. It's time to fess up on all of these little affairs of yours. It's a shame we took Heidi with us. I would have enjoyed being subjected to your taxi cab routine. I'm going to have the tuna."

"Once upon a time, I spent a week or so with Dominique before she was a de Hartogue. I fell in love with her. She went on to become a de Hartogue and she did once accompany me to DeGaulle in a taxi cab. That's all I have to offer on the matter. What do the two of you talk about in your discussions?"

"There's some US compensation work coming up with her US subsidiaries, and there's decent size acquisition on the line. Dominique's talked to me about it and she plans to talk to you. I told her where I was going. How about backing off and letting me take the work to Bowers Merrin? It will get me off to a great start."

"I have to know what I'm turning down, Monica. If it's fairly pedestrian work, you can have it."

"How about just letting me have it, Baxter? I should get a Bonnie Grow deal and I'm not."

"I have to hear from Dominique first."

"She plans to call you."

"Then I'll wait for Dominique's call. If she doesn't call, it's all yours."

"Are you angry with me for leaving, Joe?"

"It was not unexpected."

"You've lost some of your competitive fire during the last year. It's been like you were going through the motions. I know your son was a loss and that you went through a divorce. Are you all right to continue?"

"I'll be fine, Monica."

"Do you know Rob Moreland at Bowers Merrin? He says he knows you."

He had a vague recollection of someone late thirtiesh and smooth who had participated with Baxter on an executive compensation panel.

"Rob said that he would be delighted to talk to you about a role with Bowers Merrin whenever you're ready. Then we could reunite the three of us, Linda, you, and me, into a single McKenzie Barber pod."

"That just wouldn't work, Monica. Tonight's the end of it." Escargot was served in a garlic sauce.

"I don't like to see what's happening to you, Joe," Monica said after a bit of escargot. "You seem so alone out there."

"Tell me about Dominique. Is she happy?"

"She runs de Hartogue, has an acquisition chest, runs around the world in a manner fitting a monarch, and makes a little time for her children from time to time. Dominique keeps herself up and loves the discipline of measuring her life on return on capital."

"How's her marriage?"

"At expectations. Henri is a dutiful husband and spends a lot of time with the boys. He's accepted Dominique's role in running of the family interests. She's produced healthy heirs and they're comfortable in their life together. Henri is a little like the family dog. He's affectionately glad to see Dominique when she comes home, sees after the children, and loyally sleeps at the foot of her bed. He may have an occasional dalliance on the side, but

Henri does it quietly. He and Erik have been taking vacations together in remote luxury settings. I suspect they enjoy male bonding and weeks of debauchery together. Henri always picks up the tab and I'm not included. Erik is taking the long way home tonight. I suspect that he's found a friend in Miami."

Baxter finished his escargot in silence. The subject of the details of Monica's marriage had never come up before in their seven year work relationship.

"I've got to make some real money over the next few years, Baxter. You and I have always had a money issue. I want the life style I should have had as a San Francisco Graham. The problem is that I pissed all of those years away as an heiress ex-pat. I can say things now like I wouldn't exchange a day of my life, but I bummed around until I was 32."

"How did you meet Dominique?" Baxter asked as the salad was served.

"Erik announced one evening that Henri had a new girlfriend and that we would meet her that Saturday for tennis and a late lunch. We played doubles. Dominique was a very awkward tennis player, but fiercely energetic and competitive. It was obvious to me that she hated to lose and we beat them in straight sets. Dominique asked me over lunch if I was available to play one afternoon a week. We started to play tennis and after a couple of months, she could trounce me at will. Dominique developed a powerful serve and she could smash with either hand. We became good tennis friends, and I slipped to easy competition. Erik and Henri go back to university days where they were both world class playboys."

"And how did you meet Erik?"

"I was at the Sorbonne and living in a strange little apartment on the Left Bank. Erik was sleeping with my roommate, Susy Schlegal from Columbus, Ohio. I found him interesting. He dropped Susy, and I moved in with Erik. We were on and off for about five years. My trust fund began to run down. Erik's father told him it was time to get to work. We had skied most of Northern Europe. Erik got the job with the bank, and Dominique went to work for de Hartogue and began to parcel out little consulting projects to me. Erik and I decided that it would look better if we were married. Then the transfer to the US came up. Dominique and I were pretty close by that time. She offered to write a letter of introduction to her old lover, Joe Baxter, and here I am tonight at the final stage of my going away party. I have learned the trade of executive compensation consulting and will out-earn my husband in my new job. There are some messages there, Baxter. The bank regards Erik as a C plus player, and he keeps his job by being close to the de Hartogues. The bank will eventually want Erik back in France, and I don't know whether it will make good career sense for me to go back with him."

"What in hell are you telling me, Monica?"

"I'm telling you, Mr. B, that I've passed up my husband professionally and I'm getting a little tired of his periodic diversions. Tonight, I'm saying good-bye to my old boss and mentor of 7 1/2 years with whom I've enjoyed a very antiseptic relationship. I'm going to miss him very much."

"And I'll miss you too, Monica. But as of Monday morning you will be competing against me."

"What are you doing for female companionship these days, Baxter? Linda now has a fiancé."

"There's a woman in the small town where I have my country home. I generally see her when I'm up there on weekends. Your Linda Green theory is preposterous," Baxter responded.

"I have a key to Dominique's suite. Why don't you and I go up there for a night cap after dinner?" Monica proposed as the entree was served.

They made light conversation over the entree and when the plates were taken away, Monica extended a hand which was clasped by Baxter. Their eyes matched and it seemed understood that they would leave the dining room, move to Dominique's suite, and make love.

Baxter signed the check and helped place Monica's mink on her shoulders. She nuzzled against Baxter as they left the restaurant. "I have a permanent key."

The elevator took them to the 14th floor and Monica paused to kiss Baxter after the elevator door closed. It was a long wet tongue connected kiss, with Monica's coat open and her body pressed against Baxter.

"Dominique's suite is at the end of the hall. It's 1400," Monica whispered and kissed Baxter on the ear. He turned his head and shared a brief off-center mouth kiss.

Monica produced a key from her purse and turned the lock on 1400. The door opened to a chain lock and they could hear the sound of soft rock music through the narrow door opening. Baxter noted that a 'Do-Not-Disturb' sign was hanging from the doorknob. Monica gave two pushes to the door and rapped.

"No maid service, please," they heard a voice cry out.

"Maid service, hell! Who's in there?"

A face peered out at them from through the door chain opening. It was Henri de Hartogue in a bare chest. He greeted Monica in French. Monica responded in French and Baxter made out Erik's name twice.

They spoke rapidly in an interchange of French. Monica became very angry. Baxter deduced that she was demanding to see Erik. Henri appeared to be calmly denying that Erik was in the suite. Monica's voice grew more assertive and angry.

"Alles vou san," Henri kept calmly repeating.

Monica's voice grew more animated.

Finally a second male voice shouted something in French from inside the suite.

Monica spoke with fire in French and finished with a 'Go to hell, you son-of-a-bitch' in English. She placed her finger over her lips, tugged on Baxter's arm, and whispered in English, "Let's get the hell out of here! Anywhere!"

They heard the door close and latch as they waited for the elevator. "They are not in Miami," Monica said in a controlled voice. "They are shacked up in New York and I'm pissed. I've been lied to."

They rode in silence to the main floor. Baxter placed his hand briefly on Monica's shoulder only to have her brush his hand away.

"I want to walk, Baxter. Will you walk with me?"

Monica lit a cigarette when they were outside the hotel. The temperature seemed to have dropped at least ten degrees during their dinner. They walked down Madison Avenue in silence until they reached 54th Street. "That son-of-a-bitch!" Monica said to the night. "Why in hell couldn't they have settled for Miami?"

"Probably because the ladies live in New York," Baxter offered.

"This has the making of a mess, Baxter. It's partly my fault. I never should have brought you back to the Versaille for dinner and suggested a nightcap in a place where I had no business."

"And I know you had no plans other than a quick final farewell drink in Dominique's home away from home." Baxter took Monica's arm as they walked across 54th Street.

"If I hadn't gone up there, I wouldn't have known. Erik would have shown up innocently with flowers and taken me to lunch. We would have rented a movie on the way back from lunch and probably made love. I planned to cook on Saturday night and we have a Sunday brunch with one of Erik's high net worth customers. We are scheduled to spend a week at an island off the Spanish coast with Dominique and Henri beginning December 10th and we're spending Christmas with Erik's family on a skiing holiday. I'm locked into my marriage. Dominique will be my client at Bowers Merrin."

"Maybe it was quite innocent."

"I smelled marijuana in there. They were turning on with some ladies." They crossed 51st Street and Monica paused in front of Helmsley Palace. "Baxter, where in the hell are we going?" Monica demanded.

"You were the one that wanted to walk. I was simply trying to accommodate."

"What did you plan to do after we said good night."

"I was going to rent a car and drive up to my country place."

"The one in upstate New York?"

"It's in Brinker's Falls, a little better than half way to Albany."

"Let's go there together right now."

"It's 12:45, Monica."

"The Hertz on 48th Street is open all night. Let's get a car and take off. I'll drive if you're tired. I feel wired."

"Don't you want to go home and pack a few things?" Baxter suggested.

Monica shook her head and wrapped both arms around Baxter's overcoat arm. "No, Baxter. I'm prepared to rough it. I'll show that son-of-a-bitch. I'll disappear without a trace until Sunday night with my good friend and mentor, Joe Baxter."

"You may not want to wear that suit all weekend," Baxter cautioned.

"I'll spend the weekend in one of your tee shirts. I've lived off the land earlier in my life," Monica kissed Baxter on the cheek. "And you're going to be such good company."

Monica fell fast asleep just north of Tarrytown. They had paused at the all night drug store across from the Waldorf in order for Monica to acquire necessities. Baxter insisted on driving and Monica delivered a long monologue on her life with Erik. It represented new material. They had worked together professionally for over seven years without boring each other with their life stories. Monica viewed Baxter as a life-long McKenzie Barber Partner who had come East after growing up in a small town in northern Minnesota.

Baxter, in turn, had viewed Monica as an American who had turned European. She had popped into Baxter's life as a referral from Dominique with an articulate mouth and no relevant experience. Monica had always had a good work ethic on her own terms, i.e. come late, stay late. She was a quick study and always maintained one step ahead of the client. Monica had complained about her McKenzie Barber pay from her first day at the firm, and now presumably the market had begun to adjust her reward level in equilibrium with her perceived experience. She had talked Bowers Merrin into paying her a lot of money. If Monica flopped, she could well be adjusted down.

Market adjustments of compensation were not part of Monica's early Saturday morning dialogue. She talked about her life as an expatriate living off a trust with alternative residences in France and Spain.

"I liked being a student. I liked men and I loved Europe. I lived through an extended period of self indulgence. So did Erik. Henri, Erik and I wandered over Europe. Henri took up with Bibi, who was in the movies because she had a hot body and photographed well. We used to camp out together at places where Bibi was on location. She was a charming enough person but a terrible actress. Henri worshipped Bibi. He asked his father for permission to marry her was turned down and had his allowance cut off. It turned out Bibi got most of her parts by providing special favors to film producers and directors. She stopped getting film work and tried modeling. We had one last summer together in the south of France and that was the end of it."

"Henri went to the Baron, pleaded for forgiveness, and was taken back. I believe he told him a little white lie about Bibi being pregnant. Lord knows they always seemed to be trying for that result. They moved into the de Hartogue mansion and Henri was told to start paying attention to the business. My trust had damned near run out. Erik's parents had practically written him off. They wanted him to break free from that American woman. I considered going home. The Baron gave Henri some kind of a job counting the family money. It was kind of a funds custody job. The French banks started cultivating Henri and he told them about his friend Erik, who was now ready to start his business career. I got one last loan from my father to attend business school. That loan, I am proud to say, was paid back by means of those piddling McKenzie Barber bonuses you got for me. Erik was initiated into the world of private banking. I finished my degree and took a couple of loser jobs. Bibi never got pregnant, put on a few pounds, and got weary of living in the de Hartogue compound. She found a lawyer and they trumped up grounds for divorce. The de Hartogue's sent Bibi away and told Henri to never marry again without a pre-nuptial agreement. Henri had gotten a little weary of Bibi by that time. Enter Dominique as a fresh young consultant from McKenzie Barber."

"Bibi went back to her film career, was unsuccessful, and finally married some Latin passing through. A tabloid magazine traced her to Bogota. Dominique contributed two children, and became the business leader for the family interests and Henri has a free hand to do what he wants as long as he fills his family obligations. He and Erik have a lot in common. They're attractive, amusing men without much ambition. Henri comes from a lot of money and Erik comes from a little."

"And what will you do now?" Baxter asked interrupting Monica's monologue.

"I'm going to disappear until Sunday night. I'm going to play hooky from my marriage with my friend of seven years. Right now I'm going to catch a few winks. You were right, Baxter, to insist on driving."

Monica was snoring in a few minutes time, while Baxter fought off fatigue. It was a clear cold night and Baxter reckoned that they would arrive sometime between 2 and 3 in the morning. He hadn't been up to Brinker's Falls since the first week in November.

Darlene customarily had arrived in his upstairs bedroom very early on Saturday morning and positioned herself on the edge of his bed.

"Joe, I've missed you so much." She had leaned down and kissed Baxter about the eyes, cheeks, and mouth until he was fully awake. Then Darlene stood up and boldly undressed in front of him.

"We don't have much time. I have to be back to make Luke's breakfast by nine o'clock. I'll have Rob with me when I come to clean this afternoon." There had been thirty minutes of very physical sex before Darlene was off to the shower. Baxter had followed Darlene into the bathroom. She had a towel wrapped around her head and was humming something that sounded like the opening bars of Schubert's Unfinished Symphony. Darlene had stepped out of the shower dripping and Baxter had dried her with a large terry cloth towel.

"I made coffee before I came up. You're getting me very excited," she had said as Baxter worked the towel over Darlene's large Nordic body. This relationship was moving into a danger zone, he concluded. It was attractive enough when they were together, but it clearly had no future and certainly shouldn't have started in the first place. He had to figure out a way out of it.

It had been going on now in short furtive doses for better than fourteen months. Would Darlene show up on this Saturday morning for some pre-breakfast action?

Baxter turned into his moonlight bathed driveway a little after two-thirty. He could make out a note on the side door. Leaving the car running he found a sheet of letter size paper fastened by thumbtacks. The message was formed by large block letters from a newspaper and read;

DOPMAN/BAXTER!

YOUR TIME IS COMING SOON!
YOU MUST PAY FOR YOUR SINS!

GOD'S HELPER

Baxter carefully folded the note and placed it in his jacket pocket. Returning to the car, he turned off the engine and roused Monica.

"Where the hell am I?" she said finally.

"We're at my country place. You said that you wanted to hide out from Erik until Sunday night."

Monica nodded her head. "That son-of-a-bitch." She was wobbly out of the car, and Baxter steered her through the back door.

"It's colder inside than outside. Where are we? The North Pole?"

"I keep the heat turned down to 40 degrees. I'll build a fire and turn up the heat. The house will be as warm as toast in the morning," Baxter explained.

Monica huddled in her fur coat of the first flames in the fireplace while Baxter scurried around turning up thermostats.

"Baxter, if you have a St. Bernard with a brandy casket running around here, please send him by," she called out. Baxter partially filled two coffee mugs with brandy and sat down next to Monica in front of the encouraging flames from the fireplace. She leaned against Baxter and sipped from the brandy mug.

274

"I could be home in my warm bed blissfully waiting for Erik to return from Miami. I had a nice going away party and a nice dinner. But I had to get sentimental and decide to take my boss to bed for old time's sake. Boy, was that dumb!"

"I'll drive you back in the morning," Baxter offered.

"You're driving me back on Sunday afternoon, Mister," Monica affirmed. "I'm going to finish this brandy and find someplace to sleep around here." Monica leaned forward and took long smells from different spots on the bear rug. "I'm checking for sperm stains. I assume the bedrooms are upstairs. I may stay right here and move to a bed in the morning."

Baxter wrapped both arms around Monica. "I can bring you down a blanket and a pillow. You can set up down here and I'll try my luck in the upstairs cold. It's been my experience that two bodies are warmer than one."

"It's way too cold to entertain sex, Baxter. What do you do for women when you're up here?"

"I have a local who drops in from time to time," Baxter explained.

"What does this woman do when she drops in, Baxter?"

"She cleans and occasionally joins me in bed. She might show up tomorrow. I thought I would put you on the alert."

Monica took another long swig from her brandy mug. "Will this woman get emotional if she finds me here in the morning?"

"She will probably clean around you. I'll put a sign over you that says 'Unscrewed!'"

"Make that read 'Unscrewed at this time!' Baxter."

Baxter settled Monica in front of the fire and padded up the steps to the master bedroom. Was God's Helper waiting for him in the dark? He would just have to take his chance.

Darlene appeared at the side of Baxter's bed in the morning darkness. "Joe, who is the woman downstairs sleeping in front of the fireplace?" Darlene demanded.

Baxter shook his head. Was it a dream? Darlene shook Baxter's shoulder. "Who is the woman downstairs?"

"She's someone from McKenzie Barber. Her name is Monica Graham. I may have mentioned her. We're working against a deadline on a very important project. We decided to work up here," Baxter lied. "She's a very happily married woman." Baxter heard the sound of steps on the staircase. The bedroom door opened and Monica entered the room in her fur coat.

"The fire went out and my back is killing me, Baxter. Move over." Monica placed her coat over a chair and smiled at Darlene. "Good morning, I'm Monica Graham. I work with Mr. Baxter." She extended her hand which Darlene stood and accepted. "And you're—?"

"My name is Darlene."

"Well you're certainly on the job bright and early, Darlene. I'm lucky if my cleaning lady in New York shows up by 9:30. It's got to be that country air." Monica turned to Baxter's clothes chest and after locating tee shirts in the second drawer. "I'm going to brush my teeth and pop into a conventional bed. Don't worry about the noise from the vacuum, Darlene. I'm a very sound sleeper."

Monica left the room with her bag from the all night drug store.

"Joe, I got up very early to see if you had come up. I was so happy when I saw the car. I've missed you so much. And then I found that woman sleeping in front of the fireplace. I want you so much." Darlene delivered a very wet kiss. Baxter pushed her away gently.

"We must be careful," Baxter whispered. "You have a husband waiting for his breakfast."

The bedroom door reopened and Monica reappeared wearing Baxter's tee shirt with her suit, panty hose and shoes in her hands. She folded her suit over a chair placing her panty hose on top of the suit, her shoes at the foot of the chair and the drug store bag on the seat. "Well I'm already for more Z's. Nice to have met you, Darlene. Gangway, Baxter."

Monica ran across the room and jumped into Baxter's bed. She turned her body away from Baxter, closed her eyes, and hugged her pillow. Darlene stood on her feet and left the room without another word. They heard a door slam and a car engine turn over. Monica turned in the bed toward Baxter.

"She forgot to vacuum. Get your warm body, over here. My side of the bed is damned cold."

Monica promptly fell into a deep sleep with periodic snoring. Baxter showered, shaved, quietly dressed himself in a flannel shirt, corduroy trousers and donned his boots. He left Monica a note and retrieved his threat from God's Helper. Baxter decided to pay a call on Sheriff Clowson before shopping at the A & P.

Sheriff Clowson was on the phone as Baxter entered the office. He greeted Baxter with a nod.

"It sounds like kids to me, Mrs. Herrington," Clowson said into the phone. Baxter studied the wanted posters on the wall as the Sheriff talked.

"Of course I'll come out. Luke comes in at ten on Saturday mornings. He likes his wife to fix him breakfast. No, I won't send Luke. I will come myself, Mrs. Herrington. Yes, I will see that there's a report on file for the insurance company. I will make it my first stop this morning, Mrs. Herrington. Now I remember you on Bear Road just past the Scoggins on the right hand side. No, don't pick up the glass until after I get there. I'll bring my camera so you can have some pictures for the insurance company. No, I'd call Harvey's Glass in Painterville. Tell 'em that Sheriff Clowson said it was an emergency. Things will get taken care of, Mrs. Herrington. Count on it. Good-bye."

Sheriff Clowson made notes on a pad and without looking up, addressed Baxter. "What can I do for you this morning, Mr. Baxter?" His face didn't seem particularly friendly. Baxter walked to the desk and produced the threatening note.

"I found this tacked to the back storm door."

The sheriff glanced at the note and handed it back to Baxter.

"The fellow who did this has got you mixed up with Dopman. You still getting calls?"

"Not since summer. I got one call in my voice mail in New York a while back. I have a theory, Sheriff. I believe the first caller has gone away. This is a copy cat who has taken the name of God's Helper. Where number one was a batty nuisance but harmless, number two is more seriously deranged and probably dangerous."

"You can tell all that from studying those letters taped on that paper? You city fellers sure are smart," Sheriff Clowson said shaking his head.

"Sheriff, I have a whacko on my hands who won't go away, and I believe that I have a suspect."

"Who's that?"

"He sits behind that typewriter." Baxter pointed toward Luke Bohlweiser's empty desk.

Sheriff Clowson placed one leg up on the corner of his desk and leaned back in his swivel chair. He took off his glasses and stared incredulously at Baxter.

"Why would Luke do a thing like that? Do you think he's caught on that you've been carrying on with Darlene?"

"Darlene is my housekeeper. I have allowed her to come and go in the house as she sees fit. I've had the caller before I took on Darlene. I believe Luke Bohlwesier stepped in after the first caller went his way."

"What do you want me to do about it, Mr. Baxter?"

"Observe him. Keep an eye on him."

"I've observed Darlene's Chevy in your drive at some pretty odd hours when you're up here. I take it she's learned to clean in the dark."

"Would you mind if I contacted the State Police on this?"

"You can bring in the FBI and the Secret Service too if you like. I'm sure I'm not the only one that's seen Darlene's Chevy in your driveway at odd hours."

"Thank you for your time, Sheriff," Baxter said and started for the door.

"Mr. Baxter, one piece of advice," Sheriff Clowson called after him. "Why don't you list that place of yours with a realtor and get out of here. That house should be a lot easier to sell now. You can buy yourself another country retreat on the Jersey shore or up in the Poconos. I might even be interested myself in making a reasonable offer for your place."

"Sheriff, my country home is not for sale. I'm glad that we've had this talk. I will choose my own methods for dealing with the creep who calls himself God's Helper."

"I'll keep my eye out and come by anytime, Mr. Baxter," Sheriff Clowson called after Baxter as he left the office. He hoped he would enjoy a better reception at the A & P.

Monica was up when Baxter returned. It was shortly after eleven and he found Monica seated at the butcher block kitchen table sipping coffee with a burning cigarette in the saucer next to her cup. She was now wearing a pair of bib overalls over Baxter's tee shirt and had donned a pair of sweat socks. Baxter recognized the overalls as Muffin's and sweat socks of his own. Her hair was wet and there was a towel around her neck.

"Welcome back, Baxter. I thought I'd greet you in something sexy. I found these overalls in one of the other bedrooms. They must be your daughters, because they sure wouldn't fit that housekeeper of yours." She sprang up from the table after Baxter had set down the grocery bags. "I'll bet there's food in there," she said rapidly unpacking the grocery bags.

"As a host, Baxter, you leave a great deal to be desired." Monica placed two pieces of bread in the toaster. "This is to tide me over until you make me a substantial breakfast. This should be followed by a hearty lunch and an elaborate dinner. I've got a hangover and found myself alone in a foodless retreat."

Baxter poured a mug of coffee and began to leaf through the Times. He began with the Business Day section. There was a lead story about interest rates. Baxter then scanned the left hand column Business Digest of today's stories. Four stories from the top was headline that read;

BRIMMER INDUSTRIES CEO DIES IN THAILAND

Company officials announced late Friday that Paul K. Brimmer, 63, Chairman & Chief Executive of Brimmer Industries, died of a stroke in his Bangkok hotel room on Thursday, November 30th, NYSE listed industrial company names wife as Chairman. Story (34) Obituary (26).

"Jesus Christ," Baxter said aloud. "Brimmer died."

"Who's Brimmer?" Monica asked as she carved out cold butter for her toast.

"The man who should have succeeded Ernie Grey as Chairman."

"Brimmer," Monica said with a toast mouth. "He had a company in Atlanta. The last of the 1970 conglomerates," she acknowledged.

Baxter turned to page 34. There were side by side pictures of Paul and Lorna Brimmer.

BRIMMER INDUSTRIES CEO DIES IN THAILAND

Paul Brimmer, Chairman & Chief Executive Officer of Brimmer Industries, a NYSE listed Atlanta headquartered industrial holding company, died of a stroke in Bangkok on Thursday, November 30th, in the midst of an extended Southeast Asia business trip. Brimmer, 63, was succeeded as Chairman by his wife, Lorna. Mrs. Brimmer, Vice Chairman, was elected Chairman in an emergency meeting of the Board of Directors on Friday. Mrs. Brimmer joined Hruska Industries, the predecessor company, in 1979 along with Mr. Brimmer. Previously she was employed with Mr. Brimmer at McKenzie Barber, an international management consulting firm. In a separate action, the Board elected Francis X. Alvardi, a nationally known executive compensation authority and educator, to fill Mrs. Brimmer's board vacancy. Brimmer Industries which reported $3.76 per share through 9-30-89 issued a press release that record earnings were expected for FY 1989. The stock closed at 46 7/8 off 1/8 from Thursday's close.

Baxter turned to the page 24 obituary.

Paul K. Brimmer, 63, CEO, Brimmer Industries Dies in Thailand.

Paul K. Brimmer, the highly respected CEO of Brimmer Industries, an Atlanta headquartered NYSE listed industrial conglomerate, died of a stroke in his luxury hotel room suite in Bangkok on Thursday. Company sources stated that Mr. Brimmer died in his sleep early Thursday morning. He had been on an extended review of Brimmer Industries Southeast Asia subsidiaries.

Mr. Brimmer was a native of Scout's Point, Kansas. He graduated from the University of Kansas, served as a Marine Corps officer, and completed an MBA degree at Northwestern University. Mr. Brimmer joined McKenzie Barber, an international management consulting firm in 1954, was elected a Partner and named Managing Partner of that firm's Chicago Office. He became involved as a consultant to Hruska Industries, a troubled conglomerate in the mid-1970s and was invited by the Board of Directors to replace the founder, and turn the company around. Mr. Brimmer joined Hruska Industries in 1978 along with his wife, Lorna, a former associate at McKenzie Barber. The company returned to profitability after one year, and was renamed Brimmer Industries in 1981. Brimmer Industries, at the time of Mr. Brimmer's death, was a $5 billion revenue industrial conglomerate comprised of 23 companies organized into six sectors. The company has received a number of awards and citations for management excellence over the past several years. Mr. Brimmer had a reputation as a tough, demanding, results-oriented CEO who was totally devoted to his company.

Mr. Brimmer married Lorna King, a McKenzie Barber Associate in 1978. Mrs. Brimmer was elected to the Board of Directors in 1982. Elected Vice Chairman in 1985, Mrs. Brimmer was responsible for shareholder and community relations in recent years.

Private family funeral services will be held in Atlanta on Tuesday.

Monica placed her hand on Baxter's shoulder and read the obituary between chomps of toast. "They sure didn't have much to say about him," she commented.

"He was known only by his company's return on capital employed and share price. He was a total business animal."

"Was his wife a fast track Manager or Director?"

"She was Admin. Her last job was a cross between a controller and a group administrator for the Strategy Practice. She used to be Alvardi's girlfriend. She converted to a Southern socialite. Lorna's an attractive, highly intelligent woman who's probably capable of running Brimmer Industries."

"Is she still Alvardi's girlfriend?"

"I have no idea," Baxter answered although in his heart, he doubted that Lorna had ever ceased being Alvardi's girlfriend.

"You don't have a hair dryer hidden anyplace. I want to look nice for your housekeeper if and when she comes back." Both of Monica's hands were placed on his shoulders.

"I have never owned a hair dryer. Tell me what you want and I'll drive in and get you one," Baxter offered.

"My hair will have to dry stringy. I need you here to make me a breakfast. Now tell me all about this Brimmer character."

"There's not much to tell. I met him briefly on the day I was hired, had a ceremonial lunch with him as I was being promoted to Manager, got an ass-chewing once when I didn't keep him informed on something, sat next to him at a dinner in Atlanta a couple of years back, and arranged for him to meet Harwell privately. He was a cold, distant man who intimidated the people around him to perform. It was assumed that he would follow Bruce Dinsmore as Managing Partner-New York. The Managing Partner-New York would have positioned Brimmer to succeed Harvey Randolph as Deputy Chairman, and Ernie in 1984 as Chairman. Ernie, for some reason, leapfrogged Burke into the New York Managing Partner's job. Everyone expected Brimmer to go to New York and Burke to go to Chicago to prove himself as a Managing Partner. There was a natural order of progression dictated by success, and Ernie disturbed that by placing Burke to the head of the pack."

"Based on our Executive Office review, I placed your friend Burke in the schleeze class," Monica offered. "How would Brimmer have been different?"

"Brimmer would have been a law and order Chairman. He would have taken the politics out of the firm, and replaced it with tough demanding performance standards just as he did with Brimmer Industries."

"I assume you knew Mrs. Brimmer better than Mr. Brimmer." Baxter began to fry the bacon and Monica stood next to him facing the electric frying pan.

"Lorna was a friend. She and Alvardi had a relationship. I was just her drinking buddy. She started out as Clyde Nickerson's secretary, slipped into administration, and became Brimmer's secret girlfriend. This morning she is Chairman of a $5 billion revenue listed company."

"I love to hear success stories like that. It inspires me to work harder. Now if Brimmer had gone on to become Chairman of McKenzie Barber, how would that have affected Joe Baxter?"

"Positively. I did well under him in Chicago. I have to assume that I would have done well under Brimmer in New York. He would have peeled off the Walker Frederick and Clyde Nickersons of the firm and the achievers would have flourished."

"You make it sound like a regular Camelot, Baxter. Would Brimmer still have married Lorna?"

"I have no idea. I have to assume that he would have sooner or later and that Lorna would have been a very good first lady of McKenzie Barber. She's been a very good first lady for Brimmer Industries."

"Would Burke have done better than Pritchard?" Monica posed.

"Yes. I believe we would have settled down half-way through his term. He was young enough to have served two terms as Chairman of McKenzie Barber, and I believe that the 1990-96 period would have been the best in the firm's history."

"Another Camelot with Baxter as an old loyal knight seated two chairs down from the king at round table meetings. You are probably close to being the last of the great Pollyana idealists, Baxter. After breakfast, we can drink to the dear departed, Mr. Brimmer." Monica returned to the table and began to read the first page of the Times. "Let's see how the rest of the living are doing this morning."

Baxter took Monica on a complete tour of the house following breakfast. He took her through the history of the Dopman Brothers to the advent of God's Helper. He included his morning's conversation with Sheriff Clowson.

"My God, Baxter. You're doing the guy's wife. If I were you I'd turn this place over to a realtor and stay in New York until there's a real estate closing. This place is pretty isolated. You're a sitting duck out here."

"I like the isolation. A weekend at this place recharges me for the city. I'm not going to let that little creep run me off. Getting involved with his wife was a mistake. I'm considering getting a new housekeeper and paying Darlene a year's severance."

"Are you going to throw in outplacement too, Baxter?" Monica inspected Baxter's book shelves. "You have thousands of books, 33LPs, cassettes, CDs, and no TV or VCR. This is like a bachelor's pad back in the 1960s. What do you do when you're here? Read, listen to classical music in front of your fireplace, and drink Canadian Club?"

"Something like that. I find the isolation highly desirable."

"Well, I better find myself something to read in order to fit in around here." Monica began to seriously burrow through the book shelves. "Here's a couple that look interesting." She held up Baxter's 1953 Iron Creek Cougar yearbook and his father's copy of *What Means This Strike?* Monica placed the books in front of the fireplace. "I'm going upstairs and get gussied up to the best of my abilities. Be a good host. Stoke up this fire and pour me an after breakfast brandy. Put on some music but no French composers."

Baxter watched Monica vigorously prance up the stairs. He placed the 'Unscrewed at this time' sign on the mantel over the fireplace.

Baxter settled in with Monica on the bear rug with brandy and coffee. She amused herself for a time leafing through his Cougar yearbook. He pointed out Maggie's picture.

"I'll bet she got fat. You look so clean cut and uncorrupted. Here's a tough looking dude. I'll bet he didn't go on to Yale. Who'd think that a McKenzie Barber Partner would come out of this bunch?" Monica said closing the book. "What's your bet on the housekeeper coming back?"

"I believe you spooked her. I doubt whether Darlene will come back as long as she sees a car in the driveway. She'll probably come in before she starts her shift at the Brinker's Falls Inn." Baxter reassured Monica as he slid her overall straps over her shoulders. They shared a soft kiss that was interrupted by the sound of the kitchen door opening. Baxter leaped to his feet while Monica replaced her overall straps. Darlene had arrived with Rob. Baxter greeted them in the kitchen.

"I thought I'd give the place a quick clean. I'll be in and out and I'd like to take my check with me when I leave." Darlene's eyes appeared cold and angry. "I'll try not to inconvenience you from the work you're supposed to be doing." Rob stood pensively with hands behind his back. Baxter placed his hand on the boy's head. "Haven't seen you for a while. You look a lot taller. Want to go to my study and look at my globe. I've got a fellow worker with me who lived in Europe for over a dozen years."

Monica appeared in the kitchen with her hair tried in a pony tail. "Darlene, good to see you again." And bending down to Rob she asked, "And who do we have here?"

"I'm Rob Bohlweiser." Darlene's son extended his hand for Monica.

"We're going into my study and discuss world geography while Mrs. Bohlweiser cleans," Baxter said taking his hand. "How about some hot cocoa?"

Darlene stormed off without another word. "Mom's in a bad mood today," Rob explained with a whisper.

They settled in Baxter's den with Rob self-consciously turning Baxter's globe. Outside they could hear the whir of the vacuum cleaner. "Well Rob, how are things in the Bohlweiser household these days?"

"My Dad's interviewing for a police job up near Rochester next week. I heard my Mom and Dad talking. Sheriff Clowson thinks it's time for my Dad to do something else. I don't want to leave all my friends. I'll be starting sixth grade next year. My Mom's really mad about something. She got up real early and seemed so happy, but she was really mad when she came home from grocery shopping. Do you have children, Mrs. Graham?"

Darlene finished up in about an hour, and Baxter paid her through the end of the year. She had seemed to work out her anger. "When can we expect you up again, Joe?" Darlene asked as Baxter helped her on with her jacket.

"I may be up over Christmas, Darlene."

"And I'm going out of the country with my husband. You have probably seen the last of me, Darlene." Monica extended her hand and kissed Darlene on the cheek. They waved from the car as it slid down the driveway toward the road.

"You don't suppose that Mr. Bohlweiser will be our next visitor?" Monica said after the door was closed.

Baxter poured fresh mugs of coffee, and found Monica stretched out with her overall straps down over her shoulders. "Baxter, this adultery business isn't as easy as it looks. I believe this is where we left off. But I have to tell you that I'm just about out of the mood."

"We could always play scrabble," Baxter offered.

Monica stood up and stepped out of her overalls and pulled her tee shirt over her head. She was down to light blue bikini panties. "Let's go Baxter. We can play scrabble later."

Baxter was awakened on Sunday morning by Monica's kisses. She stroked him until he was firm and then mounted him from a kneeling position. It was over for her quickly and she let her body collapse on top of him. He turned Monica on her stomach and entered her from behind. Her body shook against him for better than a minute. "Jesus, Baxter, we're finally hitting our stride, and it's almost time to go home." Monica slid to the side of the bed and lit a cigarette. "It's damned near nine o'clock. We really should have tried this before. I had no idea how good we'd be together. Now who's better to be with? Linda or me?"

"I have no idea of what you're talking about," Baxter said laying back on the opposite side of the bed. Monica had long legs and rather large feet. She was quite thin with a faint hint of ribs showing. Her breasts were small and resembled inverted 1920s champagne glasses. She had turned out to be a sexual machine once Baxter discovered her ignition.

"This has been very nice. My question is, will we ever be together like this again?"

"I don't think so, Baxter," Monica said shaking her head. "It really wouldn't make much sense. I have a husband to reconciliate with. God knows what you have going. I hope it's more than Darlene, the housekeeper. Let's stay in bed until noon and head back. I saw some champagne in the back of the refrigerator. I'll go down and fix us some champagne and orange juice. It's a great pick-me-up when you're making love. Not as good as champagne and strawberries but a decent substitute. Being with you is better than I have had in a long time. Everything Dominique told me about you is true."

Monica rose to her feet and took a long puff from her cigarette. She blew a long smoke ring in the general direction of Baxter's side of the bed.

"How about some toast?"

"As long as we don't make crumbs in the bed," Baxter cautioned. He watched Monica leave the bedroom. He concluded that she had a magnificent ass. He loved Monica's gracefully curved buttocks.

He stared at the high ceiling of the bedroom. He had lain there with Bridgette, Linda, Darlene, and now Monica. In fifteen minutes at the most, Monica would return, and she would be back in his arms. With luck he could probably stretch out their time until 1PM. Monica would most likely step out of his life. He thought back to a lot of the days they traveled together, and the nights Monica had slipped away alone to her room.

Monica reappeared in an apron with a tray of beer steins of orange liquid and toast buttered and quartered. She placed the tray in the center of the bed. "Well, Baxter," Monica said raising her stein with one hand and pulling back his bed sheet with the other hand. "Here's looking at you."

"Did anyone ever tell you that you were splendid in bed?" Baxter judged on his first sip that there was far more champagne than orange juice in the stein.

Monica took a small bite from her toast square. Her brown eyes seemed trained on him. She followed with another small bite of toast. Monica had sharp teeth. She had scratched his member with her incisor early in the morning. It smarted now as it swelled. She took a long swallow from the stein while Baxter sipped from his.

"This is madness, of course," Monica announced after finishing her piece of toast. "I shouldn't be here with you, and we should have not done what we have done, nor should we do what we're about to do. You represent the best physical relationship I've had in a long time, Baxter. You're an outstanding lover."

"That's the first 'A' grade, I've had in a long time. I suspect that my sexual grade point has been hovering around 2.0. You and I seem to have gotten very comfortable with each other sexually after an apprehensive start. You said earlier that our relationship has no future after today."

"Physical relationship," Monica corrected. "I would hope that we will always be friends."

"How many lovers have you had since you married Erik?" Baxter queried. Monica nibbled on a fresh toast point.

"I was with Erik a long time before I married him," Monica explained. "Which is different from being married. I had a lot of lovers when I was with Erik. After we were married and assumed membership in the bourgeoisie, my dalliances were carefully selected. They generally ran to one, or possibly two, night stands with truly interesting people. I suspect Erik is the same way. His little party of Friday night was probably more to amuse Henri than a permanent desire to be with another woman. I was more angry with myself for finding out about their little escapade than I was in catching him in an indiscretion. I just wanted to give old Joe Baxter a little going away present. How about you, Joe? Were you always faithful to Bridgette?"

"I was once we were married," Baxter affirmed.

"That's not surprising. You've always been kind of a work machine. I used to call you 'the great horse Baxter'. It's an Orwell pun. You just worked and worked and worked for your clients and McKenzie Barber. You must have gotten pretty lonely the last two years to have taken up with Darlene, the housekeeper. I'll let you off the hook on Linda. She's going to eat up that poor cardiologist. Linda will be trying to run up my back after the first year at Bowers Merrin."

"Did she volunteer to come with you?"

"Believe me, Baxter, it was a total coincidence. Linda has been heavily hit by recruiters this last year. Your big bank job was over, and you seemed to lose interest in the practice. We both reached the same conclusion. The great horse Baxter was on his way to becoming the dead horse Baxter."

Baxter took a long swallow from the stein. "You're fairly brutal this morning."

"I've always fancied myself as a pretty politician on the outside, and a hard practical realist on the inside. It was clearly time for the two of us to part company. I believe we are concluding our relationship in an appropriate manner."

"Yeah," Baxter agreed. "With a bang."

Baxter tried his phone mail around one thirty. He was dressed and out of the shower. Monica had remained behind to smoke in the tub with the agreement they would leave within the hour.

"JOE BAXTER. YOU HAVE FIVE NEW MESSAGES."

"Message #1, Saturday, December 2nd, 4AM."

"Joe, this is Erik. Monica is missing. Do you know where she is? I'm quite worried about her. Could you call me? 288-3672."

"Message #2, Saturday, December 2nd, 10:30AM."

"Joe, this is Erik. The people who were at Monica's party said that you left with her for dinner. You appear to be the last one to see Monica. I'm very worried and tempted to report the matter to the police. Would you call me, please? 288-3672."

"Message #3, Saturday, December 2nd, 3:10PM."

"Joe, this is Erik. I have now learned that you had dinner with Monica in the Versailles and left the hotel with her around eleven. Where is she? You must call me. I have tried your home telephone and left a message there. Where is Monica." the voice demanded.

"Message #4, Sunday, December 3rd, 7:15AM."

"Joe, this is Dominique. I have some work in our US subsidiaries that may interest you. Would you call me please? My number is 49-39-26-12. It's a private line. I also understand that Monica has resigned from McKenzie Barber to join a firm that I recognize as our actuarial consultant in the US. I am not familiar with their reputation in compensation consulting. Monica wants to propose on this work. I also understand from Henri that Monica disappeared with you on Friday night and has not been seen since. Did you do something naughty with her? Perhaps you are trying to woo her back through a succession of taxi rides? My little joke. Please call me back."

"Message #5, Sunday, December 3rd, 10:30AM."

"Mr. Baxter, this is Heidi. I've had several calls from Monica's husband this weekend inquiring about her whereabouts. He was rather emotional in my last conversation with him. I believe it would be helpful if you called him after you get this message. His telephone number in New York is 288-3672. I'm truly sorry to bother you on a Sunday and I'm looking forward to working with you on the Executive Office study. Good-bye."

Monica returned to the kitchen with a strong resemblance to the lady he helped out of the cab two days earlier in front of the Versailles.

"Well, Baxter, am I presentable enough for East Side Manhattan?" There were no apparent wrinkles in the blue suit she had slept in on Friday night. Her feet appeared smaller in the blue pumps and she wore a double strand of pearls that Baxter remembered from their Friday evening dinner. Her hair remained pulled back into a pony tail.

"Next time I go away like this with a man, I'm going to make sure he has a hair dryer."

Baxter punched in his phone mail. "Listen, to this please. Your hubby sounds rather concerned and a little threatening."

"Can I erase them?" Monica asked after she heard the first phone mail.

Baxter nodded and Monica worked her way through the messages.

"The son-of-a-bitch has gotten Dominique and poor Heidi involved. It's all his fault. He should have been in Miami." Monica slammed down the phone. "The man has made a colossal ass of himself."

"Let's assume Erik would have been in Miami and Dominique's suite had been empty. What were your plans for me?"

"I was planning to provide you with a little souvenir of my affection. The idea didn't really occur to me until we were served coffee and brandy. I didn't want to end it. Seeing how compatible we are, I expect that we would have spent the night there and I would have shooed you out at first light. Now we have new business at hand, Mr. Baxter. We must select the right lies to tell Erik."

Monica seated herself at the butcherblock table and placed her hands against her ears. After forty-five seconds, her hands returned to the table. "I have it. You call Erik first and explain that you dropped me off at Penn Station and that I was headed off to see someone in Philadelphia. Then I'll call him and tell him that I'm coming back to New York on the 4:30 Metroliner." Monica dialed and handed Baxter the telephone.

"Feel free to improvise but remain true to the plan. You'll hear my voice on the answering machine but Erik will pick up when he hears it's you."

Baxter waited through Monica's voice announcement and said, "Erik, this is Joe," three times in a loud but innocent voice.

"Joe." Erik's voice came on the line. "What have you done with Monica?"

"Absolutely nothing, Erik. We had a dinner at the Versailles after her party. She took the elevator upstairs to get something from the de Hartogue suite. She came down a few minutes later mad as hell about something. She placed a call to someone in Philadelphia from the lobby phone and asked me to drop her at Penn Station. I dropped her off at Penn Station about eleven thirty or so. I'm up at my country place and haven't checked my phone mail until now."

"Did Monica say who she was visiting in Philadelphia, Joe?" Erik probed.

"She didn't say, Erik. Monica was very angry when she returned to the lobby. That's all I can tell you. I'm going to be leaving for the city late afternoon. Please leave me a voice mail when you have more information about Monica."

"I will do that, Joe," Erik said coldly and clicked off.

"That was reasonably good, Baxter. I have decided to call Erik from a pay phone half way into the city. I don't want this to look like a set-up."

Monica made her call from a Burger King off Highway 87. Their entire conversation was conducted in French. He made out the word Philadelphia at least four times in their ten minute conversation. The conversation began in angry tones and softened at the end. Monica closed the conversation in a cheery manner with a smack from her lips."

"What's in Philadelphia?" Baxter asked when they were out on the highway again.

"A man I knew in France many years ago. He's the US MD for a large French company. I see him from time to time. Erik is jealous as hell of him. The mention of his name threw him into a tantrum. You're off the hook and Erik is now very contrite, which is good because we will be traveling extensively together until January."

"Are you in love with Erik?" Baxter asked.

"We co-exist comfortably. We fit together. I don't know about this love stuff. That went out the window when I was in my twenties. For what it's worth, I've always found you a very attractive man. A little straight-laced and quite cheap, but altogether a good fellow. The memory of our little weekend together will stay with me for a long time. It's behind us now."

"And how will you handle Erik this evening?"

"I expect that we will share a bottle of wine, and he will make love to me. Combined with this morning, I will be a very sore lady when I wake up on Monday morning. Think of me tomorrow morning."

Baxter exited on the 63rd Street exit off the FDR and Monica requested that he drop her a two block walk from her apartment. He pulled into a bus stop on Third Avenue and Monica put out her last cigarette. "Well this is the end of it, Baxter. I start my new career at Bowers Merrin in January. I hope we will always be friends. You've taught me a great deal, and I hope I can call on you in the future for help when I need it." Monica pulled up the collar of her mink coat as she prepared to leave the car. Then she leaned forward and kissed Baxter on the cheek. "I've become a highly paid executive compensation consultant. Thanks to McKenzie Barber and you. What else could I have done as well at?" Monica asked leaning into the car after stepping out into the street.

"You might have made one hell of a high priced hooker," Baxter replied.

"Asshole!" Monica shouted back and slammed the car door shut.

Baxter observed Monica as she walked briskly down the street away from the car. She was a fine looking New York lady. He honked as he drove past her. She waved back and blew him a kiss.

9:46 AM, Tuesday, January 8, 1992

The Metroliner was delayed shortly after it departed from the Trenton station. Baxter's car faced the Delaware River. The conductor announced a fifteen minute delay, and Baxter reforecast his arrival time in Philadelphia at 10:30 or so. The black attendant refilled Baxter's plastic coffee cup and cleared his breakfast tray with a comment that it 'shouldn't be long'. His mind had flashed back on that strange weekend with Monica during the Trenton station stop. He really hadn't seen Monica since that wave from the street. She had called him a couple of times primarily for lunch. There was talk of meeting for lunch or drinks but neither specified a meeting date. Baxter thought he saw Monica a couple of times at LaGuardia waiting to board flights. He knew that Monica and Bowers Merrin had been awarded the US de Hartogue work and learned from Dominique that the Bowers Merrin proposal was 40% below McKenzie Barber's fee estimate. Baxter had called Monica on December 1st of 1991, the second anniversary of their weekend together. Her voice mail had flipped over to a secretary.

"I'm trying to reach Monica Graham," Baxter had explained.

"Miss Graham is no longer with Bowers Merrin. Is there someone else who can help you?" the voice asked.

"How about Linda Green?"

"Linda Green is in the Boston office of Bowers Merrin. May I give you the number?" Baxter took the number but didn't get around to calling until a week later. He left a call in Linda Green's phone mail early one morning and received a call back in the mid-afternoon.

"Joe, this is Linda Wachler returning your call." The voice was crisp, cold and professional.

"How's it going, Linda? I see you're using your married name."

"You waited two years to make this call. I'm flattered that you got around to calling me. As you may have noted, I have transferred to the Boston office. Eli made a connection with the Bristol Clinic which has a world class reputation. I am the trailing spouse. We expect our first child in February, and I'm as big as a house. The Boston office is a bit of a backwater for the Exec Comp practice. I seem to spend a lot of time on rather pedestrian deferred Compensation plans. Eli is quite happy and is trying to talk me into staying home after the baby arrives. I miss McKenzie Barber and you, but couldn't bring myself to call you."

"How's Monica doing?"

"Joe, I know you called me because they told you in New York that Monica has left Bowers Merrin. Don't play any of your Baxter games with me. Monica and Erik went back to France. I heard that she was trying to hook on with de Hartogue at the holding company level." There was a silence on Linda's end of the line. Baxter waited it out. "Monica was a flop at Bowers Merrin, Joe. The only work she could get was from de Hartogue, and she had to cut fees to get it. Monica sold Rob Moreland on all the business that she was going to bring over from McKenzie Barber. The only work she really brought in was from the foreign banks at a deep discount in pricing. Monica negotiated a lot of money coming in, with a huge guaranteed first year bonus. We hit about a third of our first year target revenues. I asked for a transfer because I didn't want to be tainted as Monica's protégé. She said it was her decision but I'm certain she was counseled out last April. She and Erik left for Paris last August."

"Well, best wishes for an easy delivery and a grand motherhood, Linda."

"I'm going to take some time off after the baby, and I plan a long visit with my mother in Long Island. I'll be down in June for sure. I'd like to hear all about the merger and see you again, Joe."

"I'll await your call," Baxter said and hung up. It always made him feel good when people who left him failed.

Baxter stared out at the sign on the bridge. It was like an old friend he nodded to on each pilgrimage to Philadelphia.

TRENTON MAKES, THE WORLD TAKES

At one time the sign must have been close to true. Trenton had been a major manufacturing town through the 1940s. Now it was a dilapidated city representing a midway stop before the 30th Street Station in Philadelphia. At one time McKenzie Barber had been the world's leading management consulting firm, and now it had been swallowed up by Robson Allen and was now called Robson Barber.

The merger with Robson Allen haunted Baxter. IPCO had held a black tie retirement dinner for Ernie Grey in mid-December of 1991. Baxter had received an invitation. He suspected that Toni had engineered his name on the invitation list. Baxter had planned to attend, but canceled when he learned of Diane Ganski's death. He decided to make one of his final trips to Iron Creek, and confront Ernie Grey another time on the unfortunate legacy he had left behind at McKenzie Barber. People around him appeared to be dying right and left. Now it was too late.

Baxter sipped his coffee, stared at the sign and recounted the two year period that separated that last week in November when the firm began to unravel. Business picked up for Baxter's New York Office Exec Comp practice in January of 1990. Baxter had the cushion of the Executive Office review to absorb expenses, and a stream of new business. He did not replace Monica and Linda but accepted junior consultants from Dilger's Benefits Practice. Bob Dilger was elated that Baxter had at last accepted his fate to be combined with the Benefits practice and wrote a memo to Pinker lauding Joe Baxter's sense of teamwork in this time of reorganization and consolidation. Baxter knew there was a clock running on his further tenure with McKenzie Barber and was fashioning his personal escape route. His major objective was to avoid a unit cut in the fall of 1990, which would affect his retirement play in the spring of 1992. His plan, regrettably, had been based on the continuity of McKenzie Barber as a separate entity.

Baxter knew what Fitzgerald and Pinker wanted from their Executive Office review. Their objective was a general discrediting of the people and jobs they identified as redundant. A project plan had been developed and approved by the afternoon of December 4th. Baxter began the review with an initial meeting with Clyde Nickerson to review the structure of Executive Office in the Pritchard Administration.

Baxter drafted up a memorandum for review by Pinker and signature by Pritchard, advising Nickerson of the review's objectives and three, two-hour time period during the weeks of December 2-8 and December 11-15 were scheduled as available dates when Baxter would be available to meet.

Nickerson responded through a secretary that he would meet with Baxter from 8:00 AM until 10:00 AM on Friday, December 8th, in the Lex level conference room. It was assumed that Baxter would come alone, and their meeting would be between Partners.

In his thirteenth year in the New York Office, Baxter could only remember visiting the Lexington Avenue level three times. His first experience was related to Walker Frederick calling what was termed an emergency meeting of New York Office Human Resource consulting Partners and was unable to book an upper floor conference room. Alvardi passed the memo to Baxter saying, "It is not my policy to attend meetings at the Lex level. You better go, kid."

Baxter had found himself in a bare room with folding chairs, five actuaries and Dilger, with Walker presiding with a pointer. The subject had been practice synergy. The second time had been several years back before the advent of word processing. The report section had been repeatedly late and the supervisor had been rude to Marveen. He was a late fifties martinet who had referred to Baxter early in their confederation as "Baxter". His name tag had read 'John' and he had referred to Marveen as 'this colored woman here'.

"I'm Mr. Baxter, John, and this is Miss Scott. Let me hear you say the names aloud. I suspect that you may have a hearing and speaking problem that's standing in the way of you doing your job. If you are unable to listen and speak, the firm should find you another less demanding job." John was a short, heavy set Italian who suddenly became obedient, servile, and complaining about his lack of staff and proper equipment.

"You would have made one hell of a Second Lieutenant," Marveen had commented in the returning elevator.

It was now December of 1989. Baxter wasn't certain of the mission of the Lex level. Time sheet data was inputted at the local office level to the Lex level, and sooner or later CARS reports were processed and slowly distributed back to the local offices. The Lex level was a place where health insurance claims and other pieces of paper were sent. From time to time there was an announcement of a firm-wide automated support system which would include automatic client billing. The Partners would rise in rebellion over the prospect of an alien group directly billing their clients, and the firm-wide automated support service was withdrawn for further customization. McKenzie Barber's Lex level represented to Baxter the last of the world's established protected bureaucracies. Pieces were chipped away from time to time, but no one had either taken the time nor had the inclination to dig into its core.

The Lex level had a uniformed desk guard, in contrast to the receptionists on upstairs floors. Baxter presented himself to the desk guard at 7:55 AM and was asked for ID. He was asked to sign in, and was escorted by another uniformed guard through a maze of rabbit warren-like offices to what Baxter estimated as the Lexington Avenue wall. The guard knocked on the door to conference room N and opened the door to Clyde Nickerson seated at a large oval table in a small room.

"Come in, Joe," Nickerson said without getting up. "Lyle," he addressed the uniformed guard. "Let's hurry up with that coffee. Be sure to bring two cups."

The guard closed the door and Baxter seated himself on a folding chair across from Nickerson in a swivel chair. There was a phone on a stand and some posters that Baxter recognized as standard items offered by lower Broadway art shops.

"This is my Elba, Joe. I was moved here in the evening of November 30th, after I was informed that I would be retiring Wednesday evening. What do you think of it?"

"It looks very cozy, Clyde," Baxter said slipping off his jacket and producing a legal pad for notes.

"You certainly represent an odd choice to conduct a review of Executive Office. I remember that you skipped the Lex level last time. When was it again?"

"1983. Burke was the administrative client."

"Another one of Ernie Grey's mistakes," Nickerson commented. "What's Burke doing now? Did he ever find a job?"

"I don't think he needs a job financially, Clyde. He'll probably go on to Burke Farms when his father dies."

"Burke's father will probably outlive Burke, you and me." There was a knock at the door and Lyle returned with the coffee.

"Milk, I like milk with my coffee in the morning," Clyde protested. "Get me some milk, Lyle."

"Yes sir," Lyle said and departed.

"When did we get uniformed guards at the Lex level, Clyde?"

"It was Brett's idea, and a good one. We were going to place them on every floor by the end of February. Brett believed the security at the New York office was unbelievably poor."

"Well Clyde, I know our time is short," Baxter began. "This is what I'd like to cover this morning." Baxter handed the twelve point, one page agenda across the table to Nickerson. He observed Nickerson scanning the page from top to bottom twice.

"This is more than two hours time. All I can give you is two hours. I'm not going to start until Lyle is back where with the milk. This firm is full of rumors right now."

"I would assume that Lyle's code of conduct, as a uniformed guard, precludes him from repeating snatches of conversation overheard in conference rooms."

Clyde picked up the agenda and scanned it again. "I see Brimmer died a few weeks back. Did you catch it in the Times?"

"It also ran in the *Wall Street Journal*. Brimmer's obituary was run in all of the national and international business press."

"Did you attend the funeral?" Nickerson asked.

"No. The Times stated that it would be a private family service," Baxter responded.

"I wonder what kind of a family Brimmer had? He had to be in his mid-60's and didn't marry until he was in his fifties. They didn't have children, did they?"

"Paul Brimmer was a very private man, Clyde."

"Tell me about it. Ernie sent me out to Chicago to work for the man. He married my old secretary, Lorna. There he was, the Managing Partner of McKenzie Barber's #2 office, a man who was on the Chairman ladder at McKenzie Barber, and he took up with an ambitious admin. Brimmer should have gone to New York as Managing Partner in 1978. He would have been Chairman in 1984, and this firm would be in a lot better shape today."

"Clyde, are you saying that Brimmer was more qualified to be Chairman than Ross Pritchard?" Baxter teased.

Lyle humbly re-entered the room with a small carton of milk. Baxter feared that Nickerson would demand a pitcher. Nickerson added a liberal milk splash in his coffee and waited for Lyle to exit. "Thank you, that will be all, Lyle," Clyde said with finality. Baxter wondered if the Nickersons had ever kept slaves.

"Paul Brimmer should have been Chairman of McKenzie Barber," Clyde snapped back after the door had closed behind Lyle. "He was qualified, and he was ready. One last seasoning step as Managing Partner of the New York Office, and Brimmer would have succeeded Harvey as Deputy Chairman in 1982, and Ernie as Chairman in 1984. This firm would have run like a top, as did Brimmer Industries. Paul Brimmer was a natural born CEO. Then he got involved with Lorna. She used to be my secretary, you know. She sang on weekends at some Mafia financed dinner Theatre. I took a risk when I hired her. Lorna's typing skills were sub-par but she was smart and attractive. Lorna made her share of sexual overtures to me. But I was a loyal married man. Frank Alvardi began to court Lorna. I could see the electricity between them. I cautioned Lorna about getting involved with a man like Alvardi. That was about the time that Brimmer needed a personal administrator. He had that fast talking Jewish girl for recruiting, but needed someone well organized and methodical to handle personnel administration. I had to talk to Brimmer into taking her. He kept objecting that Lorna wasn't a college graduate. Now she's the CEO of Brimmer and worth zillions. Joe, there was no comparison in qualifications between Paul Brimmer and Ross Pritchard, but Ernie had placed Brimmer in a position where he had no other choice than to accept that he had lost his place in line or resign. Brimmer pretended to go along with it but resigned when Hrsuka Industries came along. Sure he had some risk, but he made a go of it. What did McKenzie Barber have left? Burke! Burke, the extravagant buyer of risky consulting firms! McKenzie Barber was on the precipice of big trouble in 1984. A bunch of us senior Partners began to talk. If left alone, Burke could sink McKenzie Barber. We couldn't close the books on time one year. You were on a special task force that time, too."

"There was Pritchard standing in the wings. He had turned around FSO. I had helped pick him. More and more of the heavy unit Partners around the firm began to have real confidence issues in supporting Burke. They didn't trust him. We made a pact in blood to find another choice. We met one Saturday at the Newark Airport Hilton. It was a little like a private political convention. It was by invitation only, and nearly 100 Partners showed up. The group came together, debated heatedly, listened to speeches and at the end of the day, it was decided to support Ross Pritchard and Neil Schmidt." Nickerson paused to sip his coffee and Baxter stared at his blank legal pad. He wondered when Clyde would say something worth writing down.

"They looked to me to be the organizer," Clyde shrugged his shoulders. "No one else was really considered. Ross explained to the group that if he was going to run for Chairman, he would need me full time. So like Paul Brimmer, I put my career at risk, left my wife and family, and took and office down the hall from Ross at FSO."

"I'll bet you took a copy of the Partner's unit run with you too," Baxter commented and drew a smile from Nickerson.

"That campaign was the best piece of work I've ever done. I managed it, and got Ross Pritchard elected Chairman. We caught Burke with his pants down. He was dead when Ernie refused to support him."

"Clyde, there was always a question about outside counsel's objectivity in counting the votes."

"That's bullshit, Joe. Each side had a ballot review representative. Burke put up Walker Frederick, and we had Floyd Piper. We knew that Burke had been sleeping on and off with Angus Windom's wife. If Burke was sensitive about Windom's independence, all he had to do was come forward and request another Wellington Barr Partner. Burke's mistakes cost him the election. It wasn't a result of any ballot count rigging."

"And look what the hell has happened to the firm," Baxter pointed out.

"The US firm is turning around. Brett Williamson should have been elected Ross's successor next year. But you chose to torpedo him. Brett was the real reason FSO got turned around. Ross liked to take the bows, but Brett took the hills and won the battles. I'll admit the guy had some flaws, but Brett represented the General Patton this firm needed to get things back on track. Ross was more the George Marshall type."

"Wasn't Neil Schmidt supposed to be involved someplace in the executive office process?" Baxter probed.

"His wife was ill. It was difficult for Neil to travel."

"That is bullshit, Clyde. Admit it."

"Are we here to do a post mortem on the Ross Pritchard administration? I believe your agenda with me has to do with a review of executive office organization. Let's get on with it." Clyde made an exaggerated look at his wrist watch.

"I'm ready to get on with it, Clyde," Baxter said firmly. "But there are two subjects where I'd like to gain your perspective. As I understand it you will be retiring effective December 31st, and this is probably the last time we will have this opportunity to talk openly. You have been with McKenzie Barber for some twenty-eight years, and I have been with the firm for twenty-two years. We have never liked one another. Please level with me on two issues."

"You tell me the issues and I'll decide whether you deserve any response," Clyde answered.

"Issue number one: How could you support a sick deviant like Williamson for so long? Issue number two: Why did Neil Schmidt delegate his Deputy Chairman responsibilities to you? Nobody elected you to that job, and somehow you've held it for the last four years."

Nickerson stared coldly at Baxter for at least a minute. He calmly poured himself a second cup from the thermos container and slowly added milk.

"At first, Joe, I didn't think we had a serious problem with Brett. He made an advance on Andy several years ago after the firm Christmas party.

302

I heard a few stories about him when I was at FSO that summer of 1984. Brett traveled about half the time. On the days he came into the office, Brett would arrive very early, generally about 6:30 AM. His staff meetings were scheduled for 7:00 AM. Then he would work intensely until half past twelve. Brett would then leave the office and generally returned after four. Then he would work until eleven and be back in at 6:30 AM. I mentioned to Ross about Brett's hours and he just shrugged it off as the way Brett worked. The guy worked intensely, and he was always pushing people to do things. One day I took a drive about the same time Brett left. I followed him to a strange little motel across the street from a strip mall. There was a woman waiting for him by the side of a car. They went inside a room together."

"Brett went out of town the next day. But I followed him again the following day. This time two women emerged from a pick-up truck in shorts and high white boots. They joined him in the same motel room. I took down the number. It was 106. I called on someone in New York who was capable of obtaining information delicately."

"I learned that Brett rented the room by the month under the name, William Brett. I thought that this kind of intelligence would be helpful at some future time. So I arranged for someone to quietly and regularly take pictures. I had quite a collection of pictures accumulated by the time I returned to New York. Some of them included faces of women I had seen at FSO. A lot of the women in the pictures looked like prostitutes. Our outside source confirmed that several of the women were prostitutes. There was one confounding fact. Every now and then Brett would entertain one of the FSO women at the same time with a prostitute. It was a dark side of the world to a family man like me."

"After the election and the confirmation of Brett as Ross Pritchard's successor as President of FSO, I took Brett aside and I shared with him my picture collection. He was taken back a little at first, but admitted that he was impressed that we were able to develop that kind of information. Brett referred to the hotel meetings as his 'afternoon recreation period'. I warned him that sooner or later a scandal would develop that would embarrass the firm. After we had that meeting, Brett Williamson began to take me seriously. Brett and I developed an understanding. Ross was only going to be a one-term chairman. Brett was one of those up-and-comers who would be a candidate for Chairman in 1990. He wanted it. The challenge was for him to keep his zipper under control."

"Who would have been Deputy Chairman under Williamson, Clyde?" Baxter finally interjected.

"I would. My retirement would have been deferred until 1993. By then we would have completed the reorganization of the firm and I could retire in peace."

"And Neil Schmidt?"

"Early on, it became apparent that Neil really didn't want to change the firm. Rather, he wanted it regressed back to the 1970s. We fought with him for two years and he simply quit coming to Operating Committee meetings. Neil decided that he would be Atlanta Office Managing Partner again and keep the Deputy Chairman title. Harley Dimon resigned after we quieted down the Bonnie Grow matter back in the spring of 1988. He took a swing at Brett after the Operating Committee in Washington. They were in the Men's room of the Four Seasons. Neil wanted to know why? My severance agreement with Harley Dimon stipulated complete silence. Neil wouldn't accept that. I was trying to keep the firm moving forward under Brett, and these fools were all upset over a matter that had been put to bed. All because this Grow girl had been naive or brazen enough to go to Brett's room. Neil had been pressing Ross to bring Harley back and had gotten some Atlanta attorneys involved. Then you came in with that woman's letter of resignation and those pictures. That was that last straw for Ross 'Buzzsaw' Pritchard. And that's why we're here this morning in this Lex level conference room."

Baxter took a deep breath. "Thank you, Clyde. I appreciate your candor. I believe we had better get back on the agenda."

They talked until close to noon. Baxter's early conclusion was that Executive Office had become very bloated with marketing and planning specialists who had been recruited to McKenzie Barber to assist the new practice initiatives in Government, Healthcare, and Education.

"The vision for our internal diversification came from Ross," Nickerson explained. "Schmidt started to balk about implementation. Ross asked me to step in and implement. It called for me to use my human resources and organizational skills. Ross told me in the Spring of 1987 to 'get it fixed'. I began to juggle people around. It became obvious that Floyd Piper wasn't going to get it done for us in New York. I then convinced Ross to replace him with McMasters. After a year of McMasters in New York, it became apparent that we were not making the rate of progress that was required. That was when I engineered Brett's move to New York and McMasters as Brett's replacement at FSO. Everything was beginning to work in place. Brett appeared to have dropped his 'afternoon recreation periods' and was working sixteen hour days. Then we had your little sally and here we are."

Baxter wondered if this was the way Rasputin had handled the Romanovs. It was likely that there was more prayer involved. Nickerson was especially down on Roger White, the Chief Financial Officer. "Roger is incompetent. He was incompetent at FSO and he's big league incompetent as CFO for the firm. I shared my views with Ross and later, the Operating Committee. Ross's solution was to place Roger on the Operating Committee and hire a controller from one of the CPA firms. He would not move on Roger. A lot of it I suspect is related to Ross's congressional run in the fall of 1990. Roger is very active in a number of Afro-American business groups, and probably could deliver some Democratic votes over in New Jersey."

Nickerson went down the line on senior staff, which he claimed were Buzzsaw Pritchard's picks. Lastly, Nickerson extended his best wishes to the proposed new leadership team of Fitzgerald and Pinker. "I plan to drop them each a note and offer my best wishes and assistance. They are unlikely to make much of a difference. We really should have stuck with Brett."

"This has been very helpful, Clyde," Baxter said closing up his legal pad with a single page of notes. He rose to his feet, shook hands with Clyde Nickerson, and departed from the conference room. How, he asked himself, had this man been allowed to acquire power in a firm with the stature of McKenzie Barber.

Baxter left the building through the Lex level exit on 50th Street. He wandered up 50th Street without an overcoat across Park Avenue to Fifth Avenue. New York City was showing its Christmas face complete with decorations and ringing Salvation Army bells. How had a firm with so much talent accepted such mediocre leadership? Would Burke have done better? He moved through the streets in long strides turning east on 53rd Street and moving South on Park Avenue to the 311 Building. Baxter aggressively climbed the cement steps to the patio. McKenzie Barber evil and incompetent leadership had been at last shrugged off. It was time for

Joe Baxter, as a McKenzie Barber Partner, to step forward and do his part to salvage the firm. He owed it to John McKenzie.

The review was completed quickly with a final report delivered to Fitzgerald and Pinker on March 2nd. Executive Office was demoralized with the rapid and unexpected exit of Clyde Nickerson. The senior staff recognized their vulnerability and offered little resistance. They saw themselves suddenly at risk and talked openly. Each department pointed their finger at the other and shared previously undisclosed performance flaws and other indiscretions of their sister functions and departments. Most fingers were pointed toward Roger White's financial organization. Roger had been the most evasive in meeting arrangements and represented the second to the last of Clyde Nickerson's direct reports. Baxter early on decided that he would save Lee Heller for last.

Heidi had turned out to be an ideal support consultant. She took copious notes in meetings, spoke in meetings only when she required clarification, produced a summary document at the conclusion of each day's work.

"This is what I came to McKenzie Barber to do," she announced at the conclusion of a 7:30 PM end of a February day.

"To review Executive Office?" Baxter kidded.

"Not just to review Executive Office but to consult, Joe," she said very seriously.

Heidi had completed the transition from calling him 'Mr. Baxter' to 'Joe' just a week earlier. "This is real consulting. Meeting client personnel, gathering facts, developing conclusions, making recommendations. I love this work, Joe. And it's a privilege to work with you. I would hope that we can continue to work together like this. I believe I can develop into an effective senior associate for you." Heidi sat erectly across the desk from Baxter, a tall, plain, intelligent woman, who wore flat shoes. Baxter and Heidi had just reviewed the day's summary notes. She had placed her glasses down on the corner of Baxter's desk. "I'm just amazed at how much work you get done each day," Heidi continued. "This study is just one of several where you are actively involved. You use people, stretch them, challenge them, and they become stronger by working with you. This meeting with Mr. White tomorrow appears to be the link that will bring everything together."

"Just bear in mind, Heidi, that we're looking at organization, and we're not auditors. It's been a long day and we better get out of this place." Baxter made an exaggerated look at his watch and rose up from his desk indicating that their meeting was concluded. Heidi put her glasses back on and rose from the side chair. "I'm going to catch some supper down the street, Joe. Would you care to join me?" she asked.

"I really can't," Baxter responded. "I have some personal matters to take care of."

Heidi nodded her head and left Baxter's office. If it would have been Monica, or some 26 year old woman MBA with nice legs, Baxter would have suggested a drink. The divorce with Bridgette was now final, and Baxter had become an officially divorced lonely man. The only physical relationship left in his life was Darlene, his housekeeper.

Roger White had taken on weight since the days of the 1973 FSO review. He estimated Roger at 275 pounds distributed over his six foot one frame. Roger wore thin wire glasses and his hair was now completely grey. He occupied an executive window office three doors down from the Chairman.

He waved Baxter and Heidi to a circular table across from a large littered main desk. Roger wore an unbuttoned dark vest and his tie was loosened at eight in the morning.

"I'm sorry I've been so hard to get with, Joe. It's just been frantic around here since December. We've been tied up with first quarter reporting and Glen and Jack have some strong opinions about reserves. Now, who is this young lady again?" he nodded in Heidi's direction.

"Heidi Klein is a consultant in my practice who is assisting me in this study. She is the only consultant involved with this project and her confidentiality is unquestioned," Baxter explained.

"I understand from Jack that this is an organization review not a financial review." Turning to Heidi, Roger said, "Joe and I once did a review of FSO back in the early 70's. They asked me to stay."

"Joe informed me that FSO was a rather sweeping review involving quite a number of consultants," Heidi responded.

"Yes indeed, young lady. We had a good many people on that review and Joe was the leader." Roger rose up from his chair and pulled a letter size manila folder from the corner of his desk. He opened the folder to a three page set of organization charts. "I guess we can wrap up this meeting in a hurry if you're just here to look at people." Roger placed his gold pen on the top box of the first chart.

"Roger, we can look at the boxes a little later. We want to start with the Executive Office budgets. We want to start with FY '88 and then review FY '89, and FY '90."

"I've already provided that material to Jack. Why would you want to review it?"

"Because it's in the scope of our assignment. We've begun every functional review with mission statements and budgets. A lot of functions had neither, Roger. We want to see how the plans flow together. So let's start there."

"Have you been keeping Jack up to speed on your study?" Roger closed the folder on the organization charts.

"We provide a weekly report to Jack," Baxter lied. Actually Pinker had Baxter's calls returned through his secretary. He was instructed to prepare bi-weekly one page progress memorandums and under no circumstances should his final report be made no later than March 31st.

Roger rocked in his chair a little and made a clucking noise as he tapped his gold pen against the closed folder.

"Clyde Nickerson was not an easy person to work for, Joe," Roger began. "I came up here to be Chief Financial Officer of the firm at General Pritchard's request. I would have been content to stay down at FSO and work for Brett. The General and I have always worked well with each other. Brett was a different kind of person. The General was a gentleman. Brett could be outright abusive. But I always knew where I stood with him. I came up here as part of the Ross Pritchard/Neil Schmidt team and wound up working for Clyde Nickerson. The man could be as nice as peach pie

308

one day and mean as a snake the next. Clyde liked moving budgets that fit his mood. I had to fix a lot of the numbers to fit his ends."

"Clyde was awful close to General Pritchard. The General had a vision for the firm, and Clyde Nickerson pushed anyone out of the way who didn't support the General's vision. Neil Schmidt tried to stand up to Clyde, but the General would back Clyde every time. He said that the General's vision for McKenzie Barber was the right one, and the vision needed support. I tried to get to the general and one day Brett, when he was still running FSO, came by my office and told me 'to get with the program'. I used to make the numbers work for Brett back at FSO. Meanwhile I could see the ship taking on water. I went to General Pritchard and told what I believed was going on. He listened and told me to hire a new Controller, Phil Zufio, the old controller got the blame for all of the problems in the financials. It was like starting all over again but numbers weren't as good as everyone expected. That's when they brought McMasters in to run New York."

"Let's go through the budgets, Roger," Baxter said firmly. Two hours later, Baxter concluded that he had uncovered a case of management fraud.

Lee Heller was last on Baxter's list. His hair remained jet black which Baxter suspected was attributable to a hair treatment formula.

"Well, Joe, we meet again during times of change," Lee greeted Baxter from his Director size office in the far corner of the 38th floor. Predictably Baxter spotted Heidi's personnel file on the corner of Lee's desk.

This is Heidi Klein, my associate on the Exec Office review."

"I remember recruiting Heidi from Columbia B school. She had an impressive early career in psychiatric nursing," Heller said motioning them to take a seat at a small circular table positioned close to his desk. Baxter observed that Heller's office really wasn't that large enough to hold both a table and a desk.

"How did you happen to pick Heidi to work with you on this project? I understand you've had some recent turnover in your department."

"I believed Ms. Klein's prior experience with aberrant behavior would be useful in the review of executive office organization."

Heller responded with a nervous laugh. "You must remember, Heidi, that Joe and I go back a long while and we have our little jokes between us." They filled themselves within the narrow table space around Heller.

"Obviously everything is in a state of uproar with all of the changes. I suddenly lost a boss and a mentor. Jack Pinker called me in January and said there was a hiring freeze on. I have continued visitations to business schools, but we're going to have to start making offers in April 1 if we're going to compete in the top schools MBA market. I understand that your report is due the final week in March. As you can see, I'm swamped. Clyde always took a special interest in my job. I was his successor, you know. He regarded my function as the lifeblood of McKenzie Barber. Tell me, Joe, did you meet with Clyde during the course of your review?"

"We had a lengthy chat in mid-December."

"It all came so suddenly. Brett Williamson's health going, and Clyde retiring. Now it appears that Buzzsaw is allowing Fitzgerald and Pinker to take over the firm. I know that Clyde had turned down Fitzgerald in a campus interview when he was coming out of some Big Ten business school. They say that he never got over it. Then Gene English hired him as a direct admission IT Partner. Now it looks as though he's a serious Chairman candidate. What's your fix, Joe?"

Baxter shrugged his shoulders. "The facts are, Lee, that Ross Pritchard has stated that he will not serve another term as Chairman. Clyde Nickerson has retired. Brett Williamson's health would not permit him to continue his duties. Therefore those jobs have to be filled. Fitzgerald has been appointed by the Operating Committee as New York Office Managing Partner and Pinker has been named Partner-in-Charge of firm-wide administration. The two are likely to be supported by the Partners as a Chairman/Deputy Chairman team in the October 1990 elections. Jack Pinker wanted a quick review of Executive Office, and asked me to do it because I did the last one in 1983."

"Well, Joe, whatever team is put in place, count on my undivided loyalty. Like you, I'm a career McKenzie Barber man."

Baxter began to go through his check list of human resources functions. Over his twelve year tenure in the New York Office, he had never had a performance appraisal. Rather he had submitted a plan and was apparently evaluated against the plan. He hadn't seen a unit increase since Burke's last year in 1984. "How's the Partner Appraisal system?" Baxter asked.

"It's still in place, Joe. Originally developed by Clyde and fined tuned every other year. It's far superior to Robson Allen's system. We still have corporations around the world visit us to review our system."

"Take us through the Partner appraisal process, Lee."

"Listen to this guy," Heller looked toward Heidi. "He's been a user in the system for fifteen or sixteen years. It's not unlike the professional staff performance plan that you're familiar with, Heidi," Heller explained. "Each Partner like Joe, here, prepares an annual plan of personal and financial goals. He reviews it for approval with his Group Partner for final negotiation. Then each signs the document and it's forwarded to the Managing Partner for final review. These goals are established by firm policy no later than September 1st of each year. There is a mid-year review between the Group Partner and Partner, and any major difference of opinion on goal achievement is immediately communicated to the Managing Partner. Then, in August of each year, performance against plan is again reviewed and unit adjustments are recommended for the coming fiscal year. After yearend, when performance has been confirmed, the unit adjustments are acted on. Meanwhile a new performance plan for the coming fiscal year has been established and will go through the performance review process. On the basis of the system, we can closely monitor our business results, and build a manpower plan that will ensure continuity of the firm's leadership."

Heller provided Heidi a little condescending smile. "It's not my system. Clyde Nickerson designed it under a mandate from Ernie Grey, a former Chairman of the firm. I am but the keeper of the flame."

"Where are all of the performance plans stored, Lee?" Baxter queried.

"In a lot of places, Joe. One copy is in the Managing Partner's confidential Partners file. The Group Partner has a copy and the individual Partner has a copy."

"Does your department receive a copy?" Baxter probed.

"No, but we can obtain a copy of any Partner's file by a request to the office of the Managing Partner."

"And what evidence do you have that all of these performance reviews have taken place?"

"We receive a document from the Office Managing Partner indicating that each Partner has been reviewed and that fiscal goals are in agreement. We do receive a hard copy on all management group and professional staff reviews firm wide. Administrative staff reviews are conducted and maintained at the local office level. We only receive copies of reviews on administrative personnel with 'less-than-expected' ratings."

"Do you have an audit process to ensure that Managing Partners are in compliance with firm policy?" Baxter continued his probing.

"It's informal. My secretary has a very good rapport with the Managing Partner's secretaries around the country. Her relationships represent our best form of audit."

"For fun, this morning, Lee, let's get my evaluation form up here," Baxter requested.

"Why would we do that, Joe? I'm sure that you have a copy of your review in your personnel files."

"Lee, I've been a New York Office Partner since 1978, and I've never signed a performance review. All of my conferences with my succession of New York Office Managing Partners have been related to business plan presentation and achievement. I have never filled out a Partner's Appraisal form, and obviously I haven't signed one."

"Joe, it sounds as though you have had your review and some minor documentation has been skipped."

"Let's call New York Office and get my files up here. Send your secretary down to get my performance appraisal forms."

"You may have been a special case, Joe," Heller responded evasively.

"Well, let's review my special case."

Heller dispatched his secretary to pick up Baxter's Partner's Appraisal files. They went on to review the Benefits Plan administration.

Heller's secretary, an early thirties brunette, who was referred to as Sandy, returned with a large brown folder headed Joseph Baxter, Jr. "Well, Joe. These look like those files that you've had no knowledge of." Heller opened up the jacket and held up a form. "Your signature is on this one." Baxter accepted the folder and scanned a FY 1989 Appraisal form. The form admitted several shortcomings in performance. The signature on the form was not his. "Let's see the rest of the forms, Lee." Baxter went through each annual appraisal form. They dated back to 1985 and each one was signed with a forged 'Joseph Baxter, Jr.' signature.

"Lee, you must have a document in your immediate files that is signed by Clyde Nickerson. Please let me see one," Baxter requested.

"Why, Joe?"

"Because I didn't sign these forms. They represent forgeries. I suspect that we have other similar incidences of forgery. I believe we will require a more complete review of these appraisal forms."

"Joe, no one other than the Managing Partner has access to these files. I'm sure that this is a little administrative foul-up where a secretary signed a form to insure that compliance dates were observed."

"Lee, I suspect that we have a deeper form of corruption here. I want to conduct an audit of performance review practices. Let's get Pinker on the line."

Heidi and Baxter spent two evenings until eleven o'clock reviewing a sampling of Partner's Appraisal forms. Baxter concluded that there were approximately twenty Partner's signatures forged on the forms. The evidence against Clyde Nickerson was reasonably damning. Each Partner had a recent record which reflected declining trends of performance. Baxter reckoned that conversations had taken place between the Managing Partners relative to business plan development and achievement. Under-performance was probably noted in these conversations. Nickerson had gone one step further in forging names on his beloved Partner's Appraisal forms. Baxter considered it a major find in his study. A brutal informal system of Partner evaluation was definitely in place, but only a small amount of offices were in compliance with the documentation policies of the firm. The forged signatures appeared to be a ploy to support the negotiation of favorable severance terms. It was apparent that Clyde Nickerson had been building documentation to get rid of Baxter since 1985.

He met with Fitzgerald and Pinker on March 23rd. Heidi was excluded from the meeting by mutual agreement. Baxter had delivered draft flip chart reports the previous day, and appeared at the New York Office Managing Partner's door at five minutes before four. Fitzgerald had brought his secretary in from Chicago. She was a woman who appeared to be in her late twenties. Her name was Bernice, but she went by "Bernie". Her phone voice was bubbly and vivacious but in person Baxter observed strong traits of insincerity. He concluded that Bernie would make an ideal Managing Partner's secretary if she could hold her confidences in the ladies room. Today she greeted Baxter standing in front of the closed door to the inner office.

"I'm afraid that Glen and Jack are running long, Joe."

"Should I come back?" Baxter offered.

"It shouldn't be that long. Why don't you take a seat and I'll pour you a coffee." Bernie was long-legged in a red pants suit and dark pumps. Baxter's eyes followed her as she moved across the room to pour Baxter's coffee from the silver urn near the window of the Managing Partner's anteroom. "Cream and sugar?" she turned back to him with a smile.

"Black," Baxter answered.

Baxter's coffee was served in a cup and saucer with a cloth napkin.

"Who's in there with Glen and Jack?" Baxter asked innocently.

"I've forgotten his name. He's from outside the firm," Bernie replied in equal innocence. "There are so many new names to learn coming out to New York." Her phone rang and was answered. "Mr. Fitzgerald's office, Bernie speaking." She paused to listen to the caller. Baxter decided he liked Bernie's mouth. Her features were well sculpted and her dark hair was shoulder length. It was Bernie's mouth that appeared sensual to Baxter. She had full lips with fresh lipstick applied.

"Mr. Williamson retired from McKenzie Barber in December of last year," Bernie announced. "If this call is of a business nature, I can pass your name on to Mr. Fitzgerald who succeeded Mr. Williamson. No, I have no idea of how to reach Mr. Williamson, and it is against firm policy to provide information on the addresses of retired Partners and former employees to telephone inquiries. I would suggest that you correspond in writing with Mr. Lee Heller, the firm's Director of Human Resources in care of 311 Park Avenue, New York, 10022." Bernie hung up quickly.

"Now there's a phone line we're getting rid of on April 1st. It was Mr. Williamson' private line. I get all kinds of strange calls on it. Glen found a telephone in a teak box on the credenza behind the Managing Partner's desk. He had the extension transferred out here. I take it Mr. Williamson was quite a character."

"Mr. Williamson represented the new breed of Managing Partners at McKenzie Barber," Baxter replied. He walked up to the coffee urn. "Is this the urn that used to be in the Managing Partner's conference room?"

"Glen had it moved out here. He's a Mormon you know, and abstains from coffee drinking, although he's a sucker for diet Dr. Pepper."

"How long have you worked for Glen?" Baxter asked.

"I've been with McKenzie Barber for two years. I worked for the IT practice for a couple of months, and have been with Glen ever since. I came to McKenzie Barber right after my divorce. I also remember you calling Glen up in November and insistent that I get him out of a meeting to talk about nametags. The last few months have been very exciting."

"I'll bet they have," Baxter agreed. "Have you lived in New York before?"

"This is really the first time. I was a flight attendant before I got married, and used to lay over in New York from time to time. Then I got married, divorced, went to word processing school, and came to McKenzie Barber. Now you know my whole life story," Bernie smiled.

Baxter leaned back in a side chair and settled in with his coffee, leafing through a four week old copy of *Forbes*, while occasionally peeking at the closed door of the New York Office Managing Partner's Office. The door finally opened at 4:37. A man in a dark suit with close cropped blonde hair emerged through the doorway with Glen Fitzgerald's hand on his shoulder. Close behind Fitzgerald was Pinker. Both were in shirt sleeves with ties unknotted and collars undone. They were dressed nearly identically in blue shirts, red and blue club ties, red braces, and dark suit trousers. Baxter wondered when they would begin to look alike.

"I'll get it done for you, Glen," the man in the dark suit addressed Fitzgerald.

"You've never let me down before, Rod," Fitzgerald reassured the visitor. "We're counting on you to bring home the bacon. And we want our bacon fast."

The man called Rod shook hands nervously with both Fitzgerald and Pinker. "Bernie," Fitzgerald instructed his secretary. "Get Mr. Phillips a car for LaGuardia." He then spied Baxter sipping his coffee. "Hey, Joe. It looks like we overran our time a little. Com'on in, Joe."

Baxter was motioned to the circular table where he could remember dealing with a succession of Managing Partners ranging from Bruce Dinsmore to Burke, followed by Floyd Piper, Lon McMasters, and most recently Brett Williamson. While Fitzgerald and Pinker had seemed cordial in the anteroom, their faces turned cold after they were seated around the table. Each had a copy of Baxter's Executive Office Review in front of their table place. Baxter suspected that some portion of his report had been discussed in their previous meeting.

"This report," Fitzgerald began, "generally meets the objectives of what you were engaged to do, but falls rather short of our expectations."

"Joe," Pinker chimed in. "Glen and I were looking for more convincing evidence of the underperformance of Executive Office."

"Are you looking for a lot of excuses to fire a lot of people, Jack?" Baxter responded. "All you have to do is to read the report again very slowly."

"I believe that you gave too much space to Clyde and the Partner appraisal forms," Fitzgerald shot back. "Clyde's gone, Joe. Most of the Partners of this firm recognized him for what he was. Buzzsaw took care of business. Clyde's out of here. We want that section of the report deleted. It will serve this firm no advantage to exacerbate old wounds."

"But we do believe," Pinker added, "that you were overly kind to Roger White in your report. Glen and I would like you, Joe, to revisit your report and be a little more critical of Roger and his department's competence and judgment. We would like to inform you in confidence that we have just engaged an executive recruiter to bring in a new Chief Financial Officer for McKenzie Barber. Your report implied that Roger had tried, but was unsuccessful in informing the Chairman and the Operating Committee of the faltering financial condition of McKenzie Barber. That appeared to Glen and me, a rather editorial point of view. We had hoped that your report would properly fix the blame."

Baxter took a deep breath. He was vested in the pension plan, but what he was about to say would certainly cost him.

"Fellas, this is a draft report. We all knew going in that Executive Office was incompetently managed and over-staffed. Clyde Nickerson was the principal suspect. Now you want me to gloss over Clyde's transgressions, and there were many, and concentrate on Roger White, who makes a nice easy-to-hit target. Roger, however, is a member of a minority in our age of cultural diversity, and you two, in your wisdom, want heavy duty blame placed on Roger. Let me make a recommendation that isn't in the report. Roger is prepared to be bagged. Cut him a deal and let Roger leave McKenzie Barber with dignity. Don't go depreciating him in a report. There are a mess of people to cut from Executive Office. The report has the downsizing recommendations in Exhibit III. There is some money to be saved. The guy responsible is Clyde Nickerson. He was allowed to mess up this firm big time. Ross "Buzzsaw" Pritchard placed Clyde Nickerson in that kind of responsibility level. No one elected him."

"You missed the point, Joe," Fitzgerald countered. "Jack and I are here as a matter of accommodation with the Chairman. All of this is due to the discreditation of Brett Williamson. Our covenant with Chairman Pritchard is to avoid discrediting certain Partners who played prominent roles during his administration. Buzzsaw agreed to have Williamson and Nickerson out of the firm, but he didn't want any baggage. Williamson and Nickerson are part of the deal for General Pritchard's cooperation."

"I would add Roger to that group. You can feel free to butcher the rest, but Roger will cost you."

"Joe," Fitzgerald continued. "Buzzsaw believes that Roger had let him down. He blames Roger for a lack of financial integrity."

"How's he feel about Clyde Nickerson?" Baxter interjected.

"Buzzsaw recognizes Nickerson for what he was. Pritchard just wants to get out of here with his glowing reputation so that he can run for Congress. The man wants to look good stepping down from McKenzie Barber, and he's damned mad at Roger White."

"Fellas, you should tell Buzzsaw to lighten up. I believe that Roger White got up each morning and tried to be the best Roger White he knew how to be. He was way over his head as Chief Financial Officer of McKenzie Barber. Now, who put him there? The answer is Ross "Buzzsaw" Pritchard. Most everything that has happened since Buzzsaw was elected Chairman has gone wrong. I prepared you two a draft report evaluating Executive Office. There's really not much for me to do after this point. What other questions do you have?"

"Your draft report was professional enough, Joe, but I believe you've overlooked several obvious opportunities for streamlining and cost reduction." Fitzgerald produced some sheets of graph paper and recited his personal conclusions relative to an Executive Office downsizing plan. "Your recommendations are way too soft. We've got to trim down our bloated Executive Office costs fast. We're going to hire a new Chief Financial Officer who will lead the cost cutting plan. We expect to have a person in place within sixty days."

Baxter nodded his head. He knew that the search would be likely to last 90 to 120 days unless they made a quick hire of someone unemployed. He did not want, under any circumstances, to be named the interim project leader for Executive Office cost reduction. Someone else would have to clean up Clyde Nickerson's gigantic mess.

"I can be available to brief the new CFO at any time," Baxter offered.

"We would like you, Joe, to assume responsibility as the interim coordinator for the reorganization of EO."

"I have a practice to run, fellas."

"Your practice has been slipping and is scheduled to be merged into Dilger's Benefit practice this summer. Jack really doesn't have time to do the Administrative Partner job. That can be yours October 1st. You can stay in the job until you retire," Fitzgerald counter offered.

"We would anticipate that you would be retiring in 1993 and there would be no adjustment up or down in units," Pinker added.

"Where would the Administrative Partner report? To the Chairman or the Deputy Chairman?" Baxter asked.

"It might wind up reporting to the new Chief Financial Officer. We want to bring in some very senior," Pinker answered.

"Then do I understand that you are considering having a Partner report to a non-Partner?" Baxter probed.

"We may have to bring in the new CFO as a Partner. Roger was an officer of FSO and was elected a Partner of the firm when he moved to EO in 1984."

"Have you let a search for a Chief Financial and Administrative Officer?" Baxter questioned.

"Something like that. I'm using a recruiter that I have personally used for years. He will provide me a write-up later on this week and I'd like you to review it. Jack and I would see your role as oversight for all non-financial functions of the firm. That leads to another point. When you're in that job, there doesn't seem to be any reason to keep this Lee Heller. You were a little soft on that job in your report too. Jack is getting off a note to Heller in the morning announcing a hiring freeze. Near as I can see, all the man does is hire MBAs, review training schedules, and make a half-hearted effort to help us get rid of people. Do you know him well, Joe?"

"We were in the Chicago Office together in the 1970s. Lee moved over to the Admin side working for Dr. Barry Keller when he headed up the Strategic Planning practice," Baxter explained.

"Dr. Barry Keller," Pinker whistled. "What ever happened to him? He must have flamed out when I made Associate."

"Dr. Keller announced in 1979 that his consulting career was concluded and went to Europe where he served on a succession of Business School faculties, wrote a bunch of books, and did a little consulting on the side. I believe he died from a brain tumor about three years ago."

"Wow!" Pinker commented. "Dilger told me that you knew the Partner's pension plan as well as he did."

"I used to get assigned to special projects during the Hamilton Burke days. In each case I continued to run my practice with considerable success. I have been exposed, over the years, to a little more of the inner workings of the firm than the average Partner."

"That's where you could have a great deal of value to this new administration, Joe," Fitzgerald observed. "You're a real firm historian. You could provide a valuable counseling link to the new Chief Financial Officer. Now, how about Heller? Somehow he's gotten to be a very highly paid non-Partner. He's also closely identified as a Nickerson protégé. What would you say to immediately terminating him? We could cancel college recruiting this year."

My God, Baxter thought, these guys are as dumb as the last crew. "Fellas, answer this question for me. You have been recently appointed to your responsibilities. No one has elected you to anything. There is time for other factions to emerge and get themselves on the ballot. Executive Office needs to be pruned, but not ravaged. You can cancel college recruiting, but you are sending a message to our consulting competitors that the firm is in trouble. In addition you're going to jeopardize the firm's relationships with the college placement directors of the big MBA schools. You want them on your side to ensure the flow of new MBAs. Go through the motions, make some non-competitive offers, blame Heller in the summer. You can tank him in time to have him out by October 1st, and his severance won't hit until FY 1991."

"Would you be willing to go into that job October 1st, Joe?" Fitzgerald asked.

So that was it, Baxter concluded. They wanted him to pick up Nickerson's old job. They were going to bring in their own Finance and Admin guy and bury Baxter in the old Human Resources job.

"Fellas, I'm a line Partner. I want to stay with my practice until retirement," Baxter replied.

"That's not what we want you do, Joe. We want you to be the implementor of EO reorganization plan and then work under the CFO until you retire. Your practice is going in with Dilger. Dilger believes he has two prospects that can succeed you. You've started this project, and you must finish it."

"I'm going back to my practice, assist in the in the integration of my practice into the Benefits Practice, and will retire December 31, 1991. If you like I will drop you a note to that effect tomorrow morning."

"You're looking at a twenty-five percent unit cut October 1st, Joe, if you don't do what we ask you to," Pinker threatened. "That will affect your little retirement nest egg."

"You can't do that according to the Partnership by-laws, Jack. Once when I announce my intent to retire early, my units are frozen until my retirement date."

"Brett was going to cut your units 25% if you didn't make plan," Fitzgerald announced.

"Brett Williamson isn't here anymore, fellas. He's retired to his snake breeding farm in Mississippi."

"Joe," Fitzgerald began. "Suppose we ask you to do this in a very nice way and pay you a special bonus at year end if you get everything done. As a sweetener, you can write us a letter announcing your intention to retire December 31, 1992. That will freeze your units until your retirement."

"What are we talking about in terms of a special bonus? I'm quite willing to put a special bonus at performance risk. But I would like an idea of what kind of measurements are involved, and what kind of an award is at stake."

Baxter felt both sets of eyes burning into him. It was Fitzgerald who spoke. "We want a 40% reduction in costs and we'll recommend to the firm that they pay you a $50,000 bonus in October 1990."

"That's pretty skinny, Glen, for a forty percent reduction of EO costs."

"I believe that we would be very generous to recommend you for a special bonus. We could just order you to do it, Joe," Fitzgerald said.

"I would take Miss Klein with me on the project. You should fund $15,000 for her at year end if we hit target," Baxter recommended. "I'm not doing this job alone, and Heidi is up to speed on EO. When the work is completed, Heidi can return to another Benefits Comp practice or there may be a spot for her in the newly reorganized EO."

"Is this Heidi some kind of girlfriend of your's, Joe?" Fitzgerald accused.

"Hardly. She may be the least attractive woman at 311 Park Avenue. Based on three months on the study, I believe Heidi will be most valuable on this next phase of our EO work."

Fitzgerald drummed his mechanical pencil on the table. Pinker decided to talk. "Joe, you're taking us into negotiations that we haven't considered. We're not happy with what you've produced so far. Now we're giving you a chance to make up for your underperformance and you're negotiating all kinds of extras. You're someone with short future career expectations at McKenzie Barber, and we're giving you a chance to extend your career a few years."

"I got it," Fitzgerald blurted out. "We merge Benefits and Executive Compensation effective April 1st. Joe transfers to Executive Office as the Special Project Review Coordinator. We'll transfer that woman too. They go off New York Office payroll and onto EO." Fitzgerald pointed a finger at Baxter.

"With that transfer, you're out of your practice and New York Office forever. We'll announce Carl Miller as Joe's successor. He's the one Dilger wants. Joe, I want you to get together soon with Rod Trombley, our recruiter, on the CFO search. This will give you an opportunity to pick your new boss. Part of your bonus will ride on how fast the new CFO is on board. Also Jack tells me that you're pretty good at cutting employment deals. I want you to negotiate favorable terms with Roger on his termination."

"Then gentlemen, I believe it's time for us to get a memorandum of understanding on paper. I'll draft up what I believe our agreement to be. You review it for final form, return one signed copy and we have a deal."

"I fail to see why we have to have anything in writing, Joe," Fitzgerald said coldly. "We've got to have a little trust here."

"Glen, I know that I can trust Jack and you, but we need a little documentation here in the event that the two of you go down in an airplane. I'll draft it, you review it, and we'll sign-off."

"Bernie had better type it," Pinker said.

Fitzgerald began to tap his pencil on the table. "This is where I wanted to be after the meeting, but I'm not sure how we got here. I want you to understand that you have no sign-off to make EO changes. Jack has the sign off. You're expected to recommend for your approval, and then implement. You have no authority unless we give it to you. Buzzsaw is still Chairman until October. We're both now on the Operating Committee. I don't need to tell you, Joe. But the US firm is in trouble. We have some major receivables problems from the Government, Healthcare, and Higher Education practices. We're working out from under Gene English's follies in Information Technology. FSO may not be as golden as it was painted. McMasters has uncovered a pile of write-offs in the Middle East. It's time for all Partners to pull together."

Fitzgerald rose up from the table, followed by Pinker. The meeting was over with an exchange of handshakes. Fitzgerald accompanied Baxter to Bernie's desk. "Joe's going to bring you some confidential documents Monday morning for you to prepare. Jack and I will need copies and Joe will need a copy."

"I'll bring it in CD-ROM form," Baxter acknowledged and walked back to his office. He closed the door and sat for a long time in his swivel chair. Baxter recognized that he had just abandoned his practice and consulting career. He had agreed to finish his McKenzie Barber career at a second level administrative manager job in Executive Office. Fitzgerald and Pinker wanted him to serve as Clyde Nickerson's successor. He raised the blinds on his window and studied the lights of Lexington Avenue down to the outline of the Chrysler Building. He began to quietly rock in his chair in the darkness. Baxter wished that he kept a bottle in the office. He felt very lonely. His wife had left him and now his practice and clients were going away.

The red light on his telephone indicated phone mail. Baxter punched in his code and was greeted by the mechanical voice.

"Joe Baxter, you have three new messages. Press key 5."

"Message #1, 4:35 PM."

"Kid, this is Frank. Frank Alvardi. Dwyer is dead. We need to arrange a funeral. Would you call me right away? 714-915-6301. Got it? 714-915-6301. I would prefer not to handle this alone. I'm trying to find Dirks. It would be helpful if you come up with a current telephone number."

"Message #2, 6:02 PM."

"Joe, this is Heidi. I'm leaving the office now. I'm really interested in how the meeting went. Could you call me at home this evening, or just leave me a phone mail." Sweet plain looking Heidi. She would have no future in the Executive Compensation practice without him. Baxter knew he would have to find a place for her.

"Message #3, 6:25 PM."

"Baxter/Dopman! This is God's Helper. Adultery is a sin! Your time is getting close." Baxter saved the message.

He dialed back Alvardi. "Alvardi," the telephone was answered.

"Baxter here. I got your message. How did it happen?"

"When was the last time you talked to Bill, kid?"

"It's got to be three or four years anyway. No it was at Dirks going away party in December of 1984. He was going off to a public accounting firm. I have forgotten just which one."

"Well he had a few jobs after that one. He wound up at an upstate New York community college thirty miles north of Rochester. He was teaching Cost Accounting and Industrial Engineering. He hanged himself on Wednesday, and they didn't find him until this morning. I was listed on his forms as someone to contact. I'm going to grab the red-eye and I'll be there in the morning. There are some early morning flights to Rochester. Lorna's going up tonight to Rochester. I found Dirks. He's going to meet us in Rochester. I figure we'd get Bill buried quick and blow out of there. There's a Brimmer Industries Company that makes fire hoses up there. Lorna's got the President's secretary working on the details. You can be back in New York Sunday morning."

"Bill hanged himself?" Baxter questioned.

"That's what the Provost told me. He was pussyfooting around. His name is Dr. Thistle. My guess is that Bill was boozing pretty heavily. He used to call me from time to time leaving a lot of strange voice mails. My guess is that he slipped over the side. Wild Bill had been on a long slide since the mid-seventies. I believe that we owe him a quorum at his funeral. Anything else we should talk about, kid?"

"Where did you find Dirks?"

"He's living up on the other side of Cape Cod in a place called Yarmouth. He's living on a boat. Anything else, kid?"

"I'll see you in the Rochester Airport, Frank. There's a US Air Club. Shall we meet there?"

"Fine, kid. Got to go."

Baxter reserved space on a next morning 7:10 AM flight to Rochester with an open return. He walked reflectively to the elevator. It had been Dwyer who engineered him into McKenzie Barber. Now he was gone too. Bernie stood in front of the elevator bank.

"So we meet again," she greeted him with a fur coat over the shoulders of her pants suit. Her arms were full of Federal Express packages.

"The boys seem to be working you late," Baxter commented.

"They're still there. We missed the last Federal Express pick-up. They're getting to know me pretty well at the Lexington Avenue station. They are about the only friends I've made in New York so far."

"When did you come out?" Baxter asked.

"The second week in January. I haven't had much time to look for an apartment. I'm in an apartment hotel over on 53rd Street. Tomorrow I'm staying in to go apartment hunting. I have been going back to Chicago every other weekend."

"Can I buy you a drink tonight?"

"If you buy me a drink, Mr. Baxter, you'll also have to buy me dinner. Those are my terms this evening," Bernie responded as the elevator doors opened.

"I accept your terms. I have to catch an early morning flight to Rochester so we'll make it a fast dinner," Baxter offered.

Baxter instinctively took Bernie's arm as the crossed Fiftieth street. She flashed a smile. "That felt good. I asked Jack about Mrs. Baxter and he said you were divorced."

"I separated from my wife in the fall of 1987. Our divorce was finalized in December," Baxter confirmed his marital status.

"Mine was final in February of 1988. I was married three years. My husband was a sales manager and he used to fly on my LA's. I dated him for about three years. He asked me to marry him and wanted me to quit flying. His company was headquartered in a suburb of Racine, Wisconsin. I moved to Racine and we lived in an apartment. He sold housewares."

"Was his company called Washburn Manufacturing?" Baxter asked.

"Yes." Bernie stopped mid-block and squeezed Baxter's arm. "They were part of a British company called Henry Wiggins. Do you know them?"

"I married a Washburn."

"Now that's interesting," Bernie said entering the Federal Express station. She picked up the subject of Washburn after they had returned to the street.

"Italian, French, Chinese or Swahili?" Baxter offered.

"I'd prefer French. I ate Swahili last night."

"There's a place over on 51st Street. It's Friday night and we may have to wait for a table."

"Then you can buy me a drink and tell me about Washburn Manufacturing. You can start right now, if you like. Marvin, my ex, told me that there hadn't been any Washburns in the company for a long time."

"They all were dispersed with the sale of the company in 1967 to Henry Wiggins Plc. I was a son-in-law and resigned the first morning of Henry Wiggins' ownership. There was a fellow named Ray Schucker who stayed behind to be President of the Company. Did you ever hear that name?"

"I believe he had been gone a long time by the time Marv showed up. There was some kind of arrangement that they had with certain mass merchants that they referred to as a 'Schucker deal'. Marv didn't like 'Schucker deals' and he was trying to get rid of them. The Henry Wiggins people promised Marv he would be the next President when they hired him as VP Sales & Marketing. Marv thought if he were going to be President, he ought to have a wife to help him entertain customers and attend the trade shows with. I was tired of flying and had been seeing Marv for three years after he split with his last wife. Washburn Manufacturing looked like a promotion to me."

They settle at the front bar at Les Halles with martinis and the promise from a smiling maitre'd that they would have a table sooner or later.

"And what happened to Marv at Washburn Manufacturing? Is he still there?" Baxter asked.

"They fired him six months after I left him. They always wanted Marv to raise prices and the quality was going downhill. They had a British accountant running the company. Marv told me they hired his replacement and told him he would be groomed for President. They also closed the Deer Lake headquarters and moved to Dallas. Poor Marv. He's had two jobs since. He was a much better date than he was a husband. Now I've gone and told you much more than you've told me."

"I went there after graduate school and married the boss's daughter—". Baxter presented the abridged sanitized version of his career at Washburn Manufacturing. His story lasted two martinis before they were seated at a table in the far end of the dining room.

'This is really fun," Bernie proclaimed as she looked over the menu and returned it to Baxter. "Order me a salad and fish," she said in between chomps of French bread. "This is a god-send being with you tonight. I've been working night and day since I came out here and haven't had time for a social life. The question is, should you and I be fraternizing?"

"I believe we're okay if it's just for tonight," Baxter responded.

Bernie made a face. "Poo! I believe we should have dinner at least once every two weeks until it's not fun anymore."

"Shall we begin to slip around to quaint little restaurants where no one will recognize us and exchange confidences by candlelight?"

"That sounds very attractive to me. Are you going to show me New York City?"

"I could do that. I've never been in town before in terms of extended periods of time. It looks though I may be landlocked in New York for the next couple of years."

"I know that Glen and Jack want you in Executive Office. I guess I have to be careful, Bernie," Baxter noted. "You should be careful. If we're going to be great pals, you have to make an assessment as to how much information you're willing to share with me."

"You're regarded at McKenzie Barber as a rather clever man, Joe. As a lonely newcomer to New York, I find you very attractive. What would you want from me in a relationship?"

Bernie was beginning to remind Baxter of Lorna King during her pre-Brimmer period in the Chicago office.

"Just a passing friendship," Baxter answered innocently. "The New York office is a complex place with a lot of twists and unexpected turns. Possibly, there may be some instances where I can help you," he offered.

Bernie took a long sip from her wine glass. Then she shook her head and asked Baxter to order her some coffee.

"Joe, what can you tell me about Druanne Smithers? Glen expects me to have a lot of contact with her, and she refuses to talk directly to me. She has a snippy secretary who told me to clear any matters through her. Miss Smithers would then be directly back in touch with Glen. I'm trying to reach her regarding a number of sensitive personnel questions. Glen won't take the time to return her calls. He snapped at me on the way out. Glen wants information, and the woman will only talk to Glen. I've even sent her a memorandum signed by Glen, authorizing her to talk to me. What do I do?"

"On Monday, you will receive a draft memorandum of understanding relative to my transfer to Executive Office which will delineate my new role as Deputy Director of Administration for the firm. I expect there will be a few amendments to the language, but essentially I have a deal with Glen and Jack to implement the restructuring of Executive Office. Once Glen and I are in agreement on the verbiage, you should issue a memorandum from Glen that states I will be his personal liaison relative to New York Office personnel matters. Then I will have a little meeting with Druanne and open up communications with an ax."

"Then you're on our team?" Bernie questioned.

"I'm signing up on Monday," Baxter replied.

Baxter barely made the 7AM fight to Rochester on Saturday morning. He had bonded with Bernie and dropped her off with a handshake shortly after ten PM. Then he returned to his apartment and hammered out his first draft of a memorandum of understanding. He made his requirements reasonably aggressive, but carefully planned a series of back-up positions for final negotiations. Glen and Jack were stuck with Baxter and now he had agreed to be stuck with them. He needed the memorandum of understanding in the event Fitzgerald did not make it to the Chairman's job. Baxter's objective was to survive for three more years without a unit cut. He completed his final draft of the letter of agreement shortly before midnight and carefully placed the CD-ROM in an envelope which he tucked into the recesses of his brief case. He then called Heidi's voice mail briefly reporting that the meeting with Fitzgerald and Pinker had gone well, and they would be continuing the Executive Office project. He would provide her further details first thing on Monday morning.

Finally Baxter poured himself a Canadian Club on the rocks and played some Sondheim. There was something he had to do tomorrow. What was it?

Then it came back to him. Dwyer's funeral! His early mentor was dead. Baxter played his Bill Dwyer memory tapes back as he sipped Canadian Club. He thought back to their first meeting back at Washburn Manufacturing. Dwyer had been a reluctant consultant. Lee Heller had been assigned to the engagement and now some twenty-five years later, Heller's McKenzie Barber career was in his hands. Dwyer had brought Baxter into McKenzie Barber. It was Dwyer, after he became ill, who had arranged for Baxter to transfer temporarily to Alvardi's practice. He had survived in the Comp practice for twenty-two years. Over time Baxter had sensed that Dwyer's sarcastic banter had matured into outright resentment of Baxter and anyone related to leadership at McKenzie Barber. He regretted their alienation. Now there was no time to make it up. To top it off, poor Bill would probably not make the obituary section of the *New York Times*.

Baxter made the plane boarding with five minutes to spare and fell asleep during the taxi. Dwyer appeared to him in a dream. There were circles around his eyes and he held a highball glass in his hand. He kept lecturing Baxter. "You're not a consultant, Joe. You're a politician. Now the firm has finally got you exactly where you belong!"

Baxter tried to switch his dream over to Dominique and the weekend they had together in Paris, but his dream channel was stuck on Dwyer. 'You're dead! You cynical old drunk!' he said and willed himself to wake-up. The safety belt instructions were being issued at the time he forced his eyes open.

Baxter read the *New York Times* and drank coffee in the US Air Club awaiting Alvardi's arrival.

Baxter immediately turned to the Obituaries.

BRYAN STARWALTER, WRY POET IS DEAD AT 65

ANTONIO SAACA, 53, OWNER OF FAMED ITALIAN RESTAURANTS

HELLWIG GRASSER, 93, GERMAN FILM ACTRESS

MARGOT S. FRIER, 73, A BRIDGE CHAMPION

Bill Dwyer had obviously missed the Saturday, March 25th, 1990 edition of the Times. Perhaps Sunday or Monday would be his day.

Alvardi joined him at 9:30. "Let's go kid. Lorna's got a limo waiting for us," he greeted Baxter. Alvardi hadn't changed. His hair was jet black and he continued to resemble Joe DiMaggio. "Lorna sent down the company plane to pick me up in White Plains. She came up last night in the company jet with Liz MacReavie, Brimmer Industries, PR lady. She has Liz organizing things. Lorna has learned very quickly to direct other people who organize."

Alvardi, like Baxter, had selected a blue pin striped suit to wear with a red club tie. "I see we're in our funeral suits, Frank," Baxter observed as they walked rapidly through the Rochester air terminal.

"These things are coming a little too frequently to suit me. Good thing that you and I are indestructible," Alvardi said slapping Baxter on the shoulder.

"Do you have any more details, Frank?"

"Liz MacReavie will give us a full report in the car. She's very efficient."

A long black, stretch limousine was parked at the curb with a uniformed driver standing near the rear door. He was smoking a cigarette while carrying on a conversation with a uniformed policeman. The engine was running.

He stamped out the cigarette at the sight of Alvardi and Baxter, opened the rear door of the limo, and took Baxter's bags. Lorna was seated near the window in dark glasses with a white sable coat over her shoulders smoking a cigarette. She was now a platinum blonde. Across from her in the jump seat was a small woman with a mink coat over her shoulders and a cup of coffee in her hands. Baxter estimated her to be in her mid to late forties. She had a sharp, merry, Irish face with bright alert eyes and she extended a talon like hand in greeting to Baxter.

"Mr. Baxter, I'm Liz MacReavie, Director of Communications for Brimmer Industries." Her handshake was steel. Alvardi slid across the seat next to Lorna. He slipped his hand around Lorna's shoulder and kissed her lightly on the cheek. Baxter pushed down the jump seat next to Liz MacReavie. "Coffee?" she offered Baxter from a thermos beside her.

"Please," Baxter responded and Liz poured Baxter coffee into a Styrofoam coup.

"Frank," Lorna spoke. "Why in hell are we here? Bill Dwyer was nothing more than a lecherous old drunk, and I never liked him. Was he special to you, Joe?"

"He brought me to McKenzie Barber and changed my life. I really don't think Bill liked me very much after 1984. I'm here, I guess, because it's the right thing to do."

"We owe Bill a decent funeral, Lorna. He has no identifiable or locatable family," Alvardi said with his hand settled on Lorna's right sable shoulder.

Lorna looked directly across the back seat to Liz MacReavie. "Liz! Brief us!" she commanded.

Liz slid some 3" by 5" cards out of the pocket of her purse.

"William Dwyer had been an Adjunct Professor in Industrial Engineering at Websterville Junior College since September 1989. Previously he had been an Adjunct Professor in the Business Administration Department of St. Mark's College in Roystan, New York from 1987 to 1989. Previous to this his record indicates that he was a free lance independent consultant from 1984 to 1987 following his retirement from McKenzie Barber."

Baxter noted that the history failed to include the public accounting firm Dwyer had joined after McKenzie Barber.

"Mr. Wheeler, the President of Brimmer Industrial Bearings here in Rochester, has been of considerable help in developing information on this matter. He's very well respected in the community."

"He's generally a splendid fellow. He just has difficulty in meeting our return on capital standards," Lorna commented coldly.

"You've got tough return on capital standards at Brimmer Industries," Alvardi observed.

"Back to Mr. Dwyer, if we may," Liz continued. "Brother Matthew at St. Mark's College confided in me that Mr. Dywer's contract was not renewed at St. Mark's, but that he had recommended him to Dr. Thistle at Websterville Community College. Dr. Thistle confided to me that while Mr. Dwyer was a well liked member of the faculty, his drinking and general deportment was not consistent with the college's standards of behavior. Mr. Dwyer was advised on Tuesday, March 20th, following a previous warning by his department head, that his services would be terminated following his classroom lectures of Wednesday, March 21st, and that his duties would be assumed by an Associate Professor. Mr. Dwyer apparently conducted his final lecture, returned to his home, and hanged himself. Funeral arrangements have been made through Brunlinger Funeral Home with a reviewal this morning through noon, a service at 2:30 PM at the funeral home, followed by an internment at Cherry Wood Acres, a cemetery to the north of the city."

"Our schedule going forward is to meet briefly with Dr. Thistle at Websterville Community College, visit Mr. Dwyer's lodgings in Drolling, New York, attend a luncheon hosted by Mr. and Mrs. Wheeler at the Great Valley Club in Rochester at 12:15 and then proceed to the Brunlinger Funeral Home for the 2:30 services, followed by the internment at Cherry Woods Acres. I have a reservation for this evening at the Hyatt for you, Mr. Baxter, should you wish to stay over."

"What about Roger Dirks, Liz?" Alvardi interjected.

"Mr. Dirks is driving from Cape Cod. He expects to join us for the services at the Brunlinger Funeral Home."

"Who's going to be conducting the service at Brunlinger's?" Lorna snapped.

"They have a Catholic priest on retainer who will conduct the ceremony," Liz responded.

"I don't like that. The Catholics have a bad attitude about suicide. Joe Baxter will deliver a eulogy in both the chapel and the gravesite. Advise Brunlinger's or whatever they call themselves that we won't need their priest. We have someone who will take care of the eulogy. The Reverend Joseph Baxter. There shouldn't be much of a turn-out."

"Lorna, I don't do eulogies on Saturdays," Baxter offered.

"If I'm paying for this funeral, and I assume I am," Lorna stated. "The funeral and gravesite oratory will be done without any Catholic mumbo-jumbo. I was raised Catholic and find their ceremonies lacking." Lorna looked across the car to Baxter. "Joe is very good on his feet. He will say and do the right things."

"Very good, Mrs. Brimmer," Liz answered dutifully and produced a cellular phone from her bag.

"Liz, tell the driver, that it's time to get away. We have a number of stops to make this morning," Lorna ordered.

The limo pulled away under a sullen March sky with four resigned, silent passengers. Baxter began to think about his Dwyer eulogy assignment. 'Bill Dwyer never met a cocktail waitress he didn't like'. He would have to use those lines somewhere in the eulogy. Perhaps he'd find a Bible and quote from John 3:16. People seemed to be always waving banners at football games with John 3:16 in large letters. Baxter had assumed it was something about extra points.

The limo left the airport and entered the freeway. "Websterville," Liz recited, "is approximately 29 miles from the Rochester airport. The Websterville Community College has a two year curriculum, 1900 students,

334

and awards an Associate Arts and Science degree. The school produces a number of technicians, and nearly fifty percent of its students matriculate to colleges and universities."

"Christ," Lorna said in a low voice directed at Alvardi. "He wasn't even teaching at a four year school."

"St. Mark's was a four year college," Liz offered.

"They apparently kicked him out of there," Lorna observed coldly.

The Websterville Community College was formed by a series of rectangular yellow brick buildings that reminded Baxter of a closed H. Between the half filled parking lot and the main assembly of buildings was a two story white frame building with a large green and white sign that read:

CENTRAL ADMINISTRATION
OFFICE OF THE PRESIDENT

They exited the limo in a single line through the pathway to the sidewalk. The campus seemed strangely antiseptic and barren. It looked to Baxter like a place where one could manufacture aspirins. He stepped aside so that Alvardi could lead the party, followed by Lorna with her sable coat on her shoulders, and Liz who walked in quick short steps through the pathway to the steps to the central administration building.

They were greeted in the main reception area by a white male teen-age student with long black hair tied in a pony tail. He manned a telephone switchboard behind an octagonal grey counter. "May I help you?" they were greeted.

Alvardi announced the group authoritatively and their mission to see Dr. Thistle. There were only four folding chairs in the lobby which was decorated with posters of students working against a backdrop of immaculate industrial settings. There was one section of the wall adorned with scenes of students who appeared to be receiving awards, and group pictures of what looked to be faculty and students. Baxter looked for clues of Dwyer. There were none.

Lorna and Liz inspected the pictures and posters, exchanging silent nods as if they were in an art gallery. There was a five minute wait, which seemed to Baxter to be more like one hour, before a middle aged woman stepped through a sliding green door to the right of the reception area. She wore a sweater and skirt with glasses suspended from her neck on a leather chain. Baxter recognized the woman as another member of the great army of executive assistants who twenty years earlier called themselves secretaries.

"Mrs. Brimmer, Mr. Alvardi. I'm Eve Jenske, Dr. Thistle's Executive Assistant. Won't you come this way?"

Alvardi quickly introduced Baxter and Liz and after a fast exchange of handshakes they followed Miss Jenske through the green door to an elevator which rose to the second floor. They were ushered into a large office paneled with books. There was a large oval shaped desk set next to a computer work station and a round table with six seats. Baxter noted that two of the side chairs did not match.

Dr. Thistle appeared to be in his late thirties. He wore a grey glen plaid three piece suit and his crew cut was more grey than white. Miss Jenske introduced each member of their party and there was a solemn acknowledgment and handshake.

The round table contained three thermos jugs, a tray of mugs, paper napkins, and a paper plate of cookies.

"I really regret that we have had to meet all of you under such unfortunate circumstances, Mrs. Brimmer. We are, of course, well acquainted with Hugh Raymond and Brimmer Bearing. Brimmer Bearing is one of the most respected industrial companies in Onondaga County." Miss Jenske circled the table as Dr. Thistle talked, offering whispered choices of regular or decaffeinated coffee or hot water for tea.

Alvardi then spoke up to take control of the meeting. "Dr. Thistle, Mrs. Brimmer, Mr. Baxter and I were colleagues of Bill Dwyer during our McKenzie Barber careers. Mr. Baxter worked the longest with Bill. Roger Dirks, another retired Partner from McKenzie Barber, is expected to join us in time for the funeral. Bill retired from McKenzie Barber in—." Alvardi looked to Baxter.

"December 1984," Baxter recited. He remembered at that second the last time he had seen Dwyer. It had been at Dirks going away party. Dwyer hadn't been particularly friendly.

"Nearly six years have passed since we've seen or heard from Bill. What can you tell us about the final period of Bill's life?"

Dr. Thistle removed his tea bag, took a quick sip, and cleared his throat. "Mr. Dwyer and Websterville College represented a mismatch. I serve on a community business council with Brother Matthew, the academic dean for the business program, at St. Mark's College. As a community college, we are not always able to attract faculty with the academic and experiential depth that we need. Brother Matthew mentioned once after a meeting that a distinguished adjunct was completing his three year contract and wanted to stay in the area. That adjunct professor was Bill Dwyer. He made a strong impression on our faculty during his interviews and joined us in the fall term. By the beginning of November we heard reports that Mr. Dwyer was delivering his afternoon classes under the influence of alcohol. His classes were well attended and many students not enrolled in his industrial engineering classes began to attend Mr. Dwyer's classes unregistered, which lead to serious overcrowding. We started to monitor Mr. Dwyer's classes and found that he had abandoned his curriculum plan and was teaching in the case method. Now I have always admired the case method, but believe it is best appropriate for graduate school classes. Mr. Dwyer was exposing 18 and 19 year olds to the case method. One case was highly critical of the Eastman Kodak Company's manufacturing operations. Mr. Dwyer was counseled in December and placed on probation for the Winter quarter."

"We had an enormous registration for Mr. Dwyer's classes in the Winter quarter. He began to hold beer busts for the students at his home during the Holidays, and it carried over into Winter quarter. We heard reports that some of our young women students were spending the night at Mr. Dwyer's home. His department head filed a disciplinary action against Mr. Dwyer last Tuesday that he would be relieved of his class room effective Wednesday. Mr. Dwyer delivered his last lecture on Wednesday, said good-bye to his class and was not seen after that time. One of his students discovered his body on Friday morning. Mr. Alvardi was listed in Mr. Dwyer's records as the person to contact in case of emergency. Miss Jenske contacted Mr. Alvardi at Western Pacific University and that should bring us current. May I answer any questions?"

"Has Mr. Dwyer's death been announced at the college?" Alvardi asked.

"There will be an announcement made on Monday. I'm working on the draft now. The police coroner's report has ruled Mr. Dwyer's death a suicide. Mr. Dwyer, in death and in life, regrettably, has been an embarrassment to the college."

"Dr. Thistle," Alvardi began. "We regret that our former colleague, whom we remember as the most gifted and talented of men, has been an embarrassment to your obscure little community college. We thank you for your hospitality and time this morning." Alvardi started to rise, but Lorna motioned for him to sit down.

"The Brimmer Industries Foundation, Dr. Thistle, provides scholarships for students to attend institutions of higher learning. We would like to provide $50,000 in annual scholarship funds to deserving students of the College's choice," Lorna said. Turning to Liz, she went on, "Liz, establish the William E. Dwyer Memorial Fund on Monday. Make it effective this fall. Miss MacReavie will be back in touch with you next week regarding the details."

Dr. Thistle rose up from his chair with the others. "Mrs. Brimmer," he said when they reached the door of his office. "Could we call the scholarship, the Brimmer Industries Memorial Fund?"

"If you want the funds for your school, Dr. Thistle, you will call the fund what we tell you to call it," Lorna said turning her back on the Provost.

Dwyer lived in a rented white frame house with peeling paint which was situated next to a Shell station. There was a swing set on the creaking front porch and the inside door behind the storm door was open. A woman was in the living room packing things into cardboard boxes.

"Good morning," Alvardi greeted the woman. "We're friends of Bill's up here to arrange the funeral. Who are you?"

Baxter estimated that the woman was in her early thirties. Her face was youthful, but lined. It was round, and she wore large rimmed glasses, a red sweater, and blue jeans. Her black hair was cut short and her nose had an Irish beak.

"I'm Rose Scanlon. I was a friend of Bill's. Are you the ones who are arranging the funeral?"

Alvardi made introductions and Rose Scanlon nodded at each of them at the sound of their names as she fondled a book.

"There will be a service at a place called Brunlinger's Funeral Home," Alvardi said. "Will you be joining us?"

"I was thinking of it. I had better finish up here and go home and put a dress on. What time is the funeral?"

"2:30," Alvardi replied. "What is it that you are finishing up, Miss Scanlon?"

"I'm getting my things out of here. I used to spend a lot of time over here. I've got clothes, books, and personal stuff. You look like the McKenzie Barber bunch. You're all so well dressed. He used to talk about McKenzie Barber a lot. You said your name was Alvardi?"

Alvardi nodded. They now had formed a semi-circle around Rose Scanlon.

"He talked about you. Your name is familiar," she addressed Baxter. "He talked about a Baxter. I believe he talked about your husband, Mrs. Brimmer," she said is Lorna's direction.

"How long did you know Bill?" Lorna asked.

"I was his teaching assistant at St. Mark's, his second year at St. Mark's. I guess it's close to three years now. I don't live here full time. I was with him maybe from one third to half of the time. Bill, rest his soul, was a heavy load to be with all the time."

"Were you in love with Bill?" Lorna asked.

Rose Scanlon shrugged her shoulders. "Love sounds a little drastic. I drank with him, slept with him, and fought with him. I don't believe I loved him. He's seen a good bit of the world that I haven't seen and I learned from him. Let's just say that we had a relationship. We had a bit of a falling out around the end of the year. I heard last night that Bill had done himself in, and I figured I'd better gather up my stuff while I could. I was afraid that the police would seal the place up or something."

"What do you think made him do it, Rose?" Baxter asked.

She shrugged her shoulders again. "I guess the man was at the end of his rope. I heard they were going to fire him at the community college. Brother Matthew wanted Bill out of St. Mark's. I'm on the faculty of St. Mark's. Websterville was a big step down for Bill. But he needed a job. His students loved him. They loved him at St. Mark's and they loved him at Websterville. He would have been fine if his classes could have been in the morning because Bill never started drinking until noon." Rose Scanlon shrugged her shoulders again. "He wanted me to come back. I told him I couldn't. He called me on Wednesday night. He was drunk. Bill wanted me to come back to him and I told him I couldn't. He hung up on me. He hanged himself that night." She shrugged her shoulders again and then burst into tears. Lorna stepped forward and took Rose Scanlon into her arms. Rose Scanlon cried uncontrollably for nearly five minutes before Lorna calmed her down. She slipped off her sable coat and placed it on a chair. "We'll help you pack," she reassured the sobbing woman.

The Great Valley Club turned out to be a golf club situated off the outer ring of Highway 390 which encircled Rochester. Lorna, Liz, and Alvardi talked during the ride from Dwyer's house, while Baxter tried to organize a decent brief eulogy sufficient for a small audience. "Bill Dwyer was always a messy person. It was a miracle that he lasted as long as he did," Lorna pronounced. "And here we are, after his death, cleaning up his messes."

Hugh and Blanche Raymond had reserved a private room off the main dining room where a buffet luncheon was displayed. Hugh Raymond was a portly, energetic man in a brown suit who greeted them with a warm solemnity in the reception area.

"Mrs. Brimmer, I am truly sorry for the loss of your friend," he greeted Lorna and helped her off from her sable coat. A thin young woman in her twenties who wore a dark suit stood at Raymond's side. "This is Portia Maslin, our Manager of Communications. Portia has worked out most of today's arrangements."

Portia was honored to meet Mrs. Brimmer and extended a mousy hand in greeting. Lorna made the other introductions. Alvardi was introduced as a Board member and long-time friend of the Brimmers. Baxter became one of the senior partners at McKenzie Barber, and Liz remained the Director of Corporate Communications and Investor Relations for Brimmer Industries. Portia remarked that she read Mrs. MacReavie's internal memoranda religiously and kept them in a ring binder on the bookshelf in the office.

"Let Mrs. Raymond and I add our grief to yours," Hugh Raymond said after introducing his wife, Blanche, a heavyset woman whom Baxter concluded had been to the hairdressers that morning. A waitress in a white and blue uniform hovered near Lorna.

"May I bring you a beverage m'am?"

"I believe I could use a martini straight up with a lemon peel," Lorna announced.

"Make that two of them," Liz added.

"I'll have mine on the rocks with a twist," Alvardi joined.

"I'll join this man with a BeefEater martini on the rocks with a twist," Baxter requested.

"In the interests of efficiency and just-in-time inventory planning," a voice boomed behind them from the doorway, "Bring two shakers of Martinis. This is an 8 to 1 crowd as I remember them." It was Dirks.

The waitress looked to Hugh Raymond. He nodded his head in ascent and ordered Dry Sack for he and his wife.

Dirks wore a white oxford cloth button-down shirt, grey slacks, blue blazer, and shiny tassel loafers. His color was back and he seemed the bulldog of old.

"Mr. Dirks retired from McKenzie Barber a year ago. He served as Deputy Managing Partner for the New York Office and served on the firm's Board of Directors for many years," Alvardi introduced Dirks beginning with the Raymonds.

"The old Badger Bearing Company. You sold out to Hruska in the early seventies."

"We've been a member of the Brimmer family of companies for seventeen years," Hugh Reynolds acknowledged.

"Paul Brimmer was one hell of a good man. We served on the Board of Directors together," Dirks said and looked Lorna over. "I remember you as Nickerson's secretary in Chicago. Then you went to work for Brimmer in some kind of Admin job. You may not remember it, but I dropped you a note when Paul died. It was a real loss for your shareholders, the company, and business community at large. I admired your husband very much, and he should have been elected the Chairman of McKenzie Barber in 1984."

"Paul regarded his position at Brimmer Industries with much more regard than being a Chairman of a consulting firm," Lorna snapped back.

Baxter studied Liz's face. This was the first time she had heard of Lorna King Brimmer's early secretarial career.

"I knew him, Mrs. Brimmer, as the finest Managing Partner we had at McKenzie Barber. I bought shares in Brimmer Industries when the company traded as Hruska Industries. I have held those shares in my retirement."

"Well, it's always great to meet a shareholder," Hugh Raymond inserted into the pregnant silence.

Baxter hoped that the club bartender was fast.

Dirks started a conversation with Hugh Raymond about the bearings industry. Mrs. Raymond joined the group. Alvardi moved toward Baxter's side after he had lit cigarettes for Lorna and Liz.

"Dirks pissed Lorna off," he whispered to Baxter.

"Not something we worried about in the old days, Frank," Baxter said slapping Alvardi on the shoulder.

The waitress arrived with the drinks. "If I were you, Miss," Baxter quietly advised the waitress. "I'd reload immediately for the martini drinkers."

A middle-aged, heavy set man in a dark suit and clergyman's collar entered the room. "Jim," Hugh Raymond greeted the newcomer.

"I'm so glad you could join us." Then turning to the group. "Dr. Witzler is the pastor of our church, St. James Anglican Church in Penfield. I was informed that Mrs. Brimmer was uncomfortable with the presence of a Catholic priest at the services this afternoon, so I asked Dr. Witzler to join us and help in any way he can on this unfortunate occasion."

Dr. Witzler was introduced around and he repeated his name as "Jim Witzler" with each handshake.

"Perhaps we can bow our heads in prayer for a minute on this day of sorrow," Dr. Witzler smiled benignly.

"It will be a few minutes before we're ready to entertain any of your ceremonies, Jim," Lorna announced regally. "I want to finish my martini and my cigarette, and perhaps even enjoy a second cocktail before we move on to prayer."

"I propose a compromise," Dirks said. "Let's bow our heads for ten seconds of silent prayer for our departed comrade, Bill Dwyer."

Lorna looked at her watch. "A very good suggestion, Mr. Dirks." Heads were bowed for the same amount of time a basketball team was allotted to cross mid-court. "Amen," Dr. Witzler said softly as the other heads came up.

"Well, here's to Bill Dwyer," Dirks raised his glass. "Departed from this globe on his own initiative."

Lorna, Liz, Alvardi and Baxter raised their glasses. The Raymonds and Dr. Witzler looked on in horror.

Baxter raised his martini glass after the toast had been completed. "To Wild Bill Dwyer. A man who had a great career beginning and a bad end," Baxter toasted.

"His career middle wasn't so hot either," Dirks added.

Glasses were raised and drained. The waitress entered the room with a fresh tray of martinis.

"Ah, reinforcements!" Alvardi observed.

"Maybe we should begin our lunch now," Hugh Raymond suggested.

"On the contrary," Alvardi responded. "We will require more toasts now that we're getting warmed up."

"More toasts, less prayers," Dirks said supportively. "You're up, Frankie."

"To Bill Dwyer, a comrade who lost his way from the main road and wound up in obscurity among the philistines." Alvardi raised his glass accompanied by a glare from Dr. Witzler.

"How about it, Lorna? You're up," Alvardi said.

"I'll defer to Liz and make the final toast," Lorna said. Liz raised her glass looking around the room as she searched her mind for words.

"Here's to Mr. Dwyer. A man whom I've never met who's managed to screw up my weekend. He's now a man who's no longer hanging around." The glasses were raised and sips were taken.

"Congratulations, Miss MacReavie," Dirks said. "You have just moved to number one in our worst toast contest. Only Mrs. Brimmer has the opportunity to compete with you for number one."

Everyone looked to Lorna Brimmer standing against the wall with her sable coat on her shoulders. She was an attractive woman of 50 who looked to be in her late 30's.

Lorna had a tall trim body in an expensive suit, high priced but conservative jewelry, and a classic face with cold eyes. She could easily be mistaken for an aristocratic mistress of the manor.

"Here's to the men and women who made up the mid-1970's face of McKenzie Barber. We are here to mourn the loss of a sometimes amusing, but most of the time exasperating, comrade. Good-bye, Bill Dwyer."

Lorna drained her glass in concert with Alvardi, Baxter, Liz, and Dirks. Placing her empty glass on a table, Lorna turned to the buffet table, and quickly selected items for her plate. She was followed by Liz, Mrs. Raymond, Alvardi, Dirks, Hugh Raymond, and Dr. Witzler. Lorna seated herself at the head of the table. Baxter's watch said one o'clock. Dr. Witzler suggested that they pray after they were seated.

"We've already had ten seconds of silent prayer. There's no need to overload the channels of communications with the Lord. Might be some Nigerians trying to get through," Dirks pointed out.

"I have to admit this is the most unusual assembly of distinguished men and women I've ever accompanied to a funeral service," Dr. Witzler offered, after he had consumed a healthy mouthful of potato salad.

"I would assume that the people at this table will represent the totality of the attendees at the funeral home service," Lorna estimated.

"Dr. Thistle's wife called me just before we left for the luncheon," Mrs. Raymond interjected. "They may come for the service."

"What role would you like me to play in the service, Mrs. Brimmer?" Dr. Witzler asked.

"I'm not certain," Lorna said. "I recently buried my late husband. Bill Dwyer is another matter. Mr. Baxter will deliver the eulogy. How would it be if you would more or less convene and close the ceremony?"

Dr. Witzler looked down the table at Baxter. With two martinis down, Baxter felt a decent glow, and he was on the edge of drowsiness. "Have you given a funeral eulogy before?" Dr. Witzler asked.

"Joe Baxter," Dirks interjected, "is the Chairman of Eulogies International. He gives eulogies all over the world."

"It was my understanding that Mr. Baxter was still with McKenzie Barber," Dr. Witzler noted.

"That's his job during the week," Alvardi explained. "Joe is Eulogies International on weekends."

"How long have you been doing this work, Mr. Baxter?"

"I just started this morning," Baxter explained.

"I would like to remind you that funeral services are a sensitive religious ceremony not to be mocked," Dr. Witzler said sharply.

"And I don't recall inviting you to participate in the service," Lorna responded.

"You're totally lacking in sensitivity, Jim," Dirks explained. "The man we've come to bury was a renegade and a rounder, not the retired principal of the local junior high school. You may be uncomfortable with us, but we, in turn, are quite uncomfortable with you."

"We recognize the union card that you wear around your neck," Alvardi added. "But I really doubt that you're much needed after lunch. It might be convenient if you attended as an observer. I'm certain Mrs. Brimmer will want to recompense you for your time."

Aha! Baxter observed. The group had a fresh enemy! Poor pompous Dr. Witzler. He would dearly earn his stipend this afternoon.

The chapel of the Brunlinger Funeral Home was packed. There were some front row seats reserved for the family, but every other seat was taken. Baxter recognized Dr. Thistle and a middle-aged woman seated on the far right hand side. Every seat appeared to be occupied by a student, and there were three lines of standees behind the last section of seats. They wore sweaters, jackets, and jeans. Only Dr. Thistle, among the audience, wore a suit. Organ music played over the speaker system.

"How shall we do this, Frank?" Baxter questioned Alvardi as they entered the chapel.

"Take center stage, kid. Keep that asshole, Witzler out of this. Get up there. Give the damned eulogy and then do a brief wrap-up at the grave site. I'll buy you a drink after you're done."

Baxter walked up the side aisle to the altar. It was showtime again.

Baxter looked out at the audience. He had made some notes during the morning on the pad at the back of his week-at-a-glance book. There were words that coded memories of Dwyer before and after he had begun to slip. How had he allowed himself to be placed in this position? Lorna, Alvardi, Dirks, Liz, and the Raymonds were seated in the first row. Dr. Witzler was sitting in a chair to Baxter's right holding a Bible in his hand. Baxter assumed that Witzler was prepared to jump in should he falter. He was the safety net. What the hell, Baxter said to himself. Here goes nothing.

"GOOD AFTERNOON. MY NAME IS JOE BAXTER. I'VE BEEN ASKED TO SAY A FEW WORDS OF GOOD-BYE TO WILLIAM DWYER. I'D LIKE TO THANK YOU IN ADVANCE FOR ASSEMBLING HERE TODAY TO BID FAREWELL TO A TRULY REMARKABLE MAN WHO FAVORABLY IMPACTED SO MANY LIVES AND CAREERS. I AM PLEASED TO SEE SO MANY YOUNG PEOPLE IN THE ROOM AND ASSUME THAT YOU WERE HIS STUDENTS."

"SOME OF THE PEOPLE IN THE FRONT ROW WHO HOLD VERY RESPONSIBLE POSITIONS IN INDUSTRY AND HIGHER EDUCATION HAVE COME FROM FAR POINTS OF THE COUNTRY. THEY TOO WERE STUDENTS OF BILL DWYER AT ONE TIME IN THEIR CAREER. BILL WAS A MAN WHO TAUGHT ALL HIS LIFE, ALTHOUGH COLLEGE TEACHING ONLY CAME AFTER THE CONCLUSION OF A BRILLIANT CAREER IN MANAGEMENT CONSULTING."

"NOW, WE ASK OURSELVES, WHAT MATTER OF MAN WAS THIS BILL DWYER ANYWAY? HE WAS NEVER CONVENTIONAL, ALWAYS CHALLENGING, AND ENDLESSLY QUESTIONING. AS A CONSULTANT, BILL IDENTIFIED PROBLEMS, DEFINED THEM, AND SUCCESSFULLY IMPLEMENTED THE SOLUTIONS. HE CAME TO MCKENZIE BARBER DIRECTLY FROM WHAT WAS THEN A MAJOR MANUFACTURER OF TRUCKS AND FARM IMPLEMENTS. BILL REPRESENTED THE FIRST OF A NEW BREED OF MANUFACTURING CONSULTANTS WHEN HE JOINED MCKENZIE BARBER IN THE MID 1960s. HE WAS IN VIRTUAL COMPETITION WITH THE OLDER BREED OF TRADITIONAL MCKENZIE BARBER INDUSTRIAL ENGINEERING CONSULTANTS. I FIRST MET BILL DWYER IN 1966 WHEN I WAS A YOUNG PLANT MANAGER WITH A WISCONSIN HOUSEWARES MANUFACTURER. I WAS

ASSIGNED TO WORK WITH BILL AS HE BRILLIANTLY REORGANIZED OUR COMPANY'S APPROACH TO MANUFACTURING. LATER AFTER OUR COMPANY HAD BEEN SOLD, I HAD THE PRIVILEGE OF JOINING MCKENZIE BARBER AS ONE OF BILL'S CONSULTANTS, AND WAS HIS STUDENT FOR A SECOND TIME.

BILL DWYER HAD A UNIQUE SET OF CREDENTIALS. HE HELD MECHANICAL AND INDUSTRIAL ENGINEERING DEGREES IN ADDITION TO BEING A CHARTERED ACCOUNTANT AND PROFESSIONAL ENGINEER. DON'T ASK ME HOW HE ACCUMULATED ALL OF HIS DEGREES AND ACCREDITATION'S, BUT I ASSURE YOU THAT HE HAD THEM. BILL'S ACHIEVEMENTS FOR MCKENZIE BARBER CLIENTS WHICH RESULTED IN SEVERAL BILLION DOLLARS OF SAVINGS OVER HIS NINETEEN YEAR CONSULTING CAREER, ARE TOO NUMEROUS TO BE RECITED THIS AFTERNOON. THE IMPORTANT THING TO REMEMBER IS THAT BILL PROVIDED TRAINING AND INSIGHT TO MANY. YOU, HIS STUDENTS, LIKE MY COLLEAGUES IN THE FRONT ROW, HAVE BEEN LEFT A RICH LEGACY OF KNOWLEDGE BY BILL DWYER THAT WILL REMAIN WITH US FOR THE REST OF OUR LIVES.

OVER THE YEARS BILL DEVELOPED AN ADDICTION FOR ALCOHOL. IT WAS HIS ADDICTION THAT CONTRIBUTED TO HIS DESTRUCTION. THE DECISION TO EXIT FROM THIS WORLD WAS BILL'S. HE HAS TAKEN HIS LEAVE OF US, AND NO AMOUNT OF PIOUS PLATITUDES WILL BRING BILL DWYER BACK TO US. TODAY WE SAY GOOD-BYE AND RETURN TO OUR LIVES, BETTER PEOPLE FOR THE LESSONS BILL DWYER TAUGHT US. THANK YOU FOR YOUR ATTENTION. DR. WITZLER WILL NOW LEAD US IN THE LORD'S PRAYER."

Baxter spent a good part of that Saturday night drinking Scotch in Roger Dirks' room at the Hyatt Regency. They had endured the grave side ceremony where Dr. Witzler led the students in singing Onward Christian Soldiers.

As the casket was lowered, Dirks whispered to Baxter. "I hope to hell, Dywer's really in there."

Students awkwardly milled around the grave side. Finally, one stepped to Baxter's side. His hair was long and tied into a pony tail. He wore a soft leather jacket with Indian designs and fringe. He was at least two inches taller than Baxter. He settled in a place six feet from Baxter and lit a cigarette. "You said some good words back at the funeral home about Mr. Dwyer."

Baxter took a step forward extending his hand. "Thank you. My name is Joe Baxter." His hand was slowly accepted.

"I'm Uncas White Bear. I used to go to his classes."

The hand was moist and pumped Baxter's in two quick jerks before it was released. Baxter estimated that Uncas was in his mid-twenties. "I'm not a regular student here at the college. I'm in an apprenticed deal in toolmaking. I heard about Mr. Dwyer's class and came one day. I liked the way he talked. His classes were long. I know these colleges. It's 50 minutes and you're out. Mr. Dwyer would go on for two hours. He would talk for a long time and then he would ask the students questions to see if they were paying attention. I was thinking of going to the community college. Mr. Dwyer would tell us that we were all welcome, but that sooner or later we should step up and become regular students. I don't think the college liked the way he did things. I learned plenty of things from him. I went to his house a couple of times, and he tutored me in math. He was really good when he was off the bottle."

Suddenly the words stopped flowing. The cigarette was stomped out under a black boot, and Uncas White Bear took his leave of Joe Baxter.

Other students dribbled by. Dirks came by finally to fetch Baxter. "Queen Lorna is back in the limo and wants to get out of here. It's time for you to break off your little receiving line," Dirks said slapping Baxter on the back. They walked together away from the gravesite. Dirks stopped at the start of the path that led to the parking lot. He turned and took one last look at the grave. "Good-by, Mr. Chips," he shouted.

Baxter had planned to return to New York that evening.

"Stay overnight with me and go back in the morning, Joe," Dirks requested. "God knows when, and possibly if, we'll ever see each other again."

Lorna, Alvardi, and Liz MacReavie took leave of them when the limo arrived at the Hyatt Regency. "You did very well today, Joe," Lorna complimented Baxter. "This was an ugly experience which certainly didn't require my participation," she said looking coldly at Alvardi. "Brimmer Industries will pay for your room, Joe. Liz will take care of it."

There were handshakes all around, and Lorna's party disappeared into an elevator.

"We'll need a couple of bottles of Scotch. There's a package store down the street," Dirks directed.

"I don't drink Scotch," Baxter protested.

"Drink whatever you regularly drink tomorrow. Tonight we're drinking Scotch in honor of that great teacher, Mr. William Dwyer. Now tell me where the hell you came up with that several billion dollars worth of savings?"

"It sounded good when I said it. The number, as you know, was unaudited. It may have been slightly lower by eight or nine hundred million," Baxter explained.

"How old do you think Liz MacReavie is?" Dirks asked.

"Late forties, early fifties," Baxter estimated.

"She's coming by my room tonight after she's gotten Frankie and Lorna tucked in for the night."

Dirks' room was rather small. They set up the bar on the dresser and ordered up sandwiches and potato chips from room service. "Charge it to your room, Joe. We might as well get fed on the bounty from Brimmer Industries. It was probably impolitic of me and inconvenient for Lorna Brimmer to be reminded that she was once a secretary."

They settled back with Scotch and Dirks asked Baxter to bring him up to date. Baxter entered into a lengthy narrative describing the events that had taken place from Dirks quiet retirement to Baxter's Friday agreement to leave his practice and join Executive Office.

"Cut yourself a deal and get out of there, Joe. I barely know Fitzgerald and I never thought much of Pinker as a Partner. Those two geniuses aren't going to reverse a tide that Ernie Grey allowed to start and the team of Buzzsaw, Schmidt, and Clyde make into a torrent. McKenzie Barber was a hell of a firm at one time. It would have continued to be one hell of a firm if Ernie had either Brimmer or me take over from Bruce in 1978. Get Fitzgerald to put you on the Pension Committee. The retired Partners need an inside man."

"How do you feel about today?" Baxter asked.

Dirks refilled both Scotch glasses. "How do I feel about today?" Dirks repeated Baxter's question, pacing in the narrow space between the bed and the dresser. "Well for the first thing, we've practically got it over with. Next, Frank was right. Someone had to do something for Bill. We did the right thing for him today, and we did it our way. McKenzie Barber was probably the only employer in the world that would tolerate Bill Dwyer's shenanigans as long as they did. Ernie Grey was Dwyer's ultimate protector. There were a lot of get-rid-of-Dwyer movements when I was running New York Office. Burke wanted to get rid of him. I played that one through to a tie, and Burke lost all interest in the New York Office when he went off on his acquisition binge. Then Friedman came to New York. He started looking at people. Friedman was a decent planner and the first Managing Partner who looked hard at the future of the New York Office. They all delegated the present to me. Friedman wanted to get rid of Bill, but word came down from Ernie's office to leave Bill alone until he met vesting. Bill Dwyer was a dead man at McKenzie Barber regardless of who was elected in 1984. Bill was having far more bad days than good days at the time he exited, and his personal behavior became downright weird. He was heading in the direction that he ended. It was just a matter of time when Bill would decide, 'Enough of this'."

"I don't think Bill liked me very much at the end," Baxter observed.

"He was jealous of you, Joe. You were the protégé who slipped out of his grasp and passed him up. Do you think Ernie Grey would have trusted Bill Dwyer on the Review Task Force? He resented you. You're a natural organization man. In my book, you were a better national practice leader than Frank. Frank never worked very hard. He was always coasting. They canned Frankie and abandoned his practice at Robson Allen. You, in

351

contrast, were always a horse and a fighter. I thought you wrote a better book than Frank. I think his book is intellectual jello, but I've got to hand it to Frankie. He's a tremendous personal promoter. He's caught the eyes of the media and talk shows as the ultimate ombudsman of executive pay. He's also obviously the lap dog of Brimmer's widow. And that's not the worst fate that could befall a man like Frankie in his later days. What was Mrs. Brimmer like in the old Chicago Office days?"

"Not as she is today. That was a dozen years ago, Roger. Lorna has successfully re-invented herself. Let's leave it at that. Lorna is Paul Brimmer's widow and the Chairwoman of Brimmer Industries."

"Brimmer was an unusual man. I was on the Board with him. I more or less petitioned my way on the Board as an at-large Board member. Ernie was pissed at me when I was elected to the Board without his endorsement and permission. I used to be a burr in Ernie's side. Brimmer always played to Ernie. I knew he was my competition to succeed Dinsmore as the New York Office Managing Partner. I also assumed that Brimmer would get the job, and I would either work for Brimmer in New York or get the Chicago Managing Partner's job. I never took Burke seriously."

"Brimmer was a private man. There he was in his early forties, and no one could recall ever seeing him with a woman. That led to some low volume talk. Then one night I saw him with a woman. There used to be a very high class bordello on the West side in the mid-eighties. They had the most beautiful women in the world, the highest professional fee schedule in western civilization, and they accepted plastic. It was very private with a series of little trysting rooms stocked with liquor, snacks, a circular bed, a hot tub, and a separate bathroom and shower. I believe it was a thousand dollars for four hours, and twenty-five hundred for all night. These were 1975 prices mind you. They let you look through a picture book at reception, and you made a choice on the basis of three or four photo shots. You had to settle in advance on fees and they provided you a room key with a number. It was an old brownstone, and I estimated that they probably had twenty billets. To make a long story short, there was a key mix-up and I opened a door and discovered Brimmer and a fine looking Asian lady in the hot tub. He looked at me and I looked him in the eye and said, 'Sorry sir, there's obviously been a key mix-up.' I closed the door and found the madam running down the hall. She, apparently, had discovered the mistake. That was the night I met Nada, my Spanish dancer friend."

"That was the one who stabbed you?" Baxter queried.

"That was her. She had about nine or ten names, but I knew her as Nada. She was a part-time hooker in between dancing gigs. Nada came to the US with an Argentine dance troupe. They went back and she stayed. I looked at the picture book and saw a worldly woman of mid-thirties. One of the pictures showed her in her dance costume with a beret, a long slit skirt, and six inch stiletto black high heels. I opted for all-night, sight unseen." Dirks took a long sip of Scotch. "And she was a something. Nada was also grateful that she wouldn't be expected to do more than one trick that night. I'm getting ahead of myself. Back to Brimmer. I suspect that he was a little awkward in the courtship of women. It probably took too much time. Brimmer probably frequented very high class brothels around the country. We were in a Board meeting the next day. Brimmer shook hands with me at the start of the meeting. I don't remember him making eye contact that day. I imagine Lorna was close at hand in the Chicago office, and looked like she could keep her mouth shut. I've always stayed away from shipboard romances. How about you, Joe?"

Baxter sipped his Scotch. It was beginning to taste less and less like iodine. It was unlikely that he would never see Dirks again after this evening. "I may have slipped a few times over the years," Baxter confessed. "Tell me more about Nada, the Spanish dancer. I've heard innuendoes over the years. One story was that your stabbing cost you the New York Office Managing Partner job."

Dirks shook his head. "Ernie used the incident as an excuse to position his protégé. At the same time, Burke had never run anything as big as the New York Office. In fact, Burke had never really run anything at McKenzie Barber. He was an attractive line partner that Ernie had floating like a balloon over in Europe until he determined it was time to pull it in. My theory is that Ernie picked Burke out pretty much the same way Mr. Mac picked Ernie out. Burke was Ernie's choice over Brimmer. He cooked up that European job as a place to park Brimmer as a back-up if Burke didn't make it. Brimmer was having none of it, and took the next job that was offered him which turned out to be Hruska Industries. Hruska was a nothing company that Brimmer put his stamp on, and later his name. Now Lorna is a very rich widow."

"Can we go back to Nada?" Baxter requested.

"Christ, Joe, you're taking me back twelve or thirteen years. How many times have you been married?"

Baxter held up three fingers.

"How many of your wives are still living?"

Baxter held up the same three fingers.

"That must be expensive."

Baxter shook his head. "The funding of divorce settlements is all behind me."

"Amazing. I was only married once and she damned near sucked me dry. How old were you when you were married for the first time?"

"Eighteen."

"I was twenty-two. Mary Lou was an Art History major at Cornell, and she was a couple of years older than me. I was Roger Dirks, one of four sons of a druggist in Bentley, Vermont. My oldest brother, and the favorite of the family went off to Medical School, and the rest of us had to forage for ourselves. I managed to get into Cornell on a Naval ROTC scholarship. I was the guy who worked three jobs at a time to make ends meet. One of those jobs was in the library where I met Mary Lou. She was pregnant by the time I graduated, and I married her the week before I went on active duty. I requested sea duty and Mary Lou had an allotment check and medical benefits. I came home a couple of times on leave and concluded that I really didn't like her very much. We had a son named Robert, and he's turned out to be a pretty good young man. We both have a love of the sea, and while Robert wasn't much of a student, he's a pretty good sailor. He's a tug operator now in Brooklyn."

"Now you're wondering, Joe, what in hell does this have to do with Nada? I developed a taste for exotic women while I was in the Navy. Some of them were whores, but a lot weren't. Later I fell in with Alvardi and Dwyer who were womanizers. My first experience with Nada was sensational. Nada kept emphasizing how she was stranded in New York, and whoring was only a temporary weekend line of work until she landed another dancing job. I made a date for the following Saturday night and damned if she wasn't as good as the week before. I figured that at $2,500 a night, Nada could become a very expensive habit. That's when I asked her to move in with me for a while until she got a dancing job. I emphasized that the relationship would only be temporary, and that I traveled a lot."

"Our arrangement started off well enough, but a steady diet of Nada was not a wholesome experience. She really didn't look very hard for a dancing job, although I started paying for ballet lessons for her. Nada was really past her prime as a dancer, and in a couple of years, she could well be past her prime as a hooker. She slept until noon every day, and then drank and watched television on the afternoons when she didn't have dance class. Nada liked to get dolled up and go out for a late dinner. Except she was pretty drunk by that time and a lot of restaurants didn't welcome us back. Dirks, I asked myself. How did you get yourself into this mess? At the same time, I struck up a relationship with this lady senior editor at *Enterprise Week*."

"I started seeing her and taking the long way home. I came home late one night, and Nada was drunk and screaming at me. I turned to leave and suddenly felt a sharp pain. Nada had stabbed me. Then she stabbed me again and I turned and slugged her. I must have knocked her out cold. I pounded on doors until I woke up enough people to dial 911. I lost a lot of blood, almost died, but here I am to talk about it. The moral of the story is to leave whores in bordellos, just as you leave waitresses in restaurants. Now tell me about your McKenzie Barber indiscretions, Joe. Were they young impressionable female consultants?"

Baxter counted Hillary, Dominique, and Linda. "Just three in twenty-two years. I would call that a reasonable level of restraint."

"Any secretaries?" Dirks questioned.

"Not one."

"Was Lorna a secretary when Brimmer took up with her?" Dirks probed.

"She was in an exempt administrative manager position. As I remember it, Lorna replaced Lee Heller as Dr. Barry's admin guy when Heller moved to New York to work for Clyde."

"	"Lee Heller!" Dirks followed the name with a whistle. "Now there's a real big league empty suit. How in the hell has McKenzie Barber allowed a modestly talented consultant like Heller to stick around all of these years? Conversely, how can a man choose to stay year after year with McKenzie Barber in staff jobs?"

"I believe he's enamored with the brand name of the firm," Baxter responded. "Why did you stay at McKenzie Barber for your entire career?"

"Because I don't believe I could have made as much money or been as productive somewhere else. I was good at McKenzie Barber, Joe. So are you. And I suspect that's why you've stayed."

"And what's it like being retired? Do you miss McKenzie Barber?" Baxter asked.

"That calls for more Scotch." Dirks added to his glass. "I live alone on a power boat in a slip in the harbor of a town called Yarmouth. It's paid for, sleeps four, and it's damned cold in winter. I'm reading books that I haven't had time to read, and I watch old movies on my VCR. I've more or less dropped out. I read the *New York Times* and the *Wall Street Journal* every day, do a little pub crawling, and occasionally entertain a lady who would fall into the senior citizen category. It's a small town, and nobody has any suspicion of my past. The rumor around town is that I'm a retired tugboat captain. Do I miss McKenzie Barber? I miss the old McKenzie Barber. The contemporary McKenzie Barber is a mess, and I lay that blame on Ernie Grey. Brimmer should have succeeded him. Not Hamilton Burke or General Buzzsaw! Clyde Nickerson should have been scourged from the firm. What's done has been done. Roger Dirks and a number of other retired Partners need the firm to keep going in order to fund the pension disbursements."

"What was McKenzie Barber like under John McKenzie?" Baxter asked his favorite question.

"It was a very conservative, highly professional firm that was a little on the stodgy side. I came in 1954 after Korea. Ernie Grey came in about 49 or 50, and was Mr. Mac's errand boy. It was a solid firm, but the leadership was pretty rigid. There was no screwing of women consultants or secretaries in those days. When Mr. Mac spoke, everybody listened. Bruce Dinsmore was enshrined as life-long Managing Partner of the New York

Office, and it eventually proved my fight, right or wrong, to drive the operating plan through. Our problem at McKenzie Barber is that we installed a management structure in the early 1970s that either neutered the talent we had, or drove it out of the firm. But what really bothers me tonight is knowing that the flaky Mr. Alvardi is up there in the suite with that fine looking woman with that enormous net worth." The telephone rang cutting Dirks short. "Dirks," he professionally answered the telephone. "Liz, how good to hear from you. No, you're not calling too late. Joe and I are having a quiet libation or two and we had some sandwiches sent up. No, it's not too late. We would be delighted to see you. That's room 619."

"Should I leave?" Baxter asked.

"Jesus, Joe. You've got to stick around for at least two drinks before I position Liz to begin to entertain the idea of spending the night with me. Stay the course man! Accommodate and support your old comrade as he cleverly spins his seduction plots."

"Count on me," Baxter agreed and replenished his glass.

The knock on the door came five minutes later, and Dirks sprang to his feet with catlike quickness. Liz MacReavie had changed to pants and a sweater. She looked much shorter in flat shoes. Baxter gave up his stuffed chair for Liz, and moved to a side chair.

"I have to say right off, Joe, that I thought your eulogy was brilliant today, considering what you had to work with. I've been with Frank and Lorna for the last two hours and they were telling Bill Dwyer stories that would curl your hair. Joe, you did a marvelous job in dignifying today's proceedings."

"How long have you been with Brimmer Industries, Liz? Dirks asked.

"Three years now. I was recruited away from Georgia-Washington Paper where I was Manager-Investor Relations. I was hired to report to Paul Brimmer, but wound up reporting through Lorna. At Brimmer Industries, I have been responsible for all communications including investor relations," Liz answered. Dirks poured three inches of Scotch into a glass of ice.

"Then you must have had frequent contact with the late Mr. Brimmer?" Dirks suggested.

Liz took a sip of Scotch before responding. "I worked mostly through Lorna. I had two meetings with Mr. Brimmer in three years. They were very difficult meetings. I was very glad that Lorna was in those meetings in order to diffuse Mr. Brimmer. Lorna is demanding, but she is also reasonable. This weekend is an example of that. She called me in after lunch and told me, 'I need you for the weekend, Liz.' I had no idea of who this Bill Dwyer was. But I dropped everything to be here. It reminded me of the day when Lorna learned that Mr. Brimmer had died in Thailand. Lorna told me, 'I need you, Liz' and I worked through the weekend. Now, Roger, did I hear today that Lorna had been a secretary at McKenzie Barber?"

Baxter looked to Dirks for amendments. "I misspoke. I confused Lorna Brimmer with another Lorna in the Chicago office. I spent most of my McKenzie Barber career in the New York office."

"Roger had Lorna Brimmer confused with Lorna Shrumpfmiller, a tall blonde from Milwaukee who used to supervise the typing pool," Baxter added.

"It was my error, Liz. Joe set me straight. Lorna had a Director level position, that's one level under a Partner, with the Strategy Practice Business unit. Had Lorna stayed, she probably would have been elected a Partner at the time Paul went to Hruska Industries."

"I believe she had been deferred one year at the time, Roger," Baxter lied. "Lorna Shrumpfmiller married the African American mail room supervisor," Baxter added.

"I remember they called him 'Satch'", Dirks added to the liturgy of fibs.

"Now are Lorna and Frank settled down for the evening?" Baxter asked. The Scotch was beginning to get to him.

"Frank is such a peach. I don't know what Lorna would have done when the news of Mr. Brimmer's death reached us, if it weren't for Frank. Now he's on the Board, and I expect that Frank will relocate to Atlanta one of these days. With that said, I will say no more on the subject. Now what have the two of you been up to since we broke up?"

"I have engaged Joe to deliver the eulogy at my funeral," Dirks reported.

"Are you planning to face death soon, Roger?" Liz asked.

"I believe I will be just fine for tonight and tomorrow night. After that, I'm in the Lord's hands," Dirks explained. Baxter studied the eye contact between Liz MacReavie and Roger Dirks. He concluded that the relationship had a chance. He rose to his feet. "I have a very early morning flight and some Sunday work I have to get ready for. I had better leave."

There was an exchange of handshakes and Dirks saw Baxter to the door. "Let's get together in Boston and tie our ties to the bar," Dirks suggested.

"I'll call you," Baxter promised.

Baxter never called, and learned in the summer of 1991 that Dirks had died of a heart attack in his sleep. Roger Dirks had been buried for three weeks when Baxter learned of his death. There was no announcement from McKenzie Barber, and Dirks' death did not make *The New York Times* obituary section.

10:25 AM, Tuesday, January 8, 1992

The Metroliner was sixteen minutes late to its Philadelphia 30th Street Station stop. Toni and her brother, Jim, were waiting for him in the lobby in front of the train schedule board at the center of the station.

Toni wore dark glasses with a mink coat draped over her shoulders. Her brother, Jim, wore a blue suit with an empty breast pocket and a blue tie. Baxter concluded that Jim could pass for Toni's chauffeur.

Toni raised her sunglasses to her forehead when she recognized Baxter. Toni's eyes seemed very hard and her skin had retained its Florida tan.

She took a step forward as Baxter approached and greeted him initially with a handshake and then offered a cheek to be kissed. Jim Alter simply shook hands.

"It's been horrible, Joe. I'm so glad to see you. The reviewal was yesterday and now we're driving to Greystone Academy for the funeral service. There's a small cemetery there where the headmasters have been traditionally buried. Ernie's going to be buried among the headmasters."

Jim Alter led the way to a large white Cadillac where a uniformed chauffeur was waiting. He seemed to be dressed identically to Jim Alter.

"This is an IPCO staff car. It belongs to the General Manager of the IPCO Refinery. Tom Donohue, the CEO, arranged it. He and his wife, Eve, have been wonderful," Toni whispered as she led Baxter into the spacious back seat. Jim Alter climbed in the front seat next to the driver.

"Let me tell you about our day." Toni prodded a diary from her purse. "The funeral service will be at two in the Greystone Academy Chapel. The reviewal was yesterday, and you missed it. Over two hundred people signed the book. The service is expected to last thirty minutes. There will be six pall bearers, three from each side of the family. Tom Donohue, my brother, Jim and you will be pallbearers. Pres Grey, Spencer, the youngest Harwell boy, and a man named Lockwood Barings will make up the other set of pallbearers. Lockwood Barings is Millie Grey's attorney, and may be her current boyfriend. We had some brushes with him during the divorce settlement, and I believe that they are planning to contest Ernie's will. Be careful of him."

"The cemetery is behind the chapel, so Ernie will have to be carried about fifty yards. There will be sandwiches, coffee, soft drinks, and cake served in the school lunchroom after the burial. Next the immediate family and certain people have been invited back to a place called the Schuykill Club where cocktails and a buffet dinner will be served. I plan to skip the coffee and sandwiches at the Greystone lunchroom and proceed directly to the Schuykill Club. Jim's car is parked in a lot near the 30th Street Station and he will drive back home. I have tickets for us to the Club Car on the 8:30 Metroliner back to New York. I assume I can count on you to remain at my side the entire day."

Baxter nodded his head and peered out at the city streets of Philadelphia. He had been the eulogy giver at Dwyer's funeral and now was going to be a pallbearer at Ernie Grey's funeral. The next logical step would be for him to be the main attraction.

"It's really a very lovely ride. There's a little Inn on the way where we can stop for lunch. Ernie and I used to stop there regularly when we visited Greystone. Ernie was the Chairman of Board of Trustees for two years while the school got on its feet again. If it weren't for Ernie, Greystone might have gone under. Have you ever been there?" Baxter shook his head.

"Well the school goes back to 1820. Greys have always attended Greystone Academy. It's co-educational now. If I should ever have a son or daughter, I would want them to go through Greystone Academy."

Baxter patted Toni's hand. "I'm sorry I couldn't get there before now. How are you holding up?"

"It was the suddenness that shook me. At this time last week, Ernie and I were roller blading in Naples. We were drinking cokes under an umbrella by our pool and talking about what we would do for the rest of his life. Ernie was a very healthy, vigorous man at age 70. They had a wonderful retirement dinner for him at IPCO. I was so proud of him. We were talking about traveling around the world. We used to go roller blading in the morning before the heat set in. We had a sailing lesson in the afternoon. Ernie was determined to learn to sail. We took our short route last Saturday morning and had just started the final stretch home. The next thing I knew

Ernie was flying through the air and landed on his head. He was gone by the time the ambulance got to the hospital. Here was an air ace, who shot down 23 Japanese planes and survived the battle of Midway, killed by a pick-up truck. I shouldn't have called Pres right away to tell him that his father had been killed. I should have taken charge of the funeral and then told the Greys what had happened. They just brushed me aside and took over. Tom Donohue was in the Middle East. He didn't get back until late Sunday. He's taken my side. He called Millie up and reminded her that I was Mrs. Grey, not her."

"Isn't the objective to get Ernie buried in a dignified manner?" Baxter suggested.

"They want to humiliate me, Joe. I know that Millie Grey regards me as a young twit who stole her husband. I made him happy, Joe. She never made him happy."

Baxter patted Toni's hand again. He wished to hell she'd shut up. He had started to think about Rusty. Her plane had to be half way to LA by now.

Toni squeezed Baxter's hand. "You're very quiet this morning, Joe. Do you have a lot of things on your mind?"

"I will be finishing my career with the firm tomorrow. I'm on the list of Partners to be guillotined. I am vested at 24 1/2 years. There is no place for me at Robson Allen Barber. I've been dodging them for the last month so I could build another year into my pension. At this time tomorrow, it will be all over for me with McKenzie Barber which has dominated my life for the last twenty-five years or so."

"Ernie was upset when he read in the paper about the merger. He was angry over John McKenzie's name being dropped. He had a bad week in early November after the merger announcement. But then Tom Donohue reminded Ernie how well IPCO had done during his tenure as Chairman. Tom and his wife, Eve, have become our best friends over the past three years. Tom tends to be very blunt. He just told Ernie over cocktails one night, 'Godamn it, Ernie, you can't take the blame for the performance of a firm that you left seven years ago.' Ernie thought about it for a couple of seconds and said, 'I believe you're right, Tom.' He never brought up McKenzie Barber again. Now, what will you do after McKenzie Barber?

Ernie always felt you should have gone to work for Leon Harwell, but that it only would have worked if Leon had lived."

"I've been playing with the idea of writing a book about McKenzie Barber."

"Oh," Toni brightened. "That sounds like a good idea. Ernie always felt you were a very good writer. We saw your book on the shelf in a store in Naples. I have possession of a lot of Ernie's correspondence. He had a huge John McKenzie file in his Naples study. If you're serious, you should come down and spend the week. I could use the company. Also I could use you in my market research company." Baxter's hand was squeezed again.

Jim Alter joined them for lunch at the Alhambra Inn. Baxter was afraid he would choose to eat with the driver. Toni excused herself to make some telephone calls and Baxter sipped at a glass of white wine while Jim ordered a Budweiser.

"How are things up in Horseheads, Jim?"

"They're good, Joe. Tuesday is generally not that busy. I will be glad though when this funeral is over. I don't know how to deal with all these people. I sure like Mr. Donohue. He and his wife had dinner with us last night. I'm proud to have had the opportunity to spend time with a man like that. He's got more of a common touch than Ernie. The man has a PhD in Geology, but he started out as a roughneck when he was seventeen. The man talks plain where Ernie always seemed to be straining to say hello to someone like me."

Thinking about what he had just said, Jim Alter retracted his comment. "I mean, I admired and respected Ernie. He was obviously a great man, but he made it obvious that he was a couple of levels ahead of me. I know you two were good friends and partners in business, but that's how I felt about him. The whole family was shocked when Toni took up with him. We were afraid that Ernie would lose interest in her after a while. My father and mother wrote Ernie a letter when they were first living together that Toni intercepted. They were very upset. Toni was my big sister. She was the real smart one. She never did have many dates in high school. Toni came close to making Valedictorian, but wound up Salutatorian and getting a library science scholarship. I figured she'd go off and marry a teacher. And suddenly there she was, living with this very powerful man who was twice her age. Maybe that happens in New York City, but it isn't accepted in western New York. Once when they were married, things changed. Ernie even came by to have Sunday dinner with the folks one spring. My Dad kept on calling Ernie, 'Sir'."

Toni rejoined them at the table. "I'm starved. Let's order," the latter Mrs. Ernie Grey commanded them.

They drove into the Greystone Academy lot of twenty minutes to the hour. The semi-circle driveway in front of the chapel was filled with cars. Some students in Greystone jackets assisted by two uniformed police men directed them to a parking place in the middle of the rapidly filling parking lot. The temperature was in the low twenties under a bright afternoon sun. Baxter quickly began to recognize familiar faces as they stepped through the icy parking lot.

Baxter identified Adele Harwell holding the arm of her son, Spencer, as they moved through the parking lot in short steps. A large man in a grey coat and matching Stetson hat stood outside the car. He was accompanied by two other younger men in dark coats with somber faces.

"Hello little lady," Tom Donohue greeted Toni as she emerged from the Cadillac. "I trust you had a comfortable ride," he enfolded Toni in his arms and kissed her once on each cheek.

"Toni, say hello to Doni Ciardi and Rex Hart, two of my senior staff people. I asked them to come over this morning and get into the details." Baxter came around from the other side of the car in time to hear Donohue tell Toni in a low voice. "I had a talk with Millie Grey and her son Preston this morning. I believe I got things straightened out."

"Tom, do you remember Joe Baxter? He came up from New York to be with me today."

Tom Donohue looked Baxter up and down critically, and then extended a large hand. "I believe we've met a couple of times. You made a couple of presentations to the IPCO Board. I'm glad you're finally here. Ernie really thought a lot of you." Donohue offered Toni his arm. Baxter exchanged handshakes with Ciardi and Hart, and Jim Alter dutifully fell in step at the rear of their procession.

"We're going to be in the front pew on the right," Donohue explained to Toni. "There's room for you, me, Eve, Joe, and your brother and one more if we want. The left pew is for the other Greys. The pew behind them is reserved for the Harwells. It looks like a whole bunch of them turned out. They may require two pews. Don and Rex will direct traffic and they will pass out the programs at the door. Dr. Ensley, the President of Greystone, will conduct the service. You met him at the reviewal yesterday. I guess Ernie had something to do with his hiring a couple of years back when he chaired the Trustees. He seems a little young, but apparently is qualified to conduct the service."

"I'm quite familiar with Dr. Ensley," Toni interjected. "He and his wife, Deborah, have visited us twice in New York. Last summer they stayed overnight and we treated them to dinner and a play. They're lovely people. Yesterday was such a blur. I don't know how I got through it. Dr. Ensley is quite well qualified to conduct the service. He is an Episcopal Minister and holds a Doctorate in Education from Harvard. Ernie believed that Greystone needed fresh leadership and vision. Once he said," Toni partially suppressed a giggled, "'What we don't need at Greystone is another over the hill pompous old fart looking for a place to retire. We need someone with vision and energy who will build over five years, groom a successor, and get on with his career.'"

"Boy, I can just hear Ernie saying something like that," Donohue observed with a short laugh. "Toni, you're going to be seated last. Joe, here can escort you into the pew. Millie Grey will go in ahead of you accompanied by her son, Preston. I had breakfast with Dr. Ensley this morning. I explained a little of the history, including why there were two Mrs. Greys. Then I reviewed the outline of his sermon and made certain that we were of one mind on what was to be said. I believe we have everything worked out. Dr. Ensley really brightened up when I informed him that IPCO was sending some scholarship money to Greystone in Ernie's name. The service will probably start a little late because of the turn-out. We would have been better off holding the service in the gym and the reception in the chapel. The service should run about thirty-five minutes." Donohue turned to Baxter. "Ever been a pall bearer before?" Baxter shook his head. He had been a eulogist, but never a pall bearer.

"Rex will fill you in. He just buried his father last month. I've never been one either, but people seem to take on the job everyday," Donohue said. They were fast approaching the driveway to the chapel. Donohue paused for some final instructions to the group. "There will be a hymn at the gravesite, a few last words from Dr. Ensley, and then you will scoop the first earth on the coffin. Then Millie Grey will handle the next shovel full. There will probably be a pretty good turn-out for the reception in the gym, Toni. Joe, I want you to escort Toni from the gravesite and stand next to her at the head of the line. And—," Donohue looked at Jim Alter. "Jim, why don't you stand on the other side of Joe. We need a bit of a buffer between the other Greys. When the last person goes through, the driver will be around front to take you directly to the Schuykill Club. That's Millie Grey's show and it's up to you and me, Joe, to make sure that Toni doesn't get pushed around by the Greys. Got it?"

"Yes sir," Baxter replied. It was obvious that Tom Donohue was a man accustomed to giving orders.

There was a large ante-room in front of the chapel where people appeared to be assembling in small clusters prior to entering the main room of the building. Baxter's watch said twelve minutes to the hour. Sounds of organ music wafted through the ante-room. They took a place in the far corner of the room to await their time of entrance.

"It's Bach," Baxter said softly to Toni. She had somehow donned a black hat with a veil during the walk from the car to the chapel.

Toni nodded her head and gripped Baxter's arm tightly. She had appeared to have assumed her official grieving widow pose. At the opposite corner of the room was an unveiled Millie Grey accompanied by her daughter, Kathleen, who wore a black pants suit, and her son, Preston, who looked like a Brooks Brothers catalog model with the exception of his hair which he had tied in a pony tail.

Preston made a slight wave at Baxter and Toni from across the room. A small man with hanging spectacles and supported by a wooden cane with an ivory handle slowly made his way to the center of the ante-room. He was accompanied by a uniformed driver who supported him on his left arm. The pair stopped suddenly in mid-floor and the small man stopped to look at his watch and then shook his head. He pointed with his cane toward Baxter's corner of the room and they came to rest in a place six feet away.

"It's Charley Robson," Baxter whispered to Toni. "I flew in the next seat to London with him four years ago. He was about to retire at the time."

Charley Robson's appearance, in Baxter's estimation, had aged twenty years since their plane trip four years earlier. His hair was now a shaggy grey, and he appeared emaciated in a tweed sport coat that hung like a tent over his frame. The driver held an overcoat over his free hand.

Baxter steered Toni over to within three feet of Charley Robson.

"Charley, Joe Baxter here," he said extending his hand. Charley Robson, with the assistance of his attendant, raised his spectacles to the bridge of his nose.

"Who the hell are you?" Robson questioned.

"Joe Baxter of McKenzie Barber. We shared a plane ride to London about four years ago. You were about to retire from Robson Allen. This is Ernie's widow, Toni Grey," Baxter said presenting Toni.

Charley Robson shook his head. "Ernie's wife, Millie, is over there. I'm going to say hello to her later. I want a back pew so I can get out fast. I don't remember meeting you."

"This is the second Mrs. Grey. Millie was the first Mrs. Grey," Baxter explained.

Charley Robson nodded his head. "I understand now. You're the second Mrs. Grey. There were at least four Mrs. Robsons at last count, and I don't think I could name them all if you pressed me at this minute. My condolences, Mrs. Grey. Your husband could do two things better than I could. He could shoot down Japs, and apparently rollerblade with some limitations in success." He turned to his driver. "Let's go in now, Peter." Charley Robson pointed his cane toward Baxter. "And I don't know who the hell you are."

"What a rude man," Toni whispered to Baxter.

"He always disliked Ernie, Toni. Charley's here to dance on Ernie's grave. He had better dance fast because it doesn't look like he's going to make July." Baxter predicted as they observed the founding Chairman of Robson Allen Harbridge traverse the space next to the chapel doors.

Rex, from Tom Donohue's party, briefed Baxter on his duties as a pall bearer. There would be eight pall bearers with Baxter at the lead on the left side and Preston Grey at the lead on the right side. Baxter's watch read five to the hour.

"Do you want to go in?" he asked Toni.

"I'm going last after Millie. I was Ernie's wife. Millie used to be his wife," Toni answered in a quiet and determined voice. The side door to the ante-room opened and Baxter recognized Burke in a trench coat and Madame de Robilliard in a fur coat that looked like ermine from across the room. Each embraced Millie Grey and exchanged kisses on the cheek. Then Preston Grey offered his mother an arm and they entered the chapel at 1:58. Baxter started to follow only to have a heavy set man in a brown overcoat barge ahead of them with a muffled 'excuse me'. Baxter watched him squeeze into the aisle seat in the last pew.

He studied the man's face as he slowly escorted Toni down the center aisle. It was a weathered lined face with a bald head. He bowed his head into a hymn book.

Dr. Ensley stood at the pulpit in his black clerical robe. A full choir was assembled in the balcony choir loft. Baxter and Toni took their seats with Millie and Preston in the last seats in the front row. Dr. Ensley smiled at them as they took their seats.

"May we all please stand and sing from Hymn #37, How Great Thou Art," Dr. Ensley said with a rising hand gesture. Baxter counted the choir as twenty strong, including four young women. Their voices swelled in unison against the off-key singing from the main assembly. The voices made it through four stanzas finishing slightly behind the choir.

Dr. Ensley beamed out at the assembly of mourners.

"WE ARE GATHERED THIS AFTERNOON TO CELEBRATE THE LIFE OF AN EXCEPTIONAL MAN WHO HAS LEFT THIS LIFE TO TAKE HIS PLACE IN THE KINGDOM OF OUR CREATOR. ALL OF US ARE MOURNING THE LOSS OF ERNEST GREY III, BUT WE MUST ACCEPT AND UNDERSTAND THAT ERNIE GREY HAS SIMPLY PASSED FROM THIS LIFE AND MOVED TO ANOTHER.

ERNIE GREY WAS A MAN WHO ACCOMPLISHED MUCH IN HIS 70 YEARS OF LIFE ON EARTH. IT IS INDEED FITTING THAT HIS PASSAGE IS BEING CELEBRATED IN THE CHAPEL OF GREYSTONE ACADEMY WHERE HIS YOUNG ADULT LIFE BEGAN.

THE YOUNGEST SON OF PRESCOTT AND ANNE GREY, ERNIE WAS THE FOURTH GENERATION OF GREYS TO ATTEND GREYSTONE ACADEMY. HIS FATHER WAS AN OUTSTANDING STUDENT LEADER AND THE FIRST BASEMAN ON OUR CHAMPIONSHIP BASEBALL TEAM. ERNIE'S FATHER, PRESCOTT, WENT ON TO BECOME CHAIRMAN OF THE PHILADELPHIA NATIONAL BANK. PRESCOTT GREY'S SON, ERNIE, WAS AN OUTSTANDING STUDENT, A CLASS LEADER, AND THE STAR TAILBACK OF THE GREYSTONE FOOTBALL TEAM. I MIGHT ADD THAT THE GREYSTONE CRIMSON CRUSADERS WERE UNDEFEATED DURING ERNIE'S JUNIOR AND SENIOR YEARS, A LEVEL OF PLAY THAT HAS NEVER BEEN MATCHED IN THE FIFTY THREE INTERVENING YEARS.

ERNIE GREY INTERRUPTED HIS COLLEGE YEARS WHEN HIS COUNTRY WENT TO WAR IN DECEMBER OF 1941. HE VOLUNTEERED AS A NAVAL AIR CADET ON THE DAY AFTER PEARL HARBOR.

ERNIE GREY DISTINGUISHED HIMSELF AS AN AIR ACE IN THE PACIFIC WAR THEATRE. HE BECAME ONE OF HIS COUNTRY'S MOST DECORATED WAR HEROES. AFTER THE WAR, ERNIE RETURNED TO COLLEGE, MARRIED THE FIRST MRS. GREY, GRADUATED FROM THE HARVARD BUSINESS SCHOOL, AND JOINED THE WORLD FAMOUS MANAGEMENT CONSULTING FIRM OF MCKENZIE BARBER.

ERNIE GREY ADVANCED RAPIDLY THROUGH THE RANKS OF MCKENZIE BARBER WHEN HE WAS ELECTED CHAIRMAN AT AGE 36. HE RETIRED FROM MCKENZIE BARBER IN 1984 AND MOVED TO ANOTHER CAREER AS CHAIRMAN OF THE INTERNATIONAL PETROLEUM COMPANY. HE WAS EQUALLY SUCCESSFUL AT THE INTERNATIONAL PETROLEUM COMPANY, AND RETIRED FROM HIS SECOND CAREER IN NOVEMBER OF LAST YEAR. SOMEWHERE DURING HIS LAST YEARS AT MCKENZIE BARBER AND THE BEGINNING OF HIS NEW

EXECUTIVE CAREER AT THE INTERNATIONAL PETROLEUM COMPANY, ERNIE DISCOVERED THAT HIS ALMA MATER, GREYSTONE ACADEMY, WAS EXPERIENCING DIFFICULTIES IN ADJUSTING TO THE DEMANDS OF THE 1980S. ERNIE JUMPED IN WITH HIS CUSTOMARY GUSTO AND WORKED TIRELESSLY TO PUT THIS WONDERFUL SCHOOL RIGHT. HE WAS ASSISTED SPLENDIDLY IN THIS ENDEAVOR BY THE SECOND MRS. GREY. ERNIE GREY LOVED GREYSTONE ACADEMY AND IT IS ONLY FITTING THAT THIS FINAL SERVICE IN RECOGNITION OF THIS GREAT MAN'S LIFE BE CELEBRATED IN THIS CHAPEL WHERE HE SPENT SO MUCH TIME IN REFLECTION DURING HIS YOUNG MANHOOD.

IN ADDITION TO HIS WIFE, TONI, ERNIE GREY LEAVES BEHIND KATHLEEN, DAUGHTER, WHO IS A CORPORATE ATTORNEY, AND A SON, PRESTON, WHO HAS FOLLOWED HIS CEO FATHER'S FOOTSTEPS IN THE INTERIOR DESIGN INDUSTRY, AND HUNDREDS OF THOUSANDS OF MANAGERS WHOSE CAREERS HE INFLUENCED.

THE GREYSTONE ACADEMY SENIOR CHOIR WILL NOW SING A MEDLEY OF ERNIE GREY'S FAVORITE HYMNS."

The funeral ceremony lasted approximately forty minutes by Baxter's watch. Both Toni and Millie accompanied the coffin which turned out to be rather heavy. Baxter noted that Ernie's grave was in a plot two spaces down from the founder of Greystone Academy. The grave site was quickly encircled by the funeral assembly. The front row joined hands and sang, 'Let us Gather at the River' followed by the Lord's Prayer. Baxter looked over his shoulder and observed the heavyset form of the late comer in the brown overcoat. The casket was lowered and Millie Grey applied the first shovel of dirt. Baxter heard a voice from behind him as Toni was passed the shovel from Millie. Baxter heard the words, "Good-bye Laddie". He turned to again observe the man in the brown overcoat and there was an empty space in the next row.

He stopped the woman behind him as the assembly dispersed.

"The man in the brown overcoat who stood next to you. Did you see where he went?" he asked.

The middle aged woman shook her head. "He simply said something that sounded like 'good-bye laddie' and he started off around the back of the chapel."

"We'd never seen him before," the next man to her added. Baxter turned to Toni.

"I'll be right back." He maneuvered his way through the crowd and ran to the far corner of the chapel. He saw the man in the brown overcoat walking briskly toward a waiting car.

"Stop! Wait up! I need to talk to you!" Baxter shouted.

The man in the overcoat began to trot and he shouted some words to the car which backed up to meet him. He jerked open the rear door and disappeared into the inside. The car sped away at least fifty yards ahead of Baxter's shouts. Baxter failed to make out the license plate number. He stood puffing in the road and observed the car disappear into the bright, crisp, mid-afternoon January sunlight. Baxter was convinced that he had seen Will Harwell.

A large private room had been reserved at the Schuykill Club. It was a massive, three story stone building overlooking the Delaware River. Baxter could remember being there once before on a New Year's Eve with Stephany Hart in the late 1970s.

"I really have to get back now, Toni," Jim Alter repeated at least three times during the ride from Greystone Academy to the Schuykill Club.

"There is no need for you to spend any more time here, Jim," Toni finally conceded. "Joe can take care of me from here. Driver," she instructed the IPCO chauffeur. "You can drop Mr. Baxter and me at the Schuykill Club, and drop my brother off at his parking lot which is around the corner from the 30th Street Station."

Baxter exchanged handshakes and Toni embraced her brother. They stood outside the club and waved as the IPCO staff car pulled away. "The poor dear. He dropped everything to come down and be with me and he was so far out of his element."

"Well I bet Jim's a mover and shaker up in Horseheads." Baxter observed as he steered Toni through the main entrance to the club. They were now on Millie Grey's home turf.

A lavish warm buffet had been arranged in comparison to the coffee and sandwiches offered at the Greystone Academy gym. Toni locked herself onto Baxter's arm after their coats had been checked. The reception room was called the Philadelphia Room, and a fire flamed from the fireplace in the middle of the room. "Joe," Toni said gripping Baxter's arm tightly as they entered the Philadelphia Room. "I'm going to need a couple of very stiff drinks to get through this part of the day."

"What's your pleasure, lady?" Baxter asked.

"A quietly ordered double Scotch." Toni turned and her breast brushed up against Baxter's arm.

Baxter estimated that Millie Grey was at least a double Scotch ahead of Toni as she approached them shortly after Baxter's drink delivery.

"Well it's behind us, dear," Millie said offering her glass to be clinked.

"It's a sad day for both of us," Toni said.

"I'm really not that sad. The man was a son-of-a-bitch," Millie smiled. "We'll have to talk about this later. I have guests to greet," Millie said sliding away.

Toni took a long drink from her Scotch glass. "I'm going to ask you to get me another of these very shortly. Will you please stay at my side and not drift off, Joe?" she requested.

The guests streamed into the room. Baxter recognized Buzzsaw Pritchard and his wife coming across the room to them. They had exchanged words in the reception line at Greystone Academy. What more could be said now? Baxter questioned.

"Mrs. Grey," Buzzsaw said solemnly. "Again, our condolences. What are your plans now?"

"Ernie and I were about to embark on a round the world trip. I guess I will have to go alone now."

"Please let us know if there is anyway that we can help," Ross Pritchard said and they drew away to the large circle where Millie Grey was holding court. Toni held up her empty Scotch glass. "It's time, Joe."

Baxter returned with a fresh drink to find Toni flanked by the Donohues. Eve Donohue was holding Toni's hand.

"Well," Tom Donohue greeted Baxter. "I think this funeral went off pretty well, don't you? I believe everybody did their jobs right, and Ernie has been properly laid to rest. Here's to him." Donohue raised his glass to clink Toni and Eve Donohue ignored them and continued an animated conversation.

"Ernie Grey!" Baxter said raising his glass.

"I guess you were pretty close to Ernie," Tom Donohue said.

"Not that close, Tom. I worked with Ernie over the years but I was hardly a golfing buddy," Baxter confessed.

"I guess I'm in the same category, Joe. Ernie kind of picked me out. I spent some time with him, but we were never real close. I've always wanted to be CEO of IPCO and he got me there. This day was a day of gratitude for me."

Across the room they could hear Millie's loud laugh. "I sure as hell can see why he got rid of that woman," Donohue commented.

"I met the first Mrs. Grey three times excluding today. The first time was in the late 1970s at a fund raising dinner. The second time was at the wedding of a McKenzie Barber Partner. The third time was at a funeral reception for Leon Harwell, one of the firm's important clients," Baxter shared.

"Was it at that VanderKelen playhouse deal on the Hudson?" Donohue queried.

"Yes. It had presumably been built as a weekend place for the VanderKelen children to entertain their friends," Baxter explained. That had been the night Burke had ordered Baxter not to bring Andy Bourke and Toni had become the last minute substitute coming in her roommate's 'Auntie Mame' outfit. She had met Ernie that night and it marked the beginning of the end of Ernie's first marriage and the start of the relationship with Toni that was being concluded today.

"Eve and I were there that night. It was one of Cornie VanderKelen's command performances. He filled three tables with IPCO people. We had to fly up from Houston to be there. IPCO was a lot more political in those days. You got invited to a lot of foolishness in those days. The only thing worse than being invited was not being invited. You assumed you were on Vandy's promotable list when you got invited to one of those shindigs. Eve made me buy my first tuxedo for that one." Tom Donohue took three steps to his right away from the place where his wife and Toni were talking. He motioned for Baxter to accompany him.

"The problem with Cornie VanderKelen, Joe, is that the man could never settle down and decide who exactly he wanted to be. There were times when it looked like he really wanted to be a dynamic chief executive. Then he seemed to lose interest and he'd go off to another government appointment. Cornie had a very short attention span. I know he ran for Governor and Congress and wasn't elected. His wife was a mental invalid. I heard that she fell off a horse and had brain damage. No one ever saw her. It was rumored that he had a lot of lady friends, but nobody knew who they were."

"The best thing that ever happened to IPCO was Cornie bringing Ernie to the Board. Ernie dug in and learned the business as opposed to those high profile people who liked the director's fees. Suddenly Cornie had a Board member who was objective and willing to take him on. Ernie would take Cornie on in a calm and analytic way. Maybe it was his training as a management consultant. Ernie did a lot to keep IPCO on track. Senior management silently applauded and held its breath when Cornie installed Ernie as non-executive chairman. Without Ernie, IPCO could have been in a real crisis when Cornie died suddenly down in Argentina. Ernie had established excellent relationships with the family and controlled the board."

"He picked out three of us that he believed could run IPCO, and more or less merchandised us to the board and the family. I came out the finalist."

"I can remember going out to that fund-raiser on the VanderKelen estate. I looked around that estate and told myself, 'Here's a guy who never had a paper route when he was a kid.' Ernie did. He told me about it last year when we flew back from Kuwait. I guess his folks were fairly well off during the depression. Ernie told me he wanted to show that he could compete with the other boys at his age. He must have talked about that paper route for twenty minutes. Then he dozed off. He never talked about his first wife and said very little about his kids. He never brought up his fighter pilot days and he closed me off whenever I mentioned McKenzie Barber. But he did talk my ear off on that flight about his paper route. For a man who accomplished so much in his life, it seemed odd that his success on the paper route was so important to him. He told me that he gave it up when he went off to Greystone Academy. Ernie must have slept three or four hours and when he woke up, it was getting light and the flight attendants had started to serve coffee and juice. Ernie got up to go to the head. He came back all shaved and crisp looking in a fresh white shirt, took a sip of his coffee, and looked at me for a minute. 'Tom," he finally said. 'Are you prepared to succeed me as CEO of IPCO?' I looked over to him straight in the eye. 'I believe I am.' I told him. Ernie said, 'Okay. After this plane lands I'm going to draft up a memorandum for the Board recommending you as my successor. I will be retiring in November 1991.' I asked him what he was going to do after IPCO. 'Maybe I'll do nothing.' Then he put on his glasses, pulled out a copy of *Fortune Magazine* and I was lucky if I got twenty words out of him until after we landed."

Tom Donohue shook his head. "It's been a long time since I thought about Ernie's paper route and that flight back from Kuwait." Tom Donohue slapped his hand against Baxter's shoulder. "That's all I have to say. We had better get back to the ladies."

Baxter looked around the room and spotted Hamilton Burke coming across the room to him followed by the icy blonde wife.

"Joe," Burke said extending his hand warmly. "Good to see you but certainly under sad and unwelcome circumstances." Their hands gripped. Yvonne de Robilliard Burke had stopped to talk to some ladies ten feet back.

"Those are VanderKelen cousins that Yvonne knows from somewhere. Looks as though there may be more VanderKelen representation here than McKenzie Barber alumni," Burke commented.

"It's Robson Allen Barber now, Ham," Baxter corrected. "Ernie's been gone from McKenzie Barber for slightly over seven years. He did wonders for the family's net worth as Chairman of IPCO."

"I was surprised to see you as a pall bearer. I take it that you had become close to Ernie after his retirement."

Baxter nodded his head solemnly. "We developed a closeness in the last several years. I've lost a friend today. Toni, you remember Toni, his widow, wanted me to serve as the lead pall bearer."

"I remember Toni Alter very well, Joe. As you will, no doubt recall, I hired Toni and paid her out of my own pocket at McKenzie Barber. I also remember how that little romance started when you escorted Toni to that black tie up in Tarrytown. Now, are you still with the firm?"

"Today, yes. I'm going in tomorrow to negotiate my severance with the Robson Allen Barber crowd. At this time tomorrow, I'll be retired from the firm."

"How old are you now, Joe?"

"55. I'll turn 56 in June."

"I buried my father on Saturday. I'm leaving tomorrow morning to take over Burke Farms. I could use someone like you to come down and help me sort things out. Are you interested?"

"I'd have to think about it, Ham. Everything is so up in the air right now. I have to be out on the coast next week or the week after. Could I give you an answer then?"

"I would need a commitment from you by next Monday. You could put off beginning until mid-February."

"What exactly would you want me to do, and how long would you want me to do it?" Baxter again found himself looking into Burke's grey wolf eyes.

"I need you to do what you used to do. Look over the organization, assess the people, come back with some recommendations and then help me get them implemented. Pretty much what you've done a hundred times for me before. Oddly, I mentioned your name to Yvonne this morning. I believe that I said that I could use someone like Joe Baxter to come in for a while. She correctly predicted that I might run into you at the funeral."

Yvonne came to Burke's side. She was wearing a blue silk dress with a narrow slit bodice contrasting a diamond necklace against her pale white skin. She had to be in her mid-fifties now but her make-up erased ten to fifteen years.

"Hello, Joe," Yvonne said extending her hand. The hand reminded Baxter of smooth steel. "I told Hamilton this morning that he was sure to see you today. We seem to be going from one funeral to another. My brother died in an auto accident in Spain last week. Then Hamilton's father died at age 91 when his horse threw him. Next Ernie Grey dies while roller blading. What is this world coming to?"

"Your father died at 91 from a horse fall?" Baxter questioned Burke.

"He rode every morning of his life from the age of ten on. He had the constitution of a vigorous man in his mid-fifties. I am the sole heir and things have slipped a little the last ten years. Burke Farms has a strong balance sheet, a decent group of loyal employees, and large revenues supported by thin profits. I'm going to have my hands full, but I'm looking forward to it."

Baxter quickly calculated that Burke, other than an occasional consulting project had been unemployed for better than seven years.

"Now, Hamilton has something to do," his wife said triumphantly.

"My dear," Burke immediately corrected his wife. "I have never wanted for work. The question was the level of work I was willing to carry out. Did you see Charley Robson today, Joe?"

Baxter nodded his head affirmatively.

"Charley approached me right after I resigned from McKenzie Barber and wanted me to run International for Robson Allen. The next step would have been to succeed Charley. I turned him down. The only consulting firm I've ever wanted to run was McKenzie Barber. I wanted to run a real business with brands and assets that produced more things than reports in binders. I almost had one if the de Hartogue interests had acquired Hortense Foods. I must have looked at one hundred companies for acquisition over the past few years. Now I have the company I wanted more than anything else in the world, Burke Farms, my birthright."

"Will you be moving to Virginia, Yvonne?" Baxter asked.

Yvonne de Robilliard Burke smiled. "My home is in Paris. I have businesses around the world and an apartment in New York City. I will visit Hamilton in Virginia from time to time, but I prefer New York."

"I couldn't very well ask Yvonne to bury herself in rural Virginia, Joe," Burke explained. "I asked Joe about coming down to work with me at Burke Farms. He's going to give me an answer by next Monday."

"Your old friend, Dominique, talks of you from time to time," Yvonne added. "She said that she will visit Hamilton to look over Burke Farms." Turning to Burke, Yvonne said, "Maybe she will buy Burke Farms from you, Hamilton, and you can retired in Cannes and see me more often."

"Burke Farms is not for sale, dear. One day soon it may have some outside shareholders. But it will always be an independent company," Burke said firmly.

Yvonne shrugged her shoulders. "Maybe you could adopt someone as you were adopted and leave Burke Farms to them. Joe, how good to see you. I must say good-bye to Millie Grey and then we should leave."

Baxter exchanged a final handshake with Yvonne.

Burke and Baxter looked at each other in silence for at least a minute. Burke spoke first. "Now you know the Burke family secret. I was adopted. My mother lost a son to diphtheria at age four. I was located in a home and given the name of Hamilton. I didn't know I was adopted until I came back from Vietnam. My father told Yvonne after I brought her back as my wife. We have had some tensions in our marriage since. So much for family secrets, Joe. I'm going to get Yvonne out of here now. Burke Farms is mine now. I was always concerned that Rufus would change his will, but now he's stuck with me."

Burke pulled a card from his wallet and scrawled some telephone numbers. "I'm writing down both the headquarters office number and the manor number. Call me on Monday. It's beautiful down there and caught up in a 1948 time warp. Some how I suspect that Rufus still may have slaves hidden away someplace. You can help me find them. Ernie Grey is gone from my life. He may have sponsored my career at McKenzie Barber, but wasn't there for me when I needed him. We would have made McKenzie Barber hum forward and Robson Allen would have been our acquisition." Burke turned and walked away from Baxter without another word.

Baxter made his way through the rapidly filling room back to Toni's side. She was now in a small circle that included Adele Harwell, her son, Spencer, and Eve Donohue. Eve motioned to Baxter. "Step in here, Joe. I'm going to freshen up this drink and find Tom," she commanded.

Adele Harwell wore a small black hat with her veil pinned up. She appeared to have aged ten years since her husband's funeral. Her arm was locked in Spencer's and she held a cocktail glass in the other. Spencer wore a smart double breasted blue suit, and drank from a bottle of imported beer. His glasses were at rest across his chest suspended from silver chain. Baxter estimated that Spencer was the only person in the room drinking from a beer bottle.

"Mrs. Harwell." Baxter joined the circle and extended his hand. She studied Baxter for a few seconds and Spencer appeared to whisper Baxter's name to his mother.

"Joe," her face brightened. "Joe Baxter. Where have you been?" She took two steps forward and kissed Baxter on his cheek. He could not remember being kissed by Mrs. Harwell at any time in the past. Spencer was at her side for support.

"It's so good to see you. I was just reading through the notes I received after Leon's funeral, and yours was so special."

379

"Mr. Leon was a very special person and I miss him very much," Baxter replied. He couldn't remember what he had written.

"It's such a sad day losing Ernie. He was such a good friend and advisor to Leon over the years. You were too, Joe. I would hope that Spencer and you could develop a closeness. I know that Spencer could use your advice as much as Leon did." Tears formed at the corners of Adele Harwell's eyes. It was apparent to Baxter that Adele Harwell was on her second cocktail.

"Adele, I see two chairs over there. Why don't we sit down for a minute and get off our feet," Toni offered.

Mrs. Harwell nodded her head and Toni took her arm. "It's I who should be comforting you, Toni," Adele Harwell said as Toni steered her away.

Baxter remained next to Spencer Harwell.

"Mother took Ernie's death pretty badly. Ernie and Toni took her out for dinner in the middle of December. I guess Dad and Mom went a long way back with Ernie. She really likes Toni. It has to be a little sticky for the Greys to have Toni here." Spencer took a long swig from his beer bottle.

"So what are you up to these days, Joe?"

"I'm concluding my career with McKenzie Barber tomorrow. I'm going to take some time off and consider my options. How's Harwell Management?"

Baxter hadn't seen Spencer since the funeral reception in 1989. His blondish hair was thin, and he had his father's bright glint in his eyes. He had acquired a touch of his father's condescending arrogance in the intervening years since their last meeting.

"I have to tell you, Joe. Outside of my mother, you're not in favor with the Harwell family. The attorneys alerted me to that deal you cut with Dad about coming as General Manager. Hakim was furious. Ned and Dan were furious. The conclusion was that you took advantage of my Dad when he was in failing health and feeling very insecure about Hakim. Hakim described you as the consultant who wanted to come in from the cold. Ernie defended you to the family and offered to resign as a Director. Mother wouldn't hear of it."

"Your father was a client in the beginning. Later I regarded him with a personal interest and loyalty that exceeds the relationship that a consultant extends to a good client. Your father approached me about coming to Harwell Management as some kind of overseer. I didn't seek the job, but finally agreed to come. At the time of his death, I had a signed contract with Harwell Management that I could have litigated for a settlement. I greatly admired your father, and it is my hope that when you grew up, you will be fifty percent of your father's abilities and moral stature. You should get your mother home pretty soon," Baxter said turning his back to Spencer Harwell.

"Joe!" Spencer called after him. "I've got something else to say to you."

"Drop me a note on it, Spencer."

"Joe, please," Spencer said beckoning him.

Baxter took three steps in reverse. "Joe, I had to say what I just said. Now I have a question. Mother wants you to come on the Board to take Ernie Grey's place on the Harwell Management Board. Will you consider it?"

"Spencer, the question is, do you want me on the board? If you sincerely want me on the board, I'll consider it." Spencer took another swig from his beer bottle. "I'd like to spend some time with you and review some family issues. My mother told me to get you on the Board and technically she has control. Look Joe, this birthright stuff isn't all what it's cracked up to be. I need someone to talk to. I don't always understand Selim's motives. He's got Ned and Dan in his hip pocket and I keep popping out. I wish to hell I could be a trader or something at Broadbaker, but I have my family obligation."

"And how's my old pal, Hakim?" Baxter asked.

"He's pissed off as hell. We couldn't get him into the Gotham Club. He had a tantrum in December when I had to give him the news that the membership committee had passed on him. Selim has also got us into some things that make me nervous. My Dad's idea to bring you in wasn't all that bad. It's just that the only one he ever discussed it with was my mother."

"I'll think about it, Spencer," Baxter said. He was tempted to tell Spencer about the man at the grave site who resembled his uncle.

"Call me on Friday and we can set a date. If we should go ahead, I'll get you the same deal we had with Ernie."

"I'll call you on Friday, Spencer," Baxter said again backing away. He backed into Preston Grey.

"Hey, Joe. I've been looking for you. Mother wants to see you. She's standing over there near the door." Baxter waved across the room to Toni and followed Preston Grey to his mother.

Millie Grey wore a dark belted suit with a striped scarf. Her hair was dark brown set in a tight permanent. She stood in the center of two people. The other was Ernie's daughter, Kathleen, who was dressed in a black pants suit. Baxter entertained greeting Laura Harwell with a 'I believe I saw your old hubby in the parking lot', but decided to remain silent on the matter.

"Here's Joe Baxter, Mother."

Baxter shook hands with Mille Grey and then to Kathleen only to have Laura Harwell ignore his hand. She nodded at Baxter and excused herself.

"Well, Joe Baxter, we continue to meet each other at funerals," Millie Grey greeted Baxter. "Adele Harwell was singing your praise at the reviewal yesterday. I take it that you are squiring the grieving widow around?"

"You mean the gold digging widow, mother," Kathleen added.

"Oh, shut up, Kathleen. She's a good sort and has been through a very difficult day. Toni, or whatever the hell her name is, has handled herself with a lot of dignity today."

"I believe the whole family has conducted themselves with dignity today, in addition to that little nobody."

"Kathleen, go out there and mix. Don't let Laura Harwell run off with the life of the party award. Go find that married boyfriend of yours who snuck in here when I wasn't looking. I need to talk to Joe Baxter, the attender of funerals."

Kathleen Grey smiled good-bye to Baxter and cautioned her mother, "Be careful of your drinking, mother," and walked briskly away.

"Well, Joe, shall we raise our glasses to him?" Millie Grey asked.

"Here's to Chairman Grey," Baxter said clinking his glass against Millie's.

"How are you getting back to New York?" Millie asked.

"We have Metroliner tickets," Baxter answered.

"I've got a car and driver. It's a stretch with jump seats. There's plenty of room. It will just be Pres, me and the two of you. I'd like to spend some time with the second Mrs. Grey and this isn't the place to do it. In a lot of ways, I really admire her. I want you to go back and very quietly ask her to join Pres and me for the ride back to New York. I'll be ready to leave in fifteen minutes. I believe if the two of us left together, it would set the right tone for the conclusion of the day.'

"What if Toni prefers the Metroliner?"

"So be it."

Baxter looked away from Millie to see Clyde and Andy Nickerson enter the doorway.

"Millie," Clyde greeted her with one of his leering smiles.

"We've come to share your grief for the passing of a very dear friend."

"Clyde!" Millie responded. "Get the hell out of here and take your little tart with you! Ernie carried you for years and you betrayed him! You're not welcome here."

"Millie," Clyde continued. "I know that this day has been an ordeal for you. Our only thought was to comfort you in your grief."

"Mr. and Mrs. Nickerson," Toni's voice came from just behind Baxter. "You're not welcome here. You're not acceptable to either of the Mrs. Greys. Please leave."

Toni moved to Millie Grey's side. Millie slid an arm around her waist and kissed her on the cheek. "We Mrs. Greys should stick together, dear. Clyde, go home, you're neither needed or wanted here."

"Millie, you obviously have been drinking and may not be in a coherent frame of mind. We understand." They turned and left the room without another word.

Millie looked to Toni. "I've been waiting to say something like that to Clyde Nickerson for years. The man is an abomination."

"I totally agree," Toni said and she kissed Millie Grey on the forehead.

They left as a foursome approximately twenty minutes later. Millie and Toni occupied the backseat while Baxter and Pres Grey took jump seats. There were three bottles of champagne on ice in the bar for the drive back to New York.

"I really can't drink one more glass of anything," Toni protested as Preston Grey dutifully opened up the champagne bottle and dispensed the contents into plastic goblets.

"Pour half a glass for Toni, Pres," Millie instructed.

"Now it's time for one last toast to Ernie Grey III, my husband of twenty-five years and the father of my two children. Ernie was a smart, cold blooded, leader of men who really cared more for power than for wives and family."

"I can't drink to that, Mother," Pres Grey said. "I don't believe I ever measured up to what my Father wanted me to be, but I loved and respected him. My Dad was an exceptional man."

"Ernie was a Chief Executive at first and a husband second," Toni contributed. "I only expected to participate in a small piece of his life. I was very happy with the piece I received."

"Joe Baxter! What do you have to contribute to this toast?" Millie demanded.

"When Ernie Grey and I were contemporaries at McKenzie Barber, he was either my boss's boss or my boss's boss's boss for most of my career. Later in my career and after his retirement from McKenzie Barber, I had the pleasure of getting to know him more intimately. I admired the man for his integrity, intelligence, management abilities, and leadership skills. I never knew him well. I suspect that few of the people around Ernie Grey really knew him well. He was a man of many compartments. Those close to him were admitted into only those compartments where he allowed strangers. The remainder of his compartments remained private and locked. I admired Ernie Grey from afar. He was the Sun God of McKenzie Barber for years. Now he's gone and so is McKenzie Barber for that matter. Baxter raised his glass. "To Ernie Grey! He was a different man to each of us. None of us I suspect truly knew him well."

"I'll drink to that!" Millie Grey responded. Both Preston Grey and Toni Grey were tentative in raising their glasses. After a silence, they took small sips from their glasses.

"That was well said, Joe Baxter. You may have seen the man more clearly than the rest of us." Turning to Toni, Millie continued. "Are you aware I was married before Ernie. I met Ernie at a collegiate school mixer. I was at a place called St. Benedicts. I had been sent down from a collegiate school in Vermont. We had a dance that Spring with Greystone. I had danced once and was standing at the foot of the band stand with a friend. All of a sudden, my friend said, 'There's Ernie Grey. I wonder who he's going to ask.'"

"He kept coming and he was smiling. I looked to the right and left of me. Then he was right in front of me. 'Hi, my name's Ernie Grey. Would you like to dance? The band was playing *My Silent Night* and he took my hand and led me to the dance floor. 'My God,' I told myself. 'I got him to dance with me. How do I keep him?'"

"I kept him for a while. Maybe a year or so and he dropped me. I graduated and went out to Mills and met John. It was a blind date. I was a Freshman at the time. John turned out to be handsome, dashing in his Second Lieutenant's uniform, and he was fun. He didn't take himself seriously and liked to laugh. John had gone to Stanford and had been commissioned the year before through the ROTC program. He was stationed in the Presidio and patiently waiting for the war to start so that he could do what people expected of him. John had no great ambitions. He wanted to get his military service behind him so that he could get a good job someplace and settle down. He lived his life a day at a time. When the war came, all I could think about was to marry John before he slipped away. We eloped. I followed him through a couple of training camps in the South. We had a three day weekend in New York and John shipped out. He was a supply officer which sounded nice and safe to me. He participated in the North Africa landing and then came Normandy and Omaha Beach. Farewell, my nice decent John, the love of my life."

"I got a job at Stockbridges and read about war hero, aviation ace, Ernie Grey in the Philadelphia papers. They always liked to see a Main Line guy make good. I finally ran into him again one night just before Christmas in 1946 at the good old Schuykill Club. That was the beginning of Phase Two of my life with Ernie Grey."

"Ernie was ambitious. He wanted to go to the Harvard Business School and be President of a major company. There were no CEOs then. President was as far as you could go. Ernie was smart, attractive, and he always could talk."

Millie paused and extended her glass to Baxter.

"Fill it up, Mister. I'm on an emotional roll."

Preston Grey stared off into space. Baxter wondered if he had heard this story before.

"You summed up Ernie pretty well just now, Joe Baxter. He was a man of many compartments and totally different from my nice, open John. He knew he would be expected to have a wife sooner or later and I generally met his requirements. I was a cute little thing in those days, full of energy, and I knew all about the care and feeding of men. I had a little trust money and I got a job as a handbag buyer at Gimbel's so we could live a little better than the other consultants. Ernie used to describe us as part of a package. We were the Greys and we were going all the way to the top together."

Millie paused for more champagne intake and held her glass out to Baxter for refilling.

"We were happiest when we lived in New York City. I never wanted to give up that apartment. It has too many memories. Ernie had his John McKenzie to idolize, and I had Gimbel's to bitch about. We were busy New York people on our way up. Then Pres came along and Darien beckoned. Our life changed after that." Millie paused to look around at her audience. Her eyes settled on Toni. "So, toots, how did you get him away from me?"

Toni took a deep breath followed by a small sip of champagne.

"The Ernie Grey I met impressed me as a very lonely man. He seemed to want someone to talk with. I was very flattered when the most powerful man at McKenzie Barber took an interest in me. I assumed in the beginning that he would grow tired of me and that I would move on in life with a brief memory of being with Ernie for a short time. Instead Ernie made a place in his life for me. It turned out to be a permanent place. I didn't steal your husband, Millie. You lost him." The limo tooled along in silence for several minutes.

Baxter broke the silence. "So, Preston, how's the decorating business? I would suppose that you're chasing new business these days."

It was 11:15 when Baxter returned to his apartment. Ernie Grey was now at rest, nestled among the former headmasters of Greystone Academy. He had seen Toni Grey to the entrance of the Grey's New York Fifth Avenue building and declined an invitation to come up. Baxter had promised to visit her in Naples to review Ernie's McKenzie Barber's papers. Millie Grey was now half way to her Greenwich townhouse in the company of her son, Preston, Chief Executive of GreyWebb Designs.

It had been a long day. Tomorrow he would confidently complete his career at McKenzie Barber or Robson Barber, as it was now designated.

Baxter had widened his options since he left the apartment with Rusty that morning.

Burke had offered him consulting work at Burke Farms. Spencer Harwell wanted to talk to Baxter about taking Ernie's place on the Board. He wanted to write the McKenzie Barber book. Finally there was Rusty. Where the hell did she fit in? Or was the weekend simply another flirtation similar to his weekend of so many years past with Dominique?

He dialed Rusty's number in California and got her voice mail. Her voice was crisp, professional, and upbeat. Baxter hung up and redialed the number in order to hear Rusty's voice again.

"This is Rusty Collins. I can't come to the phone right now. Your call is very important to me. Would you please leave a message with the time and date of your call after the beep?"

"Rusty, this is Joe Baxter. I'm back from Philadelphia and in my apartment. Please call me and don't worry about the time. My number is 212-980-6031."

Baxter poured himself a Canadian Club nightcap out of habit, kicked off his shoes, turned on his sound system to some Satie, and seated himself in the Eames chair. This was his last night as a McKenzie Barber Partner/Consultant. He had buried his old Chairman, and the firm he knew was really gone forever.

Everett Faunce had been the choice of Glen and Tom as the new Chief Financial Officer of McKenzie Barber. They had promised Baxter that he would be involved in the hiring process, but immediately hired Faunce in April 1990 after a long weekend series of meetings. Baxter knew Faunce by reputation. He had been the restructuring CFO of the late 1980's.

Faunce had gone into a number of companies as the right hand man to a downsizing CEO, and in each instance participated as the hatchet man partner of the CEO in the restructuring of corporations through voluminous staff cuts and aggressive sales of assets. Each corporate entity eventually disappeared after the institutional investors had been rewarded. Baxter estimated that Faunce had been between jobs for about six months when his hire was announced.

Bernie had called Baxter on a Monday morning in early February.

"Joe, one moment for Glen."

Baxter had waited on the line before Glen Fitzgerald's voice sounded.

"Joe, we've solved our CFO problem. Do you know the name, Everett Faunce?"

"He's flitted around troubled companies over the last ten years. I would hope that McKenzie Barber isn't in that class," Baxter responded.

"We've hired Faunce. His last stop was Interstate Industries where he did one hell of a job in cleaning up that company. Ev's starting tomorrow, and we want you to brief him on your progress and conclusions to date with the Executive Office reorganization. Tom and I want you to get together with Ev for breakfast tomorrow."

"Do you want my assessment of Mr. Faunce?"

"There's no need for that, Joe. Ev spent the weekend with the Operating Committee. Ross Pritchard has approved him. He was offered the CFO job on Sunday night, and he's starting on Tuesday."

"It was my understanding that I would participate in the selection process. Where will Faunce report?"

"To Ross until he steps down as Chairman this October. Actually Ev will report through Tom and me to Ross."

"What will be my relationship to Mr. Faunce?" Baxter probed.

"We have also given Ev administration. If you decide to stay in your job, you will be reporting to Ev."

"Is Ev coming in as a direct admission Partner?"

"Ev is joining us as a management employee with officer level responsibilities."

"We're organized as a Partnership. The by-laws call for a Chairman and a Deputy Chairman. I don't recall any provisions to appoint other officers," Baxter commented.

"Joe," Fitzgerald's voice betrayed exasperation. "I didn't call you to review or debate the articles of partnership. Ev Faunce will expect you at seven thirty tomorrow morning in a private room at the Marco Polo Club. Please be prepared to brief him." Fitzgerald clicked off.

Baxter pulled up Faunce's biography from the firm's data bank. He had graduated from a third tier college with an accounting degree, and spent six years with the Boston Office of a national public accounting firm before joining a listed company as Assistant Controller. Over six years, Faunce advanced to Corporate Controller only to have his company acquired. Thereafter he moved to CFO responsibilities with a smaller company and entered into a series of two year moves in and out of restructured companies. The business press has picked up on Faunce as "the financial surgeon" who operated on sick companies.

Ev Faunce was shorter than Baxter had anticipated. He was five feet eight at best. His face was freckled, and there was an Irish twinkle in his eye. Faunce greeted Baxter with a broad smile and a firm handshake. Baxter was ten minutes early and Faunce had already settled into his private room with his suit jacket draped over a chair. There were two places set for breakfast at the far end of the table. Faunce had been working at the near end of the table which was strewn with papers.

"Joe, I'm Ev Faunce," he greeted Baxter. "With a name like Baxter, you must be Irish. Do you know what part of Ireland your people are from?" Faunce motioned Baxter to a chair at the end of the table. Baxter placed his suitcoat over a chair and seated himself to the left of Faunce's chair.

"My father emigrated from Ireland in the 1920's to work in the Pennsylvania mines. He later moved to Minnesota where he worked in the open pit iron ore mines. I've had no contact with his side of the family," Baxter stated matter-of-factly. It was not the response Faunce had anticipated. He jerked his head slightly. "I thought all the McKenzie Barber Partners were blue bloods. I'm surprised to find a miner's son."

"I've been here 23 years and have been a Partner since 1978," Baxter announced.

"This is a grand old firm, but it seems to have fallen on some hard times. How do you explain that, Joe?"

"We had a Chairman election back in 1984 which resulted in a sweeping and unfortunate change in organization and direction of the firm."

Faunce nodded his head in response. His bio placed him in his mid-fifties, but Faunce appeared to be ten years younger.

"Tell me a little about yourself, Joe," Faunce requested after the waiter had poured coffee and taken their order.

"Why don't you tell me a little about yourself first? It's my understanding that you are joining McKenzie Barber as Chief Financial Officer, but may or may not be a Partner of the firm. I'm prepared to brief you on the Executive Office functions of McKenzie Barber. My conversation with Glen was very brief, and I need to know who you are and what your charter is."

"That seems like a fair exchange to me. Do you have any idea of who I am?"

"You're public accounting trained and have gone from one troubled company to another applying financial fixes. You have been referred to by the business press as a 'financial surgeon'. While I acknowledge McKenzie Barber has slipped over the past six years, I was not of the opinion that the firm required surgery."

"Patients rarely recognize their symptoms until they are near fatalities," Faunce explained.

"And Glen and Tom have wheeled the firm into you for surgery? I wasn't aware the cancer of incompetence had spread that far?"

"I sense, Joe, that you have some facility for words. I tend to be a plain spoken man. The grand old firm of McKenzie Barber has managed to get itself in trouble. I have been working with troubled companies ever since I left public accounting. I have always cleaned up these companies for their stakeholders. McKenzie Barber is a partnership which makes you a stakeholder. Let's just say that I've come to McKenzie Barber to protect your interests and your partners' interests. Having said that, explain to me who you are, what your role is, and bring me up to date on your review of what I call the corporate staff functions."

Baxter began after breakfast had been served. He had been making presentations to business audiences for twenty-three years, but he quickly marked his presentation to Ev Faunce as one of his most arduous. He was peppered with aggressive questions throughout his briefing. Baxter concluded his points at 9:45 AM. Faunce shook his head.

"You're going way too slow, Joe. The Executive Office cost structure must be stripped down immediately. McKenzie Barber can operate without those services. Like most consultants looking at their own companies, you're too soft. I've had a man who does what you do in the last two companies I've served. His name is Ludwig Strasser. He's an organization psychologist by training, but an industrial engineer by inclination. I want Mr. Strasser to immediately assume your responsibilities. I want you to have a briefing meeting with Strasser similar to this one on Thursday. Then you can consider yourself relieved and go back to whatever you were doing before you picked up this project. You'll just be in the way of what has to be done. You're like the shoemaker's children. I have engaged consulting firms over the years and generally they are good at what they say they can do. There's one thing they can't do, however. They are quite poor at running their own business," Faunce judged.

Baxter drew up from his chair. "You're here. I'll get out of your way. But I suspect that your approach is very mechanical and you may cause more harm than good."

He extended his hand which was not accepted by Faunce. His attention was on Baxter's passouts which he was studying with a yellow highlighter.

"I'll have Strasser call you. Please have the waiter send in a small pot of coffee. I don't want you in Executive Office after Thursday of this week," Faunce said coldly dismissing Baxter.

Baxter returned to his office and placed a call to Glen Fitzgerald. Bernie's voice greeted him.

"Glen's in meetings this morning, Joe," Bernie explained. "May I have him call you later in the day?" Baxter knew this meant two days later. A coldness had come into Bernie's voice over the past several weeks. He had never followed up after their cheery January dinner.

"I have to talk to him now! Tell Glen that I have just concluded my meeting with Ev Faunce and I need to talk to him immediately," Baxter demanded.

"That's impossible, Joe. You'll have to wait along with the others who want to talk with Glen and await your turn."

"Bernie, tell Glen that I have just left Everett Faunce and he was slumped on the breakfast table with some kind of stroke," Baxter lied.

"Joe, I'm going to put you on hold. I'll get Glen out of the meeting." In times of deceit, one had to respond in deceit, Baxter rationalized.

"Joe!" Fitzgerald's voice blurted into the phone. "What's happened to Ev Faunce!"

"He's just fine. I left him highlighting with his yellow marker. He seemed in good health and good spirits. That little cost cutting leprechaun is beginning to work his magic back at the Marco Polo Club. He informed me that I was not going to be part of his magic show. If that is true, the firm is in violation of the agreement you signed with me in January when I took on this job."

"We agreed with Ev that he would have a free hand in finance and executive office administration."

"I hope to hell he has that in writing, Glen."

"Joe, I'm going to put Bernie back on the phone. She'll put you on my calendar and we can talk this matter through."

"We must meet today, Glen. Have a nice meeting."

Glen Fitzgerald canceled their first meeting, rescheduling for the following morning. Baxter appeared at eight thirty to find only Bernie and an empty office.

"Glen's in Chicago, Joe. It was an emergency meeting. He left on the 7AM flight. We expect him back this evening," Bernie greeted Baxter crisply. Baxter asked himself as he started into Bernie's cold eyes. 'What ever happened to the dinner companion who seemed to be ready for an adventure or two?'

Bernie presumably pulled up Glen's schedule on her computer.

"Now, this is subject to change, Joe. There are enormous demands on Glen's time. Could you meet with Jack instead?"

"If I meet with Jack, I want Glen in attendance, Bernie. Certain arrangements about my role at McKenzie Barber were agreed to and documented with both Glen and Jack. Now I have been given to understand that our agreement has been abrogated by a newly hired non-Partner of the firm."

"Joe, I don't want to discuss the details of your meeting with Glen. I'm just here to coordinate his schedule," Bernie admonished Baxter. "Now I can give you 4:45 PM on Thursday or it's going to have to be at the end of next week."

"4:45 will do nicely, if it's next week. I will bring my attorney along for company."

Ev Faunce took up residence on Thursday morning. A memorandum had been distributed on Wednesday morning signed by Chairman Pritchard announcing that Faunce had been appointed Senior Executive for Finance, Control, and Administration for Executive Office. It went on to say Dr. Ludwig Strasser would assume responsibility for all administrative functions including human resource administration. It concluded by saying that Joe Baxter's project team had completed their executive office review and would be returning to a consulting practice.

Strasser introduced himself to Baxter in the mid morning of Thursday. He was a surprisingly short man no taller than 5'2" or 3" who wore dark rimmed glasses. His hair was dyed jet black and was slicked down with something that made it shine. He wore a blue suit with a yellow tie decorated with green alligators. His black shoes were immaculately polished.

"You're Baxter. I'm Strasser," he said entering Baxter's cubicle. Baxter instinctively stood up and Strasser sat down across from him without a handshake pushing the door shut.

"You've been told that this is your last day in Executive Office?"

"It's been mentioned to me."

"Faunce and I have worked together twice before. We're very good at putting corporate overhead right. I looked through your review. You write well, but your conclusions are too soft. This patient needs immediate surgery. You want to fix and mend, we're here to operate. I need some hands and feet for a while. I've spent time with this woman called Heidi. She tells me she's worked with you on the review project from the beginning. We would like to keep her for a few weeks for transition. We've talked to Druanne Smithers and she's assured us that your Heidi will have a place back in consulting."

"Druanne Smithers is a personnel lady. You had better get a commitment from either Fitzgerald or Pinker."

"Miss Smithers is the Human Resources Director for the New York Office. I would hope she can handle a matter like this without having to bother Glen or Jack about it,' Strasser leaned back in his chair and placed a shoe on the corner of the desk."

"Put your foot down," Baxter commanded. "We don't put our feet up on our desks here at McKenzie Barber."

Strasser smiled and slowly removed his left foot from the corner of the desk.

"Will there be anything else Mr. Strasser? I have a lot to do today."

Strasser stood up and waved to Baxter from the door. "Any last advice, Baxter?" he asked from the doorway.

"Mess up payroll, and you're a dead man, Strasser," Baxter said with a smile.

Bernie called Baxter late morning.

"Glen can't do it again, Joe. He wants you to have lunch with Bob Dilger on Friday. You should call Bob. He expects your call."

"Bernie," Baxter protested. "Glen owes me a meeting. I have no agenda with Bob Dilger."

"Joe, Glen doesn't have time to meet with you," Bernie's voice sounded exasperated. "He wants you to meet with Bob Dilger." She clicked off.

Baxter met Dilger on Friday for lunch at the New York Actuarial Club. Dilger hadn't changed over the years. He had retained his image of a tall, sandy haired, lanky, country boy from Indiana who had become accustomed to living in the city.

Dilger greeted Baxter with a "Hey Joe, good to see you," in the small club lobby.

They were seated in a rear table. "I don't know about you, Joe. But I feel like a beer today." Baxter ordered a Perrier.

"Well, Joe, how about coming back to the Benefits and Compensation Practice?" Dilger proposed after their drinks were served. "I hear your work at EO is done."

"Bob, I have a letter of agreement with Glen Fitzgerald that I was to reorganize Executive Office and assume the role of Administrative Partner for the firm through my retirement. What are you and I talking about?"

"The decision has been made to go another way in EO. I have been told to make a place for you back in Benefits & Comp. I have to hand it to Glen. I think it's one hell of a good idea. You can keep your units and we might even get a few more for you next fall."

"Whatever would I do in the Benefits and Compensation practice, Bob? Would you have me report to Carl?"

Dilger took a long sip from his beer glass. "God, I love a beer at Friday lunch. You're not drinking today?"

"I'll have one with you after we conclude the business portion of our luncheon discussion, Bob," Baxter responded.

"How about coming back as Deputy Managing Partner of the Benefits & Compensation Practice. I'll run the overall practice and you can run the Compensation side. Carl Miller can report to you. The practice needs the stability of your leadership right now, Joe. Carl Miller is a loose cannon. Harry Devonshire is nearly out of control. I need you to step back in between me and the Comp practice to stabilize things. And," Dilger pause, "As an extra incentive for you,—there's a lot of talk about spinning out of the firm. We've got to wait until the Fall Chairman election, but I believe we will have an opportunity to spin out the Benefits and Comp practice as a separate company. You could be a key shareholder in that business. The financial upside will be phenomenal."

"This is new news, Bob. Where did you get it?"

"I'm quite close to Glen and Jack. They are going to nominate me for the Operating Committee in the Fall. McKenzie Barber got into a lot of financial trouble over the last six years. There were some major receivables problems at FSO that had been covered up for years. McMasters blew the whistle after he got down there, and that led to Ross summarily firing Brett. In addition, we tried to finance too many new practice initiatives at one time when we failed to recognize a lot of business units were bleeding. Clyde Nickerson kept covering things up and making things looking better than they were. Roger White was a big part of it. Our outside accountants should have caught it. The only option for Glen and Tom was to bring in someone like Faunce who is experienced at sorting things like this out. Joe, you are well out of EO right now. You belong in a practice serving clients as opposed to an administrative partner position. How about it, Joe?"

"I believe we should properly document our discussion, Bob. Then I would see us with a deal." They shook hands on it and Baxter ordered a Beck after he determined that the club did not carry Gellhorn Beer.

Baxter had returned to his practice a little more than 90 days after he left it.

Lee Heller asked Baxter out for a drink two weeks later. They met in the front bar of the Four Seasons. Heller had the look of a hunted man as he approached Baxter. Lee Heller had to be near Baxter's age. His hair was salt and pepper and he wore a grey glen plaid suit. There was a nervous enthusiasm about him as he made his way to Baxter.

"Joe, how are you hitting 'em?" Lee said extending his hand from ten feet away.

Baxter accepted the hand and pulled his coat off the bar stool he had reserved for Heller.

"Well, Joe, I hear you're back in harness again as Deputy Managing Partner, Comp & Benefits! Congratulations on an escape from the hell hole of Executive Office." Baxter loaded Heller up with a white wine. They made McKenzie Barber gossip small talk for a few minutes before Heller blurted out that he had been fired.

"Joe, they have put Druanne Smithers in my job. University Relations activities have been canceled. We're writing universities that we have a hiring freeze on until the Fall. Experienced recruiting has been placed on hold and consultants are leaving the firm in droves. I couldn't handle the damage that Faunce and Strasser are doing to the firm. I asked them to release me."

"What kind of severance were you provided, Lee?" Baxter probed.

"Tell me, Joe. What is the firm's policy? I believe I we should have a minimum of two years severance. I have been with the firm for over 25 years. I was always rated outstanding in my annual reviews with Clyde."

"Partners generally get a year, Lee. You're not a Partner. What were you offered?"

"Three months, Joe."

"Did you resign or were you fired, Lee? This is important."

"I resigned, Joe. I could not stay and watch them destroy the firm's human resources program."

"Then, if you resigned, Lee, three months is defensible."

"Joe, I resigned because they brought in Druanne Smithers over me. I had no other course."

"Has your resignation been accepted?"

"Joe, I have been asked to either accept a position as Druanne's assistant at a 20% paycut, or leave McKenzie Barber with 90 days severance. I need your counsel. Should I engage an attorney and fight this?"

"Lee, I haven't been at the Director level since 1978. As I recall, there was an employment agreement that placed some constraint on going to a competitor and provided a commitment of six months advance notice on both the firm and the management employee."

"That's long gone, Joe. That was one of my first projects for Clyde after the 1984 election. I redrafted the agreement and reduced the Director's agreement to 90 days."

"So then you're being treated in a similar manner to the other Director level management employees in the firm and believe you deserve better."

"Joe, I've seen the deals that have been cut over the years. Working for Clyde, I saw everything. There was a three year deal cut out for some woman senior consultant in the Atlanta Office. There also were a number of multi year deals cut for women consultants out of FSO."

"Do you know why those severance deals were cut?" Baxter probed.

Heller shook his head. "I just saw the documentation. Working for Clyde all of those years, I learned there were times to ask questions and times to remain mute."

"Lee, what are you being paid?"

"$140,000 and there were special bonuses from time to time. Clyde took pretty good care of me. He got me on the preliminary Partner nomination list on three different occasions. I was always removed without prejudice because I was senior staff as opposed to being on the line. I know Glen and Jack are after me because I was too close to Clyde. Clyde was my mentor. I know you and he had your differences over the years, but Clyde was a very special person to me. I couldn't believe that Buzzsaw trashed

Clyde the way he did. Clyde got the man elected Chairman." Heller held up his empty wine glass. "Can I get another one of these?"

"Have you talked with Clyde over your dilemma?"

"Clyde's very busy with his father's foundation. He wants no more involvement in firm matters. He's the one who suggested that I meet with you. He said that Joe Baxter would know what to do. Joe, McKenzie Barber has been my life. I've represented the firm to the external world outside of clients. I recognized many years ago that I didn't have the marketing and selling skills that would make me a Partner. At the same time, I recognized that it takes a lot of musicians to make a great orchestra. I was content with my place. 90 days severance is the ultimate insult. Shall I sue, Joe?"

"I believe the firm has a number of unfair dismissal suits on its docket. How many have been settled and how many are awaiting trial?"

Lee Heller stared at his wine glass. "Joe, I don't believe the firm has ever settled an unfair dismissal suit."

"There's your answer, Lee. I'd take your severance and run. Maybe you can hook on as a college placement director."

"I couldn't afford it, Joe."

Baxter called for a check. Poor Lee Heller. He had become a victim of the system he had helped to create.

Baxter returned to the newly merged Benefits and Compensation practice in mid-April of 1990. It was now going to be designated McKenzie Barber Human Resources Consulting Services and Baxter was issued business cards designating him as Deputy Managing Director, McKenzie Barber HRC.

Dilger sent out a firm wide E-Mail announcing that Joe Baxter had completed his work in the reorganization of the firm's executive office and was returning to HRC as Deputy Managing Partner. Carl Miller was furious. He wrote Dilger demanding to go before the firm's Operating Committee to argue for his continued leadership of the executive compensation practice. He additionally recommended that the firm engage

Frank Alvardi to perform a strategic assessment of the executive compensation practice. He concluded that reappointing Joe Baxter to head the practice would only lead to the continued decline that had begun with the resignation of Frank Alvardi.

Dilger sent the letter to Baxter with the notation,

Joe:

Better go see Carl and shut him up. You have my support if you choose to terminate Carl. Please take care of this matter within five working days.

Dilger

Baxter called Carl and summoned him to meet at the O'Hare Red Carpet Club conference room.

"What will be our agenda?" Carl asked.

"We're going to review certain aspects of your recent letter to Bob Dilger, and the prospects of your continued participation in the McKenzie Barber HR practice. I would suggest that you review the Partnership agreement in advance of our meeting. 10AM tomorrow," Baxter snapped and broke off further conversation.

"Long time, no see, Carl," Baxter greeted Carl Miller as they walked back to Conference Room B the next morning.

Carl wore a blue suit with a vest. The suit appeared baggy and his eyes appeared tired. They had started at about the same time in the old Chicago Compensation practice under Alvardi. Carl had come in from the consulting pool, while Baxter had been transferred on a temporary basis from Dwyer's manufacturing practice. Carl Miller, the quintessential quantitative intellectually arrogant "techie" appeared to have lost twenty pounds from his spare frame. His hands shook slightly as he snapped open his brief case.

"Needless to say, Joe, I'm not happy over this turn of events." He produced two flip charts and three manila legal folders stuffed with papers. Carl passed out flip charts to Baxter's side of the table. It was titled in bold letters,

Dwight E. Foster

MCKENZIE BARBER
THE EXECUTIVE COMPENSATION PRACTICE

A STRATEGIC VISION
CARL A. MILLER-SPRING 1990

"I continue to hope that I will have the opportunity to present this vision statement to the Operating Committee, Joe. I'd like to take you through it this morning."

They had been introduced for the first time in the Spring of 1970. Carl Miller had been in his late twenties then, and his baby face made him appear in his early twenties. He now looked older than Baxter with a lined face and slightly stooped shoulders. Baxter recalled that Carl's year of birth was 1945. That would place him near 45 or 46. He was well under the rule of 73 for early retirement.

"How's the family, Carl?" Baxter asked to settle him down.

"Growing. Marge is pregnant again. She's due in September."

"How many will this make?"

"Five. Our oldest is a senior in college. We're going to be tuition poor the next few years. I need more units with higher unit values. I was counting on a big jump in units this Fall when I moved up. Now that's gone. The great smooth talking shoe salesman has returned. Now I want to take a few minutes to bring you up to speed on where to take this practice. If you follow my vision outline, this practice will be a success again." Carl pointed with his pen to the flip chart in front of Baxter.

Baxter poured two mugs of coffee. He had support and he presumed authority to fire Carl Miller this morning.

"Carl, has Bob Dilger seen this material?"

"I took him through it around April 1st."

"What was his reaction? This is the first I've seen of this document."

"The man is an Actuary. Dilger is trained to deal in tables of probability. He has little concept of the nature of our work. For openers, I recommended that we separate the practices again October 1st, but continue to report to him. I further recommended that major investments in people and technology were required to make the practice competitive. You have run the practice on a shoestring for a number of years. The last two years you just appeared to be going through the motions. I thought the executive office job was an ideal way to get you out of the practice and make way for fresh thinking and new leadership. Now we're stuck with you again. It's outright debilitating."

Baxter flipped through the pages of Carl Miller's presentation document. Carl hadn't made a business plan in three years. His practice made a little money but not a lot. He considered Marty to be a better technician. Carl Miller had been a marginal Partner at best, and Dilger had written him off in three months time. He watched Carl's handshake as he nervously helped himself to a second cup of coffee.

"I believe we should talk this morning about your future with McKenzie Barber, Carl. FY 1990 is not an investment year for the Exec Comp practice. It would appear that you have a lot of fresh ideas in this presentation and I'm going to study it and discuss it with Bob. What's your service date with McKenzie Barber, Carl?"

"August 1, 1968. I will have 22 years in by this August."

"Have you ever considered leaving McKenzie Barber for a firm where your talents are better recognized?"

"I've had my share of calls over the years, Joe, just as I know you have."

"Have you returned those calls, Carl?"

"I have always been loyal to McKenzie Barber, Joe."

"I believe, Carl, that in your best interests, it may be advisable for you to polish up your resume and start returning those calls."

"What are you trying to tell me, Joe?" Carl fumbled for a cigarette. It was a non-smoking room and Baxter could not remember ever seeing him smoke before.

"Carl, I'm three years and out with McKenzie Barber. Dilger is uncomfortable with you leading the Comp practice. That's why he requested me to transfer back from EO. This is a change of power year at McKenzie Barber. There will be a lot of changes effective October 1st. It might be smart for you to actively test the market between now and the end of the summer. You're a talented exec comp consultant, and there certainly are firms out there who might value you higher than McKenzie Barber. Why don't you quietly find out?"

Carl took two puffs from his cigarette and stumped it out in his coffee cup saucer.

"I find this discussion disturbing, Joe. I talked with Lee Heller, the other day, and he's being treated in an absolutely criminal manner by the firm. I believed in McKenzie Barber. It was where I did my summer internship in graduate school, and Clyde Nickerson promised me an offer when I graduated. I didn't sign-up for another interview my MBA graduating year. Then I was assigned from the consulting pool to Frank Alvardi's practice. It was the kind of work I wanted to do all my life. I was good at it. Then you transferred in from Dwyer's practice. It was explained to me that you would remain as part of the practice until Dwyer returned from his leave of absence and then transfer back to manufacturing. The next thing, I knew, you were a fixture and became Frank's fair-haired boy. Finally you became my boss. I was ready to quit then, but you were claimed by New York. I had the job I always wanted with just one obstacle, Joe Baxter. You've been like a cat with nine lives. You always seem to survive, despite your lack of professional qualifications. Now, here you are, reclaiming the job that I had earned and implying that I should consider leaving the firm."

"Carl, over the years, you have made an acceptable contribution to the firm, but there are many who don't believe it is sufficient to retain your services. You haven't made a business plan in three years, and are ranked within the lower quartile of McKenzie Barber Partners. You have not made much of an impression on Bob Dilger. I will do my best to help you improve your standing in the firm. I am also recommending that you test the market. Starting this morning, I want you to concentrate on achieving the Mid-West FY 1990 business plan. Put national initiatives and strategic direction on the shelf until October." Baxter snapped open his brief case. "Now it looks as though you've got some work to do on your FY 1990 plan." Baxter produced the latest CARS summaries. He questioned how accurate the data was.

Carl Miller died of a heart attack over Memorial Day weekend. He had been working early morning Saturday at his desk in his study. His wife, Marge, had found him collapsed against his PC. Baxter picked up Miller's engagements and spent three days a week in the muggy Chicago summer. Dilger was unsympathetic to the budget shortfall.

Baxter had allowed Darlene Bohlweiser to develop into a problem relationship. She had been fine in the housekeeper relationship, but the additional role as occasional mistress proved burdensome. It had been fine and fulfilling to introduce Darlene to the classics in literature and music, but it had been a grave mistake to develop a physical relationship with her. They engaged in lengthy discussions about Flaubert and Dostoyevsky, and Baxter sensed what a freshman literature instructor was subjected to. Additionally, it was apparent to Baxter that Darlene was under serviced by her husband, Luke.

He concluded that Darlene's full body could be ranked somewhere between Kim Novak in her years of decline and his first wife, Maggie, when she was in her prime. Darlene had been blessed with chiseled Germanic features, muscular thighs, and generally firm bosoms. She bought her wardrobe at discount stores, and generally wore blouses and jeans with dangling earrings.

Darlene was capable of undressing faster than any woman Baxter had ever known. He could turn his back on her for a matter of seconds, and turn around to find her naked. She was quite aggressive sexually, and workmanlike in her approach to sex. In short, Baxter had become quite bored with Darlene, and she was beginning to become quite possessive in their relationship.

Darlene became reckless. Baxter's New York City life had become routine and boring. Monica and Linda were now out of his life. Bridgette was history. Baxter had become a 56 year old single man with a sliding career. He found that he was too old for the New York singles bars, and buried himself into the drudgery of repositioning a rapidly slipping Compensation practice. Every two weeks he would have an irreverent

Thursday dinner with Stephany and Beth, which resulted in a blinding Friday morning hangover. Baxter would limp through the day and board the 6:14 Metro-North train for Brinker's Falls. He was generally in his driveway close to ten o'clock after stopping at the IGA for groceries. Baxter would look over and around the back door for a communication from God's Helper after he let himself in. Then he would build a fire and settle in with Sondheim and Canadian Club until he was ready for sleep.

Baxter was ritually awakened by Darlene's touch somewhere around half past six in the morning. She would sweep his blanket away and stand before him naked. Darlene would greet Baxter with a succession of hungry wet kisses from a spearmint and flavored mouth and gently pull his tee shirt and shorts off.

"Oh, Joe. I've missed you so much this week. Friday was the longest day of my life." Her hands fondled and pulled on his member until it was firm. Then Darlene would roll over on her back to receive Baxter. She would climax very early and smile lovingly up at Baxter. Darlene generally would experience a succession of short climaxes reserving a long moaning emotional crescendo for Baxter's time. Baxter, in turn, tried to form images of other lovers as he coupled with Darlene. Dominique was his favorite although he occasionally dialed in Bridgette, Monica, and Linda when he required inspiration. Sex generally ran 15 to 20 minutes by Baxter's watch. After conclusion, Darlene would pad quickly into the bathroom and return with a warm wash cloth. She would then proceed to sponge Baxter's private parts. The sponging was capped off by a long wet kiss on the head of Baxter's member. Darlene would then pad out of the room and return with coffee and sweet rolls.

It was over coffee that Darlene delivered a lengthy monologue describing the preceding week of her life in Brinker's Falls. Baxter now knew more about the twisted ego of Luke Bohlweiser than he cared to know.

Luke had taken a second job with a private security guard firm in Albany that required him to work weekends. In this position, Luke was a shift supervisor at a Japanese manufacturing and assembly plant thirty miles north of Brinker's Falls. Darlene brought Baxter a picture of Luke taken outside their mobile home. Luke stood at parade rest in a blue uniform with sergeant stripes. He wore a side arm encased in a leather holster and his campaign hat rested squarely on his head. Luke resembled the Marine DI he had once been.

"He had to buy the uniform and the gun. Luke would kill me if he heard me use the word gun. It's a weapon. He's in charge of a whole shift from Friday night until Sunday morning. Luke thinks he might be able to work his way up to Captain if he goes to work Special Security full time. Sheriff Clowson gave Luke permission to work weekends, and has encouraged him to look at industrial security opportunities. I think Sheriff Clowson wants Luke to move on for his own good. What do you know about the industrial security business, Joe? Would it be good for someone like Luke? We had to get a small loan from the finance company for his uniform and weapon. Luke started last weekend. He'll be gone all weekend now and it will be easier for us to be together." Darlene then would go on to describe her evening school class at the Adirondack Community College. They were reading the plays of William Shakespeare, and Darlene was quite concerned over the treatment of King Lear by his children. Finally there was her son, Rob, a gentle little fellow, whom Darlene insisted idolized Baxter.

"He must ask me three times a week, Joe, about how Mr. Baxter is. He loves to talk to you when I come to clean on Saturday."

Darlene also kept Baxter well informed on the interactions of the personnel at the Brinker's Falls Inn. She worked six evenings as a waitress at the Inn and had developed unique and for the most part, boring insights into the social interaction of Brinker's Falls.

Darlene would begin to dress promptly at eight o'clock. She would step into her Sears Roebuck panties, hook on her brassiere, pull up her jeans, and rebutton her blouse within sixty seconds time. Baxter would receive a long wet good-bye kiss and Darlene would always wave from the doorway. Baxter could hear her Chevy turn over somewhere between 8:07 and 8:15. Baxter would stare at the ceiling for a few minutes and then close his eyes hoping to return to sleep.

Darlene would return to clean at 2PM with Rob. The boy was growing rapidly and he had his mother's Nordic features. Baxter made it a point to be in his study when Darlene and Rob arrived for the Saturday afternoon cleaning.

"Mr. Baxter," he would appear at the study door. "Would you mind if I talked to you while mother cleans?"

Rob seemed to grow an inch a week. Rob would be tall and tow headed, resembling his mother. "Have you been anyplace interesting this week, Mr. Baxter?" he would ask. They would talk non-stop for better than an hour. Their conversation would usually last two hot cocoas and would range from the discussions that had taken place in Miss Tomlinson's class at Brinker's Falls Consolidated School to the broader aspects of identifiable life outside the town that had housed his young life.

Baxter pointed on the map to his Iron Creek beginnings. He then tracked to Fort Gately back to the University of Minnesota, then onto Racine and finally to Chicago and New York.

"And how many foreign countries have you been to?" Rob would ask each time they met.

"Not that many," Baxter would reply and show Rob on the globe where he had been.

"I think that I will visit China and India. And of course, I will go to Germany, France, and England. I'm not certain as to what work I will be doing. My mom says that you know what people do and what kind of an education I should get. My Dad believes I should go in the military after high school, and then figure out what will be my life's work."

Baxter concluded that Rob was a nice boy, intelligent and reasonably unspoiled. He loved and feared his father, and doted on his mother.

"My mom said you changed her life," Rob said. Outside the study Baxter could make out Beethoven's Seventh Symphony above the buzz of the vacuum cleaner. "She said that you got her interested in books and music. Now she's taking university courses. My Dad says taking literature courses is a waste of time and money. He says mother should take practical courses that would help her earn more money. Dad takes correspondence courses in police work. He's really fast at it. The lesson comes in with the afternoon mail and Dad has the lesson done and mailed back by the next morning. They just made him an honor student at the World Police Training Institute. They gave him a special card that he keeps in his wallet."

"How old are you now, Rob?" Baxter asked as the boy perched himself on the corner of Baxter's desk.

"I'll be twelve in January, and I'll start junior high in the fall. I don't know where I'll be going to school though. We may move. My Dad says that we will have to move to properly advance himself in his chosen field of police work. Did you move a lot when you were my age, Mr. Baxter?"

"I lived in the same house until I got married after my senior year and moved to Minneapolis." Baxter traced his move from Iron Creek to Minneapolis on the map.

"Sometimes when I'm here with mother, I look through your yearbooks. You were a Cougar. You were an honor student, Captain of the basketball team, and were the best typist in school. Sometimes Mom and I sit together and look at the pages of your Cougar yearbooks. My Dad was a famous football player in high school. People still remember him for that. Do they remember you in Iron Creek as a famous basketball player?"

"Rob, I was not the star of the Iron Creek Cougars. We had a fairly successful team my senior year but it's pretty well forgotten by now. If I'm remembered, it's as Joe Baxter, the guy who moved to New York City."

"My Mom said that I should try to be like you. That's why I always come in and talk to you when you're here. I'm pretty smart in school but I'm not good in sports. I'm nearly always the last one picked for a team in gym. My Dad sometimes takes me out to play catch with a football in the backyard. He throws it hard and it hurts when I don't catch it. He says I'm uncoordinated and that I inherited it from my mother. Did you take after your father or your mother, Mr. Baxter?"

"My father. He was a large red-headed man."

"Was he a teacher or someone real smart?"

"He was a man of little formal education who was given to drinking and brawling."

"Was your mother real smart?"

"She was a telephone operator at the Iron Creek Telephone Company. I don't believe she finished high school."

"Then how did you get so smart, Mr. Baxter?"

"I may not be that smart, Rob. I just may have others convinced I'm smart while being quite average."

Rob shook his head. "I think you got real smart from reading books. That's what my mother's trying to do. We read together a lot. She's reading me the plays of William Shakespeare. I guess they are really good but they're hard to figure out. The characters talk funny. I try to read one book every two weeks. Mr. Baxter, what should be my life's work?"

Rob had Darlene's large innocent wondering blue eyes.

"Don't be in such a hurry to select your life's work, Rob. Spend your time learning about the world, and then figure out what kind of role you want to have."

Rob stared in silence at Baxter. He seemed to be processing Baxter's words. "That's good advice. I hope I can keep talking to you if we move away. I know my mother is more than just your housekeeper, and that she's very happy after she visits you in the morning. It's a secret we keep."

The study door opened and Darlene stood framed in the doorway.

"All done for another week," she smiled.

Baxter placed his finger on the map. "It looks as thought I'm going to have to be in Chicago next weekend and Atlanta the weekend after. I probably won't be back until the end of the month. It's the busy time for McKenzie Barber," Baxter lied.

"We'll miss you," Darlene said. Tears were forming in her eyes.

Baxter accompanied Darlene and Rob to the Chevy. "Rob, I left something in the house. You be a good boy and get into the car and mother will be right along."

With four long strides, Darlene was inside the kitchen door.

"Why didn't you tell me this morning that you were going to be traveling? Why do you have to stay out over the weekend?"

"Darlene, I have my work to do. Now don't leave Rob out in the car by himself." He placed his hands on her shoulders and kissed her on the nose.

"I'm coming back tonight after I get off my shift at the Brinker's Falls Inn. I have to see you again tonight and I'm going to stay until morning." Darlene blew her nose, smiled and was out the door.

Baxter watched the Chevy move slowly down the hill. Rob's hand waved out the window. It was obvious to Baxter that this arrangement had gone too far. Perhaps he would take an extended vacation. He certainly wasn't going to make his business plan this year.

McKenzie Barber became a very gloomy place to work during the summer of 1990. The massive layoffs in Executive Office began in May. The team of Dr. Strasser, Druanne Smithers, and Heidi Klein clinically and dispassionately handled the terminations with the cool precision of a SS death squad. They assembled employees in small groups in the late afternoon in the Lexington level conference rooms. They were summoned on the pretext of communications conferences. Once assembled in small groups in remote conference rooms, the Strasser/Smithers/Klein team informed the small groups that their positions had been eliminated. There was a niggardly severance formula related to weeks of severance pay to years of service with no exceptions. Heidi would explain the COBRA rules affecting their health insurance plans and life insurance conversion privileges. Druanne would pass out the checks in McKenzie Barber envelopes stamped PRIVATE in large block letters. Strasser would then give a little speech thanking them for their services and provide each eliminee a letter of recommendation. They were then required to sign a letter acknowledging receipt of these documents. Special appeals were to be directed within ten days to Bernice Randlin, the newly appointed Appeals Secretary in the Office of the Chairman.

Appeals would have to be made within fifteen days of termination. The termination ceremony was followed by either anger, tears, or dumb silence. A member of the newly acquired security force would then escort each terminee to their desk or office. They would be instructed to clear out their personal belongings and turn in their keys and identity cards. They were then escorted down the elevators and out the revolving doors of 311 Park Avenue.

The security force impressed Baxter as a faceless bunch dressed in cheap suits and wearing short haircuts. They were all men and had that enlisted man look as they walked the halls in silence with an occasional wooden smile. Baxter had no idea how many there were or where they went off after hours. Some of them always seemed to be around no matter what the hour. Baxter wondered if he would see Luke Bohlweiser come limping down the hall one day in a shiny, three-year-old Richmond Brothers suit.

The early stages of the cutbacks moved smoothly. Administrative Executive Office McKenzie Barber personnel accepted their fate with modest grumbling, occasional tears and passive anger. The exceptional cases like Lee Heller and Roger White had been handled separately. Both sued. Roger White received a settlement, while Lee Heller's claim was set aside for litigation.

A lull followed the gutting of executive office staff. Baxter took the elevator down one August evening with Heidi. He noted that she was now wearing make-up and earrings.

"How's it going, Heidi?" Baxter greeted her. "When are you coming back to us?"

"Oh Joe, I've been meaning to call you. I'm staying permanently with Druanne in Human Resources. This is confidential, but I expect to be placed in charge of personnel administration in September. I've learned so much from Druanne and Dr. Strasser over the past few months. I believe I'm better suited at this level than just being a consultant."

"Good for you, Heidi," was all Baxter could think of saying in response. She was sounding like Andy Bourke in her youth.

Fitzgerald and Pinker were elected by general acclaim at the October 1990 McKenzie Barber Partners meeting. The year-end financial numbers presented on the first day of the meeting were both inflated and still ugly. Ev Faunce was introduced by Glen Fitzgerald and took the Partners through the damning numbers. Ross "Buzzsaw" Pritchard gave a farewell speech that afternoon to a half empty auditorium. He took credit for a critical repositioning of the firm during a period of reinvestment. He predicted that the harvest of this investment would come under the fresh collective leadership of Glen and Jack. There was light, unenthusiastic applause at the conclusion of Buzzsaw's speech, and the Partners emptied out of the auditorium to Rancho Mirage bars and the fleshpots of Fort Lauderdale. General Pritchard was now a part of McKenzie Barber history.

Bob Dilger was not pleased with Baxter's performance for FY 1990. They met for a seven o'clock breakfast by the Rancho Mirage pool on Saturday morning. Dilger explained at the black tie dinner that Fitzgerald and Pinker had called a last minute Operating Committee for nine o'clock. He had slipped up to Baxter at the cocktail party, and placed a hand on his shoulder.

"Joe, you and I need to talk before you head back to New York. Glen and Jack want to have a kick-off meeting at nine. Meet me at the pool around seven for breakfast."

Dilger slipped away without another word. Baxter wondered if Dilger was going to try to fire him.

Dilger arrived for breakfast in a floral shirt, Bermuda shorts and sandals. Baxter, in contrast, appeared crisp in a blue button down shirt, tie, and tan trousers. Dilger plopped down on his chair and promptly drained his water glass. He propped up one long hairy leg on the adjacent chair and pulled his sun glasses up on his forehead while the waitress poured him coffee and orange juice.

"I'm afraid I over celebrated a little last night, Joe. What did you think of the meeting?"

Baxter anticipated that it was either his last annual Partner's meeting or his second to the last meeting. He certainly didn't expect to be invited to the 1992 meeting.

"It marked a passage. The end of the Buzzsaw Pritchard/Neil Schmidt/Clyde Nickerson era, and the beginning of the Fitzgerald/Pinker era. I don't expect to be around for its conclusion." Baxter thought he'd get the cards out on the table early.

Dilger nodded his head. "How much longer do you expect to work, Joe? I looked you up the other day and saw that you're going to turn 56 pretty soon."

"You and I have worked the Partners Retirement Plan numbers for a long time, Bob. You know I'm vested and that I can retire at age 58 without any discount in pension. Where do you want to go with this conversation?"

"How do you feel about this last year, Joe?"

"It was a dumb year. I got pulled out of my practice to do an executive office review. My successor was appointed, and three months later I was sent back to my practice to replace my successor who reluctantly stepped down. I've been shuttling back and forth to Chicago since Carl died, and my practice is presently in free fall."

"Joe, I have to tell you, I have reviewed your FY 1991 plan and found it very timid. You plan to lose money first quarter, break even second quarter, and complete the year at zero growth with a 10.6% net to gross for the year. That just isn't good enough. You're consolidated in our plan, but if Glen and Jack ask to see a breakout of Exec Comp's numbers, they are going to ask me, 'Why are we in this business?' What should I tell them?"

"Tell them to quit jerking me out of my practice for executive office reviews, and I'll deliver those profits for FY 91 and show 15% growth for FY 92 with a 21% bottom line," Baxter responded.

"How about 93?" Dilger asked while scanning the menu. They both ordered scrambled eggs and bacon from the hovering waitress.

"FY 93 will show 16.3% growth with a 21.4% operating net," Baxter answered boldly.

Dilger opened his arms in a questioning gesture. "Where are you getting all those numbers, Joe? You were supposed to submit a three year plan and I only got a weak one year plan. You used to be the guy who always hit plan. The last couple of years you seemed to have been coasting. I know you had some personal problems with your divorce and your son's death. My question is, where is your head at these days? Can we count on you?"

Baxter sipped his coffee before offering a response. Should he tell Bob Dilger that he planned to leave for Harwell Management in the Fall of 1988 and that he had despised coming to work each day since. "How old are you, Bob?" Baxter asked.

"I'm 49, Joe, and a long ways from being vested," Dilger responded. "McKenzie Barber is stuck with me for a while."

"I plan to stay through 60, Bob."

"If you're going to stay through 60, Joe, you're going to have to improve your performance. You're looking at a good sized unit cut this year, Joe."

"I have a paper signed by Glen Fitzgerald protecting my units for the next two years. Cut my units and I'll litigate and I promise you that I will win."

Dilger rocked slightly in his chair. "I might ask you to produce that document, Joe."

"It's in my safety deposit box, Bob. My attorney also has a copy. You can get one from Bernie, Glen's secretary. I guarantee you that the document exists. It was drafted last January when I agreed to leave my practice and take on the Executive Office review. If I don't meet the submitted plan for FY 1991, I will agree to take early retirement effective October 1, 1992."

Their breakfasts were served, and they began to collectively nibble on their eggs. "There's another alternative," Dilger said suddenly with his mouth partially filled.

"The US firm is going to slim down to a few practices. That's what today's Operating Committee is about. It's Step Two of Ev Faunce's recommendations. He's fixed Executive Office. Now Glen and Jack want him to trim down the rest of the firm."

"What in the hell does Ev Faunce know about the consulting business?" Baxter protested. "The guy is basically a cost cutter. He has no grasp of where the top line comes from."

"He makes a lot of sense, Joe. He's looked at the firm from a different perspective. Ev believes McKenzie Barber is in too many practice areas. He believes we are offering too many services in too many industries. One practice that he questions is Benefits & Compensation. I believe we could buy our practice from McKenzie Barber during 1991."

"Will they try to sell it to someone else?" Baxter questioned.

"They will entertain bids for all of the practices designated for disposal. We need to get an early bid in. Whoever buys the Benefits practice will have to take the Compensation practice. I can't very well lead a bid for the practices unless I can be sure of you, Joe."

"What's your timing on this, Bob?"

"I'm not sure. It's a major topic on the agenda of the Operating Committee meeting this morning. I would expect that we would have to have our bid in by the end of April. That means a strategic plan and financing. You and I, and the other Partners would have to commit seed capital and get the banks lined up. I know you're close to Harwell Management. Maybe they would want to take a position."

"How much of the company would I own?" Baxter asked.

"How does 12% sound?"

"Very low."

"Joe, the Benefits practice is seven times as large as the Comp practice. I believe 12% is very reasonable."

"25% sounds more reasonable to me."

"25% sounds excessive to me, Joe, taking into consideration the poor performance of the Comp practice in FY 1990. I have 12 Benefits Partners who will require a substantial equity opportunity to join this venture."

"What happens if there is no internal bid for our practices?" Baxter probed.

"Then we're going to be sold to someone else and we are likely to go as management employees. This is our opportunity to make a lot of money. If you were to come with us, I would need your commitment to stay five years and develop your successor."

"Let's talk again, Bob, after you're back in New York. I really have to give this matter some thought. It has come as a complete surprise to me," Baxter said after they had concluded their breakfast. There was a handshake and Baxter watched Dilger's lanky frame walk away in long strides to attend a meeting which would mark the beginning of the dismemberment of McKenzie Barber.

February 22, 1991

It reminded Baxter of Jean Paul Sartre's "NO EXIT". He was in a meeting with twelve actuaries planning to bid for the Benefits and Compensation practices of McKenzie Barber. They were friendly and cordial enough to Baxter. He knew most of them by face and few by name. It was Baxter's third meeting with the buy-out group.

Dilger ran all of the meetings in his relaxed Indiana manner. As a group they wanted the Compensation practice, but expressed skepticism over Baxter's performance numbers. There was a tediousness about the group that made Baxter uneasy. Minor issues required detailed and extended discussions. Dilger conducted the meetings collegially inviting input on every issue from each table member. Baxter questioned himself time and time again as to whether he wanted to be in business with twelve actuaries.

The Strasser/Smithers/Klein downsizing team had now invaded the various consulting practices firm-wide. Practices engaged in disposal discussions with McKenzie Barber were exempt from downsizing. The core practices were not. The consultants proved far more combative than the middle managers and senior staff from Executive Office. Open war broke out.

The Lexington level conference room approach blew up on the first action. Five marginally chargeable second year consultants had been assembled for a conference. Each Consultant was selected by a Partner from a separate practice group. They attended the Lexington level meeting with the expectation that their input on the management of the firm was being solicited. Two consultants had independently prepared flip chart presentations which provided a business strategy to return McKenzie Barber to its former glory. The five consultants were comprised of three women with Columbia, Wharton, and Darden School MBAs and two men with graduate degrees from Yale and Tuck.

They had been hired in 1988 by Lee Heller, and had yet to advance from the consulting pool. They were comfortable over the cancellation of the 1991 college recruiting program. They believed it provided them extra time to select a proper practice. They arrived early to the conference room with confident exuberance. Dr. Strasser began the meeting with the announcement that their services would no longer be needed at McKenzie

Barber, and that Druanne and Heidi would now brief them on severance pay and health insurance continuance. Shock turned to outrage on the faces of the assembled consultants. Brian Holden, a burly former tight end from Yale, pounded hard on the table for order.

"Hold on here. What's your name again, sir?" He pointed with a large hand to Dr. Strasser.

"Again, I'm Dr. Strasser, the Director of Administration. This is Miss Smithers, Director of Human Resources who has assumed Mr. Heller's duties, and Miss Klein, her assistant. I realize the news we're giving you is difficult to absorb, but decisions have been made that are in the best interests of McKenzie Barber and your own careers." Strasser gave the group a broad benign smile.

"This is a lot of crap," Mary Ellen Higgins, a Wharton graduate in a pin striped pants suit responded. She placed her hand over the strategic assessment flip chart that she had planned to share in the meeting. "If someone is going to fire us, we want to hear that from a Partner, not some useless Executive Office flunkies. What rock did you come out from under, Dr. Strasser? We recognize Druanne. She was brought in by Brett Williamson the firm's resident sexual harassment expert to fire secretaries. Heidi used to be in the pool with us. The only practice that ever used her was Executive Compensation. I have been rated 'Above Expectations' in every review. Now you're telling me that I'm out? You don't even know who the hell I am. I'm not going to sit here and have three obvious losers tell me there is no future for me at McKenzie Barber."

"The basic consultant's agreement clearly states that we will receive quarterly reviews from our assigned counselor and that we will have one quarter to correct any performance deficiencies," Todd Stoller, a sandy haired 1990 Darden School graduate added. "I haven't had a review since the late spring of 1990. This action is in violation of the consultant's agreement offered to all of us when we joined the firm."

"The consultant's agreement is no longer in effect," Heidi had blurted back.

"No one's ever been provided any notice to that effect," Brian Holden shot back. "I believe all of us should immediately consult our attorneys. We'll be back to you when we have an opinion on the legality of all of this."

Strasser slapped his hand on the table for attention. "All of you must understand that McKenzie Barber has no more need of your services. You were summoned here because of your low utilization level, and we have severance checks for you. Outside we have security people who will escort you back to your desks to clean out your personal effects, and are instructed to collect your access cards and personally escort your from the building. Let me repeat myself. Your services are no longer needed at McKenzie Barber! We're here to tell you that you're terminated and not to debate the matter."

Holden stood up from his chair, removed his suitcoat, placed his Rolex watch on the table, and stood up. He looked around the table at his consulting associates.

"How many of you accept this attempt at a summary execution of consultants? Raise your hands please."

His four companions shook their heads.

He then started across the room to the conference room telephone which rested on a shelf behind Strasser's chair. Strasser placed his hand over the phone protectively only to have Holden pull his hand off the phone. Holden dialed the operator and asked for Fitzgerald's office.

"My name's Brian Holden, and I'm one of five consultants who have been called to meet with some personnel people from Executive Office. What these personnel people have proposed is in contradiction with the personnel policies of the firm. We need to meet with either Glen or Jack Pinker, or some senior partner of the firm. Can you set that up? We're on extension 4914 on the Lex level in a conference room. You're going to call us right back? What's your name, M'am? Bernie? Okay, Bernie. We'll stay at this extension."

Holden glared at Strasser and took his seat at the end of the table.

Strasser offered up a smile. "Look, I know this is a shock for all of you. But the firm must cut back. This meeting was mandated by Messrs. Fitzgerald and Pinker. They have delegated this painful task to us. We don't particularly like it, but it's our job. Some one hundred consultants will be asked to leave firm-wide. There simply isn't enough work for you to do.

You are the first five. Some 95 will be following you. There is no going back and no protest. The reduction in force for professional staff is an ugly reality for the consulting business in 1991. You are obviously attractive, intelligent, and gifted young men and women. You will find new positions very quickly."

"What you are saying may be true," Mary Ellen Higgins interjected. "But you're not the people who should be telling us that we're no longer needed at McKenzie Barber. We need to hear from the Partners. If the Partners say that we should leave, then we'll leave in an orderly manner. We're McKenzie Barber consultants, not blue collar factory help."

"You're employees of McKenzie Barber," Druanne corrected the group. "The firm has too many employees to support its level of business. Executive Office and the support staff have already been cut. College recruiting has been canceled for 1991. Now it's time for the consultants to share the pain. You five were selected because of your low level of utilization during the first two quarters of this fiscal year."

"You're missing the god-damned point, lady," Holden shot back. "If we're going to be fired, we want to be fired by Partners, and not by some sub-professional personnel people from Executive Office. We're going to wait here for someone from Fitzgerald's office to phone us back. You can just gather up all of your envelopes and get back to whatever you're supposed to be doing when you're not trying to fire people." Holden looked around the table for confirmation and was answered with an affirmative nodding of heads.

Strasser rose up from the table. "Very well then. But you're just making it hard for yourselves." Druanne and Heidi followed their leader out the conference room door.

Five minutes later they received a call from Bernie, Glen Fitzgerald's secretary, who informed them that Jon Grunwaldyt, a Group Partner would meet with them as a group at 8:15 the next morning in Jack Pinker's 39th floor conference room.

It was quickly concluded that the layoff of consulting staff had to be personally handled by a ranking Partner. Fitzgerald and Pinker selected Jon Grunwaldyt as the firm's right-sizing spokesman. He sought out Baxter for a Four Seasons front bar conference on the evening before he had to meet with the initial group of five.

Baxter's phone rang shortly after 6PM.

"Joe, I need to talk to you right away in private. Glen has just given me a new special assignment. It's a bit of a sticky wicket and I need to talk to you about it privately right away. Can we meet in fifteen minutes over at the Four Seasons?"

The bar stools were taken, and they settled into a spot near the back railing.

Baxter reckoned that he hadn't seen Grunwaldyt up close for the better part of the year. He had caught glimpses of him at the Partner's meeting and at the Christmas Party. There had been an exchange of smiles and waves, but neither had made an effort to seek the other out. Baxter suspected that he had been categorized by Grunwaldyt as an over-the-hill, fast slipping McKenzie Barber Partner. Grunwaldyt, in turn, obviously ranked himself as one of the key members of the new 1990 McKenzie Barber leadership team. His call out of the blue surprised Baxter.

Jon Grunwaldyt wore a grey pinstripe suit. Hermes tie with matching braces peeking out from his open suit jacket. His face seemed a little fuller, but had retained its youthful glow. He had retained his image of Jon Grunwaldyt, the handsome young Siegfried of management consulting.

"Joe, it's been too long," Grunwaldyt greeted Baxter. He had apparently arrived early and ordered two white wines which were being served at the time of Baxter's arrival. "I really appreciate your coming over on such short notice. I have been given one of those dirty little projects that Glen and Jack like to pass out in order to test the up and comers. I need some sage advice from Joe Baxter, the old master," they clinked glasses and Baxter waited for Grunwaldyt to proceed on his agenda.

"Well, Joe, this certainly is a time of change and new challenges at good old McKenzie Barber. My grapevine tells me that you are going to be a key part of the Employee Benefits/Compensation practice buy-out group. That could be a very sweet deal for all of you guys. I'm on the Operating Committee now, and that deal looks very good for both sides." Baxter nodded and said, "I'm looking at the transaction with great interest, Jon."

"You sure made a flying escape from Executive Office. You're back where you belong now."

"I guess so, Jon. I'm quite curious about this new dirty little project you've been assigned. Can you share some details?" Baxter said pushing Grunwaldyt.

Jon took a long sip from his wine glass and motioned for the waiter to bring another round.

"Joe, how well do you know this Strasser fellow in EO?"

"I met him the morning I transferred back from EO to New York Office, Jon. He's Ev Faunce's favorite henchman. They've screwed up companies together before."

"Well, Joe, I have to tell you that I'm very impressed so far with Ev Faunce. He's exactly what the doctor ordered for McKenzie Barber. He described Strasser at an Operating Committee meeting as his expert in organization rationalization. The man and his team have certainly done a wonderful job in right sizing executive office. They stubbed their toe today in Phase Two of their mandate, and Glen has asked me to step in and give them a hand."

"Knowing Strasser, Jon," Baxter suggested. "You may have to offer his group both hands."

Grunwaldyt held his wine glass up to the light. "This is a California Sauvignon Blanc. It's a little pricey, but worth it."

"What have you been asked to do, Jon?" Baxter pushed.

"The firm is going to fire 100 consultants this month," Grunwaldyt said in a low voice. "We've out counseled consultants for years, but we did it in a very quiet way. Clyde Nickerson used to handle it. Then Clyde trained Lee Heller to take care of it. Consultants who couldn't make it were cleverly out placed so they thought it was their idea. They became friends of the firm and did everything they could do in their new careers to get us invited in for consulting work. They disappeared one by one. Now it's been decided to cut one hundred all at once. Strasser tried his initial group of five tonight, and World War III almost started. The group, which was made up of two year consultants, refused to recognize the EO group's authority to terminate their employment. They demanded to meet with a ranking Partner of the firm. Glen told me to jump in and take care of it, and handle all of the other dismissals. He knows how busy I am, but he just looked at me and said, 'take care of this Jon. Strasser's downsizing task force now report directly to you. I want this done quickly, and professionally, without any drop in morale.' Tomorrow morning at 8:15, I'm meeting with the first group. Strasser is meeting me for a seven o'clock breakfast to brief me on the five. I have to attend a Hortense Foods creditor's committee at nine."

"Where are these one hundred consultants located, Jon?"

"Strasser will provide me the specifics in the morning. I would suspect that the bulk of the redundancies will be in New York, Chicago, Los Angeles, and San Francisco. FSO is a separate culture, and they're used to sending people home. Atlanta and Dallas have always operated slightly understaffed. They should be okay."

"They're blue collar consulting practices with a lot of public sector work. Do I understand correctly that these 100 consultants are two year MBA hires in the pool?"

Grunwaldyt nodded his head. "I don't like it either, Joe. It's cutting into our bloodstream of talent. We heavily recruited for these people. They had many other choices when they chose McKenzie Barber. We competed for them with aggressive pay and glorious career visions. Then they came to us, we put them through the boot camp of the consultant's pool. Now we're going back to 100 of them at one time and telling them we can't seem to generate enough business to keep them around. There's going to be a lot of noise in the marketplace, Joe. Clyde knew how to make people disappear with smiles on their faces. These kinds of layoffs are likely to get very ugly. While I admire Ev Faunce and all the things he's doing to help us rethink the operating structure of the firm, I believe we're playing with fire here."

"So what are you going to tell this guinea pig group of five tomorrow morning?"

"Joe, I've been thinking that it might be helpful if you sat in on this meeting tomorrow morning. You could, more or less, critique me."

Baxter produced an air plane ticket folder from the breast pocket of his suitcase.

"I'm on a 7:05 Delta to Atlanta. I have a very critical meeting with Planters & Commerce Bank. Did someone suggest that you call me?"

"Glen said that I might want to get you involved."

"I don't have time for this, Jon. I'm working hard to rebuild my practice which is involved in a buy-out transaction from the firm. The best I can do is offer some advice. Now here's how I believe you should handle the meeting."

Grunwaldyt produced a small leather notebook from the breast pocket of his suitcoat.

"First, introduce yourself as a graduate of the consulting pool. Ask them to introduce themselves and make a short statement about their feelings toward McKenzie Barber. This will be the tricky part, because you only want to let them vent slightly. Then share with them a few of the shaky points in your own career. I can, for example, remember one morning back in the late 1970's when Dirks was ready to fire you. Then tell them that this is one of the hardest tasks that you've ever been asked to take on. Explain the realities of the situation. They are in the room because of their personal low utilization and this is a matter of the Partners failing to generate a sufficient amount of work for them to do. This is not their failure. Then remind them that it is not in the best interest of their own careers to remain in the consulting pool at their current low level of utilization. I assume the firm will continue to provide them phone mail services. Tell them that you will personally stand behind them on reference queries. Ask them to handle this decision on their career continuity with McKenzie Barber with objectivity and professionalism. Then thank them for their services, ask them to clean out their desks by noon, turn in their keys to Bernie, and go out and have a nice lunch on the firm to be placed on their final expense report. Wish them good luck and get the hell out of there."

Grunwaldyt scribbled notes in his notebook with a silver Cross pen. "This is going to take better than an hour, Joe."

"It shouldn't, Jon. You have made Board presentations on strategic planning issues in twenty minutes. You sure as hell can fire five pool consultants in forty."

"Should I have Strasser sit in?"

"Lock him up in a closet until ten o'clock." Baxter drained his glass.

"Another one?" Grunwaldyt proposed.

"I've got to run, Jon. I have a dinner meeting uptown," Baxter lied.

"When will you be back from Atlanta?"

"Late tomorrow night."

"Can we talk again?"

"Of course, Jon. But I can only offer advice. I don't have the time to participate in this process."

"Joe, I'm afraid this is just the beginning. This could be a tar baby for me."

"Jon," Baxter said placing a hand on Grunwaldyt's shoulder. "Just consider this a test of your leadership capacity. You could well be Chairman of McKenzie Barber one day." Baxter looked back on Grunwaldyt from the staircase landing. The waiter was serving him a fresh glass.

Baxter left the Four Seasons and walked across 52nd Street to Madison through a light spring rain. McKenzie Barber was breaking apart. It was selling off practices that were classified as no longer strategic to the core business. At the same time, it was shrinking the resources of the main practice. After this initial round of 100 consultants would come Managers, Directors, and Partners. McKenzie Barber was tidying itself up for a buyer. Every company over the past ten years that had employed Ev Faunce had been ultimately sold.

Baxter turned south on Madison Avenue walking slowly down the East side of the street. September 1991 would mark 23 years with McKenzie

Barber and he would be 56. He had hit the 79 mark in age plus years of service. If he could cut the right deal in a negotiated retirement, Baxter estimated that he would have a full retirement approximating 35% of $400,000 or $140,000 for life. If he retired tomorrow morning, Baxter would be subject to an annual discount of $5,600. His partnership unrealized receivables account was approximately $100,000. He was expected to contribute $200,000 of equity capital for five years as a founding Partner in the buy-out group. He would be obligated to spend the next five years of his life in a firm dominated by Pension Actuaries. It was time to exit McKenzie Barber. Baxter had been ready to early retire in September 1989 in order to join Harwell Management. Now the window was open again.

The rain became heavy at 43rd Street. Baxter pulled up his collar and continued to walk in slow contemplative steps. He began to plot his escape from McKenzie Barber with the stealthy mind of a convict planning a jail break. He would not make plan again this year. Baxter's senior people had a reprieve from execution as long as he appeared to be a participant in the buy-out. Baxter estimated that he had some eight to nine weeks unused vacation accumulated. He would simply disappear on an extended vacation in mid-August and not return until the Partner's meeting. On September 1st, he would write to the Chairman announcing his intention to take early retirement effective February 1, 1992. He would continue on and go through the motions, but in mid-August, Baxter was going over the wall to freedom and the world outside McKenzie Barber. When it got down to it, McKenzie Barber ceased to be much fun after the Chairman election of 1984.

Baxter stripped off his wet clothes after returning to his high ceilinged apartment. He placed a Ravel piano CD on his sound system, settled back in the Eames chair, sipped brandy, and stared at the ceiling. If he weren't a McKenzie Barber Partner, who would Baxter become? Where would he live? Would he retire or do an adjunct professor routine? Would he retire to Brinker's Falls? He'd have to break his relationship off with Darlene and put an end to his feud with God's Helper. Alternatively, he could sell the Brinker's Falls house and find another part of the country to live in. Maybe he'd find a warm weather college town and get Muffin out of that community college in Vermont and into a major university. He was 56 years old with five work experiences, the union, the Army, the University, Washburn Manufacturing, and McKenzie Barber. McKenzie Barber really had been his career, He had fed on legends of the founders, and had been a witness to its fall. Baxter had somehow become one of the historians of the firm. If the firm were merged within the year, its history as a separate enterprise could well end. McKenzie Barber needed a history. Baxter could provide that. He would review the archives, assemble the anecdotal information, and collect the data. It could be Baxter's mission to write a history reflecting the rise and fall of McKenzie Barber.

Grunwaldyt called first thing on Thursday morning to report his success.

"It went smoothly, Joe. Most of your advice was right on the mark. They were five marginal consultants with high opinions of themselves and soft performance ratings. I'm sure we can find another 95 just like them. I was finished up with them in thirty-five minutes. I'm putting together a procedure for exiting professional staff. I'd like to run it by you. I agree with you on Strasser's people. As soon as this is behind us, Druanne Smithers and Heidi Klein should be terminated. I'll have the procedure over to you this afternoon in the inter-office mail. Mark it up and send it back right away. I want to have copies in front of Glen and Jack first thing Friday."

Baxter explained his McKenzie Barber history book project over a Saturday lunch the following week to Beth Gold. She thought it was a stupid idea.

"It seems to me like a major effort that would appeal to a very small market. It might make a vanity press project if you would be willing to fund the publishing costs. Why don't you write an executive pay book first. Your little Italian friend made quite a splash with his. Put together an outline and I'll arrange a lunch with my agent. It's obvious to me that it's time for you to get out of there, but if you plan to write, do a pay book first."

"And how are you doing these days, Beth?"

"Don't ask. I'm living off diminishing royalties and doctoring some screen scripts. I have four aborted novels on discs and I owe an advance to a publisher for a book I can't seem to deliver. Everything was so much easier for me ten years ago. Now everything is drudgery. Things started to slip for me when Lester died, and they've never improved."

"And where's Stephany today?" Baxter asked.

"She's on an interview in Philadelphia. It's a small institutional firm. Stephany's been out of work since last fall when Fletcher Berwick pushed her out in a reorganization. She's becoming a little desperate. Stephany has too much energy to be unemployed this long."

"Stephany has more Hart money behind her than she can count," Baxter observed.

"You're operating on old information, Joe. Her father has Alzheimer's and he has had to be institutionalized at considerable cost. Stephany had her share of the family assets in a blind trust during her SEC years. Her idiot brother invested in some of the worst commercial real estate in America. The estate's been sold to meet debt service, and Stephany has her West side apartment up for sale. She wants $600,000, but she won't get it. I think she'd settle for $425,000 if you want to buy it. Stephany needs a job, Joe. Keep your eye out for her. Do you think the Harwell people could use her?"

Baxter coasted through the summer. Planned reductions and related anxiety were all around him as he peacefully ambled in at 9AM and retired at 5PM. Once every two weeks, Baxter would attend a meeting of the buy-out group. The venture was now called MB HRC Ltd. which was abbreviated for McKenzie Barber Human Resources Consulting. A strategic plan had been prepared, and a three year forecast of revenues and earnings had been prepared. McKenzie Barber would be MB HRC's landlord through 1996, and would provide accounting and office services on a chargeback basis. The timing of the spin-off had been set for October 1, 1991. Capital contributions were set for September 1st, and seed capital contributions by the new Partners were due July 1, 1991. Dilger was elected Chairman, and each Partner was responsible for bringing in one investor. It was assumed that Joe Baxter would deliver Harwell Management as an investor. His practice's low level of performance was ignored on the assumption that Baxter was sandbagging work which would be delayed until after October 1st.

Baxter and his 591 US Partners studied the carefully worded periodic communiqués from the Operating Committee. The firm had missed its cash plan by $33 a Partner's unit resulting in a $56,000 personal cash shortfall for Baxter in FY 1990. The 9-30-90 firm-wide accrual financial statements presented a year slightly behind FY 1989. There had been a build-up in receivables, and a substantial increase in unbilled work in process. The US share of Barber earnings were also off.

Much to Baxter's delight, the annual contribution to the Partner's pension fund had been generously funded. The presentation of the year-end financials at the October 1990 Partner's meeting might have inspired a riot in past years. Instead the Partners accepted the results with grim, silent faces. The reign of Ross "Buzzsaw" Pritchard as Chairman was over. The 1984 Partners had made their choices and were living with the results. The post 1984 Partners were collectively and suitably outraged. After giving his farewell speech to a poorly attended early Friday afternoon session, Buzzsaw was not invited to speak at the Black Tie dinner and the Partners were recipients of 'We've-got-to-get-this-firm-moving-again speeches by Pinker and Fitzgerald. The numbers were not from their watch, but belonged to Buzzsaw. Fitzgerald predicted at the close of his speech that McKenzie Barber would be number one again in 1996. There had been medium applause. Baxter doubted whether many of the Partners in the room accepted the statement.

The Future Directions 1991 plan was introduced firm-wide through the distribution and viewing of videos to all Partners, Management Group members, consulting associates and admin. employees. Partners and Director level employees received personal video tapes at their homes. Managers and consulting staff were organized into conference room groups of ten. They would view the video and provide feedback to Glen and Jack through a group moderator. The 1991 McKenzie Barber was going to be a focused, participatively managed firm which invited upstream input on how to make the firm better.

Glen and Jack came across well on the videos. They had obviously received extensive coaching and appeared relaxed and open to the eyes of the video camera. Their message was that the firm must return and concentrate on the core practices which had made the firm great. Other practices outside the core functional and industry groups would be divested with first right of refusal given to the existing Partners. It would be their opportunity to take their piece of McKenzie Barber and grow it at their rate of expectation. Jack Pinker went on to say that the bloated Executive Office staff had been already substantially right-sized. The next step would be to get the operating practices of the firm back on track. This would involve change in responsibility for many. Glen and Jack needed to hear new ideas and realities from the field.

"We need to make our firm better," Glen concluded. "If you have an idea or thought on how to serve our existing clients better or attract new clients, we need to hear from you. This is why we have asked Bernice Randlin to serve as the firm's first National Coordinator for Performance Improvement Input." A picture of a smiling Bernie was flashed on the screen along with a mail station number and E-mail number for performance improvement input.

A memorandum was distributed the next day indicating that the Government Services, Higher Education, and Healthcare practices were going to be integrated into FSO effective April 1, 1991. It looked to Baxter as though a 'For Sale' sign had been placed on FSO.

Baxter ran the business case through his mind. Who would be a prospective buyer for McKenzie Barber? What would they buy? Could they buy the US firm without also acquiring the UK firm and the splinter international practices? What would they be getting? A brand name, work in process, accounts receivable, the partner's equity, the goodwill of the firm and the unfunded pension liability of the retired and active Partners? It would have to be a good sized International services firm. It would represent a large bite for an international public accounting firm. A large computer services firm with a high PE multiple could be a bidder. Banks and Insurance companies were out of the question. The large actuarial firms were a possibility, but they would prefer to settle initially for the Benefits and Comp practice before taking up the entire carcass of McKenzie Barber. The only consulting firm near McKenzie Barber's size was Robson Allen Harbridge. After that were a grouping of fast growing firms which had climbed from boutique status into formidable competitor status. McKenzie Barber would represent a major and risky step forward for a fast growing specialty consulting firm. Lastly were the international advertising agencies, cash flow intensive with their basic businesses, markets, specialized industries, changing in concert to shrinking operating margins.

McKenzie Barber startled the business world on the 1991 July 4th week by announcing that they were in preliminary talks with Robson Allen Harbridge relative to a possible business combination. Baxter had taken the week off to spend in the quiet of Brinker's Falls. Muffin had come down from Vermont for the week, accompanied by a friend named Larry. Baxter had been fully dressed at seven AM on the Saturday morning before their arrival. He did not want Darlene to catch him defenseless in bed when she arrived in the morning for her pre-cleaning activities. He had visited

Brinker's Falls sparingly through the late spring and early summer. He had been sipping on a mug of coffee and leafing through CARS engagement statements when he heard the Chevy engine moving up the driveway. The car door slammed shut and steps were heard on the back steps before the key turned opening the door. Darlene appeared in the doorway in a tee shirt, red athletic shorts, sweat socks, and tennis shoes with her dime store sun glasses mounted on her forehead skier style. Baxter hadn't been with a woman in the three month interval since his last visit to Brinker's Falls. She looked quiet inviting this morning.

"You're up and dressed," she observed with a surprised face.

"I've got company coming today. My daughter and a friend are coming down from Vermont to spend the week. May I pour you a coffee?"

Baxter poured Darlene a mug of coffee and watched her nervously stir a general tablespoon of sugar into the cup.

"I haven't' seen you in over ten weeks. I get your checks in the mail, and there's never any note. I almost called you at your office, but I couldn't remember where you worked. I came back here to find that book you wrote, and I found one of your business cards. I keep it in my wallet now. I also cut your picture off the jacket of your book. I love you, Joe and I miss you very much. Rob always asks after you. 'Is Mr. Baxter traveling around the world again, Mom?' he asked the other day. I'd like to bring him by to see you this week."

"Darlene," Baxter began. He had rehearsed the little speech he was about to deliver in his mind on the train the night before. "We've had a relationship between the two of us since the Labor Day weekend of 1988. We were both lonely people and we reached out for one another. I've been very comfortable with you during our time together. I believe, however, that it's time for us to break this off and revert back to employer and housekeeper. There is no future for our relationship. I think the world of Rob, and I'd like to help out with the funding of his education at some future time. I know that Luke is looking for work outside Brinker's Falls. It probably would be best for you to move and have a fresh start as a family unit."

He watched the tears stream down her full tanned cheeks to her breasts. Darlene's body began to shake and she broke into a deep bawl. Baxter resisted an impulse to comfort her. He knew he had to break off this relationship and this morning would be as good as any. He calmly sipped his black coffee in waitful silence. His watch said 7:12 AM. Darlene's sobbing peaked at 7:15. She produced a tissue from her purse and blew her nose twice.

"Have you met someone?" she asked.

"No. I've been working very long hours and traveling quite a bit. I haven't had much time for social relationships. It is highly likely that I will be retiring from McKenzie Barber in January. I will probably put this house up for sale and move to a place where the winters are a little warmer. I had a former associate go off and become an adjunct professor at a university out in California. I might do something similar."

"I could join you, keep house for you and I could take courses," Darlene volunteered.

"Whatever I do, Darlene, I believe it's time for us to step back from our relationship for a while. I believe we should take the first step this weekend."

Darlene took a long drink from her coffee mug.

"It's so easy for you, isn't it?" Her face hardened. "And we go back long before Labor Day of 1988. I remember meeting you for the first time at the Brinker's Falls Inn when you were with your wife. I think it was in the winter of 1982. Coming into this house with all of your books and music was such a treat for me. I've been in love with you since 1984. I couldn't believe it when we became lovers. Living with Luke is an ugly experience. I hate him. When he gets the new job, I'm not going with him. I'm taking Rob and we're going away to start over. And I'm not telling Luke or anyone where I'm going. If you leave here, I want to take Rob with me and go and keep house for you. You can marry some woman more your style. I just want to be near you for the rest of my life."

Baxter rose from his chair and stroked Darlene's hair which was tied in a tight pony tail.

"When you're ready to leave Luke, I'll help out with some fresh start money. You can count on me," Baxter said. Darlene placed her hand over

Baxter's, squeezed it once and rose up from the chair. "When will you expect your daughter to come?"

"Muff and her friend should be here in an hour or so," Baxter lied. He was expecting them by early evening.

"What day would you like me to come by and clean?"

"How about Monday and again next Sunday after they've gone. I'll write you two checks now if you like," Baxter offered.

"Yes. I would like the money now," Darlene answered coldly. Baxter wrote one large check which Darlene carefully folded and placed into her purse.

She paused near the door. "We are no longer lovers. Is that right?"

"It's best this way, Darlene."

"Then have it your way," Darlene said and closed the door behind her with a slam. Baxter listened for the Chevy as it faded down the driveway. He concluded that it had been too easy.

Muffin and her friend, Larry, arrived in a well-dented Buick of early 1980s vintage. The engine ground to a stop in the driveway behind Baxter's pick-up truck. Muffin bounced out from the passenger seat, tall, blonde, and thin in loose fitting blue jeans and a yellow turtleneck sweater. Baxter stepped out of the side door to the cement steps, and Muffin ran to him.

"Oh Daddy," she sobbed as she threw her arms around Baxter's neck. "I've missed you so much."

Baxter greeted his daughter with kisses on her cheeks and forehead. He looked over Muffin's shoulders at a male figure emerging from the driver's seat. He was of medium height, bearded, with long hair tied in a pony tail. He walked immediately to the trunk and began to silently unload bags.

"Larry, come and meet my Dad."

Larry's hand was rough and his handshake was firm. His blue eyes seemed calm. His brown hair and beard appeared flecked with grey. Baxter estimated that Larry was easily in his mid-to-late thirties. He quickly computed Muffin's age at 21.

"I'm glad to meet you, sir. Muff's told me so much about you."

Their baggage consisted of a large metal suitcase, two large canvas bags, three boxes of paints, some brushes enclosed in a plastic bag, and an artist's easel.

"Larry's an artist, Dad," Muffin explained. "He plans to do some landscapes this week."

"Where would you like me to sleep, Mr. Baxter?" Larry asked.

"You may continue whatever sleeping arrangements you two presently have," Baxter said picking up the largest suitcase.

"I told you that would be what he'd say," Baxter heard Muffin whisper to Larry.

Baxter settled them in an upstairs bedroom at the far end of the hallway distant from the master bedroom. They returned hand in hand down the stairs after ten minutes, and joined Baxter in the living room.

"This is a wonderful fireplace in the winter, Larry. Dad and I used to snuggle up in a blanket in front of the fire. We'd either play scrabble or read while we listened to classical music and Broadway shows. Then sometimes we would go to the Brinker's Falls Inn for dinner, and Daddy would dance with me to the juke box."

They opted for beer when Baxter offered cocktails, and settled into stuffed chairs and couch facing the fireplace.

"I have steaks I can put on for dinner when you're ready," Baxter suggested.

"Dad, Larry and I both are vegetarians. We bought some groceries in Albany and I'll cook tonight. Then we can go into the IGA tomorrow to get the right kind of groceries," Muff announced.

Baxter remembered Muffin eating ham and eggs at their breakfast following Joel's funeral.

"How long have you been a vegetarian, Muff?"

"Since January. I got to know Larry around Christmas. He works at the Walnut Inn."

"I'm the maintenance man, Mr. Baxter," Larry announced with a sense of pride.

"Larry graduated in Fine Arts from Oberlin. He's an artist, but earns his regular living as a carpenter and maintenance man. Larry convinced me that eating meat was bad for me. I'm feeling much better since I became a vegetarian."

Baxter looked to Larry. His face had the smug confidence of an evangelist who had just made a convert.

"I'm on the straight meat diet myself," Baxter countered. "It's beef steak tonight, lamb kidneys tomorrow night, and horse tongue the following night. I like my meat. It keeps me alert and competitive which is a necessary state for survival in my line of work."

Larry looked at the bear rug. "Did you shoot this bear?"

"He wasn't shot," Baxter answered. "He broke in here and tried to take over. I strangled him with my bare hands."

Larry rolled his eyes in Muffin's direction.

"Dad, please don't be impossible. Larry just met you and he was very intimidated over the thought of meeting you. I told him all about the house, the Dopman brothers, and the strange man who calls on the phone from time to time. We're starved. Why don't you take Larry for a walk while it's still light, and I'll get dinner ready. I'll even fix your steak, Dad."

"I'll fix my own steak," Baxter said rising to his feet.

"Com'on Larry. Bring your beer. We'll tour the baronial grounds."

They walked down the pathway toward the creek at the far west corner of Baxter's property. Baxter narrated through a long monologue about the legend of the Dopman brothers and the history of the property as they trudged through the over run path.

"Mr. Baxter, do I represent an intruder in your reunion with Muffin? I can drive away in the morning and come back for her next Saturday," Larry finally asked after one hundred yards of listening to Baxter.

"Please call me, Joe, Larry. Obviously you're someone important in my daughter's life, even if you are a vegetarian. Let's take the time to get to know each other." They reached the creek where Baxter seated himself at the foot of a tree.

"Let's get acquainted. I'll tell you about myself and you can tell me about yourself. Then we can go back to the house, and I can eat meat while you two gobble up your vegetables. You want to start or should I?"

"She talks about you constantly, Joe. I know all about you were a poor boy from Northern Minnesota, married Muff's mother, split with her, moved to New York and became a famous pay expert. I'm very nervous to be in your presence. I wish I would have brought a second can of beer with me. You're fairly overpowering. I know you went through a divorce in the last couple of years and Muff has a real sense of loss about her stepmother. She really misses her brother who died a couple of years ago and she has a love-hate relationship with her mother."

"What did you think of Muffin when you met her?" Baxter asked. Larry took a long pull form his beer can.

"We both work at the Walnut Inn Ski Lodge in Maple Patch, Vermont. Muff works in the gift shop and writes the menus. I'm the maintenance man. I'm a pretty good carpenter and electrician, and a fair plumber. I thought that Muff was a lot older than she was. I figured she was twenty-five or twenty-six. I used to see her around the Inn, and I started taking a pottery course at the community college where she was taking a literature class. I started giving her a ride home, and you were all she could talk about. The more time I spent with her, the more I realized how troubled she was. A couple of years ago, she had an abortion. She lost this stepmother of hers that she admired so much, and her brother, died of AIDS. Muff also believes that she has let you down. She thinks you expect her to go back to college, graduate, and go off and be someone important. She's not sure she can do it."

"And who are you, Larry?" Baxter asked.

"I like to believe that I'm an artist who works as a maintenance man, as opposed to a maintenance man who's an artist on the side. I don't know what my intentions are with your daughter. I just know I like her very much, and she needs someone to take care of her. Muff moved in with me the week after Easter. It's been very good between us so far."

"Where did you come from and what did you do before your maintenance man career with the Walnut Inn?" Baxter pushed.

"I grew up in Springdon, Ohio where my Dad was the plant manager at a refrigerator assembly plant. He started as a factory worker and worked his way up to a plant manager. My mother was a music teacher who had graduated from Oberlin. We grew up in a small town of 9,000 or so where my father was a very important man. I was the youngest of two boys. We both went to Oberlin. My older brother, Ralph, dropped out, got drafted during Vietnam, and went off to Canada. I got active in the anti-war movement on campus and my father disowned me. I managed to work my way through Oberlin by playing in a rock band, and then, I just started to drift around. I did drugs for a while and lived in communes, but then went pretty legit about ten years ago. I sell some paintings every now and then and like to believe that my talent is beginning to evolve."

"How are you with drugs these days?" Baxter asked.

"Just a little grass every now and then, Joe. I'm off hard drugs for the rest of my life."

"And no meat."

"I must sound pretty silly to someone like you."

"How old are you, Larry?"

"Almost 36, Joe."

"Well, Larry, I have to ask you this. Are you the kind of person you wanted to be at age 36?"

"No, Joe. Not at all."

Baxter rose up from his seat under the tree. "Then you have some work in front of you to catch up." He slapped Larry on the back. "Let's head back and have another beer. It's almost veggie time."

The first days of the visit went well. Larry and Muffin would rise very early and eat their breakfast outside on the massive oak picnic table built by the Dopman brothers. Larry would paint with the morning light, and Muffin would sit patiently by his side reading a book. He painted a number of landscapes which Baxter judged as quite good. His artist eyes had caught the loneliness and isolation of the acreage surrounding his house.

"Could you do a drawing of the house for me?" Baxter asked Larry on Monday evening as they watched the sun go down.

"Did you want a painting?"

"Just a pen and ink drawing will do. I may put it up in my office."

"It's a magnificent house. You've got some rot beginning in eaves. How much have you put in maintenance since you moved in?"

"Only the alarm system. I moved into the house in the fall of 1979, and really haven't done anything with it or to it. I come here maybe sixteen weeks a year. It's my get away."

"Muff told me about your caller. Aren't you afraid? Muff said you had called the police.

"I'm more irritated than afraid, Larry," Baxter explained.

"Do you think the Dopmans did murder all of those children?"

"I have no opinions on the matter, Larry. All I know is that I purchased a piece of property at 30% of its appraised value and nobody's going to drive me off my bargain."

"And you don't own a television set and have wall to wall books and music. The first time I was with Muffin, she stayed up all night and told me about her life. She's really a very complex person, Joe. I'm afraid that she needs regular psychiatric help. It can be very expensive, and the health insurance benefits offered by the Maple Inn aren't much."

"I'll help," Baxter offered. "Muffin should have a trust from her grandparents, the Washburn family. Has it kicked in?"

"She told me there was an annuity that would begin on her twenty-fifth birthday. Muffin has mood swings. She takes some kind of prescription pills. I took psychology at Oberlin and have been reading some books lately. I think she might be classified as a manic depressive. If she takes her pills, she's okay. I get the impression that her mother was troubled too."

The screen door to the kitchen opened and Muffin appeared in the doorway in bare feet, shorts, and wearing one of Baxter's tee shirts.

"Did I hear you two talking about me?"

"Larry has agreed to draw the house for me," Baxter said breaking the conversation off.

Muffin handled the cooking. At lunch, she would set up a buffet with breads, cheeses, carrots, celery sticks and avocado slices. In the evening, Muffin would prepare vegetarian dinners, and twice they went to town for dinner at the Brinker's Falls Inn. They drank beer and took turns dancing with Muffin to tunes from the juke box under the watchful eye of Darlene in her waitress uniform.

Sheriff Clowson joined them the first night, sitting down with his mug of coffee.

Baxter introduced Larry and Muffin suddenly recognizing that he didn't know Larry's last name.

"How's everything at the Baxter place?" Sheriff Clowson asked. "Nice and quiet, I hope."

"No calls and no letters, Sheriff," Baxter answered. "That's what I call peaceful."

Darlene came by the table for their order.

"Don't worry about me, Darlene. I'm just here to finish my coffee with Mr. Baxter and his family."

Larry and Muffin ordered salads while Baxter ordered a ranch steak.

"I may have an opening for a new clerk and you may need a new housekeeper, Mr. Baxter. Looks like Luke has an offer to be Lieutenant in charge of security for the Jap plant up in Hillmont. I guess there aren't many Japs working there. Maybe two or three at the most."

"I would like to come to clean tomorrow, Joe," Darlene said glumly.

"On July 4th?" Baxter questioned.

"Luke wants to drive to Hillmont in the early afternoon and look over housing. I'll come back on Sunday to clean."

"That's fine. When will you be by?"

"I'd like to come at eight o'clock."

"Do you want me to look around for another housekeeper, Mr. Baxter?" Sheriff Clowson said while rising to his feet. "I guess with Luke and Darlene moving, you will be starting all over again up here." Sheriff Clowson tipped his hat to Larry and Muffin and left the Inn.

"Dad, why would you have her clean twice? Next Sunday will do."

"Because she needs the money, Muff," Baxter explained.

The first five days of their visits had gone smoothly. They went through two cases of beer and carved out their pieces of privacy. Baxter read books, played endless scrabble games in which he trounced his competition, and he listened to at least half of his library of classical music. He found that Larry liked Gustav Mahler and they listened to all ten symphonies. He enjoyed a number of long walks with Muffin, and Larry produced a first class drawing of the house. Baxter concluded that he was a young man of gentleness and talent.

Darlene arrived at 8AM on Thursday morning accompanied by her son, Rob, to clean.

"Your daughter has taken up with a hippie," Darlene commented privately to Baxter. Baxter took Rob for a walk while his mother cleaned.

"Mom's in a real bad mood these days," Rob shared with Baxter. "She's been real cross since Saturday morning."

"And how's your Dad doing?"

"He might quit Sheriff Clowson to become a full-time Security Supervisor for that Japanese company. If he does that, we will have to move. Mom doesn't think she'll be able to be your housekeeper anymore. I shouldn't tell you this, Mr. Baxter, but I don't think my Dad likes you very much."

"Well, Rob," Baxter explained. "Sometimes it's hard to have everyone in a family like you."

Baxter found himself sitting at the butcherblock table in the kitchen after Darlene left.

"So she's still hanging around here, Dad," Muffin commented as she opened two beer cans. They could see Larry from the kitchen window beginning to clean his brushes.

"She's been a very reliable housekeeper."

"Dad, what are you doing for women these days?" Muffin asked.

"I'm a bachelor again, Muff. I'm very busy in my work and really don't have much opportunity, nor do I have the inclination to start up with new relationships."

"Dad, you've always been a lady's man. I just hope you haven't taken up with Darlene. I saw her eyeing you up just now."

"Well, Muff, for the purposes of discussion, what's wrong with someone like me taking up with someone like Darlene?"

"Oh, Dad. First she's married. Second, how would she ever fit into your world? She's so backwoods."

Baxter nodded his head. "I believe you have several points there. Now tell me where Larry fits into your world? Do you plan to marry him?"

"Dad, you're not being fair. Larry is a very talented, sensitive person and he's good to me. I was a lost soul before I got together with Larry last December. I was having a real problem adjusting to my life. I know you invited me to move in with you in New York, but I'm not ready to return to that kind of life."

"What if I asked you again right now, Muffin, please come back to live with me in New York. Let me help you get back into college and finish your education."

"You don't believe Larry is good enough for me? Is that it, Dad?"

"He's a very nice, young, sincere man, but you have your whole life ahead of you and you're just marking time right now."

"Dad, Larry's been very good for me. I was considering suicide last fall. You're not really my father. My mother assured me of that. Rather you're someone who has taken care of me because you believed it was your duty. You're someone that I could never live up to. My mother's a bitch, and my brother's dead. I killed my child in an abortion. There were a lot of mornings when I woke up and didn't want to live through the day. Then I met Larry. He takes care of me. I need him. I'm ready to marry him when ever he gets around to asking me. I know one thing is for sure. The one thing I don't want to do is move in with you in New York and pass myself off as your daughter."

The kitchen door swung open and Larry entered the room. "How is everybody?" he greeted them.

Muffin stood up from the table with tears in her eyes.

"It's time to pack up and go back to Vermont, Larry. Our time here is over."

They were gone within the hour.

"What the hell happened between you two?" Larry asked Baxter twice.

"It was a father/daughter thing," Baxter passed it off.

Baxter tried to persuade Muffin to stay, but she was having none of it. "I want to be away from you," she said at the doorway. "It's not good for me to be around you. You're well meaning enough and I'll always love you, but I don't want to be with you anymore this week."

Larry shook hands as Muffin sobbed in the car. "She gets like this every once in a while. Muff will get settled down in twenty minutes and want to come back. If she does, are we welcome?"

"Of course," Baxter agreed.

Larry backed his car down the driveway honking good-bye as he reached the road. Baxter watched the car pull away and reckoned that he was unlikely to see his daughter again for some time. It was July 4th, 1991, and he had three more days to kill on his vacation. That's when Baxter decided he had two more places to visit that summer. Paris, France, and Iron Creek, Minnesota.

There were two letters among the bills and junk mail awaiting Baxter when he returned late Saturday to his New York apartment. One was a bulky letter from Muffin, and the other was from E. Ganski, 267 Hill View Drive, Iron Creek, Minnesota. Baxter opened Muffin's letter first. It was written in large block letters across Walnut Inn stationery.

Dear Daddy,

I behaved very badly during my visit. Can you ever forgive me? You were so nice to Larry, and he admires you very much. Could we come again next spring after ski season? I just have so many feelings churning around inside of me. I miss Joel very much. He was a very good brother and I loved him very much. I know that my mother is a selfish and wicked woman, but I will always want her approval. I keep thinking about the baby I gave up to be murdered. The baby would have been three now. I dream about that child. Sometimes it's a little girl on a swing, and sometimes it's a little boy running through a field. Then there is Bridgette who seemed to have abandoned me at the same time she abandoned you. Last there is you, the good wonderful Dad who is not my Dad, but who has been my Dad. The big question is who am I? I don't know and I need time to figure it out. I'm in analysis and taking anti-depressants. Some days are better than others. I snapped that last day we were together. I'm so very sorry but sometimes I just lose control.

Larry and I have talked about how good it was to be with you and how much fun it was until I spoiled everything. Just give me time, Dad. I will get right again. I've got to get right before I can decide on my life's work. Please love me and be patient with me. I love you.

Martha

P.S. Larry has written you a little note which is enclosed.

Larry's note was written in pencil on ruled paper and enclosed in a small Walnut Inn envelope. The Inn appeared to Baxter to be the major source for stationery.

Dear Mr. Baxter or Joe as you told me to call you,

Muff and I really enjoyed our time with you. I hope you liked the drawing of the house. Muff felt pretty bad after she left, and was ready to go back after an hour on the road, but it didn't seem to be the right thing to do. As you could see, Muff has a lot of emotional problems, but she's working with some good people up her to get her right again. The health insurance coverage at the Inn isn't much. Muff could use some financial help. $600 a month ought to do it. I assume you're up to that kind of money for year or so. I feel very close to your daughter, and I'm trying to take care of her as best I can. I could use some help. Good luck in your work and I hope we meet again real soon.

Your friend,
Larry

P.S. Muffin has moved in with me. She can be reached as Martha Baxter, #171 Pinetree Trailer Park, Mountain Edge, Vermont 05402

Baxter wrote a check on the spot with a note that read:

445

Dwight E. Foster

Dear Muffin:

There's nothing to forgive. You are my spiritual daughter if not my biological daughter. Sort out and neutralize your demons. This is a task for everyone. It is easier for some than others. I will be sending you a check in the middle of every month. Keep good financial records, and claim a tax credit on your Federal and State returns. Write or call from time to time. I expect to be doing some overseas travel this summer.

Much love and support,
Your only Dad

Ganski's letter was a downer.

Dear Joe,

I'll come to the point quickly. Diane has been diagnosed with cancer and not expected to last out the year. She asks about you from time to time, and I'd like to see you myself. Is it possible you could visit Iron Creek this summer? There are some things I'd like to talk to you about.

As you know, I was appointed to Feike Smetinan's seat in the State Senate last January after Feike died in November. Feike had held that seat for the DFL for 24 years. I believe I should run in the Fall of 1992. There are others in the DFL who want to run for the seat, and I'm going to have to fight hard for party support and designation. A couple of those guys competing with me are young university types. I want to talk things through with you. You're a man of the world and you see things a little differently than I do.

My other news isn't so good either. Carl, Maggie's husband, has some kind of brain tumor and can't work anymore. She's still working at the K-Mart where they made her some kind of Supervisor. She's even lost some weight, but her teeth are lousy. I'm rambling. I need some time with you this summer and have no plans to visit New York. My office number is 218-411-0001. I need you right now, Joey.

The Right Honorable Edward Ganski
1953 Cougar

Baxter read the letter twice. Diane was dying and it sounded as though Ganski was fishing for campaign funds. He decided to visit Iron Creek and then go on to Paris. It would represent his first extended vacation from McKenzie Barber.

Baxter wrote Dilger a memorandum stating that his physician had recommended that he take an extended vacation and he would be unlikely to return until Labor Day. He went on to cite that he had accumulated eight weeks in unused vacation, and wanted to use it prior to the merger. He designated Marty Dunlap as the interim leader of the New York Practice during his absence. Baxter briefed Marty first thing and then announced his absence in a poorly attended Monday post July 4th staff meeting.

"You look quite healthy, Joe," Marty had observed.

"I need to get away for a while, Marty," Baxter explained.

"We're going to miss plan by about 30%, but life will start over again with the spin-off which is scheduled for October 1st. I have some personal matters to take care of which I won't have time for after October 1st."

"Is the merger with Robson Allen really going to happen, Joe?"

"It would appear so, Marty."

"Then the only choice for the Comp practice is to go with the spin-off firm."

"That's about it, Marty."

"You've always fought to keep the Comp practice independent from the Benefits practice. Why are you giving in now?"

"Because it's the only road open. It's a safe road for you, Marty, and the rest of the consulting staff. The most substantive parts of the pre spin-off discussion with our Benefits consulting colleagues have to do with the protection of their pension benefits. Robson Allen is not going to take a lot of prisoners. There's a soft landing ahead for our people," Baxter reassured Dr. Dunlap who nodded his head in return knowingly.

Baxter concluded that there would be a minimum of four stops on his holiday. His first stop would be at Iron Creek via connecting flights to Chicago and Duluth. Then he would return to Chicago and board an international flight to Paris. Following Paris, he would head for Milan to see Jennifer for one final visit, and then he would go to London and try to see Fairbrother. He sent faxes to Dominique de Hartogue and Richard Fairbrother, a cable to Jennifer, and he called Ganski.

"You're really coming! That's great, Joe!"

"Put me up in the Pennsylvania Hotel, Ed."

"Can't do it, Joe. It closed in December and is scheduled for demolition the week before Labor Day. There's a new Days Inn at the end of Railroad Street that's pretty nice. I'll have my Executive Assistant, BJ, book you in. Damn, it will be good to see you."

Baxter's plan was in place. He was going to withdraw from the buy-out group on Labor Day and finesse his way into the severance arrangements which were sure to be his right after the merger. Remaining on the payroll through 1-1-92 should enhance his retirement benefits by 4% since the severance would certainly carry him past 9-30-92. Every 4% increase per annum would make an easier life in the post McKenzie Barber period of his life.

July 10, 1991

Ganski was officed in the Glossett Building. Penn-Mine now only occupied two of the first two floors and leased the rest of the office space. Baxter parked his rental car in front of an empty storefront which had once housed the Greek restaurant. Six nickels in the meter gave him ninety minutes time. Baxter never had been in the Glossett Building. He could remember his father railing against the evil Penn-Mine predators as they stood on the outer side of Broadway with his brother, Gordy, in the perambulator.

There was a large reception area in the entrance way with a uniformed guard at the front desk. To the left of the desk was a plaster bust of Charles Glossett, who had apparently served as President of Pennsylvania Steel from 1919 to 1925. He had a large forehead and wore sideburns with a bushy looking mustache.

"My name's Joe Baxter. I'm here to meet with Senator Ganski," Baxter announced solemnly.

"Ed's up on the 6th Floor, 611," the middle-aged guard said and began printing a name tag for Baxter on an adhesive badge.

"I remember you, Joe. I was two classes behind you at Iron Creek High. My name's Orv Bungo." He extended his hand which Baxter accepted and shook.

The sixth floor was the top floor, and offered a view of Iron Creek. There was a law firm, an accounting firm, an insurance broker, and the office of Edward C. Ganski, Member of the Senate, State of Minnesota. Baxter opened the clouded glass door and faced a pretty young woman in her mid-twenties.

"You have to be Joe Baxter," she said, standing up from her desk and extending her hand. "I'm BJ, Mr. Ganski's executive assistant." She wore a white dress with a vee showing a hint of her bosom. BJ was full bodied and energetic. "Ed's on the phone with the Capital right now, but he shouldn't be much longer. Can I get you some coffee? It's fresh brewed."

Baxter took a seat in a chair facing the view of Broadway Avenue. Coffee was served in a plastic cup. BJ seated herself in an adjacent chair. Baxter looked around the room. There was an empty conference room behind him and the closed door of a private office facing him.

"Boy have I heard a lot about Joe Baxter over the past year," she said crossing her legs. BJ wore white stockings and white pumps. She had brown hair, smooth skin, and a large but attractive, red mouth heavily applied with lipstick.

"How long have you been with Ed?" Baxter asked.

"Right after he was appointed State Senator last January. I was working for Senator Joe Blatnik out of Duluth. He had two assistants and I was the junior one. So I got matched up with Ed. He needed someone who knew their way around the Capitol. I'm not that seasoned, but I had been with Senator Blatnik for two years and knew some of the ropes in St. Paul. We're developing into a good team, and now our objective is to get Ed nominated and elected in the fall of 1992."

"And how long have you been in political work, BJ?" Baxter probed.

"I've grown up in the DFL. My mother was a precinct chairman in West Duluth, and my Dad was a shop steward for the Steelworkers in the Duluth Iron and Wire works. He was a delegate to the State convention six times, and a delegate to the national convention three times. I started out as a block worker when I was a junior in high school, and graduated from UMD in political science. I love what I'm doing."

Baxter nodded his head and sipped his coffee. "I understand that Mrs. Ganski hasn't been well," Baxter offered.

"You'll have to discuss that with Ed. Diane's in chemo and he's taking it pretty hard," BJ shot back.

Baxter looked out at Broadway Avenue in silence.

"I suppose you're a Republican. Ed told me that you were the leading management pay expert in the country. He also told me that your Dad was killed in strike violence."

The closed door opened and the summer 1991 edition of Ed Ganski stepped into the reception room. At age 56, Ganski still wore his hair in a crew cut. He remained stocky and broad shouldered in a short sleeve shirt, an unknotted tie, and grey slacks. Ganski wore wire rimmed glasses and his face appeared tanned and square.

"Joey!" Ganski enthusiastically clasped Baxter's hand and then overlapped his left hand over Baxter's. Was this new two-handed DFL political handshake? Baxter asked himself. Ganski led him into his office. "BJ, hold my calls. Only the governor."

The office had a large oval desk stacked with papers, two side chairs, a PC on a metal table behind the desk. On the wall were pictures of Ganski in the company of what appeared to be various Northern Minnesota luminaries. In addition, there was an autographed picture of Walter Mondale and a team picture of the 1953 Cougars.

"This is wonderful, Joe. How long are you going to be in town?"

"I'm heading out Saturday to Paris out of O'Hare. I have some overseas stops in Milan and London. I was really disturbed about your news about Diane. I'd like to look in on her as soon as possible."

"She's looking forward to seeing you, Joe," Ganski brought his hands up over his ears and stared at the carpeting for a few seconds. "She's not going to make it, Joe. The Docs give her December at the outside. I'm trying to get her into a hospice where she can get some good care, but Diane's not having any of it. She's lost a lot of hair through the chemo treatments. It's not a good time for either her or me."

"Where are your sons these days?"

"Joe lives out in Long Beach. He's a Supervisor in field engineering for Lockheed. He's married with three boys. I guess they play a lot of soccer. Mort joined the Marine Corps and has got 21 years in. He's going for three more and out. He wants to make Sergeant Major and thinks he can do it. Mort married this woman from Egypt that he met on embassy duty. We haven't met her yet, but have talked to her on the phone. Her English is pretty good. Mort followed his namesake and has done pretty well in the Marines. Ronnie's been another story. He's been a bit of a disappointment to his mother and me."

"I figured Ronnie would be the star of the family. He was the best athlete and the smartest, but it never seemed to come together for him. He didn't get along with his coach at the Cougars, didn't get much playing time, and finally quit the team. His grades were so so. Ronnie tried community college and that didn't work. Finally I put him through bartender's school and he's been drifting ever since. He married and divorced some cocktail waitress he met in Reno, and has settled into Las Vegas. I'm trying to bring 'em all back for Labor Day for one last family reunion. Diane isn't going to make Christmas. So, how are your kids?"

"Joel is dead. He died of AIDS last year. Martha, his sister, is going to school in Vermont."

"And you got divorced from that little number you had out here for the 30th anniversary? Her name was Bridgette and I kept calling her Gidget to piss her off. That was eight years ago this summer. That brought a lot of dollars into town. I've been thinking of engineering a 40th in two years that would honor me. It will only work if I can get re-elected to the State Senate."

"Do you still have a connection to Penn-Mine?"

"I retired from Penn-Mine after I got elected Mayor."

"You were Mayor of Iron Creek, Ed?"

"One term only. It only paid $24,000. I used to attend a lot of Mayor's conferences and got myself known around the state. It helped me get appointed when Feike died. I like being a state senator. It's six months a year in St. Paul and I've got this printing business on the side that's making some money printing computer forms. It's called the Northern Press. We get a lot of work from the unions and people who do business with the state. We've got a bunch of Indians working in the plant, so we're a preferred supplier. I'm listed as an Advisory Board member, but I own 95% of the stock. Some people got me into this when I was Mayor. It's working out very well. I may get into some other things after I'm re-elected. You met BJ just now. For a kid of 25, she has enormous political moxie. She really knows her way around the DFL. BJ, by the way, stands for Betty Jayne. She hates her name and shortened to BJ after she graduated from UMD."

"She seemed very capable," Baxter responded. Were these two an item?

"So where are you off to from here, Joe?"

"Paris via Air France out of Chicago. Then to Milan, on to London, and then back to New York."

Ganski whistled. "I've been promised that I would be a delegate to the 1992 convention and I'm going to be getting out to Washington more. Is this the kind of travel you do all the time?"

"This is a kind of a close-out trip, Ed. It looks as though McKenzie Barber will be merging with another firm late this fall, and I will probably retire in January."

"You're my age, Joey. You're way the hell too young to retire," Ganski protested.

"I'll do something else, Ed."

"Why don't you move back here? I've got a lot of business opportunities that come my way. Maybe you could run them for me and I'd be the silent partner?"

Baxter peered out the window at mid-summer Broadway Avenue. He remembered the old days when he ran the street in the early morning and would turn up on Pine Hill. So much had changed but nothing had really changed. Iron Creek was still an ugly Iron Range town caught in a 1950's time warp.

"The range is coming back, Joey. It's been at its low point but it's going to be coming back strong. There will be jobs coming in here in 1992 and 1993. Right now there are a number of service businesses to be acquired from people who are pretty desperate. It would be a natural holding company deal. Joe Baxter, the world famous executive consultant, retires from his New York City life and returns to his home town. Baxter buys a number of businesses under something called Baxter Holdings. I provide the investors. You put a little of your own money and we'll be the kings of Iron Creek. What do you say we go over to the Lion's Club and have a beer. Then we'll go back to the house for dinner. Diane can't cook much anymore so we have a woman who comes in and prepares meals. She's making corned beef and cabbage tonight."

On the way out, Ganski and BJ disappeared into the conference room to go over a few matters. Baxter studied the closed door. Were they in a clandestine lover's embrace? Or were they discussing campaign contributions?

BJ emerged first. Her lipstick looked fresh.

"Joe, it's been wonderful to meet you after all I've heard about you from Ed. I hear you're leaving us for Paris tomorrow. I hope you'll think of us back in Iron Creek when you're walking down the Champs Elysees." BJ shook Baxter's hand firmly. Ganski said he would call her later.

Ganski settled them into the back room of the Lion's Club which was situated at the far end of Railroad Street. The back room was dimly lit with candles placed at the center of formica covered tables. In the far corner of the room there was a bright light shining over a large pool table. Baxter could make out the muted voice of Frank Sinatra over the sound system.

"Well, Joey," Ganski asked after the beer had been served. "What do you think? Do I make sense with my proposition? You could join the Country Club and I'll stay with the Lions Club. I could use some help with the business community in my 1992 election campaign. I also will have BJ call you when you get back for a contribution. The big battle will be to get the DFL nomination. If I get the nomination, I will be elected. I can probably last as long as old Feike did."

"Ed, what you've outlined doesn't sound like it's something I really want to do at this time in my life. It's been almost forty years since Mort, you and I used to sit up on the hill and watch the goings-on at the Iron Creek Country Club. Mort's gone and you and I have gone on to be different people."

"Come back, Joe. You never should have really gone away in the first place. This we can finish out our lives as best friends. You know Mort planned to come back after he had his twenty years in. I named my sons after you guys. The three of us had a very special relationship from first grade on. You were always the smartest kid in the room. You always beat the girls in the spelling bees. I figured you'd go off to college and come back to Iron Creek and be a teacher who coached and go on to be the Principal of Iron Creek High School. Now you've done your big business bit. I would think it would be time for you to come home."

"Ed, give me a couple of months. I've got some unfinished business in Europe. I'll give you my answer after Labor Day. For now, let's drop this subject and get caught up." Baxter knew his answer would be an unequivocal NO.

Ganski nodded his head in agreement.

"Joey, is it true that the Tweetmans have split?" Ganski began.

Diane Ganski wore a turban at dinner. Ganski had explained in advance that his wife had lost most of her hair in the chemo treatments. She was very thin and wore what Baxter suspected was her best black dress with pearls. Baxter, from the living room, spotted candles on the linen tablecloth spread over the dining room table. A large woman clad in a sweat shirt, denim jeans, and athletic shoes rose up from the couch to greet Baxter.

"Hi, Joey," the woman greeted Baxter with a Rolling Rock beer bottle in her free hand. Baxter concluded it was Maggie.

He accepted her moist hand. "I came by to help Diane get set up."

Baxter embraced Diane Ganski kissing her on the forehead and then on the cheek.

"I'm so glad you could come by for dinner, Joe. We're having corned beef and cabbage, Joe. I hope you like it."

"Can't get it in New York and certainly smells good." The smells from the kitchen were wafting into the room.

"I have help these days. Mrs. Moltke from the next block looks in on me and handles my meals. Ed is so busy with his political work, and spends a lot of time in St. Paul." Diane Ganski had the tired smile of a dying woman. She had always reminded Baxter of an energetic teenage girl. Now her energy seemed gone. Diane's face was pallid, and her voice was raspy. She formed her words slowly. Ganksi kissed his wife dutifully and disappeared through the swinging door to the kitchen to fetch beer.

"Will you be joining us for dinner, Maggie?" Baxter asked his first wife.

"I'd like to, but I gotta look out for Karl. This is one of my days off from K-Mart. I don't work Thursdays or Sundays. When I heard you were coming to town, I wanted to catch up on all the doings. I suppose you want a report on Lenore to start off with." Ganski delivered Baxter a can of Budweiser. "I'm sure you remember her."

"I last heard from her in April," Baxter responded. "She had finished her degree in nursing and was named Associate Director of Nursing at St. Andrews Hospital," Baxter recited. "I helped her out with the tuition."

"Well, she still wants to go off and be a nursing missionary. There they are with a nice cozy little home in Duluth Heights. Her husband's got a steady job and they have money in the bank, and Lenore wants to go off in the jungle for two years. They can't seem to conceive children, and Duane won't adopt. Are you going to see her while you're out here?"

"I think not," Baxter answered.

"Joe has to be in Paris in a day or so," Ganksi defended him. "He made a special stop to spend some time with Diane and me."

"You never have really cared for Lenore have you?" Maggie went on.

"That comment is beneath response, Maggie," Baxter said sternly. Maggie's face flushed and she stared down at her athletic shoes.

"Joey," Ganski cut in. "What everybody wants to hear about is the inside track on the break-up of Iron Creek's marriage of the century. First confirm it. Have Tommy and Lucy really split?" Maggie looked up from her shoes and was at full attention.

"Yes, they have broken up. I don't believe that they are officially divorced, but they are clearly headed in that direction. Lucy has returned to Indianapolis and has a relationship with a man who runs a large insurance brokerage. They both must finalize divorces before they can marry. Lucy sent me a wedding invitation with a late September date. Tommy is living in Washington where he is now President and General Manager of a promising software division of Belt Way company. I believe he is seeing someone, and his oldest daughter had moved in with him. That's all I can tell you about Lucy and Tommy."

"She was a queen bitch," Maggie observed. "Does this guy she's marrying in Indianapolis have a lot of money?"

"He's rolling in it. Lucy has traded up significantly."

"I remember their wedding. I got quite sick on champagne." Diane Ganski's head shook as she formed her words. "You left with that girl from Duluth. She was very nice, and Mort had said something awful to her."

"That was a while back. Nearly 25 years ago. I was still a student. The girl's name was Nancy and she was in the wedding party. Mort asked her a very direct question that she hadn't been asked by the boys at UMD," Baxter recollected. "She gave me a ride back to Minneapolis and I saw quite a bit of her until I graduated and moved to Racine. She was a very nice person."

"And Mort was very drunk and obnoxious. Rest his soul," Diane said.

"What happened to all of your wives, Joey? I hear you're single again," Maggie blurted out.

"One is living in Italy, and the other is in New York occasionally. I'm officially a free man."

"You had some kids. What happened to them?" Maggie demanded.

"I had a son who died, and my daughter is in the hospitality business up in Vermont. We spent July 4th together."

"What did your son die of?" Maggie continued.

"AIDS," Baxter responded.

"Jesus," Maggie reacted and looked at her watch. She was on her feet and drained what was left in the bottle of Rolling Rock. "I've got to get Karl's dinner. Good to see you, Joey. Keep piling up those wives." Maggie kissed Diane affectionately on the forehead and brushed by Ed Ganski without a word. She paused in front of Baxter and took his hands.

"I really wish that things would have been right with us." Tears formed at the corners of her eyes. "Got to run. Good-bye all." Baxter stood at the front door and watched Maggie's bulky figure ease its way into a battered ten year old Buick. The engine made a long grinding sound before it finally started. Baxter exchanged waves with his first wife.

"Her husband, Karl, has a brain tumor and can't work anymore," Diane Ganski announced after Baxter had returned to his chair.

"Maggie has been my best friend for twenty-eight years. She was my first friend in Iron Creek. Ed and I came back to Iron Creek after Germany. I was only 19, and Maggie was so good to me. She always talked about you, Joe. And she was a very good mother to Lenore. Maggie knows that she never would have fit into the life of the person you have become. It's the same way with Ed and me. Ed's become a State Senator. When Ed got interested in politics, I never believed in my wildest dreams that Ed would go on to become a State Senator. Now I've got to get my health back so that he can be re-elected next fall. Of course he has BJ to help him if I'm not around." A short squat woman in an apron emerged from the swinging door to the kitchen.

"Mrs. Ganski, I've got supper on the table."

It was a hearty dinner comprised of tough corned beef and overcooked vegetables. Conversation was painful. Diane Ganski was convinced that her chemotherapy would be successful and her recovery would be full. It was obvious that Diane knew about her husband's relationship with his executive assistant.

Bridgette had been a major disappointment to her. "I had never met anyone like that before in my life. We spent an entire day together, and she had seen so much and done so many things. I wrote her so many times over two years and she never wrote back once. We were such good friends for that one day. We bought identical dresses together. If something should happen to me, I'd like to be buried in that dress," Diane said with finality.

It was a long tedious dinner. Ganski seemed attentive enough, but his mind seemed off in a distant place where he was no doubt sorting out political intrigues. Baxter was confident that his old friend was not contemplating conflict of interest issues.

"When I get well, I'd like to travel. My parents are buried back in Oklahoma. They died over ten years ago. Did you know I was the youngest of ten children?" Baxter could not recall talking to Diane Ganski previously on any subject longer than three minutes. She talked on slowly forming words in a dry voice. Diane seemed determined to at last share her life story with Baxter. "Ten is too large a family. All I got in the way of clothes were hand-me-downs from my sisters. My folks used to have a farm, but we moved into a small town called Renfrow where we lived on the edge of town and raised chickens on the side. I went to work in the Kresge's when I was fourteen. I did stock work in the beginning, and the management asked me to help out in the soda fountain at the store. Some soldiers from Fort Sill rented the high school gym, and they used to stop in for coffee and cokes before they'd play. Then they would drink beer at Snoop's Tavern after they were finished playing. Do you remember that, honey?" Diane addressed Ganski.

"I remember it well, my little Oklahoma Rose. We rented this gym so that we could have a home floor. They had great facilities at Fort Sill, but we wanted a gym that would be our home floor. We used to beat teams in Renfrow that we would be lucky to get within twenty points of back at Fort Sill. We used to meet at the counter of Kresge's and there would be my little Oklahoma Rose behind the counter."

"I was just a junior in high school when they started coming in just about every Saturday. I told Ed that I was a senior so that he wouldn't think I was too young for him. He was always asking me to come out and see the game and go over to Snoop's after the game. They played at six o'clock so I went home, put on my best dress, high heels and my sister's earrings. I got there in the third quarter and stood all dressed up in that smelly gym for better than an hour. Then after the game, Ed came out with a white shirt and a tie on and I thought he looked so handsome. We went to Snoops and I drank coke while they drank beer. They were all nice guys like Ed but they had all these floozies with them. I didn't want to be seen with those floozies so I asked Ed after an hour if we could go somewhere and eat. We went down to the Oldcrafter's Diner and I was so proud to walk in there holding hands with Ed. We got a booth in front and we stayed there until midnight talking. That was the first time I heard about Iron Creek, the 1953 Cougars, and Ed's best buddies, Joe and Mort. After that night, Ed would pick me up properly and we'd go to a movie and then on to Oldcrafter's. Then I started to take a bus on Saturday to Fort Sill to see Ed. And that's how I got pregnant with Joe."

"We got married one month after my seventeenth birthday. I said good-bye to my family one month later, and went off to be with Ed in Frankfurt. I didn't go back to Renfrow until the family started dying in the 1970s. Iron Creek has been my home. It's a nice place too. Sure, the winters get cold and there's a lot of snow. But the people here are terrific and it's really pretty with all of the pine trees. After I get well, I want to put this house up for sale and move up to Pine Hill."

Baxter looked around the room and observed the well worn furniture and predictable pictures.

"This has always been a nice homey place," Baxter commented. The house had been one of the early real estate tract developments in Iron Creek. Approximately sixty homes of similar design had been put up in the mid 1970s. The Ganski boys had grown up in this house and Diane was highly likely to die in this house.

"What makes you want to live up on Pine Hill at this time in your life, Diane?" Baxter asked.

"I've always wanted to live in Pine Hill. Those houses have always seemed so fine. This house has been good for us, but when Ed is elected State Senator, we'll need a house that we can properly entertain in. I just have to get well so that we can get on with our lives. We've done all right by our kids, and Ed has some investments now. I'd like to travel again. I have so much to live for and I'm going to live, Joe."

They left just before ten o'clock after the dishes had been cleared and the dishwasher had been activated. Ganski helped Diane into the bedroom and closed the door behind him. Baxter waited out on the front step and studied the neighboring houses. It was a warm, July, Iron Range night with a full complement of stars. The houses were identical with driveways, cars abandoned for the evening, bicycles and tricycles. Baxter could spot the glow of television sets through the front windows of the living and family rooms. It was ten o'clock news time in Minnesota. Who would he be if he had come back here after the Army? Would he be living in one of these homes watching the ten o'clock news awaiting the pension and the long contemplated life after work?

The front door suddenly swung open. "Let's go, Joe. BJ is meeting us for drinks back at the Day's Inn."

Baxter expected that they would meet in the bar. Instead they proceeded to the Bridal Suite which was two up from Baxter's rear first floor room.

"I got a deal with the Manager, Joe," Ganski explained as he turned the key in the door of a corner room marked "suite" in script print.

"Hey, BJ, I got Joe with me," he called out from the door. BJ appeared wearing a blue top, white Bermuda shorts, and sweat socks. She was wearing glasses and cradling a diet coke.

"Hi, Joe. How was dinner?" she nodded her head toward the wet bar to the left of the doorway. "The bar's all set up, Ed. There's Scotch and Canadian Club along with some beer and wine. You've got some St. Paul calls to return, Ed. They all expect to hear from you tonight," she said handing Ganski a clip board.

Ganski studied the clip board. "Shit! Something must be up for Riley to call. Keep Joe company, BJ, and bring me in a tall Scotch. This may take a while."

"I hear you're a Canadian Club man," BJ smiled at Baxter. "On the rocks?"

"On many rocks and all the way up," Baxter requested.

Baxter made himself comfortable on the couch and found himself listening to George Winston on a portable tape deck. BJ joined him on the couch after delivering the Scotch through a far door that Baxter deduced was the bedroom.

"Politics is a 24 hour game. I just gave him some surprises he's got to handle." BJ pulled her feet up on the couch and perched Indian style. "How was Diane tonight?"

"A little grey looking. She talked a good deal and seemed in good spirits. Diane talked about her plans after she gets well."

"Good luck. Diane isn't making it past the end of the year according to her doctors. This has been a tremendous strain on Ed. He has a tough year to get through before the Fall 1992 elections. His whole political future in on the line. He doesn't need a dying wife right now." BJ took a long sip form her diet coke. She had large muscular thighs and heavy calves. Baxter concluded that BJ would be a wonderfully athletic bed partner.

"What is Ed's future if he's not re-elected?" Baxter inquired.

"Not real good. The DFL might find him something to do, but it's unlikely he'll ever be endorsed again for public office. On the other hand, if Ed gets party endorsement and wins the primary, he's in. One full term in the legislature means bigger things for Ed. We could use you to come back here and help in the primary campaign. Ed's going against these University professors. One's a UMD Poli Sci type and the other's a smart young gunner teaching at a community college in Grand Rapids. Neither of them is particularly popular with the party up here, but they've made an impression on the folks back in St. Paul. The odds are good that Ed will prevail."

"What kind of risks do you two run by meeting for political rendezvous in this suite, BJ? Is there likely to be talk?" BJ sprang up from the couch. "I'm going to fix myself a drink. Does your's need freshening?"

Baxter followed BJ's body across the room. She took a pose in front of the wet bar after mixing a drink in a tall glass.

"Diane is dying. I was told she had a year to live when I came to work for Ed. Everybody in town knows that Diane is dying. She hasn't left the house since January. Ed needs me and knows I can help him. We eat and sleep Minnesota politics. Any personal relationship between Ed and me is understood by the right people in the party. The UMD professor is gay. We don't want to use it unless we're forced to. Ed and I are not seen together in public. For a guy who's been married to three different wives, you sure come on sanctimoniously."

"I'm just an out-of-towner making some observations, BJ. Tomorrow I'm long gone for Paris."

"Is it true you were married to that tub of lard at K-Mart called Maggie?"

"Many years ago. She was just a slip of an illiterate girl then. My later wives were far more impressive, BJ."

BJ returned to the couch and took up her Indian fashion position.

"Did Ed ask you to consider coming back here and becoming his business partner?"

"The matter was discussed, but I have a number of options to consider. Returning to Iron Creek is at the very bottom of the list."

The bedroom door opened and Ganski returned to the room with an empty glass.

"All false alarms, BJ," Ganski announced and handed BJ his glass for a refill.

"Some people were nervous over things that have been already taken care of. What have you two been talking about?"

"We discussed Diane's health, the vulnerability of your clandestine relationship with BJ, and the overall improved qualities of my wives following my starter marriage with Maggie. It's been a lively exchange."

BJ returned with a fresh Scotch for Ganski and slid onto the couch to his right. Ganski immediately extended his right arm around BJ's shoulder and she moved close to him.

"Good old sharp-eyed, Joe. Let me set the record straight for my best friend. BJ and I have been getting it on since last January. It's been damn good for both of us. I outgrew Diane fifteen or twenty years ago. She's been a good wife and mother, but she's been slowly dying for a year. What the hell would you do, Joey? I'll tell you what you'd do. You'd find someone like BJ and you'd hang onto her as long as an old man can hang on to a young woman."

"You're not an old man, Ed. You're a young man with some age." She kissed him on the mouth and Baxter prepared to excuse himself for the evening.

"There's no sense in pussyfooting around, Joe. Diane is dying and BJ's in my life now. She's going to help me get elected and when it's time for her to move on, she'll move on."

BJ shook her head. "I'm yours as long as you want me, Ed." She kissed him again in front of Baxter. Baxter stood up.

"I really should go, Ed. I've got to make connecting flights tomorrow out of Duluth and Chicago in order to make Paris."

"BJ, fix Joe a topper," Ganski commanded. "God knows when I'll see him again. Tell me again what Tweetman's doing?" Baxter provided a narrative report on the Tweetman and Lucy's forthcoming remarriage.

"Tell me, Joey. Were you finally able to screw Lucy?"

"It wasn't worth the wait, Ed," Baxter replied.

Ganski guffawed. "You should have seen this guy thirty-eight years ago, BJ. He was the smartest and funniest guy in Iron Creek High School. Now what was the name of that girl who came down to stay with Lucy Christmas vacation of 1952? She went on to become a famous writer according to Diane."

"Her name was Beth Gold," Baxter answered.

"Beth Gold! Beth Gold was here in Iron Creek!" BJ was incredulous.

"It was her only visit. I see her from time to time in New York," Baxter explained.

"Beth Gold was here. My God, I have read nearly all of her books," BJ continued.

"Continue to buy them as gifts for friends. Beth can use the royalties. She's going through one of her dry periods," Baxter urged.

"She's a very good and famous writer, Ed," BJ confirmed. Ganski shrugged his shoulders. "You never can tell where people will end up. By the way, Joe, I think the Duluth police have given up looking for your brother. I suspect that he's weighted down at the bottom of Lake Superior."

Turning to BJ he explained. "Joe's brother, Gordy, developed into a minor figure in Duluth organized crime. One day he disappeared and was never found again. They finally got Fu, the Chinaman, on tax evasion, and he's in some minimum security prison. Your old pal, Kawalchek, died last Fall. He had some kind of brain hemorrhage and they had a sparsely attended funeral of which I was one of a dozen mourners. I always show up for Cougar funerals, even if they were assholes." Turning again to BJ, Ganski explained. "Kawalchek was a big bad guy who Baxter beat up when he insulted Lucy Albright's honor. It was the only fight I can remember Joey being involved in. He's a lifetime one and O. Maggie had the hottest body in six counties."

"Maggie, the fat check-out girl at K-Mart?" BJ questioned.

"She was delectable in those days, BJ. She had strictly restrained herself to upper classmen before Joey broke the code."

"I found her highly experienced, BJ," Baxter added. "It was a time before abortions when young men did the honorable thing when young women became pregnant. I did the right thing."

"I did the right thing by Diane back in Oklahoma. We've lasted 36 years, and produced three sons who are okay. Now, tell me, Joey, how did your son get AIDS?"

"He was gay and he wasn't careful, Ed," Baxter responded.

"How could a son of your's be gay, Joey?"

"I have no idea. He was my son by Jennifer and it was his choice. Maybe I should have spent more time with him and developed Joel into a womanizer, but I didn't and he's gone."

"Christ, I just don't understand shit like that, Joey. BJ always tells me I'm out of touch with Generation X. I just want to represent the people in law making, that is, the ones like me. I don't know what the hell to tell you about gays and Generation X."

Baxter stood up again. "I've got to go, Ed."

"Come back in December, Joey," Ganski said and shook hands firmly. BJ kissed him on the cheek. "I hope you'll forgive me if I got a little sharp a while back. I know you and Ed are like brothers. When you see Beth Gold, will you tell her how much I like her books. It would be fun to have her autograph."

They waved from the doorway with their arms drawn over one another's waist. "Fuck her for me, Ed," Baxter said silently as he entered the elevator for the first floor.

July 13, 1991

The Iron Creek Holiday Inn seemed several planets away in the star system as Baxter walked down the Champs Elysees on a Saturday night. It was eleven o'clock and the streets were teeming with people. Baxter had arrived late morning, checked into the California Hotel just a half block off the Champs and plunged into a heavy sleep. He experienced a succession of short dreams which included Maggie, Jennifer, Bridgette, and Luke Bohlweiser, alias God's Helper. Baxter had tried to dial in Dominique but his personal dream factory failed to comply with the request.

He walked down the Champs Elysees to the large park that encircled LeNotre. He knew nothing about the restaurant's history. He had been there just once in his life in the company of a young Barber consultant named Dominique Beaufort. That had been fifteen years earlier, and they had been different people. Now they were to meet for a Sunday luncheon.

They had communicated through phone mail. Most of Dominique's messages stated that she was quite busy but would try to make some time for him during his visit. Perhaps he could come out to the de Hartogue chateau. She would send a car and driver to pick him up.

Baxter replied that he wanted to have lunch with her at Jardin Elysees LeNotre to commemorate the fifteenth year of their acquaintanceship and to provide Dominique her long awaited performance appraisal on the United Pharmaceutical engagement. Baxter picked up Dominique's final confirmation on his voice mail when he dialed in from the Air France lounge at O'Hare.

"You win, Joe. I will meet you at 1PM at Jardin Elysees LeNotre on Sunday, July 14th. The reservation will be in the name of de Hartogue. I will allow you to pay the check. I am quite interested in receiving my long awaited performance appraisal on the work we did on United Pharmaceutical. Most of the Managers in the study are either retired, deceased, or have been fired. Ironically, we are in negotiations to buy the Italian subsidiary. I have Monica down this weekend. She sends you her regards. Au revoir until Sunday."

It was Bastille Day in Paris, and a long weekend for most of the French. Baxter leisurely made his way down the Champs Elysees through the July heat. Families thronged past him brandishing French tri-color flags and balloons. They appeared to be moving in the direction of the Arc de Triomphe where a celebration was to be held. Baxter cut through the park to the receiving door of Jardin Elysees LeNotre. He was ten minutes early. The matire'd came to attention at the sound of the "de Hartogue" name.

"We have a very private table overlooking the garden reserved for Baroness de Hartogue. She called and said that she would be a few minutes late. Would you like to be seated now or would you prefer to have an apéritif in the bar?"

Baxter chose the table and was led by a tuxedo clad head waiter to a table situated in a large alcove at the rear of the restaurant. The next table was easily ten feet away and Baxter could look out at magnificent rows of flowers. He ordered a martini for the hell of it.

They had been seated in the main dining room for their Friday luncheon some fifteen years earlier. Dominique had been 23 or 24 then. They had four days together, and he had wanted her forever. There had been no mention of any barons that weekend. It had been obvious to Baxter that Dominique knew her way around men, but at the same time she had the intensity of a sweet loving animal. They had been Paris lovers, and he could pull distinct snapshots of that weekend from his memory scrapbook. Walking up the stairway to Dominique's apartment for the first time sensing that she would be in his arms the minute the front door had been closed, making love for the first time with the cat patiently observing them from a chair across from the sofa bed, dinner that evening at a neighborhood brasserie knowing they would return to bed in a few hours, the last taxi ride in the rain to Charles DeGaulle Airport. Tucked away in Baxter's memory were four days that would haunt him the rest of his life. The girl in the French rain coat at the airport was gone forever.

She had been replaced by the chic young baroness Baxter had met at the 1983 Barber alumni reception in Paris. The chic young baroness had in turn evolved into the Wall Street predator of the late 1980s. Baxter wondered which model of Dominique de Hartogue would appear today at lunch.

Dominique arrived at twenty-five minutes after one. She was escorted to the table personally by the maitre'd. Dominique arrived wearing dark glasses under a broad brimmed black hat. She wore a white belted dress and black Ferragamo pumps. Baxters stood up from the table and extended his hand. She accepted it with a gloved hand and was seated by the maitre'd who asked her something in French with apéritif in the sentence. Dominique ordered a sherry.

"Well, Joe, what brings you to Paris?" she said removing her gloves and resting her dark glasses on the table. "I apologize for being late, but there were many traffic tie-ups. This is equivalent to the Fourth of July in the states."

The 1991 model of Dominique Beaufort de Hartogue was tall, elegant, exquisitely dressed, and rather self possessed. She impressed Baxter as a woman who was accustomed to giving orders.

"I'm taking a little time off, Dominique. I'm here to celebrate the approximate fifteenth anniversary of our engagement for United Pharmaceutical Corp. As you may recall, we had a luncheon here after we sent the report draft into typing."

"I recall that luncheon and that weekend quite well, Joe. I also remember the weekend I spent with a gorgeous boy from Stanford who took me to the California-Stanford football game. I spent the weekend with him in Palo Alto. I have memories of four or five brief romantic interludes over my life and you represent one of them. It's a lot like recalling old playmates." Dominique took a small sip from her sherry glass. Baxter was on his second martini when the waiter left menus.

"This place is an over priced tourist trap, Joe," Dominique said scanning the menu. "McKenzie Barber and Robson Allen appear to be merging. Does this mean you will be out of a job?"

"I expect to retire in January 1992. I will be 56 1/2 and young enough to start a second career. 25 years of McKenzie Barber is quite enough for Joe Baxter."

"Is this a job hunting trip?"

"It's a one-last-look-trip meeting with some people I haven't seen for a while. You were high on my list of people I wanted to see and I'm very grateful you made the time for me today."

"You're a very manipulative man, Joe Baxter. You're older and heavier, but still an attractive man. Monica and I have had some good talks about you."

"And how is Monica?"

"She's well. I have her on retainer as a permanent internal consultant. She didn't do very well out on her own away from the guiding hand of Joe Baxter. Erik remains a junior officer with his bank, and he is sometimes useful for us. He remains Henri's comrade in adventure and travel. Burke is also on retainer to me. He has been most helpful on acquisitions. Apparently he learned much from making so many bad ones for McKenzie Barber."

"And how is Ham?"

Dominique quickly scanned the menu. "You order for me, Joey. I will have the consommé and the frog leg salad. If you order wine, I would favor a white Bordeaux."

"Burke," he reminded her.

"Hamilton, I think, is a sad man. He awaits his father's death, and no one has asked him to run their company. If we had won Hortense Industries, I was prepared to install him as a caretaker CEO as we sold off assets. We walked away with a lot of money when Hortense Management made their foolishly high offer. Your late friend, Leon Harwell, did very well, also. Burke, as I said, is a permanent consultant, and I must say that he has contributed. His bitch of a wife resents that Hamilton is our consultant. The hire of her husband amuses me. Madame de Robilliard has few friends. I also suspect that her husband isn't particularly crazy about her. I love to refer to her as Mrs. Burke when we meet socially. There's nothing else really to say. Hamilton is the man who wasn't elected Chairman of McKenzie Barber in the mid-1980s."

"And how is Monica?"

"Monica is my best friend. We have no secrets, and she serves as my personal representative in a number of matters relating to people and organization. She would have liked to be here today, but she is very badly needed at one of our Italian investments."

"And she and Erik remain together?"

Baxter was interrupted by a hovering waiter and ordered.

"They will always be together with occasional separate holidays. Just as I will always be with Henri. He is an affable man with little mind for the family business interests which are most complex. I have my people in place and am in firm control of the de Hartogue interests. I will prepare my sons for the passing of leadership when I'm ready to relinquish it."

"I would estimate you at forty, Dominique. Do you plan to remain CEO for twenty to twenty-five years?"

"I'm 38," Dominique corrected him. "I am a woman who was in the right place at the right time. The old Baron trained me well. There were some retainers who resented my youth and inexperience, but they have come around. The ones who didn't have been disposed of."

Baxter drained his second martini as the waiter delivered the wine. Dominique gestured for him to display the wine bottle to her and shook her head.

"He tried to serve us an 88. That was a terrible year. He's gone back for an 85."

"You should have asked him for a 76," Baxter suggested.

"1976 remains on your mind, Joe?"

"I think about it every day. What ever happened to your cat?"

"You remember the cat?" Dominique broke into a smile.

"I believe the cat will remember me and I'd like to look in on her this visit. Would you have her current address?"

"Celeste was a very old cat then, Joe, and I am certain that she is now sitting in cat heaven someplace regaling the other cats with stories about the redheaded American her mistress brought home one weekend."

This time the headwaiter returned with the wine and what sounded like profound apologies in French. He poured some wine in Dominique's glass for tasting and she passed the glass across the table to Baxter.

Baxter held up the glass to sunlight and studied it for several seconds. Then he ran his nose all the way around the glass.

"Well," he concluded to the headwaiter. "It will do, but it's certainly not a 76."

The headwaiter agreed solemnly and instructed their waiter to pour the wine.

"Joe Baxter, you remain a very outrageous man," Dominique laughed. "You must bring me up to date. Four years ago you had just separated from your wife, and you brought this young woman to our private little dinner. She couldn't take her eyes off you. She appeared to be a sweet ready to be sampled. Monica implied that you had gone well beyond a few samples."

"That Monica is such a gossip."

"She also gave me quite an account of a weekend trip to your country dacha."

"I understand that you had swapped an earlier account of our 1976 taxi ride to DeGaulle."

"Monica and I are like sisters. Everyone must have a confidante. Monica is my confidante. Who is your confidante, Joe?"

Baxter searched his mind for a designated confidante. He really didn't have one, and recognized for the first time how alone he was in the world.

"I'm presently confidanteless, Dominique," Baxter confessed.

"Oh, poor unfortunate, Joe." Dominique extended her right hand across the table and Baxter extended his left hand to meet it. Their fingers touched briefly and withdrew when the appetizers were served.

"Do you presently have a woman in your life, Joe?"

"Not a one. My divorce from Bridgette is final. There is a woman I see from time to time at my country place, but the relationship which was incidental is quite over."

"Are you traveling to Europe to seek a new relationship?"

"I have a space in my life coming up that marks the conclusion of my McKenzie Barber career and the beginning of something else. I've never taken much vacation and everything is certain to be washed in a merger. I thought I'd take this time to see some people I don't have the opportunity to see every day. Dominique de Hartogue is high on that list."

"Is your objective to arrange a consulting relationship with me?"

"My objective is to make love to you again."

Dominique slowly finished her consommé. Then she took a sip of the Bordeaux as if to clear her palate. "You are a very outrageous man, Joe Baxter, to make such a proposition to a married woman who is the mother of two sons. Can you give me any reason why I would consider such a distasteful act?"

The Dominique de Hartogue across the table seemed calm and unemotional. It was almost as if Baxter had asked to acquire a money losing smelting plant in Gary, Indiana. His proposal had been rejected because it lacked merit.

"I can give you several reasons, Madame de Hartogue. Let's suppose I can provide you more reasons why we should than you can identify as objections?" Baxter offered.

The entrees were served. Baxter picked at his monk fish while Dominique sampled her frog salad.

"You want to make this into some kind of contest. Is that it?" Dominique's eyes were cold and beautiful. "Then begin your game."

The head waiter returned with the wine steward. "We have located a bottle of the 76. Compliments of the house, Monsieur, Madame."

"My favorite year," Baxter smiled. "Merci."

"Now you are plotting to get me drunk in your contest. You are, indeed, a most wretched man, Joe Baxter. Please start with your arguments. My rebuttal is complete."

Baxter took a long sip of the Bordeaux and began his oratory. "Once, some fifteen years ago, two consultants fell very much in love. They were different people then as they are quite different people today. Yet each of them carries a memory of a wonderful four days, and each carries a question of how their lives may have progressed if they had continued their love. Now one lover, many years later, has asked the other for one final tryst."

"That's a flimsy argument. These lovers are different people today. What they had in common some fifteen years ago has long since rotted away. I certainly hope you can do better than that."

"My doctor has told me that I have contracted a very rare, nearly incurable disease. I will die within the next 48 hours unless I have sexual intercourse with a French woman CEO. My life is in your hands."

"Now, there's an argument. I will locate you one old and fat woman CEO so that you can continue your life."

"I want to go on record that I would prefer you to make the sacrifice. I have still another argument. I believe that the vigorous pace required of you as the CEO of the de Hartogue interests may deprive you of suitable sexual relief. I can guarantee you an outstanding pleasurable experience."

"I have heard those kind of grandiose claims before," Dominique dismissed him.

"On the other hand, I have references. Find a young woman called Dominique Beaufort. She's 23 years old, thin with long legs, a subtle smile and wonderful hands. Reference Joe Baxter."

"If I can find this Dominique Beaufort, she will only know the Joe Baxter of 1976. The Joe Baxter of 1991 is quite different. What insight can she give me as to the Joe Baxter seated across the table from me on Bastille Day 1991?"

474

"Find her! She will remember the Joe Baxter of 1976 who loved her more than anything in the world. She is the one who chose to desert their relationship in favor of career development."

"Are you saying that she should be up to one final tryst for old time's sake?" Dominique questioned.

"I'm saying that the man across the table from you wants to take you in his arms and kiss you about the face, neck, and shoulders. Then he wants to untie the belt and unbutton your dress. After the dress and the underthings, he wants to plant a kiss on every square inch of your body. Finally he wants to unite his body with your body for one last time."

Dominique's right hand extended across the table to Baxter where their finger tips touched briefly and then withdrew.

"You have made a series of very convincing arguments, Joe. Your life is obviously at stake and old friends must do what they have to. We keep a suite at George V. I have things to do this afternoon. I will plan to meet you at the suite at 19:30 hours. The concierge's name is Antonio. I will leave a message that Joe Baxter is to be admitted to the suite. Ask for Antonio and Antonio only. Tell him you have a business meeting with me. It's on the sixth floor. I'm going to finish this glass of wine and get up and leave you in a few minutes. I'll meet you at half past seven. You stay for dessert and settle the check."

Dominique was predictably late. Baxter was settled into the suite at 7:15 and was two drinks down when a key turned in the lock. Dominique appeared in the doorway and bolted the door behind her. She sailed her broad brimmed hat across the room at Baxter.

"I am late, but I'm here, Joe. Pour me a gin on the rocks and do all of the things you promised at lunch. Let no square inch of my body go unkissed."

Baxter went to the wet bar and poured two drinks of Beefeater over ice cubes and followed her into the bedroom. Her dress was off and hanging in the closet and she stood before in a white body garment. Dominique accepted the glass from Baxter and proceeded to take a long sip.

"Now, Joe, darling, help me get free of this contraption. You're not the only one that has added weight in the past fifteen years."

Dominique's body had gained between 15 and 20 pounds during the intervening years. Her breasts were larger and her thighs thicker, but she had remained the willing lover he remembered.

"You are too heavy, Joe," she protested. "Let me come on top."

They were good together, Baxter concluded at 9:30. Dominique walked naked out to the wet bar and refilled her glass. Baxter had remembered Dominique as thin and lithe. She was now a full bodied, handsome woman. She returned to the bedroom with a tray of crackers, cheeses, and a can of pate.

"I could have room service send something up, but I don't want any unfamiliar suspicious eyes to see us. Antonio is the only one here that I trust."

Baxter toured the suite in his boxer shorts. The suite contained a large sitting room, a conference room with eight chairs, a wet bar which included a well stocked refrigerator, and an enormous master bedroom. There were splendid suspended glass chandeliers in every room. The art on the wall, which he had assumed were prints, turned out on close inspection to be originals. He returned to the bedroom and heard soft Gershwin music playing from an invisible sound system. Dominique was spreading cheese and pate over crackers.

"Joe, I feel like champagne." She handed Baxter her glass. "Throw this out! You will find champagne in the refrigerator."

They settled into champagne and crackers on the bed as the opening strains of Gershwin's Concerto in F came over the sound system.

"How long have you had this set-up at the George V?" Baxter asked.

"Nearly five years. I needed a place for business meetings in central Paris. I have similar arrangements in New York. I believe Monica was going to show you the New York suite one evening when she found it occupied by Henri and Erik and two unidentified ladies. Henri has no idea of this place's existence. If he did, he and Erik would be bringing women up here for one assignation after another."

"So Henri's continued to be a lady's man," Baxter observed.

Dominique made a shrug of her shoulders jiggling her breasts attractively.

"Henri has always been a lady's man. It was the old baron, Arnaud, who picked me out for Henri. He wanted legitimate heirs. God knows how many bastards Arnaud had fathered over the years."

"I got to know Arnaud when I reviewed headquarters administrative costs. We were quite busy at the time, and it was considered a paltry consulting project for a prestigious client. I worked for a manager named Pierre who was very busy on a big project at Renault. 'There is nothing to this. Just be careful of the politics and keep me informed' I was told. I was taken out to the chateau and introduced to Monsieur Chardin, Arnaud's Secretary General."

"I found out quickly that he didn't want the project done. He considered it a waste of funds, and told me that I was too inexperienced. I insisted on meeting with the Baron. He arranged for fifteen minutes in the middle of the following day. I came into Arnaud's study at 5 minutes to ten and I was there through lunch. After that I spent everyday at the Chateau for five months. I discovered after one month that Monsieur Chardin was stealing from the de Hartogues. They were small sums, one thousand francs here five hundred francs there. I carefully documented these thefts and presented my finding to the old Baron."

"He scanned my report twice and said, 'Very good. Chardin is not stealing as much as he used to. Give me your opinion if I paid him more money, would Chardin steal less?' I exploded. I told the old Baron that the de Hartogue headquarters offices were run very poorly, and that I imagined that the subsidiary businesses were run just as poorly. Budgets were needed. Perhaps I should set up a theft budget so that he could have an annual plan for the amount that he would allow his employees to steal from him in a given year. He nearly rolled over in laughter. 'I will call McKenzie Barber today and ask for permission for you to work with us over an extended period of time. Have you spent much time with my son, Henri?' I told him, the Baron, that I had been introduced to his son and had seen him in the halls. The Baron smiled at me and patted my hand for the first time. 'Then my dear, you should seek him out, interview him, and find out exactly what he does around here. Then I would like you to recommend what he should be doing in order to one day succeed me.'"

Dominique paused for a cracker which was washed down by champagne. Baxter reached across the bed and stroked Dominique's left breast.

"Big, aren't they? I have considered a breast reduction operation. The old Baron insisted that I breast feed both of my sons. That's when I got so big. Please don't neglect the other breast. I like your touches very much. Now where was I?"

"You were on your way to interview Henri and figure out what he did all day." Baxter kissed Dominique's right breast.

"Henri drove me off to a magnificent lunch at a chateau somewhere between Paris and Lyon. Over a charming two and one half hour lunch, I found that he did practically nothing nor that he ever been assigned specific duties. He disliked Monsieur Chardin and refused to work for him. Henri had a very short attention span on matters related to business. He talked a good deal about his good friend, Erik and his American wife, Monica, and his unfortunate marriage. When lunch was concluded, Henri asked if he could see me sometime outside of business hours. I found him the most attractive man I had ever met, and I was in his bed within a week."

"You can learn a great deal from men when you share their bed. The Baroness had died when Henri was nine. They had sat out the war years in Montreal, and returned in 1946. Arnaud, the old Baron, had a succession of mistresses, but never married again. Henri had much encouragement from the old Baron to see me socially. It was the old Baron's idea for Henri to charter the yacht for a tour of the Greek Islands. He allowed Henri to bring Erik and Monica, and at the last minute decided that he would join us. I believe he wanted to make certain that Henri proposed marriage in front of witnesses before the boat docked."

"Then the opportunity to work with Joe Baxter came up. I was through with the de Hartogue work and I had three weeks before we sailed. The assignment fit my schedule perfectly. Then you came into my life. Regrettably, I hadn't planned on you. I was very confused. My life's direction had been set on a course. Suddenly I found myself very much in love with a big handsome red-headed American who wanted to bring me to Chicago. Once when I was out on the boat, my decision was clear. I was going to become the Baroness de Hartogue, produce an heir, and perhaps have some ongoing role in the family businesses. I did not anticipate that I would be running the family interests as early as it happened."

Dominique paused for a sip of champagne and placed her free hand on Baxter's cheek and ran it down his neck over his shoulder down his arm to his fingers.

"In the beginning, I spent all day with Arnaud, the old Baron, and we would try to involve Henri. He would always have commitments that required his being excused. Henri was quite interested in several charities. The old Baron used to shrug his shoulders and smile. 'If Henri is determined to give away some of our money, you and I should determine just how we can make some more.' The old Baron and I visited every de Hartogue business in the world during the first year of my marriage. Henri went with us in the beginning, but begged off when we began to visit the North African subsidiaries."

"de Hartogue SA was a terribly messy assembly of companies. There was an informal process for repatriating a minimum dividend to maintain the family member's lifestyle. The company was managed through the review of a series of auditor's reports, advice from aggressive billing attorneys, and the inspired hand of Monsieur Chardin. I developed and installed the first business planning process and systems. Next I fired Monsieur Chardin and assumed his responsibilities. Then I reorganized a central staff capable of providing oversight for the some 40 companies de Hartogue operated or participated world-wide. It was a wonderful job for a business school trained 26 year old. The old Baron wanted an heir and I had a playboy husband who found excuses to travel. So I started to spend some of my nights with the old Baron. Soon I was pregnant. Arnaud became a doting grandfather and Henri suddenly became highly attentive, and then I produced a second son. I was now running de Hartogue, and had met my heir production goals."

"de Hartogue provided income for a great many uncles, aunts, cousins, nieces, and nephews. It wasn't unlike the situation your old friend, the late Mr. Harwell, had. They were highly critical of me. They complained to Arnaud that I was too young and very power hungry. They were outraged after I fired Monsieur Chardin, even after I explained what a dishonest old thief he was. I presented a plan to Arnaud showing which businesses we should keep and which we should divest."

"He agonized over my plan for a week, and then presented it to the family board as his own plan. I was to be the implementer. In the course of the divestitures, I was introduced to Hakim Selim when he was at Broadbakers. He represented buyers, and while I had people representing us as sellers, I was always personally involved in the final negotiations."

"Then Arnaud had a stroke in 1985, and he was dead within the year. His will left me in charge. The family members, however, formed little cabals and hatched plots criticizing my decisions and lack of experience. I won the war finally on the Hortense takeover. Hakim had gone to Harwell Investments through your efforts, and he brought the Hortense deal to me."

"Were you serious about installing Burke as CEO if you had acquired Hortense?" Baxter asked.

"Burke was my back-up position. Hakim and I concluded early that de Hartogue would make an initial bid and then a secondary bid, and then let a higher bidder take the company. If we would have been stuck with Hortense, I would have installed Burke as CEO, we would sell off assets, and let people go. Then we would have cleaned up the company for sale or an IPO. Then the management buy-out offer came through financed by the Double G's debt offering. They overpaid considerably on the premise we were going to make a third offer. McKenzie Barber helped the MBO group develop the offer. It was very amateurish strategy work. The McKenzie Barber Partner's name was Grunwild or something like that. Do you know him?"

"I do know him and his name is Grunwaldyt," Baxter acknowledged.

"Management overpaid for Hortense Foods, and we walked away with a good deal of cash. The family was astounded. There hasn't been any criticism of me since." Dominique drained her champagne glass and slid across the bed into Baxter's arms. There was a long open-mouthed kiss, followed by a push and she slid her body on top of Baxter. "So now you know how I have been spending my time since our last meeting."

She rubbed her body against Baxter and then began to kiss him about the chest, his navel, and finally took his member in her mouth. Then they coupled again with Dominique perched on top of him.

"Let's not be in such a hurry this time," she cautioned.

Was he dreaming? Baxter questioned. Would he suddenly wake up and find himself alone in the room at the Iron Creek Holiday Inn? He was making love to Dominique after all of these years. It was not the same Dominique he had known fifteen years ago. That Dominique had been a 24 year old girl with a loving innocence about her. This Dominique was a mature, worldly woman accustomed to power and having her own way. Loving innocence had gone its way over the intervening years. Her eyes were closed as they moved and gently gyrated their connected bodies. Was she thinking of a previous lover?

Baxter placed his hands on her breasts and Dominique became quite animated. Her time came quickly and she rolled off Baxter to his side. He cradled her head under his arm and she stared at the ceiling in silence for several minutes.

Finally she turned to him. "Shall we take a shower?"

Dominique wrapped her head in a towel and they shared a long hot shower.

"It's 10:30 and I have a very important decision to make," Dominique announced as Baxter dried her.

"I must call my driver and tell him when and where to pick me up. He is on call until eleven. I can stay here tonight with you or have him pick me up very early in the morning. Which do you prefer, Joe?"

"We do this so infrequently, Dominique. I would prefer that you stayed over," Baxter said and she turned her head and kissed him lightly on the mouth.

"That is my preference also." She called from the phone on the wet bar and spoke in French to someone in polite but firm tones. He could make out 6:30 and George V.

"He is a good man. Devoted and discreet. He was Gabriel, the old Baron's driver. Now he is my driver."

Baxter followed Dominique into the bedroom. She slid open a closet door revealing a full inventory of clothes. Dominique produced two night gowns. One was long and white and the other short and crimson.

"Take your pick," she said holding them up for Baxter's inspection.

"The red one. The other one has too much fabric to suit me."

"Another predictable answer," Dominique acknowledged and slid the shorty night gown over her head. The lower hem barely brushed the top of her thighs and a V neckline revealed her breasts. "There, now I am more respectable. Not fully respectable or as respectable as I would have been in the long white gown, but more respectable. You remain reminiscent of Adam. Regrettably there is nothing your size. Therefore you must continue as you are." Dominique rubbed Baxter's belly. "I propose we have a brandy for a night cap and return to bed. My memory of you is that you could be quite entertaining in the morning."

Baxter nodded. What could he tell his long lost love? I'm not the cowboy I once was. Don't expect too much.

He followed Dominique out of the wet bar where she produced a bottle of twenty year old Armagnac and half filled two snifters. They took places on a couch which looked out on the street. Baxter extended his arm and Dominique slipped into place. She brought his hand down across her breast.

"There, now I am settled and more comfortable." Baxter noted that the Gershwin on the sound system had turned into Brahms.

"This is so comfortable, Joe. I want you to know that I rarely spend an evening like this."

"Do you have lovers?"

"There is a lover from time to time, but I must be very careful. Henri has had many affairs. His favorite playmate is Erik. They seem to collect girls together, and I believe they sometimes exchange them. I travel a good deal and there are friendships that I have developed."

"I would hope that I made the friendship list. I'd like to make application for the Dominique's frequent friend program." Dominique kissed Baxter on the cheek. "You are on fifteen year intervals. We will met again in 2006."

"I don't suppose you'll free up tomorrow night. I'm used to you in four day doses."

"Tell me about your life, Joe. You are divorced again?"

"Fully divorced. I had a son who died two years back and a daughter who's living up in Vermont. I plan to announce my retirement from McKenzie Barber in September. My retirement date will be in January. I'll be able to pick up a stub year's Partnership distribution."

"What are you plans then?"

"I'm thinking about writing a book about McKenzie Barber. The firm's going to disappear after the Robson Allen merger. I believe that the writing of some kind of history is appropriate."

"Why is the merger necessary?"

"Because the firm got off course in 1984."

"Would the firm have a different outcome if Burke had been elected Chairman?"

"I'd like to think so. I fault Ernie Grey. He should have engineered his succession seamlessly. He didn't and the firm faltered under the misdirection of the new group."

"It's been so long ago for me, Joe. I had the summer internship in the San Francisco office, and a job offer from the Paris office after I graduated. If I hadn't gone to work for McKenzie Barber, I never would have had the assignment with de Hartogue. I wouldn't have met Arnaud and Henri, and it would be unlikely that I would be running a major French company today. I would be, today, at best, a senior middle manager if I had joined a large French company. McKenzie Barber is not an organization for me. Rather, it is an old memory of a place I used to live. With Hamilton Burke, it is something more. He almost climbed to the top and was pushed back down the mountain. He expected that he would be in demand for CEO jobs, but none have materialized. I was ready to give him one but the generous offer came. Now he waits for his father to die so that he can assume his birthright. He is married to a very difficult woman who has a very big ego."

"And are you happy, Dominique?"

"I have secured a good place in the world where I can generally control matters to my advantage. I have two very bright sons, 11 and 13, an attractive, fun-loving husband and nearly unlimited funds. I am very good at business and will make my mark in the world of commerce. My mother and father are very proud of me and they are naming a school after me in my village. Tonight I have taken licentious liberties with an old lover. Tomorrow I'll be back into my routine, and Joe Baxter will be a memory again."

"So we have tonight, and then it's good-bye again? Is that it?" Baxter questioned.

"How could it be more than that? I just planned to have a lunch with you, and now I'm spending the night with you. What more could you expect? I'm a married woman and the mother of two."

Baxter tilted Dominique's head and she freely offered an open mouth. He could feel her hand on the back of his neck. He broke off and followed up with a series of brief kisses.

"Where will you be tomorrow night at this time?" he asked.

"In a five star hotel in Barcelona. But I will be alone. I will not have a large red-headed American touching me and giving me such pleasure. I have a business review Tuesday morning, and it will not be a very pleasant meeting for our general manager who is turning in a very poor performance. Then I'm off to Abu Dhabi to meet with our Arab partners. That should take two days because they have so many lies to tell me. Then I'm connecting through London back to Paris. There will be no Joe Baxter in my room in Abu Dhabi either. I will arrive back in Paris late on Friday night and we are spending the weekend in our country chateau. The boys have friends down for the weekend, and I believe Erik and Monica will be down. So it will be a madhouse. That's my life, Joe. We couldn't very well do what we've done tonight five nights in a row. It's nice for tonight. I will be sore for a few days which will reminded me of my Bastille Day rendezvous with Joe Baxter, but I may not think too much of you the following week. I'll be in Frankfurt negotiating with the Germans."

"When will you visit the US again?"

"November. I can let you know in advance when I'm coming and perhaps we could fit something in. But there is no real future for us. Tonight, Bastille Day 1991, is what we have. It is very unlikely that you and I, no matter how pleasant all this is, have any future beyond tonight."

"How would you like to conclude this historic meeting?" Baxter queried.

Dominique pushed herself up free from the couch and drained her brandy snifter.

"I believe I would like to take two aspirins and sleep in your arms. I will pretend I'm Dominique Beaufort, a 24 year old Barber consultant, and you can be Joe Baxter, the American who has come to Paris. Then when I receive my wake up call, we can make love one more time, and get on with our lives." Dominique called the desk for a wake-up call at 5 AM. She slid under his arm after they walked into the bedroom. Then Dominique pushed him away. She pulled the red night gown over her head. "I certainly won't need this to get in the way of your touches." Baxter noted that the Brahms had turned into Chopin as their bodies came together under the sheets.

There was no encore performance in the morning. Dominique seemed to sleep in fits and starts. She got up once and padded her way out to the living room. Dominique returned to bed only to spring up again an hour later. This time Baxter followed her out of the room. He found her on the phone and smoking a cigarette and speaking to someone in Spanish.

Dominique waved to Baxter. The conversation impressed Baxter as calm, controlled, but intense. He took a seat on the couch and observed Dominique taking notes on the telephone pad. The conversation was concluded with an 'adios'. Dominique took a long drag from the cigarette and stumped it out in the ash tray.

"Barcelona?" Baxter asked.

"No. Mexico."

"I don't remember you as a smoker," Baxter observed.

"I enjoy a cigarette from time to time. It sometimes relaxes me. I think I'm through sleeping for the evening."

Baxter's watch said 4:15.

"I'm going to take a shower now, then fix us some coffee and get dressed. Please go back to sleep if it suits you. I'm being picked up at 6:30 and it is important for you to be out of here no later than nine which is the maid's general time to make up the room."

Baxter followed Dominique into the massive bathroom. "This is a shower I take alone," Dominique said. "The coffee pot is on a shelf under the wet bar. I plan on three or four cups." Dominique stepped into the shower stall and turned the water on. Baxter fumbled through the percolator set-up and discovered a small bathroom and shower stall adjacent to the wet bar. It appeared that he would be showering alone this morning.

Dominique dressed quickly into a blue linen suit with matching pumps. Between gulps of coffee she left a series of phone mail instructions in French. Her voice inflection was even and crisp. It was obvious that she was issuing commands as opposed to requests.

"These were matters I should have taken care of last evening, but I was distracted," she explained to Baxter adding a naughty wink.

The clock on the wet bar wall showed 6:23 AM. "I must leave now, Joe. Let's defer any further embraces until we meet again."

"In 2006?"

"Maybe sooner." Dominique ran a hand from the top of Baxter's head down over his ear to his shoulder. "It's good-bye for now without embraces." Dominique walked away from him in quick steps, turned at the door, and blew Baxter a kiss. "Be sure to be out of here by 9AM," she reminded and exited through the door.

There was a cable from Jennifer waiting for Baxter at his hotel.

JOE

WILL BE IN LONDON JULY 15-19. STAYING AT SOMERSET HOTEL IN MARBLE ARCH THROUGH FRIDAY. LOOK ME UP THERE IF YOU WANT TO SEE ME.

JENNIFER WASHBURN

Baxter was tempted to go on to Milan anyway. His appointment with Richard Fairbrother had been set for nine AM on Wednesday, July 17 and his return flight was scheduled for mid-day on Thursday. Maybe he would just continue to wander about Europe for the next several weeks. For the first time in his McKenzie Barber life, Baxter was not consumed with making his practice plan. He was not going to be close, and he had composed and edited his resignation/retirement letter in his head at least a dozen times. Baxter could easily float through Europe accompanied by his American Express card and an inventory of traveler's checks.

He spent July 15th meandering through the streets of Paris trying to retrace the route and places of his weekend fifteen years earlier. He came to rest in mid-afternoon at a sidewalk cafe on the Champs Elysees and sipped cognac and coffee while observing the endless flow of people parading up and down the boulevard. Baxter could remember holding a younger Dominique's hand as they made their way up to Fouquet's for a late lunch after mid-afternoon lovemaking. He saw a tall American man in a Wharton sweatshirt holding hands with a Gallic young woman stop near the matire'd's stand to study the restaurant menu. The man appeared to be in his early thirties with close cropped hair, and wire rimmed glasses. His companion appeared to be in her twenties, and wore a blue tee shirt, white shorts and low cut tennis shoes.

The man's arm was extended around the woman's shoulder and his hand brushed her breast as she talked about the menu. She raised her hand and playfully scolded the man. Then she shook her head and they walked away, arms clasped at the waist. Baxter's eyes followed them until they passed from view into a swarm of people.

He had just turned 40 that summer of 1975 and Dominique had been twenty-four. Public displays of affection had been limited to holding hands and an occasional kiss on a remote side street. Now they were quite different people, former lovers who had come together for one last reunion. Baxter raised his cognac glass in a silent toast. Hail and farewell, Dominique Beaufort de Hartogue.

Jennifer proposed that they meet for tea at the Somerset. The Somerset was nestled between the Churchill and the Portman two blocks off Marble Arch. It was a smaller, quieter, gentile hotel, in contrast to its bustling multi-cultural neighbors.

Jennifer was now going by Mrs. Washburn. A bellman escorted Baxter to the far corner of the lobby where a tea service had been arranged on a coffee table between two stuffed chairs. Jennifer was lounged in a chair reading the Herald Tribune. She wore a striped top and white pants that were tucked into black boots with buckles.

"Mrs. Washburn, your guest is here," the bellman announced Baxter.

"Joe." Jennifer extended her hand in greeting which Baxter clasped briefly and released. He wondered if she expected it to be kissed. "I remember you as a coffee drinker. Coffee is it then?"

"Coffee will be fine," he ascended. Jennifer had continued to be what many men would regard as beautiful. She remained a classic beauty with high cheek bones and saucer eyes. Baxter estimated Jennifer to be in her early fifties, and capable of passing for ten years younger under accommodating light. She offered Baxter a plate of biscuits which he declined.

"What brings you to Europe, Joe?"

"It's half vacation and half research. I'm in London to visit with the Chairman of Barber, and I met in Paris with a former consultant who has gone on to other endeavors. I thought I'd include you in my visit and bring you up to date on Muffin."

"Martha," Jennifer immediately corrected him. She produced a cigarette from her bag and waited for Baxter to provide a light from the matches on the serving tray. "Muffin is the nickname that Tom's dreadful old housekeeper gave her. My daughter was named Martha after my mother."

"Heard from her lately?"

"I wasn't particularly encouraged by her last letter. She mentioned she was going to see you over the July 4th weekend with her boyfriend. I understand that she's still going to some rural community college and working at that resort. Martha will come into some money from a Washburn family trust on her 25th birthday." Jennifer took a long pull from her cigarette. "I haven't talked to you for a while. There really is little for the two of us to talk about. Our only common link is Martha and she's not even your biological child."

"But I have appreciated the opportunity to raise her," Baxter interjected.

"Both my parents are likely to pass away in the next few years. There were some trusts arranged for Joel and Martha. Now Martha's trust will be considerably larger. She will not be well off, but will have a comfortable supplementary income stream. There was a lot of talk about a Larry in her letter. What kind of a young man is he? Is he from a good family?"

"He's a decent enough fellow. Larry's a struggling artist who earns his living as a handyman. Muffin, or Martha as you call her, is still fragile. You might try to do a little on the mother side if you can squeeze it in."

Jennifer rested her cigarette in the ash tray and sipped some tea. She looked around the room to catch the waiter's attention. "You may bring a check," Jennifer commanded.

"If you dislike me so much, Joe, why did you seek me out?"

"First, I wanted to remind you that you are a mother to a young woman in Vermont. Second, I sense that I'm going around the game board one last time, and I was curious to see you one more time."

"You and I were a terrible mistake and a waste of each other's time, Joe. Getting together with you was Tom's idea. He saw you as someone who could run the company and produce a Washburn heir. You and I have never really had anything in common. You seem to have somehow made your way in the world. I see Basil Crowley from time to time. He tells me that you've become a famous executive pay consultant. I'm amazed."

"Tell me about your life, Jennifer. Why are you in London, for example?"

"I'm here to buy and sell art. I have an interest in a small, but very successful gallery. My Partner's name is Antonio Piscotti. He's well known in art circles. He's also asked me to marry him. I'm giving it some thought. I may ask Martha to visit me. If I do, would you pay for her airfare? You can book her on one of those cheap fares. Martha could live with me quite comfortably after she comes into her trust."

Jennifer signed the check and looked at Baxter. "Do you and I have anything else to discuss?"

Baxter rose from his chair. "Good-bye Jennifer," he said and departed from the room without looking back.

9AM, Wednesday, July 17, 1991

"Joe, what brings you to London?" Richard Fairbrother greeted Baxter cordially. They met in his private conference room, a circular room with an imposing oil painting of John McKenzie and Erik Barber. Fairbrother was larger framed than Baxter had remembered him. He appeared jacketless in a blue shirt, with a white collar, school tie, and braces. Fairbrother had a thick, leonine head of brown hair that reached the edge of the back of his shirt collar. There was a dynamism about him as he listened to the reasons Baxter recited for his visit.

"A history of McKenzie Barber. Now that's an interesting project. It might also be a timely project with the merger hanging over our heads." Fairbrother poured Baxter a coffee without asking whether he wanted on and then filled his own cup. "Have you talked to Ernie about it?"

"I plan to a little later this Fall," Baxter added. "Ernie will be retiring from IPCO this December and he should be able to provide me some time in January. I would like to be introduced to somebody at Barber who is the equivalent of an archivist."

"Archivist? I'll be damned if I know if we have a bloody archivist? I'll get Miss Quigley, my assistant on it. She'll find out who's got what hidden away where. Now is this an official US firm sponsored project, Joe?"

"No, Richard, it's a matter of my personal initiative. I'm on holiday right now. I haven't decided whether I want to be a part of the divested practice. I may choose early retirement. Should I retire in January, I plan to proceed immediately on the book. I believe we owe it to them." Baxter gestured to the oil painting on the wall.

"That's a fake, you know. I had it painted from old photographs. If this merger goes through, I just may have the same painter add Charley Robson on the end. I certainly don't want him in the middle. I was thinking of maybe adding Ernie, but I always heard that Ernie and Charley didn't care much for one another. They might object to sharing a painting."

"We appear to be dealing with what we always considered the unthinkable," Baxter commented. His real objective had been to draw Fairbrother out on the merger status.

"What's your status these days, Joe? I know you were well placed in the old Burke crowd, but what are you doing these days? That is other than being on holiday and planning to be firm historian?" Baxter detected skepticism in Fairbrother's eyes.

"I'm the National Director for the US Executive Compensation Practice, although I was pulled out of the practice this spring on a study of Executive Office. As you may be aware, my practice and others are planned to be spun off to the Partners to be operated independently outside the firm. McKenzie Barber US is trimming down to be an easier match for the Robson Allen combination. Do you have similar issues in Europe?" Baxter asked innocently.

"Robson Allen is a very distant second to us. According to the preliminary agreement, Robson Allen will be merged into Barber and we will sort out the organizations. The US is another matter. Robson Allen will be left out to sort out the US firm and the two surviving firms will become the industry leader. Your firm has been in a muddle since those 1984 elections of yours. We both are experiencing serious 1991 recessions in our respective countries. We were prepared for ours, but the US firm had been in total confusion. We don't like this man named Faunce. I haven't been impressed with the US Robson Allen people we've met to date. The merger may or may not happen, but it had better happen for the good of the US firm." Fairbrother glanced at his watch. "I have another meeting, Joe. Get me a proper authorization letter about your project and I'll have Miss Quigley drum up our archivists." Fairbrother stood up and offered Baxter his hand.

"How long are you over for?"

"A couple of weeks," Baxter answered.

"Well, you have a project that should be addressed." Fairbrother slapped a hand against Baxter's shoulders. "Get us some formal authorization and we'll cooperate."

Baxter continued traveling. He took a train to Dublin, flew to Frankfurt and leisurely took trains all the way from Vienna to Zurich. He drank in wine stubes, took bus tours, exchanged pleasantries with prostitutes, ate well, and walked the streets each night until after midnight. He read the

Herald Tribune, Financial Times, and the *Wall Street Journal Europe* each morning over an extended breakfast. Baxter loafed through Europe through mid-August and then concluded that it was time to return to whatever he had left to do at McKenzie Barber.

6:15 AM, January 8, 1992

Baxter sat at his desk in his shorts and replayed Rusty's phone mail message to him.

"Yesterday, guy, was a very long day in the consulting career of one Rusty Collins. The flight was forty-five minutes late in getting out of Kennedy and there was fog in LAX. I took my bag to the office and worked until midnight. My career's on the line tomorrow with CCCS. That's California Credit Card Services, my client who wants to make me a job offer, if you don't remember. I'm presenting our report at 3PM, Wednesday, and I expect to have an offer by Friday. I should have been back Saturday and leisurely finished my report but I was seduced and kept prisoner by a middle aged roue whom I miss very much. How was your funeral? Is today the day you're going to quit? I'm unreachable until the evening on Wednesday. How about a telephone date? Can you call me at 11:30 your time? God I miss you! All I wanted to do was to have a drink or two and talk about my career. Now look at me. It's all your fault. Come to think of it, Joe Baxter, I just may have fallen in love with you."

Rusty was out there. A week ago at this time, she was a notation in his week-at-a-glance book. Now she was someone who had come into his life and was waiting for him on the other end of the country. He was fortunate to have someone out there. He would fly out to see Rusty on the 18th and determine how much of the magic between them had been retained.

Today was Baxter's last day in his McKenzie Barber career. He would dress, walk to 311 Park Avenue for the last time and make his settlement with Dr. Ranglinger, the Robson Allen hatchet man. At the top of his right hand drawer was Baxter's good-bye McKenzie Barber file. It contained copies of all pertinent documents including his petition for retirement and the exact computation of his severance payout and pension. The back up trailed back to his original offer letter from Clyde Nickerson, and the first day forms he had filled out with Andy Bourke Nickerson and Naomi on the Tuesday after Labor Day in 1968. The McKenzie Barber Baxter had joined some 23 1/2 years earlier had turned into another animal and it was time to leave the zoo forever.

Near the top of the pile was a copy of the letter he had written to Bob Dilger on September 1st. It read,

Dear Bob,

It is with deep regret that I must inform you of my intention to withdraw from the Dilger Group of Partners.

As you are well aware, I have had a great deal of enthusiasm for the formation of this partnership from its inception. Regrettably my health and certain events in my personal life dictate that I petition for retirement effective January 31, 1992. You have assembled a fine group of professionals in the Dilger Group and I am confident that you will be very successful.

Best wishes,
Joseph Baxter Jr.

The letter had been timed to reach Dilger's desk around September 4th. He wrote a similar letter to Glen Fitzgerald dated September 1, and sent it registered mail. This letter read,

Mr. Glen Fitzgerald
Chairman
McKenzie Barber & Co.
311 Park Avenue
New York, New York 10154

Dear Glen:

I am writing to declare my intention to retire from McKenzie Barber effective January 31, 1992. My years of service and age exceed the requirements for retirement eligibility. My present state ill health dictates a lengthy convalescence and I have advised Bob Dilger that I will be unable to assume my Partnership responsibilities with the Dilger Group.

My McKenzie Barber career has meant a great deal to me. I regret that I must withdraw prematurely from my great many friends and Partners during this period of great change and opportunity.

Yours very truly,
Joseph Baxter, Jr.

Baxter estimated that he would hear from Fitzgerald's office via Bernie by September 10th.

Now that Baxter had announced to the world that he was in ill health, he would have to come up with an illness. He had gotten the illness idea when he contracted food poisoning in Amsterdam on his European tour. He had spent two days in and out of his hotel bed where he listened and stared at the ceiling. He reflected long and hard on his life during those two days and reconfirmed his conclusion to make as hasty an exit as he could from the firm.

Illness would be his exit excuse. He had never taken a sick day in his twenty year career with McKenzie Barber. He purchased some medical books. He settled in on a brain tumor. Baxter reasoned that if you told someone you had a brain tumor, they would pretty much have to take your word for it. He developed a scenario of describing meetings and scans with leading specialists which could be described in vague terms.

Baxter came into the office on Labor Day morning 1991 to sort out his correspondence and the thirty-five items of voice mail that the system would accept. His incoming correspondence had been arranged in three large piles approximating 12 to 15 inches in height. Two piles of envelopes had been opened, while a third pile marked private remained sealed. The executive compensation practice revolved around Baxter and he disappeared for two months in the merger confusion. Had he been missed?

Baxter drank coffee from a thermos as he sorted through his mail into piles on the floor beside his desk. His piles were divided into approvals, new business, ongoing business, billing and receivable matters, McKenzie Barber communications, and universal garbage. Baxter was half way through his mail when Marty appeared in his office doorway.

"Joe, I hoped I'd find you here." Marty shook Baxter's hand jubilantly. "It was like you dropped out. You're the guy who never took vacations and suddenly you're gone two months without any warning."

"Close the door, Marty," Baxter said somberly. It was as good a time as any to try out his ill health story. "Sit down Marty." Baxter rocked slightly in his chair for effect.

"I have a medical problem. I extended my time off to consult with some physicians overseas. It looks as though I'm facing some serious surgery. I have just announced my intention to retire effective January 31st. I expect to be in and out of the office through the end of the year."

Marty's jaw dropped open. "What happens to the practice? You were the only Partner in the Dilger Group. What happens to the rest of us, Joe? We were counting on you to see us through."

"Now, you'll have to have someone else see you through, Marty. My life is on the line."

"What do you have, Joe? You look great."

"I don't want to get into details and I don't want you to repeat it to others. I have a brain tumor that may or may not be operable."

"Jesus, Joe," Marty said. Tears were forming in his eyes. Good old gentle Marty. This brain tumor stuff was obviously a little harsh, Baxter concluded.

"It's got to be our secret, Marty. I've informed Bob Dilger and Glen Fitzgerald in writing that I wish to retire for health reasons. You're the only one I've told about the tumor and I'm counting on you to keep the matter in confidence," Baxter cautioned.

Baxter was more circumspect in his discussion one week later with Bob Dilger. He was summoned by Dilger's secretary to meet his designated leader.

"What does this letter mean?" Dilger greeted Baxter brandishing Baxter's letter.

"It means, Bob, that I've developed a health problem and that I have decided to take early retirement from McKenzie Barber. I have this option under the Partner's agreement and I have elected to exercise it. Under the Partnership agreement I have given my six month advance notice in writing to the Chairman of the firm. I'm willing to shorten that period to the end of January. There's no way I am prepared to participate in the Dilger Group. Therefore it's best that I drop out now."

"Would you still like to be an investor in the Dilger Group? Your capital contribution could be worth a lot of money in a few years time." Dilger leaned forward placing both of his elbows on his desk blotter. It was a $500,000 question.

"I don't believe so, Bob. I would only invest if I were a participant."

Dilger's dark Indiana eyes grew cold and mean. "Where the hell have you been the last two months?"

"I took an extended vacation and had the time accumulated. As you will recall, I dropped you a note stating that I was taking a long vacation."

"Your practice will lose money this year. I was the one that took you back after you screwed up in the executive office review. I took you back on trust, and now you come in my office and give me some cock and bull story about some mysterious health problem and that you're going to cut and run out on your obligations to the Dilger Group and the firm."

"Bob, I'm retiring. That's my call."

"The firm will require some documentation on this illness of yours."

"The firm will receive documentation when I put in a claim. All McKenzie Barber has to know at this time is that I have chosen to take early retirement."

"You don't have AIDS do you? As I recall, you had a son who died of AIDS," Dilger commented.

Baxter stood up from his chair, reached across the desk and pulled Dilger up by the necktie. "That was in poor taste, Bob." Baxter released Dilger and pushed him back to his chair and stepped to the doorway.

"I'll be in and out of the office over the next few months and I'll keep you current on my whereabouts."

"I'm sorry, Joe. I apologize." Baxter heard Dilger's voice call after him.

Predictably, Bernie called Baxter on the morning of September 10th.

"Joe, Glen asked me to call you on your retirement note. We're all concerned about your ill health. Is there anything you can share with us?"

"Not really, Bernie. I'm in the midst of a lot of tests and may require surgery. I thought it best to announce my retirement. It's one less Partner to account for in the proposed merger."

"You know I can't comment on that, Joe."

"I didn't ask you to comment, Bernie."

"Glen wanted me to ask you if you expect to be honored with the retired Partners on the dais at the October Partners Meeting?"

"It is my understanding that I meet the requirements for retirement. Therefore, I should sit on the dais with the other retiring Partners. I promise not to give a speech."

"It's just that you seem so young to retire. We're all going to miss you very much."

Baxter's retirement was accepted and Harry Devonshire was designated as his replacement in the Dilger Group. He requested that Baxter visit him in Atlanta and provide him a complete briefing on the practice.

Harry Devonshire was officed on the 34th Floor in the center city Atlanta office tower that housed McKenzie Barber's four floors of offices.

Harry's speech patterns had softened over his three.year stay in Atlanta.

"Come in, Joe," he greeted Baxter with a cold handshake and gestured him to take a seat at an oval table which faced the north side of Atlanta. "It looks to me that you have left me a good sized mess to clean-up," he opened their discussion.

Harry had a point, Baxter quickly agreed. The leadership ranks were totally depleted with Carl's death and Baxter's retirement. Harry's Atlanta practice would be the most profitable unit in the executive Compensation practice during FY '91. 25% of his practice volume was from Planters & Commerce Bank, the legacy client Baxter had left for him. Baxter went over the history of each office with Harry in dispassionate detail. Harry asked questions and took notes. They concluded the review in slightly less than two hours.

"Dilger promised me that I would be invited into the Partnership after one year if I met objectives. He also promised me that I could run the practice from Atlanta. Can I trust him?"

"Bob's a solid citizen actuary from Indiana. He's only fibbed over the years when he had to."

"He told me that he asked you to retire. That I assume is a euphemism for being fired."

"Call it what you want, Harry. I'm out of here," Baxter agreed.

"You work for me now. It's my understanding that you're at my beck and call through January."

"You may beck and call to your heart's content, Harry. If you present yourself sympathetically enough, I may respond to you in a timely manner," Baxter countered.

"Still the same arrogant Joe Baxter. I used to have to humble up to you. We met some people who know you at a fund raiser. They asked me to say hello."

"Did they have names?"

"One was Mrs. Brimmer. Paul Brimmer's widow. She's the CEO of Brimmer Industries and has just gone on the Planters & Commerce Board. She's a very powerful figure in the Atlanta social scene. Now did you know her when she was in the Chicago Office of McKenzie Barber?"

"Very slightly. Lorna was an MBA from some Eastern school and was on Brimmer's staff. I used to talk to her at the office parties. Now I run into her some at funerals."

"She was with Frank Alvardi, whom I understand was your old mentor. He certainly wasn't very kind to you in his book. I believe Alvardi is on the Brimmer Industries Board. He told me that he was moving to Atlanta. Do you talk to him regularly? I was thinking of putting him on retainer to the

Dilger Group. The man has a world of contacts and his book has made him rather famous."

"Frank should be a very valuable addition to your practice, Harry. He may have some baggage from his Robson Allen days but Dilger Group would be an independent equity. Frank has always admired the actuarial mind. He regards it superior to humans."

"Did I hear a rumor that you were in ill health, Joe?" Harry asked as Baxter was readying to leave.

"I've never felt better in my life, Harry," Baxter responded. "Dilger believes that fresh leadership is needed and I've been pushed into early retirement. My health has never been in question. I'm retiring because it's the right thing to do."

Baxter attended his final Partner's meeting at the Boca Mirage Club during the final week in October of 1991. The meeting convened on Wednesday, October 30th and the ballot for the merger was the first order of business on Thursday, October 31st.

The merger talks with Robson Allen Harbridge moved through a jagged, twisting course to the day of the ballot. The business press reported periodically on the merger talks with the *Wall Street Journal* publishing a left hand front page column in September headlined, *The Fall of a Giant*. The theme of the article was the inept stewardship of Buzzsaw Pritchard. It stated that Ernie Grey had refused to be interviewed for the article but the criticism sounded as through Ernie had dictated the article to the reporter. It referred to the Fitzgerald team as well meaning lightweights. There were numerous internal memorandums published to reach the various audience levels that made up McKenzie Barber.

There was a Partner's Update that was published every other Friday to update the Partners on the merger progress. It even contained little squibs about Robson Allen. The management group letter came out in three to four week intervals and generally carried a watered down version of the Partners Update. The employee letter was one back-to-back page describing the job security that would come with the linking of the two most powerful consulting firms in the world. Baxter was in the rear of the elevator one early October evening reading the *Wall Street Journal* when what appeared to be three young consultants got on from the 35th floor. The group was comprised of two young men and one woman in their late twenties. One had a copy of the latest Partner's Update.

"Can you believe this swill? Great opportunities in a giant merged firm. Robson Allen people will be taking over. We should just send them our resumes now."

"Just sit tight and get involved in a long assignment, Gerry. Your Partner will protect you," the young woman advised.

"That's all very nice, but who's going to protect my Partner. He's one of those fogies in his mid-fifties who helped screw up McKenzie Barber. He'll be gone if this merger ever gets done." The elevator opened on the lobby floor and Baxter lingered in the rear until the trio cleared into the hallway. What once was pride had been replaced by cynicism.

The business press stated twice during the month of September that talks had been suspended. The final agreement was reached subject to ballot on Friday, November 1, 1991. Opposition in the Robson Allen ranks continued over the funding of the McKenzie Barber Partner's pension fund. It was the final and major negotiating issue.

Robson Allen demanded that the retirement benefits be partially funded by contributions from the future earnings of the remaining or surviving US McKenzie Barber Partners. This was totally unacceptable to the US Partners. They presently received half their retirement from an annuity which had been funded from firm earnings, with the other half funded by a contributory fund from the active Partners. It worked a little like social security, the active Partners made contributions to fund the retirement of the retired Partners.

Baxter's plan for survival was predicated on McKenzie Barber meeting its retirement commitments. Now that plan had been clouded by the merger negotiations. Baxter was floating through his last days of McKenzie Barber with only occasional client contact, and little participation in the practice. It was not clear to anyone what he was actually accomplishing and no one seemed to care much. Harry Devonshire was in and out of New York conducting the Monday morning staff meetings and taking his place on the leadership council of the Dilger Group. Everything was in limbo until the conclusion of the merger negotiations with Robson Allen. The Dilger Group could not be launched. Robson Allen and McKenzie Barber continued to compete for the same clients in the consulting marketplace. The accounting firms and specialist consulting firms subtly discredited McKenzie Barber in the marketplace as a failing firm that required a savior merger partner in order to survive. The FY 1991 results were 25% off plan, resulting in a corresponding reduction in Partner's unit value.

It was a grim group of Partners who gathered at the El Mirage Hotel & Yacht Club on October 31st, 1991, for the final meeting of the Partners of McKenzie Barber. It was a two day meeting with a first day's agenda of briefings. The merger ballot was scheduled to be turned in no later than 10PM on Thursday evening when the ballot boxes were to be sealed. The results of balloting were to be announced at the beginning of the Friday morning meeting. A Dr. Millet of the Millet Group was then scheduled to deliver a presentation on Management Teamwork in the 90's. Dr. Millet was to be followed by Glen Fitzgerald who would adjourn the meeting, leaving the Partners a free afternoon. The meeting would be concluded with the black tie dinner where Baxter would sit on the dais with the retired Partners.

The Partners of McKenzie Barber began arriving in the late afternoon of Wednesday, October 30th. They somberly checked in at the front desk exchanging quiet greetings with familiar faces. Baxter arrived shortly after 6PM, and following check-in he was ushered to a remote grouping of two story stucco buildings that the hotel referred to as the luxury cottages. The cottages were located in an area beyond the parking lot situated on a street facing the high wire fence off the golf course. The cottages were located on the far end of the club property. Baxter had always wondered who was housed in this street of dwellings situated more than two hundred yards from the main hotel building. As a newly elected Partner, Baxter had been housed on the second floor of the main building. Later, as he advanced in status in the early 1980's, Baxter had moved to the tower overlooking the bay. Now for his final meeting, he had been relegated to the cottages.

Baxter noted that he had been assigned a roommate. There was a suitcase on the bed and a golf bag against the wall. One side of the closet was filled with clothes in plastic dry cleaning bags. It looked as though his roommate was planning on staying for a week. Baxter noted that the laundry bags had a Dallas address. He concluded that his roommate was a first year Partner from the Dallas office.

Baxter walked leisurely down a pathway that led to the bay and looked out at the water. Would he ever return? He then cut across the lawn to

Mirage Lounge and took up a stool at the far end of the bar where he could overview the room. He fastened his McKenzie Barber name tag over the breast pocket of his blazer and ordered a draft beer. Many of the faces around the room appeared familiar to Baxter and nods of recognition were exchanged. They formed conversation groups of three and four. There was some occasional forced laughter at someone's joke but the faces seemed uniformly grim to Baxter.

A heavyset man in a yellow golf shirt seated himself on the stool next to Baxter. He wore a name tag that said ABLEY "Brad" Cleveland.

"You're Joe Baxter aren't you?" he said after ordering a martini straight-up.

"And you're Brad Abley, Cleveland," Baxter responded and they exchanged handshakes.

"We're sitting next to each other on Saturday night. They've got the retirees seated in alphabetical order on the dais. You look a little young for retirement, Joe," Abley said taking a short sip from his martini. His hair was a brownish grey and he wore bifocals.

"I'm vested, and this is as good a time as any to retire from McKenzie Barber."

"Boy, I couldn't agree more." Abley raised his glass in a toast. "You probably won't remember this, but we were both in the Manufacturing practice back in the late 1960's under Bill Dwyer. We once worked together on an inventory control; system for a bicycle manufacturer in Ohio. The job lasted six weeks. We had dinner a couple of times at the Sheraton."

Baxter studied the face next to him. It didn't connect with his memory bank.

"Of course I looked a lot different then. Take fifty pounds away, and I'll bet you'd recognize me. You look a little heavier, but you don't look a day over forty-five. Dwyer got sick right after the job, and you wound up in the Comp practice. We were both in the group that Dwyer insisted on hiring directly from industry to round out all those apple cheeked MBAs."

"And you spent your entire career in Cleveland, Brad?"

504

"I spent my entire career in plants, airplanes, and motels. I used to visit the Cleveland office to get my mail. I was good at project management, and I ran jobs for McKenzie Barber all over the world. I wasn't a big seasoned type but once when I was into a client I could see a lot of other ways where we could help them. Bill Dwyer drummed that into me. I was a Manager for four years, a Director for five years and finally Barney Ingram added up all the work I was managing and put me up for Partner. I made it at fifty. I'm probably the oldest Partner the firm ever elected, if you exclude all those high priced direct admission Partners that came in under Pritchard. I never got a lot of units once when I got in as a Partner and I was a little worried about a pension reduction but it looks okay now. I assume you're voting affirmatively for the merger."

"I don't see a lot of options right now," Baxter responded.

"Joe, I used to love this firm. It gave me a chance to be someone I never thought I could be. I was Chief IE for a family held caster company in Lejune, Indiana. The family had Dwyer in for a couple of days to do a preliminary study of productivity. Bill liked to review standards methodology and I spent the better part of the day with him taking him through our MTM standards. He told me at the end of the day that I was doing it all wrong but had a good head on my shoulders. He made a presentation to the family on overall productivity improvement study. He quoted them a fee that made them choke. I ran into Bill in the plant parking lot and he was getting ready to leave. He gave me a business card and told me that I could have a future in consulting and to call if I was interested. I waited a month or so and then I called him after I read about McKenzie Barber in a *Fortune Magazine* article."

"I had to get by Clyde Nickerson, who was the biggest pompous ass I ever met in or outside the firm, and I wound up getting hired anyway. I kept changing over the years with what was hot. I started as kind of a manufacturing floor specialist and then I became a Material Requirements Planning specialist. Then when MRP slowed up, I became a Manufacturing Rationalization specialist. Then came activities based costing. I'm bowing out as an activities based costing expert. I've seen solutions and people come and go over the years. When solutions topped out on their life circle in the US, we would take them overseas. Now I'm going."

"What will you do in retirement, Brad?"

"I've got a horse farm in Kentucky. The house in Cleveland has been sold. My kids are through college and working, and I'm catching a plane out of here Saturday morning that will take me to Lexington. Soon as I get home, I'm going to start a fire and burn all my McKenzie Barber cards. I might catch up with Bill Dwyer and invite him down for a weekend. Do you know where he can be reached these days?"

"Bill passed away last year, Brad," Baxter explained.

"Did he drink himself to death?"

"That was part of it."

"Well here's to him." Abley raised his glass. "Wild Bill Dwyer!" They touched glasses and Baxter signed his check.

"I'll see you on Saturday night, Brad," Baxter said rising from his bar stool. It was time to work the room.

He edged into a threesome standing in the center of the bar room. There were two late thirties, early forties men in blue blazers, flanking a thirtiesh woman in a red pants suit.

"Hi, I'm Joe Baxter," he announced himself as he stepped into the group. The woman extended her hand first. She wore granny glasses and her handshake was aggressively firm. "Lila Burgess, IT Practice LA."

"Jim Hunt, Financial Services LA." The second acknowledgment was from a man of medium height with intense eyes.

"Jerry Chowman, IT, Dallas." Chowman was tall and thin with close cropped salt and pepper hair.

The waitress took fresh drink orders and they stared at each other for a moment. Lila Burgess spoke first.

"You're the one in Exec Comp aren't you? Rusty Collins is a good friend of mine and she talks about you from time to time."

"You look pretty young to be retiring, Joe," Hunt observed. "I see in the program that you're on the retirement dais this year."

"It's time," Baxter confirmed.

A fresh round of drinks were delivered, and Baxter signed the check.

"Joe," Lila began. "I've been with the firm for ten years and have been a Partner for three. Robson Allen has always been the enemy and now we're proposing to merge with them. We have a large LA office. They have a large LA office. Their IT practice has always appeared stronger than ours. What does the merger mean for my career? Or Jim's or Jerry for that matter?"

Baxter had switched to white wine. He studied his wine glass before responding. He had stood in this room seven years earlier when the Partners had voted for their choice of leadership. Now the Partners who had been admitted after 1984 were living with those choices.

"First the merger will happen. Retiring or near retirement Partners will vote for the merger. The units are weighted in their favor and with the pension matter presumably resolved, that grouping of Partners has only one choice. The Barber Partners have already affirmed the merger. As young Partners, your option is to go along with the merger and assess your opportunities with the merged firm. A year from now you can assess whether you want to continue with the merged firm," Baxter responded blandly.

"The rumor, Joe," Hunt interjected, "is that Robson Allen is going to ask certain Partners to sign five year stay agreements and offer retirement terms for the Partners that don't fit. As Partners we question why this Ev Faunce, who is not a Partner, has been leading the negotiations for Glen and Jack. The rumor is that Faunce has negotiated long term deals with Barber for Glen and Jack. The rest of us will either have the opportunity to sign up as Robson slave Partners, immediately sever from the firm, or if we're vested, take early retirement. Some of the practices, like Benefits & Comp will be spun off but the three of us are in core businesses of the merged firm. We're getting calls from other firms about jobs with more pay and more stability. Our careers are ahead of us. We have no significant retirement stake. If this merger is approved on Friday, I'm going to begin to take interviews on Monday. What do you think of that?"

It was the first Baxter had heard of five year contact demands. "Is this a soft rumor or a hard rumor?" Baxter probed.

"We have it on good authority that it will be disclosed tomorrow in the Robson Allen afternoon presentation," Chowman, the Dallas IT Partner interjected. "It's going to be presented in a take-it-or-leave-it proposition. The heavy unit Partners like you, Joe, are going to vote for the merger and this firm will belong to Robson Allen by mid-morning or Friday. Then Robson Allen will come back by the end of November and tell us if they want us to leave or stay. If we stay, it will be on their conditions. They got a guy named Dr. Gilbert Ranglinger that the Robson Allen guys refer to as Dr. Death. He reports directly to Al Carmichael, their Chairman. He's going to be their designated hatchet man after the merger."

"You seem to have a lot of inside information, Jerry," Baxter observed.

"My roommate from SMU B School went to work for Robson Allen and is a Partner. We stay in touch. He's given me what he understands to be the skinny."

"Does your friend like working for Robson Allen?" Baxter asked.

Chowman shrugged his shoulders. "What I can decipher is that we're paid about the same. We both like doing client work. They have always been ahead of us in IT, and Robson Allen has been better managed than us. My friend goes up and down on Robson Allen but he's still there."

"So what makes you think you're at risk in the merger?" Baxter questioned. "You fit into Robson Allen's core competency. The five year contract certainly has a clause that will allow you to move to a client and out of consulting. It wouldn't appear that you have a problem," Baxter said slapping Chowman on the shoulder. "It's been nice chatting with you." Baxter departed from the group with a wave.

Grunwaldyt was outside the bar at the edge of the pool in a cluster flanked by Fitzgerald and Pinker. A fourth man, whom Baxter didn't recognize, competed the group. They were all wearing suits.

Baxter walked through the glass door to the outdoor pool court. He paused near he diving board and looked at the bay. Baxter stood in full view of the group sipping his wine while he awaited some kind of acknowledgment. They shared a large laugh together that concluded with Fitzgerald, Pinker, and the third man drawing away together in the direction of the tower. Grunwaldyt recognized Baxter with a wave and walked over to Baxter.

"You're too young to retire, Joe," Grunwaldyt greeted him.

"I'm just the right age to retire from McKenzie Barber, Jon."

"You look like you're ready for a refill, Joe. It's not the Four Seasons, but how about letting me buy you a drink at the Beach Club Bar?"

"That would be peachy, Jon."

The Beach Club was across the bay via a five minute launch ride. "Do you have dinner plans, Joe?" Grunwaldyt asked when they were on the water. "I'm staying at the Beach Club this year. Where are you? The Tower, I suppose."

"I'm in the cottages."

"The cottages! My God, Joe, what did you do to wind up in the cottages?" Grunwaldyt seemed shocked.

"I'm only staying two more nights, Jon. It's a bit of a walk but I can endure that. I've had my share of nights in the Tower."

"Still though, Joe. To put you up at the cottages at your last meeting is an offense."

They left the boat and walked up a winding lighted asphalt path to an outside elevator.

"Have you been to the Beach Club, Joe?" Grunwaldyt asked.

"Just for drinks."

"They opened up for senior people a couple of years ago. Glen and Tom are staying here, as are the Robson Allen people. I stayed here last year. It's an improvement over the Tower."

They were seated at a dimly lit table in the center of a noisy room where a trio played *Fascination*.

"The Beach Club is filled with civilians. The firm has been quietly placing certain people over here for the past three years. The firm has gotten too big for the El Mirage. I don't know what we'll do next year. Robson Allen has held their meeting at the Wintersage in Arizona, and they have capacity problems. What resort do you know of, Joe, that's big enough to hold all of us?"

"The matter of headcount, Jon, doesn't appear to me to be resolved."

"The merger will happen, Joe. And it will be good for all of us, including the retired Partners," Grunwaldyt said with resolution. The waitress took drink orders.

"I'd recommend the pompano, Joe. I had that last night," Grunwaldyt said as he scanned the menu.

"You came yesterday, Jon?"

"I'm part of an advance party to serve as liaison to Robson Allen during the meeting."

"I saw you at poolside, Jon, with Glen and Tom and a stranger. Was he a Robson Allen man?" Baxter asked.

"That was Bart Messilli, their Director of Communications. He's going to be handling the press for the meeting. There's a private dinner for Robson Allen and McKenzie Barber senior management tonight. Richard Fairbrother has come in for the meeting. Robson Allen has a presentation tomorrow but then they will stay out of view until after the ballot. Friday mid-morning, we will be one firm."

"And how do you feel about that, Jon?" Baxter asked as the drinks were served.

Grunwaldyt took a swallow of white wine before answering. "To be frank with you, Joe, I'm sad that McKenzie Barber has come to an end. You and I go back a long ways, Joe. We met at that training conference back in 1975. You came across as a leader in that training conference. I walked out of there believing that McKenzie Barber was the number one consulting firm in the world. We lost our way. I've moved up and I have been assured that I have a place in the merged firm but I have been given no guarantees. I'm 44 years old and making $600,000 a year. Will I be of the same value to the merged firm? I was assured of a career track with McKenzie Barber. I don't know where I stand with the Robson Allen people."

Jesus! Baxter thought as he assumed his listening position with head slightly projected forward. How in hell had Grunwaldyt moved to a unit level of $600,000?

"We have a bondholder law suit on Hortense Foods. Since the bankruptcy this Spring, the creditors are looking for any party with deep pockets. We worked with management to develop the projections for the underwriters. Do you know Ed Bassonette at Robson Allen?"

Baxter shook his head.

"He worked for Al Carmichael, the Chairman. Bassonette is some kind of senior operations Partner. I've been involved in a lot of the Robson Allen discussions, and I have been asked to develop a bunch of special analyses for Ev Faunce. We were in a meeting two weeks ago with Robson Allen and Faunce brought up Hortense Foods. 'Jon,' he said. 'I believe it's time that you reviewed your litigation on Hortense Foods.' It wasn't McKenzie Barber's litigation, rather it was Jon Grunwaldyt's litigation. I wound up being grilled after the meeting by Bassonette. He told me that we should have left the prospective reporting to their public accounting firm. The next day I was summoned over to Robson Allen's law firm and instructed to send over the working papers. I told the law firm that I would be glad to visit with them with our attorneys present, but all documents would stay at McKenzie Barber."

"Bassonette told me that the Robson Allen policy manual clearly precluded a single Partner putting their firm to that level of risk. Then Glen dropped a note that he was very disappointed that I hadn't kept him better informed on Hortense's Foods litigation. I think I'm being set up, Joe."

"They seemed friendly enough at the pool court," Baxter observed.

"They didn't ask me to join them for dinner. In the last two weeks, I sense that people in the firm have been avoiding me."

"What's the litigation number, Jon?"

"$5.3 billion. Management should have let that French woman buy the company and cashed out their options. Our projections were thoroughly caveated. Our attorneys, Wellington & Barr, are recommending that we should offer a small settlement funded through our liability insurance before the merger date. I'm going to come out of this stained in the eyes of Robson Allen."

"Jon, this will blow over for you. Be positioned with a good book of business in January and all will be forgiven."

"That's just it, Joe. I don't have much in the way of clients right now. I've been involved in making all those videos for the management group and professional staff for Ludwig Strasser. Glen asked me to support Ev Faunce on special projects. Jack wanted me to do a special independent study on staff reduction to see if I agreed with Faunce. I got caught right in the middle of that one. Now I have the Hortense Foods litigation. I haven't made a client presentation since the beginning of August. Joe, I'm vulnerable. This could well be my last Partners meeting too."

"Jon, how long have you been attending meetings with Robson Allen?"

"Since late April. Pinker believes that I have a sense of history of the New York Office. I think he got that from all the years I worked for Dirks. Merging with our largest competitor was one of Ev Faunce's early alternatives.

"What differences have you identified between the two firms?"

"Robson Allen is more bureaucratic than we are. I know the literature about their founders being smart young math whizzes right out of the Army after MIT, but they have a rule and procedure for everything, and their people can access it on their PC's. Robson Allen has always been well ahead of us in IT. McKenzie Barber has the advantage in International. Robson Allen has never been successful overseas. They were going to sell or spin-off FSO but lately they have been having second thoughts, Joe.

Other than those differences, Robson Allen isn't that much different from McKenzie Barber."

Baxter and Grunwaldyt picked their way through dinner in between bottles of Sauvignon Blanc. Grunwaldyt traced their relationship back to the 'train the trainers' in 1975.

"There was a lot of talent in that room. And there I was a second year consultant assigned at the last minute. That was over sixteen years ago, Joe. Alice Dungler was in our group. Do you remember? She really had eyes for you. Who'd believe that she would found the largest software company in the world? I was still single but Amy and I were living together. You were my idea of a seasoned guy on the verge of being elected a Partner. Joe, can I ask you a sensitive question?" Grunwaldyt did not wait for an answer. "How many times have you been divorced?"

Baxter held up three fingers.

"Is it hard to do?"

"It's as hard as you make it, Jon."

Grunwaldyt held up his wine glass and stared at it in the candlelight. He appeared to be about to make a very serious statement or pronouncement. The band had started to play again and Baxter leaned forward to hear Grunwaldyt above the soft rock sounds from the band.

"Joe, I've been having an affair with a young woman for the last four months. I've always worked hard to be a good husband to Amy, and a good father for our children. It's very difficult to maintain a McKenzie Barber career in balance with a marriage and family. The travel demands and time commitment for a successful consulting career are close to excessive. Amy has tried very hard, and been very patient over the years. She's built a separate life with the children and her community activities, and we try to make time for each other on weekends. But things aren't what they used to be."

"Jon," Baxter interrupted. "Are you seeing someone at McKenzie Barber?"

"No, Joe. Amanda's not with McKenzie Barber. She's with an outside firm that made our employee communications videos. We worked together for a week, and I started to spend one evening a week at her apartment. Amanda's coming down tomorrow to video the Partner's meeting, and we're going to spend the weekend together. Amanda wants a commitment. I told her that I would give her an answer this weekend. I'll introduce you to Amanda at the meeting tomorrow. She's young, bright, attractive and quick. Amanda makes me feel alive. Joe, you're the only one at McKenzie Barber I could talk about this with. You've been through several divorces. What would you recommend that I do?"

Baxter looked across the table at Grunwaldyt. There he was, McKenzie Barber's ambitious young Sigfried role model in early middle age with large cracks in the substance of both his career and marriage. He tried to draw up a picture of Amy Grunwaldyt from his memory archives and drew a blank.

"Jon, how long have you been married to Amy?"

"Fifteen years."

"And how old are your children?"

"Thirteen, eleven, nine, and seven. The two oldest are boys, and the youngest are girls."

"Then take my advice. Screw the hell out of Amanda this weekend, and tell her that it's all over Sunday morning breakfast. Then grab a mid-morning flight back to New York, and surprise Amy with a dozen red roses. Limit your hanky panky to road games with safe sex on one night stands. Listen to an old sinner who has raised a lot of unneeded havoc over the years. And now it's getting late. We've got a big day tomorrow at the funeral of McKenzie Barber." Baxter reached for the check but Grunwaldyt quickly claimed it and scrawled his name and room number on the back.

"That's the kind of answer I expected from you, Joe. And it's very sound advice," Grunwaldyt acknowledged gravely standing up from the table. Grunwaldyt accompanied Baxter to the elevator that would take him on the path to the launch.

"Joe, having you to talk with this evening has really meant a lot to me. I hope that we can remain friends for the rest of our lives. Before we break up, level with me on two matters." Grunwaldyt stood in front of the elevator blocking the button panel. "How's your health?"

"It's better, Jon. I'm in remission," Baxter lied.

"Did you really take a swing at Bob Dilger?"

"I've never hit an actuary in my life." Baxter reached around Grunwaldyt and pressed the down button.

Baxter ran into Bernie, Fitzgerald's secretary, in the pool area after he had climbed up the step from the dock. She was sitting in a plastic rope chair with her legs crossed, accompanied by a man wearing a University of Virginia tee shirt and purple running shorts.

"Good evening, Joe Baxter," she called out to him.

The man waved. Baxter knew the face. He was a middle level Partner from either Chicago or Dallas and his name was either Ray or Roy. Bernie wore a white skirt that exposed her legs mid-thigh.

"Joe Baxter," he greeted the man in the running shorts.

"Roy Benton, Joe. We've met lots of times. I'm a government services practice Partner from Atlanta. I hear you're retiring."

"This is my last Partner's meeting, Roy."

"Roy runs five miles every night before he goes to bed," Bernie explained. "He's just back from his run and he offered to buy me a drink after he has his shower. I was just beginning to explain that I was waiting here for you with some forms to be signed."

"Well maybe we can have our drink tomorrow night, Bernie," Roy said. "Joe, good luck in retirement." He extended his hand to Baxter again, waved to Bernie, and started off in a sprint to the main building.

"Boy, am I glad you came along, Joe. I couldn't get rid of that man. He used to stalk me when I was in the Chicago Office. This is so pretty and quiet this time of night. I was going to have a quiet nightcap and cigarette out here, and along came good old Roy. He considers himself a real bon vivant with the admin people. Now, Joe, where are you coming from this time of night?"

"I had dinner with Jon Grunwaldyt at the Beach Club," Baxter explained.

"Oh, Jon. He is one of my favorites. He's such a cutie. Did you ever see that picture in his office of his wife and kids? They are such a perfect looking family and Jon's so devoted to them."

"Yes, Jon has always been top notch," Baxter said supportively. "I thought he came across sincerely as a firm spokesman in those firm communications videos."

"Glen always says that all of our consultants should come across like Jon. Amanda Wasserman, our video consultant, spotted Jon's picture in a Partner's directory. I was with her at the time and she said, 'If this Jon Grunwaldyt looks 75% as good as he does in this picture, we've found our spokesman!' I set them up for a lunch, and she called back and said, 'He's beautiful.'"

"What's this Amanda Wasserman like?" Baxter asked innocently. Bernie shrugged her shoulders.

"She's like all those media people. Attractive, frenetic, a little disorganized and full of herself. She'll be here tomorrow to film the meeting. Glen wants to send copies to every client and employee of the firm. I believe Robson Allen will do the same. They are bringing in some Hollywood actor to do the voice overs after they have the video in final form. I believe she will be videoing interviews with certain retired Partners but I don't think you're on the list. Meet me by the pool tomorrow at the lunch break, and I'll try to introduce you to Amanda. You'll like her." Bernie pushed herself up from her chair. "I'm not quite tired enough to go to bed. I know where there's some cold beer if you want to have a nightcap, Joe."

Baxter studied Bernie as she stood beside him. A beer could gain him some additional information, but did he require additional information at this point in the short remainder of his McKenzie Barber career?

"Well, just one," he agreed. "It might make the perfect night cap on the historic evening."

Bernie led Baxter to a chest on a grassy spot behind the Tower facing the dock. She unlocked and opened the chest which contained an equal amount of ice and imported beer.

"Help yourself, Joe. It's Glen's private stock."

"I thought that Glen was a disciplined Mormon," Baxter said selecting a Heineken.

"Glen has an occasional beer. Tomorrow afternoon there's a boating outing with the Robson Allen people. It will be Glen, Jack, and Richard Fairbrother and the three top Robson Allen people including Carmichael. A cruiser is picking them up at one-thirty and they're scheduled to be out until 7:30. The only beer that Glen has ever tasted is Heineken and my job was to see that he had a supply on the boat. They will never miss two."

Bernie led Baxter to a path that encircled the Tower and faced to a group of maintenance buildings. They stopped for periodic sips of beer and Bernie's body brushed casually against Baxter as they walked. "Are you in the Tower or the main building, Joe?"

"I'm out at the cottages."

"My God, you're retiring and on the dais. You should be in the Tower and reasonably high up. I had very little to do with the meeting arrangements this year."

"Three nights in the cottages won't kill me, Bernie." They walked in silence. They could hear some bursts of laughter from the pool but at five minutes to eleven, Boca Mirage had grown very quiet.

"I heard that you had a fist fight with Bob Dilger. Do you suppose that you were placed in the cottages because of that?"

Baxter clasped Bernie's arm bringing a halt to their walk.

"Bernie, I have heard from three different people tonight that I assaulted Bob Dilger. To put the record straight, Bob and I had a spirited discussion and he said something unfortunate and in poor taste about my son's death. I picked up Bob by the necktie briefly to make a point. He immediately apologized, and that was the end of it. Bob has to be the source of these stories because there were just the two of us. What was between us certainly didn't rate my violent classification. I suspect there are other agendas here at work. I'm preparing a deposition for my attorney."

Bernie placed her hand on Baxter's upper arm.

"Joe, are you implying there's some kind of firm conspiracy against you?" Bernie's breast brushed against Baxter's arm.

He pulled away. He didn't trust Bernie. "I've got quite a walk ahead of me if I'm going to make bed check."

"Joe, what are you going to do after you retire from McKenzie Barber?" Bernie asked. She was holding his arm now. Baxter suspected that they weren't having this walk by accident.

"I'm from a place called Iron Creek, Minnesota. I have a long time friend named Ed Ganski who's a State Senator. Ed has a number of business interests that he wants me to get involved with. I plan to get out of New York and move back to Iron Creek," Baxter lied.

"May I share that with Glen and Jack?" Bernie asked.

"I'd prefer that you hold off until January. Just tell Glen and Jack that I have no intention to go off to a competitive firm."

"Well, I know there was more than a little concern on Bob Dilger's part when you announced your retirement. I know that he's not very happy about Harry Devonshire leading the Exec Comp part of the practice. He really wanted you, and it was a real blow when you said you weren't going to join the Dilger Group. Bob thought your health problem story was a cover for another agenda. You look awfully healthy to me."

Bernie seemed to Baxter to be in possession of a great deal of information. Did she have an intimate connection with Dilger?"

They walked in silence to the front door of the main hotel entrance depositing their empty beer cans in a trash container.

"What will happen to you after the merger, Bernie?" Baxter probed.

"I expect to follow Glen, Joe. He will be given a major practice area to run, and I expect to be his admin person. I might look at some things outside the firm."

"You could be awfully valuable to someone like Bob Dilger when they launch the Dilger Group," Baxter suggested.

They had reached the front revolving door entrance of the hotel.

"Well, Bernie," Baxter said extending his hand. "It's time for me to head off to my villa in the cottages. Thanks for the beer." Baxter turned and walked away quickly after they concluded a hand clasp. Bernie was dangerous.

Baxter entered his room and observed the form of a man in his shorts watching a television basketball game. He was a broad shouldered muscular young man in his early thirties with close cropped blonde hair and a heavily tanned face. He set down his can of Budweiser and rose to his feet after Baxter entered the room.

"Bryce Herrington," the young man said extending his hand. "They call me Bingo. I much prefer Bingo to Bryce. I'm a first year IT Partner from Dallas."

Baxter accepted a powerful handshake. Bingo wore only a pair of striped boxer shorts.

Baxter repeated his name and seated himself on the edge of the bed.

"This is Dallas/Lakers. It's an exhibition game. I'll turn it off if you like," Bingo offered.

"No need for that," Baxter said. "Is there another beer in the mini-bar?"

"I've cleaned out the Budweiser but I think there's a Strohs in back."

Baxter located the Strohs and took up his place on the edge of the twin bed closest to the TV.

"You look like a big fellow, Joe. Did you play ball sometime back?" Bingo asked.

Baxter sipped beer and watched the players line up for a free throw. It was a different game than the game he had played in the early 1950's. "I played some in high school, but that was a ways back," Baxter offered.

"I played varsity three years at Texas Lutheran. I was a shooting guard. I read the program and saw your name, Joe. I guess this is your last meeting."

"And this is your first."

"Yeah. Here I am an elected Partner of a firm about ready to be merged into another firm. This may be my last meeting too."

"Do you have an industry specialization?" Baxter asked. He sipped his beer in silence and observed the players lining up for a foul shot.

"I'm in the Government practice. State & Local Government IT engagements is my playing field. I don't take on a job less than a million in fee and I deliver. I billed out ten million dollars in fees this last year, so the big powers decided they better make me a Partner. Robson Allen has been trying to recruit me for two years, and now it looks like they got me. There's a lot of folks in consulting trying to talk to me these days. I've gone on record with Glen Fitzgerald that I carry a big piece of the Dallas Office and the firm had better start paying for what I've been throwing down to the bottom line."

"I talked with one of your Dallas IT Partners during the cocktail hour this evening. Jerry Chowman was his name. He brought up something about five year contracts with Robson Allen. Have you heard anything about that?" Baxter probed.

"I'm not signing one. For a nice average low unit Partner, like Jerry, a contract would be a hell of a deal. It would represent job security. For someone like me, it would be millstone around my neck."

Ah hah, Baxter observed to himself. 'A young Turk!'

"So what have you been doing all these years with McKenzie Barber, Joe? I don't recall ever hearing your name before."

"I've been in the Executive Compensation practice," Baxter explained.

"That's an itty bitty practice. I heard they were throwing the Comp practice in with the actuaries and getting out of the business. Maybe you're bigger in New York, but Comp has been a pretty anemic, little or no growth practice in Dallas. I caught this guy Alvardi on C Span the other night. I understand that he used to run the firm's Exec Comp practice. I guess things headed downhill after he left."

Baxter took a long swig of beer. He wasn't certain as to what could be gained from continuing this conversation.

"So when did you make Partner, Joe?" Bingo continued.

"Some time in the mid 1970's," Baxter replied.

"How come you're in the cottages? I would think the firm would have you up high in the Tower. I was having beers with some guys from the Dallas office tonight, and they were kidding me about being stuck out in the cottages."

"I didn't plan to attend this meeting. This is the best that could be done for me at the last minute."

"You should have gotten to that lady they call Bernie. She's Glen's secretary. Have you ever met her? She's a real looker and seems to have her hands around everything. Ever met her?"

"I've talked to her a couple of times," Baxter responded.

"Tell me, Bingo. As a young Partner, how do you feel about Glen and Jack's performance in running the firm in the post Buzzsaw period?"

Bingo flipped off the TV. Dallas was losing with less than a minute left.

"I thought Ross Pritchard was a pretty good man. He sure as hell championed the State & Local Government practice. I don't believe we ever had the right national leadership, but I made out pretty well on my own

521

in Dallas. I met Clyde Nickerson a couple of times, and he impressed me as a pretty slimy operator. He was some kind of an executive office admin guy that Pritchard gave too much rope to. I really liked Brett Williamson. He made a lot of sense to me. I guess the poor guy had problems keeping his fly zippered. Glen's okay, but he's never been my idea of outstanding. Jack Pinker's a guy Glen brought along for the ride. I know Glen inherited a lot of problems when he took over as Chairman, but I have to believe that Williamson would have gotten them fixed faster. If Williamson had been allowed to move up, I have to believe that we would still be independent. I sure hope that Robson Allen has better senior management than we do."

"What do you think of Lon McMasters?"

"Oh hell, Joe. You're taking me back to the beginning of time in the Dallas office. McMasters moved up to New York sometime in the mid-1980s. I must have been a first year Associate at the time. He dressed sharp and everybody in the office was scared shitless of him. I thought Williamson and McMasters would have been a good team to run McKenzie Barber. But they didn't get their chance. This firm has been too damned political to be successful in today's marketplace."

"Can you remember Ernie Grey?" Baxter asked.

"Yeah," Bingo responded with a shrug of his bare shoulders. "He was the guy between John McKenzie and Ross Pritchard. He retired and went off to some big oil company as Chairman of the Board. The old timers in the Dallas Office say nice things about him. Was he the one who left his wife to marry some young lady consultant? I was a first year Associate when he retired. That's the way it is in firms like this. You make your mark for a while, and then you're history and pretty soon you're ancient history."

Baxter drained his beer can. "I'm going to hit the sack, Bingo."

"I'm going to have another beer, Joe. I might read for a while. I've got an early tennis date in the morning. Nice to talk to you."

"Bingo, it's reassuring that young Partners like you will be taking over this firm."

"If I stay," Bingo said after Baxter turned off his bed light.

That night Baxter had a long dream that placed him back to the 1984 Partners' meeting. He was by the pool with Burke when his dream was broken by Bingo's 6AM wake-up call.

8:45 AM, Thursday, October 31st, 1991

The Rancho Mirage auditorium filled slowly. Baxter had taken an aisle seat at 8:20 AM armed with a cup of black coffee and copies of the *New York Times* and the *Wall* Street Journal. He turned to review the obituaries. Perhaps a Partner had dropped during the first of the week.

FELIX SCHWARZCHILD, POET AND TRANSLATOR, 78.
HERBERT SINGER, 87, LONG TIME LAWYER FOR THE SEC.
IRVING GREEN, A MYSTERY WRITER OF LOGIC, DIES AT 75.
MICHAEL F. KELLY IS DEAD AT 93.   TOP POLICE
COMMANDER IN THE 60'S.

Baxter was now 56. How much time did he have left? Ten, perhaps 15 years of life. He was facing, for the first time a life after McKenzie Barber.

There was a full day agenda for Thursday, October 31st. Baxter sipped coffee and re-studied the agenda.

1991 ANNUAL MEETING OF THE PARTNERS OF MCKENZIE BARBER & CO.

Thursday, October 31st, Great Hall
Boca Mirage Club

8:30 AM Greeting	Glen Fitzgerald
8:40 AM Review of US Operations	Jack Pinker
9:30 Report from the Chairman of	
Barber & Co.	Richard Fairbrother
10:30 AM	Coffee Break
11:00 AM Report from the	
Chief Financial Officer	Everctte Faunce
12:00 Summing up Questions and	
Answers	Glen Fitzgerald
12:30 to 2:00 PM	Adjournment for Lunch
2:00 to 3:30	
Robson Allen Harbridge Presentation	Alan Carmichael-Chairman

3:30	Coffee Break
4:00 to adjournment	Questions and Answers
Closing remarks	Glen Fitzgerald

FRIDAY, NOVEMBER 1ST

9:00 AM Results of balloting	Glen Fitzgerald
Going Forward, Agenda	
contingent on ballot results	Glen Fitzgerald/Dr. Armand Millet-Management Teamwork in the 1990
12:00 Adjournment	
Free afternoon for golf, tennis, fishing, bridge, etc.	
6:00 PM	Cocktail party
7:15 PM	Partners Annual Dinner (Black Tie)

Glen Fitzgerald stood with his hands clasped behind him at the far corner of the stage. He was dressed in a proper blue suit and appeared to be calmly looking out at his growing audience in the slowly filling auditorium. Bernie, wearing a red suit, walked across the floor with several folders clasped against her breast. She said something to Fitzgerald and he shook his head and she returned in brisk steps to the near end of the stage where Everette Faunce in a tan suit, struck a pose with his arms folded. Bernie said something to Faunce accompanied by a headshake and offered the folders. Faunce dismissed her with a sharp movement of his hand. Bernie walked smartly off the stage and down Baxter's aisle. She was obviously angry over something and walked half way up the aisle before disappearing out a side door. Bingo was right. Bernie was most certainly a looker.

The auditorium was filled shortly after nine o'clock. Glen Fitzgerald calmly snapped on his lapel speaker and walked amid the din in the podium. The lights were dimmed.

"Good morning Partners!" Fitzgerald's voice firmly responded throughout the auditorium. "It's time to get on with our meeting." The audience of Partners grew quiet with the exception of a few coughs and whispers. The final meeting of the Partners of McKenzie Barber had begun.

"We are beginning a historic two day meeting that will have a lasting impact on all of our careers. The Partners of McKenzie Barber are facing a unique opportunity to participate in the formation of the largest and most powerful management consulting firm in the world. You will be asked by the end of the day to decide whether you, as my partners, want to continue to compete as a single entity, or choose to be part of a stronger, more formidable firm capable of dominating any selected segment of the world-wide marketplace. You will hear briefings this morning from Jack Pinker on US operations, Richard Fairbrother, the Chairman of Barber will address you on world-wide operations, Everette Faunce, our Chief Financial Officer will bring you up-to-date on financial performance and certain balance sheet matters, and then a panel comprised of Jack, Richard, Ev and I will take questions from the floor until we break for lunch."

"After lunch, Alan Carmichael, of Robson Allen Harbridge, will be with us to present his firm's case for the merger. Richard, Jack, and I have spent a great deal of time with Alan and his senior Partners beginning in the late spring and through the summer. I have come to regard Alan as one of the premier business leaders in the world. I, for one, would be pleased to be part of a firm under Alan's overall leadership and vision. Following Alan's briefing, we will break for coffee, and after our return, Alan will take questions. We expect to adjourn around five o'clock. All of us plan to circulate this evening at the cocktail party in the Tower Club room, and the card room. We will be available to answer any questions you have. Each of you received a ballot in your advance materials package last week. If you have lost or misplaced your ballot, please see Bernice Palmer, my executive assistant. Bernie will be stationed at a help desk outside the Great Hall. Should we have some unexpected rain, the help desk will be moved into the lobby of the Tower."

"Mitchell Hilton, a Partner from our law firm, Wellington Barr, will be on hand to provide oversight to the balloting. Your ballot must be placed in one of the ballot boxes by 10 PM. The polls will close promptly at 10 PM."

"The ballot results will be tabulated, audited, and retabulated. The results will be announced as the first order of business in Friday morning's meeting. Now, Partners, please give your attention to Jack Pinker, our Deputy Chairman."

Baxter felt the impact of a body plopping into the seat on his left. He turned and recognized the bulky form of Brad Abley, his early evening cocktail companion of the evening before. "Good morning, Joe," was whispered.

Pinker began to talk his way through a series of graphic slides depicting the FY 1991 operating performance of McKenzie Barber. A theme of continued improved and successful operating performance, marred by the costs of discontinued practices and down sizing, was presented.

Abley nudged Baxter and whispered. "You can't paint shit white." Pinker concluded that McKenzie Barber had taken the steps necessary to build toward an outstanding FY 1992. The unit value was off 4.5%.

"Boy," Abley whispered. "I heard they had to pull out all stops to get it that high. Unit value was supposed to be off 18%. What the hell. We can take our money and run."

There was weak applause after Pinker stepped down from the podium. He was followed by the leonine erect figure of Richard Fairbrother. His hair was longer than Baxter remembered. His glasses hung from a gold chain around his neck, and Fairbrother carefully fitted the bridge on the furthest point of his nose. He seemed to possess a leadership presence about him that made Fitzgerald and Pinker seem like middle managers in comparison. He raised his hand and requested. "May I have the first visual, please. Following the example set for me by Mr. Pinker, I will try to dwell on our good news and go very quickly over our less good news. First of all, we had an event that began in January and carried through the spring called the Gulf War. It negatively impacted our UK business, killed our Middle East business, and generally pushed Europe with the possible exception of Germany, into a recession. Now that's the good news—."

Fairbrother was an entertaining speaker, and his presentation drew several belly laughs from the audience. The Barber story presented a scenario of a strong and proud firm which was completing a calamitous, never to be repeated performance year. There was loud and sustained applause when Fairbrother stepped down.

"God, I would have liked to have worked for that guy," was Abley's critical comment.

"Yeah," Baxter whispered back. "He knows how to paint shit white."

Baxter got up from his chair for the coffee break, leaving his *New York Times* to mark his seat. Abley followed close at his heels. They found a coffee urn next to the ballot table and Baxter drew up to the table where Bernie was flashing her best plastic smile. Baxter perched on the far end of the table with his coffee.

"Good morning, Madam. Gotten any good ballots lately," Baxter greeted her.

"Joe, don't go away. I need to talk to you," she gestured to a middle aged lady in a sun dress. "Molly, can you spell me for a coffee break?"

Molly dutifully took Bernie's place in between the two large ballot boxes. Baxter introduced Bernie to the trailing Abley and gave her his coffee. The line at the urn was longer this time. He returned after five minutes to find that Bernie and Abley had been joined by an attractive blonde wearing tight fitting white pants, a blue blouse, and flat white slippers. He read her nametag as he entered the trio. Her first name, AMANDA was in large letters at the top of her badge. Her last name was WASSERMAN was in small letters. The company affiliation 21st Century Media. It was Grunwaldyt's girlfriend.

"Amanda, this is Joe Baxter," Bernie introduced him. Amanda pulled her sun glasses up on her forehead and extended a hand. Amanda's grip was firm and Baxter observed that her nails were long and brightly polished.

"I have been looking for you, Mr. Baxter." Amanda had a throaty voice. "I understand that you are one of the retirees. I'm working on a couple of production themes at this meeting. One has to do with the retired Partners. Can you give me some time on camera?"

"Brad, here, is also a retiring Partner. I assume you will want to talk with him too," Baxter offered.

"Wow. I have a list of retired partners I want to talk with and I've found two of them at the morning coffee break. Brad, could we get together for a few minutes by the pool after the meeting today?"

"I believe that can be arranged," Brad answered with dull satisfaction.

"How about you, Joe?" Amanda turned to Baxter. He could catch a wisp of her perfume in the air as she stood in front of him.

"I can do it right now. Brad, here, can take notes for me relative to the rest of the morning meeting." Baxter produced his ballot from the inside pocket of his blazer. "I have made my voting decision." He offered the envelope to Bernie.

"I can't accept it, Joe. You must personally place the ballot in the box under the eyes of an observer. That's Wellington & Barr's election rules," Bernie responded.

"Then why don't I place the ballot in the box right now and then link back up with you, Amanda? Brad can carefully record the epic comments of Ev Faunce and report them back to me at lunch time."

"I'll find my camera man. Meet me back at this very spot in ten minutes," Amanda commanded.

Brad followed the Partners returning to the auditorium while Bernie accompanied Baxter to the ballot box. "Are you certain that you don't want to wait with your ballot, Joe?" Baxter once again felt Bernie's breast against his arm.

"No, I heard enough this morning, Bernie. My mind is set. I have no need to listen anymore to Ev Faunce or listen to Glen to respond to predictable questions with predictable answers. I'm voting now and putting that task behind me. I may vote again later in the day with a dead Partner's ballot. It is my plan to continuously vote throughout the day. Just consider this an opening ballot," Baxter said as he dropped the envelope into the large hole in the wooden ballot box in full sight of Molly. Baxter started to pull away, but Bernie caught his arm.

"I haven't finished my coffee yet, Joe." They walked back to the spot between the table and the coffee urn to await Amanda's return.

"I observed your little pre-meeting interaction with Mr. Faunce this morning. What the hell was all that about?"

"He's a very difficult man, Joe. I don't know if he'll be here after the first of the year regardless of how the ballots turn out," Bernie said. Her body seemed to tense at the mention of Faunce's name. The Partners were beginning to queue for their return to the auditorium.

"Are you sure you don't want to go back in, Joe? Glen regards Ev's presentation as key to the meeting."

"No, Bernie. I far prefer Amanda to Ev Faunce. All he's going to explain to the Partners is that our balance sheet is lousy, and the firm's only choices are to merge with Robson Allen or to downsize and cut the unit value in half for FY 1992. Nobody in that room wants to take a 50% paycut so the balloting will be a slam dunk in favor of the merger" Baxter reasoned.

Bernie took a step backward and surveyed the immediate area for possible listeners. "Joe, there is another choice. Richard Fairbrother has proposed that the US firm be formally merged into Barber. He would be Chairman of the combined firms. Glen was afraid that Richard would announce his proposal during his presentation. Glen believes he's waiting for the question and answer period after Ev Faunce's presentation. He told Glen and Jack last night that he has the English banks lined up. We could have a no merger vote and in that case, Glen says Robson Allen will walk away forever."

Amanda returned with a mustached camera man named George.

"We can do our interview under the umbrella with a background view of the bay."

Baxter started to follow only to have Bernie grip his arm.

"Joe, first, please don't mention to anyone my Richard Fairbrother's story. Second, I have to be on duty until 10:30. Will you have a late dinner with me tonight someplace outside the grounds? I have a car at my disposal and I need to talk to you."

"Glen and Jack are going off on their evening cruise and the ballot counting will be the exclusive responsibility of Wellington Barr."

"I'll see you under the moonlight between the ballot boxes," Baxter agreed and briskly followed Amanda to their appointed rendezvous at the white table facing the bay.

Amanda had a waitress setting up a coffee and iced tea service as Baxter drew up to the large white metal table. Some lapel microphones were resting on a napkin. Her cameraman was smoking a cigarette two tables beyond them.

"Joe, I thought we'd take a few minutes to get acquainted before we tape our talk," Amanda greeted Baxter and motioned for him to take a chair at her left.

"Now, Joe," Amanda opened with a supporting broad smile that displayed even white capped teeth. "Are you feeling a lot of emotion at today's meeting? That is with your retirement meeting combined with a Robson Allen merger vote decision?"

Baxter studied Amanda Wasserman's face. Did she have a live tape recorder concealed in her purse?

"Amanda, I have enjoyed a rich twenty-five year career with McKenzie Barber. It's now time for Joe Baxter to do something else. I'll leave the merger decision to the active Partners," Baxter responded blandly.

"I've gotten to know Jon Grunwaldyt pretty well over the last six months. We initially worked together on the Human Resources communications videos. Jon is one of the most camera ready executives I've encountered. He shared with me a number of stories about McKenzie Barber's history. You were in most of them. Now do I understand that you were a prominent figure in the 1984 Chairman election campaign?"

"I was hardly a prominent figure. Ernie Grey, the long time Chairman of McKenzie Barber had announced his retirement, and rightly or wrongly, did not endorse a successor. There was a run-off election between Ham Burke, the Deputy Chairman, and Ross Pritchard, the Chairman of the firm's FSO subsidiary. Mr. Burke had been instrumental in introducing me to McKenzie Barber. I had worked on several special assignments for Mr. Burke over the years. Mr. Burke asked me, among others, to take on certain tasks during his election campaign, and expressed his interest in my serving as Senior Administrative Partner for the firm following his election."

"Mr. Pritchard was chosen as Chairman in the 1984 election. Mr. Burke resigned from McKenzie Barber, and I returned to the position I've held through my retirement." Baxter noted that the clasp was open on Amanda's black purse. He would continue to measure his words carefully.

"It's my understanding that you were trained under Frank Alvardi at McKenzie Barber and succeeded him after he left McKenzie Barber for bigger things."

"If bigger things means failing at Robson Allen, and running a very small moderately successful, boutique consulting practice, mean bigger things, you're absolutely correct, Amanda," Baxter responded in a clear easily recordable voice.

"Do you plan to do something similar to Frank Alvardi? He appears to have established himself as the critic of excessive executive compensation practices."

"I have always considered Frank to be the father of excessive executive compensation practices. His current standing is a testament to Frank's nimbleness of mind in identifying the vulnerability trends of greedy American business executives and their executive compensation consulting accomplices."

Now that was quotable! Baxter silently complimented himself.

"You sound like you're ready for the talk show circuit, right now, Joe," Amanda commented. "Any predictions on the merger vote today?"

"I assume these two firms will be one big happy family after today, and combine to become the colossus of the management consulting world."

"Jon told me that among all of your many consulting skills, you have mastered the art of insincerity."

"Did he tell you that in bed, Amanda?" Baxter asked.

Amanda snapped her purse shut and called her cameraman down.

The cameraman was a bearded young man called Fred. Baxter sipped coffee and leafed through his newspapers while they set up. Then Amanda clipped Baxter's microphone on his breast pocket and swept away his coffee cup.

"This is Amanda Wasserman, at the 1991 McKenzie Barber's Partner's Meeting. I'm here with Joe Baxter, one of twelve retiring Partners at this year's meeting. Joe, you're looking back at a twenty-five year consulting career with McKenzie Barber. What would you consider the real highlights of your career.

"Well, Amanda, there have been several—," Baxter began.

Baxter did not return to the meeting. Instead he went to the pool area, drank more coffee, and leisurely read the *Wall Street Journal*. He made his way back to the door to the great hall where Bernie was manning her ballot station. His watch read ten after noon.

"The meeting seems to be running a little long, lady. Do I have time to vote again?" Baxter asked.

"My bet's on 12:30, Joe. My informant told me that Mr. Fairbrother put Mr. Faunce on the stand and was highly critical of the latitude that Glen and Jack had allowed him. He had plenty of time to say that in private, but he seemed to want to do it in front of an audience."

"If Fairbrother turns out to be Chairman," Baxter whispered. "I may retract my retirement."

The doors to the great hall suddenly swung open and Partners began to loudly stream out of the conference room. Their faces seemed upbeat. The portly figure of Brad Abley sought him out.

"Until we meet again under the stars," Baxter said taking leave of Bernie and the ballot table.

"Brad, what did I miss?" Baxter asked after they had settled in corner bar stools at the pool bar.

"Well, everybody got pretty fed up during Faunce's presentation. Then Richard Fairbrother went to a mike and started grilling him. He made Faunce go through his slides twice and had the room in stitches. Then other guys went to the mikes and asked questions. The room was damn near out of order a couple of times. Glen tried to calm the room down and Fairbrother went to the mike and said that he regarded Faunce's presentation the most amateurish he had ever encountered during his professional career. He said something to the effect that Glen should get this fool off the stage and we should get on with the business of the meeting. It was obvious to everyone in the room that Glen had no idea of how to handle Fairbrother. I guess Jack and Glen were the ones who hired Faunce and gave him all of his power. There was quite a buzz about that." Brad took a long slug of beer from his schooner glass. "Now, how was your interview with that fine looking blonde? I can't wait for mine."

Baxter floated among the Partner groups during the luncheon break. The only thing he seemed to have missed was Ev Faunce's come-uppance. There had been no coup d'etat move by Fairbrother. The last meeting of the Partners of McKenzie Barber appeared to be proceeding on schedule.

Baxter was in his seat at the Great Hall fifteen minutes in advance of 2:00 PM. He selected a seat on the aisle in the second row of the middle section and was promptly joined by Brad Abley.

"Boy, did I lose track of you out there. I had my interview with that Amanda. She seemed to be in a hurry and we only talked for about five minutes. What do you really think of Robson Allen, Joe?"

"They have been better managed and more focused in the US. They've never gotten off the ground overseas. I once flew to London back in 1988 with Charley Robson, their founder. He was on his farewell trip. He told me that McKenzie Barber had tried to buy them a couple of times. Now they are proposing to buy us."

"I've never been that impressed with them in the marketplace, Joe," Abley said shaking his head. "They were always trying to sell engagements 3,4, and 5 before they completed the first assignment they were hired for. They also staffed their jobs with junior people."

Baxter saw Glen Fitzgerald appear from backstage accompanied by a tall man with thinning brown hair wearing a grey suit with a red tie.

"That's Alan Carmichael, their Chairman," Abley said. "I've heard him speak before. He's a pretty good speaker. He's supposed to be a no-nonsense guy."

Carmichael towered over Glen Fitzgerald on the stage. Baxter estimated that Carmichael was easily 6'4 or 6'5. He placed his hands on his hips and looked out at his audience. Carmichael's pose reminded of an

Army Sergeant drill instructor looking over a company of new recruits and draftees.

Abley made nervous conversation with Baxter which he only partially absorbed as the room rapidly filled. Richard Fairbrother walked on the stage and was warmly greeted by Carmichael. Fairbrother, Baxter noted, was nearly Carmichael's size. They both dwarfed Glen Fitzgerald. Glen made his way to the podium and the din of the room silenced.

"Good afternoon, Partners. This is the moment we have been waiting for. Alan Carmichael, the Chairman of Robson Allen Harbridge, has come here today to address us. At this time last year, Alan was the last person in the world I expected to be introducing at a McKenzie Barber Partner's Meeting. Let me share with you the road we traveled to get here. It was obvious to Jack and I after you elected us in the Fall of 1990 that McKenzie Barber had to go through much transformation and change. The strategic plan initiated by the previous leadership had proved to be a failure. I don't mean to be overly critical of this leadership group. They had inherited a poorly conceived acquisition strategy of under performing practices, and made a concerted effort to repair the damage that had been their legacy. Jack and I formed a new operating committee to look hard at our business units and concluded that we had to streamline and focus. We concluded that a number of our practice units would be better off operating independently while maintaining their membership in the global network of McKenzie Barber. These plans for change were initiated by mid-April. Then on April 19th, Wellington Barr, our outside counsel contacted me to inform me that they had been contacted by Robson Allen Harbridge's attorney, Wilkenson Spear, to arrange a meeting with Alan Carmichael to discuss certain management consulting industry matters."

"I met with Al for breakfast on the following Friday morning for the first time. He came very quickly to the point. Al believed that our two firms were an excellent fit. I agree with that today. But we were not an easy fit and our discussions took a great many detours down side streets before we reached today's meeting. Jack and I, and the Operating Committee's believe that Robson Allen's term of merger are very fair and in the best interests of the Partners and employees of McKenzie Barber."

"Now let me brief you about Al Carmichael. He has some thirty years of service with Robson Allen Harbridge. Al is a MIT graduate where he completed BS and MS degrees in Mathematics. He was twice a summer intern in the office of Charley Robson, the founder and Chairman of the firm. Al joined Robson Allen in 1962, and was elected a Partner in 1970 at age 29, which made him the youngest Partner in the history of the firm. He served as Charley Robson's chief troubleshooter for two years, and then was given the assignment of opening up Robson Allen's Boston Office. This office grew to over 600 consultants and was regarded as Robson Allen's second largest practice behind New York. In 1978, Al was asked to take over the Chicago Office of Robson Allen, which he quickly turned around to be our most fierce competitor. We were relieved to see Al transferred to London in 1981 to head up Robson Allen's European Operations. Al was transferred back to the US in 1983 as Deputy Chairman and planned successor to Charley Robson. In 1986, Charley Robson announced his retirement, and the two worked closely together to position the leadership transition. Al was elected Chairman of Robson Allen Harbridge in December, 1986. Al is described as a man of vision, competence, and results at Robson Allen. Partners please welcome Alan R. Carmichael, the Chairman of Robson Allen Harbridge."

Alan Carmichael stepped to the podium in long strides. He looked over his audience for approximately ten seconds and then rested his arms on the side of the podium.

"I talked to Charley Robson, our founder, this morning, and Charley said to say hello," Carmichael spoke with a distinctive Boston accent. "I asked him if he wanted to join me this afternoon. Charley said, 'Hell no. I'd just screw things up. This combination is good for everyone concerned.' There are a great many similarities between our firms and some disparities. If you choose to join us today, I guarantee you that the disparities will be corrected rapidly."

"As most of you know, McKenzie Barber had a twenty-five year head start on Robson. John McKenzie formed McKenzie Barber in 1921, while Charley Robson convinced Jason Allen and Abner Harbridge to go in business with him in February 1946. The three of them graduated first, second and third in the class of 1942 from the Massachusetts Institute of Technology. They enlisted in the Army together, and were assigned to one of the early think tanks in Washington. A number of their projects involved working with personnel from FSO."

"Their military experience provided Charley, Jason, and Abner early exposure to the first generation of computers and the intricacies of mathematical modeling, the forerunner of a discipline which came to be known as operations research. After the war, the three young bachelors returned to New York and tried to hire out as a team. Charley received an offer from McKenzie Barber, but Jason and Abner were turned down as being too naive and inexperienced."

"Charley liked to refer to himself as the social chairman of the three young men. It was Charley who got them dates. He came to them on one Sunday night and announced, 'If I can get you guys girls, I sure as hell can get you work.' And that was the beginning of Robson Allen Harbridge."

"Robson Allen Harbridge, in its early years, had the reputation of an upstart firm. Its three founders matched youth, brilliance, ebullience, and energy against the experience and twenty-five year headstart of McKenzie Barber. And they held their own!"

"John McKenzie, the founder of your firm, first approached Charley Robson about coming to work for McKenzie Barber in the early 1950s. According to Charley, your Mr. Mac offered him a Partnership and said that he could bring his firm along with him. 'What about Jason and Abner?' Charley asked. Your Mr. Mac replied that Jason and Abner were fine young men but certainly not mature enough to be McKenzie Barber Partners. Charley then reminded Mr. Mac that he was the youngest of the three founders."

"There were additional merger discussions over the years. Mr. Mac introduced a new McKenzie Barber face into the talks during the mid 1950s. The new face was Ernie Grey, who went on to become John McKenzie's successor. Charley Robson took an instant dislike to Ernie Grey. Charley once described Ernie Grey to me as follows."

"He's one of those bigger than life types. You know, Philadelphia Main Line, World War II Naval air ace, married to a department store heiress, movie star handsome, and Chairman at age 36. All the qualities of a lower class Jewish kid from Brooklyn can really learn to hate. The merger discussion broke off in 1956 and were not resumed until this summer. Every Christmas season, Charley would carefully select a card to be sent to Ernie Grey. He would have Abner and Jason reluctantly sign it and send it off with a pledge to pass up McKenzie Barber over time. A pledge that was ultimately fulfilled."

"Charley Robson established McKenzie Barber as the enemy of every consultant at Robson Allen. We awoke each morning with McKenzie Barber on our minds. They were the enemy who stood between us and our goals. When a consultant strayed to join McKenzie Barber, they were ostracized and became non-persons. When someone from McKenzie Barber came to us, they were greeted as delivered souls from hell. We were brought up to hate McKenzie Barber."

"Over time, the firms became somewhat similar, but there were some gaping differences. Robson Allen's roots were in information technology. Robson Allen grew organically. McKenzie Barber made a number of acquisitions in the early 1980s. We wanted them too, but McKenzie Barber paid more. These acquisitions turned out to be troubled businesses. McKenzie Barber, following their 1984 Chairman election, pursued new industries and new directions. Robson Allen stuck to its knitting i.e. providing IT solutions to functional areas and to the forward strategic drives of our clients. Our US practice flourished and your practice floundered. We were focused and you were not."

"Overseas, it was another matter. Barber continued to dwarf our International practice. Barber was more focused than the US firm." Carmichael paused to look over his audience.

"When the opportunity developed to resume merger discussions after some 26 years, the combination made an awful lot of sense. Now I'd like to show you some performance comparisons of our two firms from 1984 to present."

The lights were dimmed and a series of comparative revenue and profitability charts were displayed simultaneously on three screens behind and to the right and left of the speaker. 1984 showed McKenzie Barber substantially ahead world-wide with what appeared to be a ten percent lead in the US. Barber was easily double the size of Robson Allen International. Partnership income for the two firms had been about equal in 1984. The years moved forward with the Robson Allen revenue line intersecting and proceeding to gap the McKenzie Barber revenue line. The McKenzie Barber Partners were well acquainted with their firm's performance after 1984. It was the first time they had seen the comparable performance of Robson Allen.

"Boy, he really knows how to hurt a guy," Abley whispered to Baxter.

Robson Allen International had fallen further behind Barber in 1991, and the McKenzie Barber Partners broke into applause accompanied by a few shrill whistles.

"I heard Barber cooks their books," Abley commented to Baxter.

"As you can see, the combination of the two firms makes a good deal of business sense. Our counsel has assured us that the probability of a regulatory body interfering with this merger is remote. Upon the completion of our merger, I will serve as Chairman, and Richard Fairbrother will serve as Deputy Chairman world-wide and Chairman of International Operations. Our Ed Bassonette, who has been my right hand man for Operations, will serve as Deputy Chairman for US operations. I am now prepared to take some questions from the floor."

The lights went back on and the US Partners studied one another's faces. Fairbrother went to one of the aisle microphones.

"Al, I believe it would be helpful if you could share with the McKenzie Barber Partners, the plan for integrating the two firms. I believe this is a time for absolute candor."

"Richard, as you well know by now," Carmichael replied. "At Robson Allen Harbridge, it's always time for complete candor. We're light on hyperbole, high on measurement, and demanding on goal achievement. Let's start with International. We expect you to sort the combined operation and will look to you and the management group you select to determine which Partners and consultants fit and which Partners and consultants are redundant. I would also look to you as a key resource in running the combined firm. We are going to operate with nine board members, four from McKenzie Barber and four from Robson Allen. I will chair the board. Then official date of the merger will be January 1st, 1992. The target date for the completion of the integration of the two firms will be April 1, 1992. This should provide us ample time for a timely, but thoughtful reorganization of the two firms."

"Thank you, Al," Fairbrother acknowledged. "I thought it best for you to state the leadership and transition plan on record for the Partners in this room."

Baxter then observed Jerry Chowman, the Dallas Partner and cocktail hour companion of the evening before, advancing to a microphone.

"Al, I'm Jerry Chowman from the Dallas Office. What will Glen and Jack's role be in the merged firm?"

Carmichael smiled. "Glen and Jack will continue in their present roles through March 31st. We will identify leadership positions consistent with their experience in consulting practices. They will assume these responsibilities effective April 1st."

"May I ask you another question?"

"You may ask as many questions you like, Jerry," was the reply from Carmichael.

"There's a rumor that after the merger is approved, we will be asked to sign five year contracts. Can you comment on that?" There was silence in the room.

"As I told you previously, candor is one of the hallmarks of Robson Allen Harbridge. Many of you will be asked to sign five year contracts. Some of you will be offered severance arrangements and early retirement. We plan to assess every McKenzie Barber Partner following the approval of the merger. Dr. Gilbert Ranglinger, our senior Human Resources Partner will lead the assessment process. We call him Dr. Gil. We are a people business, and are very proud of our human resources management skills. I pledge to you that every Partner in this room will know their career path with the merged firm by March 31, 1992."

"Sounds like they got themselves a Clyde Nickerson too," Abley whispered to Baxter.

Baxter's roommate, Bingo went to the microphone. "Mr. Carmichael, I'm Bryce Herrington, first year Partner, also from Dallas. My question is this. Suppose the Partners in this room vote to stay independent? Then what will Robson Allen do."

"I assume you were in the room for the graphic presentation. Should this merger initiative be rejected by the McKenzie Barber Partners, life will go on for both firms. We believe that Robson Allen will continue to open the gap in the US and will make up the gap in international. Our Partners will out-earn McKenzie Barber's Partners. Our growth will provide the capacity to make more Partners and McKenzie Barber will continue to slip. If this merger is rejected, we are unlikely to pursue this initiative again."

"Mr. Carmichael, I'm whipping Robson Allen's ass in my segment of the Southwest market. There are others in this room who can deliver the same testimony. Maybe we should talk to Mr. Fairbrother into coming over here to be our Chairman. We can throw out all those old farts who have screwed up this firm and show you another set of charts in 1998." The room burst into applause.

"Who in hell is he?" Abley asked Baxter.

"A first year Partner with good numbers who obviously believes they will continue," Baxter answered.

"Mr. Herrington, with your attitude and self-confidence, you sound like a pretty good prospect to run this combined firm by the year 2010. I would hope that you would stick around and go for it."

Light applause followed Bingo's return to his seat.

The lanky figure of Bob Dilger advanced to a side aisle speaker.

"Al, Bob Dilger, National Director of the Benefits and Compensation practice here. As you are aware, we have plans on the drawing board to separate our practice out as an independent firm. Our spin-off has been delayed by the merger discussions. In the event of the merger, will you honor the commitment for practice's independence?"

"Yes. Any previous discussions to separate out non-core businesses will be honored, and any new proposals will be promptly studied and acted upon. We will set the combined firm right in ninety days time from the effective merger date."

A woman partner whom Baxter didn't recognize advanced to a center mike. "Mr. Carmichael. What will the combined firm be called?"

"This is not final, but our preliminary thoughts will be to call the combined firm, Robson-Barber." There were some gasps in the room. "As we see it, we're giving up two founder's names and you will be giving up one."

"There goes old John McKenzie," Abley commented.

The questions continued through four o'clock, well past the scheduled coffee break. The question of Partner job security was repeated with assorted phrasing. Carmichael finally appeared to lose patience with his questioners. He made an exaggerated look at his watch.

"I'm afraid I've run over my time and shortchanged you on the coffee break. Let me make a summary statement that will address the last five questions."

"One, the merger is logical and will create a larger and more successful combined firm. It is in your best interests and our best interests for this merger to happen."

"Two, liabilities of McKenzie Barber pension plan will be assumed and honored by the combined firm."

"Three, this is not quite a merger of equals. We will determine within the first ninety days whether Partners fit into the plan for the combined firm. Those who fit will be offered the security of five year employee agreements. Those Partners who choose not to be part of the new firm will be provided a standard severance arrangement consistent with your McKenzie Barber Partner agreements. Those Partners for whom we don't see a future will be provided a similar severance arrangement."

"Good people do well with Robson Allen Harbridge. Mediocre people and politicians don't last. We have expended a good deal of management time over the past four months in the study of this merger. We have committed on assuming the liability for the pension plan and traded off on some other issues. Management control of the new firm was a non-negotiable item. It is our conclusion that this merger will work to everyone's benefit. The choice is in your hands. I look forward to shaking your hands as my Partner in the most powerful professional services firm the world has ever known. Thank you."

Carmichael strode from the podium where Glen Fitzgerald greeted him with a handshake on his way to take his place.

"Thank you, Al. All of us appreciate your candor. Partners, let's take a fifteen minute coffee break and have a wrap-up session. Remember your ballot must be in by 10PM."

Baxter studied the Partner's faces during the coffee break.

"What do you think, Joe?" Abley asked.

"I believe we are retiring at exactly the right time, Ken. The merger will be approved."

Bingo joined him for dinner. He was showered, dressed in the standard blue blazer, white shirt, striped tie and grey slacks combination and nursing a beer in front of the six o'clock news when Baxter entered the room.

"I heard a few things about you today, Joe," Bingo greeted him. Baxter quickly undressed and showered without a reply. He returned to the room in a towel and opened a beer from the mini-bar.

"People told me that you used to be the right hand man of Ernie Grey, the old Chairman, before Pritchard. That was before the firm started slipping in 1984. Boy, according to those slides, we sure slipped under Pritchard. The guys at lunch talked about this personnel guy named Clyde Nickerson, who practically ran the firm for Pritchard. I concluded that if we could shed ourselves of all these incompetents, we could, over time, make this firm pretty successful again. I was very impressed with Fairbrother, the Brit. I loved the way he undressed Faunce. I just don't think Glen and Jack are up to running this firm. They know it too. That's why they went off running to Robson Allen looking for a merger. What do you think, Joe?"

"I think it's time for McKenzie Barber to merge with Robson Allen. My ballot was in this morning."

Bingo accompanied Baxter to the cocktail party which was held in the grassy quadrangle across from the entrance to the Great Hall. After the bartender poured him a Canadian Club, he found himself facing Grunwaldyt and Amanda. Their faces were sullen as Baxter moved in front of them. Then they forced smiles of greeting.

"Well Jon, what did you think of today's presentation?" He noted that he had Bingo at his side and had been joined by Abley.

"I liked Carmichael's candor," Jon responded predictably. Bingo stepped forward and introduced himself to Grunwaldyt and Amanda. "I thought you made a very bold statement, Bingo. Some one had to make the case for remaining independent. In the old days, Joe would have been the one to go to the mike."

"It's my last meeting, Jon. I want to get my watch and leave peacefully." He turned to Amanda. She was still wearing her blouse, white pants outfit of the morning. "How's your retired Partner's interview schedule proceeding? I understand you met with Ken." Abley waved from his position at the rear of the group and Amanda forced a smile.

Grunwaldyt looked at his watch. "I have to attend a joint Partner dinner on the yacht."

"Don't miss your boat, Jon," Amanda reminded. "And don't forget to call your wife tonight."

Grunwaldyt set his glass at the edge of the bar. "Well, I guess I better go." He brushed by Baxter and whispered, "I'm going to be grilled again on the Hortense Food litigation. I just may wind up in that group that have no future."

"I really must get changed," Amanda said excusing herself.

"That is one fine ass," Bingo observed as Amanda worked her way through the crowd. "Anybody around here taking care of that?"

"I believe she's a single parent and a devoted mother of three," Baxter commented.

"She looks in mint condition to me," Bingo said. "What do you say we try some dinner, Joe?"

They settled into a table in the center of the main hall room. A ten piece band clad in blue tuxedos played Deep Purple.

"How many women Partners do we have?" Bingo asked.

"Maybe 30," Baxter estimated.

"The band comes with the Club," Abley explained. "I remember the years before we had any women Partners. I guess Alice Dungler was the first one back in the late 70s, but she resigned the day after they confirmed her election."

"Alice Dungler used to be with McKenzie Barber?" Bingo seemed astounded.

"She was a Director level in the LA IT practice. She started her own software company on the side and decided that she preferred running her own business to being a McKenzie Barber Partner," Baxter explained. He ordered a bottle of red wine to go with their steaks.

"Did you guys know Alice Dungler?" Bingo asked respectfully. Baxter allowed Abley to answer first.

"Not well. She came out once to consult on a systems planning engagement with specialty steel company in Pittsburgh. Pittsburgh was her home town, I guess. She gave us three days and told Ted Banzhoff, the Partner, that we were doing it all wrong. They wound up yelling at each other. She was a big woman and had a foul mouth on her, but she was brilliant. And she turned out to be right. The job blew up and really set Banzhoff's career back. Nobody had any confidence in him after that."

Bingo looked to Baxter. "I knew her reasonably well. I met her at a Manager's meeting in 1976 and we stayed in touch over the years. She asked me to come in as her Admin guy in the summer of 1977, but that was the year I was elected a Partner."

"You picked a Partnership with McKenzie Barber over an opportunity to get in one the ground floor with a company like Dungler Technologies? Have you ever estimated the kind of money you would be worth today? What was the specific job she offered you?"

"Vice President Finance and Administration. I've never bothered to calculate my capital appreciation because there's no sense in looking back. I am the person you see across the table, Bingo. And for better or worse, this is my last Partner's meeting and probably the last meeting of the Partner's of McKenzie Barber."

Bingo shook his head to Abley. "I'd jump at a chance like that. There's an ex-McKenzie Barber Partner running Dungler Tech now. Did he take the job you were offered?"

Baxter took a drink of water to clear his throat and then began to deliver a history lesson on the 1984 election which included Bob Friedman's run for Deputy Chairman. His narration extended through the wine service, dinner order, and the serving of salads.

"So this Friedman was dead in the water after he missed getting elected as Deputy Chairman? He then goes to work for Alice Dungler, and now he's CEO of the largest software company in the world, and he wasn't even an IT Partner. This is a screwy world. Being good may not be good enough to get a guy ahead. What happened to Burke?"

"He's been living in Europe providing occasional advice on major transactions. If the de Hartogue investment group had been successful in acquiring Hortense Foods, Burke would have been named CEO. Instead the company was acquired by management who overpaid."

"We're getting sued over that. I heard the Partner on the engagement could wind up taking the fall for the pro-formas the firm put together."

"That Partner will be nearly retired by the time that case is settled. The firm can't fire him because that would imply a performance problem. They are unlikely to promote him, but need him around for depositions. That poor devil will spend the rest of his active career in medium limbo and when the dust is settled, he is likely to be early retired," Baxter pronounced.

"There had to be someone over him who approved the scope of the work from a risk management perspective," Bingo countered.

"Any proposal in the Dallas Office over one million has to have a second partner review."

"The New York Office was in chaos. McMasters had just been installed as Managing Partner. The Partner was ambitious, was given encouragement to steam ahead by Clyde Nickerson, and got himself in over his head. He was the hero of the New York Office in 1990."

"You're talking about Jon Grunwaldyt, aren't you, Joe?" Abley interjected.

"Jon Grunwaldyt, the firm spokesman on the videos?" Bingo was aghast. "I thought he was on the way to becoming the next Chairman after Glen."

"Careers can become a little fragile around McKenzie Barber when a guy gets too full of his own juice," Abley commented.

They talked for another hour with Baxter and Abley exchanging folklore relative to the McKenzie Barber of the past.

"It's ten to ten," Abley announced finally after a series of furtive glances at his watch. "The balloting will be done and my prediction is that the Partners of McKenzie Barber will vote themselves out of existence."

"I've got to meet a lady at the ballot box," Baxter got up from the table.

"I'm going off to the poker game in the tower," Bingo announced.

"I'll go with you, Bingo," Abley followed. Bingo gave Baxter a how-could-you-stick-me-with-this-guy-look and departed with Abley at his side.

The ballot boxes were being sealed in the presence of two Wellington Barr attorneys when Baxter drew up to the table. Molly, Bernie's heavy set companion of the morning was chattering with the lawyers as the ballot boxes were placed on a dolly.

"And where's my friend Bernie?" Baxter asked.

"She went off with Mr. Fairbrother about an hour ago. I believe he was taking her to dinner," Molly replied cheerfully.

"Well I'm certain that she left for dinner with a good appetite. Was the evening balloting heavy?"

"The last ballot I can remember was around seven o'clock," Molly said.

Baxter was not ready to return to his modest room in the cottages. It was the night that McKenzie Barber had voted itself out of existence. He started in the direction of the Tower and encountered Amanda smoking a cigarette on a lounge chair facing the pool.

"Joe," she called off to him standing up from the lounge chair. Amanda had changed into a white suit with a skirt that settled at mid thigh. Baxter decided that Amanda had great looking legs. "Have you seen Jon?"

"I believe he was whisked away by the Robson Allen entourage." Baxter drew up within two steps of Amanda and could smell her perfume. Had she made love with Grunwaldyt the night before? Baxter wondered.

"I need a favor, Joe. Could you escort me up to the Tower cocktail party? Jon may be there, but I don't want to go up by my myself."

Baxter extended his arm and Amanda locked a hand around his bicep. "I understand that Jon told you about us," Amanda said as they crossed the concourse to the door to the Tower.

"I said something indiscreet this morning," Baxter confessed. "You angered me when you were trying to surreptitiously record me this morning. I thought it was a cheap journalist's trick."

"Journalists, these days, are expected to gather and deliver information, analysis, insights, and opinions. I do what I have to. What made Jon tell you about us last night?"

"Jon has serious concerns about his future right now. We go back a ways. He needed someone to talk to last night and he told me all."

They stood in front of the elevator bank. Amanda looked a little hard in the bright lights of the lobby. Baxter concluded that she was in her very late thirties.

"I assume that you're not going to compromise Jon and me with others."

The elevator opened and three middle-aged Partners emerged exchanging handshakes drunken pleasantries with Baxter. They looked over

Amanda and Baxter encircled her waist possessively with his arm and steered her into the elevator.

"We'll confuse them. Now they'll think I'm hitting on you," Baxter said after the elevators closed.

"Are a lot of people at McKenzie Barber sleeping together?" Amanda asked as the elevator floor lights popped forward toward the 36th Floor of the Tower.

"No more than any business or government organization of comparable size. McKenzie Barber may be at the norm. Perhaps the Robson Allen merger will provide a real shot in the arm for increased hanky panky."

The elevator came to a stop on the 36th floor, and they stepped into the roar of a large cocktail party crowd. Baxter's arm remained around Amanda's waist and he pecked her quickly on the neck in full view of the group waiting to board the elevator. "I'm just trying to throw people off the scent," he whispered to Amanda.

The 36th Floor Cathedral Room encircled the elevators. As they edged through the crowd, Baxter's mind went back to the 1984 Chairman election. The faces were different, but the noise seemed to be the same volume.

"I believe this best course of action is for us to secure a drink and work our way around the room three times. If we haven't located Jon by then, he's not here."

Baxter had been attending Partner's Meetings since 1978. The 36th Floor Cathedral Room had high ceilings, cathedral windows, and a panoramic view of the Boca Raton area. Baxter estimated on the basis of tradition that forty percent of the Partners had left the resort reservation in order to explore the fleshpot bars of Fort Lauderdale. Fifty or sixty assembled in the downstairs card room for the annual bridge tournament with a somewhat smaller group of two dozen poker players playing into the night for high stakes. A smaller group was scattered in the front bar lounge off the main dining room or across the bay at the Beach Club.

Sooner or later all parties assembled at the 36th Floor Cathedral Room for a nightcap. It was generally half filled at the post 10PM, pre-11PM period. Tonight the room was packed. Baxter recognized old faces and new faces as he maneuvered Amanda to the bar.

"We'll load up here and move west," Baxter instructed Amanda. The faces of the McKenzie Barber Partners seemed somber and resolved. There was no absence of smiling and laughter, but it seemed forced and shrill to Baxter. The people in the Cathedral Room appeared to be working hard at having a good time.

He armed Amanda with a white wine spritzer, and himself with a Canadian Club and they proceeded to edge their way around the room. Every few feet someone greeted them. The opening questions ranged from,

HOW DID YOU FEEL ABOUT TODAY'S MEETING?

to

COULD YOU WORK FOR THOSE GUYS?

There was an occasional 'Why didn't we just combine the two firms and make Fairbrother the Chairman instead of setting up those two lightweights?' There was a general bitterness toward Fitzgerald and Pinker, and outright hate for Ev Faunce. Baxter introduced Amanda at each stop as a journalist covering the meeting and inquired as to Jon Grunwaldyt's whereabouts. Midway through the room, they encountered Bob Dilger who was standing framed by one of the cathedral window surrounded by his actuarial Partners.

"Joe!" he called out to Baxter.

"Do you know who he is?" Baxter whispered to Amanda.

"I do and I'd like to say hello to him. The Dilger Group could well become one of our clients." Amanda flashed a smile and waved.

The group accepted Amanda and Baxter into their center and closed around them.

"Well, Joe, there's still time to reconsider," a scholarly actuary named Barstow said with a smile.

"There's a lot of folks who want to sign up with us after today's chat from Mr. Carmichael," Dilger announced waving his glass of Scotch at Baxter. Baxter noted that Dilger was well ahead of him in alcohol assumption.

"I'm retiring, Bob. I may teach and write," Baxter responded.

"Teaching and writing is fine, Joe. If you go off consulting after retirement, you have to have the firm's permission or you'll be in violation of retired Partner's agreement."

"Which firm is that, Bob? McKenzie Barber is going to vote itself out of existence tonight. The Dilger Group is unlikely to be in operation before April 1. I would expect that there will be a lot of forced early retirements this Spring. The new firm will get themselves sued if they try to tie up people's ability to earn a living." Baxter exchanged glares with Dilger.

"Joe and I were trying to locate Jon Grunwaldyt," Amanda interjected. "Have any of you seen him?"

"Jon's over with the Robson Allen people. Al Carmichael wanted a personal report on the Hortense Foods litigation. We've some litigation pending, and I think Jon's about third in line after McMasters, who's got the Federal Government after FSO, and a Los Angeles IT Partner who has been implicated in some kind of computer fraud," Dilger blurted out.

"Carmichael's been briefed on the litigation by Ed Bassonette, his number 2. Now he wants to personally review the legal problems."

One member of Dilger's group raised his finger to his lips.

"The Robson Allen people are very thorough, and Al Carmichael is supposed to run a tight ship. I'm sure that they have had their fair share of litigation over the years."

Amanda passed out business cards. "We should talk as the time gets closer to launch the Dilger Group. We'd like to help you to build your marketing communications strategy."

"We'll have to look at a long lunch, Amanda," Dilger acknowledged.

"Please send Jon Grunwaldyt our way," Baxter said steering Amanda away from the nucleus of the Dilger Group.

"Jon told me that you slugged Bob Dilger," Amanda said after they plodded ten feet forward.

"That story has been embellished and exaggerated. I haven't hit anyone since I was a junior in high school. I have had the pleasure of watching Bob grow from a well meaning, country boy actuary from Indiana into a flaming, self important asshole. Wait until he has his Chairman cards printed. Bob will move his game up to a new level of pomposity."

Amanda locked Baxter's hand into hers and pushed forward through the crowd.

"This is hopeless. Why don't we bring our drinks down to my room and wait for Jon to call," Amanda proposed.

Even Amanda Wasserman had a room in the Tower. It was a small third floor facing the concourse. Amanda motioned for Baxter to sit while she played her phone mail. He took a seat on the edge of the bed leaving ample room for Amanda to join him after she concluded reviewing her phone mail.

"Eleven calls and not one from Jon." Amanda remained at the desk and lit a cigarette.

"How much trouble is Jon in, Joe?"

"I wasn't aware that Jon was in any kind of trouble until dinner last night. He's been the New York Office golden boy for two or three years now. He is unlikely to be fired, but he will not be entering the merged firm in a favorable light. Jon has moved pretty fast over the last four years. His days of moving fast may be over. He's going to have to live as a shelf-sitter for a while. Jon might have to learn to live with a compensation adjustment."

"Do you know his wife?"

"I've talked with her briefly over the years at McKenzie Barber gatherings. Her name is Amy. I believe they were engaged when Jon was a senior in college. She's very much the attractive young Greenwich matron."

"I've seen the pictures of Amy and the kids. He showed them to me in our first meeting. She bores the hell out of Jon. He knows he's in a rut. Jon needs to be with someone who can help him with his career. He has the potential to be a CEO someplace."

"Behind every great man is a woman," Baxter said patting the space on the bed beside him.

The phone on the desk rang sharply. Amanda answered it on the third ring. "Jon, are you all right? I looked for you all over 36. Someone said that you had to meet with the Robson Allen people. Have you eaten yet? Come by my room. It's 316. I'll have a sandwich sent up. A bottle of champagne too? You're making this evening sound very promising. Give me ten minutes, my darling."

Amanda Wasserman stood up from the desk. "Jon will be here shortly. Thank you for everything, Joe."

Baxter pushed himself up from the bed and blew Amanda a kiss. "Give my best to Jon."

Baxter walked slowly back across the grounds to his room in the cottages. There was no Bernie, and certainly no Amanda to share his bed. Tomorrow morning would mark the announcement of the end of McKenzie Barber. He would sit on the dais the following evening as a retiree and then run out the clock on his consulting career. He started to call Ernie Grey's New York apartment number, but hung up two digits short of a connection.

Baxter took his place next to Abley on the retired Partner's dais shortly after seven o'clock on Friday evening. The chairs in the Great Hall had been rearranged into a dining room, and a dais for the retired Partners had been formed on the stage to face the dining audience.

"Didn't see much of you today, Joe?" Abley commented as he slid into the seat on the aisle next to Baxter.

"I stayed long enough for Glen to confirm the ballot results, and then I rented a bicycle and toured the area. Now I'm back for my watch," Baxter explained.

"Boy, that roommate of yours has a high opinion of himself," Abley commented.

"Bingo is a young Turk. You give this new firm a chance and they'll drain that confidence right out of him." Baxter did not mention that Bingo's bed had not been slept in Thursday evening.

The dais was now filled. There were fourteen retiring Partners on the stage and a booklet had been prepared with bios and head sketches of each of the retired Partners. The Partner on Baxter's right turned out to be a Barber Partner named Cyril Cardwell. He was bald, heavily tanned, and wore a white dinner jacket. Baxter scanned Cardwell's biography in the booklet.

Cyril Cardwell was born in 1931, and had an Eaton/Cambridge pedigree. He had served in the Cold Stream Guards, joined Barber in 1954 and was elected a Partner in 1963. He had held a succession of Group Managing Partners positions with a 1986 Managing Partner posting in the Middle East in Bahrain. He had returned to England as a Group Managing Partner in 1990, and was retiring after 36 years of service. He had been knighted in 1991. Cardwell had been a Barber Board member since 1975.

Seated on Cardwell's right was a fast talking Chicago Office Banking practice Partner named Seymour Dworkin. Dworkin had a well deserved reputation for messing up large scale Banking IT jobs. Pinker had engineered an early retirement for him shortly past Dworkin's 50th birthday. Baxter reviewed the other retired Partners names on the list. Each possessed a flawed reputation. The group represented a strategic thinning out of the Partner herd. Baxter wondered if he was the only one lodged in the cottages.

Cardwell sized up Dworkin after a minute of conversation and turned to Baxter.

"Baxter," he said scanning the program. "You were the top remuneration man for a time. You replaced that Italian chap."

"Cyril Cardwell," he said offering Baxter his hand.

"Brad Abley, Cleveland Office." Abley's hand reached across Baxter at the prospect of having someone new to talk with. Cardwell took quick note of Abley's rented tuxedo and coldly joined the handshake.

"You're retiring at the US Partner's meeting?" Baxter asked.

"We're indeed honored, Sir Cyril."

"It was Fairbrother's offer. He called me in and said that with all the conflicting year ends of the merged firms that if we were going to get it done properly, I should sit with the Americans. It was Bruce's way of getting me retired by the end of the year. We've been treated like royalty. First class travel, penthouse suite in the Tower. Private dinner with the Robson Allen people."

"According to the program, you certainly have had an illustrious career with Barber," Baxter pandered.

"Yes, it's been quite a ride. Some 37 years long and here I am retiring on the Yank Partner's dais. Life's full of ironies and ambiguities, and we're cast to make the most of it." Cardwell took a long sip of his white wine. "A cheap California. I hope they do better on the red. I believe I met you, Joe, briefly back in the 1980s. You were a remuneration man and traveling with Burke."

"It was at a dinner at Simpsons in 1983." Baxter could not recollect meeting Cardwell.

"I remember you as Burke's man. Burke was Ernie Grey's man, and you were Burke's man."

Abley turned his chair and was facing them with his elbows resting on his knees as if he were part of the audience to a historic conversation.

"I see Burke from time to time. He serves as some kind of an advisor to that de Hartogue woman. Do you know the name? She was a consultant in our Paris office briefly in the 1970s, married her way into the family, and now she's running the whole bloody place."

"She was on one of my international engagements back in 1977. Dominique came across a highly intelligent young woman."

"She has been dubbed the dragon lady of French industry by the European business peers. This, of course, makes Burke's wife, Madam de Robilliard, quite jealous because she believes she has earned the designation."

"What sort of things does Burke provide advice to Madame de Hartogue on?" Baxter asked.

"Mostly M & A matters. It's surprising that anyone would engage Burke to help on M & A matters after his track record at McKenzie Barber. Are you in touch with Burke?"

"From time to time."

The soup course was served with Cardwell waving off his soup.

"Were you close to Ernie Grey?"

"Somewhat. I see him from time to time. He's Chairman of IPCO and due for his second retirement next month."

"I saw Ernie several times during my Middle East stint. He brought Toni, his young wife, with him once. We entertained at our villa. I have a similar model. The two of them still correspond, and we will be looking in on them at their Naples place before we head back. I understand that Ernie has taken up rollerblade skating. We may be treated to an exhibition of his newly acquired skills on Sunday. I, of course, will provide him with a complete report of the meeting."

"Did you ever meet John McKenzie?" Abley asked Cardwell across Baxter. Cardwell made Abley repeat the question before he consented to answer.

"He was pointed out to me once in the 1950s. He was the man who kept Barber in business in the 1950s. The least Richard could have done was to fight a little harder to keep the old man's name on the door. He made a magnificent figure, a large man with flowing white hair and a handle bar mustache. The young man who was standing next to me in the hallway

555

whispered to me, 'I'll bet that's what God looks like.' Mr. Mac smiled at us as he walked by. And that's as close as I got to him."

A salad course was served, interrupting their stream of conversation. Cardwell waved off the salad dressing service.

"You never can tell what they put in the banquet dressings. They had a big sendoff for me after I came back from Bahrain. I became quite ill and it was tracked back to the salad dressing. I'm very careful what I take in these days."

"How long were you in the Middle East?" Baxter asked.

"The better part of four years. There were two of us who represented Richard Fairbrother's competition to succeed Sir Thomas as Chairman. Fairbrother reorganized as Chairman. He shipped his two principal rivals out. Archie McCload was sent off to Hong Kong, and I drew the Middle East. Fairbrother wanted us out of sight so that he could slip his boys in place. Archie has two years left before retirement in Hong Kong before he gets his watch."

"How did you like the Middle East?"

"We loved it as a life style. It was a very comfortable backwater to end my Barber career. I went there prepared to make the most of it. Then we had all that funny business with the FSO people."

"Funny business?" Baxter questioned.

Cardwell arched an eyebrow. "I don't suppose you New York people were very close to the FSO people?"

"FSO has always represented a distinctly separate business. It was organized as the single subsidiary of an S Corporation owned by the Partners of McKenzie Barber. Mr. Mac had acquired FSO as a favor to the Federal Government shortly before the Korean War. The US Partners had no contact with FSO other than financial statements. There was an occasional modest profit distribution to the US Partners, but FSO really didn't make much money until General Pritchard was hired," Baxter recited.

"I had inherited some major operations services contracts with the Arab states. My predecessors had positioned the work with FSO people. Your General Pritchard and our Mr. Fairbrother were closely involved in originally selling the business. We were the prime contractor and FSO was the sub-contractor. The contracts represented an increasingly larger percentage of our Middle East business over time. That fellow Williamson took over in 1985, the year before I came out. My instructions from Fairbrother were to provide gentle administrative oversight of the FSO contracts, and make certain that we were taking our fair share of the income. I was to concentrate my efforts on developing Middle East work for our core services. Therefore, I took one long initial look at the contracts and relationships."

"What I found was bloody appalling. FSO was overcharging us. We were overcharging the client, and FSO was paying bribes. I went to Fairbrother straight on and presented my findings. He agreed to review it with Pritchard, but asked me to take it up quietly with Brett Williamson."

"Williamson, of course, maintained that he had no idea of what I was talking about. I demanded a meeting and he agreed to meet me in London. The meeting was postponed three times, and we didn't meet until the summer of 1987. I kept Fairbrother informed, and he said that he had reviewed the matter with General Pritchard, and it was up to Williamson and me to quietly and amicably work the matter out."

"When we finally met, Williamson took the position that the contracts had been structured to benefit all parties. He said that we had the option of exiting with one year's notice, but that might be unwise for the client. The contracts were primarily related to defense communications. We managed the systems, supplied the technicians, and trained their personnel. The Middle East was heating up. The Arab States were not well positioned to change their service providers. Williamson told me that I should sit tight." Cardwell shrugged his shoulders and began to pick at his salad. "I asked Fairbrother to get me out of there. He took his time, but I came home in the Spring of 1990, about three months in advance of the Iraqi invasion of Kuwait."

"Williamson was moved up the New York Office Managing Partner position, and then mysteriously left McKenzie Barber at a time when there was talk of him succeeding General Pritchard. I assume the funny business has been corrected by now. Williamson's successor was a fellow named McMasters from the New York Office. You probably know him."

Baxter nodded.

"I offered to brief McMasters, but he wrote back and said he had enough information already. I assume the matter has been disclosed to the Robson Allen people in some form. And you, Joe," Cardwell said patting Baxter's hand. "You are the first one I have ever told that story to. Here I am sitting on a retirement dais a long way from home observing the firm where I spent my career being consumed by its most avaricious rival."

Cardwell raised his glass and clinked it against Baxter's glass. He said little else for the remainder of the evening.

The speeches started shortly after the dessert had been served.

Glen Fitzgerald read a prepared speech honoring the career achievements of the retired Partners. Baxter suspected that Bernie had drafted the speech. An abbreviated bio of each Partner was read by Glen Fitzgerald in a monotone. Each retiree would then walk to the rostrum where they were presented with their retirement watches. Abley went first, followed by Baxter. Richard Fairbrother took Fitzgerald's place for presentation to Cardwell which he accompanied with a splendid little speech. The remaining Partners bowed out to Fitzgerald's monotone. A long applause followed the watch presentation to the fourteenth retiring Partner, a greying managerial accounting consultant from the San Francisco office named Wilkenson.

Glen then returned to the podium.

"Well, Partners, we have assembled here at the Boca Mirage to decide the future of McKenzie Barber. We have listened, discussed, and voted. A majority of the Partners have voted for the combination of our firm with Robson Allen Harbridge. We will go through a transition period that will begin on December 1st and will be concluded at the end of March. Many of us will hold different responsibilities within the new firm. I ask each of you to patiently support this combination of talent. When it is completed, you will be Partners in the largest and most powerful professional services firm in the history of man. Your opportunities for personal growth and increased income will be boundless. I ask each of you to raise your glass to toast

McKenzie Barber one last time. To McKenzie Barber!" Fitzgerald said raising his glass. It looked like coke to Baxter. Several hundred Partners stood and raised their glasses.

"To McKenzie Barber," came the shout.

A voice from the center of the room began to sing "Auld Lang Syne" and was quickly accompanied by others until the room swelled into a gigantic choir. The song was repeated three times and Baxter could make out tears in the eyes of many of the tuxedo clad Partners seated in the front row of tables. Glen Fitzgerald raised his hands.

"Thank you! Thank you! With that impromptu musical tribute to our firm, I move that we conclude the seventy-second meeting of the Partners of McKenzie Barber. Do I have a second?"

Baxter estimated that some twenty voices offered a second.

"Voice vote for affirmative?"

"Yeas," came back scattered from around the room.

"Against?"

The Partners were circulating around the room and many were filing out of the ballroom. Fitzgerald tapped his gavel twice. "The seventieth meeting of the Partners of McKenzie Barber is concluded. Good luck to all. Please travel safely."

Cardwell stood up from his chair looking resplendent and aristocratic in his white dinner jacket. "Nice to talk to you, Joe. All the best." He shook Baxter's hand and quickly walked away ignoring Abley's extended hand.

"It's been good to spend time with you, Brad," Baxter said squeezing Abley's hand.

"I'll drop you a note with my address, Joe. Look me up."

"I'll do that, Brad. I have to catch up with some people right now." Baxter slipped his watch into his tuxedo jacket pocket and quickly departed the ballroom. A bar had been set up on the concourse facing the water. Baxter found himself in the bar line directly behind Lon McMasters.

He tapped him on the shoulders. "Hey, Joe," McMasters greeted him. "Saw you up there getting your watch. I'm not far behind you."

McMasters had aged since the time of the last drink they had shared in the front bar of the Four Seasons. His face seemed lined, and he appeared to have physically aged ten years in three.

"How about grabbing a private drink together?" Baxter proposed.

"That's one hell of an idea," McMasters agreed.

They located a bench around the corner of the Tower building that faced the water.

"Well, Joe, you left some money on the table, but you made it through. Here's to you." McMasters raised his Scotch glass against Baxter's Canadian Club.

"I managed to survive Williamson and made it to the dais."

"Shhh," McMasters raised his forefinger to his lips. "That's a name we don't talk about anymore."

Baxter looked out on the water at the lights from the Beach Club. He questioned as to whether he would ever return?"

"How did it happen, Lon? How could a firm as successful and powerful as we allow this merger with Robson Allen to happen? Where did we go wrong?"

"You know damned well when things got out of control, Joe. We could have made it under Brimmer. Ernie never should have put up Burke. You had a front row seat for that back in 1984. The alternative was for Ernie to stay another three or four years and groom Burke. Ernie has done real well with IPCO. He knew how to run a company. Brimmer showed he could run a company. We elected a General who made some money at FSO. Ernie should have stepped up to the plate in 1984 and said that Pritchard and Schmidt and that turd, Nickerson, were unacceptable. But he didn't. He was busy shacking up with that research consultant. Ernie became an absentee Chairman and he let us all down."

"How could people like Fitzgerald and Pinker get in power?"

"We had a big time vacuum. Things were falling apart and Brett had his Middle East problems."

"I thought that Brett had sexual harassment problems," Baxter interjected.

"Shit, Joe. A third of the Partners in this firm could qualify for sexual harassment. I was transferred down to FSO to clean up a mess of problems that Buzzsaw and Brett had developed on some work in the Middle East. I've signed stuff that precludes me from talking about it. But it was messy. It was a time when we needed an Ernie Grey to step in and we didn't have one. Buzzsaw's main resource was Clyde Nickerson, and the only things that Clyde was really good at were lying and covering up."

"I sat next to Cyril Cardwell tonight on the dais. He baited."

"Cyril Cardwell was part of the problem. He certainly wasn't part of the solution. I had nothing to do with the man and he was a real tar baby for Fairbrother. He's signed the same non-disclosure documents as I have. Robson Allen wanted to review the firm's Middle East contracts, and Fairbrother decided that he would retire Cardwell after he let him talk to them."

"And what's going to happen to you after March 31st, Lon?"

"I'm going to be with FSO until it's sold, or I reach retirement age. I will tell you one thing, Joe. FSO isn't what the Partners thought they had in 1984 when they voted in Pritchard as Chairman."

"How much longer will you stay, Lon?"

"Two or three years maybe. Maybe I'll be on severance April 1st. What in hell are you going to do? The Dilger spin-off looked like a good deal to me. You look pretty healthy to me. Why aren't you going with them?"

"I don't want to be in a business dominated by actuaries."

"Did you really slug Dilger?"

"No. I pulled him up from his desk by the knot of his necktie. That's as far as it went, Lon. Let me ask you a question. What do you think of Fairbrother? Could he have kept the firm independent?"

"Fairbrother is a lot of talk. He probably will be the next Chairman of the combined firm. He would never have put himself on the line to fight the takeover. I believe Fairbrother screwed Fitzgerald's secretary last night. You know, the tall one they call Bernie. I'm next door to him in the Tower and damned if she didn't pop out of his room at six in the morning when I opened my door to get the *USA Today*. I sure hope that she didn't get harassed in there. Near as I can see, Joe, it's okay to screw 'em, but you can't harass 'em."

"Did Bernie have a smile on her face?"

"It's my theory, Joe, that she was being interviewed for a job as Fairbrother's US secretary. The man may be given to long interviews. She's got no future working for Glen. They're going to be around a few months as front men, but I suspect they're ultimately going to be assigned as Group Partners with a good sized pay cut. Fitzgerald was pretty good at one time, so he ought to do pretty well."

"Pinker never was more than mediocre. I don't expect that he's going to adjust real well. Now tell me, Joe, what are you going to do? Near as I can see, you've slipped some since the days we were together in New York. I know I don't see your name in the paper anymore. Are you gonna be another Alvardi and take shots at all the plans you designed?"

"Lon, I just want to break away from McKenzie Barber and do something else. I'm prepared to scale down my standard of living. I'm thinking hard about writing a book about the firm something equivalent to the Rise and Fall of McKenzie Barber."

McMasters stroked his chin in reflection. "That's not a bad idea, Joe. There's enough people who have come and gone with this firm who would want to read the book. You ought to give it a try. Come down to see me in Washington one weekend. I've got a lot of stuff packed away that might be

562

helpful. I never really could bring myself to throw anything away. Somebody's got to write a book about this. McKenzie Barber's taken up twenty-six years of my life, and it looks as though I might last a full thirty. Maybe you're the guy to be the firm historian. I sure wouldn't want someone like Clyde Nickerson to take on that job."

McMasters rose up from the bench and slapped Baxter affectionately on the back.

"Joe, you were a god damned good McKenzie Barber Partner. You always put back more than you took out, and I can't say that about too many people. I got an early morning tee time. I thought I'd play the course one last time. You have a good life!" He walked to the corner of the building and turned back to face Baxter. "You come down and see me?"

Baxter wanted a refill, but the bar had been wheeled away. The front bar was still jammed. He did not want to be in a noisy room. Instead he walked slowly down the sidewalk pathway to his room in the cottages. There were clusters of Partners in the dark saying their farewells. He paused to listen to the words around him. The Partners of McKenzie Barber were taking leave of one another. McKenzie Barber was over.

Baxter returned to New York on an early morning flight from Miami. He unpacked his suitcase, sat down at his desk, and made a list of the matters he had to resolve in the time period before his official retirement date of January 31st, 1992. He had removed himself from all day to day accountabilities at McKenzie Barber, and really hadn't expended much effort after returning from his European odyssey. He was expected to be on call for consultation relative to past and future client relationships. A young actuary named Hannigan had been named as his interim successor. It was expected that Harry Devonshire would be named as Baxter's replacement at the time of the Dilger Group divestiture. Baxter made a list headed Unfinished Business As of Saturday, November 2, 1991.

A fluid exit from McKenzie Barber.

A trust provision for Muffin. Trustee? Beth Gold? See lawyer.

Close off Darlene. Provide funds for her to exit relationship from whacko husband. Clean break personally.

Make Go/No Go decision on McKenzie Barber book.

Move permanently from New York to Brinker's Falls no later than 3-31-92.

Figure out what to do with the rest of life post McKenzie Barber.

Develop low risk financial plan for the final years of life through closure.

Baxter studied the note pad carefully scanning the items in his post McKenzie Barber life plan issue. He knew he would require income over and above his retirement plan. While Baxter was prepared to cut costs, he knew his lifestyle would require additional income of approximately $100,000.

The question was where Baxter would pick-up the incremental income?

Baxter searched his mind for other items. He considered adding 'closure with Ed Ganski' as an item. But he had already eliminated returning to Iron Creek as a viable alternative. Baxter concluded, after scanning his list three times that the action items were estate planning with Zach Blum and closure in his relationship with Darlene. The former was more easily resolved than the latter.

Baxter first arranged a luncheon with Beth Gold.

"You want me to do what?" she asked after they were one martini down in their luncheon at the Edwardian Room at the Plaza.

"I'd like you to be the alternative fiduciary for my estate if something should happen to me. You would have oversight over the distribution of the assets of my estate," Baxter explained.

"Why me? Why not appoint an attorney or a banker?"

"I'm just an account number at my bank, someone that they can send direct mail to regarding credit cards and home equity loans. Zach Blum has been with me through my divorce from Bridgette, and I have him drawing up a will which will name him as a legal advisor. I want a caring person to be the executor. I have a daughter out there who needs some guidance. I want to limit her full access to the funds until she reaches age thirty. You can approve things like college tuition, room and board, but I don't want her to have full access to any funds until Muffin decides who she is and who she wants to be. Lastly, I don't want her mother to have access to any funds in my estate."

Beth drained her martini. "Are you going to buy me another drink?"

Baxter reordered with a wave.

"Joe, you appear to be interviewing me for a stepmother job. What are the pay and benefits?"

The martinis arrived, and the waiter paused at the table. "The ladies seated at the table against the front window have asked if you are Beth Gold, the writer."

"I am Beth Gold, the famous late 20th Century authoress." Beth placed a fresh cigarette in her holder and assumed an Auntie Mame pose while Baxter fumbled with a matchbook light.

"I believe the ladies would like an autograph."

"Please advise those dear ladies, I'll pop over to see them in a minute. I have just solicited a proposal of marriage from this aging redheaded cad, and can't be disturbed just now."

The middle aged, tuxedo clad waiter quickly stepped away from their table.

"Beth, I have proposed that in the unlikely event of my death, to have you serve as the executor of my estate. I am in good health and the probability of your having to assume the role of my executor is remote. I was not suggesting marriage."

"I was," Beth said, sitting back in her chair. She was wearing dark granny glasses and a striped top, black ski pants, and long black boots that extended over her knee.

"How old are you, Joe?"

"I'm 56."

"I'm 57 and I'm alone. You are about to retire from McKenzie Barber and I understand that you are alone. We have known each other since we were seniors in high school with some lapses of time in between. I enjoy a reasonably good income, although it is not what it once was. I believe you're in the same boat. I have a good sized apartment in the city and a time share in Colorado. You have that place in upstate New York. You could be a house husband if you like. We could finish out our lives together and you could help me work the *New York Times* crossword puzzles. At my time of life, there's really not much out there. You could well be as good as I can do."

Baxter was dumbfounded. He had just wanted Beth to serve as executor of his estate. The estate wasn't going to be very large, but he wanted someone other than Zach Blum with the final say until Muffin was mature and stable enough to handle the money.

"I'll give you some time to think it over," Beth said rising up from her chair. "Order a salad with oil and vinegar and the snapper for me. I'm off to meet my public. They may represent my last two readers in the world."

Beth departed with a martini in one hand, and her cigarette holder in the other. Baxter's eyes followed Beth across the room. She was tall and thin with narrow hips and small breasts. The women at the table appeared to be well dressed and fiftiesh. Baxter observed Beth stand over the table and then slide into a chair with an exaggerated crossing of booted legs. There was a round of laughter and then Beth begin to address her audience who were in rapt attention. After five minutes had elapsed, she had concluded writing something on paper for each and returned to her feet following an exchange of handshakes. Beth rapidly retraced her path to the table where Baxter rose and held her chair. Beth quickly pecked him on the cheek as he pushed her chair in.

"Well, do you want to marry me?" she asked.

"I'll have to think about it. Give me until the end of January. Be my executor for openers, but don't go off and buy me an engagement ring just yet."

The resolution of Baxter's relationship with Darlene Bohlweiser required sensitivity, tact, and cash. It would have been so simple to have maintained his relationship with Darlene back at the housekeeper level. But he had crossed the line and placed himself in the range of her crazy husband. Baxter chose an isolated coffee shop/truck stop in Stockport, New York for a final rendezvous. They met by agreement at 10:40 AM on the second Tuesday in December. It was a sullen, overcast, grey winter day that was threatening snow.

Baxter arrived ten minutes early and spotted Darlene's battered Chevy parked in the outer ring of the snow crusted parking lot. It was one of nine cars in the lot, which assured Baxter of the opportunity for a private discussion. Darlene was seated in a back booth reading a newspaper. There was a large pot of coffee on the table, and a mug and a sweet roll facing Darlene. Her eyes were intensely reading the newspaper stretched out in front of her. Darlene wore a blue knit cap with her satin jacket rested on her shoulders.

"Hi," Baxter greeted her and slid into the opposite side of the booth. He noted that Darlene's eyes appeared to be red from crying.

"I cried on the way over here, Joe. But I'm all right now." She extended her hand across the booth to Baxter. He accepted it for a second, patted the hand, and poured himself some coffee.

"I will be retired from McKenzie Barber by mid-January. I may take another extended vacation. How are things with Luke and you? How's Rob?"

"Luke has taken the security supervisor job, and expects us to move with him to Binghamton on the first of February. He's going to put money down on a new trailer home this Saturday. I'm supposed to sell our old trailer home and come up and join him. I'm not going with him. I know there isn't a place in your life for someone like me. I remember your wife, and I've seen the women you bring to your house. They are beautiful and sophisticated. I'm someone who was convenient for you when you were up here alone. There are no men like you up here. I have become a new person because of you. I used to have a dream of going to a new place with you and becoming your housekeeper. Men like you treat women like me much like this diner. There's really no other place for you to go in a small town, so you try a small snack. But you're really used to eating at fine restaurants around the world. No, Joe. I'm going to take Rob and run away."

"Have you mentioned the possibility of divorce to Luke?"

"Luke is a strange, violent man. Sheriff Clowson wants him gone and out of Brinker's Falls. He also thinks I should take Rob and run."

"Where do you want to go?"

"I have been reading books and studying maps at the library. I have decided on Cedar Rapids, Iowa."

"Why Cedar Rapids?"

"Because Luke will never look for me there. There are two community colleges, one four year college, and it's on a lake. I don't think Rob and I will fit into a large city. I don't want to move to a small town like Brinker's Falls. There are always waitress jobs open, and I know how to do that. I owe Luke to be here long enough to settle the trailer house rented or sold. I have some suitcases packed out from K-Mart. Then I will pack up three suitcases with everything that Rob and I will need to get started in Cedar Rapids. We will take the Greyhound bus south to New York, and change at a place called the Port Authority for a bus to Chicago. Then we'll change buses in Chicago for Cedar Rapids. I'll find us a cute little apartment and slowly furnish it. I can work two shifts in the beginning. Then in the fall, I can start community college. Maybe I'll become a teacher. Rob and I will start all over again in Cedar Rapids, Iowa."

Baxter nodded his head as Darlene described her escape plans. How old was she? Mid-thirties? She had led a hard, dismal life and wanted a better one. This was her opportunity to make a break for a better life. He considered suggesting Iron Creek as an alternative. Ganski could watch over her there. He would have to leave the next morning for Laura Ganski's funeral. The timing would certainly be right.

"Do you need money?" Baxter asked.

"Yes. I want you to lend me five thousand dollars, and I will pay you back every month at the same interest the bank charges. I will start paying you back in July. Can you help me?"

Five thousand was five thousand, Baxter calculated. Iron Creek was not an alternative. He had to get Darlene out of his life. Cedar Rapids was the answer.

"I will. When do you want the money, Darlene?"

"I need the check by a week from Friday. I've opened up a special account at the Brinker's Falls Trust. I've saved some money on my own and I have a plan."

"Have you discussed this plan with Rob?"

"I have told him that we might take a bus trip to see my aunt in Rochester the first week in January, and that it was to be our secret. He liked the idea. Rob is going to miss you, Joe. It would be nice if you could write him one or two times. He always asks about Mr. Baxter."

"Darlene, is there anyway you could put your life back together with Luke?" Baxter asked.

Darlene began to cry. "How could you ask me such a question, Joe? Luke is a mad man. What kind of a man calls himself God's Helper and leaves threatening notes on doors? Sooner or later Luke will try to kill Rob and me. My life was lonely and I was very unhappy until you came into my life, Joe. You have changed my life for the better, but I know there is no place in your life for someone like me. I'm grateful for the time you gave me. I'm grateful for your help in getting me away from Luke. You must promise me to stay away from your house in Brinker's Falls for a year after I leave Luke. He won't come to New York City to bother you, but he might try something crazy up here. Promise me, Joe, you will stay away for a year after I run away."

Baxter nodded his head, and made a mental note to have a discussion about the menacing, dangerous Luke with Sheriff Clowson.

"Is there anything else, Darlene?" Baxter asked.

"This may be the last time I see you, Joe. I have a request. There is a small motel in back that the truck drivers use. I rented a room this morning. Can we make love one last time there this morning?"

Darlene's hand was again extended across the counter top to Baxter. He had planned to have a supportive discussion with Darlene and contribute some going away money. He hadn't planned on either the five thousand dollars or sex. Darlene left two dollars on the table for the check.

"We can go out the back door."

They made their way down a dimly lit hallway past the men's and ladies rooms to a back door that opened into a row of white motel cabins.

"I have a six pack of beer on ice," Darlene announced as they walked across the icy driveway to number 115.

Darlene had brought classical cassette tapes and flipped on her portable recorder to Erik Satie. Then she opened up a half-quart can of beer for Baxter and bolted the door. Baxter sat on the edge of the bed. It was eleven-fifteen in the morning and he held a cold beer while he watched Darlene pull her turtle neck over her head.

Darlene had again gained some weight since the last time they had been together. She peeled off her sweat socks and stood before him in a black bra and black pants. Darlene was blonde and full bodied, a truck driver's sexual fantasy.

"Please take off your clothes, Joe," she requested.

Baxter ranked his own performance as half-hearted at best. There were a number of beery kisses and several couplings of naked bodies. Darlene repeated that she loved Baxter over and over again, as he listened to the piano works of Erik Satie. Finally, Darlene fell asleep in his arms and soon began to snore. Baxter stared at the ceiling and followed the movements of a spider until she stirred.

December 17, 1991

Baxter bowed his head and sang the words to "Amazing Grace" as the casket of Diane Ganski was lowered into the frozen ground of the Iron Creek Cemetery. Ed Ganski's entire family had turned out for the funeral, along with several of Diane's kin from Oklahoma. Maggie stood next to Baxter gripping his arm as tears streamed down her cheeks.

There was no sign of BJ, Ganski's able executive assistant, although the funeral events had her organizational touch. Baxter had arrived too late for the reviewal the day before. The funeral service was at ten-thirty AM at the Calvary Lutheran Church.

Ganski embraced Baxter outside the church.

"Joe, thank you so much for coming." There were tears in his eyes.

Baxter quickly exchanged handshakes with the Ganski sons, which included his namesake, Joe. They appeared sober and middle-aged. Ganski's hair had a distinguished salt and pepper quality. He wore a somber blue, three piece suit without an overcoat. Baxter suspected that Ganski's hair had been colorized by BJ as part of his candidate image orchestration.

The temperature was around five degrees, and there was a bite to the morning air that Baxter had long forgotten. A large woman came to his side and pulled on his arm. It was a full faced Maggie with reddish brown colored hair. She was accompanied by a tall red-haired woman in a dark ski jacket. Her hair was straight, pulled back and tied with a red ribbon. She wore no make-up, and crow's feet were beginning to form around both eyes. It was Lenore, the daughter of his brief marriage with Maggie.

"God be with you, Father," she greeted Baxter. "Mrs. Ganski is off with the Lord now. And we must properly say good-bye to her."

"Carl don't get out of bed no more. That's why he ain't here," Maggie explained.

"Shall we go in?" Baxter offered.

"Duane was unable to come because of his responsibilities," Lenore explained.

"We'll miss him," Baxter said and led both women through the open church door.

Lenore immediately fell upon her knees in prayer after they had taken seats at the far corner of the third row. Maggie offered Baxter a stick of gum.

"She was my best friend, Joey. I've lost my best friend. Do me a favor, stick close to me through the burial. I just might not make it."

The minister's name was Mucha. He appeared to be in his early forties, and at ease in the pulpit.

"That's Eddie Mucha's oldest boy," Maggie whispered. "He was a couple of years ahead of Lenore at Iron Creek High. Carl is Catholic, but he quit going after we got married. I started going here with Diane. She was the church member. The only time Ed would show up was when he was running for office."

The Reverend Mucha conducted an orderly up-beat funeral ceremony with one accommodation. Ed Ganski spoke to the assembly from a side pulpit. He made a short reading from the Book of Isaiah and then launched into a brief speech.

"Diane Randling Ganski was my wife for 38 years. I met Diane during my military service with the US Army. I was stationed to Fort Sill, and Diane was a senior in high school. We fell in love, and stayed in love throughout our time together. When I learned of my transfer to Germany, I proposed to Diane that we get married. The furthest she had ever been away from home before had been Oklahoma City. Diane came with me overseas to Germany, and returned with me to Fort Campbell, Kentucky, where I mustered out of the Army. We had talked many times on where we wanted to settle after my military service. Diane always had the same answer. 'I'm your wife, Ed. I want to live in your home!' Diane returned to Iron Creek with me in 1957, and made this community our home. She and I raised three sons together, who have gone on to become responsible citizens in their communities and blessed us with three grandchildren."

"When I considered leaving Penn-Mine to go into a political career, it was Diane who provided the courage and support to move forward with my political career. In her last days of life, I pledged to Diane that I would win the 1992 election and hold my seat in the State Senate. I intend to honor that pledge and with God's help, I will. As a Lutheran and a member of this church, I know that I will rejoin my Oklahoma Rose in the life hereafter when God calls for me."

Ganski wiped a tear from his eye, stepped away from the side pulpit, and returned to his place next to his sons in the left front aisle.

Maggie shook her head in disbelief. "Going for votes at his wife's funeral," she muttered loudly enough for the row ahead of her to hear. The assembly was then instructed to sign Hymn #126 which was followed by Hymn #79. Reverend Mucha made some closing remarks, quoted more scripture, and led a recitation of the Lord's Prayer. Baxter noted that the service had been completed in 49 minutes.

The grave-site service was even more rapid. Baxter estimated that approximately half of the service attendees made it to the grave-site at the Hill View Cemetery. The cemetery was located on a far hill across the Iron Creek Valley from Pine Hill. He arranged to face Pine Hill during the internment ceremony.

Across the grave stood the Ganski boys along side their father. A cold wind had risen, and Maggie shivered on his right while Lenore appeared to be intensely praying with her eyes closed. Baxter listened to make out her words, but couldn't make them out. He wondered if his daughter was talking in tongues.

The casket was lowered into the grave. Each Ganski emptied a shovel full of dirt over the coffin, and Reverend Mucha led the singing of "Amazing Grace". Baxter was beginning to remember the words. Three or four more funerals and he would be at the top of his game.

Baxter had offered to drive Maggie to the cemetery in his rental car, but she declined to ride with Lenore.

"Joey, do me a favor and drop me at the K-Mart," Maggie whispered as they drew away from the grave. "Lenore needs to get back to Duluth."

Baxter nodded is agreement. "Lenore, honey, your Dad is going to drop me back at the K-Mart. I know you got to get back to Duluth for your shift at the hospital."

Lenore nodded her head in agreement. She extended her hand to Baxter. "One day, Father, you must come to Duluth and visit us. I understand that you will be retiring from your work in a short while. I want you to know that there will always be a place with Duane and me in our home if you should want to move in with us. We can show you how to get back on God's path."

"That's good to know, Lenore. Thank you," Baxter responded. They exchanged kisses on the cheek and Lenore turned away from them. Ganski appeared at Baxter's side. "Thanks for coming, Joey. We've got a buffet set up at the Sky-Line Motel. Please drop over. You too, Maggie. Diane always considered you as one of her best friends."

"I got to get to work, Ed," Maggie said with tears starting to stream down her cheeks. Ganski reached out to comfort Maggie but she pushed him away.

"Leave me alone! God damn it!" she protested.

"Maggie's very upset," Ganski said placing a hand on the shoulder of Baxter's topcoat. "When are you planning to go back?"

"I'm connecting on a 6 o'clock flight to a Northwest LaGuardia flight," Baxter explained.

"Drop over to the Holiday Inn this afternoon. I need to talk to you," Ganski said.

"I remember that Mort's buried here. I'd like to see his grave."

"It's up there about 100 yards and to your left," Ganski gestured with his hand.

"Com'on Maggie. I want to take a look at Mort Himmelman's grave before I drop you." He extended his hand and Maggie gripped it tightly.

"I hate that phony son-of-a-bitch," Maggie said when they were several rows beyond the grave site. "He's been two-timing Diane for years. There's talk about him and that snooty assistant that he's got."

The wind was now very strong and Maggie turned her back from the wind. It blew through her long, dyed brown, stringy hair. The headstone had a view of Pine Hill. It read simply,

MORTON L. HIMMELMAN
MSGT USMC
BORN JUNE 22, 1935
DIED MAY 19, 1966
MEMBER 52-53 COUGARS

"Shit! He's got 'Cougars' on his headstone," Maggie commented. "Are you going to put that crap on your gravestone, Joey?"

"It's a thought, Maggie." Baxter bent down and ran his are hand over the marble gravestone. "Mort was reported to have died at his desk. A Viet Cong mortar shell was lobbed in with no specific target in mind and landed on Mort. He had been scheduled to return stateside in three weeks."

"Do you miss him?"

"I saw him for the last time in December 1963, just before I got married to Jennifer. I don't think about Mort much anymore. But at one time, Ed and Mort were the best friends I had in the world. We went different ways. Now Mort's below the ground, and Ganski and I continue to be above it. We'll join him sooner or later. So long, Mort," Baxter said to the headstone.

Baxter extended his arm around Maggie as they walked down the hill. He had once in his life been married to this ugly, obese, but sincere, woman and they had produced a child who had turned out to be a fundamentalist religious robot.

"I'm glad you're driving me back to K-Mart, Joey. I know I shouldn't say this, but I really don't like to be around Lenore much anymore."

"How's that, Maggie?"

"You've always been the checkbook father for her, Joey, but Karl and me had to bring her up. In some ways, Lenore was just perfect. She never got into any trouble, always got good marks, and always had part-time jobs. She got in with the Baptists around eighth grade, and after that Lenore started to become superior to the rest of us. Our other kids can't stand her. She and Duane wanted to go off and become missionaries, but it has to be a country with elevators to be maintained. Lenore wants me to bring Karl to a service in Duluth. She thinks her minister can faith heal him. I told her that the man has an inoperable brain tumor. But Lenore says to bring him next Sunday. This is a man who can't make it out of bed anymore, and has to be in diapers. Lenore stays that her Minister heals people all the time. I asked our doctor and he just shook his head."

Baxter opened the car door for Maggie, and she hoisted her girth into the car wheezing slightly.

"Karl's never going to get well. He may die a year form now or ten years from now. I'm a supervisor now at K-Mart. I like the work, and the benefits come in handy. Diane always envied me and my job at K-Mart. Ed wouldn't let her work. He always told Diane that it reflected poorly on his position in the community. Diane and I could have had a lot of fun together working at K-Mart."

Baxter drove around the city to reach the K-Mart. Maggie talked continuously. "I heard that the queen bitch Lucy Albright Tweetman split from Tommy and just got remarried to some guy in Indianapolis. It was in the Iron Creek Telegram."

"I believe Lucy married a Carl too. He runs a large insurance agency in Indianapolis. I once had a Sunday brunch with them at the Plaza," Baxter recalled and then remembered his audience.

"What's Tommy doing?"

"I believe he's running a company in Washington. Their children are grown."

"What did Lucy look like when you had this brunch with her at the Plaza, or whatever the hell that place was?"

"She hadn't changed a lot. She was still petite and pretty."

"I wish to hell you could have told me that she had gotten fat or something. What happened to that wife of yours that you brought back to the 30 year reunion? Diane really liked her."

"We've been divorced three or four years. I've lost track of her. Her name is Bridgette."

"Diane used to write her. She used to send her fashion reports. She'd be in the car and visit all the mall stores, grill the clerks, and send off these fashion reports. She did it every week for about a year, and Diane never heard back. She even tried to call her a couple of times, but her secretary said Bridgette was either in meetings or traveling. Diane finally gave up. What went wrong between you two?"

"She was always traveling or in meetings," Baxter answered.

"Are you going to get married again."

"I really doubt it. I'm married out." He turned on to the freeway. He wanted this ride to be over.

"Would you have married me if I hadn't been pregnant with Lenore?"

"No," Baxter responded.

"I always figured I was better off with Karl," Maggie countered as they pulled into the Iron Creek strip mall. Baxter parked the car in front of the main entrance to the K-Mart store. "I don't guess I'll see you after today, Joey."

"I have no immediate plans to return to Iron Creek, Maggie."

"Then how about coming out of the car and give me a nice kiss good-bye?"

It became apparent to Baxter that Maggie wanted to be kissed good-bye in front of the K-Mart. She threw her arms around him and opened a juicy-fruit mouth to receive Baxter's kiss. He turned his head and deposited a kiss on her cheek.

"There was a time when I could get you to kiss me anywhere, Joey," Maggie said as Baxter stepped away to the driver's side.

"That was one hundred pounds ago, Maggie. Good-bye!" Baxter started the car and quickly exited the mall without a wave.

Baxter joined Ganski in his Holiday Inn suite in mid-afternoon. BJ opened the door.

"Come in, Joe. Ed should be over from the Sky Line shortly." BJ's brown hair was tied in a bun, and she was wearing dark rimmed glasses. Her high necked black dress would have made appropriate funeral garb. They had talked of Diane's death in the same room and now it was conveniently behind them.

"Ed hoped that you could make it by. I'm supposed to pour a drink."

"Coffee will do," Baxter said as he crossed the threshold. He noted that a can of diet coke was open next to a glass on the coffee table.

"How was Ed's talk at the funeral?" BJ asked.

"It seemed to be received well. There was no applause, of course," Baxter responded.

BJ crossed her legs after she seated herself in the chair across the coffee table. She appeared to have matured since their mid-summer meeting.

"I planned the funeral. How was it?"

"It worked. A lot of people came out. Some words were said, scripture read, hymns were sung, and prayers were recited. Diane has had her send-off, and after the luncheon meat sandwiches, everyone can get on with their lives."

"Is everyone out in New York as cynical as you, Joe?"

"I'm at a time in my life when I attend a lot of funerals. Weddings are down and funerals are up. Can I anticipate another Iron Creek wedding in the near term, BJ?"

"We have to get Ed re-elected this fall. After that we can look at his marital situation. Can we count on you to help us? Ed tells me that you are about to retire from McKenzie Barber. I believe he outlined a business proposition when you were out in July."

"BJ, this is my last visit to Iron Creek. I came out to pay my last respects to Diane Ganski out of respect for Ed. I'm going to catch the six o'clock commuter back to Minneapolis, and it's unlikely I will ever return. I will, however, send a political donation to Ed to help with his State Senate campaign. And you can count on me for contributions on future campaigns."

"What will you do now?"

"I'm not certain. But what ever I do, it won't be done in Iron Creek, Minnesota."

A key turned in the lock and BJ was on her feet. Ed Ganski appeared in the doorway.

"I need a Scotch, BJ," he commanded.

"Jesus, Joey, it's almost over. I just have a family dinner to get through. I know that Iron Creek is a long way from New York City, and I really appreciate your coming to the funeral. How about coming to dinner tonight with me and the boys?"

"Joe's leaving on the six o'clock flight to Minneapolis so he can make his connection back to New York," BJ chimed in from the wet bar.

"You have to go back?" Ganski pressed.

"Yes," Baxter lied. There was no need to return that evening, but he wanted Iron Creek behind him.

"What did you think of the funeral? How was I up there?"

"You came across very sincere, but I don't believe you have Maggie's vote," Baxter responded.

Ganski took a long drink of Scotch. "That woman's a mess. I tried to comfort her and she pushed me away. She's got a lot of problems. Her husband's an invalid."

"Which one is she, Ed?" BJ interjected.

"The big sloppy woman who works at the K-Mart and used to hang around Diane. Joey used to be married to her."

"That was over thirty years ago. I have been married to more presentable women in recent years. I will say, however, that Maggie is a good soul and was very loyal to Diane. She made a few comments about your relationship. If you're not careful, Ed, you'll lose the family vote."

"We're being very careful, Joe," BJ said. "These last months have been very hard on Ed. He's been a saint, and Diane cooperated by dying on schedule. Ed will be freed up for the January session of the Minnesota legislature."

"I've got a new environmental bill I'm going to be introducing. Did you bring it, BJ?"

"It's in my brief case, Ed. Shall I get it?"

"Not now, BJ. I just want to relax and talk to Joe a while. The bill was written by some hotshots on regulatory staff. I've got to study it and make sure that we're regulating the right parties. Have you read it, BJ?"

"Three times, Ed. I have prepared an executive summary and five pages of comments."

"Good. I'll review it tomorrow. Will you be here?"

"I will if you want me to be here, Ed.

Ganksi raised his glass. "Freshen this up for me, BJ." He observed Baxter's coffee cup. "You're not drinking, Joey?"

"It's too early in the day, Ed. I ought to check in by five fifteen for the six o'clock commuter out of Hibbing. I had better be on the road by 3:30 at the latest. Coffee's fine for me. I told BJ a little earlier that I was not interested in participating in business opportunities on the Iron Range or related places. I'm going to be a New Yorker for a while longer."

"Joe said that he will be a campaign contributor and will come to help next fall," BJ said bringing Ganski a refreshed Scotch.

"I appreciate that, Joey," Ganski took a long swig of Scotch.

"I may take a nap after Joe leaves. Christ, it's been a long time since the old 53 Cougars. I hear Tweetman and Lucy split up. You got any details, Joey?"

"It was a career thing for Tommy. Lucy wanted to stay in Indianapolis. Tommy said no to a couple of transfers. He's running a logistics systems company in Washington now. It may represent the big opportunity he's looked for all his life."

"Lucy is Lucy Albright," Ganski explained to BJ. "Her father ran a couple of stores downtown. He was kind of an establishment civic leader in those days. They lived up near the top of Pine Hill. Joey was crazy about Lucy, and she took up with Tommy Tweetman, who, in his own opinion, was the hottest thing ever to hit Iron Creek. We were the starting guards. I'd pass, then Tweetman shot. He may have been the original shooting guard. They play the game differently now, but the game we played, we loved. We probably had the most incompetent coach who ever wore a whistle around his neck, but we were one shot away from going to the State. How far would we have gone in the State, Joey?"

"If Tommy was hot, we might have made semi-finals," Baxter estimated. "Otherwise, we would have been knocked out in quarter finals. We weren't that good, Ed."

"Do you still think about the Cougars, Joe?"

"From time to time. I remember us clearing it out for Tommy on the right side. I thought he'd take a jumper, but he drove and took the hook shot. He wanted to at least draw the foul. I followed, the shot curled out right to me. I should have gone for the net, but Rychek always wanted us to go for the bank shot down deep. I banked it and it came out. I will remember that moment until my dying day."

"Jesus, I'm tired. Maybe I'll take a nap right now. BJ can keep you company."

"No, Ed," Baxter said rising from the couch. "I'm going to take off now."

Ganski emptied his Scotch glass and rose to his feet. "BJ, why don't you get your dress off and climb in with me. I need company."

"Ed!" she admonished Senator Ganski. "I know Joe's your best friend, but you should be careful the way you talk in front of others."

BJ shook Baxter's hand and began picking up the suite. Ganski saw Baxter to the door.

"Well she's gone, Joe. It's time for me to get on with my life."

"Fuck her for me, Ed!" Baxter whispered as they shook hands.

He drove back through the downtown area. The old house on Mine Street, along with the neighboring houses had been demolished to make room for a mini-mall. The mini-mall housed a convenience store, laundromat, dry cleaner, and an empty store front with a For Rent sign. Baxter turned off on Truck Street and on to Broadway. He proceeded slowly down Broadway Avenue. The Christmas decorations and banners were hung. They appeared shabby and Baxter suspected that they were the same decorations used in the 1950s. The stores had been replaced by bars, liquor stores, adult book stores, and fast food franchises. The Hotel Pennsylvania had been torn down.

Baxter turned up Pine Hill. The Dutch and American colonial houses had been preserved in a time warp. The street seemed long now. Was it possible that he once ran up this street? Baxter paused for twenty seconds in front of Lucy's old house and then proceeded to the top of the hill. He had kissed Beth Gold there in December of 1952. He stepped out of the rental car and took one last look at the view of Iron Creek. Baxter knew that he would never be coming back.

December 20, 1991

"I don't know why I'm being included in this little holiday luncheon," Beth Gold protested as Baxter steered her on the elevator to the Sunset Club. They had come from Zach Blum's offices where Beth had signed the documents to serve as the executor of his estate. He had arranged lunch with Mr. and Mrs. Godfrey Bain to celebrate Godfrey's recent appointment as Headmaster at the Middleville Collegiate School.

"I haven't seen Laura in a good 35 years. She's given up trying to coax me into speaking at ladies literary groups in New Jersey or serving as a commencement speaker."

Beth was conventionally dressed wearing a mink top over a dark suit. In recent weeks, she had developed a rash on her face that she covered with a layer of powder. She wore dark glasses and reminded Baxter of pictures he had seen of silent screen stars.

Headmaster and Mrs. Bain were waiting in the lobby area of the Sunset Club. Godfrey's hair was more grey than black and he sat with long legs crossed reading an ancient copy of *Enterprise Week*. Laura Bain was seated next to her husband reading a paperback book. She appeared middle-aged and full faced in a red knit suit.

"You beat us," Baxter greeted them.

"One never can be certain about the traffic flow through the Lincoln Tunnel and the time spent in finding a parking spot on a holiday Friday in New York. We've been here since the doors opened at eleven-thirty. Laura, fortunately, brought a book to read written by her favorite author." Godfrey had remained tall, erect and trim. Baxter observed that Bwana should photograph well for the Middleville Class Bulletin. Laura stood up holding her book for Beth to see. It was entitled the MacMoreland Legacy. Beth had written it in the summer of 1977 when Lester, Stephany, and Baxter had grouped together. Beth had been under control to produce a novel and privately admitted to the group that she modeled the book after Thomas Mann's *Buddenbrooks*. It had been produced as a made-for-TV movie in the late 1980s.

Laura embraced Beth as she might a long lost sister.

"Oh Beth, you look so good."

Beth exchanged kisses on the cheek and patted Laura on her shoulder. Godfrey stood behind them and Beth stuck out her tongue in Baxter's direction.

They were quickly seated in a window table which overlooked the west side of Manhattan. "Oh, this is magnificent!" Laura gushed. "We usually have lunch or dinner at the Princeton Club when we visit New York."

The waiter hovered over the table for a cocktail order. Laura ordered a white wine spritzer.

"Do you serve martinis here?" Beth asked the waiter.

"Of course, madam."

"Then please make me the largest martini that the club has ever served. You may use a bowl if you like."

"We'll do our best, madam."

Bwana predictably ordered a Dry Sac. Baxter ordered a regulation martini straight up with a twist.

"Now as I remember it," Laura began. "The last time the four of us were together was back in Fort Gately, Georgia in 1956. It was the night that Godfrey proposed. Joe, you had escorted Beth off to a party very diplomatically, leaving Godfrey and me alone. Then we left early the next morning to drive to Miami to visit your mother, Beth. Beth and I had spent the year together as students in France. We had driven all the way to Fort Gately with one stop in Northern Georgia. As I recall, we met you in the motel bar on a Friday night and small world, Joe had become friends two years earlier when she visited northern Minnesota on her Christmas vacation."

"As I've always said," Beth commented. "It's truly a small world out there."

The waiter served drinks and included a dessert glass size martini for Beth Gold.

"Don't lose the way," Beth called after the waiter.

"Isn't it wonderful to be back together again?" Laura said raising her glass. "Godfrey and I went down the same road together, and you, Joe, and Beth have gone down separate roads and we've come together for a festive Holiday luncheon some thirty-five years later."

"Congratulations, Bwana, on your election as Headmaster at Middleville. Here's to success as Headmaster! May you survive your trustees!" Baxter said raising his glass.

"Bwana! Joe, you are the only person in the world who calls Godfrey, Bwana. God forbid the students ever hear that name. That goes back to when the two of you were in the Army," Laura said opening her menu for study.

"Godfrey had the name Bwana when I came to Fort Gately. He will always be Bwana to me."

"You used to call him Yerfdog," Beth reminded Laura. "Now there's a name that you don't want the students to get a hold of. I find Bwana a most respectable name. You should have cards printed up that read Godfrey 'Bwana' Bain. Headmaster. That would be a real attention getter. As Headmaster, you have to develop some color so they will put up a statue or at least a plaque in your name when you step down." Beth raised her glass. "Good-bye, Mr. Chips!"

"James Hilton," Baxter added.

"Where were you this morning when I was working the *New York Times* Crossword puzzle, Baxter?"

"Godfrey's appointment as Headmaster was not an easy time for us," Laura said. "They had a year long search for a Headmaster. The search committee interviewed a great many headmasters and deans. They finally settled on Godfrey because of his ability to raise funds and attract students. It's been Godfrey's life-long dream to be Headmaster at Middleville."

"It would have been no contest if Godfrey had been known as Bwana. Aim for the stars, I always say," Beth said followed by a long sip from her oversized martini glass.

"Now Beth, I'm really enjoying reading the *MacMoreland Legacy*. I read it in hard back when it was first published back in the early 1980s. I remember I liked it very much. I did not like the movie at all. I picked up the paperback edition back in the Princeton book store. You're in the late twentieth century American writers section."

"I'm pleased that I haven't been placed in the early twentieth century American writers section. I probably would have nestled next to Fitzgerald. With the late twentieth century crowd, I've got to be just on the other side of William Goldman. I just hope to hell that Erica Jong isn't on the shelf next to me."

"Are you still writing, Beth?" Laura asked innocently.

"Yes," Beth responded and took another long swallow from her oversized martini glass. "I stay at it. I have some screen scripts to complete and a major piece of non-fiction when I am under contract to write. I very definitely am continuing to write. I'll be at it easily as long as you're Headmaster wiving it."

"And Joe," Bwana interjected. "I understand that McKenzie Barber is merging with a larger firm called Robson Allen Harbridge."

"I will be retiring in January, Bwana."

"You're very young to be retiring, Joe. What are your plans?"

"I have proposed marriage to Mr. Baxter," Beth announced with a leer. "He's very good with *New York Times* crossword puzzles and hopefully can bring other skills to our union."

"Marriage? You two!" Laura said. "How very wonderful for both of you."

Godfrey turned to Baxter with a skeptical face. "I have not responded to Miss Gold's offer of marriage. Rather I am weighing it against contrasting offers from several sympathetic ladies. Beth and I will always be good friends. We just left my attorney's office where we arranged for Beth to serve as the executor of my estate in the event that I should expire suddenly. Other than you, Bwana, Beth is the person whom I trust more than any person in the world to do the right thing with any money I have left over after I move to the bar scene in the next world."

Beth placed her hand over Baxter's. "Good old Joe Baxter, the pride of Minnesota's Iron Range, has entrusted me with his family fortune."

"Joe, I would hope that you might entertain Middleville in your plans for deferred giving," Bwana suggested.

"Joe has already sponsored three inner city students through Middleville. They are in their senior years at Ivy League schools," Laura offered.

"You might want to establish a memorial scholarship in Joel's name, Joe," the Headmaster suggested.

"I'll have to think about that, Bwana. Joel never really accomplished anything other than contracting AIDS."

"Your son died of AIDS. That's the first I've heard of it. That has to be tough for a homophobic like you, Baxter." Beth flagged down the waiter and held up her glass. "I'd like another just like this. We may have some other thirsty people at this table. I suggest that you poll them."

Baxter ordered another martini while Headmaster and Mrs. Bain stood pat.

"My husband, Lester, died of AIDS," Beth announced. "He was a very decent and thoroughly lovable man who liked occasional sex with men. He's been gone a dozen years now and I miss him."

"So many gifted people have been taken away from us by that terrible disease," Bwana offered.

Beth stared in silence at her oversized martini glass for a few seconds. "You're reading the *MacMoreland Legacy* for the second time, Laura? What do you think of it? Has it held up?"

"I just love it, Beth. It's a timeless plot. The decline of the MacMoreland family. It reminds Godfrey of *Buddenbrooks*. The Thomas Mann novel."

"First novel, 1900," Baxter inserted. "*The MacMoreland Legacy* has little similarity to *Buddenbrooks*," Baxter defended *The MacMoreland Legacy's* origins.

"Let me try you on another one of my books. Have either of you read *An Interlude of Discontent*?" Beth asked. The table became silent. "I consider it to be far and away my best book and either people didn't like it or didn't bother to read it at all. The critics were unmerciful to me."

"I tried Beth, but I couldn't make it through," Baxter confessed. "It was my second wife's great cause and I was never sympathetic to the Stop the War Movement."

"I'm in the same boat with you," Headmaster Bain admitted.

"I read the book all the way through," Laura said. "It was not your best book, Beth. You were like an Ayn Rand in reverse."

"Well, so much for *An Interlude of Discontent*. I spent five years writing it and dedicated it to Lester. No movie offers for Interlude."

Baxter patted Beth's hand and kissed her on the cheek. "That was in the late 1970s, Beth. It's December 1991. Looking back doesn't help a lot. We need to look ahead. We've gone through periods of our life to get where we are this afternoon. Let's savor what we have and not look back."

Beth nodded her head. "Godfrey, now that you're Headmaster of Middleville, do you intend to stop there, or do you plan to move onto the Presidency of a major university?"

They broke up lunch around two. The Bains left first after good-byes with Beth lingering behind for an extended visit to the Ladies Room.

"Oh God, Joe, are they really gone?" Beth asked when she returned from the Ladies Room. "Why don't we go back to my place, have a drink and do a post mortem on lunch?"

"I have to be back at the office for a meeting," Baxter begged off. "I'll buy you a drink in the bar while I have a coffee," he offered.

Beth talked animatedly after they had been seated in the far corner of Sunrise Club Bar.

"What a pair of losers! I'll bet they're Republicans who crossed over for LBJ. Godfrey has become a placating pompous ass. Laura has become the bulky, self-centered American Club woman that we both used to ridicule as exchange students."

"You were also once lovers," Baxter reminded her.

Beth produced a cigarette holder from her purse and lit a cigarette. She took a puff and slid back in her bar stool.

"That was thirty years ago, Joe. Laura had a wonderful body in those days, and a manipulative mind. I cultivated her, befriended, seduced her, and, more or less, made her my consort. She never lost her love of her precious Yerfdog. My God what a bore he is. They deserve each other."

"Laura is one of your loyal readers, Beth," Baxter reminded.

"She probably is equally loyal to Dr. Seuss." Beth took another long drag through her cigarette holder. "I believe we should get married, Joe. Should I have my accountant send you a copy of my balance sheet?"

"I'd like three years back and proformas for '92 and '93," Baxter responded.

"You're an impossible man. I'm leaving for Barbados tomorrow. How would you like to go with me? I'm coming back on January 6th."

"Can't do it, Beth." Baxter opened his week-at-a-glance book. He could do it. His only commitment was to have a drink with Rusty Collins, the LA based consultant on January 5th.

"Let's have a lunch after you get back. I expect that January 10th will be my last day ever with the firm. Why don't you round up Stephany and the three of us can have one last outrageous lunch together?"

"Stephany? Why Stephany? I would hope that she hasn't proposed marriage too. She's run through her money."

"She'll be one hell of a lot more fun that the Bains. Tell me, Beth, has Steph read *Interlude*?"

"No comment." Beth had her appointment book out. "Lunch on January 10th. I'll invite Stephany. There's a new place in the village I'd like to try. It's called Bull Finches. 12:30. It's somewhere around 4th Street. You find it. I'll buy."

Baxter signed the bar tab and accompanied Beth to a cab stand.

"Let's have a kiss, Baxter," she commanded.

It turned out to be an open mouthed kiss with a nicotine tongue brushing Baxter's tongue.

"Are you sure you don't want to see me to my door?" Beth asked.

"I've got a meeting," Baxter lied.

December 23, 1991

Baxter checked into the Walnut Inn Hotel and Ski Lodge at mid-day on the second to the last Monday of 1991. He had made the reservations in September after his return from Europe. Baxter had written Muffin that he had planned to be a guest at the Walnut Inn from December 23 until December 29. There was no reply or acknowledgment until late November.

Dear Daddy,

I checked this morning and learned that you remain a confirmed guest for the Christmas week at the Walnut Inn. Larry and I have had some problems. We're still good friends, but I have moved out of his trailer home and have a room at the staff house. I don't know what made you decide to come to the Walnut Inn, but I will be very glad to see you. I got your post cards from Europe and the one from Florida. It's hard to think of you as retired.

Will you be bringing a girlfriend with you? The Walnut Inn is a family and couples place. There are very few unescorted ladies who stay here. Thursday is my day off. What are your plans for Christmas dinner? I am so excited over the prospect of seeing you again. You can reach me most evenings between 7 and 9. The number is 603-696-9600 extension, 71. Please call me on the Saturday evening before you come up.

> Your loving daughter,
> Martha

Baxter called Muffin promptly at seven on Sunday night.

"Oh Daddy, I'm so excited you're coming. I've told everyone at the Inn that my famous Dad is coming. Edna at the front desk has a lovely room with a double bed on the third floor rear with a wonderful sunset view of the slopes. I assume you're bringing a woman with you. Tell me about her."

"Muff, I'm coming alone. Can we have Christmas dinner together?"

"If you don't mind, Dad, can we eat together at the staff dinner? I would so like to show you off."

"I'll look forward to that."

"Dad, you might get bored up here. I don't ever remember seeing you on skis, and the town of Maple Patch is just a bunch of shops, a grocery store, and a beat-up movie theatre. There really won't be a lot for you to do if you don't ski."

The Walnut Inn proved to be a more formidable place than it appeared on the drawing on the hotel letterhead or the color picture on the post cards. The main building was a four story maple colored wood frame edifice with a huge horse shoe drive. The Inn was ringed with modern two story villas that stretched at least a quarter of the way up the mountain.

Baxter had pictured the Walnut Inn as a place well past its prime years in the early stage of dilapidation. Instead, he discovered a bustling going concern with a front drive busy with at least fifty skiers visible in the entrance quadrangle. Baxter was greeted by a uniformed young man wearing a blocked ski cap.

"Reservations?" he greeted Baxter.

"Baxter. I'm staying the week."

"First initial?"

"J." The attendant wrote Baxter's name on a yellow tag and tore off a receipt. "Mr. Baxter, the valet will park your car and Archie will see to your luggage. Welcome to the Walnut Inn."

Archie appeared in a bellman's uniform complete with a pillbox cap. The pillbox cap was a little small for Archie's head and his red hair protruded over his forehead.

"Welcome to the Walnut Inn, Mr. Baxter," the greeting came again. "Just one bag and the brief case, Sir?"

Archie produced Baxter's baggage from the trunk. "You're Mr. Joseph Baxter from New York City?"

Baxter nodded.

"Then you're Martha's Dad. Martha's busy right now, but she's very excited to see you. Your daughter is a good friend of mine," Archie announced leading Baxter in the front entrance into a massive atrium lobby. The front desk was gleaming maple and had four reception stations. Baxter was escorted to a woman wearing a light brown blazer.

"Here's Mr. Baxter, Miss Grace."

"Welcome to the Walnut Inn, Mr. Baxter." Miss Grace extended her hand. She was white haired, sixtyish, and appeared efficient. Her name tag read Grace Dewing, Asst. Mgr. She brought up Baxter's reservation on the screen.

"You're going to be staying with us through Sunday, December 29th. And you're the only guest?"

"Just me," Baxter reassured her.

"I have you in a third floor rear room, double bed, American plan which includes breakfast and dinner in the grill room. The rate is $325 per evening, plus tax. I could put you in a smaller room at $275 a night."

"Hang the expense. I'll take the room you have reserved for me," Baxter said producing his credit card.

"I understand that you're Martha Baxter's father. She's requested that you join the staff dinner on Christmas Day. That dinner will be included in your American plan. Will you require rental equipment?"

Baxter shook his head. "Breakfast is served in the coffee shop on the lower floor. Dinner will be served in the Grill Room. You may eat in the Matterhorn Room at your own expense. Please be reminded that there is an entertainment cover charge in the evening at the Matterhorn Room. The staff here is discouraged from fraternization with guests. An exception will be made in the case of Martha and you." Miss Grace pressed a bell which was answered by a grinning Archie.

"Archie, please escort Mr. Baxter to room 330." She passed a large key to Archie. "Enjoy your stay at the Walnut Inn, Mr. Baxter."

"You can walk up easily enough, Mr. Baxter. I recommend that we take the elevator for your first trip to the third floor. The Inn is only three stories high but it's at least ten stories long. It went up in 1924, operated through 1947. The Inn is owned and operated by the Dewing family who were Innkeepers in Germany. Miss Grace has been with the Inn for over forty years."

"And always at the Assistant Manager level, I bet," Baxter commented as they entered one of the two operating elevators. Archie suppressed a giggle. "Tell me, Archie, do you suppose you could persuade Miss Grace to stop by my room tonight for a drink?"

Archie guffawed. "Martha told me you were a real funny man, Mr. Baxter." Baxter followed Archie down the hall to a corner room number 330.

The door was opened into a dark room. Archie quickly snapped on the chandelier light and pulled open dark green drapes to a view of one of the ski slopes.

"That's Pumpkin Hill over there and you're facing west. The sun goes down about a quarter to five these days, and you'll have a wonderful view. Martha has instructed me to deliver a bottle of your favorite brandy no later than four o'clock." Archie placed Baxter's bags on a luggage rack. "Will there be anything else, Mr. Baxter?"

"How well do you know Martha, Archie?" Baxter asked.

"We're very good friends."

"Is this your life's work?" Baxter asked searching his wallet for tip money.

"I work here during the ski season. I'm in my third year of Mechanical Engineering at RPI."

"Do you know Martha's friend, Larry?"

"He works here as a maintenance man. He can fix most anything." Baxter passed a five dollar bill to Archie.

"Thank you, Mr. Baxter. Enjoy your stay. There's time for a late lunch in the Grill Room, and the cafeteria at the lower level is open until ten o'clock."

"How about the vaunted Matterhorn Room?"

"That's open, but it's very expensive."

"How do I find Martha?"

"She said she'll find you when she gets off work at eight. She's got a lot of stock work to take care of. Martha's very conscientious about her job. She does all the buying for the gift shop, and handles all the records for the rental shop. Martha has a very good head for business. I guess she takes after you."

Baxter exchanged handshakes with Archie, and took up a seat by the window. The ski run was a good one hundred yards away. The figures appeared small and graceful. Now what was he to do? He was in an isolated place killing time until he could see his daughter. There were no women currently in his life. Darlene was scheduled to take her escape bus to freedom on Friday night. Baxter had decided to stay clear of Brinker's Falls until Thursday, January 9th. Then he would gather up the things he wanted to take back to the city and not return until the Fall. By then the Luke Bohlweiser issue should be resolved. Perhaps he'd put up the house for sale. The Dopmans had been gone a long time.

Baxter's only real choice for lunch was the Matterhorn Room. It was located on the second floor with its entrance facing the atrium. The view from the maitre'd's station was a large, half empty room with a large stone fireplace at the center surrounded by two long paneless windows offering panoramic mountain side scenes. Baxter was greeted by a youthful blonde man in a blue blazer.

"May I help you," Baxter was greeted.

"One for lunch."

"Do you have a reservation?"

"No, I'm a guest in the hotel, and I'd like a little lunch please."

"Come this way, please." Four tables into the room a man in a white turtleneck sweater waved. "Joe Baxter!"

Rising to his feet was Hakim Selim. "Joe, come join us." It was a large round table with capacity for six. Selim had been seated between two attractive women. Their outer garments were strewn over two of the chairs and Selim pulled the empty chair at his side open for Baxter.

"We're just in from the slopes and settled in with some Bull Shots. Come join us. Joe Baxter, this is Aiysha and Danielle. Ladies, Joe Baxter, a Partner from McKenzie Barber, the famous management consulting firm."

Aiysha made a little wave of recognition with her hand. Danielle offered a smile.

"Excuse me for not getting up, Mr. Baxter, but I had two bad falls."

"And how was the skiing?" Baxter queried politely.

"Skiing was shit," Aiysha responded. Her face was Middle Eastern, with heavy dark eyes, dark bangs, and a graceful swanlike throat extending up from her dark turtleneck sweater.

"The runs were icy in spots," Danielle reported.

"This is our first of the day," Selim said. "You might as well drink what we drink." Selim snapped his fingers at a youthful waitress. "Bring this man a hot Bull Shot like ours." Turning to Baxter. "We're drinking doubles and the skiing was not very good."

"The skiing was shit," Aiysha repeated. "The invitation was for Colorado and we're stuck in Vermont in this very second-rate place."

"I have to be close to Boston this week to conclude an investment transaction," Selim explained.

"This place is within an hour and fifteen minutes of Boston by car with a little acceleration and thirty minutes by charter plane. Colorado is a day away at the least. I've been up here before and it's been okay."

"Have you skied here, Mr. Baxter?" Danielle asked.

"I have never had a pair of skis on in my life. I'm up here to see my daughter."

"Daughter?" Selim shook his hand. "By Bridgette?"

"No. One wife back from Bridgette. She's twenty-two and has been working up here for a couple of years. The plan is to spend Christmas together."

Baxter's Bull Shot was served steaming hot. Selim raised his mug. "Here's to good times." Baxter and Danielle raised their glasses and clinked. Aiysha lit a cigarette.

Danielle's white hair was cut in a butch. "Is your wife with you, Mr. Baxter?"

"I'm divorced," Baxter explained.

"I saw an investment offering on some high priced mail order luxury goods venture that listed Bridgette as the senior merchandising officer. She's using Morgan again. It was a private placement convertible deal."

"Hakim, I let Bridgette off at the World Trade Center two years ago, and haven't seen or heard from her since."

"And how are you two acquainted?" Danielle asked. Aiysha blew a large smoke ring across the table in Baxter's direction.

"Joe recruited me from Broadbaker to Harwell Management. He was a long time consultant to Mr. Harwell, the CEO of Harwell Management. I respect Joe as a friend and I'm very glad to see him this afternoon."

"And how long will you be staying here?" Danielle continued.

"I plan to head back to New York on Saturday, the 28th," Baxter replied.

"How will you keep occupied all week if you don't ski?" Danielle asked.

"I understand there are hiking trails. I'll take some hikes, read, and get caught up with my daughter's life."

There was a muffled buzzing and Hakim produced a mobile phone from his knapsack. "Selim!" he greeted his caller.

Aiysha stood up from her chair and consolidated outer garments into a single armchair.

"Hey, Joe Baxter. Come over here and keep me company." Aiysha was tall and appeared slender under layers of sweaters. She pulled out a chair and patted the seat.

"This way you won't have to listen to Hakim's boring phone call. It's probably from one of his mistresses." Selim had walked away from the table and was now standing alone in front of the fireplace. Aiysha hoisted one leg on Baxter's thigh. "Do you know how to remove a ski boot?"

"I'm better at unhooking brasseries."

"Start with the boots. We can always move on to other things if you should exhibit some skill here."

"Hakim had us in the chair lift before sunrise. We are very tired, chilled, sore, and quite hungry. I regard myself as a very good skier, and I took two bad spills today."

Baxter solved the riddle of unclasping Aiysha's ski boot. He massaged her foot after the ski boot dropped to the floor. "And did you fall today, Aiysha?" Baxter asked.

"Aiysha never falls," Danielle volunteered.

"Now do one more and we will be friends for life," Aiysha said lifting her other leg across Baxter's thigh. Hakim continued his telephone call in front of the fireplace. He was speaking rapidly.

"I think we need more Bull Shots," Danielle said waving to the waitress.

"Change me to Remy. I don't want anymore beef broth."

"Make mine an Armagnac," Baxter said.

"Change that from a Remy to an Armagnac. When a man takes off my ski boots, I drink what he drinks."

The second boot dropped and Baxter massaged Aiysha's left foot.

"You're good with feet. What else are you good at?" Aiysha teased.

"Feet are about it for me. I've never had much luck above the ankle," Baxter responded.

"Luck can change," Aiysha observed.

"I know this kind of call. Hakim could be on the phone for an hour," Danielle said.

"Let's order. He can eat later. Hakim deserves it. Bringing us to this shit place." Aiysha scanned the menu while Danielle ordered the next round of drinks. Both feet were now resting on Baxter's thighs. She wiggled them and Baxter placed a hand around each athletic socked foot.

"That feels so good to me. Danielle, you should try Joe after he's through with me."

"Explain a few things to me, ladies," Baxter began after the additional round of drinks had been served. "What are the arrangements here? Are there more to your party?"

"There were to be four of us, but regrettably, we have turned out to be three," Danielle explained. "And if Hakim goes to Boston, there will be just two until he comes back. This is a very unfortunate way to spend Christmas. Perhaps the three of us can sing carols together."

Baxter looked around the room. The clientele appeared to be solid citizen families and couples. He had innocently walked in the door to grab a lunch, and had joined the international jet set.

"And you ladies live in New York?" Baxter asked.

"You're beginning to sound very investigating, Joe. I don't know what this world is coming to. You innocently let a man play with your feet and he begins to ask probing questions," Aiysha commented.

"Joe," Danielle proposed. "I'll bet that you cannot guess my profession?"

"If you guess the oldest profession, I'll kick your balls off," Aiysha threatened.

"You're nuns on holiday. You're Catholic and Aiysha's Coptic."

"Bad guess, but clever," Aiysha commented. "I'm glad you joined us. Have you ever helped a lady out of her stretch pants?"

"Not in a restaurant," Baxter answered.

"He's mine, Aiysha," Danielle said. "He must guess what my occupation is?"

Baxter leaned forward on the table to take a closer look at Danielle. Frosted silver hair, pierced ears, dangling gold earrings, thin athletic body.

"You are a professional acrobat on vacation from a touring circus," Baxter guessed.

"My God!" Danielle screamed and then placed her hands over her ears. "How did you guess?"

"It was a guess. I deduced that you were not a professional skier, and I know that Hakim has a far reaching taste in his lady friends. You have an outgoing entertainer's personality and a remarkable innocence about you," Baxter said.

"You are a good talker," Aiysha observed and pulled her legs off Baxter's thighs.

"Now guess what Aiysha does," Danielle requested.

Aiysha's hand brought Baxter's hand against her thigh.

"According to the information provided me, this is as high up on a woman's leg as you have ever been," Aiysha challenged.

"I lied. And you're a foreign exchange trader."

Aiysha pushed Baxter's hand away.

"I believe I'm ready for a clubhouse sandwich. How about you ladies?"

Hakim had completed his call and replaced his mobile phone in his knapsack. "We're getting close to a deal. I may have to leave. You may come to Boston with me or stay here," Selim stated.

"Take Aiysha," Danielle suggested. "I'm too sore right now to travel. Joe guessed that I'm a circus performer. He also helped Aiysha off with her ski boots. He's been very helpful in your absence, Hakim."

"Let's eat," Hakim commanded.

"Answer me, Hakim," Baxter interjected. "Is Aiysha a foreign exchange trader?"

"Half right, Joe. She used to be," Hakim signaled for the waitress.

"It's a complex deal, Joe," Hakim explained half way through the lunch. "It has to do with a change of control matter. We're ready to finance with the right partners and your old friend, the Baroness, has interest in participating in a piece of the financing. The deal, however, must be structured by December 31st."

"You're in contact with the Baroness?" Baxter questioned.

"Let's order," Hakim commanded. Aiysha and Danielle ordered steaks, while Hakim settled for prime rib. Baxter ordered a club house. Turning to Baxter, Selim said, "I'm on the phone with the Baroness on a weekly basis. Harwell Management and de Hartogue have been very good for each other over the past five years. Hortense Foods was our first deal and we can continue to deal. The Baroness could have been a hell of an investment banker. She mentioned you had lunch with her in July."

"What Baroness is this?" Aiysha demanded.

"Just a Baroness, Joe and I know. Joe's known her longer, but I've done a more deals with her."

"Does she have a name?" Aiysha probed.

"Not in this conversation," Selim ruled.

Aiysha replaced her foot on Baxter's lap.

"Have you known Hakim long?" Baxter asked.

"A couple of weeks," Aiysha responded with a shrug of her shoulders.

"I win. I met Hakim in July," Danielle added.

"We were invited to Vail, and here we are in Nowhere, New Hampshire. Hakim's friend, at the last minute, couldn't come. We're a man short if you haven't noticed." Aiysha's foot made a circular motion over Baxter's crotch.

"I think we should change places, Aiysha, after the food comes," Danielle suggested.

Aiysha and Danielle devoured their steaks. Danielle changed places and seated herself next to Baxter.

"Are you good at massage, Joe. I'm feeling quite sore. We have one of the villas. Why don't you come back and give me a massage. Aiysha usually gets most of the attention from Selim."

Baxter looked around the Matterhorn Room. They represented a table of sybarites in contrast to the conservative appearing couples and families distributed about the room.

"You're welcome to join us in the villa, Joe," Selim said as he signed the check.

"Maybe just one drink," Baxter consented.

There was a line of mahogany stained A frame villas set in a flat are behind the main lodge. They entered through a deck staircase into a three story building with a sauna and hot tub on the lower floor, a living room and master bedroom on the main floor, and two smaller bedrooms located off a balcony on an upper floor.

"It's a thousand a day, Joe," Hakim said as he took Baxter on an abbreviated tour of the villa.

"It's a shower and the hot tub for us," Danielle announced.

"Come join us, Joe."

"Let's have some Scotch," Selim said producing a bottle of Chivas Regal from the wet bar.

"You seemed to be overstaffed," Baxter commented after accepting the Scotch glass.

Hakim took a deep breath followed by a sip of Scotch. "This is a bit of a misadventure. I have a good friend from Broadbaker who likes a little sport from time to time. I had these two set up to go to his place in Vail. On Friday, he calls me and tells me that he's going to reconciliate with his wife. Meanwhile the strike date in a major transaction has been moved up. This villa is rented for the winter by another friend. I've never been here before in my life, and probably will never come back. So who do I run into? My old friend, Joe Baxter. This adventure is overstaffed, and you are invited to join us. You seem to have made an impression over lunch."

"Tell me about the Harwells," Baxter asked.

Hakim shrugged his shoulders. "I make a lot of money for them. But they are not very grateful. I report to both Ned and Spencer. They don't get along very well. The two sides of the family quarrel a lot. Mrs. Harwell doesn't believe that we should participate in unfriendly takeovers. Spencer's suddenly become a risk management expert. Ned thinks I make too much money. So does the brother-in-law, Dan. The whole family wants access to what they believe is their birthright money. Wilson wants to take his money out to make films and has got some shyster LA lawyer bringing suit against Harwell Management. Leon used to make them toe the line. The whole family was scared of Leon. I got creamed on one deal last summer, and the whole family took turns pointing fingers at me. Leon Harwell was a great and truly exceptional man."

"To Leon Harwell," Baxter said raising his glass." Hakim clinked glasses.

"I found out about your proposed General Manager arrangement with Leon. Looking back, the idea really had a lot of merit. You could have handled the family, while I managed the money. Leon Harwell was a brilliant stock picker, but he belonged to another time. He saw the financing opportunity on the deal side. He didn't want to be a gorilla, but he saw them multiplying around him. The family has a large financial appetite. The first transaction I got Harwell into was Hortense Foods. That deal made Dominique too."

"Dominique and I are kindred spirits. Her husband is a well mannered, charming empty suit. Your friend, Ernie Grey, should have stood up to the family and told them Leon wanted Joe Baxter in as the General Manger. With you in place, my job would be one hell of a lot easier. I'll probably finish out my contract, and either retire and run my own company, or go back to work for Broadbakers."

Baxter could hear giggling from the lower floor. Where did you get those two?"

"I collected them. I like women. They both seem to like you, Joe. You could probably take your pick. Danielle would be better company. Aiysha can be a little moody."

There was a padding of feet on the staircase and Aiysha appeared draped in a towel. "I need a drink. We're going into the hot tub now. Come and join us." She filled a glass with ice and poured a great deal of Scotch in it. "Danielle is waiting for her backrub, Joe." Aiysha kissed Hakim on the cheek and then shared a longer open mouthed kiss. "Hurry along," Baxter heard her whisper.

Baxter's watch said six-fifteen. Where had the afternoon gone?

"I had better pass, Hakim. I'm meeting my daughter at 8 o'clock. She's on staff here. I expect we'll be having dinner out," Baxter said rising from the stool facing the wet bar. "Maybe the three of you could be my dinner guests tomorrow night."

"You'll be missed this evening. But I understand." Hakim walked Baxter to the door. "Until tomorrow then. We'll probably be on the slopes by seven and in for lunch around two." Then placing his hand on Baxter's shoulder. "You should come by the office in January. Spencer can take us out for lunch at the Gotham Club. I don't have much luck with the membership committee."

"Please send my best and regrets to the ladies."

"They'll have to accept your regrets. You aren't going to be around to show your best." Selim smiled and closed the door behind Baxter.

Baxter trudged through the winter night back to the main lodge. Had he been inclined to stay, it would have likely represented an all night affair. Baxter speculated that it would have been only a matter of time before the controlled substances would have emerged from their hiding places. Twenty years earlier, he would have stayed and met his fate.

Baxter was showered, shaved, five minutes into a book when he answered Muffin's knock on the door of his room.

She stood tall and thin in a red sweater and dark stretch pants.

"Oh Daddy, what am I going to do with you?" she greeted him. Her face was taut.

Baxter offered her a drink. "There's coke in the mini-bar, Dad. I'll have a coke."

"What's wrong, Muff?"

"Dad, I have told people around here for weeks that my famous father is coming to visit me over Christmas week. Now it's all over the lodge that you were in the Matterhorn Room with this fast group of Euro-trash. I heard that you took off one woman's ski boots and were massaging her feet. Then I heard she had her foot on your crotch. Dad, that sort of behavior is not condoned in the Matterhorn Room. Tell me honestly, Dad, are they drug dealers?"

"Muff—," Baxter began.

"And please don't call me Muff or Muffin. I'm known as Martha up here."

"All right, Martha," Baxter responded firmly. "The man or host of the table, Mr. Selim, is the money manger for one of the leading family fortunes in the country. One woman is a distinguished foreign currency leader. The other woman is one of France's leading aerialists. They were a little playful following a long run on your ski slopes and I joined them for a late lunch. I find your comments priggish at best, and more than a little foolish."

Martha entered into a long sigh. Baxter could remember the sigh. It was her way of regaining control. He remembered first observing the sigh

605

back in the house on Palmer Street. It was usually after Agnes, the housekeeper, had ordered her to go to bed.

"Dad, I'd like to buy you dinner tonight."

"The vaunted Matterhorn Room?"

"Staff do not eat in the Matterhorn Room, Dad. Would you mind going into town for a pizza?"

Town was called Old Granby, and a roadside sign claimed 1239 inhabitants. It was a bleak town of white frame houses, a supermarket, a coffee shop, two gas stations, three bars, a drug store, and a pizza parlor called Eddy's. Eddy's greeted its customers with a large neon sign portraying a beer mug inside a pizza. Muffin insisted on driving and transported them in an ancient battered Chevrolet to Eddy's crowded parking lot. She delivered a running monologue during their drive.

"I felt very badly about this summer. You've been so nice to send me money. I'm not spending all of it, and what I haven't spent on therapy I've put in a bank account. I moved out from Larry in October. I'm back in the Walnut Inn staff dorm where I share a room with two other women. Dad, I believe I'm ready to go back to college."

"I'm running the gift shop this year. I've just been a clerk in past years. The gift shop manager quit in April. The Inn ran some ads, but couldn't find anyone who would come for what they were willing to pay, or that they liked. Miss Grace asked me to take over."

"Dad, it was like a job that I've been waiting to do all my life. I planned the merchandise, negotiated with the suppliers, picked people and we're having $2000 days compared to $500 last year. I'm good at retailing."

"It was just a mess when I took it over and I remembered most of the things that Bridgette taught me. I used to listen to her handle charge backs to the suppliers. I even threatened some the way she used to do. I worked night and day to get the gift shop turned around. All of a sudden I wasn't feeling sorry for myself, and I didn't have a lot of time to go to therapy. I suddenly saw Larry differently. He was a maintenance man and I was a Manager. Dad, I want to take the entrance tests this spring and to apply for admission into Retail or Hospitality Management programs. I hear Cornell,

Michigan State, and Penn State are very good, and I'm sure that there are others. I'll be lucky to get in as a sophomore and I know it will be very expensive for you. But this is what I want to do and I will work very hard to take on part-time jobs to earn my keep. Then after I graduate, I will travel around and live in other parts of the country."

Muffin suspended her soliloquy to park the car at the far end of Eddy's snow covered parking lot. "This is the place where the kids like to hang out. I'd like to show my Dad off. Please don't help anyone off with their shoes, and act like a good establishment, Dad," she implored as they entered a noisy room that resembled a beer hall. There were long tables facing the door and smaller tables at the rear of the room. Muffin led Baxter to the rear of the room exchanging waves and smiles with young, boisterous, laughing Eddy's patrons. "Martha" was called out at least ten times before they reached a small table at the far end of the room. Baxter spotted Archie, the bellhop, clad in a dark turtle neck sweater waving from across the room.

"Will we see Larry this evening?" Baxter asked after he had settled in with a mug of dark beer.

Martha shook her head. "I don't see Larry any more, Dad."

"Are you seeing anyone now?" Baxter asked.

Muffin squeezed her shoulders. "Sometimes I'll catch a movie with Archie. There's a boy named Roy who goes to Boston College. He's working in the kitchen this winter. I see Ray, the tall, dark-haired bartender who works in the Matterhorn Room. He's working on a Masters in Theatre Arts at Yale. Roy's the one who told me about your escapade this afternoon in the Matterhorn Room. How about you Dad? Are you seeing anybody? You've always been a ladies man. Are you planning to remarry?"

"My marrying days are over, Muff. I will be retiring from McKenzie Barber in January. I expect that my life style will change dramatically. I may do some traveling, and I have a writing project. I saw your mother in London this summer. What do you hear from her?"

"She wrote me in September. Mother is usually good for a letter around Labor Day. Her letter sounded a little lonely. I think she's quarreling with Uncle Chuck over Grandfather's estate. Tell me Dad, were you ever really in love with Mother?"

"I was very strongly attracted to her. The attraction was so strong that I overlooked a lot of her flaws. Your mother has never been wired together correctly, but her exterior was magnificent."

"Mother told me that she was abused by her grandfather."

"It was an abuse that she grew to love. She became mentally unbalanced and then presumably cured. She was awfully spoiled and was used to having her own way. Nothing has really changed over the years. The Washburns wanted her married and I looked like a good prospect to take over the company one day. I think I fell in love with the thought of being part of the Washburn family, and eventually running the company. Every lad of modest means dreams of marrying the boss's beautiful daughter and living comfortably ever after. If I hadn't done it, you and I might not be sitting here together this evening."

"But you're not really my father."

"I'm your father for all practical purposes. You bear my name and I raised you. I love you. Lastly, your mother slept around a little, but on a probability basis, you're my kid. Get on with your life and quit speculating about your specific genetic origins."

"Aren't you concerned about where you came from and what made you what you are?"

"My father emigrated from the mining country in England and never talked about his people. My mother came from a farm in Proctor, Minnesota and, from what I saw of them, they were a pretty dull bunch. My mother and father were unhappily married and my father was killed when I was eleven or so. My mother always favored my younger brother."

"He was the one who had the wedding reception in the Chinese restaurant in Duluth. I love to tell that story. His name was Gordy and he married a black night club dancer. He disappeared. Did they ever find them?"

"No, and I believe they quit looking for him a long time ago."

"Aren't you concerned about what happened to him?"

"Not especially. I never really liked him."

"You were married before you met mother. She was fat. You had a daughter with red hair. Do you love her?"

"Lenore is a good person, but I don't especially care for her."

"Dad, am I the only family member you care about? You seem so alone. Were you in love with Bridgette?"

"Bridgette and I had something going between us. Now looking back, it may have been love."

"What made Bridgette leave you?"

"Bridgette came to the conclusion that she had outgrown me." Muffin shook her head. "I loved Bridgette, Daddy. I know that Joel hated her, but Bridgette was someone very special for me. I guess she dropped both of us at the same time. Do you get lonely, Dad?"

"A little. That's why I thought it would be nice to spend some time with my daughter over Christmas."

Their conversation was interrupted with the serving of their pizza. Muffin had remained a vegetarian.

"Dad," she asked after two bites of pizza. "Do you remember that woman from McKenzie Barber who drove up to see us in Racine. We had a picnic with her. Were you in love with her?" Baxter hadn't thought about Hillary in a long time. Like his brother Gordy, Hillary Stone had disappeared over the horizon. It had been a brief flirtation with a staff member. She had been engaged, but ready to leave her fiancé for Baxter.

"We knew each other briefly."

"Did you have an affair with her, Dad?"

"A very short one."

"Have you ever been madly in love with someone?"

"Just once."

"Tell me about her, Dad."

"Muff, fathers don't discuss their love affairs with their daughters."

"You're hardly a regulation father and I'm certainly not a customary daughter. Tell me about your one great love affair."

Baxter provided a sanitized version of his two weeks in 1977 with Dominique. He omitted their meeting in Paris last summer.

"She should have chosen you, Dad. You would have made her happy."

"But she is very rich and very powerful today. That might not have happened if she had chosen me," Baxter pointed out.

"Any others?" Muffin asked.

"There is a lady whom I have asked to look after you if something should ever happen to me. I have made a new will and she will be the executor. Her name is Beth Gold."

"Beth Gold. Beth Gold," Muffin repeated the name. "She's a writer isn't she? I believe there are some of her books in the Inn Library."

"Beth Gold is a well known American writer. She is also an old friend whom I trust. I'll arrange for you to meet with her after the holidays."

"Is she a girlfriend, Dad?"

"Just an old friend. We go back some 39 years. I met her back in Iron Creek over the Christmas holidays during my senior year at Iron Creek High School. She's a highly intelligent and caring woman."

"Is she married?"

"She's a widow."

"Maybe you ought to marry her," Muffin suggested.

"She's just a friend."

"Maybe there's someone at the Inn who would be right for you."

"I have my eyes on Miss Grace. I hope she's not taken." Couples were dancing to the juke box in a six by nine foot clearing in the tables.

"Let's slow dance, Dad." Muffin led Baxter to the dance floor exchanging smiles and waves with her friends. They moved onto the dance area and swayed fluidly to a Frank Sinatra song. "I estimated this morning that you were 56 years old, Dad. And you are a very young 56 who looks like he's 45. You're too young to retire. Men retire when they're in their sixties."

"I'm retiring from McKenzie Barber, not from earning a living. I have a daughter to put through college so that she can take care of me in my old age."

"Am I a burden to you, Dad?" she asked with small tears forming in the corners of her eyes.

"You're a delight to me, Muffin, alias Martha."

They broke off the evening near midnight in the parking lot of the Walnut Inn.

"I have a big day tomorrow. Can you keep yourself occupied until tomorrow night? There's someone I want you to meet for dinner," Muffin said after hugging Baxter.

"Make it the night after. I may be having dinner with my friends from Matterhorn Room tomorrow night."

"That's Christmas Eve, Dad."

"I don't believe they observe the Christian holidays."

"The night after Christmas night. I want you to get Christmas dinner at the staff house. When do you go back to New York?"

"On Friday, the 27th."

"Then there's someone I want you to meet for dinner on Thursday. It will be my surprise."

Baxter accompanied Muffin to the steps of a side entrance. He kissed her once on the forehead and then on the cheek before Muffin closed the door behind her. A slight snow began to fall and Baxter crunched his way on the path around the building to the luxury villas. Hakim's villa was dark and soundless at midnight.

Baxter wondered what he had missed. Would the moment still be there tomorrow?

He took a long walk, following breakfast, around the entire Walnut Inn compound. The temperature was in the low teens, but the sun was bright. Baxter concluded that it had to represent an ideal day for skiers. He paused to watch the skiers. This stage of the trail was near the end of the hill. He tried to make out the forms of Hakim, Aiysha and Danielle on the slopes, but all of the skiers looked alike.

Baxter turned up the path to the Villas. The door to Hakim's villa was open, and a young cleaning woman was emptying considerable trash.

Baxter started up the steps and faced a woman with red hair protruding from under her stocking cap. She wore bib overalls over her sweatshirt.

"Is there anybody home here?" he asked. Perhaps Danielle had stayed behind to rest her sore body and Baxter could keep her company.

"They're all gone. They checked out first thing this morning," the cleaning lady reported from a gum filled mouth. Baxter noted that her sweatshirt read Green Mountain College.

"Checked out?" Baxter repeated. "We're talking about Mr. Selim and his lady companions." Perhaps he was at the wrong villa.

"The Arabs were here with the French girl, if that's who you mean? I guess they had a car pick them up first thing this morning. We'll have someone new coming in by noon." She stepped back into the open door and emptied an armful of towels into a canvas cart which sat in the corner of the deck. "They sure used a lot of towels," the cleaning lady commented as she added another armful of towels to the cart.

"I was with the Hakim party yesterday and dropped by for a drink. I may have left a notebook inside."

"You're welcome to look inside, Mister."

Baxter entered the room and walked quickly through the bedrooms, the bathroom and the sauna, finally hovering for a minute at the wet bar. There were towels everywhere and Baxter spotted condom wrappers in the master bedroom waste basket.

"I guess I didn't leave that notebook here," Baxter said over the hum of the vacuum cleaner. He received a nod in reply.

Baxter located Miss Grace at the front desk.

"Do I understand that Mr. Selim's party has checked out?" he asked after capturing Miss Grace's attention.

"A car and driver came for them first thing in the morning. They have checked out and certainly won't be welcomed back," she commented sternly.

"I was their guest for a drink yesterday afternoon. I'd be interested in renting a villa. If not on this stay, perhaps a future stay."

"The villas are owned by private investors. It is quite difficult to rent to just anyone unless they are acceptable to the villa owners. There is a waiting list for the C villa and a very nice family from Hartford will be moving in from the main lodge to the villa by noon today."

"And who is the owner of Villa C?" Baxter asked.

"That particular villa is owned by a prominent family in Boston and Mr. Selim was their guest."

"Can you identify the prominent family by name, Miss Grace?"

"That sort of information is confidential, Mr. Baxter," she responded brusquely.

It was ten-thirty on Christmas Eve Day. His room had yet to be cleaned. Baxter decided to drive off the grounds and visit some of the other nearby towns. They showed as small dots on the map on two lane highways. The Walnut Inn appeared to have three neighboring towns with Old Granby as the closest some ten miles south. Pleasant Rock was fifteen miles north while Taft was twenty miles east. Baxter selected Pleasant Rock for his visitation. He had concluded that ski resorts could be quite boring for guests who don't ski.

Pleasant Rock was located in a small valley thick with pines and birch. There was a large logging operation next to a railhead. The town seemed drab, and lacked the minimal glitter offered by Old Granby. He parked his rental car on the main street and began to walk.

Pleasant Rock was four streets deep and ten blocks long. There was a scraggy Christmas banner drooped across the main street. The A & P supermarket parking lot was filled with cars and seemed to be the busiest place in town. People on the street nodded to one another, but Baxter detected no smiles. They made brief eye contact with Baxter and looked away. Pleasant Rock was a lonely place on the edge of the world.

Martha was right, Baxter had become a lonely man without family, and without a great deal of close friends. He had spent his life as the charming visiting consultant without roots.

Two of his three career principal employers had been acquired. Only the US Army remained intact. He purchased a cap with earflaps from a vintage variety store and looked for a place where he could stop for a single beer before returning to the comfort of the Walnut Inn. He had his choose of three places on the main street and selected The Nutmeg Tap Room.

It turned out to be a rustic place where the locals passed time and strangers were carefully observed. The Nutmeg Tap could have been located in Brinker's Falls, New York, or Iron Creek, Minnesota. It smelled of stale beer. There was a pool table, two slot machines, and an ancient 1950s juke box. Behind the far corner of the bar was a grill with hamburgers frying. In the middle of the bar, two men in plaid flannel shirts were perched on bar stools engaged in Indian wrestling. The bartender was a woman wearing a New England Patriot sweatshirt.

"You guys break anything and you bought it," she said sharply to the Indian wrestlers.

"Help you?" she greeted Baxter.

"I'll have a bottle of Samuel Adams," Baxter ordered after observing a Samuel Adams neon sign in the back of the bar.

"Need a glass?"

"That would be nice."

The men in the middle of the bar appeared to be in a standoff. His father would have put both of them away at will.

"That's one dollar."

"Truly a bargain," Baxter said planting a five dollar bill on the bar in return for a beer bottle and glass.

The juke box played 'Here Comes Santa Claus'. The wrestlers unlocked their hands. "Two taps down here, Mary," one said. "And some ice water too," the other added.

"Mary, take the taps out of here," Baxter said pointing to his collection of dollars on the bar.

"Hey, where the hell did you come from?" one of the wrestlers looked Baxter over. He was short, pot bellied, fortyish and wore a crew cut. His companion was younger and had shoulder length hair, and full beard.

"I came in from outside to have a beer today." Baxter stepped off his bar stool so that they could take note of his size.

The bartender was a hard looking blonde in her forties who in her tight fitting blue jeans presented herself favorably as she served schooners of beer to the wrestlers.

"He paid for them," the bartender credited Baxter as she placed the beer in front of her other customers.

The younger man stepped down to Baxter and looked him over. The sleeves of his flannel shirt had been rolled up and revealed a succession of tattoos on each arm.

"Thanks for the beer, buddy. Why did you buy it?"

"I had an old memory when I saw you two Indian wrestling. My father used to be one hell of an Indian wrestler. I thought back to my father," Baxter explained.

"How are you as an Indian wrestler?"

"Sons of Indian wrestlers rarely equal their fathers."

"Let's see your hands," he demanded.

Baxter held out his left hand and allowed the man with the tattoos to run his hand over Baxter's. It was rough with calluses and the tip of his little finger was gone.

"You do office work?" he sneered.

"I work with my mind. My father worked with his hands." The shorter man with the crew cut stepped between them.

"It was very nice of you to buy us beers, Mister," he said in a conciliatory tone. "I don't recall seeing you before."

"This is my first visit here. I'm doing a little exploring. I'm staying at a place called the Walnut Inn."

"That's a very nice place," Mary, the bartender, commented.

"What are you doing now, Mister? Slumming?" the younger man demanded.

"Now, Marv, just settle down," the older man said. "This stranger here is just being neighborly. It's Christmas Eve, and it's clear to me that neither one of us is going to beat the other. Let's have a Christmas beer with this kind gentleman and go home."

"You want to arm wrestle me?" Marv challenged Baxter.

"I'd prefer to arm wrestle, Mary," Baxter offered. Marv raised the beer schooner to his mouth and drained it.

"You got a smart mouth. Next time I see you, you and I are going to have a little action," he said using his sleeve to wipe his mouth. "Merry Christmas, Vern," Marv said to his companion and he pushed his way out the front door.

"Marv, can get mean from time to time, Mister," Vern said after taking a sip from his beer. "We both do logging work and got off early today for Christmas Eve. What brings you over here?"

"I wanted to take a look at the world outside the Walnut Inn," Baxter explained.

"You a New York fella?" Vern asked.

"I'm from Minnesota originally, but I've lived in New York a number of years."

"You're also pretty sure of yourself. I thought Marv was getting ready to take you. Do you think you could have handled him?"

"I really can't comment on that," Baxter replied.

Vern finished his beer and slipped into a vest that had been placed over a bar stool. "Thanks for the beer, Mister. Keep your eye out for Marv if you come this way again. So long, Mary." He waved as he went through the door.

Mary was applying fresh lipstick in front of the bar mirror.

"I'll have one more Samuel Adams and I'm on my way, Mary," Baxter requested.

"You don't look to me like a bar room fighter," Mary said serving Baxter his beer.

"It has been a slow afternoon."

"I may close up pretty soon. It's half past four on Christmas Eve."

"I'll drink quickly," Baxter offered.

"Take your time. I'm going to close up now."

Baxter remained on his bar stool and observed Mary move about the room turning down lights and finally opening the front door where she tied a 'Closed Christmas Eve' sign on the front door.

Mary poured herself a glass of bar scotch and seated herself on the stool next to Baxter.

"So, how's the bartending business going, Mary? Is this your full time occupation?"

"It's my uncle's bar and I'm watching after it while he's in Florida. He comes back in January, and I'm out of here. I grew up here and left. I came back here in December, and my uncle asked me to take the tap room until he got back from Florida. Now who in the hell are you?"

"Joseph Baxter, Jr." Baxter extended his hand for Mary to grip. Her hand was a smooth in some places and hard in others.

"Mary Burchek. What do you do when you're not staying at the Walnut Inn?"

"I'm a world famous management consultant who is in the process of early retirement. I'm visiting my daughter who runs the gift shop at the Walnut Inn. I'm heading back to New York on Friday. I have been married and divorced three times, and am currently a single man. Your turn, Mary."

Baxter had hoped that he would be in bed sometime that evening with either Aiysha or Danielle. Now he had been reduced to pursuing a lady bartender in a small town for his evening's sport? Was this to be his fate in middle-age?

618

"I used to work at the Walnut Inn. I was a maid there a couple of winters right after I left high school. It's a very snooty place. Have you met Miss Grace? She fired me. It was okay by me. They didn't pay worth shit."

"What were you fired for?" Baxter asked.

"Fraternization," Mary Burchek carefully sounded out the word in syllables. "I kept a little company with one of the bartenders, and a couple of the guests. The guests tipped me a little. I'm not welcome there anymore."

"How long ago was that?"

Mary Burchek shook her head. "Twenty, twenty-five years ago. I quit high school when I was sixteen. I figured I was hot stuff. After Walnut Inn canned me, I took a bus out to Los Angeles. I settled there for a couple of years and moved on to Nevada. I was in Stateline, Reno and Las Vegas. Had some good times and some bad times. Got married a couple of times, pushed on to Denver, wound up in Chicago. My uncle asked me to come out and take care of the Nutmeg until he got back from Christmas vacation. I'm getting the hell out of here in January."

"Where will you go?" Baxter asked.

"Probably Atlantic City. I know some people there. I sure as hell aren't' going to stick around here one more day. I don't have to. How about you, Joe?"

"I'm going back, to New York on Saturday, the 26th, and I'm unlikely to come back here for a long time."

"So you're passing through." Mary placed a cigarette between her lips and waited for Baxter to light it.

"I'll drive back to New York City on Saturday morning and will be unlikely to return for at least a couple of years," Baxter responded by lighting Mary's cigarette with book matches he located on the bar.

Mary took a long drag and exhaled through her nose. "So what made you come to Pleasant Rock?"

"I don't ski and thought I'd visit the neighboring towns. I thought Nutmeg Tap appeared to be as likely a place as any to have a beer. The arm wrestling reminded me of growing up in northern Minnesota."

"Let me come to the point," Mary said. "Are you looking for a little action"?"

"No, I was looking for a couple of beers. I've seen my share of action."

"Twenty-five bucks would come in handy this close to Christmas." Mary stood up from her bar stool and stroked Baxter's face with a rough hand. She had a compact body and a hard face. "I'd earn it."

Baxter opened his wallet and produced two tens and a five. "Mary, I'm not interested. But here's twenty-five dollars for your Christmas fund."

"But I haven't done anything to earn it," she protested mildly and swept the money down the bar nest to her cigarette pack.

"Consider the offering in the spirit of Christmas, Mary."

Mary went back around the bar and drew a fresh glass of beer. "This is on the house," she said placing her elbows on the bar. "Here's to Christmas Eve," she toasted.

"Do you have family in town, Mary?"

"Just my uncle, and he's off in Florida. He's got a trailer home down there. I'm staying at his trailer home up here. He took his waitress and her kids down there with him and left me to run the bar. I've got a cleanup man and two waitresses on over the weekend. My uncle Eddie pays me off the books, and he knows I won't steal from him. The man's sixty something and he's talking about staying in Florida an having me run this place for him." Mary shook her head. "Pleasant Rock is the end of the world."

"Then why did you come back?"

"I was in New Orleans living with this guy, and he started beating me up. Uncle Eddie was the only one I could think of who could help. He sent me down a money order Federal Express. I left with my purse and all the clothes I could get in a suit case and caught a bus. Now here I am back where I started from twenty-five years ago after I was canned from the Walnut Inn."

"Do you have children?"

"I've been pregnant." Mary counted on her fingers and stared at the ceiling closing her eyes. "Six times. I always gave them up for adoption. I had one abortion and I never want another one. The oldest one has to be twenty-four now, and the youngest has to be twelve. A woman today has more things to her disposal so she can stay away from pregnancy. A lot of times I wish to hell I had been born a man so I could have been the abuser instead of the abusee. What about you, Joe?"

"I made a girl pregnant in my senior year of high school. We were divorced when I was in the Army and she married someone else. Then I married a very beautiful and evil woman, and had two children before we divorced. My most recent wife was a very powerful retail executive who out-earned me. I fathered a son who died a few years back, and I have a daughter who dropped out of college and is running the gift shop at the Walnut Inn. I will be retiring from my firm in January and will essentially be a free agent."

Mary pulled the bartender's stool to a place across from Baxter's stool. Then she went to the juke box and deposited several coins. "What we need is some atmosphere," she announced. *Love Me Tender* sounded.

"The words just roll off your tongue, Joe. I don't know if they're all fibs and lies, but I sure like the way you talk. This is a lumber town. There are a lot of hard talking, plain people here. The smart ones leave town and the slow ones stay. I love sitting here and talking to you. You handle yourself so confidently." Mary extended her pack of Marlboros to Baxter. He shook his head.

"How about dancing with me, Prince Charming?"

Baxter looked at his watch. It was pushing five o'clock. He had already stayed beyond his one or two beer and out plan.

"Com'on," Mary held out her hand. "We'll have a Christmas Eve dance. Just one."

Mary led Baxter to an empty place on the far side of the pool table and switched off the light. She was five feet five or six in her athletic shoes and danced on her tiptoes.

"God, you're tall," she said as she slipped into Baxter's arms pressing her body aggressively against his. "You're a smooth dancer. Let's have a Christmas kiss."

Mary pulled Baxter's mouth down to meet hers. Her mouth tasted of stale beer and cigarettes. Mary rubbed her body strategically against Baxter. He hadn't remembered *Love Me Tender* as such a lengthy song.

He kissed Mary on the forehead at the conclusion of Elvis Presley's final whole note and pushed her gently away.

"This has been great fun, Mary, but I've got to catch up with my daughter." Baxter quickly stepped away in the direction of the door.

"Come back here, you smooth talking son of a bitch!" Mary demanded.

Baxter unbolted the front door.

"Come back! You cocksucker!" she shouted as he closed the front door.

Mary ran out into the empty street after Baxter's car and shouted obscenities into the early evening Christmas Eve quiet. He reached the Pleasant Rock city limits quickly, and turned into a two lane road that was crowded with slow moving pick-up trucks and battered Chevrolets. Baxter edged his rental car forward at an average speed of twenty-five miles an hour. He found himself thinking about his father for the first time in a long time.

It was probably the Indian wrestling that triggered Baxter's memory. The Nutmeg Inn was his father's kind of place. He would have quickly disposed of Marv and Vern in Indian wrestling and would have ravished Mary Burchek on the pool table.

The memories flashed in Baxter's mind in a series of snapshots. He was walking down Broadway with his father back in Iron Creek pushing Gordy in the stroller. He was in Spike's room learning about Tchaikovsky and unionism. He had won his first, last, and only fight with Kawalchek defending Lucy Albright's honor. How odd that the Joe Baxter of 1952 had become the Joe Baxter of 1991. What would the Joe Baxter of 2001 be like. He could have regressed into his father's model of behavior on Christmas Eve afternoon. Baxter was the son of the town brawler drunk and a slow-witted country woman. Where was his genetic legacy?

Admittedly he now had a lonely life. His long time acquaintances were either retiring or dying around him. Now Baxter was leaving the bedrock of his professional career. His lone sexual partner in 1991 had been poor Darlene Bohlweiser. There had been a great many overtures but no first acts.

At his daughter's invitation, Baxter joined the Walnut Inn "kids" for Christmas Eve dinner. They dined in a lower floor room presided over by Miss Grace.

Baxter was seated at a long table on Miss Grace's right and Muffin was on her left directly across from her father. Archie, the red-headed bellhop was seated next to Muffin. The room was filled with young men and women in their very early twenties. They wore sweaters and sported good complexions. Only the girls wore earrings.

Wine, beer, punch, and soft drinks were served in pitchers. The room was trimmed extensively with banners, wreathes, colored lights and elves suspended from the ceiling. Christmas music was piped into the room.

Baxter's adventurous luncheon of the previous day in the vaunted Matterhorn Room had been the talk of the staff. He was now Martha's legendary father.

Miss Grace and Baxter shared a small pitcher of white wine which he estimated, on first taste, had a retail value of $3 a bottle.

"And are you enjoying your stay here?" Miss Grace asked.

"The Walnut Inn is truly a handsome facility, Miss Grace. The staff is obviously very professional and well trained and I expect that many of the young people who begin their careers at the Walnut Inn take the value system they have learned here and use it as a platform to sustain them in their future careers."

Miss Grace broke into a broad smile. "I believe I would be the first to agree with that statement. Most of the young staff people who get their start here go on to enjoy exceptional careers in the fields that they choose."

Baxter toyed with the idea of introducing Mary Burchek's name as a worthy alumnus who was applying the simple truths she had learned in her Walnut Inn days.

"Martha showed me your book, Mr. Baxter," Archie chimed in. "Have you written a lot of them?"

"Just one. But I may start another the first of the year."

"Martha informed me that you are a famous pay consultant. I would imagine that your work is quite interesting," Miss Grace went on. Baxter found himself locked into a continuous conversation with Miss Grace. Muffin brought her friends one by one to meet her father. One was the blonde haired maitre'd from the Matterhorn Room.

"Who were those people, Mr. Baxter?"

"Just your average jet setters. Mr. Selim is a well-known investment manager who prefers to travel with a pair of ladies. He always brings a spare with him," Baxter explained.

"Oh, Mr. Baxter, how you talk," Miss Grace said suppressing a giggle.

Later she patted his hand to make a point. The room began to thin out after the main course of turkey had been served. There were some attempts at caroling, but the singing gave way to table clearing. Baxter was left with Miss Grace who began to launch into her life story.

"I just planned to stay out of school one semester. I was a sophomore at the University of Vermont. It was the winter of 1948. I was asked if I could stay through the summer. Then they gave me a raise for staying through the ski season. The Neisner family owned the Inn. The generation that ran the Inn were very active. They were succeeded by a generation who hired Managers to run the Inn. Now we have a hospitality firm running the Inn. We seem to have a new General Manager every other year, and they get younger and younger while I become older and older. The gift shop has suddenly become a real money maker around here. Martha has come into her own."

"Martha came to us a few years back as a very fragile young woman. She was attending the community college and in therapy. She was in a zombie state her first year but then she took hold. I assume you have been informed about Larry."

"I met him this summer. He seemed like a nice young man," Baxter commented.

"Larry has been the Inn's handyman for the past five or so years. Competent help is hard to come by up here. Larry appeared out of nowhere one day when we had a plumbing problem. He fixed the plumbing and proved to be a whiz electrician. He is a nice young man, but he is going nowhere. Larry befriended your daughter, and this spring Martha moved in with him. I was beside myself. If she settled in with the Inn handyman, Martha Baxter's life could mirror my own life. Her therapist, Dr. Erlich, is a good friend of mine. I asked her to intercede as best as she could to persuade Martha to move out from Larry. I'm sure you will agree, Mr. Baxter, Martha needs to be with rising young men and women her own age, not with hotel handymen who do a little painting on the side."

Martha returned with Archie and they took up chairs around Baxter and Miss Grace.

"You two seem to be getting along famously," Muffin proclaimed.

"I am about to invite Miss Grace to the Matterhorn Room for a nightcap," Baxter said rising from the table and offering his arm.

"I will have one drink with you, Mr. Baxter," Miss Grace said rising to her feet. "But I must make a brief stop to the powder room." Her words came out slightly slurred.

"Mr. Baxter," Archie offered. "You are truly an amazing man."

Baxter's final evening at Walnut Inn was spent at a dinner in a place called the Evergreen Lodge. It was to be Muffin's treat. She brought a boy named Nick, who turned out to be an MIT senior who worked Christmas holidays as a waiter in the Matterhorn Room. Baxter's surprise date was Dr. Erlich, her therapist.

Dr. Erlich arrived at the Evergreen Lodge twenty minutes late.

"I know she'll be here, Dad," Muffin had assured her father during the wait. Nick wanted to know about the Matterhorn Room incident.

"I'm on the evening shift, Mr. Baxter. But the report was that those women were absolutely gorgeous. You were massaging their feet and it looked like you were all going off to the sauna together."

Dr. Erlich turned out to be a slight woman with short black hair, and high bangs. She wore bluish tinted glasses and spoke with a slight accent, and appeared to wear little in the way of make-up. Dr. Erlich wore a red sweater with a single silver chair and black stretch pants.

"So this is the famous father," she greeted Baxter. He accepted her hand and seated Dr. Erlich to his right.

"And you're the world famous therapist from Vermont."

"I have been brought up-to-date on your activities by Grace Dewing, a long time friend. It appears that you have taken the Walnut Inn by storm without ever putting a ski on."

Muffin fairly bubbled in front of her therapist. She wanted to make a favorable impression. Dr. Erlich apparently was serving in a surrogate role for Muffin.

A trio consisting of an accordion, bass, and drummer played to a small dance floor at the Evergreen Lodge. Nick escorted Muffin to the dance floor after twenty minutes of chatter and Baxter found himself alone with his daughter's therapist.

"It's very interesting to meet you after so many sessions with your daughter. I formed an image of an overpowering taciturn man, and you appear to be very charming."

"Your approval is obviously important to my daughter."

"Your daughter was very fragile but she is growing stronger. She has come to recognize that you are her father, regardless whether you are her biological father. Her mother appears to be a very destructive person. Her image of you to me was some kind of Daddy Warbucks who has unstated standards that Martha can never meet. You are very important to Martha. Martha believes she has been abandoned by both her mother and her stepmother. The death of her brother, of course impacted her deeply. The abortion continues to haunt Martha."

"Was the Larry relationship good for her?"

"No. It was comforting, but Larry is a charming but unstable young man. I agreed with Grace Dewing that she break off this relationship. Now she has a number of relationships with young men like Nick. Martha is very sensitive about physical relationships with men. She never wants to be pregnant again."

Dr. Erlich took a sip of Perrier and stared at Baxter through her tinted blue glasses. "Do you have any questions you would like to ask me?"

"Sure," Baxter responded. "Would you like to dance?"

Baxter left the Walnut Inn for New York City very early on Saturday morning, December 28th. On balance, Baxter concluded that he could have had a better time with Beth Gold in Bermuda. Muffin appeared to be on the mend, and we would have some costly tuition and residence bills to pay over the next four years.

He checked his phone mail and found the Rusty Collins message. He remembered the tall red-headed consultant who was now officed in Los Angeles. He had shared a room with her one evening in Chicago the winter before. He remembered her as a bright, independent lady who obviously was concerned with her career direct on. His phone mail contained a series of broadcast announcements from Glen and Jack concerning the merged firm transition. One message, which was no surprise to Baxter, still stunned him. Effective Tuesday, January 2, 1992 all offices would use Robson Barber as the official firm name in all written and telecommunications. New letterhead and business cards would be distributed on Friday, December 27th. Hail and farewell, John McKenzie!

Baxter continued to periodically dial the switchboard number of the New York Office throughout the weekend. He would listen to the sweet sound of the firm's name and hang up.

YOU HAVE REACHED THE NEW YORK OFFICE OF MCKENZIE BARBER. OUR OFFICES ARE NOW CLOSED. IF YOU KNOW THE EXTENSION OF THE PERSON YOU ARE CALLING, YOU MAY ENTER IT NOW. FOR GENERAL INFORMATION, THE NEW YORK OFFICE OF MCKENZIE BARBER IS OPEN WEEKDAYS FROM 8:30 AM UNTIL 5:30 PM.

Baxter donned his overcoat and walked through the streets of New York. It was a crisp late Saturday afternoon with full darkness at five o'clock. Baxter walked up Fifth Avenue through the retail shops and stopped into the Stanhope front bar for a drink. Sitting at the bar watching a college basketball game was the unmistakable profile of Tommy Tweetman. He was accompanied by a blonde lady in a dark pants suit who resembled Dr. Horgcost's former executive assistant, Elyssa.

Baxter seated himself two stools down. 39 years earlier they had been Iron Creek Cougars. Tom Tweetman sat erectly on his stool. His body appeared to be in the game. His shoulders tightened and his fists clenched as he watched the game. Elyssa was smoking a cigarette and appeared bored.

Baxter waited for a commercial. "Nothing but net, Tom," he announced himself.

Tom Tweetman turned his head in Baxter's direction. Baxter moved down the bar to the neighboring bar stool. Tom Tweetman's face was fuller and slightly lined, but continued to resemble his 1952-53 Cougar teammate.

"Joe Baxter," Tweetman acknowledged. "Elyssa, do you remember Joe Baxter?"

"McKenzie Barber," she said stuffing her cigarette out in the ash tray. "Tom, I may go up to the room and take a nap." Elyssa stood up from her bar stool. Baxter stood up to shake her hand. He remembered Elyssa's short skirts and long legs from their 1987 meeting. Now she appeared tall, thin, and leggy in high red boots and a tight fitting pants suit.

Elyssa accepted Baxter's hand. "We've come a long way since you came to see us in Washington, Joe. I know Tom will fill you in." She kissed Tom Tweetman on the cheek.

"I'm really exhausted, Tom. Please remember dinner reservations are at eight."

Tweetman placed a possessive hand on Elyssa's thigh and patted it. "I'll be up in a half hour or so. I could use a nap, too."

Baxter and other men in the bar observed Elyssa's exit.

"She's a fine looking woman, Tom," Baxter offered. It was half-time and Duke was playing UCLA in some kind of holiday tournament.

"I love the Duke teams," Tweetman said as the camera showed the players warming up for the second half. "I could have been one hell of a point guard for Coach K."

"I believe shooting guard would have been your natural position, Tom."

"This is amazing. Ten million people running in and out of New York City every day, and I stay in a small hotel on the upper East Side, and who comes sauntering in the door but my old 1953 Iron Creek Cougar teammate. Do you live around here, Joe?"

"I was taking a long way and got thirsty, Tom."

A buzzer sounded and the teams prepared for the second half.

"Last time we were together, Joe, we had words. You were catching the shuttle back. What was that about? Refresh my memory."

Baxter refilled his beer glass. "I told you that I had gone to bed with Lucy."

Tom Tweetman held up two fingers for the bartender. "One more all around, Bart," he instructed the bartender.

"I like this hotel, Joe. Elyssa and I have been coming up weekends. She likes to hang around in the Metropolitan Museum across the street. Ever stayed here?"

"I had a couple of glasses of wine here six years ago."

"You're the consummate New Yorker now, Joe. I could get used to this place. Ask me how it's going?" Tommy's request seemed like a challenge.

"Gee whiz, how's it going, Tom?"

"It's fantastic. Dr. Horgcost has resigned, and the company has been named Replen-o-link Corp. I am CEO, and we are operating at 55% rate of growth. We are no longer a beltway bandit company but a NASDAQ listed growth company headed for the NYSE. You were the guy who told me to call Horgcost and worked out my employment deal. For that service, I forgive you for screwing my ex-wife. Lucy is remarried to my old customer, Howard Brunger, in Indianapolis. You know Howard. Lucy told me the three of you had lunch one time in New York."

"He was a great catch, Tom."

"A fucking great catch. He inherited his grandfather's insurance agency, and it's still profitable. Lucy can blend right back into her Indianapolis social leader routine and I hope to hell that she's ready to put out often enough to maintain Howard's attention."

"Adaptation is the key to survival, Tom."

"Here comes a back door play, Joe," Tommy predicted and a UCLA guard glided in for an uncontested lay-up. "How would you like to be playing today, Joe? I know I could have made it. But how would you have done. You couldn't be a 6'4" center, and you'd be pretty small for a forward. You couldn't have made it as a guard."

"Tom, then was then and now is now. I might have had to give Ladies basketball a try or have gone to a very small high school. The point is that I played, and I wasn't all that bad. If I would have hit that last shot against Darwin, we would have gone to the State. I never should have tried to bank that rebound. My instinct was to shoot for the net, but Coach Rychek wanted everything in close banked."

"Coach Rychek!" Tom Tweetman raised his glass. "What an incompetent asshole! We had a hell of a coach at Ginter Lakes. Cory Dunlap was his name. He went on to be a successful college coach in Missouri. The Ginter Lakes Indiana team went to the semi-finals of the State in 1953. There was no comparison between the talent we had at Ginter Lakes and the Cougars. I took the Cougars about as far as I could have taken them. I always wondered how my life would have turned out if my Dad hadn't taken the job at the Iron Creek Clinic."

"You might have never met Lucy," Baxter jabbed.

"Shit! There was a career mistake I could have avoided. She was probably the best looking woman in town, but there really wasn't a lot of talent in Iron Creek."

"Ginter Lakes, of course, is a major source for Miss America candidates," Baxter commented.

"What the hell was the name of the one you knocked-up that got so fat?"

"Her name was Maggie. She's continued to expand. I was just back for a funeral. Diane Ganski died."

"That's too bad, Joe. I don't remember her that well. What's Ganski doing? Is he still a small town politician?"

"Ed is now a State Senator. He may be headed for Washington one of these days," Baxter offered.

Tom Tweetman shook his head. "You never can tell where people will wind up. I never figured for Joe Baxter to become a big time New York Partner with McKenzie Barber?" Tweetman paused. "Did I just read that McKenzie Barber has just merged with someone?"

"Robson Allen Harbridge," Baxter affirmed. "The merger is effective January 2nd."

"Are you out of a job, Joe?"

"I am retiring, Tom."

Tom Tweetman's face broke into a large grin. "So the great Joe Baxter is a merger victim."

"We're all victims, Tom. I have chosen to retire and proceed on other options."

They watched the game in silence until a foul was called.

"Lucy has pointed to you for years as the great success model She'd read about you in the *Wall Street Journal* and say, 'Look how well Joe is doing!' Then Lucy would tell me that she believed you'd had always been in love with her."

"I always had a fondness for Lucy, Tom. It was never a matter of smoldering passion. How are your kids doing?"

Tom Tweetman nodded his head as he watched a Duke guard bury a three pointer. "I could have averaged 35 points a game with a three point shot rule, Joe. I have Kevin in the business. He's a sales rep in Atlanta for Replen-o-link. I'll move him up to home office in a year or two as a product manager. Kevin's got a lot of upside. I got Jill transferred into Indiana where she has just been accepted in the women's basketball program. She'll be on full scholarship starting spring semester. Jill has her old man's touch. How about your kids, Joe?"

"My oldest boy, Joel, caught a bug and died last year. I just finished a holiday visit with my daughter, Martha. She's working a posh Vermont resort called the Walnut Inn."

"That's too bad about your son," Tommy said nodding his head as he stared ahead at the televised basketball game.

"Elyssa and I have a ski weekend planned for February in Vermont. What's the name of the place again?"

Baxter replied Walnut Inn and Tommy wrote the name down on a small pad he produced from an inside pocket of his blazer.

"Do you and Elyssa do a lot of traveling together, Tom?"

"She's my main squeeze, Joe. She was a big help when I landed at FRS and helped me take out Horgcost when the time was right. Elyssa's our Vice President for Administration now. I couldn't operate without her."

"How do your kids get along with her?"

"They don't. Elyssa's a good business head, which their mother was not. She also is an accommodating woman which Lucy was not. So right now, Joe, Tom Tweetman has pretty near everything he wants. I'm running a hot company. I've got a couple of million dollars net worth based on the fair market value of my shares. And to top it off, I'm rid of Lucy Albright Tweetman without any damned alimony. We broke up for a while after I came back from Kentucky and went off to Bay State. You should have moved in and swept her off her feet. How different my life might have been."

"But then, Tom," Baxter said rising from his bar stool. "You might not be in the Stanhope front bar waiting to go upstairs to have a nap with Elyssa. It all evens out over time, Tom," Baxter said. He slapped Tom Tweetman on the shoulder and departed from the bar without looking back.

Baxter, on impulse, tried Stephany from the pay phone in the Stanhope lobby. He felt quite alone. The phone rang five times before transferring to voice mail.

"THIS IS STEPHANY HART," her arrogant crisp voice answered. "I'M OUT OF THE COUNTRY UNTIL JANUARY 5TH. IF YOU'RE A RECENT OR FORMER LOVER, I'M DOUBLY SORRY I MISSED YOUR CALL. IF YOU'RE A BURGLAR, FORGET ABOUT IT. MY BUILDING IS THE MOST SECURE IN NEW YORK. NOW PLEASE LEAVE A MESSAGE AFTER THE BEEP."

There was a low shrill beep. "Steph, Joe Baxter here, wandering around the neighborhood on a Saturday afternoon. It's been a while since you, and I, and Beth, got together. My last day at McKenzie Barber, Robson Allen as of 1-2-92, will be Wednesday, January 8th. I propose that the three of us get together for a final outrageous lunch before I embark on the next stage of my life. Call Beth and give me a call. 938-4924. I hope you have a lot of calls waiting from your second category."

Baxter crossed over 82nd Street to Park Avenue and then started off to the apartment he once shared with Bridgette. From a distance the entire penthouse floor appeared to be lighted. Baxter entered the lobby where he was greeted by a grey haired uniformed doorman. "Good evening, sir. May I help you?"

It was a new face to Baxter. He had been gone from the building for over three years.

"I believe you have a Miss Morgan in PHA. I'd like to drop in on her."

"We have a Miss Morgan in PHA, sir."

"Miss Bridgette Morgan?"

"Miss Bridgette," the doorman corrected Baxter.

"Would you call Miss Bridgette and tell her that I'm in the lobby and that I'd like to see her for a few minutes. My name is Joe Baxter."

The doorman went to the house phone and dialed. There was a long interval before a response came. He passed the phone to Baxter.

"Hi Bridg, I was in the neighborhood, saw the lights in the penthouse, and thought I'd drop in and say hello."

"Well aren't you sweet, Joey. I haven't heard from you since that day with the lawyers and here you are in my very own lobby on the first Saturday night after Christmas. What a surprise."

"I was with Muffin over the holidays. She sends you her best. Muff's developed into quite a capable little merchant."

"Well isn't that something. I'd love to hear all the details but I have company. I'm sure you understand. Call me some time, and we'll get together. I'm in the book, Joey. It was so nice to hear from you. Bye."

The line was dead. "Miss Bridgette has company. Thanks for your help."

The doorman looked Baxter up and down and then tipped his cap as Baxter exited through the revolving door of the high rise which had once been his home.

Baxter walked slowly down Madison Avenue to his apartment. It was pushing six-thirty. There were so many good memories of Bridgette. They had had something together at one time. Where had it gone?

At 64th Street, Baxter remembered the night with Monica following her discovery of Erik and the Baron de Hartogue in an indiscretion. She had been planning one of her own with Baxter, but became furious after discovering her husband had gained the initiative on her. Good old Monica who had played her role in the destruction of Brett Williamson. Where was Monica now? They had checked out of Baxter's life. Today was the day for Darlene Bohlweiser to board the Greyhound bus to a new life. It was time for Baxter to invite some new people into his life.

Wednesday, January 8, 1992

Baxter's alarm buzzed him awake at 6:30 AM. Today was a very special day in his life. He was going to meet with Dr. Gilbert Ranglinger and settle up on his twenty-five year career with McKenzie Barber. It had been his first night without the body of Rusty Collins comfortably positioned in bed with him. It was 3:30 AM in Los Angeles. Baxter had left a message in Rusty's phone mail the evening before. He had instructed her to call anytime. Had he missed her call?

Baxter padded his way into his living room office area. A red light was flashing on his phone. Baxter punched in his ID number and pressed the play button.

"JOE BAXTER, YOU HAVE TWO NEW MESSAGES."

"Message #1, 2:25 AM, Wednesday, January 8th."

"Baxter! Where are my wife and son? They belong with me! Your life is forfeit unless they return to me by January 15th."

Now there's a phone mail for you. Luke Bohlweiser talking through a handkerchief. He wrote on his desk pad. Call Sheriff Clowson and save the message.

"Message #2, 3:02 AM, Wednesday, January 8th."

"Joe, Rusty here. It's after midnight coast time and I'm still on New York time and quite exhausted. I'm also quite pleased with myself. I finished the final draft of my report to CCCS and it's pretty damned good. If I don't say so myself. I'm presenting it on carousel slides at eleven tomorrow. I believe I will knock their socks off. As I said, they will make me an offer on Friday. If it's VP, I'll pass. SVP, and the right money, I'm gone. I need a more full report on that funeral. They really had the flag at half mast in LA. This Ernie Grey must have been quite a guy. Everybody in the LA office had an Ernie Grey story this afternoon. I have been invited to a Manager's Forum this Friday afternoon about the new firm. I'd love to be in a position to announce that I'm quitting in the Q & A session. I suppose I should refrain from quitting until I have the offer letter in my hands. So much for the business news. God, I miss you!"

636

"I had only wanted to meet you for a drink or two and wound up in a very heavy and totally unexpected relationship. I shouldn't' tell you this, but I can't get you out of my mind. I am faced with the prospect of crawling into bed alone. You've spoiled me. Right now, I fear that I have fallen hopelessly in love with you. As I remember, you're coming out here next weekend. Tomorrow, I'm making reservations at a great little hideaway for us. I can't wait to get my hands on you or vice versa. Leave me lots of phone mail. I love you, Joe."

Now that's more like it, Baxter said pressing the save button on his phone. He shuffled through his address book and located the number of the Brinker's Falls Sheriff's office. He dialed Sheriff Clowson's direct line.

The call was answered on the third ring. "This is Bohlweiser may I help you?" Baxter immediately hung up. He'd have to get directly to Sheriff Clowson. His plan was to drive up in the early evening, gather up all of the McKenzie Barber historical data and return to New York to start his book. He would then stay out of Brinker's Falls for the rest of the year until the whole matter had blown over. Possibly he'd put the house up for sale.

Baxter put the coffee on and examined the New York Times obituary section. Today's entries included:

HANS SEJNA, 89, WROTE SPOOKY TALES

MARGO KENDRICK, ACTRESS DIES AT 81

ANITA JOYCE, 64, PROLIFIC ACTRESS IN STAGE ROLES LARGE AND SMALL

WADISLAW HOMOLKA, 70, EX-POLISH GENERAL AND DEFECTOR

So long ladies and gentlemen, he commented to the Obituary Section.

Joe Baxter remained prominently among the living and was ready to begin the first phase of his next career. He had the possibility of a long engagement at Burke Farms and some hints of interest from Hakim Selim. His agenda for January 8th was simple enough.

Baxter would finalize his retirement in his meeting with Dr. Gilbert Ranglinger, meet Beth and Stephany for his retirement lunch, drive to Brinker's Falls to collect his files and documents and return to the city. Baxter selected a blue pinstripe suit, white shirt, a wine Hermes tie with horses, burgundy braces, and black wingtips for the final day of his consulting career.

Dr. Gilbert Ranglinger was officed in a fortieth floor corner office. He had quietly moved in on December 2nd, some four weeks after the Partners meeting, and four weeks in advance of the January 2nd merger date. A memo signed by Glen and Jack, announced that Dr. Ranglinger had taken office space as part of an advance Robson Barber human resources team. McKenzie Barber Partners visited Ranglinger's office and were never seen again. Baxter received his first call from Ranglinger's office on December 3rd and weekly thereafter until he agreed to the nine-thirty meeting on the second Wednesday in January.

Baxter was well prepared for the meeting. All of his retirement documents were neatly organized in file folders in his brief case. He had an opinion letter from Zach Blum and supporting memoranda signed by both Glen Fitzgerald and Jack Pinker. As of January 9th, Baxter had used every day of his accumulated vacation.

He arrived ten minutes early, and was greeted by a tall bony woman wearing a grey gabardine suit, strappy shoes, and oversized dark rimmed glasses. Her desk was located in a small ante-room outside a closed door.

"Hi, I'm Joe Baxter. Dr. Ranglinger expects me at 9:30. I'm a little early."

"Oh goodness, Mr. Baxter, we've been looking for you for over a month. Please have a seat. Dr. Ranglinger is just finishing up with someone. You've been AWOL. Have a seat," she said gesturing to a pair of hardwood chairs backed against the radiator vent. "There's coffee there," she said gesturing at a large metal urn resting on a cube table.

"Madam, I've hardly been AWOL. I have, however, been using my unused vacation time prior to my retirement."

The woman, remaining un-introduced, returned to her chair.

"They certainly ran a country club around here. You're going to see a lot of changes that you're going to have to get used to."

Baxter filled a Styrofoam cup with coffee and began reading his *Wall Street Journal.*

John McCarthy emerged from the office. Baxter hadn't seen him in years. John was obviously angry and waved a menacing finger back into the open door. "You're going to hear from my attorney, Ranglinger."

"Good morning, John," Baxter greeted the aging one time Bill Dwyer protégé.

McCarthy's face broke into a grin. "Good morning, Joe," he greeted Baxter with a handshake and whispered. "Be careful of this slippery son-of-a-bitch."

Ranglinger appeared in the door of his office. He was a tall rangy man, easily three inches taller than Baxter. His black crew cut provided Dr. Ranglinger a military look. He wore a white button down shirt, dark tie, blue suit pants and gleaming black military shoes.

He grinned at Baxter from the office doorway. "You must be Joe Baxter. I've been trying to catch-up with you for a long time. Come on in."

Ranglinger's hand appeared to be much larger than Baxter's when they gripped hands.

"You make me sound like one of America's most wanted men," Baxter said taking a seat across from Ranglinger at a large oval desk. Baxter could see his Partner's personnel file folder resting in the center of the desk.

Ranglinger leaned back in his swivel chair and placed one large foot on the corner of the desk. "Well, Joe, looks like you got tired of coming to work about half way through the year."

"Dr. Ranglinger," Baxter interjected. "I would prefer that you call me, Mr. Baxter." Then Baxter snapped open his brief case and arranged his file folders across his side of the desk.

"So you're a formal kind of guy. And well prepared too, I see." Ranglinger delivered a broad white toothed smile that reminded Baxter of a dog flashing his teeth.

"I had a health problem which has been since corrected, and I have used up my accumulated vacation this summer in anticipation of my retirement."

"Bob Dilger, your Group Partner, stated that you just walked away from your responsibilities and took off."

"Bob was informed of my intent to take the summer off. I have a memorandum here that documents my request for leave which is initialed by Bob Dilger."

"You were to be part of the Dilger-led spin-out firm and then withdrew last September. Nobody has had much luck in finding you since, Baxter."

"Make that, Mr. Baxter, Dr. Ranglinger. I have my whereabouts well documented and expressed my intention to retire in an October 1st memorandum to Glen Fitzgerald. I sat on the retired Partners dais in the October Partner's meeting. This is my last day at McKenzie Barber, and I expect pension checks to start arriving March 1st. Now what's on your agenda, Dr. Ranglinger?"

Ranglinger rocked silently in his chair for a few seconds.

"There are some people around Robson Allen who are of the opinion that you may be worth saving. How would you like to hang around for a few years more and boost your pension benefits?"

"It's too late for that. I've been on the dais and have my watch." Baxter held up his Baume & Mercier for Ranglinger.

"How about as a 1099 consultant?" Ranglinger proposed.

"What would I be expected to do?"

"You know McKenzie Barber and its Partners and it's my understanding that you are very knowledgeable and up to date on the Partners pension plan." Ranglinger was now staring intently at Baxter. "From the acquiring firm perspective, we've got a 90 day period to sort out the personnel from our recently acquired firm. Someone told our Chairman, Al Carmichael, that there was a McKenzie Barber Partner named Joe Baxter who could be very helpful in sorting things out. It's taken me a month to catch up to you. I'm thirty days behind schedule."

"What would you want from me?"

"I want you to objectively consult with me on Partner retention matters. We can either rescind your retirement providing you an opportunity to earn some additional pension credits, or you can consult on a 1099 basis. If you want to consult, I can use you full time for the next 120 days and am prepared to guarantee you up to 1000 hours for 1992."

"My billing rate for this kind of work is $250 an hour," Baxter responded.

"That's a little high for a 1099 consultant," Ranglinger reacted.

"I'll give my good customers a volume discount. $225 an hour for a guarantee of 1000 hours beginning January 21st."

"$200 an hour starting on Monday, the 13th," Ranglinger negotiated. "We'll provide you an office over on Sixth Avenue. It would be in our best interests not to have you office at 311 Park Avenue."

"And you want me to help you sort out the keepers from the non-keepers? And you want me to consult on severance terms and pension liabilities for the non-keepers? Is that the planned scope of my consulting activities?" Baxter was reminded of the Racine, Wisconsin conference room at Washburn Manufacturing Company when Sir Basil wanted him to plan the redundancies.

"Let me be frank with you, Joe. And for God's sake, call me Gil. We, at Robson Allen, had to give away a lot to do this merger. Let's be objectively frank. McKenzie Barber was a floundering firm. It's been a floundering firm since your former Chairman, Ernie Grey, retired. We have agreed to honor the Partner's pension plan which, I might add, is richer than Robson Allen's plan. But we held out for the ninety day transition period to accomplish the needed surgery. A lot of cancer has spread through your old firm."

Ranglinger stared at Baxter.

"What was McCarthy so upset about? He was in your office before me and looked very upset," Baxter asked.

"We found that John McCarthy had a six month service break in 1971. He left McKenzie Barber to join a client and returned six months later. He has twenty years of service, not thirty-one. And he's being pensioned for twenty years."

"Has anyone nominated a fellow retired Partner named Clyde Nickerson for this consulting assignment? It sounds like the kind of work he'd thrive in. He'd probably do it cheaper for sheer love of the work," Baxter suggested.

"We, at Robson Allen, Joe, knew all about Clyde Nickerson. He wouldn't have been allowed to last more than a year at Robson Allen."

"You're kidding yourself, Gil," Baxter said using Ranglinger's first name. "Every organization has their share of Clyde Nickersons. The good ones never let them advance out of middle management."

Ranglinger began to rock again in his chair.

"You've heard our offer, Joe. Are you interested?"

"Why don't I think about it over the weekend and have a proposal letter on your desk on Monday morning? I'll want $200,000 from Robson Allen to do what you propose. I have a very important seminar to attend on the West Coast next weekend. The 21st would be my first on-site day. Once when you and I have finalized and documented what is expected of me, I can accomplish a lot off the initial work out of the office. I am prepared, of course, to sign all of the required confidentiality and non-disclosure agreements."

"Then do we have a deal?" Ranglinger asked.

"We do when I have a signed engagement letter," Baxter confirmed.

Ranglinger extended a hand across the desk to Baxter. His hand was larger than Baxter's.

"Now can I ask you about a couple of McKenzie Barber people outside the Partner Group?"

Baxter nodded his head.

Ranglinger opened a folder and read three names. "Dr. Ludwig Strasser, Miss Heidi Klein, and Miss Druanne Smithers. I believe you are familiar with these people."

Well, well, well, Baxter thought to himself. There were aspects of this proposed assignment that were attractive.

"Strasser came in with Ev Faunce. Do you know that name?"

"I terminated him January 2nd," Ranglinger answered. "Al Carmichael wanted him fired no later than 9:15 AM, and wanted me to call him after it was done. Strasser has been campaigning to do what I've asked you to do, Joe. I should add that he and Miss Klein are recently engaged."

"Strasser is a horror. He led a downsizing effort that got messy. He's both articulate and dumb. Heidi worked for me. She had a good work ethic. It would all depend on what you wanted her to do."

"Employee Benefits Administration."

"A great fit. Strasser will make a wonderful house husband."

"Druanne Smithers?"

"She's very good at firing secretaries. After that she falls off."

"They have been on my payroll since January 2nd. Is there any reason for retaining them?"

"I'd give Heidi a shot at Benefits, and send the other two home fast."

"That's what I plan to do," Ranglinger announced. "Do you see how well we can work together, Joe?"

"Where do you report, Gil?"

"Office of the Chairman, Joe. I'm on Executive Committee. If we work well enough together, there could be a steady succession of projects for you."

Baxter waited in silence for additional questions and comments. Ranglinger stood up indicating the meeting was over.

"I'll look for your letter on Monday, Joe. I've enjoyed this meeting. I believe you can provide a lot of insight and benefit to our new firm."

There was a final handshake and Baxter winked at Ranglinger's surly secretary as he exited from the office area.

Baxter returned to his office for the last time. He had accumulated four corrugated boxes in the area between his desk and the wall. Baxter had anticipated being required to pack in front of security guards. He had heard tales from other Partners who were watched as they packed. It had been a Nickerson procedure that had been continued under Strasser. The guards would approve every item that was packed. When the packing was completed, the boxes were sealed and shipped off UPS to an address of the Partner's choice. The Partners were then relieved of their access cards and keys and escorted to the glass revolving doors of the main lobby. It was suspected by some departing Partners that the boxes were re-opened for a final inspection before they were shipped.

Baxter had expected the worst from Robson Allen avoiding Gil Ranglinger as long as he could. He had, in turn, been treated professionally, and offered a lucrative consulting contract. Robson Allen, the upstart consulting firm of 1946, had overtaken and swallowed McKenzie Barber. Leadership had been the difference. Charley Robson had developed a competent successor, while McKenzie Barber's Partners had rebelled against the choices left for them, and installed alternative leadership that was incompetent. Who was to blame? It really got down to Ernie Grey, the Chairman, who stayed too long.

Baxter stood over his assembled boxes and looked around the room for a place to start.

"Can you use some help?" a Bronx accent called out from Baxter's office doorway. It was Rose Marie, his shared secretary. "I got nothing to do out there. The whole Benefits and Comp practice is off on some day long wing ding meeting that Mr. Dilger organized. I typed up the agenda and they are going to be gone all day."

Rose Marie was a heavyset, outspoken woman who wore too much make-up and earrings that nearly brushed her shoulders.

"Come in and join the fun," Baxter invited.

"I've seen you take stuff out of here in small batches for the last month," Rose Marie commented.

"Yes. I've been preparing for my retirement. I seemed to have accumulated a lot of paper over my career. Some I'll want to throw away and some I'd like to take with me."

"You're not doing anything the security people would get upset about. Are you?"

"I just left Dr. Ranglinger's office, and I assure you that I'm free as a bird to begin my retirement."

Baxter opened his credenza and began to stack folders and reports on his desk. He emptied out the credenza, all of his desk drawers and his bookshelf onto his desk. A series of stacks ranged from three to four feet high.

"Boy, you sure have a lot of stuff." Rose Marie picked up a copy of Baxter's book. "*Executive Pay*," she read. "*Management Realities and Shareholder Expectations*. The McKenzie Barber Press." Rose Marie began to leaf through the pages. "Was this book sold to people in bookstores?"

"It was sold in bookstores and given away to clients. Now in retirement, I may write a second edition."

"Is the McKenzie Barber Press still around?"

"It disappeared with the publication of this book. Mr. Nickerson assumed responsibility for the McKenzie Barber Press, and he was always good at making things disappear. Let's put it in the bottom of the first box."

Rose Marie passed the book to Baxter and gently placed it in the box. He suddenly had old memories of his nooners with Sybil McCarthy back in the McKenzie Barber Press days. He would have to bring up her name at lunch today with Stephany.

The debris from Baxter's career was stacked in large piles across his desk. There were old client reproofs and presentations. He carefully gathered all of the Penn Steel reports and presentations and encircled them with heavy strength rubber bands."

"Are those things that you should be taking out of the firm?" Rose Marie questioned.

"Rose Marie, leave my office at once," Baxter said with conviction.

"I'm going to call security," Rose Marie threatened and stomped out of the room.

Baxter dialed Ranglinger's extension.

"Dr. Ranglinger's office," the officious secretary answered.

"Joe Baxter here. I'd like to speak to Gil."

"He's in conference."

"Get him out. I need to talk to him this very minute."

"His door is closed," the voice protested.

"Then go to the door. Knock and tell Gil I'm on the phone."

"I'll put you on hold."

Ranglinger's voice came on the phone. "What's up Joe?"

"I'm cleaning out my office, and some secretary is calling security because she believes some six year old client reports may represent client sensitive information. If you and I are going to work together, I want you to call security right now and head off those goons. I have a luncheon to make and I want to pack quickly without interruption."

"You're not walking out with anything you shouldn't?"

"Be adult," Baxter came back.

There was a silence at the end of the phone before Ranglinger responded. "I'll look forward to receiving your engagement letter, Joe. I believe that you and I will work well together. I will call security personally."

Baxter hung up the phone and continued the sorting of his effects. He filled two boxes with papers and files that he wanted to retain and filled four boxes with scrap. Baxter sealed the boxes with tape, printed his name and address on an adhesive label, and pushed the boxes into the hallway. It was 12:15 and he could see Rose Marie applying lipstick at her secretarial station.

"Rose Marie," he called out authoritatively. "These boxes are security cleared and to be shipped to my home address. The boxes inside the office are scrap."

She nodded her head. Baxter donned his topcoat and waved as he walked past her desk on the way to the elevators. He boarded an elevator packed with youtfuly lunch-bound consultants.

"I can't get used to Robson Barber," commented a dark haired young man in his early twenties. "I got new Robson Barber cards, but they misspelled my name."

His blonde companion added. "I heard that they were going to change the pictures in reception and take down McKenzie's picture and replace it with Charley Robson."

"Weren't there three of them? You don't suppose they'll want to put up pictures of all three of them?" a tall young man with glasses contributed from the rear of the elevator.

"Somebody just died who used to be Chairman of McKenzie Barber. Did you see the obituary?" a boyish appearing man with red hair added.

"That must have been John McKenzie," a voice added.

"Oh God, Morton, Wake up. John McKenzie's been dead for fifty years. There was someone between John McKenzie and General Pritchard."

"The only people I can remember are Glen and Jack, and I guess they're going to have different jobs now."

The elevator door opened to the ground floor, and the consultants streamed out of the elevator. Baxter walked briskly through the lobby to the revolving doors facing 311 Park Avenue and pushed his way through for the last time.

Baxter was fifteen minutes late for the luncheon at Bull Finches. It was a new restaurant on 4th Street in the Village, and Beth had given him the wrong address. His turbaned Sikh driver lost his bearings several times.

Bull Finches was situated in a loft two levels above the street. The maitre'd was a woman in a tuxedo who wore her hair in a pony tail. "The Gold party please," Baxter requested. He was escorted to the rear of the restaurant where he found Beth with a cigarette holder accompanied by Stephany waving a martini glass as she talked. They were in animated conversation when Baxter arrived.

"You're late Baxter," Beth greeted him.

"The cab driver got lost," Baxter explained.

Beth waved down a waitress. "Immediately bring this man a Beefeater martini on the rocks. He's recently retired." Stephany greeted him with a wet off center kiss. She was well girdled into a blue knit suit.

Beth kissed him on the cheek. She was wearing a ski sweater, dark stretch pants, and tall high heeled boots.

"Baxter, have you really retired from McKenzie Barber?" Beth asked.

"I just cleared out my desk and have left 311 Park Avenue for the last time. I have completed 24 years of service, and am 56 years of age. That foots to 80 in a rule of 73. I leave the payroll officially on 3-31-92, and will have a check for the balance of my capital account at the end of March. Robson Barber has even offered me a transition consulting opportunity.

Other people are suggesting consulting work to me. I have a new relationship. Ladies, you're looking at a very happy man."

"New relationship?" Beth snorted. "What new relationship is this?" Turning to Stephany she explained. "I proposed marriage to this man shortly before Christmas. Now three weeks later, he's talking about new relationships."

"I said I'd give it some thought. Someone drifted into me life, and I'm going to play the next hand with her. She's a California lady."

"How long have you known her, Joe?" Stephany asked as his martini was delivered.

"Make up a separate check for this man," Beth commanded the waitress.

"I've known her for a couple of years. But I got to know her a lot better this weekend," Baxter explained.

"What did she do? Shack up with you for the weekend?" Beth shot back.

"Is she someone from McKenzie Barber, Joe?" Stephany asked.

"No. She's from Robson Barber and I enjoyed a nice long weekend with her. She returned to California on Tuesday morning. We have been exchanging passionate phone mail ever since."

"Is she over thirty?" Beth asked.

"Yes."

"Is she over forty?"

"No."

"She's too young for you, Joe," Beth ruled and looked across the table to Stephany. "Joe has appointed me the executor of his estate. I am very concerned with his life style decisions."

"Beth, give this latest amour 90 days before you get concerned. Joe wears out relationships with women like we go through shoes," Stephany advised. "Let's get off this dreary subject of Joe's relationships. Let's talk about our Christmas holidays."

"Stephany had a good time, so she should go first," Beth proposed.

Stephany sipped from her martini glass and waved at the waitress for more drinks. "Drew came back into the fold. He finally ditched his wife. His children are through college. Some of them even have jobs. Drew is returning to Washington as "Of Counsel" to a major law firm. It will be announced at the end of the month. He has written a book called *Washington Lies* and I'm to help him edit it."

"Drew?" Baxter questioned.

"Drew Farmer. A presidential hopeful of the mid-1980s. He was Mr. Clean and good government. Then the Washington paparazzi caught him on a boat with this long legged model who had a day job with a special interest group. Drew was never caught with Stephany," Beth explained.

Stephany raised her left hand which had been resting under the table on her knee. She was sporting a large diamond ring. "This was presented to me on New Year's Eve among other vows."

"Now there's a man with commitment," Beth commented.

Beth looked to Baxter. "You're next, Romeo."

"I visited my daughter. She works at a Vermont ski resort called the Walnut Inn. It was good to see her, but if I had to do it all over again, I would have gone off with you to Bermuda. It got a little boring up at the Walnut Inn. The high point was a long luncheon with Hakim Selim who showed up accompanied by a pair of world class lady friends."

"Selim!" Stephany interjected. "Did he disappear off to Boston?"

"That was the rumor. They pulled out early on Christmas Eve morning," Baxter responded.

"He and that French bitch have both taken 4.9% positions in International Brands. They want to put the company in play or be paid to go away."

"International Brands?" Beth said. "That's such a nice company run by very proper Boston people. Are you talking about some seamy takeover attempt? And who is this French bitch? My God, I'm always looking for material. Fill me in, please."

Baxter allowed Stephany to answer. "Hakim Selim runs the money for the Harwell family. He's a former banker from Broadbaker, and he loves to make strategic investments. The French bitch is a little number named the Baroness Dominique de Hartogue. She heads the de Hartogue holding company. She's been chasing takeover deals since the Hortense Foods transaction back in '87. The two like to team up. Needless to say, our friend Joe knows both of them," Stephany said patting Baxter's hand. "He helped get Hakim hired at Harwell Management, and the Baroness is a Paris Office McKenzie Barber alumnus."

Beth reached out and stroked Baxter's other hand. "Joe Baxter, the red headed boy from the Iron Range certainly has gotten around over the past 39 years. Now tell me about this French bitch, Joe."

"She was a support consultant on an engagement for US Pharmaceuticals back in 1976 or 77. We wrote the draft report together, and she was off to a boat cruise with the Baron. The story is that she came back a Baroness and never returned to McKenzie Barber. She was very intelligent, hard working, and quite intense. I saw her a couple of times over the years, met her husband, hired her best friend, Monica, and I had lunch with her in Paris last summer on Bastille Day."

"Did you ever sleep with her, Joe?" Beth asked.

"My God, Beth. You certainly give me more credit than I deserve as a lover."

"If Marquand hadn't used the title, I might try a book entitled Women and Joe Baxter. Tell me, Joe, were you one of Alice Dungler's lovers?"

Baxter shrugged his shoulders. "You're giving me credit for exploits that are simply beyond my capacity."

"Your capacity may be slipping, but 100% of the ladies at this table are former bed partners of yours."

Stephany asked the waitress for another round of drinks and menus.

"On my first date with this man, I asked him what his hobbies were," Stephany recalled. "He told me he liked to drink and fuck."

"What did you do, you poor thing?" Beth inquired.

"I got him upstairs to my apartment as fast as I could. Joe was a real stallion in those days."

"He may have gone lame. I'd get him to a vet before I put him into my stables."

"Ladies, you are embarrassing me. Now let's hear about Beth's vacation. It's her turn."

"I had a marvelous suite with a wonderful view of the bay. I gave three talks to literary clubs, and signed autographs one afternoon. The only men who paid attention to me were black gigolos. I even paid one to take me to bed one evening. I felt disgusted with myself and then I couldn't get rid of him. I could have used you, Baxter."

"Let's look at menus," Stephany suggested. "I can't let this lunch last over three hours. I need to get back in time to tell them that I'm quitting."

Baxter looked from his menu to Beth. She was crying. "It was so humiliating," Beth said shooting up from her chair. "Excuse me," she added and walked quickly away from the table in the general direction of the ladies room.

"Poor Beth," Stephany commented after a sip form a fresh martini. "I wish to hell she could find someone to settle in with. You ought to marry her, Joe. She'd be good for you and also has built up a pretty good estate. Beth has excellent business instincts."

"And how is your family, Steph?"

"Thank you for asking. My Dad's in a long-term care facility down in Florida. He's been bedridden for two years. I have to hand it to Audrey. She's stuck it out. There isn't a lot of money left after my idiot brother's real estate investment ventures. Audrey has taken a job as a cocktail waitress to make ends meet. The house has been sold, and the horses are long gone. I'm putting my apartment up for sale, and moving down to Washington. Maybe I'll go back to one of the regulatory agencies. We could well have Democrats back in office next fall. This recession has killed Bush."

"What ever happened to Sybil McCarthy?"

"She married Chet. Chet was pushed out with a big settlement. They moved to Jackson Hole, Wyoming where she wears blue jeans three sizes larger than the size Sybil wore in New York. She wanted security. She got security. Was Sybil McCarthy another notch on your belt, Joe?"

"Our relationship was strictly professional, Steph. We worked together on the McKenzie Barber Press. She helped me publish my compensation book."

"Speaking of compensation books, why don't you write a book like your old friend, Frank Alvardi?"

"That's a maybe. I'd like to write a history of McKenzie Barber." Beth returned to the table with fresh make-up.

"Who on earth will want to read that book other than former employees? It's just another consulting firm that's been merged into another," Beth said seating herself. "By the way, I saw that Ernie Grey died. The obituary was rather interesting. A World War II flying ace who died roller blading at 70. I interviewed him once in the mid-1970s. He was a charming man, but I sensed a great deal of cold power behind those merry blue eyes of his. Did you know him well? Were you at his funeral?"

The waitress took orders before Baxter answered.

"I got to know him after he retired. Toni, Ernie's second wife, worked at McKenzie Barber and became a friend. Both his first wife, Millie, and Toni rode back with me last night from Philadelphia in a limo. The funeral service was held at the Greystone Academy Chapel."

"Greystone Academy," Stephany interrupted. "My Dad went to Greystone. That school was filled with insufferable little snobs in the late 1930s. They used to haze my Dad and call him 'trucker'. Ernie stepped up and told the hazers to back off. My Dad idolized Ernie Grey."

"Well, Joe. Was Ernie Grey a great man?" Beth demanded.

"He was a gifted man who impacted a lot of people lives. I've met two great men in my life. One was a black sergeant named Wilson whom I met in the Army. The other was Leon Harwell. They both were spiritual fathers to me."

"My goodness. That's outright Joycean. Spiritual fathers indeed," Beth reacted. "I remember your Sergeant Wilson and I remember that evening we spent at Fort Gately."

"And you wrote *A Sergeant's Tale*," Baxter reminded Beth.

"Joe has been very helpful over the years. He provided all the material for my first published short story. It was called *The Strike*."

"You're not going to make me sit through another recitation of the winter of 1952," Stephany protested.

"Retold stories are the best stories, Stephany," Beth countered. "Joe was such a bright, witty effervescent young man and he had a sensational young man's body in those days."

"And you bought me my first suit at the Glass Block Department Store. Later I visited you in Duluth and you brushed me off."

"You looked like such a dear baby at the time, Joe. How was I to know that you would go on to make love to 4% of the women in the world and 100% of the women at this table? You looked so innocent in your warm-up jacket. You were such a dear boy."

"I think the two of you ought to get married," Stephany recommended. "Let Joe complete his fling with this mysterious California lady, and he should be ready to settle down to marital business by this summer. I believe the two of you would be very good for each other."

Baxter waved across the table at Beth. He wanted her as a friend for life, but he did not want her for a wife. Why not? She was gifted and had assets. What a premium was paid in this world for striking features?

"So what ever happened to your last wife of record?" Stephany asked when the entrees were served.

"You're referring to Bridgette?"

"I saw her name and bio on a couple of fund raising prospectuses. It would appear that she's all finished in the retailing big leagues," Stephany commented.

"I have no idea of what Bridgette is doing. We're divorced and she has the penthouse. Bridgette is part of my past. She grows a little fainter in my memory with each passing day," Baxter lied. As he said the words, he recognized that he still loved Bridgette and missed her very much.

"All right, Joe," Beth said after coffee had been served.

"You have retired from McKenzie Barber. What is the next step in your life plan outside of pursuing this foolish relationship with this young woman in California?"

"I plan to drive up to my country place, clean out the possessions and files that I need, and return to the city."

"Clean out?" Beth probed. "Are you moving out?"

"I may eventually. But for the moment, I've decided to close the house. I have a bit of an awkward situation up there," he explained.

Beth and Stephany watched him quizzically. Baxter began his tale of the Dopman house and the early and trailing evening callers.

He described all of his country characters including Sheriff Clowson and the Bohlweiser family. They listened in rapt attention as Baxter spun his tale.

"This has been going on for a dozen years?" Beth questioned.

"Easily that. I believe I'm on my second caller who is the Sheriff's clerical assistant who is about ready to move into his chosen career of industrial security. Luke is scheduled to move fifty miles north and I'm going back one more time to clean out my McKenzie Barber files, and that's the end of it. I may put the house up for sale."

"This woman, who was your housekeeper," Stephany queried. "You gave her money to take her son and run away from her husband. Does this Luke have any idea that you financed her flight?"

"I believe he suspects."

"You weren't' sleeping with her, were you, Joe?" Beth demanded.

"Com'on ladies. Darlene Bohlweiser is a nice country house wife married to a whacko. You would have done the same, Beth," Baxter said refolding his napkin and placing it on the table with finality. "So ladies, I'm going to make one last trip to my country dacha in Brinker's Falls, New York. Another chapter of my life will be closed."

"You better make sure it's not your last chapter, Joe," Beth said solemnly.

Beth shared an uptown taxi with Baxter. He pledged several times to be careful in the cab.

"You're going tomorrow?"

"Thursday."

"Will you call me just before you leave and call me the minute you're back in the city?"

"You sound like my mother, Beth."

"And you're going off to your country scene of unpredictable crazies, leaving his nice city of predictable crazies. Why don't you take me with you? When do you plan to leave?"

"I have a Hertz car scheduled for a 7:30 AM pick-up."

"I'll meet you. Hertz 48th Street or 76th Street?"

"48th Street."

"Then it's settled. I'm coming with you," Beth announced.

Baxter was a recipient of a poorly aimed open mouthed kiss from Beth as he exited the cab in front of his apartment. He collapsed into his bed and slept until the telephone began ringing shortly after six.

"Baxter," he greeted his caller.

"This sounds like the real Joe Baxter," the voice belonged to Rusty.

"This is the newly retired Joe Baxter."

"This is the almost resigned Rusty Collins. I'm so excited that I had to call you. They have already pulled out your voice mail at 311 Park. You belong to the new grouping of non-persons. Ask me how I did with CCC this morning?"

"You wowed them and they made you a fantastic job offer."

"That's very good, Joe. Jim Wagoner, the CEO, and Cary Binger, the COO, took me to lunch after my presentation and offered me a position as SVP Product Management. $200,000 to start, first year bonus guaranteed at 35%, 5000 shares on option, and a crack at EVP Marketing by this time next year."

"Did you ask for time to think it over?" Baxter asked.

"Hell, no. They brought an offer letter to lunch and I'm starting February 3rd. Which is why I'm calling. How about meeting me in Chicago tomorrow? I really don't want to go another eight days without seeing you."

"We're making a presentation to the Card people at Central Illinois National Bank Thursday morning. I'm in there to sell the job for the Chicago Office, but it's been understood that I won't be available to do it. After I hang up, I'm going to see Rod Porter and resign. I'm going to a client so the firm will be nice to me. I'm going to ask for January 15th as my exit day. That would give us two weeks together. But I'll be damned if I can wait two weeks to see you. I have a plan. Remember that brother and sister snowbound night we spent at the Blackford? I'm catching the Chicago red-eye tonight and have upgraded to a mini-suite at the Blackford. We're on at 9 o'clock at the bank and should be over no later than eleven. You could catch a mid-morning flight to Chicago and be downtown by noon to buy me lunch at the Blackford. We could have a relaxed freedom-from-McKenzie Barber lunch and then you could take me back to my suite and ravish me. We can spend the weekend in Chicago, much as we did in New York City and plan our two weeks together in California. How's that for an engagement plan?"

"Very promising, if we can make our critical action dates," Baxter responded. "I did have a commitment to run up to my country place tomorrow to pick up some materials. I told you that I had a country place didn't I?"

"A Dutch colonial in the snow. I assume I will get a chance to study the ceilings one of these days. How far away is it?"

"About ninety minutes by car. I planned to go first thing in the morning."

"Any chance of delaying it? You're clearly needed in Chicago." Baxter ran the idea through his head. He certainly wasn't required to go to Brinker's Falls. Baxter could leave his McKenzie Barber files there for a year."

"Well?" asked the voice on the telephone.

"I want to start the McKenzie Barber book. I'll run up tonight, collect my files, and get on a 9 AM flight to O'Hare. Count me in."

"Spoken like the man who put me in a cab two days ago. It's going too fast for us, Joe. But I'm loving it. This thing we have going is very special and I want to keep it that way." Baxter wanted to say many things, but they could be saved for the bedroom in the Blackford.

"If I'm to be at the Blackford for lunch, I had better get going. I had a long alcoholic lunch and want to get some coffee down. I can't wait to be with you, Rusty."

"Joe, I've thought long and hard about us. We're so right. I love you. Good-bye my love. I'm going to resign from this fucking place." The phone clicked off before Baxter could say good-bye.

Baxter drank from a thermos as he hurried up Taconic Parkway to the Brinker's Falls exit. He turned off at ten minutes to nine. His neglected pick-up truck remained parked at the Texaco across from the train station. He hadn't driven it in four years. Each month he received a billing from Falls Texaco changing Baxter $20 month for parking which he dutifully paid. The light was out at Sheriff Clowson's office and there were five cars parked along side the Brinker's Falls Inn. Baxter proceeded up the backroads to his country home calculating what the resale value would bring him. It was time for him to put the house and its memories behind him.

Baxter didn't turn on the heat. Rather he quickly went through his files to determine what would be helpful as background for his McKenzie Barber book. He filled three corrugated boxes and carefully packed them into the rental car trunk.

Baxter had closed the trunk when the figure of Luke Bohlweiser came into view. He was wearing his campaign hat along with his security guard uniform and carrying a rifle.

"Where in hell are my wife and son?" he greeted Baxter.

"I have no idea," Baxter said advancing to the driver's seat car door.

Luke Bohlweiser stepped in front of the windshield with his rifle raised. "Don't get in that car," he threatened.

"Luke, you're in my way and I have things to do. Please leave my property this instant," Baxter said calmly.

"I'll ask you one more time. Where are my wife and son? I know you gave them money to run away. You have violated the laws of God with my wife and taken my son away. I want them back. After they've been punished, they will be welcome back in my home."

659

"You're sick, Luke. Both Darlene and Rob were scared to death of you. Sheriff Clowson knows you have been making those calls to me over the past year. You need psychiatric care big time and fast." Baxter stepped away from the car door and faced Luke Bohlweiser. Maybe he'd jump him. He hadn't hit anyone since Kawalchek, but maybe he'd have enough of the old touch left. It's a shame Beth wasn't there. She could have stared him down.

"People like you need to be destroyed, Baxter. I know what you do. You make rich men richer. You steal away men's wives and corrupt their children. I will consider giving you your life if you tell me where my wife and son are. You must, of course, be punished first."

Baxter took a step forward. "Let's talk, Luke. I believe you have some misguided perspectives here," Baxter addressed his Luke in the manner he had developed for argumentative clients.

"You're a fancy talker who got my wife a lot of foolish ideas with your high brow books and music. People like you don't belong here with regular working people."

Baxter sized up the situation. He had a crazy with a gun in front of him. Baxter had information that he needed. Luke couldn't pull the trigger until Baxter provided him the whereabouts of his wife and son. It was a leverage point that could be used in their relationship of threatner and threatnee.

"Now turn around and face the car." Luke had produced some clothes rope from his belt. "I'm going to tie you up."

"No, you're not," Baxter said. "You're going to drop that weapon and get the hell out of here. If I ever see or hear from you again, I'm going to Sheriff Clowson."

"Sheriff Clowson can't help you. He's a dead man. I killed him yesterday. Darlene had adultured with him too. I think he gave her money too. I tied him up and punished him. He didn't know where Darlene and Rob went, so I shot him. You're next."

Oh dear, Baxter thought. There wasn't a lot of back-up in Brinkers Fall's. He'd have to move to Plan II. He'd insult Luke and then jump him. The first part was fairly easy. The second was quite risky.

"You're a misfit, Luke. You're an under-educated bully who has been a loser in everything you've done. If you were a real man, you'd set down that gun and we could settle our differences man to man in personal physical combat. But you're a coward! A man who couldn't satisfy his wife and liked to bully his children. Certainly the world would be a better place if you never had lived."

Luke's eyes appeared enraged. Now for the hard part, Baxter told himself. He lunged forward at Luke's legs and knocked him off his feet. The gun discharged into Baxter's belly. Baxter summoned all his strength and delivered a blow that landed on Luke's nose. He believed he shattered the cartilage of his nose. Not bad for forty years between fights. The gun fell within Baxter's reach. He pointed it at Luke Bohlweiser. Now how do you fire one of these things? Luke turned and ran down the driveway. It turned out to be a pump action. Baxter fired one shot into the night and propped himself up against a tree to study the situation. He heard the sound of a car starting at the foot of the driveway. Would he come back?

Blood was seeping out of his wound. The bullet must have hit an artery. He was fifteen yards away from the back door of his house.

Baxter would have to crawl up the back steps, unlock the door and get to the kitchen phone. Who would he call? 911 could well ring in the late Sheriff Clowson's office. Baxter began his crawl. Perhaps he could drive the rental car to a neighbor.

Baxter crawled to the car. The blood was streaming from his belly. He turned his body to face the sky and placed his hands over the wound. Baxter's hands were wet with his blood. There was a brilliant half-moon over him and a chill had come up in the air. He was bleeding and shivering at the same time. He gathered his strength to pull open the car door only to have his hand slip off the handle. He tried again and couldn't make it. Baxter turned over on his back again to gain strength for one more surge.

The stars seemed very bright and he could make out the dipper. It came to him for the first time that he might not be able to make it. The morning flight to O'Hare was now out of the question. This kind of situation

661

certainly make a logical case for having a mobile phone. Baxter tried to raise himself up once more but couldn't do it. He was starting to feel tired. Maybe he'd sleep for a while He tried to summon images into his mind. He called up Dominique but wound up with the Iron Creek-Darwin game of March 1953.

Tommy Tweetman's hook shot had come out, but this time Baxter rebounded the ball and softly shot for the rim. The ball swished through and he was mobbed by the team. The Cougars were going to the State!

Joseph Baxter, Jr. passed into unconsciousness and died somewhere around twelve-thirty. It could be said that Joe Baxter's death was very much similar to the death of his father.

Epilogue
April 10, 1992

Beth Gold took her seat in the first class section of the American Airlines JFK flight from San Francisco. She boarded first and instructed the male flight attendant to bring her coffee and a Remy. It had been a long day. But it had been a productive day. She had gathered a great deal of research information relative to the late Alice Dungler. The next task would be to seal herself up and churn out the first draft of *Computer Amazon.*

Beth had held two days of interviews with former McKenzie Barber and Dungler Technology associates of the legendary Alice Dungler. Her final meeting had been with Bob Friedman, the current CEO of Dungler Technologies, and successor to Alice Dungler. Beth had, what she classified, as four decent interviews and two helpful discussions. Beth, concluded, that she really wasn't cut out for the life of a reporter. She was writing against a deadline and was over four months delinquent. MacNalley House, her publisher, also published Enterprise Week and wanted to publish an Alice Dunlger book in the fall of 1991. Some snip named Sandra, who had been described as a hungry free lance sports writer, was also rumored to be writing an Alice Dungler book. She was doing her research by telephone probably backed up by internet research. Sandra would probably beat her to the finish but Beth's book would be better. It would have to be better. Beth Gold, was at a time when she couldn't endure another flop.

Today had been eerie. The shadow of Joe Baxter seemed to be hovering over Beth. He apparently had enjoyed some kind of relationship with the late Dr. Alice Dungler. His name had come up in three of the six interviews Beth had held.

The last three months had been impossible. Beth vowed that she would never consent to be someone's executor again. It had started so innocently. Here was this strapping, virile and often witty man sitting across the table at lunch in the Edwardian Room.

Beth had often considered marrying him. After all, there really wasn't that much around for a woman well north of fifty. Here was an apparently indestructible man with a good twenty years ahead of him requesting that Beth take care of things on the remote possibility that some accident should happen. He hadn't informed her of his telephone stalker. And if he had, Beth probably wouldn't have taken him seriously.

Beth Gold had relived Thursday, January 9th, a thousand times. Sometimes the scenes would come back to her in dreams. She was waiting on a bench facing the Hertz counter. Beth had prepared a thermos slightly laced with brandy and had dutifully arrived fifteen minutes early. She had occupied her time re-reading the first page of the *New York Times* and glancing up at the large clock located behind the counter. At ten minutes to eight, Beth had begun to get concerned.

She called Baxter's apartment and got his voice mail. Then she checked with the reservationist and learned that a Joseph Baxter Jr. had checked out a car the evening before at 8:15 PM.

The son-of-a-bitch had gone up the night before and hadn't told her. Had Baxter stayed the night in Brinker's Falls? He was scheduled to return the car by 6 AM. Beth rented a car on impulse. She had a twenty minute wait for a car and left the Hertz station shortly after 9 AM.

Beth had made the Brinker's Falls exit at ten thirty. It impressed her as a dreary little town with streets lined with ugly frame houses either covered by siding or revealing flaked paint. At the center of the town was a train station facing a Texaco station, a large A & P, and a restaurant called the Brinker's Falls Inn. Across the parking lot was a grey frame building with a large sign that read;

LAW ENFORCEMENT
HOMER CLOWSON
SHERIFF & CHIEF OF POLICE

There were three police cars parked in front of the building. Two had their engines running and red warning lights whirring. Beth parked the rental car three spaces away from the empty police car. She heard a siren behind her and watched an emergency vehicle pull into the space next to the police cars. People were streaming out of the Brinker's Falls Inn into the parking area. Two men in medical whites hurriedly exited the emergency vehicle and walked quickly to the front door of the Sheriff's office. A uniformed man in a broad brimmed hat merged from the doorway after the medical attendants crossed the threshold of the Sheriff's office.

Beth deduced that the man was a state trooper. He opened the door of the running vehicle positioned closest to the door, turned off the ignition and emerged carrying a bull horn. Beth stood in front of the hood of the car as spectator. The state trooper faced the people from the street and the restaurant who were beginning to collect.

"Please stand back, folks," the trooper's voice came over the bull horn. "We have a law enforcement emergency here. We ask your cooperation in giving us some room here."

"Where's Sheriff Clowson?" a middle aged man in a red jacket with matching earflaps called out.

"Sheriff Clowson's had an accident. We're getting him some help. Give us some room."

The Sheriff Office's door reopened and the two attendants returned to their vehicle and produced a stretcher from the rear door of the ambulance.

They rapidly returned through the Sheriff Office's door. The state trooper observed Beth for the first time. "That applies to you too, lady."

Beth calmly lit a cigarette and walked toward the trooper.

"I plan to leave as soon as I get some directions. I'm visiting a friend and I have some concerns for his safety. His name is Joe Baxter and he lives at a place that was formerly owned by some brothers called Dopman. Do you know the place?"

The trooper, on closer inspection, turned out to be a stocky young man in his late twenties. "Ask over at the Brinker's Falls Inn, lady. Somebody over there will know. I live two towns north of here. I'll just get you lost."

"May I ask what happened here?"

"It's law enforcement business, lady. Please remove your car from the parking lot.

The attendants returned to the parking lot carrying the stretcher. The body on the stretcher was completely enclosed. The stretcher resembled a body bag.

"I'm very concerned about the safety of my friend, Mr. Baxter. That wouldn't be him on that stretcher? Would it?"

The door opened again and another trooper called out. "We're bringing him out, Josh. Clear the way."

"Lady, I'm going to ask you one last time to get the hell out of here. If you don't go, I'm placing you under arrest," the trooper threatened.

Beth blew a smoke ring and backed her way to the car. The trooper opened his holster in preparation for some upcoming event.

Two state troopers escorted a man in handcuffs through the door. He was dressed in a blue uniform and wore a military campaign hat. The man limped as he was guided forward to the rear seat of the second police car. He looked back toward Beth as he was placed in the back seat of the police car. There was blood on his face and his nose appeared to be swollen.

"Get out of here, lady. Right now!" he commanded.

Beth started her car but waited to allow the emergency vehicles to leave. The ambulance led the way followed by the pair of policed vehicles with their sirens and whirring lights. Josh, the state trooper posted himself in front of the Sheriff's Office.

Beth maneuvered the rental car across the parking lot to a spot near the Inn. A number of customers stood outside holding mugs of coffee.

Beth approached a large man wearing a red sweatshirt under bib overalls. The name "Bob" was stenciled across the front of his luminous yellow cap.

"Good morning, Bob," Beth greeted him. "Can you help me out with some directions? I need to find the old Dopman place."

"What in hell do you want to go there for?" Bob spit on the ground beside Beth's boot.

"I have a friend named Mr. Baxter who lives there. I'm here to visit."

"Big red-headed fellow?"

"That's Mr. Baxter."

"He bought the Dopman place a while back." Bob took another sip from his coffee cup. "Darlene Bohlweiser used to clean for him. A lot of us think that she did more than clean for him."

"Was the man that left with the state troopers, Mrs. Bohlweiser's husband?"

"That was Luke all right. Looks like he killed Sheriff Clowson. That was too bad. Sheriff Clowson was a good old boy. Looks like Sheriff got Luke a good one before Luke got him. Buddy Hilger over at the Texaco was talking to Luke when the troopers picked him up this morning. He said Luke's nose was broke." Bob motioned to a man in a Texaco uniform who held a paper cup. "Hey, Buddy, this lady wants directions to the old Dopman house. She's come to visit that Baxter fellow."

Buddy was clad in his Texaco uniform and tipped his cap to Beth. "Good morning, Ma'am. Mr. Baxter keeps his pick-up truck with me. I ain't seen him lately. This here is Center Street." Buddy began, and he illustrated a series of turns with his hand which Beth took down in her pocket notebook.

"Very good, Buddy. Now do I understand there had been some violence here this morning?" Beth queried after pressing two dollars into Bob's hand.

"All I know, Ma'am, is that I open up at six every morning and this morning I found Luke sitting out in the cold on my bench with his nose all busted up. I asked him 'Luke, why don't you go off to the Sheriff's office and get out of the cold?' He just shook his head. Then I could see Bernie from the Brinker's Falls Inn walk across and pound on the door. Sheriff Clowson used to keep a spare key with Bernie. I was opening up the pumps when I saw Bernie go in and then run out back to the Inn. 'Something wrong over there, Luke?' I asked. He looked at me and said, 'God's will must be done.' Then the state troopers drove up. I asked Luke if he shouldn't' go over there and see what the trouble was. He looked at me and said, 'They'll locate me soon enough.' A little later two state troopers drove their car over and took Luke away."

"And Luke was the Sheriff's Deputy?" Beth asked.

"Luke wasn't no Deputy. He just helped out in the office. He tried to pass himself off as a law man. He used to be one hell of a football player..."

"Thank you, Buddy, you've been most helpful." Beth broke him off and returned to the rental car. Joe was going to be all right. Luke Bohlweiser was in the hands of the state police.

Beth saw the house from the driveway. It was a magnificent white Dutch colonial with a green roof and green shutters. She saw the car in the driveway and honked five times. Baxter was probably sleeping. The inconsiderate rat had had stayed over and hadn't been considerate enough to telephone her.

Beth parked the rental car on the far part of the driveway and saw Baxter's body after she emerged from the driver's seat. He was facing the sky and there was a long trial of blood.

"Oh my God!" was all that she could think of saying and she repeated twice before walking to the side door of the house. The door was slightly ajar and Beth opened it into a large kitchen with a butcher block table in the center of the room. She took a handkerchief from her purse and cradled the telephone. Should she dial 911? Instead she called Stephany?

"Miss Hart is in a meeting," Stephany's secretary reported.

"Get her the hell out of the meeting," Beth shouted. "Tell her that Beth Gold is on the line and I need her right now!" There was a brief silence before Stephany's voice came on the line.

"What's up?" Stephany's voice greeted Beth.

"I'm in Brinker's Falls. Joe has been murdered. Get the hell up here right away. I'm at his home and his body is out in the driveway. I don't know quite what to do. Stephany, get the hell up here!"

After painfully providing the directions to Stephany, Beth took steps to get herself organized before calling the police. She located the tea, heated the kettle, and began to survey the house. Joe needed to be covered. She located a bed sheet in a master bedroom chest and took it outside to place over Baxter's body. He had died with a cherubic look on his face. Joe Baxter appeared at peace with himself. He had apparently turned himself over on his back resigned to die. The sheet failed to cover Baxter's body from head to foot. Beth settled for covering his head and allowing his boots to protrude from under the sheet. The sky was clouding up. Snow would be coming.

Beth calmly poured hot water into a cup and swirled her tea bag thirteen times for luck. She asked herself, 'Beth, how do you get yourself into these situations?' and dialed 911. She reached the phone mail of Sheriff Clowson. No help there, Beth concluded and she moved on to the state police.

They arrived in two cars with whirling lights within fifteen minutes. Beth put on her jacket, poured a fresh cup of tea.

"Good morning officers," she greeted them. "I'm so pleased that you could respond so quickly."

Beth concluded that while the state police contingent appeared competent and efficient in their well pressed military like uniforms, they were fundamentally controlling and not very bright. She had, in her mind, prepared a five minute situation briefing which was interrupted with a "We'll ask the questions, lady," by the lead trooper.

There were a great many 'Who are you?' and 'What are you doing here?' questions. They pulled the sheet back from Baxter's body again revealing his peaceful cherubic face. The rifle had been retrieved and placed in some kind of protective bag.

"Did Mr. Baxter have any reason to take his own life?" the lead trooper asked.

"In the stomach? The man was bloody murdered?" Beth protested.

A third emergency vehicle arrived. This one reminded Beth of a late black station wagon. The attendants took a great many pictures of the body and the trail of blood. Then they scooped up Baxter's body and carried him off to the vehicle. Beth waved as they passed by her.

"So long, Joe. See you in the mortuary."

The troopers asked Beth to accompany them for a statement. She left a note on the side door for Stephany and entered the back seat of one of the sedan cars as the emergency vehicle pulled away.

Beth returned two hours later in the company of a woman trooper named Alma. She had read one of Beth's books but couldn't recall the title. Beth identified it as *Mornings Ago*, one of her early books written in the mid 1960s.

"Where did you purchase this book, Alma?"

"I got it out from the Nevenburg Library. After having met you, I'm going to read more of your books."

"Tell me, Alma, were you acquainted with this Luke Bohlweiser?"

"I can't discuss the case with you, Mrs. Gold."

"I wouldn't presume to ask you about the case, Alma. I would like to ask you about this Luke Bohlweiser."

"He worked for Sheriff Clowson, did typing and filing, and tried to act like a law enforcement person. He tried to hang out with some of our people. He could never pass the State Police Physical. He might have gotten hired as a clerk with veteran's preference. He had a nice wife who worked in the restaurant at the Brinker's Falls Inn. That's all about I can tell you, Mrs. Gold."

There was a new car in the driveway when they pulled in. Beth took down a mortuary recommendation and waved to Alma. It was now three in the afternoon. Twenty four hours earlier the three of them were breaking away from a long lunch. Beth discovered Stephany drinking Scotch out of a coffee cup in front of the fireplace.

"I take it I'm up here to plan the funeral." She wore a fur hat, ski pants, and short boots. "I wonder how many women our old friend, Joe, did on this bear rug? Were you ever up here with him?"

"This is my first visit. And you?"

"I haven't shared a bed with Joe Baxter in ten years. I believe your experience is more recent," Stephany countered.

"How did he look as a corpse?"

"Very peaceful. He had a large wound in his stomach and probably bled to death," Beth reported.

"Should we be crying?" Stephany questioned.

"No. We should be drinking and planning his funeral. I'm the executor of his estate. We'll set up a command post here and organize his funeral. This is a Thursday. We should have him buried by Saturday or Monday at the latest. Now where did you find that Scotch?"

They worked well together into the night with Stephany taking the administrative lead. She laid out a chart listing the steps and actions to be taken, along with assigned responsibilities. Stephany located some large spread sheets from Baxter's den and Beth built a fire. They worked together for any hour or so developing a task force to carry out the various activities required to support Baxter's internment.

"Let's get Godfrey Bain involved," Beth declared. "He's a headmaster at a boy's school. I just know he's good at funerals."

Beth later described Godfrey Bain's participation as a Godsend. It was Godfrey who identified the Unitarian Minster who taught English at a nearby community college and made arrangements for a service at the Middleville School Chapel. Stephany negotiated with a New Jersey mortuary, and Beth met on Friday with Zach Blum, Baxter's attorney. Beth discovered a mailing list in Baxter's computer files and sent out several death announcements by e-mail. The phone calls were the most difficult part of the funeral communications.

Beth reached Martha Baxter in the gift shop at the Walnut Inn.

"Good morning, Gift Shop. Martha Baxter, speaking," had been the crisp answer on the telephone.

"Martha, this is Beth Gold calling. I'm a good friend of your father's."

"Oh yes, you're the famous writer. Dad has talked about you and he wrote me that you were going to be the executor of his estate." There was a silence. "Has anything happened to Dad?"

"I'd like to drive up and get acquainted. I have some time today. It looks like a three hour drive. Can I come by?"

"Is my Dad all right?"

"He seemed very cheerful the last time I saw him. I should be there by late afternoon."

Beth quickly concluded that Martha Baxter did not resemble her father. She was tall and fair and wore clothes well.

"Can we talk a walk together? I've never been here before." Martha accepted a cigarette from Beth and they were twenty feet from the building on a pathway when Beth came to the point.

"Your father was murdered yesterday at his country home. The police have apprehended a man who is likely to have been responsible. Your father's funeral is planned for Monday afternoon at the Middleville School Chapel in New Jersey."

"That's where my brother's funeral service was held," was all the girl said as she walked along side Beth in silence.

"Martha, I'd like you to pack a bag and come with me."

"I'll have to see Miss Grace about this," she said in a daze.

Beth settled into a table with a mug of coffee among the skiers in the downstairs cafeteria. A middle-aged woman in an open ski jacket at the next table was reading *Night Friends*, a piece of trash Beth had written just before she returned to the city from her New Hampshire exile. It had sold surprisingly well in paperback. Beth suddenly looked up from her *New York Times*, to a grey-haired lady in a blue suit facing her table.

"Miss Gold, I'm Grace Dewing, the Assistant Manager." Her bearing reminded Beth of a Mother Superior.

"Do I understand that Martha's father has had some kind of accident?"

Beth motioned for the woman to sit down.

"Mr. Baxter was shot to death in the driveway of his country home late last night. There will be a reviewal on Saturday and the funeral will be at the Middleville Collegiate School Chapel on Monday afternoon. Martha appears to be Mr. Baxter's closest blood relative. He appointed me executor of his estate a few months back. I'm going to drive Martha to the home of Godfrey Bain, the headmaster of Middleville. Mr. Bain and Mr. Baxter served in the Army together and were life long friends. Mr. Bain's taking charge of the funeral arrangements."

Miss Dewing shook her head. "He just visited us. Mr. Baxter was such a handsome and charming man. Who would want to do such a thing?"

Martha Baxter had changed into a blue blazer and grey slacks. She stood sadly in front of the table with her suitcase at her side.

"I'm ready to go now," she announced in a flat voice.

Beth stood up and announced that she was going to call the Bains. She watched Grace Dewing and Baxter's daughter from the pay phone. Martha appeared to be in a catatonic state. Grace Dewing was stroking her hair. They looked like a grandmother daughter combination. Laura Bain answered the phone.

"Laura, Beth. I've got the daughter and we're going to start out. Give me the directions one last time."

Laura dragged out the directions for at least five minutes providing a series of landmark directions that included strip malls, Standard Oil stations, fast food restaurants, churches, and New Jersey jug handle turns recited in a sing songy voice. What an insipid creature, Beth concluded after hanging up the phone. What had she ever seen in her?

They drove for the first half-hour in silence before Martha began to talk in a monotone.

"Mrs. Gold, how long did you know my father?"

673

"It's Miss Gold. I'm a widow but I've always kept my maiden name. I write books for a living. I first met your father during the Christmas holidays of 1952. That's practically 39 years."

"When did he make you his executor?"

"Shortly before Christmas. It wasn't a task or an appointment that I particularly wanted."

Five minutes of silence followed.

"Who killed my father? Are there suspects?"

"The state police are looking into it. I found him dead in his driveway yesterday morning. I haven't seen a dead man since my husband died. I liked your father."

"Were you one of his women?"

"Your father was a long time friend. I was hardly one of his women. I did suggest to him over lunch in December that we consider marriage. I believe we would have been good for each other."

"Have you ever been to the house in Brinker's Falls?"

"I was there for the first time this morning," Beth answered. She drove concentrating on the twisting roads and made no effort to make eye contact with Martha.

"Did he ever tell you about the man who used to call him up on the telephone in Brinker's Falls?"

"I heard about him for the first time at lunch in New York on Wednesday. It disturbed me. I volunteered to drive out with him on Thursday morning, but your Dad decided to go up on Wednesday evening instead."

There was an extended silence as Beth studied the highway exit signs.

"Did the police suspect that the man who called up killed Dad? I think I know who he was. Do you know Darlene, the housekeeper?"

It was a new name to Beth.

"Tell me about Darlene, Martha."

"She was the housekeeper. She really had eyes for Dad. Her husband worked for Sheriff Clowson, but he wasn't a policeman. He kind of took care of the office. I suspect that Dad and Darlene became intimate. I think he got lonely after Bridgette left him."

New information, Beth concluded. Had Joe developed a relationship with his housekeeper that led to his execution?

"Darlene really wasn't much," Martha continued. "She was always hanging around playing Dad's music and reading his books."

"I don't know about Darlene, Martha. I knew your father from his New York life. He was a good friend of my husband, Lester, and me. He used to date a friend of mine named Stephany who is helping with the funeral."

"I know that name. Dad used to see her in Washington. She mailed him back his necktie once. Was Dad a ladies man?"

"Your father was popular with the ladies. He was an attractive man and quite witty."

"Are the police going to arrest Darlene's husband?"

"I believe he's already in custody."

Martha Baxter reverted into silence and didn't talk again until the car crossed the Connecticut border.

"Are you aware that I'm not Dad's daughter? My mother told me that I'm a love child from one of her relationships in the Peace movement. My mother was very active in the stop the Vietnam War movement. She met someone who was supposed to have fathered me. Can you remember the Vietnam war?" Martha asked innocently.

"I am somewhat familiar with the Vietnam War issues," Beth responded.

"Mother wasn't getting along with Dad and I guess she developed a lover. I didn't know it for years and years until my mother told me when I visited her in Italy. When I told my Dad, he said 'Forget about it. I signed for you in the hospital.'"

"I agree with your father. You're his heir."

"Has my mother been told about Dad?"

"We're not sure how to reach her."

"I'd like to call her. Once we were a family. We lived in Racine, Wisconsin, in a big old house on Palmer Street. It had been Grandfather Washburn's house. We moved in after he died. Grandfather Washburn sexually abused my mother and she was mentally ill for many years. Dad didn't know about mother's problems—"

Beth pushed in the car lighter. It was time for a cigarette. More new information was coming her way. Martha Baxter talked non stop for nearly twenty minutes. Martha had been given the nickname, Muffin, by the housekeeper, a woman named Agnes. Their mother was rarely home during the week and Baxter traveled during the week. He would spend his Saturdays with the children, and they would have a family diner together on Sunday afternoon. Her mother had held a role in the Peace movement a level below Joan of Arc. Beth could never remember meeting or seeing the name, Jennifer Washburn on any of the organization rosters. She'd have to check through her archives if she ever managed to get this weekend behind her. Beth had her 'stop-the-war years' and Joe Baxter had his McKenzie Barber years.

Martha remembered the Bains from her brother's funeral

"Mr. Bain was a good friend to my brother, Joel. He took care of the funeral. Dad didn't know what to do. Mrs. Bain is very nice. I could have gone to Middlebury, but I wanted to go to prep school in Connecticut. Do you know the Bains well?"

"Mrs. Bain and I were exchange students in France during our Junior year in college. Your father became acquainted with Mr. Bain in the Army. Mrs. Bain and I dropped in to see Mr. Bain at Fort Gately, Georgia, and there was your father again."

"They had become quite good friends in the Army. That was the weekend when Mr. Bain proposed to Mrs. Bain."

Beth thought back to the weekend. How beautiful Laura had been in those days. They had been lovers for a month when they stopped off in Fort Gately. Godfrey had claimed Laura. And there was Joe Baxter with his good looks and smart mouth. Now Laura was a dowdy headmaster's wife, and Beth was caught in the center of Baxter's funeral arrangements.

"Did you know Bridgette?" Martha asked ten miles later.

"No. Stephany knows Bridgette. I haven't had the pleasure of meeting her."

"I loved Bridgette. Joel hated her. She taught me a lot about retailing. We used to go roller skating together. Then she dropped Dad and she dropped me too. Did my Dad tell you about my abortion?"

"Your father told me he had a daughter. He provided no further details. After that weekend in Fort Gately, I didn't see your father for twenty years. I might have never run into him again if we hadn't been seated together on an American Airlines red-eye flight in 1977. He was just moving to New York then. I was married to a very nice young man named Lester. We arranged to introduce your father to Stephany Hart. They dated for about a year or two and broke off when Stephany moved to Washington with the Securities & Exchange Commission."

"Beth, I appreciate everything you're doing," Martha said and patted Beth's hand. Five minutes later, Martha Baxter was sound asleep.

The reviewal was held from two to five p.m. on Saturday afternoon at Restful Arms Mortuary in Morristown, New Jersey. Martha Baxter spent Friday night with the Bains. They had arrived shortly after eleven and Martha was suddenly wired with energy. Laura Bain made the sandwiches and Beth was poured a tall glass of Scotch.

Godfrey produced a picture album with Army pictures from the days he had spent with Baxter at Fort Gately.

"Your father very quickly became wise to the ways of the Army. The black sergeant was named Wilson and your father became Sergeant Wilson's protégé. And Beth wrote a very wonderful story about Sergeant Wilson that was called *A Sergeant's Tale*."

"It won best short story award by a new writer in 1955. It's still in print in anthologies," Beth stated between sips of Scotch.

"Your father was very skilled at moving ahead whether it was in the Army or in the world of business," Godfrey Bain said.

"Was my father famous?" Martha Baxter asked.

"Your father was well known but hardly famous," Godfrey commented. "Let's say that he made his mark in the business world. He wasn't famous in the sense that someone like Beth here is famous."

"And Beth isn't as famous as she used to be," Beth added.

"Were you in love with my Dad?"

"Your father was a very dear man. He was my friend for nearly forty years. I even proposed marriage to him in the Edwardian Room this December. I believe we would have been excellent marital companions."

"Did you have sex with my father?"

"My dear, I was at best a very minor participant in the sybaritic life of your late father."

Beth submitted what she regarded was a well written obituary draft to the Times. It wasn't the best piece of writing she had ever done but it was adequate. They butchered her copy. The obituary appeared abbreviated in Sunday's *New York Times*.

PAY EXPERT MURDERED

Joseph Baxter, Jr., a well known expert in executive compensation matters, was shot to death in the driveway of his country home in Brinker's Falls, New York. Baxter, age 56, had recently retired as a Partner of McKenzie Barber, a management consulting firm. Baxter, as National Director of Compensation Consulting for McKenzie Barber, had been the architect of complex senior management incentive plans for companies such as Pennsylvania Steel and Planters & Commerce Bank.

Mr. Baxter was highly regarded in executive compensation matters and was described as the 'witty and ebullient' leader of McKenzie Barber's executive pay practice in John Baker's book, *The Paymasters*. Somewhat less flattering comments on Mr. Baxter were contained in Frank Alvardi's *The Overpaid Executive* where Mr. Baxter was described 'a great boardroom salesman with shallow technical skills.' Mr. Baxter was the author of a book entitled *Executive Pay-Management Realities and Shareholder Expectations* which was published by the McKenzie Barber Press in 1985 and enjoyed several reprintings.

Mr. Baxter was a native of Iron Creek, Minnesota. He served for three years in the US Army, and completed undergraduate and graduate degrees from the University of Minnesota. Mr. Baxter joined McKenzie Barber & Co. in 1968, and was elected a partner in 1977. He was appointed National Director for Executive Compensation consulting in 1979. He chose retirement following the merger of McKenzie Barber and Robson Allen Harbridge in January of this year.

Mr. Baxter was shot to death by an unknown assailant late Thursday evening in the driveway of his country home. It is believed that he may have interfered with a robbery in progress. Mr. Baxter was married and divorced three times. His first marriage to Margaret Sadowski ended in divorce in 1958. A later marriage to Jennifer Washburn ended in divorce in 1976. A third marriage to retailing executive, Bridgette Morgan ended in 1991. Mr. Baxter is survived by Lenore Burchek, a daughter from his first marriage, who is presently serving as a missionary in Ghana, and Martha, a daughter from his second marriage who resides in Maple, Vermont. Memorial services will be held at 2 PM on Monday, January 13th, at the Middleville Collegiate School Chapel in Middleville, New Jersey.

Beth knew that Baxter had a brother who was some kind of local hood and who had disappeared several years ago. But she was pleased that the obituary had come out reasonably tidy with the exception of that quote from that Alvardi character. Baxter's place on the obituary page was shared with the following;

BRAD RUSSELL, FILM DIRECTOR IS DEAD AT 85.

DR. ROSWELL BENTON III, RESEARCHER ON IN-VITRO FERTILIZATION.

BONITO REPGHI, MAFIA ASSOCIATE WHO BECAME AN INFORMER IS DEAD AT 55.

Beth drove into the city on Saturday morning to meet Baxter's attorney for breakfast. Zach Blum was a fiftiesh man who specialized in divorces and estates. He seemed congenial and solicitous in their quickly arranged breakfast.

"I lost both a friend and a client," Blum began the discussion.

The turnout for the reviewal had been predictably light. Stephany had wanted Baxter laid out in his tuxedo. "Joe always suited up well."

"He'll look like a bloody headwaiter," Beth countered. "Blue pinstriped suit, pinstriped shirt, and a Hermes tie. That's our Joe," Beth ruled.

A guest book was displayed in the foyer to the reviewal room. Beth and Martha Baxter were joined by Stephany to greet the mourners.

"You really don't have to be here," Beth offered.

"Drew is coming in this evening. He's going to take us to dinner at a place called the Canoebrook Club. I have nothing else to do. Besides I'm rather curious as to who will take the time out to see our man, Joe."

The reviewal was two to five. Martha wore a dark pants suit, while Stephany and Beth had donned dark glasses.

"It will be interesting," Stephany whispered to Beth when Martha was out of ear shot. "To see who shows up. Our old friend, the late Joe Baxter, had a broad range of friends."

The first griever was an awful little man named Ganski from Minnesota who showed up at ten minutes before two. He was accompanied by a thick-featured blonde pony-tailed young woman whom Beth pegged as either his daughter or his girlfriend. The man demanded that Baxter's body be returned to Iron Creek, Minnesota, for burial.

Beth had already secured a burial plot, through Godfrey Bain, in a New Jersey cemetery.

"Look here, Beth. Joe expressly told me that he wanted to be buried in Iron Creek. He wanted to be buried right next to Morton Himmelman who died in Vietnam. There's a spot for me on the other side of Joe when my time comes."

"Mr. Ganski, I am the executor of Mr. Baxter's estate. His will did not specify a burial place preference. He will be buried in a New Jersey plot on Monday. I've had to make certain decisions very quickly, and his daughter, Martha, fully supports these decisions." Martha took a place beside Beth to the right of the open casket.

"Mr. Ganski, my father will be buried in New Jersey, not in Iron Creek, Minnesota," Martha said with finality. Beth looked toward the open coffin. There was Baxter resting peacefully in his blue suit, striped shirt and Hermes tie. There was no way this man was going to be shipped off to Iron Creek, Minnesota. New Jersey was bad enough.

The girlfriend whispered something into Ganski's ear. Beth thought she made out, 'Ed, give it up.' She stepped forward to the casket and looked Baxter over. "He certainly was a handsome man," turning to Martha, she clasped both of her hands. "I'm Betty Jayne Koski. I'm Senator Ganski's assistant. I met your Dad last summer for the first time and he was back in December for Mrs. Ganski's funeral. His death was a real shock to all of us. Mr. Baxter was a very impressive man, whom Senator Ganski regarded as his best friend."

She moved to Beth. "Miss Gold, I have read a number of your books. It's regrettable that we should meet under such unfortunate circumstances."

Beth smiled. It was good that this Ganski had this girl around. "Thank you so much for coming. Be sure to sign the book on the way out."

Stephany was less diplomatic. "You have to be a state senator. I'm acquainted with most of the US Senate. Drew Farmer is my fiance. Perhaps his name is familiar to you."

"Senator Ganski and I are going off to Washington on Monday night to confer with DFL leadership following the funeral." Ganski seemed to snap to attention at the mention of Drew Farmer's name.

"I have admired Senator Farmer for many years," Ganski commented reverently. "We represent different parties of course, but he is, in my opinion, a great American."

"Unfairly abused by the American press," the blonde assistant added.

"Will Senator Farmer be returning to public office?" Ganski appeared impressed.

Stephany responded with a hard, cold smile. "Drew needs some time to think things through. He's returned to the law. He's coming up this evening and will be at the funeral on Monday."

"I'll look forward to meeting him," Ganski responded and there was no more talk of burying poor Baxter in the remote wilds of the Iron Range in northern Minnesota.

Ed Ganski and his pony-tailed consort left after ten minutes and they were followed by a steady dribble of mourners throughout the afternoon. There was a white-haired lady with her hair in a bun accompanied by a vigorous black woman.

"I'm Charlotte Bunker," the white haired woman greeted Beth and Martha. "I worked with Mr. Baxter at McKenzie Barber for many years, and this is Marveen who was his secretary for a number of years."

"Do I understand that Joe was murdered?" the black woman asked bluntly.

"I believe the killer is in custody," Beth responded.

"Was it that crazy who used to call him up at his country place?" Marveen asked. The black woman had a powerful presence about her. The older woman named Charlotte Bunker reminded Beth of an ailing mouse. Her movements were slow and her hand shook.

"Your father was a fine man," Charlotte Bunker offered to Martha Baxter. "He truly cared about people."

"Did Joe tell you about his caller?" Beth asked Marveen.

"Joe Baxter and I had no secrets. I even knew some things he didn't think I knew. He told me about the crazy who called him. Joe didn't take him very seriously. I understand that he was shot. What time of day was it?" Marveen demanded.

Now here was a woman who was accustomed to neighborhood violence, Beth thought. Friends and neighbors of this Marveen had been shot before. She wanted details to compare with previous shootings.

"The police theorize that Joe was killed disturbing a burglary in progress. I suspect that Joe was killed by someone who wanted to kill him."

"It doesn't really matter," Martha Baxter observed. "My father is dead. Just who killed him is the police's problem. Finding his killer won't bring my Dad back."

A tall man wearing a red V neck sweater edged his way into the reviewal room. He was accompanied by what appeared to be a late teen age son and daughter. Beth estimated that he was late forties early fifties with a slight stoop to his shoulders.

"I'm Marty Dunlap," he greeted Beth with an extended hand. "This is my son, Bill, and my daughter, Nan. I wanted them to see the man I worked for so many years," Marty announced and paid his respects to Martha. Beth could sense that Stephany was beginning to become bored when she excused herself to make 'some critical phone calls.'

"He was a very handsome man, Dad," the daughter remarked as she looked into the casket.

"He was very good on his feet and really did his best to take care of his people. None of us realized this until he dropped out last summer."

"Dropped out?" Beth questioned.

Marty Dunlap shrugged his shoulders. "Joe kind of lost interest in McKenzie Barber last Spring. Our practice was scheduled to be spun off with the Actuarial practice. The merger slowed things down, but the spin-off is set for April 1st. Joe had a way of always landing on his feet. He also protected his people. A lot of us figured that Joe would start something else this spring and make a place for us. He was still a young man. But now someone has taken Joe away from us."

More new information, Beth observed.

Dunlap lingered after his children moved to the outer foyer. "Your name is familiar, Beth. Are you related to Joe?"

"Jut a long time friend whom he asked to be the executor of his estate."

Marty nodded his head. "I know Joe had been married a couple of times. We never socialized much. I would have liked to have attended the service on Monday to pay my last respects but there are a lot of organizational meetings. I may not have a job on Monday night. Joe's successor is a guy named Harry Devonshire. He was never in Joe's class, and the only one he has ever cared about is Harry Devonshire. Joe could always find a way." Dunlap shrugged his shoulder. "Beth Gold. Boy that name is familiar. Who do you work for?"

"I'm an occasional journalist," Beth explained.

She watched Dunlap lumber out the door with his children. A large gentleman who was obviously lost without the guiding cunning of Joe Baxter.

"Do you think we can go right at five?" Martha asked Beth at 4:20. "I think everyone who's going to come has been here. I don't like everybody coming in and staring at my Dad in that coffin. Wouldn't it have been better to have just had him cremated?"

"It wasn't specified in his will."

"I'm starting to remember you, Beth. You used to have two adopted Vietnamese children. We met them at lunch right after Joel and I first came to New York. What happened to them?"

"They grew up. After under performing at school, flunking out of college, they drifted away. Periodically, they write for money. Sometimes I send them small amounts. The boy, whom Lester and I renamed Jim, is parking cars at a Miami hotel. The girl, Lea, married an American Indian and is living in a mobile home in Phoenix. She sends me photographs of unusually featured children with her Christmas card. It's really more of an annual appeal than a season's greeting. Motherhood has never been my thing. Lester and I were well intentioned 1970 liberals."

"Will you have control over my father's estate?"

"Until your thirtieth birthday according to your father's will."

"So, I will have to go to you for money?"

"I understand that you want to return to college. There will be plenty of money for that."

"Is there money for me to visit my mother in Milan?"

"There should be."

"Has Mr. Blum contacted my mother about Dad?"

"He promised me at breakfast this morning that it would be taken care of today."

"I want to call my mother first thing tomorrow. Is there a chance that she could be changed to executor of Dad's estate?"

"That would not be in keeping with your father's wishes," Beth answered coldly and motioned with her hand toward the casket. 'Joe Baxter, how could you get me into this situation? Your sweet little daughter and I are unlikely to get along.'

The Associate Funeral Director was an insipid young man in his early thirties who masked his youthful face with a goatee. He would appear periodically with a serene, bland smile and inquire how things were.

"Your guest book is filling up," he complimented them.

Beth began preparing to leave at ten minutes to five. She located Stephany on the telephone in a small windowless office just off the main foyer. Beth knocked on the door and announced that they were going to leave shortly. Stephany acknowledged her with a wave.

Beth gathered the coats and returned to the reviewal room. Martha Baxter was standing in front of the open casket. She appeared to be whispering something to her father's body.

"Is this the Baxter reviewal?" a firm commanding woman's voice sounded behind her.

Beth and Martha turned simultaneously to face the door. The voice belonged to a woman in a dark pants suit who was wearing a fur hat and dark glasses.

"Bridgette!" Martha called out excitedly and ran across the room to the woman. She opened her arms and received Martha into her arms. "Oh Bridgette! Dad's dead!"

So this was the famous Bridgette Morgan Baxter, Beth observed to herself. She had an oval shaped Irish face and wore make-up well. Her voice was well modulated and she appeared to be 40 or so. There was a stinging freshness about her.

"There, there, Muffin dear. Crying won't bring Joey back. Let's go see him." They walked to the casket with arms extended around each other's waists. Bridgette kissed Martha Baxter twice on the cheek as they advanced to the casket.

"There he is. The pride of Iron Creek, Minnesota, in a New York City uniform complete with a Hermes tie. Your Dad was always one handsome dude. He looks so peaceful there with that little boy smile."

"Oh Bridgette. He was murdered! Who would want to murder my Dad?"

"Probably that creep who used to call him up in the middle of the night. Have they nabbed anyone yet?"

"Beth knows. Ask Beth."

Bridgette looked Beth up and down. "I didn't see you when I came in. I'm Bridgette Morgan, dear."

"Beth Gold," Beth introduced herself.

"Beth Gold, the writer? Joey used to talk about you. I read the obit. But what the hell really happened?"

"Joe had just retired from McKenzie Barber. He went up to his country place Wednesday night to gather up some things for a book he planned to write. He was apparently packing up his car and someone shot him. He died on the driveway. The police believe that he had interrupted a robbery. He also told me about the caller and they are apparently checking into it."

"Beth is the executor of Dad's estate. She's been taking care of things."

"I drove up Thursday morning and found him in the driveway. The funeral will be at two on Monday in the Middleville Collegiate School Chapel."

Bridgette shook her head. "I have meetings on Monday. That's why I thought I'd drop by this afternoon. He dropped by my building over the holidays. He called me from the lobby. I had company, and it would have been awkward to introduce my former hubby to my current company. He sounded a little lonely." Bridgette placed her hands on Martha's shoulders.

"My God, you're getting tall. What have you been up to?" Martha Baxter placed her arms around her former step-mother.

"Bridgette, I missed you so much! Why haven't you called or written?" she sobbed.

Bridgette looked to Beth. "I have a car and driver. Where should Muffin be next? We could have a quick bite and I'll drop her."

Beth explained that Martha was staying with the Bains.

"Know 'em," Bridgette acknowledged. "I'll need directions to find them. That's a nice wholesome place for you, Muff." Stephany returned to the room carrying her coat.

"Well, look who's here. The great retail industry genius!" Bridgette greeted Stephany. "Were you ever able to find a job again?" Turning to Martha she added. "Never bought or sold a blouse, negotiated with a resource on chargebacks, hid a mark-down, and sold her soul for 49.5 mark-up. But people who buy stock occasionally read her crap and make buy and sell decisions on stock."

"It's nice to see you again, too," Stephany replied.

On the basis of their dinner at the Canoebrook Club, Beth concluded that Drew Farmer was a generally likable Washington egomaniac. She estimated him to be in either his late fifties or early sixties. He had been a Senator/Presidential hopeful in the early 1980s. His handsome face had graced the covers of all the major national magazines. Stephany had apparently been one of his several relationships that Farmer maintained outside his marriage. Scandal had knocked him out of his Senate seat and Presidential consideration. The Drew Farmer at dinner was a man with thinning grey hair, twenty pounds heavier than his coverboy days, with square yellow teeth, bright eyes, and a name dropping confident presence. 'Not really that much of a catch,' Beth concluded.

"Now, who again was this Joe Baxter?" Drew questioned.

"He was an old friend of Beth's whom I dated for a while in New York," Stephany explained. "In fact, he used to come to see me in Washington. Joe was a Partner with McKenzie Barber. He was an executive pay expert."

"Don't recall the name. I've read Frank Alvardi's book. That was a doozie." Drew's voice was resonant and commanding. The man could read the Canoebrook dinner menu and get attention, Beth decided.

"Joe used to work under Frank Alvardi. He's mentioned in his book," Beth responded.

Drew Farmer passed his hand over his forehead. "Was Baxter the super salesman guy who was the board room operator?" Beth thought back to the tall, red-headed Iron Creek boy of 1952. An unlikely board room salesman candidate at best.

"Joe was very glib," Stephany remembered. "He had a quick mind and fast tongue. He was very engaging."

"Ever sleep with him?" Drew Farmer probed.

"Joe wasn't quite my type, Drew," Stephany responded. "But he was a lot of fun."

"I did have the pleasure of Joe Baxter's company," Beth confessed. "I once proposed marriage to the man. He even made me the executor of his estate. He was a charming, good looking, clever man who was fun to be around. He was married three times, and left two daughters behind."

"And someone murdered him?" Drew Farmer questioned.

"You have a lot of high level contacts in the FBI, Drew. Neither Beth nor I have a lot of confidence in the local police," Stephany offered. "Joe had a night caller who periodically threatened his life. The local police don't appear to be pursuing that clue with much enthusiasm. Do you think you could make an inquiry, Drew? Beth and I are at quite a lost on how to follow up on this. Joe bought this house in the country. The people before him were suspected child killers. Joe used to get threatening calls identifying him with them. He went to the local police and they promised to investigate. The calls continued on for more than ten years. Now after Joe's death, the local police seemed to be sticking to this interrupting a burglary theory. The local Sheriff appears to have been murdered. Joe's former housekeeper, was married to someone who worked for the local sheriff."

Drew Farmer produced a notebook from the breast pocket of his suitcoat. "Give me all of these times and dates again. I'll call Halliday at the Bureau on Monday."

'Joe Baxter was dead,' Beth told herself. She needed to get a good night sleep and get back to her word processor. The vengeance or retribution efforts clearly rested with someone else. Beth's objective was to get through the weekend and put Monday behind her.

The Bains organized an early afternoon Sunday brunch at the local Hilton to introduce Michael Larian, the Unitarian Minister who was to conduct Monday's funeral service. He turned out to be a tall, handsome man in his early forties who wore a reassuring black suit and white clerical collar. He took an empty chair between Beth and Martha facing the Bains.

"Good morning, Michael?" Godfrey Bain asked after beverage orders had been taken

"Today's sermon addressed the issue of capital punishment. It was entitled 'An eye for a life'. We had quite a discussion period. We must have run until 12:25. Customarily, the church empties out by five minutes to twelve."

Dr. Larian patted Martha's hand. "Dr. Bain told me quite a bit about your father and he provided me a copy of the *New York Times* obituary. I would say that your father lived quite a rich life and he certainly touched a number of other lives. Are there some special memories of your father that you would like to share with the mourners tomorrow?"

Martha took a sip from her water glass. "I really never saw much of my father. He took this job with McKenzie Barber, the big consulting firm when I was very little. He had to travel quite a bit, but he came back every Friday night and my brother and I would spend the weekend with him. We lived in my Grandfather's house on Palmer Street in Racine. My mother became very active in the Stop the Vietnam movement and her work required her to be out of the house during the week, and she had a lot of weekend meetings. My brother Joel and I had my grandfather's housekeeper take care of us. Then Dad took an apartment where he could be closer to the airport and the McKenzie Barber Chicago Office. Finally they got divorced, and my mother moved to Milan where she lives today."

Martha rambled on. "Then my Dad transferred to New York and we moved with him. After a while, he married Bridgette, who was a famous retail executive. She came yesterday and took me out to supper, and bought this suit at Bloomie's in Riverside Square. My Dad was a nice person and

690

very good to me, but he was always too busy in his work. I used to do a lot of things with Bridgette when they were married. Every Saturday afternoon when it was nice, Bridgette and I would go roller skating together in Central Park."

Turning to Beth, Martha added, "I talked to my mother today in Milan. They're six hours ahead of us. She can't be here for the funeral, but will be here next week. She wants to meet Mr. Blum, Dad's attorney. She asked if there was to be a reading of his will."

"Mr. Blum will arrange for that very soon."

"And Godfrey, I understand that Joe Baxter and you go all the way back to your Army days," Dr. Larian turned the conversation.

"Beth goes back further," Bain corrected. "She met Joe over Christmas vacation in Iron Creek, Minnesota. And that as in December 1952."

All eyes turned to Beth.

"I must say that it is an honor to meet you, Miss Gold. I've enjoyed your books for years. I looked at one of your book jackets this morning. It stated that you were a native of Philadelphia. What brought you to Iron Creek, Minnesota?"

"My mother was Catholic and had graduated from a prep school in Duluth operated by nuns from a holy order. I endured three years there. I was unexpectedly alone during the Christmas holidays and my junior year roommate, Lucy Albright, invited me to Iron Creek."

"I looked up Iron Creek on the map, and concluded it wasn't that far away if I didn't like it. I met Joe at a party that first night and we saw each other every day for two weeks. Lucy had a boyfriend named Tommy who played on the basketball team with Joe. It was the four of us in the beginning, but then it was just the two of us. Joe, at the time was a radiant young man who seemed rather young for 17 in comparison to the young men I knew in Duluth. He was good looking, rather funny, naive and altogether quite refreshing."

"He told me enough about the history of Iron Creek and their great labor strike of 1950 to inspire me to write my first published short story. Perhaps

691

some of you have read it. It was called *The Strike*. It's still in print in anthologies. I had a wonderful time with Joe. He came to see me once in Duluth when he was up to play in a basketball tournament. Joe seemed so young in his high school warm-up jacket. I didn't see him again until Laura and I visited Godfrey in Fort Gately. Joe had become Godfrey's best friend. Twenty years later I met Joe again on a flight from LA to New York. We became reasonably good friends in New York. I was a married woman, and Joe had his girlfriends. I didn't meet any of his wives and didn't meet Martha until Friday when I went up to tell her of her father's death. Joe Baxter was a talented young man from the heartland of America who made his way forward in the world with aggressive long steps. He was a fearless man who learned how to play the games that are required in the sophisticated, competitive world of commerce. In some ways, Joe Baxter was what America is all about. He was a man with limited advantages who through his intelligence, good looks, hard work, and wit managed to compete and build a business career competing with the very best. Joe had a daughter from an unfortunate first marriage named Lenore. He met his obligations to this daughter. She and her husband, Duane, are serving as missionaries in Africa. Joe may not have been a conventional parent, but he was a good one. He cared about his son, Joel, who died of AIDS, and his daughter, Martha, who is with us today."

"Joe Baxter was the eldest son of a miner and an ungifted woman who worked as a telephone operator. By Joe's account, his father was a hard drinking bar room brawler. His mother was a devout Lutheran, and he had a younger brother who became a petty criminal in Duluth and ultimately disappeared from sight. Joe Baxter traveled a good distance from his humble beginnings in Northern Minnesota to be senselessly murdered in the driveway of his upstate New York dacha."

"Should the individual who murdered Mr. Baxter pay with his life?" Dr. Larian smugly asked.

They polled the table and came to agreement on life imprisonment. Godfrey went on to talk about his days with Baxter in the Army. Old tales were repeated that Beth did not want to hear again. 'Joe Baxter,' Beth said to herself. 'You owe me one! Big time!'

The Middleville cafeteria served coffee, sandwiches, and cake following the funeral service and the internment. The Chapel had been filled to capacity. A great many well dressed couples sat through the upbeat

Unitarian ceremony which was completed in thirty-six minutes. A talented young man from the Middleville School played some Gershwin, Satie, and Sondheim, which had been identified as Joe Baxter's favorite composers. There was some handholding around the gravesite and a recitation of the Lord's Prayer. The closed casket was lowered away and Beth whispered 'So long, Joe.' It was 3:25 PM on a Monday winter afternoon and there was one final reception for Beth to muddle through. Baxter had been laid away, and there was one last ceremony to endure before Beth could escape from these people.

Beth, Martha Baxter, the Bains and Dr. Larian formed a reception line to greet the strangers. Beth had expected no more than a dozen, but counted thirty-eight.

At the beginning of the line was a couple called the Nickersons.

"How do you do. I'm Clyde Nickerson and this is my wife Andrea," they introduced themselves to Beth and Martha in their lead positions in the reception line.

The man named Clyde was balding and had the look of a mean spirited high school principal. His wife had the fleshy look of a woman on the decline. She reminded Beth of Laura Bain.

"Your father and I started on the same day at McKenzie Barber," Andy Nickerson announced to Martha. "Your sorrow is our sorrow."

The mourners moved quickly through the reception line and repeated near identical condolences. They proceeded to the coffee urns, nibbled a little, and more or less lingered for what could measure as an adequate commitment of time. A tall red-headed woman in dark glasses and a smart black leather coat with matching boots introduced herself as Rusty Collins.

"I need to talk to you," she addressed Beth.

"I should be free in ten minutes. Wait for me by the table beyond the coffee urn," Beth responded.

The woman settled into her place at the table with a mug of coffee. She had slipped off her coat and displayed a long body in a red knit dress. Beth quickly sensed that this woman could well represent one of Joe Baxter's last relationships.

"He was supposed to meet me in Chicago on Thursday," the woman greeted Beth. "I've been calling through Friday and then I saw the obituary in the Times. I stayed with him last weekend and saw your books on his bookshelves. I'm devastated. Can we get out of here and have a drink? I have to know more details than were in the obituary. We had four days together. I left him Tuesday morning to go back to the coast. He was on his way to Ernie Grey's funeral in Philadelphia. We were forming a relationship that we both believed had a future. Now he's been taken away. I'm leaving my job at McKenzie Barber for a new career. All I can think about is that Joe is gone. I was strong when I met Joe. Now I feel very fragile. Joe told me that he was going to meet with you for lunch on Wednesday. You were probably the last one to see him alive."

Beth patted the woman's hand. Did the executor's job description include comforting the former girlfriends?

"There really isn't a lot to say," Beth responded. She paused when a third person joined them.

He was a grey-eyed man with a trench coat draped over his shoulders who held a coffee mug. "My name is Hamilton Burke," he introduced himself. His voice was haunting. It had a southern lilt and there was a superb rhythm to his words.

"I saw Joe six days ago at Ernie Grey's funeral. He was going to come down and do some work for me. Do I understand that he was shot?"

"Joe was shot in the driveway of his country place. He had gone up Wednesday night to gather up some files. Joe had been planning to write a history of McKenzie Barber, and wanted to centralize all of his files in New York. He had a threatening, stalking caller who had been calling him up there for ten years or so. The state police believe that Joe had interrupted a robbery in progress. I wouldn't rule out the telephone stalker. My friend, Stephany, has a fiancé who has senior level contacts at the FBI. He's going to try to get them involved."

"Where was the wound?" Burke asked bluntly.

Burke was the first to ask where Baxter had been shot.

"He was wounded in the stomach."

"Not good. A head wound goes more quickly. At one time in my life, I saw a lot of men die in the field. Joe must have died slowly."

The woman called Rusty broke into sobs. Beth placed a comforting arm around her.

"Here's my card," Burke said, producing a business card. "If the FBI doesn't seem to make any progress, I'll get some private operatives on it. Let's make sure we get the son-of-a-bitch who killed Joe." Burke ran his hand across Rusty's cheek, lifted up her dark glasses, and kissed her once on each eye.

"Joe Baxter and I go back some twenty-five years. I met him when he was with that housewares company in Wisconsin. I arranged for Joe to join McKenzie Barber. He used to work for me. Joe Baxter always got the job done. No matter what he was asked to do, he got it done. He'd argue some in the beginning and then he would go out and get it done. I had big plans for Joe at McKenzie Barber. But I lost the Chairman election and they threw me out. They tried to trash Joe, but he stood up to them. I had hoped we'd serve together again at Burke Farms, but it was not to be. The world has lost an exceptional man, before his time and someone must pay for this crime."

The man had the eyes of a wolf, Beth concluded. No life in prison for Baxter's killer with this man.

"The Nickersons are here. You must be acquainted with them from McKenzie Barber," Beth pointed to the couple who were talking with the Bains and Dr. Larian.

"The man is a horse's ass. And his wife has learned to closely model her behavior after her husband. I had enough of those star crossed lovers when I was in the New York office of McKenzie Barber," Burke said.

Two more people were advancing to the table bearing coffee cups. One, Beth immediately recognized as Frank Alvardi. He still resembled a middle-aged Joe DiMaggio with his shiny slick backed black hair. He was accompanied by a handsome woman with platinum hair who wore a magnificent mink coat.

"Ham, how are you?" Alvardi greeted Burke. "I made out the word horse's ass. You must be talking about one of our former colleagues. This is Lorna Brimmer."

"Paul's widow," Burke acknowledged. "I remember you from the Chicago Office."

"You used to be Clyde Nickerson's secretary," Burke added after they had exchanged hand clasps.

"That was a long, long time ago, Ham," Alvardi jumped in. "Lorna is now CEO of a diversified multi-national company a year away from joining the Fortune 200."

"Joe and I were very close back in the 1970s, and we stayed in touch over the years. Both Frank and I were shocked over Joe's death and the way he died," Lorna added. Beth was taken by her crisp speech delivered in a hard Southern accent. Lorna Brimmer, may have once been someone's secretary once, but she had moved several spaces forward on the career game board and had grown accustomed to the distance between her and the other players.

"Miss Gold, I understand that you are the executor of Joe's estate." Lorna Brimmer held eye contact with Beth. She was a woman who had grown used to giving commands.

"I have that task."

"I would like to offer a $25,000 reward for information leading to the arrest and conviction of Joe Baxter's murderer or murderers." She proffered a business card to Beth. "Please have Joe's attorney contact me. I'll put him in touch with my personal attorney. I want justice."

"I'll match that amount," Burke added. "I want that son-of-a-bitch locked up and hopefully electrocuted. He shot Joe in the stomach."

Rusty put on her coat. "I'm going to go now. Good luck to all of you with your plans for vengeance. It won't bring Joe back."

Beth squeezed Rusty. "I'm sure the money will turn to memorials over time," she whispered. "The McKenzie Barber people are an 'eye for an eye' lot."

Beth excused herself from the group and walked with Rusty to the door. Rusty paused at the main conversation group. That Ganski from Minnesota had joined the group comprised of the Nickersons, Bains, Dr. Larian and Martha Baxter.

Rusty approached Dr. Larian. "I'm Rusty Collins. I became a good friend of Joe's over the last few weeks. We expected to be in Chicago together this last weekend. I thought your eulogy was wonderful."

Dr. Larian gripped both of Rusty's hands. "I understand, my dear, and I'm flattered that my hastily drawn words had meaning for you. I was just explaining to these nice people that Dr. Bain had the ceremony taped. I'm sure that if you wrote to Dr. Bain, he could arrange for you to receive a duplicate cassette tape."

Ganski took a step forward to Beth. "I thought that Drew Farmer would be here today."

"He was here for dinner on Saturday night. He and Stephany went back to Washington first thing on Sunday."

"I expect that I'll be getting out to Washington more frequently. I'd like to look him up sometime. Do you suppose Stephany could arrange a meeting? We're in different parties, but I'm confident that we believe in the same America."

"Have your little friend call me. I'll give her Stephany's number in Washington," Berth answered and slid away to face a new trio of mourners.

There was a young man with thinning blonde hair and steel rimmed glasses. He wore a brown tweed suit that seemed a little large. "I'm Spencer Harwell from the Harwell Management Company. Joe Baxter was a consultant to my late father for many years. My mother could not attend the memorial service, and I'm representing the family. This is Hakim Selim, our Chief Investment Officer. Can we be introduced to Joe's daughter?"

697

Dwight E. Foster

"Martha," Beth gestured. "Here are some more of your father's friends who wish to say hello."

A third young man stepped forward. He had dark hair and flashing black eyes. He wore a smart-looking blue double breasted blazer, blue button down shirt, grey slacks, and a red and navy striped club tie. He could well be attending a wedding.

"I'm Preston Grey. Joe was just with us last Tuesday at my father's funeral. My mother couldn't be here this afternoon and I'm representing the Grey family."

Hakim Selim was a short, attractive, obviously polished man in his early forties. He reminded Beth of a successful Baghdad merchant.

Beth introduced Martha who shook hands and maintained a wooden expression on her face. "Thank you so much for coming," she greeted each of the new mourners.

"We stopped to make a few phone calls after the burial ceremony, so we're a little late," Spencer Harwell apologized.

"Your father was a highly valued consultant to my father for many years. My father, Leon Harwell, looked on Joe Baxter equally as a personal friend and a retained consultant. I was looking forward to beginning a similar relationship with your father this year. Hakim and I planned to engage him on a regular retainer. Should a memorial fund be established in Joe's name, the Harwell Management Company would be pleased to be included."

"Both Spencer and I are deeply saddened by your father's death. It's truly ironic. I just encountered your father at a New Hampshire ski resort. We had a very enjoyable luncheon together."

"I know," Martha replied. "You were in the Matterhorn Room."

Preston Grey spoke next. "I also was just with your father at my father's funeral. His service was also conducted in the chapel of a prep school. My mother is still in grief over the loss of her husband, and chose not to join us today. My father's second wife, Toni, is in Florida and asked me to express her condolences. That looks like quite a spread over there. I'll just help myself to a sandwich."

"You look very tired, my dear. Perhaps, it's time for you to lay down and rest at the Bains," Beth suggested.

"I'd like that, Beth," Martha agreed. "Thank you for coming to remember, Dad," she said in the general direction of the three men.

Beth guided Martha back to Laura Bain. "I believe it's time for Martha to get off her feet. Can you take her back to your place and I'll come over after things are cleared up."

"Mrs. Bain said that she'll drive me back to New Hampshire tomorrow," Martha offered.

"Good," Beth agreed and stepped away into the path of Zach Blum, Baxter's attorney.

"Looks like I've missed everything. I had a divorce settlement conference that ran over. Then I got lost in New Jersey. Can I pay my respects to Joe's daughter?"

They caught Laura Bain and Martha at the side door.

"Martha, this is Mr. Blum, your father's attorney. He wants to pay his respects," Beth introduced Blum to Laura Bain.

"I know that this has been one hell of a day for you and don't want to keep you. I got to know your Dad about four years ago and have done personal legal work for him. I have a lot of clients that I really don't care for. Your Dad was a client that I really got to like. He was so fair and caring that a lot of people took advantage of him."

"I talked to my mother this morning. Her name is Jennifer Washburn and she lives in Milan, Italy. She will come to New York in the next week or so. Mother wants to talk to you about Dad's will. Her lawyer will be calling you. I believe she wants to be named executor."

"I'll look forward to meeting her. Please accept my condolences. Your father was a fine man."

They stood in the doorway and watched Laura Bain lead Martha down the walk to the Headmaster's house through the failing light of a January day.

"What the hell was that all about?" Blum asked Beth.

"I believe her mother wants to contest the will. The daughter wants to change executors. I don't believe Martha likes me very much."

"No way," Blum shook his head. "This is the way Joe wanted it and this is the way it's going to stay."

"How about letting me resign and appointing Godfrey Bain as executor?" Beth suggested as they returned to the reception.

"No way. Joe was counting on me and counting on you when he made up that will. We're going to hold our ground. I did some calculations this morning. Martha is entitled to Joe's pension. He's got a million in term insurance and there are some other assets including his house that will bring his estate to over $3 million. Martha is set for life, but she won't have access to all of the money until she's thirty. Joe and I tied our ties to the bar a couple of times. I talked about my wives and he talked about this. I didn't know the first one. Bridgette was a tough negotiator, but reasonably fair. His middle wife, by Joe's account, was a selfish whacko."

"Did Joe ever discuss with you his reason for appointing me his executor? Why not you?"

Blum shrugged his shoulders. "Maybe he thought we would be a pretty good team together."

Blum's hands clasped Beth's hand She squeezed in response.

"Let me introduce you to some of Joe's friends. We'll meet the capital punishment crowd first."

"You live in the city, don't you?" Blum asked as they approached the group comprised of the Chicago Office period of Baxter's life.

"East Seventies."

"How about letting me buy you dinner tonight?" Blum offered.

"I'm very tired."

"We can talk and maybe strategize a little. It won't be a late night. When Joe told me about you being executor, I started reading your books. You're a very fine writer."

Beth introduced Blum to Mrs. Brimmer, Alvardi, and Burke who had been joined by the younger Harwell and Selim. Rusty Collins had disappeared from the room. One less ex-girlfriend/mourner to contend with. She was probably the last love Baxter had been alluding to at Wednesday's luncheon.

Beth observed Blum with the group. He was a man in his mid-fifties, good with words, with grey curly hair, a soft gut, Semite features, and a quick mind. He seemed interested in her. They were being united as the defenders of Joe Baxter's will. She was obligated to spend some time with Blum over the next year. There really wasn't a lot out there for a woman Beth's age. He might just do.

Alvardi was telling a story. "So Joe got up on the pulpit and delivered the eulogy for Wild Bill. And he was damned brilliant—"

April 10, 1992, 4:57 PM

Beth rapidly inputted her notes into her computer pad. They would make the electronics device announcement shortly and she wanted to get her notes on the disc quickly. Her final meeting of the day had been with Bob Friedman, the CEO of Dungler Technologies, and the successor of the late Alice Dungler. He agreed to meet Beth following his late afternoon tennis session.

Beth met Bob Friedman during the late afternoon that day shortly before five o'clock. They met on the balcony of his corner office in the corporate headquarters of Dungler Technologies. Friedman greeted Beth in his tennis clothes. They took seats at a white metal table under an umbrella that shielded the late afternoon sun.

Friedman was a handsome, athletic man with jet black hair. Beth knew from his biography that Friedman was in his early fifties, but he appeared at least fifteen years younger. He was a sexy man with a heavy tan and muscular arms and legs.

"Hello, Beth," he greeted her. "I had to play a little customer tennis this afternoon. Please excuse my appearance. My wife Becky says hello, and she sent some books with me to be autographed. I believe she's read just about everything you've written. I have to confess that the only book of yours I've read is *Interlude of Discontent*. I found it quite moving. I arranged for our archivist to send material over to your hotel. I hope you had a chance to review it."

"I did and it was most helpful. The note said that we could include the pictures in the book."

"You have a competitor out there. Sandra Maven. She has written some unflattering things about Dungler Technologies. I, for one, would rather see your book out come first. You're a far more talented writer and I believe you will report on Alice's life more fairly. Now I understand that you have had other meetings in the Bay area about your book. Can you share with me whom you talked with?"

Beth used a steno pad to take notes. She opened the pad to the names. "I had a meeting with Fred Tabor of Robson Barber. Mary Chin, the retired

Treasurer of Dungler Technologies, and Bruce Fox, the CEO of Datascape. His company appears to represent your major competitor. He told me he left Dungler Technologies about the time you came."

"Now that's a well rounded group. I still don't like the sound of Robson Barber. How's Fred doing?" Friedman asked.

"He told me that he expects to retire at the end of this year."

"Alice used to intimidate the shit out of Fred. How's Mary?"

"She's operating a restaurant in Sausalito called Bloody Mary's."

"Did she tell you about her drug dealer boyfriend?"

"We concentrated on Alice. Bill Fox sends you his best."

"Good old Bill predicted doom and gloom for us. He told you our technology is dated and how Datascape will bury us. He and Alice are remembered to be in a continual state of mortal conflict. Well, Beth," Friedman said looking at his watch.

"Let's get on to Alice. Let me begin by saying that Alice Dungler was brilliant, a superior visionary, an inspiring leader, but she was hardly a saint."

Friedman was glib with sound bites, and proved eminently quotable. He was a wonderful interview. Friedman described Alice's early days in the Los Angeles office of McKenzie Barber where she dwarfed and intimidated the talent around her. Beth learned for the first time that Alice had actually been elected the first woman Partner of McKenzie Barber only to decline to form Dungler Technologies."

"The name, Joe Baxter, came up during my interview with Mary Chin. Do you remember the name?"

"Joe Baxter! The most unforgettable of the former McKenzie Barber Partners. I've lost track of Joe. Do you know what he's doing now?"

"He's dead. He was murdered last January in the driveway of his country home."

Friedman rose from his chair and stood on the balcony in silence facing the San Francisco Bay. He turned back to Beth after a ten second interval.

"That was some unexpected information." Friedman took a long drink of mineral water and returned to his chair across from Beth.

"We're a little isolated form the rest of the world out here on the West Coat. The old gang is dying off. The firm is gone. Swallowed up by Robson Barber! You expect to hear about former associates dying, but you expect the deaths to take place in some logical sequence. When I heard that Ernie Grey had died, I could generally accept that. The man was seventy years old. I would have bet on seventy-seven, but who would have predicted that Ernie would turn into a roller blader? Wild Bill and Dirks were about right. They were both good solid abusers. I figured Dwyer would go first and gave Dirks two years on top of that."

"I don't know those names," Beth interjected.

"They were Partners of McKenzie Barber. They were three levels ahead of me when I started. Legends of the firm. Then I drew even with them. Shortly thereafter, I passed them up and they pretended to work for me. But Joe Baxter is another matter. I have problems accepting Joe's death. Joe was the ultimate survivor at McKenzie Barber. His death is out of sequence. I expected Joe to be hanging around until his seventies. Who murdered him?"

"No conclusion has been reached. They suspect a Sheriff's assistant. He's on trial for killing the Sheriff, and they seem unwilling to charge him with another crime until his trial on the first charge. They seem to have their own way of doing things in Brinker's Falls County, New York."

"Well that's too bad. Have they set up a memorial fund? Perhaps I could send a check."

"In due time there will be some kind of memorial. There's some silly litigation going on. His second wife is contesting the will. Joe named me his executor. I too, thought he would live to be seventy-five when I agreed."

"Wives? The only wife of Joe, I could remember was that little peanut from retailing. She had an Irish name and she was a hot media ticket when I was in back in New York. How many wives did he have?"

"Three," Beth answered.

"Did he have kids?"

"He has an older daughter who is serving on a two year church mission in Africa. His son died a few years back. His other surviving daughter is a 22 year old college drop-out who is ready to return to school. Joe hired a competent estate lawyer who will see that Joe's estate goes to where it was intended. But it's been more time consuming for me than I expected."

"Were you one of Joe's lady friends, Beth?"

"I was a friend," Beth corrected him. "Mary Chin intimated today that Joe Baxter and Alice Dungler were close. I went through his papers and found an offer letter to Joe from Pacific Technologies, the predecessor company to Dungler Technologies."

"I know about that. If Baxter had accepted, he probably would have become a very rich man. He would have had to manage his relationship with Alice which was far from easy, but Joe, over the years, worked for a lot of unusual characters including the notorious Hamilton Burke. He might have survived and possibly held a job similar to mine. I have to tell you, Beth, my job is not very easy."

"I met Hamilton Burke for the first time at Joe's funeral. He was disturbed by Joe's death. He even hired a private investigator who built the case against the Sheriff's Assistant. I had dinner with him one evening in New York. I had no idea that Burke Farms was such a large and complex business."

"He's been waiting to inherit it as long as I can remember."

"Tell me about Burke. He seems to have led a fascinating life."

"Is Burke another one of your book projects? Are we through talking about Alice?" Friedman looked at his watch.

"One last question about Alice. How large an impact did Alice Dungler's sudden death have on Dungler Technologies?" Friedman shrugged his shoulders. "Dungler Technologies is trading at the same multiple today as it traded the day before Alice's death. We had some ups and downs in between, but Dungler Technology remains the world's leader in software products. What people forget is that Alice Dungler and I were trained at the same place, McKenzie Barber. We saw the fundamental business processes through the same pair of eyes. Alice was the brilliant visionary who conceived the company, attracted the people, set the course, and I was the one who relieved the captain on deck. Alice had assembled a well trained crew at Dungler Technologies. It was my job to successfully guide the ship to port. I have done this for five years now. I may be a lousy software engineer, but I'm a pretty decent ship's captain. I've demonstrated to the financial world that Bob Friedman can navigate."

"Now, how about Burke?"

Friedman shook his head. "Not just Burke. I'll provide you a package comment. It will be an assessment of what I believe went wrong at McKenzie Barber. You may feel privileged, Beth. You've awakened some old memories in our brief meeting."

"I believe that companies, business organizations, and firms pretty much form an individual's career expectations, life habits and values. They are, in my opinion, far more influential than the over-rated universities who provided us the ticket to attend the career dance," Friedman lectured. "Take me for example. Why and how did I find my way to McKenzie Barber?"

"I heard that they didn't hire Jews. I went to school on a tennis scholarship, and recognized that tennis skills would help, but wouldn't carry me where I believed I could go. I tailored my thesis on the profession of management consulting before anyone wrote about it. I even sent a copy to Ernie Grey. The rumor was that Ernie browsed through it and wrote a note off to the LA office. Someone told me that his comment was:

'Pretty shallow stuff. Have this Friedman in for an interview and hire him if he looks all right. Maybe we should alter our mould a little.'

"Ernie kept an eye on me after that. I didn't know he was watching until he gave me fifteen minutes once in the mid-sixties when I was a hotshot young manger. Then all of a sudden I was the youngest Partner in the history of the firm and the first Jew Partner. My wife Becky liked to refer to me as the 'Jackie Robinson of McKenzie Barber!' A couple of years later, I was made the Managing Partner of the Los Angeles office. It was a growth market for consulting services, and I wanted to be king of the hill. I was not an insider, but I was a USC graduate instead of Stanford or Harvard. Bob Friedman had broken the mould."

"Burke and Joe were outsiders. Burke came first. He was old for a new hire. Almost 30, I believe. Those of us who ran across him figured that he'd stay a couple of years and go back to the family business. Guys like Burke were classified as 'politicals'. Burke also caught Ernie Grey's eye. Burke was more Ernie's model than a tennis playing Jew from California. Ernie developed his own training program for Ham Burke. He parked Burke overseas for five or six years and brought him back as some long range planning Partner in a job where he could see the whole firm. Burke was upon us as Ernie's chosen one before we could see him coming."

"Burke brought Joe Baxter to McKenzie Barber. He was an outsider who didn't come close to fitting the traditional McKenzie Barber mould. He graduated from a state university, and didn't even have a straight business degree. He had worked at some little housewares company someplace in Wisconsin. He shouldn't have lasted two years. But Joe was smart and he had the ability to assimilate and sell. He also proved to be a very good writer. Joe, after having established himself as Alvardi's protégé, in a small practice and eventually became Burke's protégé about the time Burke returned from overseas."

"Ernie passed over a guy named Paul Brimmer, who really was the best qualified successor. Brimmer had come up through the system and was a successful, demanding, and frequently terrifying leader. Paul Brimmer was Ernie Grey's rightfully and logical successor. Ernie followed his gut and went with Burke as crown prince. Brimmer quit in disgust, and built a major industrial company."

"Then Ernie matched me with Burke. Joe became part of the troika. He was Burke's man whether he liked it or not. The next thing I knew, I was running for Deputy Chairman on Burke's ticket. As it turned out, Burke accumulated a lot of baggage from bad acquisitions. Ernie withdrew his support for Burke, and a dissident partner group elected some figurehead General as Chairman. Burke was persuaded to resign, and I was exiled overseas. This left Joe hanging mid-career. He managed to stick it out as the firm headed into a nose-dive. Joe had been both a witness and a victim. He managed to hang on four seven more years."

"Now, by this time, you're asking yourself, 'What is the lesson to be learned from all talk?' It's simple. The leader, whether founder or non-founder, of any organization has an obligation to provide leadership transition. John McKenzie did it with Ernie Grey. Ernie Grey failed, and the rest of us had to live with the consequences. My obligation to Dunlger Technologies is similar, and I have vowed to pass the leadership baton gracefully. Like McKenzie Barber and Ernie Grey, I was willed a very successful company. The test of my business career lies with my ability to transition leadership. Ernie Grey failed at McKenzie Barber. By all reports he did far better at IPCO. I believe Ernie learned from past mistakes. It's a shame Joe Baxter isn't with us. He saw it all and understood the business case." Friedman rose from his chair.

"Well, that's enough pontificating for one day. I've got to shower and change for a dinner. I am speaking tonight on the future of the Software Industry. I hope to hell someone has written something intelligent for me to say." Friedman shook Beth's hand. "My secretary's name is Lois. I'll see that she gets you a car for the airport. Good-bye."

Beth closed her computer pad and settled into the seat. Bob Friedman had been more than she had anticipated. There was a story there worth writing. But with all of the egos and political structures involved in the world's commercial business structure, would the lessons be accepted? The grand old firm of McKenzie Barber had been digested by its upstart competitor and life would go on. Now it was time to return to Alice Dungler.

Beth settled back in her aisle seat after the seat belt sign had been turned off. The American Airlines red-eye flight to New York was filled to the gunnels, and the flight attendant had been slow in delivering her Remy. She began to leaf through the *New York Times* in the general direction of the obituaries, her eyes to rest on one obituary.

MILLICENT STOCKBRIDGE GREY
INTERIOR DESIGN EXECUTIVE
DEAD AT 68

Millicent Stockbridge Grey, interior design executive, and Connecticut socialite, died on Wednesday in her Greenwich, Connecticut home following a stroke.

Mrs. Grey was Chairman and Chief Executive Officer of GreyWebb Studios, a well regarded interior design studio with offices in Greenwich, Boston, and New York. Mrs. Grey was the daughter of Bickford and Nadia Stockbridge of Philadelphia and heiress to the Stockbridge Department Store chain in Philadelphia. Mrs. Grey, who was frequently called "Millie" attended Miss Benedicts Prepatory School and Mills College. She was married to James Randolph, an Army Officer in 1941. Mr. Randolph was killed in 1944 during the Normandy Invasion.

Mrs. Grey was next married to Ernest Grey II in 1948. Mr. Grey, a decorated war hero, went on to become a management consulting industry executive with a firm then known as McKenzie Barber. Mrs. Grey divorced her husband in 1986. She joined GreyWebb Studios in 1985 and acquired the company a year later upon the death of Arthur Grey, the founder. GreyWebb, under Mrs. Grey's directions, developed a strong market following with wealthy customers in Northeast. Her son, Preston Grey, will succeed Mrs. Grey as Chief Executive Officer of GreyWebb. Mrs. Grey is also survived by a daughter, Mrs. Kathleen Goldman of Fort Lee, New Jersey.

In addition to Mrs. Grey's business leadership in the interior design industry, she was active in a number of social and political activities which included the Hudson Historical Society, the League of Woman Voters, the Republic Party, and the Greenwich Garden Club. Mrs. Grey served as a senior fund riser in the 1980 VanderKelen for Governor campaign, and was regarded as a close confidante of the late Cornelius VanderKelen. A small family funeral is planned for Sunday, followed by an open house at GreyWebb Studios in Greenwich.

Hm, Beth observed. This Millicent Grey sounded like a thousand other obituaries of Connecticut matrons she had read over the years. Joe must have known her. She caught the attention of the flight attendant. "My dear," Beth said firmly. "Will you please fetch me a Remy?"

The End

About the Author

Dwight Foster, the author of Shattered Covenants, is a native of Minnesota who transferred to New York City in 1980. He retired as a consulting partner from an international public accounting firm in January 1990 to form an executive search firm.

Shattered Covenants is a first novel, which represents an eight year writing project dealing with the passing of leadership in a professional services firm. Twilight & Endgame is the final book in a series of free standing novels narrating the formation, rise, decline, and fall of McKenzie Barber, a fictional global management consulting firm.

Earlier books in the series include:

> **Present & Past Imperfect**
> **The Road to McKenzie Barber**
> **The Consultant**
> **The Chairman**
> **The Partner**
> **The House of Harwell**

Shattered Covenants deals with the passing of CEOs (i.e. kings) and their ultimate effect on the careers and lives of the courtiers, and rank and file professionals who follow the leadership of the CEO.

The author has spent his business career in the consulting industry, and for the past twelve years, has headed up a well-recognized executive search firm. Dwight Foster has published previously in management studies and magazine articles and is quoted from time to time in the national press. His experience in the practice of executive search and familiarity with organization and business models over the past thirty years provided the motivation to write a sweeping novel. The primary narrator of Shattered Covenants, Joseph Baxter, Jr., is the son of a labor martyr from Minnesota's Iron Range who rises to a Board Room world traveling, executive compensation consultant.

Baxter is a modern day Candide who develops the cunning to survive in a ruthlessly competitive business world.

Dwight Foster is a University of Minnesota Alumnus, the father of two adult children, and is married to Dorothy Choitz Foster, a well-known journalist and consultant to the cosmetics and fragrance industry. The Fosters make their home in the Pocono Mountains of Pennsylvania.

Printed in the United States
1446700001B/165